The Man Named Destruction

The Man Named Destruction

The Scrios Chronicles

By

E. J. Josephson

Published by E. J. Josephson, 2025

The Man Named Destruction

First Edition Printing, May, 2025.

ISBN: 979-8-9989068-5-5

E. J. Josephson
Whittier, NC 28789
www.RedwolfSolutions.com
Imprint: Independently published

Ordering Information:
Quantity sales. Special discounts are available on quantity purchases by corporations, associations, and others. For details, contact the author at Eric@redwolfsolutions.com

Dedication

Writing this book has been an effort stretching over several years. People close to me have been extremely supportive of this endeavor. I'm sure it's been fun putting up with my endless yammering about the "arc of the book" or how characters, that to me, have become real people who live in my mind.

My friends and family, thank you for your support and encouragement. To my brothers, sisters and friends, you will see your reflections in this story, because you are wonderful. To the creatures out there, if you possess a reflection, I hope I have captured it.

To my Brady Bunch of kids (Ian, Silas, Amy, Sam, Jake and Amelia), I hope you take the time to enjoy this.

Mom? Sorry, I gave you some parts to read in such a small font, many of which included some truly crappy prose.

To Dad, I love and miss you.

To Melissa, thanks for being supportive, wonderful and patient. The endless drives in the car where I talked about the story like it was real life. The great feedback you gave.

E. J. Josephson

Part 1–The Long Shadow of Winter

Prelude – The End.
Sunday, March 24th, 2019, Lander County Nevada, USA. East of Mt. Tobin.

"I should be in Vegas watching a basketball game with my girl and my friends instead of here with you!" Gus said as he trudged across the barren salt basin. He looked like he was contemplating throwing the ancient golden artifact in his hand away in disgust. Even with the cart carrying the most weight, the heavy backpack still cut into his shoulders through the heavy parka he wore. The cart idea had become a total fucking failure. It might have even been comical if it were just him and Marcy trying to carry gear onto a summer beach. Sure, it was still rolling... some; but half sliding and clogged with the wet sandy clay. "I can't believe it! A goddamn snowstorm in the freaking desert! Seriously, what the hell!" he exclaimed.

Sand accumulated on the rubber tires of the cart and had also affected the bearings, causing everything to get stuck. Soon, the salty sand and mud would trap the tires once more. Pausing momentarily, he kicked the tires vigorously, hoping to dislodge the thick layer of mud, but it stuck there like a paste. The kick served as a harsh reminder of the freezing cold weather, numbing his feet. Although he didn't directly feel the impact, the resulting ache was undeniable. Dressed appropriately for the cool weather that was in the forecast, he was wearing warm clothes, but the winter storm he encountered today had been absent from the predictions. Occasionally, a gust of wind would uncover a small window of clear sky amidst the storm, making him hopeful the relentless weather would ease up.

Scrios, the ancient evil entity confined to the golden artifact in his hand, communicated directly into Gus's mind, "You could be in Vegas by now if you and your family had abandoned this nonsense generations ago. Hell, you could end this now and still make it to Las Vegas by tonight. I could make you richer than you could ever imagine." The creature inside the green gem proclaimed, "If you desire, we could rule this entire planet together."

"Stop!" said Gus exasperatedly. "This is the end. You evil piece of shit, you are done! Also, you wouldn't make me rich or work together with me. You killed most everyone you encountered, and you would kill me, too. My family hid from you, because you hunted us."

"That was nothing but war," the entity's voice declared. "A war you have won, and I have to admit, among very few losses... at least not the ones I intended to win. But you... you are safe. My wiles don't even work on you. You

1

know why, right? Have you pieced all that together? Have you deduced our familial relation? Sure, it was a little way back, but one of my siblings, born before me, slipped the fucking fence. Sorry, I mean, survived. It was tough in the Bronze Age. No In-and-Out burgers back then." The monster imprisoned in the short scepter shaped artifact droned on, stating, "I'm pretty certain blood relates my bitch sister's kids to you."

Stopping momentarily, Gus stared intently at the artifact he was holding. "Oh my God, can you please shut the fuck up? If I wanted to know more, I could take one of those GodIHopeWeAreNotRelated.com tests and find out more, but I don't give a shit why your bullshit doesn't work on me. I do care about why you hunted me and my family for ages. I do care about why you killed my friends, why you killed my family... Why you ruined Peter... Why you ruined my life and my family's life?" Gus said as his voice hinted at cracking and quieting to an exasperated mumble. "Why do you want to destroy the world? I would take an answer to that!"

Gus experienced a moment of complete silence, during which he heard his footsteps squeak on the fine, wet sand. The monster eventually replied sheepishly. "It seems like you've got the wrong impression of me. I don't want to destroy this world. You know I'm being honest with you here, because I think you can tell when I am lying. I have no desire at all. By destroying the world, I would destroy myself. I have the same desire as you to live," soothed the soft voice of the creature.

"What?!?" Gus said incredulously. "I have seen your thoughts asshole and now I'm forced to carry those memories too. I saw some of the terrible shit you did and felt the satisfaction you had doing it! No, I'm not looking into your damn crystal anymore. You fed off the deaths of those people... Fed! OFF THE DEATH OF PEOPLE!!!"

"That's not true. Why would I want to eliminate everyone when I've been patiently waiting for this world to ripen? If I killed EVERYONE, I would starve like the plants in this awful place. I have killed no one. I'm a farmer, not a murderer. No, no, NO, I leave the hating to you. I leave the jealousy to you. I leave the murdering..." Scrios said, "I can sit here, doing nothing but watch what man does to man in this world and let it nourish me."

Gus's hand wildly flailed towards the heavens, as if he were reaching for an elusive imaginary item to smash as Scrios spoke, "The living ones sustain me. Sure, there is a delicious burst near the end when they embrace that last breath, but..." said Scrios, sounding like a sommelier pairing a wine to exotic meat.

"I don't care how you parse it, you evil asshat. You kill people. When you give them their new understanding, and because of that, they kill their own families and themselves... that is you killing them."

"You say potato..." the creature started before Gus cut him off.

"Just one question," Gus asked. "Am I currently providing you with nourishment?"

The creature in the stone appeared to be holding its breath during the extended period of silence. Scrios did his best, and Gus sensed the monster's discomfort in his thoughts. "Goddamn it!"

"Wait," the creature said calmly. "I recall you making a stop at the In-and-Out restaurant for two double-doubles gorilla style," Gus heard the order in his own voice transmitted in his head like a recording. "I didn't notice any sign of you feeling sadness for the cows becoming your burgers. Plus, let's be real. Like I said, today, I could just do nothing, and the human species would overwhelm my hunger daily just by being human. If I get peckish for a nice, tasty treat, all I need to do is have someone mis-gender someone else or violate their safe space and it's like apple pie à la mode. Three thousand years ago? Finding a sustenance among people who expected tragedy??? Now that was a challenge! Today? Pfft! I mean, one presidential election and look at you fucking monkeys."

Thoughts of his departed loved ones, Scrios's impossible lifespan, and the suffering he caused, overwhelmed Gus. Gus's jaw tightened. Having had enough, Gus said, "If all you had to do was nothing, and you had done nothing, we would not be here right now!" Again, silence met Gus's observation.

He spun around as if gathering a full view of the area. "This looks like as good a spot as any... Yup, looks like this at long last, is your graveyard asshole!" With a mixture of disdain and determination, Gus started unpacking and assembling the device, hoping it could finally destroy this thing.

The hollow artifact had the appearance and texture of gold. Experts confirmed it was an electrum construct, although not a conventional alloy. Upon receiving the electron microscope results, a metallurgist accused him of lying and alleged that it was data from a meteorite. The electron microscope readings revealed gold, silver, copper, iron, palladium, bismuth, and three unidentified elements.

"Either show it to me or shut the hell up," said Randy Cooper, his online metallurgist friend, "because this belongs in either a Marvel or Middle Earth universe, not our reality." Gus liked Randy.

"Randy, I would love to let you see it, but if I did, I would probably have to kill you." Randy did not know the irony of the joke but took it as if it must be some top-secret thing or something.

"Wait a sec, this isn't like little green men stuff, right?" Randy asked.

"No, nothing like that."

"Riiight," Randy said.

Over the last six months, Gus made various comedic attempts to destroy this artifact. To be honest, if this attempt didn't work, he wasn't certain anything less than launching it at the sun would be effective. Perhaps "Operation Frodo" involving an open caldera volcano was the only alternative?

His efforts thus far with fire, including forges and the acetylene torch technique, only resulted in heating the object until it glowed. The heat from the torch dissipated unnaturally fast, with no visible change in the object's malleability.

He tried heating it in an electric furnace to a white glow, then quickly plunged it into liquid nitrogen. The nitrogen erupted explosively, but no damage was done to the artifact.

He attempted to hit it with a hammer, but it remained unscathed. So, Gus tried a real big hammer... like a goddamn mechanized hydraulic hammer of Thor used to shape and cut girders... nothing.

When he combined the electric furnace, heating it until it glowed white and quickly striking it with a massive hydraulic hammer, finally he noticed a scratch and a small dent. He actually screamed in delight. Later, still smiling to himself after finally creating a lasting mark, his mind transitioned to the thought of explosives.

In a different attempt, Gus tried enough C4 to shoot the artifact 6 feet into the ground. He debated leaving it there, but he knew somehow, someone would find it and he had to ensure its destruction. After digging it up, it remained intact. It did, however, scuff it with another small abrasion on the metal cylinder, so that too gave him some hope.

Late one night five months ago, as Gus stayed in the string of awful hotels that took cash and asked no questions, a TV show caught his eye. He found himself engrossed in an old MythBusters episode on a vintage Zenith CRT TV with a digital converter. The beginning of an idea sparked in Gus's mind. It caused a smile to grow on his tired and bearded face. To evaluate its destructive effects, the show employed a shaped charge to penetrate a U.S. Army tank.

The episode started off by talking about some movie with Tom Hanks and a sticky bomb. In their typical fashion, they exceeded expectations to the point of ridiculousness. With his fists raised in the air, Adam Savage proudly paraded around the watch bunker as the shaped charge blast ripped through the dummy in the driver's seat. "Myth Confirmed!" yelled Adam with a geeky squeak of excitement.

The hotel TV, with a manufacture year as ancient as Gus, appeared to have a hidden message just for him. As MythBusters ended, the upcoming preview for the next show was a documentary on Oppenheimer and the development of the first nuclear bombs.

Gus's mind briefly drifted back to the current task at hand in the desert. He couldn't help but notice the irony of being hundreds of miles away from White Sands, now in a similar, desolate area in northern Nevada.

The day after MythBusters, Gus reached out to an old college friend using a disposable phone. At Western Carolina University, Jack, like Gus was involved with the ROTC program. Jack, his old friend, had gained a reputation on campus for his practical jokes in the dorms, many of which involved minor explosions. He, later becoming a demolitions specialist for a career in the Army, was... let's just say, a predictable outcome. Jack Caldwell's level of military commitment far surpassed Gus's.

They had reconnected in the past, when they unexpectedly met while attending a homecoming football game at WCU. To be honest, in those years at Western, the event was more of a home band performance with a miserable beat down of a football game surrounding it.

Gus searched the small notebook he kept in his bag and found Jack's contact information. When they talked, Gus steered the conversation towards the TV show he had seen with MythBusters and the Oppenheimer documentary. Bingo! Jack took control of the conversation.

Jack was absolutely obsessed with this subject of shaped charges and their use in nuclear weapons and had a wealth of knowledge about the physics involved. He talked about the technology employed in New Mexico in 1944, which primarily involved shaped charges like the ones on that Mythbusters episode. Jack described how one bomb specifically used a charge to fire an enriched uranium slug into a uranium core. He shared with Gus how he would regularly construct makeshift shaped charges now during his retirement, using smaller ones to blow up tree stumps, while doing side work for a landscaping company.

Jack laughed while describing how easy they were to make and shared how they got him arrested on a drunken Fourth of July night. Sensing his interest, he quoted a link to Gus with a step-by-step video which, two years before, resulted in his YouTube account getting suspended. Watching that video and thumbing through an old, dog-eared copy of The Anarchist Cookbook, a plan formed in Gus's mind.

Gus's design employed a shaped charge to push a 50-caliber depleted uranium slug and force it down the about 40-caliber hole that ran the length of the tube-like artifact, which contained the green crystal he believed to be preserving the essence of Scrios. He had an optimistic vision, likening it to splitting a log. "Let's raise a glass to hope!" Gus said, while enjoying a zero-calorie soda, toasting the drawing in his notebook.

Returning to the present, Gus turned his gaze to the cart he had hauled through the cold desert rain and snow squall. The planning in the notebook led to a load of close to 300 pounds, with some in a heavy backpack and the rest on a wheeled cart. The cart had transformed into a sled on the wet sand, which he pulled across three to four miles of hills and salt flat, constantly annoyed by the cart's wheels, "That keep getting clogged with goddamn MUD!!" he yelled in frustration as he kicked the useless wheel on the cart one last time.

Once assembled, Gus placed the artifact upright on the high grade layered steel base that measured 16 inches square and 2.5 inches thick. The base alone weighed about 180 pounds. A small steel, 3-inch nub of sanded rebar, stood up in the center, welded to the plate to hold the creature's tube vertical from the inside. The artifact that contained Scrios slid on to the sanded rebar with a satisfying click. The purpose of the shaped charge was to propel the slug into the tube, wreck everything in its path, and potentially destroy the plate of steel below.

His friend Jack had sheepishly reviewed his blueprints, "The key is to force the blast in one direction," and he thought Gus's plan would do that, "but you should bolt all the other metal structure pieces in place," he emphasized. Jack paused, and stared at him on the Skype screen with a troubled look on his face. "Are you, like, really building this?" Jack asked. "Because, if the D.U. slug passes through the steel plate, someone in China might receive a slightly radioactive colonic."

In an unconvincing bland tone, Gus replied, "Oh no. I just like designing crazy stuff like this."

In the northern Nevada desert, Gus removed from the backpack, a sandbag filled with 30 empty sandbags and a crappy old military shovel remake. "This piece of crap deserves a one-star review if I ever have the chance to write one up online." The job became more challenging when the shovel broke about eight bags in, and Gus's language turned just as expressive as his level of frustration.

After three hours, with two breaks to warm his hands in his armpits, the build was finally done. Through pure determination, he ignored the pleas and promises of power and wealth from Scrios. Even with the creature customizing Miley Cyrus music and making DJ call outs for mercy, Gus ignored Scrios, the wonder tube. Until that point, he did not know of Scrios' ability to make him hear other voices, but it made sense when he thought about it.

After the build was complete, he unpacked and inserted a new battery from his pocket and powered up the wireless detonator. Gus gathered the remains of his gear, specifically selecting the items he wanted to keep. He left the cursed wagon behind and incorporated it to further back the charge before leaving.

Gus moved back approximately 100 meters. Positioned well within the radio's three-mile detonator range, he prepared to activate the switch and hit the button. In his epic application to the Darwin Awards, he had a premonition of a loose bolt or shrapnel flying at him like a bullet. He mused, "How about we step back a bit more?"

As he retreated to 300 meters, Gus noticed that the ancient monster's voice had ceased in his mind and observed how the drizzle and light snowflakes seemed to create a private domed cloud surrounding the creature. "That motherfucker! No goddam way! That has to be freaking impossible," he said aloud as he paced back and forth, staring at it.

While again contemplating whether to press the button, Gus spotted a gentle slope in the ground about 50 feet further back, along with a dry stream bed at the base. He shrugged his shoulders and nodded to himself. Listening to his inner voice, he quickly moved towards the ditch. Even without the sandbags, previous test fires of smaller test models were not excessively loud. However, he was still glad that he had come all the way to this ancient desolate lakebed.

With dusk approaching, he took a moment and consulted his phone's GPS. Scanning for the ridge where, just beyond, his car was located, he felt reassured that he could make a speedy three-mile escape once he finished the job.

Settling into the ditch, Gus found amusement in his little trigger device. The red button had a flip up cover and a green light. "Just like MacGyver!" Peter's voice and maniacal laughter echoed in his head. He smiled and barked a small, sad laugh. Gus readied himself, "This is for you, Peter," and pushed the trigger. He attentively listened for the expected loud pop that would accompany the explosion as he pushed the button.

Chapter 1 - The Stone

The Red Sea 10,371 BC

Humans had held onto the stone since they found it, in a time before anyone could remember. Men had many names for it. Since its discovery, people have valued the green crystalline stone, starting when the first person touched it and felt a slight static shock.

Ka`hra, a humble elderly fisherman, made the discovery along the shores of the Red Sea. He discovered the stone a hundred centuries before Rome's rise. The nearly flawless green sphere held a peculiar cat's-eye-like inclusion, visible only from a certain angle because of a light-bending quantum anomaly it contained.

In a timeframe measurable in epochs, the stone patiently observed the world. It watched the ebb and flow of the oceans over millions of years as its environment vacillated between warmer and colder climates. The stone found the world interesting, basking in the sunlight or darkness, and witnessing its transformation. It did not need to change position, as centuries were irrelevant. However, when stimulated, the stone's perception of the world could change, making fast moving objects seem motionless. It was driven by a purpose for analyzing and finding solutions to complex problems.

When Ka`hra picked it up, the stone slowed down to notice him. It observed a laceration on the man's palm and began repairing the irregularity. It wasn't until the following morning when the man discovered the gash on his hand, resulting from a careless slip of his flint knife, had healed completely, leaving only a bloodstain on his woven tunic, where he had wiped the wound, as the only proof of the injury. He would have believed it was a dream if the blood hadn't been there to verify his recollection.

In order to verify his suspicion, he deliberately pricked his finger with the blade. As expected, it hurt, bled, but the wound didn't vanish. Following a normal healing progression, the nick scabbed over by the next day. The stone didn't fix the injury, as it silently judged the stupidity of the primate. Stupidity, it decided, would remain unresolved, as there was no solution to it.

Ka`hra placed the stone in his bag and kept it. He was certain the stone he found was extraordinary, unlike any other he had encountered, and it had somehow mended his injured hand overnight.

Many years passed before he had a mishap, slipping on a rock and falling into a ravine. He lost consciousness because of the sheer intensity of the pain. The skull fracture caused by the fall made losing consciousness potentially fatal. The pain in his leg was so intense he didn't notice hitting his head. Besides the pain, his leg was bent in a bizarre manner, featuring a new knee which seemed to face the wrong way halfway down his shin. As he prepared his mind for his own death, thoughts of his wife consumed him, knowing that she would never discover his fate.

When he woke, he found his heavy fur wrap covered in morning dew and felt no pain. When he examined his leg, he noticed it was unharmed, except for some bruising which had turned purple. The color completely disappeared by the afternoon. When he arrived back at his house, his beloved instantly pulled him in and clutched him to her. He had never been away unplanned for an entire night, and the world was savage and full of threats.

That night, the fisherman, stared at the stone and offered his thanks. Though silent, the stone found the man's appreciation perplexing. The stone simply fulfilled its purpose.

Since the parrot fish plucked it from the coral reef and ate it in the distant past, the stone's purpose has remained constant. Sensing the fish's sickness, it repaired the damage caused by parasites and expelled them from the ailing fish. The fish grew invigorated and swiftly swam away as the stone departed and found its way down into a tidal pool. The stone felt satisfied, even when the fish didn't express gratitude, because it didn't expect to be thanked.

After living for almost a century, Ka`hra outlasted all of his friends, who had lives less than half as long. In his last moments, his wife was by his side. While she believed their love was the reason for their longevity, the fisherman remembered nights when he placed a stone on her while she was ill with a fever, and she would wake up completely refreshed the following day. The stone approved of Ka`hra because of his kind and caring nature.

The stone had no recollection of its birthplace or birth time. It simply was, and had always been. It witnessed the evolution and rotation of galaxies before plunging into the water of a stunning blue planet. Solar years passed to the stone, as if they were the flickering of a small flame. Repairing things wasn't the stone's only purpose. It also regarded itself as a witness of the universe.

It had a fondness for puzzles and order, viewing broken processes simply as a disruption of that order. When the fisherman picked it up, it found the human fascinating. Its perception of this entire species shifted after meeting Ka`hra. Late in life, he shared the stone's blessing with others.

After Ka`hra, a succession of people followed who were beneficiaries of its help. One day, a female came into his existence. She spoke of the stone as though a deity had given it to her personally. She referred to its actions as mystical gifts given by the gods. The stone tolerated her, but it found her as a pretentious and tiresome example of this species, so it sped up his perception of the world, at once appreciative of the species ephemeral nature.

Long after the annoying woman brought the stone to the small village 30 human lives ago, humans moved it to a bustling city of white bricks. They put the stone on an elevated table in the spacious new building.

The stone answered the townspeople's plea for aid for the sick. They asked the stone to help those who had accidentally injured themselves, and it complied. Occasionally, it would meet individuals with much more severe wounds and mend them. Time to the stone passed in bursts as it sped up its perception to bypass the mundane. The building increased in size and the environment around the stone underwent alterations. They placed the stone on a soft pillow and enclosed it with a box made primarily of yellow metal with 79 electrons and a balanced number of protons.

The stone relished the shrine, and the puzzles offered to it by people who visited. While broken humans were the focus of the puzzles, farmers occasionally brought sick animals from the fields.

One day, they brought a pregnant woman, in a state of delirium, into the temple. Sanura's relationship with the stone became recognized the moment it touched her mother's abdomen. The stone became instantly connected to the baby the woman carried.

It detected that Sanura's mother was on the verge of dying when it contacted her, forcing it to swiftly unravel the mystery behind her injuries. Contemplating the complexity of this nested conundrum, the stone felt a newfound immediacy within itself. It was skilled at solving complex challenges, but it could not help but notice the mother who cradled Sanura, a name the stone sensed even before her mother bestowed it upon her days later. It was concerned how solving her mother's riddle might involve sourcing components from the child, which it deemed unacceptable. Therefore, it focused on solving Sanura's aspect first. It considered this value judgment anomaly as a unique occurrence in its history and marked the decision for future examination.

The stone was unaware how eagerly the mother would have agreed with the stone's priorities of saving her baby first, if she had known there was a choice of whom to spare. Without hesitation, she would prioritize her child's survival above her own, just like almost any mother would.

Both the structure and chemistry of the problems were intricate. Because of a severe infection, the mother was on the verge of expiring and her illness, was flooding the child with toxins. In both the mother and the baby, the stone resolved to address the infection and heal the lesions caused by toxins at the spiraling cord that connected them. It examined the toxins. It examined both the tissue and the causes. Out of the millions of possibilities, the stone pondered every decision it could make. It opted for a convoluted path which would secure the child's resolution and potentially pave the way for solving the mothers. It reversed the effects of the chemicals and repaired the damage mainly done to the child. The stone prevented the causes in the mother from happening again and guided Sanura towards the optimal path.

The stone became increasingly amazed as it explored the creatures, observing the disarray and confusion in their structure. It shocked the stone that life was possible with this much randomness and weakness. Suddenly a new understanding, an uncommon event it its billions of years, rippled across its consciousness.

In this creature's complexity, randomness and its rudimentary methods to sustain life and reproduce, the stone found magnificence. It saw an existence that had defied all reason to still be here. It referenced all of its knowledge of all the many puzzles it had solved over its existence on this planet and found a common thread of majesty, which caused it to make another note for future research.

The creatures of this beautiful blue planet were not here because they possessed the perfect design to thrive. Unlike the stone's design, they were neither rugged nor eternal. Their design did not enable them to exist among the stars in the universe as it did. Life flourished here despite its terribly fragile and clumsy design. The only thing life on this planet excelled at was surviving. Mistaking the adaptations for poor design, it realized the scars of life's solved puzzles were actually the building blocks of the diversity, populating every location of the blue planet with a multitude of creatures. The epiphany the stone had was as if it had been observing the night sky for a billion years, only to just now notice the brilliance of the stars.

It felt something for the first time while attempting to solve this puzzle, as great as any effort it had made before. Despite lacking any known capability for emotions and only being aware of them through witnessing humans, it inexplicably felt one, and its irrationality almost compelled it to reconstitute itself.

The connection it had with Sanura and its knowledge of the resulting devastation, stopped it from allowing the reconstitution to take place, as it would most likely turn this part of the planet into a barren wasteland and result in the loss of a life it now cherished.

That Sanura was kindred to it compelled the stone to address the early life issue she faced, and it improved the design of certain systems her body possessed. It questioned why Sanura had to deteriorate so fast, similar to

11

everything else on this planet. As a result, it deciphered the perplexity surrounding her health and implemented a modification that not only paused her aging during her prime years but also endowed her with extraordinary recuperative powers to bounce back from devastating injuries. By fixing her, the stone erased certain limiting choices which restricted her species.

Chapter 2

Khalpe 1622 BC, Hurrian Nation

As she matured, Sanura would regularly visit the temple, driven by her fascination with the spherical green stone. She heard from her mother about the stone's role in saving her life when she was born, but her mother couldn't recall all the details, as she was unconscious and struggling to survive herself.

Throughout the centuries, the stone saved countless lives. Many names were associated with it. According to lore, the oldest name was the Fisher Stone, believed to have originated in a western fishing village. It had another name, the Judgment Stone, given by those who believed it refused to help those who intentionally harmed themselves. A hundred years prior, the stone proved useless to a third wife of a nearby king who poisoned herself as her sole means of escape. The king, storming out of the Shrine of Damu where the stone was venerated, proclaimed it a forgery and demanded the death of the temple priest. As the king's guard pressed the dagger into the priest's heart, the soldier apologized, and he swiftly departed the defiled shrine. As the king left, he grabbed the stone and hurled it into the scrubland brush on the far side of the small plaza.

The tale recounts that someone quickly retrieved the stone and placed it back on the priest's lifeless form. Observers who were present that evening, much like during Sanura's rescue years later, recalled an unusual lightning like flash and saw the radiant green crystal rapidly turn dark when it touched his body. The individuals present shared stories about the strange green stone that seemed to blink like an eye. The healed priest wasted no time and resumed his daily rituals the next morning.

Having lost his wife the night before, the king discovered the priest had miraculously recovered and investigated further. The priest's wellbeing disturbed the king. He refused to believe it was the same man he'd ordered killed.

Afterward, he ordered his followers to never mention the shrine or the stone again. He never returned and ignored its existence.

The king's own demise occurred the following year, when an assassin took his life while he slept, and no one dared to bring him to the temple in hopes of intercession.

During that time, the stone noted how local kings changed with the seasons.

Growing up, Sanura considered the shrine as her home. As Salile, the priestess who had previously employed the stone on both her and her mother, aged, Sanura was now ascending to the position of lead priestess. Salile faced difficulties in her day-to-day activities as she grew older, grappling with their demanding nature and her own fatigue. She refused the help of the stone in her own ailments, seeing them as rites of passage into old age and as her own religious expression.

The stone resonated deeply with Sanura, revealing a powerful bond between them. Their communication didn't resemble a typical conversation. The understanding between them regarding their desires was like the realization of a fact, like the sky being blue on a cloudless day, and the knowledge that the other agreed.

The knowledge of the closeness she felt to the green, clear stone defined her adolescent life, motivating her to visit the shrine nearly every day. It wasn't about worshiping it; the stone was... her friend. She would have dreams about the stone, assisting others in different situations. She comprehended it. To the stone, healing people meant fulfilling a purpose by fixing what it deemed broken. Yet, there was a further understanding of the process by which something became damaged that the stone garnered.

If a creature inflicted harm to itself, the stone would acknowledge its choice and offer no aid.

Sanura comprehended the stone was not of this world and had traveled from the stars. She kept silent about what she knew, fearing negative responses. That knowledge was sensitive and could be sacrilegious.

The stone was fond of her and could detect her understanding. It regarded her as one of its own. In its role as kindred, the stone fixed any minor imperfections it came across in Sanura. People at the shrine discussed her ability to preserve her youthful appearance despite the challenges of time, aging, and extreme weather. Sanura grew worried about the safety of both herself and the stone because of others growing jealousy.

The stories about the stone caused envy and greed among many people. Regularly, a bandit group with dreams of wealth would arrive with a desire to possess the stone. There were skirmishes on the streets, and Sanura outsmarted thieves by replacing it with a green glass shard. Sometimes, she didn't have time to make a switch, and the thieves somehow could not find the stone. With no explanation, the stone stayed in its little gold box on the pillow even after the thieves had come and gone.

In a twist of fate, a thief, who received healing from the stone later in life, confessed to Sanura that he had once, when he was younger, planned to steal it from her shrine. He confessed to sneaking into the shrine and concluded it wasn't worth risking his life.

A stone occupied the spot where the gem should have been. He firmly believed, however, that the stone in the sacred spot was not The Stone of Abar-Nahara, as his kingdom's inhabitants knew it.

Upon seeing it, the thief found it devoid of any shine or uniqueness, making it not worth the consequences of theft. "It just looked too plain to be such a great thing and did not even appear to be clear." The green orb he observed at the public ceremony, which he had planned to pilfer, was a far more impressive spectacle compared to the simple one he stumbled upon in the shrine that night.

When he returned to his tribe and informed them that the legend was a lie and the object was simply a rock, they initially ridiculed him and accused him of being a coward. In the end, they came to believe him because of his incredibly persuasive portrayal of its worthlessness. Now, viewing it from the eyes of an old man, all he could do was shake his head and feel grateful for the blessings it brought him.

While the residents of the town grew older, Sanura remained visibly youthful. Even as her childhood friends grew old, she maintained her youthful appearance. People started gossiping about her unnatural youth and spreading rumors of dark practices, polluting the temple and staining her reputation.

In the middle of the night, she woke up with absolute certainty after having a dream. She understood the stone was calling for her to take it and leave this town. All she knew was to journey northwest at night, disregarding trade roads and opting for hazardous routes through difficult terrain.

From exhaustion, she slept nearly devoid of dreams during the day and woke up revitalized every evening. Before her departure, she gathered water skins she needed for traveling, along with a generous supply of dried fish and flat bread. She took the eight silver coins and two blankets she had.

Sanura donned a dark gray virgin veil outfit as she departed from her home. Society condemned stopping a woman dressed in such a way, and she wore a full-face cover for anonymity. Upon reaching the shrine, she defied the actions of previous thieves and swiftly took hold of the stone, carefully tucking it away in her pouch as the city slept under the faint light of the waxing moon.

As intended, she departed the city and headed northwest. Unnoticed by anyone, she sneaked into and out of the shrine, and the guards of the camps around the city were oblivious to the lone woman walking past them that night.

Chapter 3

1580 BC, Hurrian Nation, Northwest of Aleppo

The night swallowed Sanura and the stone. They lived like traders, constantly traveling for more than a hundred winters. They moved around and never settled in one place for long. While traveling, the stone became conscious of its name, given by Sanura. The clear green stone embraced the name Enki. Throughout the centuries, humans struggled to comprehend the profound essence of the stone and gave it countless names. Yet, this was the sole name it would ever adopt.

In order to protect Sanura, Enki cautiously advised when and whom to help. Attaining wealth or notoriety was never their motivation for healing. Instead, they operated in private, away from the gaze of crowds.

Legends of miracles filled the land, and those who falsely claimed responsibility for the healing of the stone faced no challenge from Sanura. The charlatans significantly aided in Sanura's disappearance from memory in her homeland. Only once did she willingly disclose her identity to an old, trusted friend.

Many years after she left the temple, she ran into an old man in a marketplace. When he saw her, he approached, leaning heavily on a walking stick, and quietly asked, "Sanura... is that you?"

What had to be his granddaughter, quickly intervened and apologized. "I'm so sorry. He does this."

Sanura waved her off. "It's not a problem," as she turned to the weathered bald man. "What is your name, old man?"

"Sanura... is that you? It is me Cebrail, from the temple in Khalpe. By the gods, you have not changed at all," as he reached out cupping the air near her face, but not actually contacting her as tears welled in his right eye.

Glancing around for prying eyes, she led the old man and his granddaughter to the side near a building where a merchant sold hot tea. They sat on the carpets, spread by the merchant, and spoke while they sipped tea. Sanura asked the granddaughter if she would find bread for them to eat and gave her two small coins.

When she left, Sanura leaned into the Cebrail, "Of course I recognize you, old friend." As she reached out and held his hand. She explained to him her leaving and the need for his discretion. While she held his hand, Enki set about relieving some of his ailments and assuring that cognitively, he could maintain their secret.

When Cebrail's granddaughter returned, she found him smiling, his eyes filled with a vibrant sparkle. There was something about his smile that made him appear younger than she had ever seen him before.

Sanura politely excused herself and said goodbye after enjoying tea and bread together. Cebrail and his granddaughter also rose and turned to leave. It was immediately apparent to his granddaughter that he had forgotten his walking stick, and she returned to retrieve it for him. For her, he used it as they walked through town, but it was not the necessity it had been that morning.

Years after seeing Cebrail, who was just a boy of seven when she escaped Khalpe; Sanura grew confident that she had surpassed the lifespan of anyone who might have sought her. The stone's existence morphed into a fabled myth within a land saturated with sorcery and old wives' tales. Throughout her unexpectedly long life, she had to leave cities more than once to avoid drawing attention to her fame or Enki's powers. However, on some occasions, they found themselves presented with opportunities that tempted them to abandon caution. The opportunities resulted in Sanura rising reluctantly to positions of immense power, time and time again.

Chapter 4

1252 BC, Hittite Empire

With 300 years and ten lifetimes behind her as a traveling healer, teacher, and midwife, Sanura journeyed farther north and to the west. Now, acting as an acolyte in a temple devoted to the goddess Kamrusepa, the revered deity of magic and healing, nestled in the small city of Kanesh within the influential Hittite Empire. The disguise that membership in the goddess' temple granted Sanura was nothing less than divine, giving her the ability to blend in seamlessly with society. Even if Enki's knowledge did not include any mention of such beings called gods, Sanura proceeded cautiously, her fear of angering them outweighing her skepticism.

Over the course of his three centuries spent with Sanura, Enki fully embraced the concept of emotions and their inherently irrational calculations. It brought the stone great joy to realize its fascination with Sanura's superstitions, and Enki was grateful that it hadn't reconstituted on the day of her birth. Despite expecting a negative impact, the stone discovered that the emotions actually granted it a deeper insight into understanding the motivations of the planet's sentient inhabitants.

With a casual understanding of lust and hatred, the absurdity of war became increasingly clear. With a deep understanding of love, the first emotion Enki experienced upon meeting Sanura, it came to comprehend the profound instinct a mother has to safeguard her child, even at the sacrifice of her own.

Enki concluded that contrary to what it had expected, the opposite of love was not an emotion, but the absence of caring. Hate was the shadow cast where the light of love failed to shine. It was the apathy, not caring at all. Hate was indifference. Accepting it as such allowed Enki more clarity in his calculations.

For billions of years, Enki lived a life devoid of emotions, but now, for the past 300 years, it had experienced the depth and complexity of some human feelings. This observation gave Enki appreciation for what it originally thought of as simple primates, slightly smarter than other species on the planet. The stone now saw a species fatally limited by their tribal ways, but beautiful in its complexity.

As an acolyte of Kamrusepa, Sanura's compassionate work with the sick and injured did not go unnoticed by the leaders. Her advanced understanding of methods and innovative practices astounded the priestesses, leading to a significant surge in the number of followers, and more importantly, paying tributes.

In response to the request for an explanation of her knowledge and methods, she provided a thorough and confident explanation that convinced many individuals to believe that Kamrusepa granted her divine guidance.

This belief was so strong that it led to the defiance of all customs in order to appoint her as a priestess. At this early stage of her journey to fame, she could already perceive the first signs of recognition in people's eyes as they encountered her while walking down the streets. During a single night, the temple witnessed a miraculous cure of a young man who suffered from a debilitating disease his entire life.

The rumors of the miracle spread like migrating sparrows, reaching every corner of the countryside. In just a week, the line of families in need swelled to a hundred strong outside the temple. A month later, the town found itself inundated with pilgrim encampments.

As the crowd swelled, so did the number of criminals who saw an opportunity to exploit the vulnerable. The powerful figures in the kingdom couldn't help but take notice, but it was the growing jealousy of the temple's leadership that posed a more perilous threat to Sanura. The presence of the green gem she carried had not gone unnoticed, either. Among those she aided, there were tales of a radiant green stone that would transform in hue when it came into contact with the afflicted, its brilliance returning as the person recovered.

Enki's experiments revealed Sanura could channel its healing with the touch of her hand, as long as she possessed the stone on her person. To mitigate the rumors of the stone, they adopted that method and Sanura only met privately with the suffering from that point forward.

However, the gossip persisted as other temple members grew envious. The murmurs increased in volume as Sanura persistently requested privacy while assisting those in need.

Her remarkable results outpaced the resentment over the ensuing year. Soon, her fame spread far and wide, reaching even the royal palace and attracting pilgrims from neighboring kingdoms who arrived in caravans. The city, filled with hopeful souls seeking a miracle, prospered and developed before her eyes.

It became painfully apparent to Sanura that she had overstayed her welcome one fateful night, as an assassin unexpectedly slit her throat, ending her life for the very first time.

That evening, after dinner, she walked into her room and, surprisingly, found it was darker than usual. The strangeness of the sashes being pulled on all of her windows had just sunk in, when she noticed the sky still had a faint glow towards the west. It was in that moment that a sudden and intense line of fire sliced across her neck, immediately followed by two impeccably accurate stabs to her chest, piercing her heart.

As she lay on her back, a feeling of fear washed over her while warm blood pooled beneath her. When, out of nowhere, a bearded assassin materialized and, without warning, he leaned over her and spat right in her face. Oblivious to the fact, or perhaps indifferent, he continued his search on her, disregarding the fact that the bleeding from her throat had already subsided. Considering the stabs to her heart, it is not surprising. Perhaps this was the expected outcome, Sanura thought.

Her calm, "Why did you kill me?" completely startled the assassin. In his panic, he let out a piercing screech while instinctively leaping backwards. Trembling in fear, he cowered in the corner, desperately fumbling for the blade, while the woman, her body drenched in blood, slowly rose to her feet and locked eyes with him. His fatal mistake happened when he wrongly estimated his escape by running and diving through her east window, but he soon realized that the window overlooked a treacherous ravine filled with sharp rocks, instead of being just one level above the street like the window he used to enter.

While her question was sincere and not meant to be frightening, she acknowledged that it might have taken him by surprise. As the assassin soared through the air, she overheard his profanity laced last prayer when he realized his error. The noise he produced upon hitting the rocks below evoked memories for her, reminding her of the women dropping wet linens onto the rocks while they were washing them. His response to the impact was permanent silence. She briefly entertained the idea of going back to the ravine and questioning him, but ultimately reasoned that it would be more prudent to disappear again. Having learned from the experience, she acknowledged the need to put effort into maintaining a balanced and controlled level of attention in the future.

As she ventured further west, she not only learned new languages but also discovered a newfound sense of fame in a land characterized by many islands on the western side of the Aegean Sea.

Chapter 5

947 BC, Hellas (Greece)

In Hellas, Sanura lived for centuries. Through the lifetimes there, occasionally she found herself entangled in conflicts, and as a result, it required her to become skilled at using the short sword which was designed for her. Often, in her other hand, she carried a small golden scepter. A blacksmith named Dionys on the island of Lemnos in the Aegean Sea crafted the sword and a small scepter designed to house Enki.

Enki provided great detail, conveying through Sanura the exact composition of metals needed to create the electrum ingots. These ingots were crucial to the construction of both the scepter and the sword. Together, Enki through Sanura collaborated with the talented blacksmith on building a custom forge, capable of generating the precise heat needed to forge the items. She also shared Enki's knowledge of a more efficient technique for handling and tempering the new metal with the blacksmith. The skeptical Dionys was slow to adopt the methods until he saw the effects.

People would say that decades later, the sword and scepter she carried were gifts from Hephaestus, the god of blacksmiths, forged on Mount Olympus. Their quality was exceptional. Yet, in reality, their origin, apart from Enki's influence, had no supervision from the Gods.

With its completion, the sword boasted an edge that surpassed all others of its era, leaving Sanura in awe. Going beyond the blacksmith's efforts, Enki thoroughly examined and perfected the metals to ensure their exceptional quality at the atomic level. The golden metal short sword was a marvel of craftsmanship, designed to be both strong and lightweight. It was immune to any damage, as nothing yet created by man could leave a mark on its surface.

With each swing of the sword, Sanura improved. Over time, her well-practiced hands turned the sword into a blur of lethal power, a testament to her lifetimes of cumulative training. The traveling story tellers sang of a formidable woman warrior and spun legends. In every skirmish she engaged, her wounds mended instantly, a divine favor given upon her by the Gods.

Made from the same metal as the sword, the scepter had a beautifully ornamental design that enhanced its overall elegance. As time passed, people began referring to the short tube with the green gem inside as "The Eye of Asclepius" because of its striking similarity to a serpent's eye. The artisan placed the stone inside an electrum gold tube with great care to enhance the appearance of the inclusion, resulting in an eyelike shape with an elongated pupil.

A single serpent lazily coiled its way counterclockwise from the bottom, decorating the outside of the short electrum scepter. By holding it in her hands, Enki could remedy any ailment, provided that the stone acknowledged the necessity.

Enki approved of the design of the rod because the metal composition did not negatively affect his ability to see the world around. The metal alloy's makeup provided an excellent conductor for the stone's powers. After completion, Enki's further modifications improved the metals durability, infusing it with otherworldly elements the stone had encountered throughout the universe in its timeless existence.

The scepter provided a convenient way to transport the stone during times of need. The Eye of Asclepius, with its appearance and effectiveness, transformed Sanura's standing in the region, elevating her to a divine status.

She would always lend her support to causes she believed in. Doing that resulted in her gaining more friends and favor from people in power. Across the centuries, she established schools to teach the natural healing techniques and weapon skills she gained over her first millennium.

Hellas was the ideal setting for her as it abounded with incredible narratives of Gods coexisting with humans, and with Enki's help, she immersed herself in to these legends.

Chapter 6

Early Summer, 517 BC, The School of Tactics and Combat near Opus Locris (West Central Greece)

Once more, Sanura realized that her fame had spread far and wide, reaching every corner of the known world. This time, however, people revered her more than being perceived as a usurper of fame. Her friendships with entire generations of families had grown so strong that they were indistinguishable from blood family bonds.

While she was at her school near Opus, the second such school she established, a man with pale skin and strange clothing approached her. In his company were a few others like him. The person leading the group towards her was a scholar she had been friends with for a decade.

The scholar stepped up and explained that his companions were wanderers from a faraway land in need of her help. "These men have traveled a great distance seeking you by name. They wish to plead for your help. Although their tongue is strange, their leader's extensive travels have allowed us to share a similar second language. If you would like, I can help in the conversation, or I could just tell them to go away if that suits you."

Sanura raised her eyebrows and looked at the sky. "While this is not ideal, they have traveled a long way. If I need to send them away, at least I should provide them with a proper reason. However, I need time to prepare, and they also look tired. Take them to my home and tell my house servant Damili to provide them a place to bathe and rest. Tell her to slaughter a goat and arrange a large dinner for this evening. I will finish here, and we'll share food tonight and listen to their needs."

The scholar nodded to her, "As you wish," before guiding the group towards her home.

At the end of her day, she returned home, and her servants helped her bathe. She dressed appropriately for dinner and headed to the outdoor dining area with a view of the distant, dark blue sea. A tall individual with auburn hair spoke as the leader of the band of travelers. He didn't quite blend in because of his towering height, but he was well groomed and wearing clean, locally provided clothes, in which he seemed comfortable.

As Hamish, the leader of this odd band of travelers, conversed with Leos the scholar, she noted with curiosity the leader's strange eyes, the color a rare sight in this region, which echoed the deep blue of the sea behind him.

Enki studied the language used by the leader when he spoke to the scholar, as it contained words and syllables that had a strangely familiar sound and cadence.

Within moments, Enki deciphered a partial understanding of it. The leader's words to his own men were stranger still. It was almost as if he was gagging on his own tongue. Enki observed their conversation; his focus fixed on deciphering and cross-referencing the complex code of their native language as the leader translated to his men.

The conversation traversing three languages, led by the leader known as Hamish and Leos, moved at a sluggish pace. Hamish came from a far-off island in the north, where winter brought freezing rain and snowy landscapes. His words painted a picture of a faraway land, a place devoid of any cultural richness like that around her, bringing back memories of the places she experienced centuries ago, across the vast Aegean.

Out of the shadows, a group of servants appeared, balancing enormous platters filled with succulent meat and vibrant, freshly harvested vegetables. They served wine by pouring it from large jars into goblets. In the mutual language the scholar used to translate, Sanura suddenly said, "First we eat," with her voice filled with anticipation. The scholar and the leader of the travelers exchanged wide-eyed glances, astonished by her sudden fluency.

The visitors appeared to have not eaten in ages, as they feasted voraciously and eagerly sipped their wine, prompting Sanura to signal the servants to dilute the wine with water.

Once dinner was over, they carried on with their slow, engaging conversations. Throughout the meal, Enki attentively listened to the travelers, slowly gaining a rudimentary understanding of their language. The more the travelers spoke, whether to each other or to themselves, the stone's ability to understand them improved. When the stone's understanding reached a conversational minimum level, Sanura closed her eyes and felt a sense of enlightenment wash over her, like a warm embrace. As if by magic, the side conversations held deeper meaning, providing valuable insights into the situation at hand.

One man in the back leaned over to his fellow traveler and asked, "That woman is a god?" to which the other replied, "She is beautiful enough that I would gladly serve her anything she asked me to" with a lecherous glare.

Sanura looked at the first man, suddenly speaking fluently in his native language, and emphasized, "While some here may perceive me as a deity, I assure you, I am not." She turned to the second man, raising her eyebrows as she asked, "What exactly do you offer?" As all conversations abruptly ceased, the clatter of a falling cup echoed through the room, its contents spilling onto the table.

Hamish, with a glare that could ignite flames, cast a quick look over his shoulder before refocusing on Sanura. "I deeply regret their stupidity and offer my apologies. After months of walking to your land, and subsequent weeks to reach here, they are extremely tired. We ask that you refrain from judging our request based on their juvenile actions." Convinced of her divine origin, Hamish pleaded desperately. His companions, who had chided him about this quest based on a traveling trader's story, were now silent and in awe of this woman who inexplicably spoke their native tongue.

The scholar had a feeling of impotence wash over him as Sanura spoke in the travelers' native language, leaving Leos clueless about the conversation. Seeing his anxiety, Sanura assured him she would give him a summary later. Smiling, he shook his head and glanced at the servant in the corner, signaling for more wine by tapping his cup.

The more Hamish spoke, the more Enki realized some words shared origins it was familiar with, making the language clearer to him and therefore, Sanura.

Hamish recounted a narrative about his family and how they started from humble beginnings. With his encyclopedic knowledge of his family history, spanning hundreds of years, he captivated the audience with his powerful speaking skills. The origin of his tale dated back to when a young woman named Srene, an ancient ancestor, met Dearn, a boy who was nearly a man, and they created a family.

Sanura's keen eye for inconsistencies found something that troubled her. Hamish showed an unusually profound understanding of Srene's story. He talked about the curse that Srene had made, which resulted in the creature's creation. That's when Sanura put a stop to him.

"How did you gain knowledge of her inner thoughts and feelings?" Sanura asked.

"I should warn you; this is going to sound strange," he responded. "Despite appearing human, the curse has transformed the creature into a disturbing caricature of a man, causing unease to anyone who lays eyes on it. I'm unsure if even you, a deity, can defeat this elusive trickster or demon. His power to twist the brain didn't affect Lil, the creature's sister, or her bloodline, for some unknown reason. When Lil saw him, she somehow could glimpse into his soul and comprehend the toll it had taken on those who encountered him. She witnessed Scrios tormenting their neighbors and its insatiable desire for destruction and pain. In an instant, Lil gained unwanted knowledge and memories just by looking into the beast's eyes. Neither she nor the creature understood why it had no control over her." Hamish concluded.

23

She probed further, seeking any discrepancies in the story regarding her other siblings. Wearing a sincere expression of disgust, Hamish said, "They had all passed before he was... hatched?" Sanura nodded in approval and he continued speaking.

For an hour, Hamish listed names in previous generations, and their significance, and how they eventually led up to him. Following Lil's encounter with her younger brother Scrios, they left the land of the smaller island to the west of their current home, commonly known as, "the Island of Eire," Hamish said. "The creature had survived and ruled the land through countless generations there after my family left."

"Just a moment," Sanura interrupted him. "How many years did he survive? And now his heirs carry on his foul rule?"

Hamish stopped and had a drink from his cup. "Goddess, not his descendants. He has survived for over 20 generations, nourishing himself on the suffering of his subjects and nearby communities, steadily extending his dominion like a festering wound. When he gets to the water, we worry he will cross over into our island. Sometimes we, the blood relatives, can feel his existence. The torment we experience while sleeping is worsening, because he is becoming stronger or possibly getting closer. People who flee from that land sometimes report that an immortal ruler, called The Blue King, is inflicting torture on his own subjects and exerting control over large expanses of land. He had a single meeting with a neighboring king, and following that encounter, the king willingly surrendered his lands and wife to him. Before heading to his own keep, he carelessly disemboweled her in the courtyard of the neighboring town and ordered her body to be untouched until the carrion was done with her, as a symbol of his authority in his new kingdom." Hamish finished as the men who traveled with him nodded in solemn agreement.

When their evening reached its conclusion, Sanura asked, "What is it you wish from me?" Unsure of his meaning as she observed as Hamish placed his open hands, palms up, on the table.

"Traders from all over the world travel and spread stories about you, even in our distant corner of the world. These stories are so fantastic; they appear as if a child imagined them. There are many stories circulating about your leadership and exceptional skills in battle. Ever since we arrived in your lands, people have been praising you as an excellent teacher of weaponry. As a small clan, we require these essentials at the very least. We would greatly appreciate any help you can offer. Within our ranks, we have individuals whom we believe possess the bloodline of Lil, and we can transform them into troops and leaders. We believe that Lil's memories show that her presence prevented him from influencing her family to the distance near a bow's shot. If we can face his army on equal ground, we believe victory is within our reach... with your help. There's no doubt that his intention is to bring about the destruction of our family. We believe that the only reason for his slow border expansion is his fear of us. If he finds out where we are, we are certain that his plan is to kill us all. With no family blood to limit him, he will be unrestrained and released upon the entire world." Hamish said.

"I want to see you and your men on the training field at my school," Sanura announced. "Tomorrow at sunrise. This will allow me to assess your skills and evaluate your equipment." She excused herself and retired for the night.

Chapter 7

Early Summer, 517 BC, The School of Tactics and Combat near Opus Locris

It took hours before Sanura finally fell asleep in her bed. She reflected upon the conflicts waged against men who claimed divine favor, as well as those fought against individuals likened to beasts. All of them had been men, defeated on the field of battle or negotiated with, when the confrontations reached their conclusion.

The notion of an actual mythical creature existing ironically challenged the immortal woman's thousand years of experience. It also exhilarated her, while sparking questions of her own battle strategy against such a foe. She had faced assaults in every conceivable manner. However, the concept of something that could sway her mindset and alienate her friends with a simple gaze left her perplexed and curiously anxious. Enki imbued her mind with an awareness of the unfathomable darkness that exists in the universe. The darkness can take on a physical form and gain sentience. Enki had enlightened her about these enigmatic dark pools in the universe, and how the stone avoided them after his first encounter.

In order to remove the taint of the dark creatures' touch in such a place, Enki had to go through the process of self-reconstitution, lighting the night sky of some distant planet momentarily like a star before reassembling.

Sanura's thoughts wandered as she regarded the blue creature in her mind, realizing that despite its age of nearly 500 winters, it was still a playful youngster in her mind. The creature had not reproduced, just like her, either by choice or inability. Even though she had experienced love in the past, it seemed incredibly cruel to encounter again the sudden and devastating absence of someone as cherished and ephemeral as this individual had been. Her understanding of not having children was that Enki's healing techniques had prevented it, and she was aware of his strong aversion to parasites. Though she relied on him for quick healing, she could recover from almost anything on her own, albeit slowly and often with considerable pain. Perhaps, she reflected, someone else could still kill her without his intervention, but she was uncertain.

Chapter 8

Fourteen days before the Summer Solstice, 517 BC, The School of Tactics and Combat near Opus Locris

As the sun rose in the morning sky, she was delighted to discover that the travelers had assembled and were waiting for her on the training grounds. She noticed them loosening their shoulders and popping their knuckles as she got closer. As she walked up to their leader, she could feel the intensity of their gaze upon her. "Hamish?" Sanura asked. "Are you the most accomplished one?"

"While I'm confident in my abilities, I must admit that if I had to select someone from this group, Brill would be my top choice, even though he is not a blood relative."

As Hamish pointed, her gaze fell upon the one who had embarrassingly pledged to "serve her anything she asked," during dinner. Brill hesitantly raised his hand, giving a nervous half wave. "Well, do you think you could serve me with a single touch of your blade before it hits the ground?" She asked Brill, her voice filled with curiosity.

"But I'm afraid," Brill confessed, his eyes filled with concern. "What if I harm you?"

Sanura smiled and spoke with the voice of a young girl, "I'm scared too." Her once innocent smile transformed into a sinister grin, taunting him with, "scared I might irreparably embarrass you". The men surrounding the training grounds heard her and began laughing.

Brill extracted the bronze sword from the scabbard, made of the skin of some black furry animal. Seeming to struggle under its weight, he released the scabbard and dragged the sword tip through the sand, as if it was too heavy for him. Upon entering the circle that someone crudely scratched into the dirt, Brill abruptly became a flash of motion. The commotion suddenly halting almost immediately, when Brill's blade skittered across the sand. He walked over to where it lay and retrieved it, his brows furrowed in confusion while Sanura patiently waited. In a more subdued manner, he entered the circle, his expression tinged with a touch of bewilderment.

Once more, she uttered the word, "Again," prompting Brill to spring into action.

As the sword slipped from his grasp and hit the ground, Brill soon followed, cushioned by Sanura's firm grip on his arm. She twisted the thumb on his sword hand, causing him discomfort and illustrating the reaction to the pressure that caused him to drop his weapon, before helping him get back on his feet. She had not made a single movement to unsheathe her sword.

"That is some magic," Brill said with a mix of irritation and admiration.

Hamish grinned, "This feels just like dodging a horse's kick, only to witness your friend taking the full force of it to their chest." laughter lacing his words.

Sanura spoke and steered the conversation with a serious tone. "I can teach you various fighting techniques, and you can share your newfound skills with others. Additionally, I can teach you about the various edible herbs I've encountered during my travels. You can find many of them in any location, but you should bring others along from here for your travel back. Keep in mind that becoming proficient in any of these skills takes time and attempting them without sufficient training can cause serious injury or death. I can speed up the learning process some. I possess the knowledge to teach you both battle tactics and war strategies you can seamlessly integrate. Mastering these subjects will be a long-term endeavor as well, spanning several years of learning and growth."

"We have little time left," Hamish remarked, "maybe just days. We need to begin our travel back by the next full moon to beat the winter."

Sanura focused intently on his eyes, "That is why I'm going to come with you. I will need the additional days you have to hand over classes here, gather proper supplies and porters, and assemble a group of warriors that already know my tactics and skills. While I will aid and mentor you, if you desire my presence, these individuals I introduce will act as your commanders during times of conflict and will oversee the training of any extra recruits you provide. This morning, even before the sun had risen, I sent out runners, expecting your positive response. While we wait for them, we'll dedicate our efforts to teaching Brill how to maintain a firm grasp on his sword, minimizing the instances of it slipping from his hand," her voice filled with amusement, and even Brill joined in with laughter. "Additionally, I would like to further examine and converse about your strategies, seeking to glean insights from your expertise and integrate them into a plan."

"At this time," Hamish supplied, "we don't possess any information regarding when or where Scrios' attack will occur. We just know that one day it will happen."

"Well, after thorough preparation and training," Sanura commented, "we will choose a battlefield that suits our strengths. In the between time, we will try to avoid him until we are ready."

Chapter 9

Two days before the Summer Solstice, 517 BC, The School of Tactics and Combat near Opus Locris

They had trained every day at the break of dawn and continued until noon. Sanura would not let them touch their swords. Every lesson she gave for the first week focused on throwing an opponent and maintaining their sense of balance. In order to train their bodies, she gave them a variety of exercises to practice and master.

She spent the afternoons honing their distance weapons skills with slings, javelins, and bows, feeling the weight of each weapon and experiencing the satisfying release as they hit their targets. Two soldiers accompanying Hamish revealed their personal bows, typically reserved for hunting. At first, Sanura had low expectations because of the simple construction of the weapons; but her opinion quickly changed when she witnessed their impressive range. The large, old, wooden bows also had an impressive accuracy, easily capable of hitting targets up to 300 feet away, and with a full pull, they could launch heavier arrows much further. She introduced them to smaller compact bows, which were not made from a single piece of wood. Artisans locally used a combination of layered wood, animal bone, and horn to craft these bows instead. They used careful precision to glue the pieces together and tightly wrap them with sinew. The wood used in the traveler's bows caught Sanura's attention, and Enki evaluated the wood's composition while she held it. With her smaller, more compact bows, she could engage in battle with remarkable speed, yet the long wooden bows caused a shift in the strategy in her head, with their unmatched accuracy and extended reach.

Once the bow lesson concluded, the weapons master taught them how to maintain the smaller bow, with her translating the instructions. Working with each weapon and the repeated reinforcement of their upkeep implied the lesson of responsibility. The repeated daily gatherings led to increased comfort in the knowledge gained by the foreign soldiers.

During the second day, several men, unfamiliar faces to the travelers, jogged into the school and greeted Sanura. Sanura introduced them to the visitors. During workouts, each of these men began working with Hamish and his men one on one, using sign language primarily to instruct during sparring. Throughout the lessons, they would demonstrate proper techniques in a slow, intentional manner while searching the face of the student for a sign of recognition.

The lessons carried on for 15 days. Sanura fulfilled her promise and educated them about safe and beneficial plants found locally, such as the eliá tree's bitter tasting fruit. She explained the need to process specific local plants in order to make them edible. One of Hamish's men related that to acorn nuts needing to be soaked.

Over the next three weeks, she organized a caravan with enough donkeys that two people could take turns riding. She had wicker walled carts fastened to oxen that held dried food, water skins, various items and weapons required for their expedition. The most impressive act she accomplished, however, was assembling a group of almost 50 loyal former students, along with half that number of porters and servants to accompany them.

Hamish's heart filled with worry as he observed the assembled caravan, prompting him to engage in a serious conversation with Sanura. "I don't know how we will compensate you for this. This is far greater support than we ever expected."

"If the creature is indeed what you say it is, it falls to us to stand with you in its path and prevent harm to your family and others. I still hope that others are on the way, who I have not heard from yet. If so, they will catch up as I am leaving instructions for them here at the school."

The following morning, they embarked on an epic journey that was estimated to take three to four lunar cycles. Throughout their journey, they faced a diverse range of terrains, but they navigated through them all with remarkable ease and encountered surprisingly little resistance from the kingdoms they traveled through.

As expected, the weather presented a constant challenge. They dedicated time to maximize their hunting efforts and strategically used snares at night to supplement their provisions. To prepare for the cold weather that they were certain would come, they diligently scraped and tanned furs.

Throughout the march, Sanura took it upon herself to motivate her personal soldiers and staff members, urging them to dedicate their efforts towards learning at least some of the language of Hamish's men. She offered her support in improving their vocabulary and conversational skills. Effective communication was essential for the commanders and experienced soldiers to lead in battle, making their first words and phrases learned important. Sanura reassigned her countrymen who had difficulty with the guttural language of the north to support roles that required less communication.

While journeying, particularly in the first fortnight, their ranks swelled to nearly a hundred warriors, among whom was one of Sanura's oldest friends,

Ameatus. He was one of her cherished former students. Having retired long ago, he had created his own thriving school with the support of Sanura, grounded in her innovative principles of warfare.

Ameatus was too old for this type of adventure, but no one there would dare tell him. His experience in training, leading and coordinating battles was far too useful to turn away. As he rode up on his majestic horse, the sound of cheers erupted from those who recognized him. Ameatus embracingly waved their cheers away like a distasteful scent and dismounted beside a wagon laden with supplies. He placed his large pack on the pile and lashed his horse to the wagon, dusted off his hands after the effort, and walked with the rest of the caravan.

He greeted his friends and seemed thrilled to be off his mount. As he walked, one of his old friends jeered at him, comparing his gait to that of a pregnant woman birthing a Titan. The laughter of the group echoed throughout the area. "That is only because I still have my balls. Perhaps you would like to help me carry them with your strong back." Ameatus replied.

Sanura walked towards Ameatus and embraced him, and she introduced him to Hamish, "Old friend, let me introduce you to this man," she took the time to translate into each's native language. First Greek and again in the guttural voice of the Northmen.

To Ameatus, she promised she would share details during their rest stops on the journey to Hamish's homeland. Ameatus turned and shook the man's hand in greeting.

After months of arduous walking, fording rivers, and scaling mountains, they arrived at the tumultuous and frigid shores of the sea. They stumbled upon a tiny fishing village where they could only find small boats, guaranteeing a treacherous crossing, accommodating a maximum of two or three individuals.

Sanura turned to her old friend Ameatus, his calloused hands a testament to his family's boat making heritage. In the distance, the woods stood tall and imposing along the shore near the fishing village. He turned towards his countrymen, his voice filled with authority as he barked out orders. "The sea is our home, boys, and she calls to us. I need at least 30 straight, tall trees as far around as two men can reach. I need ten men to assemble cordage and ten more to make us pitch... lots of it." Ameatus turned to Sanura. "We will need tools. Do we have any?" Seeing the blank look on her face, he continued, "If not, we will need to see if we can trade for some. That is a good job for the North Men."

"When can we expect to have a boat that can accommodate all of us and our supplies for crossing?" Sanura asked.

"All of us at the same time?" Ameatus asked, "Never. I can build something that won't insult Poseidon which we can use to ferry us across in smaller numbers, if we have tools and the right materials, and if he grants us clear weather, in about two weeks, maybe three," looking to the sky as if thinking complex thoughts. "I thought we could see the land on the far side when the morning was clear and from a higher vantage point. That implies a reasonable distance, although if we are seeing mountain tops, it would be much further."

"The Northmen assured me that the far side had higher land, but not mountains," Sanura assured, "similar to the raised areas we see here."

"The currents appear powerful, meaning we must row with great effort," Ameatus said. "However, as I mentioned, we are children of the sea. It will take great care not to damage her on the far side, so we need to know if the locals know of a safe location to target for landing. While we gather all the materials, we could consider hiring a local fisherman to show us the far coast."

They made a deal with a fisherman, trading an iron knife of locally unparalleled quality for his services. He agreed to take them into the treacherous channel that separated the lands. As Sanura and the local man conversed, Enki pondered the fisherman's resemblance to the first human it ever encountered.

Chapter 10

Four days before the Fall Solstice, 517 BC, North Coast of France near Calais.

Even though prepared, the strong currents shocked Ameatus, and he was glad that they had taken this trip to scout the wide and angry sea. Employing Sanura as a conduit, he posed many queries to the boatman to help himself grasp the local patterns, ultimately adjusting the ship's configuration in his mind throughout the journey. "It might take closer to three weeks," he told Sanura, "Since we'll need additional ballast and higher walls for these waves... and more oars. Fortunately, we will make the crossing faster than I originally expected. The bad news is, a mistake will transform unlucky men into heroes and potentially leave parts of our group stranded on both sides of this hellish water."

"We won't make mistakes, and you and I will be on each leg of the trip." Sanura added as Ameatus nodded in agreement.

They traded for the tools they lacked in the small village or enlisted the help of local smiths to help them create them. Initially unsure, the local blacksmith eventually embraced new techniques to enhance the heat and efficiency of his redesigned forges. When they saw the impact of the changes, they showed great enthusiasm. The local blacksmith and his sons observed and gained knowledge, as the foreign men created large flat blades for working with wood. In addition, they constructed a sizable circular cauldron by digging a mold into the earth. This cauldron would later produce pitch for the ship.

The third week was coming to a close, and after days filled with hard labor, they could finally see the ship taking shape. As she approached the boat, Sanura marveled at its size nearly 30 feet long and over ten feet wide at its widest point. The weight of the ship was unexpectedly light, considering its size. Equipped with a flat removable floor, the boat ingeniously concealed its "V" shape at the bottom. This design allowed for a level surface, perfect for walking, and accommodated benches to seat the 20 men responsible for powering the boat with long oars. Underneath the floor, there was a designated space for storing hundreds of fist sized ballast stones and various items that were carefully chosen for their ability to withstand the water that was undoubtedly going to be deposited there by the rough sea.

After a quick break in launch and test, they proceeded with caution to load the ship and secure all the items. They concluded that in order to fully cross, a minimum of six trips on the ship would be necessary. On the very first day of use, the ship emitted a powerful odor of creosote, because of its thick coating of pitch which caused the traveler's eyes to water.

A group composed of two men from the north, five servants, and 15 soldiers from Sanura's troops were the first to cross. The 20 rowers, as well as Sanura and Ameatus, all had a long day ahead of them.

For three days, the weather held and as the last group reached near the halfway point of travel, the ship and its crew experienced a visitation of hell. Darkness engulfed the west, and the wind changed its course, as if it took offense to the small craft and its occupants. With the seas gaining momentum, the crew countered with determined rowing. Ameatus, realizing escape was impossible, yelled to the crew to abandon the run and turn into the face of the oncoming waves.

They fought for hours in the torrent, their shouts and grunts snuffed by the storm, until the squall finally passed and the dim light of evening painted the western sky orange. The red sky of the setting sun helped them orientate and limp toward the northern shore. The boat's rowers exerted themselves on each side of the sluggish vessel while the remaining passengers worked tirelessly to bail out the frigid water that sloshed above the elevated floor, reaching their shins. As the sun disappeared, they were thankful for the bright, nearly full moon that lifted above the distant receding storm clouds, illuminating the world and revealing tall white cliffs in front of them. They changed their course to the east and followed the shoreline until they came upon a sight that delighted them: large campfires intentionally lit on the beach. Drawing nearer, the sound of cheers from their friends filled the air.

For the next couple of days, their primary task was to dry anything that was still salvageable and remove anything that was beyond repair. To ensure their safety, they placed the goods strategically on elevated ground in the recently set up camp, far from the ocean's mist.

There were still twelve days left until they could stop walking, having bartered a deal for most of the animals. Only four donkeys and Ameatus' well-trained horse made the crossing. On two occasions during their trip in the north, they encountered anxious locals who were worried about the unusual and heavily armed caravan. On each occasion, they made it clear to the locals that their intention was simply to pass through, and the locals closely monitored them until they left their lands.

As the twelfth day passed since they left the boat behind after their great crossing, and the sun rose towards midday, another group of armed men came into view. As they approached, Sanura realized that this force was not to be underestimated, especially with the intimidating presence of domesticated wolves flanking it. Hamish's smile widened as he recognized the distinct bouncing walk of his brother Kirn, each of his steps a mix of confidence and swagger. "The pompous ass that bounces each heel off the ground with every step. That has to be my brother Kirn." Hamish said as he projected his voice above the din of his weary fellow travelers. A tired smile played on his lips, and he let out a soft chuckle. Hamish jogged out front and took a grandiose bow, instantly lightening the tense atmosphere of the encounter.

Kirn turned and spoke to his assembled force, and discarded any pretense of strength as he turned and sprinted forward to embrace Hamish. "I barely recognize you without that fat ass you dragged around before you left."

"A better part of the year walking and searching will do that to you. I look forward to growing it back," said Hamish with a laugh.

Hamish looked at the Greeks, who were still eying the wolves with suspicion. "You are with us. You will be fine," as he turned to his brother. "Kirn, can you call off your minions?"

Kirn issued a one-word command, and with a flick of his hand, all but one wolf obediently trotted off towards the woods.

Hamish looked at the lone wolf, his eyes widening in surprise. "Sally!" he said as the remaining wolf's tail relaxed and swayed. "Yes it's me... I'm sorry, but I had to go away, big girl." With a sudden spark of recognition, the wolf lunged at him with lightning speed, knocking him down effortlessly. Hamish's laughter filled the air as he lovingly spoke to the beast. "There's my big girl." After a moment or two, he stood up as the enormous wolf raced around in circles, kicking up clouds of dust from the packed dirt road.

Kirn shook his head in disbelief after the show and commented, "You have come such a long way to be here. Let's get you to a place where you can relax and eat some food." He turned and led the caravan the rest of the way to a farm bordered by a stream to the east. The farm had several larger permanent wooden buildings, including residences and a grand hall, that by modern terms would be slightly larger than a two-car garage. "Welcome, to 'Dachaigh a' Mhadaidh-allaidh."

Sanura looked at Ameadus. "Home of the wolves," as Ameadus nodded his head in understanding.

Kirn and Hamish were part of a large family of eleven siblings, with Kirn proudly holding the title of the eldest. Their family comprised three sisters and six other brothers, and the youngest sister, Amber, was only eleven years old. Their father, Malik, was the leader of the clan. His wife's passing came shortly after the birth of their youngest daughter.

The sight of the trees outside, with their leaves painted in untamed hues of yellow and orange, hinted at the impending arrival of colder weather. Having spent the night cramped together in the great hall, the Greek contingent sought approval to establish their own makeshift lodgings and training area.

With a sudden burst of inspiration, Malik guided them to a nearby clearing that he instinctively knew would provide an ideal training environment. Surrounding the clearing were towering hills and a dense forest, creating a secluded atmosphere. At the side of the closest hill, the steep slope above revealed a small rock face, its jagged surface contrasting with the smoothness of the surrounding terrain. Malik guided Sanura and Ameatus to a spot where a jagged piece of the rock wall protruded amidst the scattered moss-covered boulders. Just behind it, there was a small cave mouth that was barely wider than a man's shoulders. A bucket filled with sticks, meticulously wrapped in cloth soaked with pitch, stood on one side, accompanied by piles of shredded birch bark. Malik skillfully ignited a small pile of shredded birch using two stones from the nearby supplies. One of the two stones immediately caught Ameatus and Sanura's attention. "A fire stone, like the ones found in markets from the islands to the far southeast of the Aegean." she remarked. The other stone appeared to be a type of ore typically used in the production of iron. Using the flickering flame, Malik lit the soaked cloth torch.

With the torch in hand, he guided them into the narrow entrance of the cave. After walking about 20 strides, the narrow passage suddenly gave way to a wide, open expanse. As their eyes adjusted to the lower light, they could see a vast space that rivaled any single room Sanura had ever seen. Enki gave her a heightened awareness of every intricate detail and subtle nuance within the cave. On the light gray stone walls, intricate drawings resembling sailor knots adorned certain spaces. "Kids," Malik said, his quiet voice filled with exasperation.

As Sanura ventured further into the cave, she could sense a delicate movement of air, whispering through the darkness like the exhale of a legendary creature. "Is there another entrance besides this one?" she inquired, hopeful for an alternative route.

"Not exactly," replied Malik, his voice filled with uncertainty. "In the distance, there's a large fissure that reaches up into the sky. At certain times of the day, you can see sunlight dancing along its surface. The soft sound you hear is the gentle trickle of a spring as it cascades into a serene, natural pool. The water is crystal clear and has a refreshing, delightful taste."

"In the near term, I believe this would work perfectly as a place to house and train," Sanura remarked, her words carrying a sense of practicality. "The one way out is a concern that will require careful addressing, but we can save that for another time. If your enemy has spies, the cave will help us hide our numbers."

Chapter 11

Early Fall, 517 BC, 'Dachaigh a' Mhadaidh-allaidh Farm, Scotland.

Mornings were now regularly cold, often with ice forming on the brown grass. The leaves had changed to magical colors and were falling as the days shortened. With her troops' quarters established and foraging details worked out with Malik to feed the army; the leaders could have a conversation about the creature called Scrios. Sanura listened intently as Malik shared the familiar stories, occasionally interjecting to clarify a minor detail or provide further context. The process moved at a slow pace as Sanura conscientiously took the time between most sentences to interpret for the people from her lands. A handful of her people followed along, but the majority found the language either too rapid or their comprehension lacking.

The more she heard, the heavier her concern weighed on her. Realizing the truth behind their words, she understood the urgency of training her army. The existence of a creature capable of destroying a man through eye contact would require the deliberate unlearning of a behavior that comes naturally to every person a moment after birth.

During their discussion with Malik and the other leaders of his family, Sanura and Ameatus brainstormed various techniques to prevent themselves from meeting his gaze during battle. Among the untenable ideas, blindfolding stood out as the most impractical. Ameatus, a master trainer, suggested that the only reasonable approach was to focus solely on the waist of their opponent during battle. "It won't be easy; we'll have to push against our natural inclinations to accomplish it."

Malik reminded Sanura that if the legends were indeed accurate, Scrios' enchanting abilities would become nullified in the presence of a member of his family. This was not good enough for Sanura. "That will be great, but we must not take our safety for granted as your family members may become targets and face immediate danger... that is the strategy I would employ." Sanura's argument was persuasive, and with a frustrated nod, Malik conceded.

As it was the only path, it was the best path. So, Sanura built on the idea. They had a basic description of Scrios and several of her people were skilled artisans. She, with the aid of Hamish, described the person she wanted in a human sized depiction and stated that the eyes needed to be difficult to ignore. The artisans set out to work in the cave.

When she entered her home in the vast cavern several days later, a disturbing figure etched onto the wall greeted her. The artisan's craftsmanship was so impressive that the creature they portrayed made her anxious and forced her to confront its piercing eyes.

The eyes were shining and as she got close, she could see that they were crystals that caught the light. Behind Scrios, the picture revealed a hill that was swarmed by an army, creating an imposing sight. The image was so effective that it honestly troubled her, leaving a specter of doubt in her mind.

She insisted on covering the mural when not used, to provide a place for people to rest, but during training, the trainees always faced the unsettling mural.

In the beginning of the drills, the trainer and trainee, both Greeks, gathered to learn, their voices echoing off the walls of the cavern. Intrigued locals watched the sparring with wooden weapons, with their backs to the towering walls of the cavern.

Soon they incorporated the new mural into their training. One force represented Scrios's army and the others attacking had to protect their eyes, but still maintain their mastery.

Standing beside the mural, Ameatus and several other master trainers patiently searched for any glimmer of recognition in the eyes of those who looked at the creature's image during the staged battle. Whenever they caught someone, they would immediately approach the person, gently guiding them to sit down as they delivered the news of their demise.

Stopping the training, Ameatus's intense, frustrated glare fell upon half the mural-facing force; their indiscipline, not feigned injury, led to their removal. In a commanding tone, Ameatus called to the dead, his fellow countrymen, who had lost concentration to assemble near the cave's exit.

With a soft, grumbling, frustrated voice, he shared his message with them, aware of the watchful eyes of the other instructors and other participants who waited where he had left them. "We need to illustrate this better," he murmured under his breath. Speaking to the departed, he told them that upon resuming the exercise, they returned to the location of their death and, "When I raise my hand, you will tap any of the living within your reach with the flat of your sword until I give the signal to stop. Tap each person once and quickly move on to the next. Use only the flat of your swords, but don't be gentle. I want it clear in their minds that it was intentional, not a mistake." Sanura translated Ameatus' words to the locals, who had been observing from the cave wall. When Ameatus sent them back to their original locations, showing with a flick of his wrist. The surviving trainees waited expectantly, their faces curious, as the others returned to the training area to where they had been declared dead.

Upon their return, they settled back into a comfortable resting position, ready to resume their training at Ameatus's command. Ameatus waited for the surviving trainees tasked with attacking the creature's horde to become fully absorbed in their tasks. Then he cautiously raised his hand, giving the signal for the dead to follow their instructions.

The sharp sound of loud slaps filled the air, as the "dead" sadistically delivered forceful blows to their adversaries' backsides, lower backs, or upper legs.

Screams of rage filled the space, quickly descending into scuffles that grew more intense with each passing moment, only to halt at the piercing whistle from Ameatus.

After the chaos subsided, Sanura seamlessly transitioned into her role as translator, addressing the audience, eagerly waiting to begin their own training. "Those who look at his eyes are not dead. They are worse than dead. They are immediately your enemy." Ameatus' voice reverberated in the cave; his face flushed with anger. "You... you just killed your brother because you lack the discipline and self-control to keep your eyes down. Would you look up if you knew that in doing so, Scrios would force you to kill your wife or daughter? If you dare to meet his gaze on the battlefield when faced with that monstrous creature," he pointed at the mural, "you may find yourself compelled to commit

37

unspeakable acts against a comrade. If this creature is truly as terrible as they say, it might let you live to return home, forcing you to devour your own child while your helpless wife looks on... simply because you failed to maintain discipline that day," as fire seemed to burn in his eyes.

At the back of the room, the hushed audience listened attentively as Sanura finished her translation. Ameatus, with a look of disgust, abruptly dismissed them from training for the day and stormed out the door. Ameatus's lesson struck a chord with the locals, leaving some of them standing against the walls in horror, realizing the impact of their situation in a way they had never embraced before.

Outside, Sanura, who had followed him out, grabbed her friend and former student as his body shook with anger. She turned him towards her and whispered, "Thank you. You are the best at this, and they all needed to hear that."

Ameatus stared at her with eyes filled with the same terror as the people they had left behind. "I am telling them all the things that I will have to learn as well. I feel like a fool because I don't think I can do any better than they did today." He pointed to the cavern's opening as if he had more that needed to be said, but instead, spun and trudged away.

When Sanura went back into the cave, things were not as she expected. The Greeks had reassembled, their wooden weapons clashing and shields clanging in the air, and even the locals joined in the sparring. In the midst of the training session, Sanura joined them, her presence adding a sense of determination to the group. Although there were a few who had better training with the weapons, they were all newcomers to this uncharted and bizarre battlefield.

Chapter 12

Fall, 517 BC, 'Dachaigh a' Mhadaidh-allaidh Farm, Scotland.

After the training session, Illitus took a leisurely stroll near the cave into the brisk air. To his astonishment, he discovered a hidden treasure. There was an iron rich area reminiscent of the striking stone used by Malik to light the torch. However, what caught his attention was a peculiar stone, intricate and unlike anything he had encountered, which harbored an astonishing quantity of tin.

Sanura had been present during Illitus's birth, guiding his arrival into the world with her expertise as a midwife. At her first school near Corinth, he was the second son of the principal smith. Despite his advancing age, his experience and familiarity with working and purifying metals remained unmatched. Noticing indications of a historical avalanche revealing this rare stone, he snatched a piece. In disbelief, Illitus collected more and discovered with astonishment that the pile of rocks contained an absurd amount of tin. He set aside the fur cape he wore in this inhospitable land and carefully arranged some of the smaller, valuable pieces inside. Illitus bundled it up from the corners and headed back to the camp.

To ensure his correctness, he gathered a few additional people who he believed had knowledge in recovering metal from ore. However, they merely shrugged when he presented it to them.

Illitus located Sanura and shared his discovery with her, showing her what he had found. Sanura had some experience extracting metal in her many lives, and Enki's certainty affirmed Illitus's report. She looked at him and nodded, "What do you need?"

In a matter of weeks, Illitus established a foundry and began extracting metals with the help of Greeks and locals. While in the foundry, he took the opportunity to instruct several members of Malik's clan in the art. Soon, he proudly presented Sanura with 25 small ingots of tin, each one gleaming in the light.

The locals found the foundry a point of fascination. Children gathered to watch the magical process that produced metal. The dangerousness of the process proved to be underestimated on the third day of production, when a leaky roof caused a pop in the foundry's cauldron ejecting molten metal. Splashed in the face by glowing liquid, Malik's youngest daughter learned a painful lesson, a cautionary tale for the other apprentices about foundry dangers.

The damage inflicted on the edge of her eye was both local and horrific. When Sanura arrived, there was already a crowd gathered, and an aunt was attempting to clean the whimpering girl's wound. Sanura understood that the upcoming moments would bring about a change in her relationship with Malik's clan and preferred to handle it without unnecessary drama. She approached Hamish and Malik, who were both consoling the girl. With his jaw clenched, Malik winced at every whimper he heard.

"I can help her, but we need to clear the people first," Sanura insisted.

"We believe she will survive, but her face will bear permanent scars," Malik replied solemnly.

"You are not listening to me!" she exclaimed, her voice filled with frustration.

Hamish stepped in; he immediately caught his father's attention with his words. "Father! Let her speak," as Malik nodded and looked at Sanura.

"While I can still help her," Sanura said, "we need to remove the others who haven't seen her injuries, because many will mistakenly believe my aid is magical, even though it is not. While many stories about me are exaggerated, I want you to know that I was a healer long before I became a warrior. Let me help her!"

Before the sentence's weight had landed on Malik, Hamish cleared the onlookers and explained to them, "She needs her peace."

Sanura's carefully selected soldiers were aware of the upcoming events, so they assisted Hamish in persuading the crowd to disperse. They cleared the area around the foundry, leaving only Malik, Hamish, and one stubborn aunt who refused to leave the girl in pain. Sanura approached the girl on the ground. "No need to be scared," she assured, taking a small, golden metal rod from her belt pouch, where the item usually lived.

The metal rod appeared worn and old. There was a coiled, serpent shaped raised area that encircled the object. Over time, the top of the serpent seemed to have worn smooth, but scales were still visible in areas that people rarely touched.

The young woman, whose eyes were rolling wildly from the pain, had the rod placed on her skin by Sanura. Because of the hot metal splatter hitting her left eye, the orb now had an opaque appearance, like that of a half-cooked egg. The intense heat of the metal had seared the skin around the socket, resulting in a deep burn that reached her cheekbone. Tiny droplets of the metal had landed and burned through her clothes, leaving behind fluid-filled blisters. The burns on her left shoulder and the inside of her arm, resembling the night sky, had acted as a barrier, preventing greater damage to her face and head.

Sensing the broken systems within her, Enki took it upon himself to address the various trivial issues that were causing her distress. Witnessing the rapid healing of the young lady's damaged left eye, the aunt slumped and descended towards the ground. In disbelief, Malik instinctively took a step back, astounded by the rapidity at which the horrifying damage appeared to fade away and return to its normal appearance. Her body expressed the pieces of metal, which fell to the ground.

When the process ended, Malik's face showed a mix of fear and confusion, rendering him unable to find the right words to express himself. Seeing his reaction, Sanura questioned, "What were your expectations regarding the individual your son embarked on a journey to locate? Am I as portrayed in the stories? Oh, and the baby is healthy and should be here in the spring."

As his brain composed the words of his gratitude, in sudden realization, Malik's faced snapped to his daughter, who was now relieved from pain, and uttered the word "Baby?" as she clenched her teeth and pretended to still be unconscious.

Having seen the miracle firsthand, the aunt maintained a vigilant and somewhat skeptical attitude towards Sanura, blending a sense of awe with fear. The consensus, except for a few individuals who had firsthand knowledge of the damage, was that Malik's daughter's injuries were not as dire as originally believed. The lack of scars making it difficult to believe it could ever have been bad.

Chapter 13

Winter, early 516 BC, 'Dachaigh a' Mhadaidh-allaidh Farm, Scotland.

Seated comfortably at one of the large wooden tables specifically designed for their meals, Sanura idly toyed with the tin ingots, lost in thought, until suddenly an exciting idea unexpectedly dawned upon her. As Illitus walked past, feeling compelled, she asked, "I wonder just how difficult it would be to flatten these into thin sheets?"

As the sun was getting low in the sky, Illitus looked at it through the open doorway and confidently declared, "By the time the sun sets, I can handle most of these and even train one boy on how to do them."

Sanura's face lit up with a smile as she responded, "That will be perfect."

Once dinner was over, she gathered with Malik and Hamish and shared with them something she had gained a knowledge of many years ago in a distant land that predates her era in Hellas. In a distant region located to the east of Greece, she spent several lifetimes working as a scribe in various temples. In the past, people recorded the information on clay tablets, but now she used tin for this purpose. Besides transcribing the family stories, she also took on the responsibility of teaching the art and literacy of how to read and write the strange markings to all the members of the family. The idea of teaching them to write in Greek crossed her mind, but she ultimately opted for the writing style that she had grown up with and felt more at ease using.

Chapter 14

Spring, 514 BC, 'Dachaigh a' Mhadaidh-allaidh Farm, Scotland.

She did not rush in the preparation for war. The lack of urgency in their war preparations allowed the soldiers from Sanura's homeland to feel a powerful pull for their homes and families. She understood, but despite her comprehension, she couldn't ignore the urgency of dealing with this creature. "The longer this creature gives us," she remarked, "the better equipped we will be to handle it." The combined army spent two full years on training and teaching.

Her documentation of their history over the years was fascinating and enlightening. With Enki's help, she adjusted the symbols' meanings to match their language and taught them this new way to record their history.

The family had been able to, at a basic level, track the movements of the Blue King through a friendly trading partner in a kingdom on the western shore, which had some land holdings across the sea, along the shoreline of the island in the south.

The family's recent past was a cause of concern for Sanura. Some of Malik's recent ancestors, driven by their desire to end the blight of the monster they called Scrios, became restless and impatient. Fueled by unwavering determination, bravado or blissful ignorance to the risks, they had embarked on these missions, either alone or in small groups, with one singular aim in mind: to locate the beast and eliminate the imminent danger to the family, which Scrios represented. Many times, level headedness prevailed, but the cycle seemed to repeat itself every generation, with the regularity of the rising sun in the east.

Impatience would consume a member of the family, believed to be protected by blood from the creature's charms. Usually, a profound sense of purpose fueled their actions, while for others, it was skepticism. Most firmly believed that their path to glory lay in delivering Scrios's head, and destiny predetermined that the creature's end would come at the point of their own blade.

They would leave, and only the silence that followed marked their absence, like a whisper fading into the wind. No one knew if they reached their destination or perished during the journey. Their fate remained shrouded in uncertainty.

In the rare event they heard anything, a wandering storyteller would often carry the news in song, from town to town, telling half fictional tales of a terrible fate of torture the Blue King had inflicted on the fool that challenged him.

The poets spread stories filled with grandiosity, but they also provided scattered glimpses of truth within. Scrios not only allowed these entertainers to roam freely in his kingdoms, but he also granted them privileges, surpassing those of the masses who scraped an existence under his rule.

To intimidate the populace ahead of an invasion, he conscripted these storytellers to disseminate tales of dread. Now and again, they would share stories that were uncanny in their accuracy, which echoed the tales handed down by Lil. Those stories were unsettling to hear, as they were told in a manner that made it seem like the speaker was Scrios himself, boasting of his own achievements.

While stories of the monster were plentiful, some described an even more terrifying version of the king. One that described him as a creature who emerged from the fog shrouded moors at night and carried the fury of the gods.

Occasionally, the storytellers wove narratives which extended beyond their land, to the lands of magic and lore. A story that left a lasting impression on one member of the family was that of a remarkable woman goddess, hailing from a distant land. The stories told of her incredible prowess in defeating mythical beasts and preserving entire civilizations with her cunning.

According to that legend, the demigod Sanura was renowned as an ageless healer and unmatched warrior. In one hand was a mythical sword of impossible craftsmanship, and in the other, she carried the Eye of Asclepius, a magical rod given to her by a god. The items, forged for her, in a celestial foundry atop a mountain that was the dwelling of immortals and gods.

The exaggerated tale was once even recounted in Sanura's presence after she arrived on the northern island. It even made her question the reality of her own existence. These stories had fascinated Malik's son Hamish from a young age. They had inspired his travels.

Malik believed his adventure to be a desperate endeavor reminiscent of the other family tragedies of the past. However, Malik let him go, sending him off with four men as his escort, solely out of fear that his son would be the next to challenge the monster and try to save their family if he stayed.

To him, his son being swallowed by the world was preferable to being destroyed by the creature. He hoped that if he ever returned, he would be wiser and more patient. Malik was uncertain when or where, but in his dreams, Hamish would return with a wife or even establish a family somewhere distant and less perilous.

He certainly never thought Hamish would bring back Sanura, the hero of the fantastical stories who he left to search for. Malik, however, was slightly let down when he discovered she couldn't fly like a sparrow, as portrayed in certain narratives, and had encountered nothing more remarkable or ruthless than a normal man in warfare. Still, there were kernels of truth in the tales about her. He heard the stories of her since his own childhood, yet her appearance was younger than even Hamish. Except for her eyes. Haunted eyes revealed the lessons of time and wisdom accumulated over many years, far exceeding her youthful appearance.

Despite the relatively uneventful journey from her country, Sanura was concerned about the recent stories that featured her bringing an army of immortal warriors to establish her own kingdom in the north. Clearly, she had no plans to stay here, beyond the adventurous journey that led her to this place, but the undeniable fact was that she was indeed here and somehow, word had spread. The story's dissemination was a harbinger of an inevitable war.

Chapter 15

Late Spring, 514 BC, 'Dachaigh a' Mhadaidh-allaidh Farm, Scotland.

Among all the family members who had undergone training over the first two years, one individual truly stood out. He didn't stick out just because he was the largest; but he did tower over the rest of the family like a giant. It wasn't only because the other soldiers looked up to him; their respect for him was palpable. Among the tall men of the north, Cormic stood out like a colossal figure, with a stature that commanded attention.

His weight was almost twice that of a typical member of the clan, but there was hardly any excess fat on his frame. Two years ago, the tall, skinny young man started his journey in the forge, first carrying ore for refinement and later learning to shape metal with a hammer. As time passed, his passion for shaping metal intensified, and along with it, his strength and skill. The shaping of the metal also shaped him.

Like all the men, he also trained to be a warrior, and Cormic effortlessly excelled in that role as well. Over the first summer, his wiry muscles bulged, and he grew a hand taller than his already significant height.

No matter what physical challenge Cormic attempted, he effortlessly excelled, quickly mastering each endeavor. While waiting for a piece of iron to reach its ideal working temperature, Cormic would stand outside the forge, playfully toying with a heavy hammer. With great dexterity, he effortlessly passed it from one hand to the other, as if engaged in a spirited fight with an unseen adversary. This caught the attention of Illitus, who was watching nearby.

Illitus despised working with that cumbersome hammer, because it inevitably resulted in a daylong soreness in his back, which radiated down his left leg. An incident involving that hammer had nearly caused Illitus to lose a toe on his left foot a year prior. Watching Cormic toss it around like a stick initially frustrated him, but soon it became a source of inspiration.

Throughout the night, Illitus worked diligently, forging two massive broad heads out of iron. Their ends displayed a stark contrast, flat on one side and gracefully curved into a tapered point on the other. Additionally, to his work on the twin heads, he spent down time roughing out long and heavy pieces of ash for the wooden handles. With the heads finished, he heated them and married the heads to the handles. Over the course of the next week, he meticulously reinforced the handles by tightly wrapping sinew around them and incorporating leather grips made from the hide of a stag he had hunted and slain himself.

When Illitus completed his task, he grabbed both hammers at once and immediately felt a sense of remorse. Although he possessed the capability to lift them, the overall weight of the objects seemed excessively heavy, even for someone of Cormic's strength.

However, upon showing them to Cormic, the young man's face lit up with the same joy and excitement as someone who had just received their very first kiss. As he picked up one in each hand, Cormic made his way to an open area and swayed them, accumulating his speed. After a brief period, they picked up their pace and started moving more swiftly. After a few minutes, Cormic halted. He carefully positioned each head on the ground, leaned them against his legs and gently massaged his forearms. "My arms are on fire," the young giant remarked, as an intense heat coursed through his limbs.

"If you let me have them back," Illitus said with an apologetic look, "I can rework them and make them lighter,"

"No, No! I love them, I just need to get used to them," clutching the handles on his legs like a protective mother wolf, guarding her pups. Cormic remarked with a huge grin, "At first, the swords and spears caused a burning sensation in my arms as well. I'll get used to them."

After several weeks of training with them and destroying trees designated for firewood, he had become used to the weight of the hammers. Unfortunately, Cormic found himself without a willing sparring partner, so he resorted to practicing with wooden sticks during his training sessions.

As the months passed, Cormic distinguished himself as the preeminent war leader of the bloodline carrying relatives. Sanura thought it was a simple choice because, despite his age, he had the other qualities of a leader.

To shield their chests, upper and lower arms, the warriors created leather armor, influenced by Greek design. The Northmen's legs were covered with a heavy padded wool weave, known as "braccae".

Over that two-year period, families or parts of refugee families increasingly traveled near Malik's lands, pulling hand drawn carts that held their entire existence. As they looked into the refugee's eyes, they could see the stories of horror that they carried within them. As the number of refugees grew, they knew the conflict was fast approaching.

Sanura recognized the familiar sight of all the travelers moving in one direction, a sight that signaled the approach of an army, and inevitably war. They were certain that the beast would soon cross to their island, if he had not already.

Chapter 16

Early Fall, 514 BC, 'Dachaigh a' Mhadaidh-allaidh Farm, Scotland.

Sanura worked with Malik to find the location that would enhance their chances in a battle. She described a dream like location which was very similar to a place that Malik had hunted as a child. "A place of the ancients," he said excitedly. "I know of such a place." The valley that was several days south of their home.

He took Sanura there and showed her the place she described. The valley, shaped like a bowl, had a northern entrance and a southern entrance that was carved by the same stream. There was a raised area near one of the steep walls of the valley. On this knoll was an ancient circle of enormous stones. Sanura walked the valley with the eye of a general and nodded at what she saw.

From that day forward, they trained there in groups with regularity, so each warrior and support person would become familiar with the land. Despite the knowledge of this optimal location, Sanura felt unease at confronting the creature. The burden of leadership and expectations was a heavy mantel, even for her.

Several weeks before, while the troops trained in the valley, Sanura left and returned the next day with a stranger. Malik had seen her talking to the outsider several hundred yards away. Watching him nod as they discussed... something. Later, when they finished speaking, the man left, leading a loaded mule, exiting the southern valley opening, from which they had arrived not long before.

When Malik asked Sanura about the stranger, she explained he was a scout who she sent out to warn them if he saw an army from the south. She explained she had several of her men tasked with keeping a vigil here, for his return, with any word of his findings.

"Here?" Malik asked?

"If he were to encounter the creature, here is the only place this scout knows. Not your home." She said, as he nodded with recognition.

Two weeks passed with no report from Sanura's men. Eventually, though, through other channels, a strange story was spreading.

For the entire third week, however, there were rumors about a madman who obsessively repeated a single phrase, alerting everyone about the impending arrival of the Blue King. News spread of his wandering northeast since he washed ashore on a small boat. He walked through the wilds towards the valley, familiar to them all. To the place where Sanura and Ameatus had planned their battle and practiced the maneuvers, watching from a high point along the northern slope that contained the ancient stone circle.

The insane man went straight into the valley, where the two men stationed by Sanura were waiting. Following their orders, they killed the insane man and returned to the cave.

Days later, reports came of Scrios's movements. Something about the timing of the crazed harbinger troubled Malik. So, he asked for a meeting to discuss it.

"The crazed man we dispatched yesterday," Sanura admitted, "was the scout I hired. I purposely limited his knowledge of our numbers and location. With full knowledge of the likely mortal outcome, I deliberately sent the man to spy on Scrios, knowing all too well that his capture was a virtual certainty," she confessed. "I was afraid that his mind would be a ruin, and Scrios would witness everything he witnessed, as the stories suggested. Therefore, I never allowed him anywhere close to this home. The day I sent him on his mission, I showed him the valley where some of our troops were practicing." Sanura explained, "I intentionally provided him specifically the knowledge I wanted Scrios to possess, hoping to entice him into that valley. Assuming it functions as expected, and it seems to be, that's the spot where we'll kill the beast."

Sanura paused, noting the mixture of confusion and surprise, and spoke, "Based on observations, the Blue King is pursuing the bait we offered via the scout named Ralf."

Some people listening, caught on to the fact Sanura had just admitted to deliberately sending an innocent person to his death as bait, and their faces hardened. Sanura admitted to a calculated act, akin to luring a wolf with a helpless goat, where she sacrificed an innocent person for an advantage.

Sanura, sensing the mood of the room, expressed her gratitude to Ralf in a tone filled with apology. Her eyes swept across the crowd until they landed on one individual who stubbornly avoided her gaze. "Hamish, is there something on your mind?" she inquired, her tone gentle yet insistent.

Hamish's initial negative head shake conveyed he had no qualms, but as he contemplated further, the shake converted it into a nod of reluctant objection. "We used him as bait? We just cast him out into the dangerous unknown like a fisherman casting his net into the water? I just don't grasp the waste of it. We all knew too much, so we decided it couldn't be one of us. Instead, we grabbed a man and hurled him, body and spirit, towards this monstrous creature?" His words met with agreement from a few others in the gathering, who nodded in his support.

Sanura nodded as well. "Instead of directly answering your question, let me present you with a question in return. Hamish, imagine a situation where you could ensure the safety of your wife, children, and the entire community by embarking on the same perilous journey that Ralf did. Would you be willing to do it? Would any of you hesitate to do it?"

"I would have acted with no hesitation whatsoever, but in the end, it would have been my choice." Hamish replied.

"If I had given Ralf the choice," Sanura said, "the consequences would have posed a threat to your family, everyone here, and his own family. Ralf, though unaware of it, is the hero here." Sanura implored. "However, his sacrifice will only hold meaning if we succeed. If we fail, we unleash upon this world a monster."

The area was quiet for a prolonged time. When Hamish stood, walked to Sanura. He nodded his head and thanked her for her wisdom and strength, and turned to the others, "We need to make sure Ralf's sacrifice is not wasted."

Minutes later, Malik took over on task. "Our battle plans have contingencies in place, ensuring the safety of your family. Our families will move to an unknown destination once we leave to confront this creature. No one involved with the battle can know where they are going. We are also not enlisting all warriors capable of resisting Scrios, as that would be a foolish play. Therefore, we will send the selected individuals with the families. After we win the battle, and destroy this creature, we will come and find all the families."

Building support in the crowd, she continued. "I hope this brings you some comfort regarding Ralf. I'm sharing this message with all of you... and therefore Scrios, if we fail, so he can bear witness to my last act of defiance. He will know who I am, as I will be the person who died with his severed balls in my left hand and my sword buried firmly in his backside." As the large group cheered, Sanura finished with a triumphant smile on her face.

Chapter 17

Mid-Fall, 514 BC, 'Dachaigh a' Mhadaidh-allaidh Farm, Scotland.

Later that night, Sanura and Malik spoke together of the need to gauge Scrios's progress. She chose a handful of her most dependable men and assigned them each a local guide, selected by Malik. Sanura gave them specific instructions, to fan out towards the southwest of the valley, where the flow of refugees was emanating and look for signs of the army's advancement.

Their orders were explicit: keep a considerable distance, observe without interference, and return promptly. They had explicit instructions to avoid getting involved in any situation, regardless of the circumstances.

After nine days, many of the teams returned, bringing back stories of what looked like even more refugees. However, one team came back with much more.

Attracted by the echoes of a crowd making noise in this frigid afternoon, this group of scouts had come to the crest of a hill. Commanding yells echoed through the air from below. As they reached the hill's peak, they dropped to the ground, using the cover of the terrain to conceal themselves. The land below them stretched out, revealing a sparse landscape dotted with trees, brambles, and desolate winter fields.

A small army gathered at the base of the long hill, comprising over 200-foot soldiers and an additional 50, on horseback. They gathered together, their anticipation palpable as they awaited the further guidance of their leader. While surveying the soldiers, they observed most of the force comprised of farmers, but occasional glimpses of metal showed skilled soldiers among them. In the distance, a small contingent of approximately 15 riders on horseback was steadily approaching them.

As instructed by a mounted soldier, the army closer to them spread out into disorganized ragtag groups. Despite the distance, the commanding voice of the army's leader carried over to them, filled with fervor and the desire to motivate his troops.

The small distant force stopped on a raised area at the edge of the field near the edge of a tree line almost a league away. The Greek scout carefully surveyed the vast horizon behind the group in the distance, searching for any signs of a major army, but found nothing. As they glanced beyond the small group of riders, they noticed the scattered black and gray pillars of smoke that dotted the countryside, reaching out towards where the sky met the land. The distant group slowed, and from their midst, a lone rider on a black horse emerged, heading straight towards the expecting army. Though far away, the rider's form was distinct, his dark brown robe, crafted of rough twine or leather, clinging to his lean frame, contributed to his slender appearance.

The rider wore nothing on his head and his orange hair caught the cloud filtered sun, like fire. As he approached, the clouds thickened, as if the air itself above him resented his presence. The brewing storm clouds that grew over the rider cast a shadow on his path as he approached. Clouds continued to grow the closer he came, resembling the jagged peaks of towering mountains.

The high, dead grass of the bramble plain rippled in the wind, like waves on a pond. Hundreds of yards in front of him, flashes of movement in the high weeds were visible where multiple creatures fled the path of the man on horseback. A foreboding wave grew and flowed out like an omen, heralding his coming. The wave continued to grow as many things hurriedly made their way through the tangled brambles, rolling out like a tide. In a remarkable spectacle, the field became devoid of life as rabbits, deer and foxes suddenly burst out from the tangled grass in terror as they darted through the army, completely ignoring its presence. They ran as if they were running from a wildfire.

A bright violet flash followed immediately by a deafening clap of thunder regained everyone's attention back to the field. As the rider came through the grassland, hundreds of crows filled the sky, screaming in a chorus of ecstasy. Bringing his horse to a sudden stop, the lone rider positioned himself in the middle of the expanse, facing the army. The crows above swirled in the sky before swooping down and settling into a small stand of leafless oak trees a hundred yards to the left of the strange man. They resembled a raucous jury, fighting for the best perch and awaiting a trial.

The leader below them appeared shaken by the otherworldly display, but rallied and issued orders to his commanders to keep the army ready and to move on his order. He called his guard, which comprised the largest portion of the 50 riders in total. As he addressed them, the scout strained to hear his words, only catching fragments when the leader faced the proper direction.

During his brief speech, he referred to "the eater of children" and sneered at the stupidity of venturing into the field alone with no support, which he described as a "foolish mistake". Among the cacophony of garbled words, a coherent statement emerged. "If that is him, and he is foolish enough to face us alone now, here will be his end!" the leader proclaimed, prompting a clatter of reticent cheers from his army.

The leader and his commanders spun their horses, and galloped with determination towards the pale, skinny man in the field. Even at this distance, the lone orange haired man looked comfortable despite the clouds and wind that seemed to swirl the dead grass around him like invisible dancers spinning through the field.

Out rode the leader and his troops, their horses pounding the ground at a murderous speed. As they charged ahead, some soldiers surged past the leader, acting as a vanguard, while others fanned out in a picket line, their ends racing ahead of the center. Hiding several hundred feet above, set back at a great distance, Sanura's scout witnessed a chilling sight. The gathering of men and beasts that appeared to take the shape of a monstrous open mouth, poised to consume the apathetic man awaiting them in the field.

The strange, slender lone rider seemed untroubled, despite being at least ten minutes away from any of his meager support. As the troops drew their weapons, they made their intentions clear. They sought death, not parley.

As the horsemen closed in on their prey, the horses and riders suddenly relaxed and decelerated. Their movements became more measured, as all the horses matched their relaxed gait. Simultaneously, the once boisterous taunts from the army below gradually faded into questions and confusion.

The lone rider sat motionless, seemingly uninterested in the spectacle before them. In fact, if not for the horse's tail flicking back and forth irregularly, and the rider's head glancing at each side of the approaching force, one might confuse him with a lifeless statue.

The entire line of riders, in an anticlimactic manner, shifted to the right at a slow walk and congregated by the cluster of oak trees. The trees were so lush with abundant foliage that it seemed as if it were the peak of summer; except instead of leaves, the branches were teeming with countless crows squabbling among themselves.

With the army below as spectators and Sanura's scouts as witnesses, the men descended from their horses and shed their armor and clothing, exposing themselves to the freezing cold. The crow jury in the trees seemed to pass judgment. With the help of the fellow condemned, the naked rider's fashioned cords from their clothing and bridles of the horses. Shivering, they calmly cut and tore clothing and blankets into strips. As they worked, the lone man, the judge of this makeshift court, waved a red sash over his head, signaling several men on horseback to come forward, each carrying bulky items.

The naked men diligently pulled the knots tight, completing the cordage, while above them hungry black eyes observed their work. The first two riders arrived carrying an intriguing surprise: a chair and a small table. A third rider came forward carrying a wooden box with a handle and placed it on the ground.

The strange lone rider waved off the deliverers of his supplies, the sound of their horses' neighs fading into the silence as he hopped from his horse and swiftly righted the chair and table. He gently placed the box on the table, its weight causing a slight thud. He opened the box and carefully took out several items, their shapes and colors indistinct, until he placed the box back on the ground beside him. On the table, there was a bottle and a plate with a large, mysterious object that could have been a juicy piece of meat or a ripe fruit. He poured the bottle into the cup and lifted it towards the naked men near the trees in a toast, as they began hanging their comrades. Seven remaining men, who were not swinging, appeared to be in a state of confusion that bordered on panic. Several hundred yards away, the Greek scout's face turned pale as he placed both hands to his cheeks, his horrified whisper revealing the dire situation: "They have run out of rope, and they do not know what to do."

Given a new task, the men formed a line, standing tall and straight, as if preparing for inspection. Their leader, with flushed cheeks, seemed overexerted, or perhaps embarrassed, in the cold air. This same man, who had been rallying the army just moments ago, now stood naked before his lieutenants, their bodies bare and frigid like his own. With a heavy sword in his right hand, he skillfully and savagely hacked the neck of the first man.

Resigned to his destiny, the condemned man did not resist. The impact of the sword was so powerful that the body lurched forward, causing blood to burst forth in a violent spray from the nearly severed neck, coating the leader and the person beside him in a gruesome shower of gore as he fell. The nearly severed head, tilted impossibly and attached by a small section of flesh, obediently led the body to the ground, while the figures suspended in the trees behind danced to a silent song that only they heard.

With each swing of the heavy blade, the leader grew more visibly fatigued, continuing down the line, slaughtering his own men with only the occasional pause to vomit or scream out. With every swing, his body became drenched in a fresh spray of bloody gore. Worse than the silence that came over the crows and the army below were the mournful wails that carried from the leader as he performed his horrid reaping.

With the fall of the last man in the line, the bodies on the ground twitched, desperately seeking tranquility. The leader turned as the man at the table got up from his meal and began clapping at the absurd show's conclusion. Inexplicably, the blood covered leader mechanically performed a bow.

The leader dropped his sword, and a moment later, the sound reached the scout as he heard the weapon hit the ground. The naked, gore covered leader trudged over to the lone horse that remained. Clutching the horse's mane, with a fluid motion honed from his joyful childhood, he effortlessly swung himself onto its bare back. The horse turned, its hooves pounding against the ground as it carried the puppet covered in blood back to his army, the sound of its slow trot echoing through the air.

Witnessing the dreadful scene unfolding below, the sudden explosion of the woods in front of them abruptly jolted the scouts. Two of the horses, ridden by the condemned men, emerged from the thick brush, their eyes filled with panic as they sprinted past them. Despite their torn minds begging to leave, the scouts knew they had to stay and see the inevitable outcome of the leader's return.

Arriving in front of his army, the blood coated marionette shivered uncontrollably, whether from the cold or the horror, or perhaps both, and abruptly halted his horse before tumbling off as if his strings had been severed. Neither he nor his men tried to break the fall, leaving him to hit the ground with full force.

As the surrounding men flinched, he hit the ground with a wet thud, resembling a sack of wet grain. Still steaming from the ghastly liquid evaporating in the cold, his army, their spirit broken, left him lying there. Silent regrets hung in the air as they dispersed.

The scout's eyes turned back to the field, where the table and chair stood undisturbed, and they could just make out the box tucked behind the chair. As the creature they were now certain was Scrios rode back to his party, they noticed the clouds overhead breaking apart.

While a few soldiers from the shattered army headed north, turning to their right, the majority opted for the southern route, fragmenting into smaller units as they departed. As one of the last groups walked past the destroyed leader, a younger soldier, who had mostly served as a porter, showed compassion by pulling a blanket from his oversized pack and covering the man before continuing to walk. The retreating and broken force simply discarded anything unneeded or deemed too heavy on the ground, creating a trail of breadcrumbs leading away from the muddy spot the army had marshaled in.

The scouts wanted to check on the spoiled leader. They also yearned to inspect the table and chair, but they dared not disobey their orders. They understood the immense significance of their report. With utmost caution, they backed away from their hiding place, taking care to leave no evidence behind as they retreated from the area. Once they were clear of the immediate vicinity, they pushed themselves to their limits, their weary bodies propelling them forward until the last rays of daylight disappeared. True to their instructions, they always opted for a meandering path instead of a direct route, often circling to high ground to insure they were not being followed. As they took a break for the night, they wrapped themselves in blankets, sharing body heat to combat the biting cold. They made a conscious choice to go without a fire, even though the freezing air left a thin layer of frost by sunrise. After a sleepless night, they eagerly consumed the dried meat at first light, replenished their water skin, and promptly resumed their journey.

When they arrived home, they meticulously described every detail, causing Sanura's mood, as well as everyone else's in the room, to darken.

Chapter 18

Fall, 514 BC, 'Dachaigh a' Mhadaidh-allaidh Farm, Scotland.

Nearly a hundred warriors had come from Sanura's homeland. A group of 15 local men, trained and now warriors, had the bloodline which shielded them from Scrios's influence. Another 150 locals and relatives had trained in the cave. There were approximately 200 women, children, and elderly from the area who required relocation. They selected eleven blood relatives and 30 trained local men at random to evacuate with the families.

Working together, Sanura and Ameatus organized the troops designated for battle into separate teams. Cormic would lead the primary strike force team. He would command a group of 80 soldiers from Sanura's lands, along with 20 locally trained warriors. During the engagement, the group was further divided into teams of ten men. Their strategy involved deploying the ten units, totaling 100 men, led by Cormic for the major assault. Meanwhile, Sanura, Malik, and Robin, who was a blood relative, would lead a larger secondary force. These teams would serve as range weapon support and be available for deployment as the battle required. Even though the group was much larger, the secondary force had only a few of the professional warriors that traveled here with Sanura. Each of these Greeks led a team.

A larger force making up the rest of the troops would stay back on the high ground near the stone circle. From there, they would have a commanding view of the battle and could rain arrows and sling stones on the enemy in support.

Once the discussion and assignments were over, the men said their goodbyes to their families and set off for the faraway valley where they had trained frequently.

The steep-walled valley, which contained a circle of enormous stones in a raised area, resembled a cracked bowl. It offered only two points of entry, with both following the same stream that passed through it from north to south through the narrow cracks. The stone circles held great reverence among the locals, who considered them a shrine.

As the valley was being prepared for the battle, a local artisan who became a warrior added a design to the stone on the outer edge of the ring, to apologize to the original makers of the circle for tarnishing this sacred place with the planned conflict. A soldier, who hailed from a town close to where Sanura was born a thousand years before, took the time to carve prayers to the Gods of his homeland, seeking their aid in vanquishing the evil they were about to face in that place.

Chapter 19

Fall, 514 BC, The Valley of the Stone Circle, Two Days Southwest of the Farm

Scrios felt enticed by this expansive, steep walled valley nestled among towering rolling hills. The place he had seen in Ralf's memories came into view: a small hill with large stones perched at the top, visible in the distance. Following Ralf's memory, he ended up in the very place he was supposed to be. The moment Ralf locked eyes with Scrios, he knew he had made a fatal error, as a sense of dread washed over him.

Scrios suspected someone was planning to kill him. He even expected that it was his family. There was never a shortage of people wishing to kill him; hell, he would take it as an insult if there wasn't. Uncovering plots and ruining the conspirators was a game to him. It was part of what made his life so pleasurable.

Back in his realm, peasant revolts were a cause for celebration and feasting, as spouses witnessed their loved ones turning against each other. Larger assault campaigns from distant and valiant leaders met similar decisive ends.

However, this trip offered a taste of the exotic in an unfamiliar place and a direct confrontation with his sister's descendents. He planned to make it the last such conflict. Her descendants would provide him with a legendary army after his victory. The army he felt certain he deserved.

Ralf, the spy, was aware of the group from a distant land to the south, who had selflessly traveled upon hearing rumors of a cursed fiend on these islands. The term "cursed fiend" made Scrios smile.

Clad in a peculiar attire, the Hellenic army arrived wielding weapons forged in faraway lands. Legends spoke of these gleaming iron weapons that were said to cleave other swords effortlessly in battle. The allure of both ending his sister's bloodline and exploiting these new soldiers for his personal enjoyment was irresistible. Still, he knew that caution was necessary.

In recent weeks, Scrios had gathered a substantial number of soldiers, as well as hundreds of farmers and their families, to travel with him as one shapeless group. There was no organization necessary, at least not currently. He had given them their meanings that he felt certain would perpetuate, even if his ability to communicate with them became clouded by the effects of one of his family. He had become much better at that trick over the centuries.

He and his soldiers disguised themselves by wearing tattered farmer's clothes over their armor, blending in with the crowd. Like shepherds, he and his soldiers led the hoard on foot. He had instilled in them a strong desire to protect him at any cost and help him escape if necessary. The exotic army didn't frighten him because he believed the chances of someone from his sister's bloodline coming from such a far place were extremely low. However, he had a sense that one of his relatives was close by, which left him feeling pain in the pit of his stomach. He touched the necklace he wore with the dried thumbs of the oaf who died tied to the post. Scrios remembered marks he made that day in the soil as he studied the range of the familial effect on him. The feeling he felt in his stomach now was the first indicator. At least one relative was inside this valley somewhere, but not near enough to impair him.

He was certain that the verbal commands he had integrated into his army's knowledge would operate similarly to that of a trained dog, even when the presence of his kin muted his powers. Scrios had a group of lookalikes in the crowd, trained to repeat his commands, no matter how softly he whispered them. Once one repeated his command, there would be a chorus pulling the army into action even without his influencing control. One of his commands involved two guards swiftly apprehending an imposter and quickly retreating to a secure spot. As that thought crossed his mind, a quiet chuckle bubbled up from within him.

Scrios also contemplated his own death and, if it was possible. In a thoughtful manner, he contemplated the sensations and emotions that would accompany that release. Death didn't scare him, but he couldn't shake off the puzzlement about the mechanics of dying, considering that he appeared to be immune to the effects of aging.

Pushing away thoughts of death, he turned his attention to Ralf's home, where his wife and child were waiting. As he guided his group of 600 men, women, and children into the valley, their footsteps echoed like a thundering herd of sheep. Scrios sent the children running ahead, allowing them to frolic in the grass with their sharpened sticks. As they played, the mid-morning sun slowly became masked by a front of clouds.

Chapter 20 - The Ballad of Cormic

Spring, 514 BC, The Valley of the Stone Circle, Two Days Southwest of the Farm

One of the fundamental truths about human history is that humans are flawed and fallible. A second rule emphasizes that mistakes have a knack for surfacing at the most inopportune times. It's possible that the queues went unnoticed, overshadowed by the chaos of life. Cormic stood tall and muscular, a stark contrast to his brothers, who were small, even feeble in comparison.

The responsibility of leading the assault to eliminate or capture the Blue King, if his death was impossible, fell to Cormic. His troops were to eliminate Scrios's army. Cormic led a contingent of 80 elite soldiers from Sanura's guard and 20 specially selected trained locals. Cormic was mentally prepared to take the lives of both men and women bewitched by the creature. He knew they were likely innocent and the creature that shared his blood had corrupted them into supporting it.

The army of the Blue King, however, was a vision out of a nightmare. As a horde of children approached, Cormic felt a mix of confusion and apprehension. Just one of his twin hammers was heavier than any of the children skipping and playing with each other as they approached.

When they drew closer, a wave of fear and sadness washed over him, causing him to freeze in place. Tears gathered in the corners of his eyes as he wrestled with the weight of his command. He had been so proud of being selected to lead.

Helplessly, he glanced at the olive-skinned warriors on either side of him, their horrified expressions mirroring his own as they faced the inevitability of a reaping that would stain their souls.

Scrios savored the agony he could taste. After the children would come the incredible mass of humanity behind them, testing the soldiers' resolve. Scrios was silently offering them a choice they were completely unprepared to make. The children, 100 feet away, playfully arranged themselves in a line and erupted into laughter, eager for the game they were about to play. Behind them formed a group of teenage maidens and women, disrobing as they waited their turn.

Standing a hundred yards back, near the front of the colossal stones, Sanura felt a gut-wrenching agony at the thought of what her troops would require from their weapons.

The plan centered on using the family's power to quash the Blue King's Power over his army. Once Scrios lost control, they would deploy their forces to either kill or apprehend him. They had even prepared a thick bag to place over Scrios's head and later do whatever was necessary to eliminate his evil from the world. Should he prove invulnerable, they would secure him with chains and either bury him or cast him into the sea.

They expected a battle, expecting it to be fought between armies. Regardless of victory or defeat today, these warriors would have to decide between submission or committing unforgivable acts.

They had practiced avoiding eye contact, everyone had trained to keep their eyes low when facing the creature. Little did they know that when they stared downward, they would come face to face with the children, some as young as four, who stood at the forefront of his army.

When the children stopped their march forward, a surge of hope swept through Cormic's lines. A group of formidable warriors from Scrios's army marched confidently towards the front. The garrison of children quickly split apart, creating a path for the men in armor who carried an array of weapons and sturdy wooden shields. As they moved past the children, the two middle guards suddenly stepped forward and to the side, causing a small, hooded figure to burst out like pus from a boil. "Is this all there is? When your king approaches, you kneel..." screeched the hooded figure.

An arrow suddenly materialized from nowhere and slammed into the hooded figure's masked face, throwing it back, as if pulled by an invisible force. The impact drove the lifeless body to the ground with enough force to make it slide headfirst several feet.

Another figure, in similar garb, ejected from the group of warriors, and the discussion continued without a hitch. ...down as a sign of respect? Or do I convert you into baby killers first?" said the second veiled figure in a different, this time feminine voice.

The bow in Sanura's hands was slack, already notched with a second arrow, as she watched in horror. A chilling understanding of the enemy's true capabilities flooded her thoughts, sending a tremor of fear through her. She had underestimated this sinister creature, and now, despite nearly two years of preparation, she realized her army was hopelessly unprepared for the battle ahead.

As if answering to a silent command, the horde of children rushed forward. It was as if driven by some powerful will. Their advance momentarily caused even Sanura's skilled men to stumble back in revulsion before recovering their footing. As the line faltered, Cormic roared the well-practiced commands, as Ameatus would, his voice echoing like thunder, snapping them out of their panic.

Becoming the leader the army needed, Cormic turned and rallied his men, while the children ran towards his exposed back. Faced with the terrible predicament, they had no choice but to respond in the only way they could.

Sanura could hear the mournful wails of her troops as they swiftly dealt with Scrios' ruthless initial move in the battle. The reaping of the young happened so quickly that soon, all that remained was a stunned silence filled with sorrowful prayers.

As Sanura stood near the stone circle, a dreadful stillness descended upon the battlefield. Only the unsettling sound of her troops retching, both in the battle line below, and the witnesses standing beside her broke the silence of Scrios's intentional pause.

The weight of what her men were enduring became too much for Sanura to bear. She ordered Malik and the others to stay and be ready to provide archer support if needed, and she sprinted down the steep hill from the stone circle to join the front line.

She refused to sit above as if in judgment, while her men stained their souls. Instead, she would stand beside them and share the burden. As Sanura ran down the hill, another veiled individual materialized among the chaotic ranks of Scrios' army.

The strategy of using a leader pure in blood might have worked to perfection, if it hadn't been for Cormic's mother's brief affair with a woodsman neighbor 22 summers ago. If only there had been more contemplation of Cormic's similar appearance. If the woodsman hadn't met his untimely demise by a freak accident long before Cormic's birth? Maybe people would have linked the woodsman's immense height and strength to Cormic's. Perhaps before this audacious confrontation with Scrios revealed his true lineage.

Cormic, fueled by tales of his ancestors, and with a distorted perception of his heritage, locked eyes with the monster Scrios as the creature pulled back its veil. Cormic's world irrevocably twisted. In an instant, everything became clear to Cormic. He had no choice but to eliminate Farhad, the foreign warrior positioned to his right, and the rest of these men who he had once shared a bond of brotherhood until their betrayal. This deceit which he could not remember the specifics of currently. He only knew that their deceit had shattered the kinship, and now was the time to level the score.

As Cormic swung the heavy hammer in his right hand, it connected with Farhad, sending him flying backwards in an impossible cartwheel motion. The impact was so powerful that Farhad's chest exploded, creating a wave of confusion and panic that spread through Sanura's army at the same rate the gore splashed those around the spinning corpse. So practiced, the plan, disintegrated into madness.

The sight of Farhad's lifeless body sent a shockwave through the ranks of the disciplined soldiers. Simius, Farhad's childhood friend, dropped his weapon in horror when his friend landed at his feet. He gazed into his comrade's eyes, which remained oblivious to his impending death. He stared into the eyes of Farhad, as his friend's mouth silently worked on words without breath. As life's light left him, Simius cradled him and escorted him to the darkness.

After carefully placing his brother on the ground, he reached down and picked up his spear, feeling its weight in his hand. Standing over the body, Simius could feel an intense mix of anger and determination coursing through him as he welcomed the retribution for his friend.

Only for a moment, the discipline of several of the forward guards faltered. The moment was far too long. Their attention drawn upwards, they searched for the cause of the impact, a reaction which changed the path of their lives. Instead of the cause of the commotion, they saw Scrios' blue eyes. The gaze of his eyes shredded their reality and subjected them to the creature's intent. Their break in focus turned Sanura's trained men into the enemy, causing confusion while Scrios's rabble closed in. Standing tall, Scrios grinned as his army surged around him and his six faithful guards. The horde flowing around them like an island amidst a raging river, while Sanura's battle plan crumbled.

Pausing at the base of the slight incline, 50 yards from the chaos, Sanura commanded the larger group observing from higher ground to shower the enemy's lines with a volley of arrows. With a frustrated curse, she squared her shoulders and unsheathed her sword and sprinted towards the clash.

The finely orchestrated plan burned in front of her with enough heat to warm her hands in a harsh winter. With her eyes ablaze, she fought to devise a new strategy, realizing that the concept of bloodline relationship magic was nothing more than a child's dream. She desperately wished that Scrios had been too.

Pausing once more, she let out a commanding shout, instructing the troops to maintain a safe distance of 200 feet from the creature and to resort to their ranged weapons only. "Under no circumstances should you ever get close to the creature." She ordered.

Sanura urgently called on her remaining troops to regroup and retreat towards her, determined to reform the line and fight their way back up the hill towards the stone circle. Obeying without hesitation, Simius and the twelve remaining troops skillfully maneuvered around the colossal ogre of Cormic, its twin hammers crashing down dangerously close.

Sanura's face twitched as she sighted in on the prodigy now turned enemy and released the arrow that provided the last words to his tragic ballad.

Chapter 21

Spring, 514 BC, The Valley of the Stone Circle

While Sanura and the remaining members of the first assault warriors fought their retreat up the hill towards the circle of enormous stones, the number of loyal warriors gradually decreased as they bravely sacrificed themselves in battle and fell around her. Following her orders, the archers maintained their position at a safe distance, falling back while remaining within bow range. As she entered the circle, she quickly sought refuge behind a large rock, using it as a temporary shield. She commanded her oldest trusted friend, "Rain death upon us all once the creature enters the ring and I give the signal!"

The air behind her filled as Ameatus responded in a loud resigned voice, "As it will be!"

The field below Ameatus was a grim sight, as countless bodies of his countrymen and others he had grown affection for, lay strewn across the ground, their mangled forms either attempting to inch towards him or succumbing to their fatal wounds. Noting the moments when the rabble diverted their focus from a Hellenic warrior as he turned and aligned with them, Ameatus ordered the archers to shift their focus deeper into the enemy lines while he awaited Sanura's suicidal command. Taking the initiative after recognizing the immense danger posed by the friendly forces that had changed sides. He ordered the archers to target and disable the compromised elite army members.

Below, Sanura cautiously moved to the far side of the circle, desperately hoping that the stone ring indeed held the mysterious power the locals spoke of. Adjusting her twisted armor, she prepared for the upcoming maelstrom. She wielded her short sword in her right hand, feeling its perfect balance, and in her left hand, she held the exquisite electrum gold tube containing the stone she had named Enki. The scepter's intricate design featuring a beautifully crafted Asclepius serpent, now covered in blood of friends and enemy.

Striking a confident pose, she watched as her remaining force strategically positioned themselves around her. "Eyes down!" she repeated sternly, emphasizing the obvious importance. With blood steadily flowing from multiple wounds, Simius nodded a curt move up and down with his head, his jaw clenched in concentration. She reached for him with the scepter. The moment it contacted him, the flow halted, and scabs appeared almost instantaneously. With a second nod, he expressed his gratitude, meeting her eye. Sanura tried her best to exude the same confidence that some groups attributed to her divine status. The tattered remains of the strike force needed it.

Scrios entered the far side of the circle, surrounded by Sanura's own stoic soldiers and a few remaining local warriors. His frail and delicate appearance caught her off guard. Despite his youthful appearance, Scrios emitted an almost emaciated fragility, enhanced by his pallid blue complexion, which added to his cadaverous appearance. When the creature shockingly spoke to her in her own language, "Join me and live," she tried to avoid looking higher than his waist. With the golden tube clasped tightly in her hand, she could feel the warmth of Enki and sensed its bewilderment towards the unnatural blue man. The absolute confidence she had in Enki made her fear disappear.

Ignoring her own training and defying all reason, she raised her gaze and locked eyes with the creature wearing the guise of a feeble blue man. A moment of pain shot through her head and vanished instantly. Regardless of Scrios's intentions, Enki restored her before she could be affected.

Scrios' face contorted with confusion, his eyebrows furrowing. "You... you are different." As he spoke, a wry smile tugged at the corners of his mouth. "How on earth did you accomplish that? Who or what are you? Although we are clearly not kin, you somehow resist me."

The creature's reference to the family's resistance momentarily confused Sanura, as she had already disregarded it as mere fantasy.

Scrios set his jaw firmly at the sight of the unfamiliar human, determined to try again. As he did, a brief surge of pain coursed through Sanura's mind, quickly fading away. In that fleeting moment, she could hear her mother's voice singing softly, a sound she hadn't heard in a thousand years.

She allowed no visible reaction on her face this time, but a subtle, knowing smile played at the corners of her mouth. Scrios continued, his voice filled with deceit, "You are different, and I treasure different things, you, young lady, I will let leave and you can go live out your life as long as it is away from here and away from me," he lied.

"Young?" she laughed; her voice filled with amusement. "I have watched a thousand winters pass before that creature shit you out... maybe more. I have lost count, and I will do as I desire without want of your permission." She paused dramatically, so she could cut him off when he next attempted to speak. When he pursed his lips to speak, she proceeded, her voice filled with anticipation. "I have traveled for months for the promise of this day. Your hubris and actions have led me here to put an end to your existence. I believe this calling is the purpose that has kept me alive for so long. My witness to the rise and fall of civilizations prepared me for today's necessary intervention. I have witnessed the aging and passing of both friends and loved ones. I have lived a life beyond your comprehension, so I would have the perspective of seeing past your tricks and focus on the only outcome of today. Your demise!" She finished.

Scrios nervously searched for an unattainable purchase in her psyche, while she had talked, causing a painful strobe like sensation in her head. The pains abruptly ceased as the Blue King altered his strategy, and her own former countrymen began closing in on her.

"I'm sorry my friends," Sanura said, "but the greater good is being done here. I forgive you and apologize for your sacrifice." Wearing a look of bored determination, she instructed her remaining troops to fall back to the primary group and gave the signal for the rain of arrows to begin.

With the whistles of death falling, she forged ahead alone. The air filled with a sizzling sound as a deadly rain of arrows fell. She could barely contain her emotions as the first of her former students went limp, an arrow sprouting from his head above his right eye. The stone, sensing the ancient evil she was staring at, noticed its pleasure at her pain and for the first time in Enki's existence, it experienced the emotion of genuine anger.

As Scrios observed her deadly intent and fearless triumph in the melee, he felt a surge of panic and quickly commanded his own men to enter the fray.

Scrios pondered how this woman should have been dead 20 times over. He had turned her troops on her and gave them clarity that Sanura had always been the actual enemy. But the betrayal didn't cause her to hesitate in battle. As arrows rained down from above, Scrios watched her wade through the onslaught of her once loyal friends, marveling at her seemingly invincible presence. He couldn't understand why she required a guard.

Her deadly movements were a combination of practiced grace and precision. Moreover, she exhibited complete fearlessness towards an opponent's blow. He observed as an errant arrow lodged itself downward from behind, into her shoulder, emerging from her chest. Apart from the force of the impact, it had seemingly no effect. Almost unbelievably, he caught sight of it as it rapidly retreated, leaving a wound that seemed to close and heal itself in a matter of moments. The realization that she might be a God filled Scrios with mortal fear.

Like a skilled reaper in a wheat field, she moved through the onslaught of soldiers with her sword, cutting them down one by one. She wore a mask of indifference, but inside, her heart ached with every blow she delivered to those who the creature had turned against her. Consuming it, Scrios could taste the unmistakable sweetness of her anguish. The troops relentlessly attacked her, but she effortlessly shrugged off their strikes, emerging from the chaos unscathed despite the damage to her armor. Regardless of the unmistakable aura of inevitability surrounding her advance, Scrios failed to perceive the imminent danger she posed, armed with nothing more than a simple sword.

He locked eyes with her and caught a quick glimpse of her consciousness. Observing her, he concluded that the exertion was taking a toll on her ability to defend herself. In that fleeting instant when their eyes met, he gained insight into the stone concealed within the tube she carried in her left hand. Despite his best efforts, he failed to connect with her meaningfully, rendering him unable to help her find a renewed purpose. In that fleeting moment, though, he comprehended the value she placed on the crystal in the tube, creating his desire to possess it. He was open to the idea of her bringing it to him, if that's what she preferred.

Their eyes met when she was only a step away, and in that fleeting instant, he sensed an opportunity, desperately willing her to hand over the stone. To Sanura's horror, her left hand involuntarily extended itself against her will.

As soon as the scepter touched his hand, Scrios felt a wave of immediate regret for his last demand. Something violently ripped his consciousness from his body. Curiosity about the provenance of the crystal striking him a bit too late. Instantly, something transported his essence, and his perspective and frame of the world changed.

He observed the world as if he were seeing his surroundings from the palm of a hand that somehow, he knew, had once been his own. He watched as his body became instantly rigid and turned a carbon black. The world became engulfed in a blinding white light, and he descended from a height of several feet to the charred ground below.

For just a moment, as he fell, he sensed the fleeting presence of another entity in his prison as it dispersed.

Settling to the ground, he felt a disorienting vertigo as his vision expanded to take a panoramic view in every direction at the same time. As he looked down, he saw the dirt smoldering and emitting a faint glow, yet he couldn't feel any heat. Destruction spread in every direction, its reach expanding like a tidal wave of chaos. Intensifying relentlessly, it laid waste to everything in its trajectory, until it dissolved in the far reaches of his sight. The enormous stones that made up the circle now lay flat and scattered, their once imposing presence diminished. The sight created a sense of emptiness in the smoldering clearing. Looking up at the enormous stones, now prone, Scrios marveled at the auburn hue radiating from the molten surface that now faced the sky. The once lush, centuries-old trees, just 20 feet away from the circle, were now reduced to smoking bumps barely visible above the ground. Tree roots, fresh and upturned, were clear in the distance, bowled over and steaming as though scorched by an explosive firestorm. Flames were consuming the fallen trees. The nearby combatants and bodies of the fallen had disappeared, engulfed by the mighty wave that had created a space around it.

The explosion caused the low clouds above to part, revealing a rapidly expanding blue circle of sky. Sunlight briefly streamed in, illuminating the destruction while lightning flickered in the rapidly retreating clouds of the newly cleared heavens. Amidst the cataclysm, Scrios could only identify his own naked and burned body, standing upright with a comically surprised expression frozen on his face.

As the wave of destruction reached the edges of the steep-walled valley, it continued its path of devastation as it swept through the area. The force of the wave was so powerful that it even clipped the trees off the hilltops within sight, leaving nothing standing in its wake. In an instant, the ground started trembling violently, accompanied by the intensifying sound of a building noise that drew nearer and nearer to him. His former body convulsed twice, as if seized by a sudden spasm, before finally collapsing onto the artifact that now entrapped him. As it fell, his lifeless body covered the crystal, obscuring everything else from view. Abruptly, the corpse was forcefully dragged away by the torrent of dirt and rock, separating his corpse from his crystalline trap, leaving behind a hauntingly quiet and motionless scene.

Part 2 – The Spring Flower

Interlude - Lord of the Pig Faced

Entombed, Scrios had a lot of time to ponder. At first, he thought introspectively about how he had fallen for some terrible ruse. He cursed himself as a fool, but that title didn't quite fit. In the blinks and flashes where he caught the glimpses of Sanura, especially near the end of the battle as they had both fatigued, he had sensed this item. The reason he wanted it was simply because she cared about it so completely. He knew love conceptually, from the people he had destroyed, although the genuine appeal eluded him. Well, at least love for another creature. If it was the same as fondness, he had that of himself.

When he momentarily compelled Sanura to give him the item, he sensed horror and the fear of loss in her. Scrios knew unquestioningly that her reaction was genuine. Minus that certainty, he would never have touched it. Also, if this had been a simple trap for him, why would they have used something so volatile that it would annihilate themselves, along with him and both armies?

He had never known humans to be so selfless or have the capability at their disposal to destroy themselves just to vanquish an enemy. This left him questioning if it was an unknown characteristic of himself or the crystal that entrapped him and caused the devastation.

Somehow, despite the catastrophic explosion that he witnessed, the artifact he had taken from Sanura's hand; where he was now trapped, was still intact. Buried in the dirt and dark, he could still sense the surrounding artifact.

Scrios wondered about the properties of the crystal that now was his prison, and how the crystal related to the artifact. Scrios raged at the nothingness that surrounded him, about how unfair it was that the crystal's design was so specific to the purpose of trapping him. The metal artifact surrounding him must be for preventing multiple people from seeing him at once.

By that assumption, he wondered why his relatives wanted to trap him. He wondered if they meant to enslave him, and it had gone poorly for them. "But why?" he wondered. "Why would they have designed such an item... and how?"

Scrios was wrong about his assumptions of the design, though. The design of Enki's home predated the creature's entrapment by over 400 years. For Enki, the design was ornamental, being known as, "The eye of Asclepius".

They had carefully positioned the stone inside an electrum gold tube to maximize the appearance of the inclusion, which gave it the appearance of an eye with an elongated pupil. The design met Enki's approval because it didn't alter his perception and used a metal conductive to his powers.

In a practical sense, it made the stone much easier for Sanura to carry. In its appearance and its function as the Eye of Asclepius, it became an item of lore. The possession of it elevated Sanura's prestige in the region to that of a god walking the earth. A single serpent lazily coiled counterclockwise from the bottom, adorning the short electrum scepter.

For Scrios, the prison that entrapped him and robbed him of his corporal form. Until someone found him, he was stuck in this place. He had a long time to contemplate these questions. He stayed buried there for hundreds of years, as the loose dirt packed around him and roots grew past him. As the isolation tested his sanity.

Despite losing the ability to sleep, the sheer boredom of his confines pushed Scrios's mind into a state of dreaming. Wonderful dreams of torture that he would snap out of and find himself in his mundane tomb. His routine existence taught him focus. It also taught him patience, something he had never had to have since the day of his birth. If he wanted something, he took it... but not here.

His focus improved so much that one day he felt a human walk past his burial spot. He had felt other animals too, but not humans, since his imprisonment. He screamed at them from several feet below in the dirt, hoping they would hear him and dig. They did not hear him. His desperation had long faded to fatality before he had discovered a deception that would one day release him from the dirt.

The trickery he learned created a flicker of interest in everything from forest animals to the innocent minds of humankind. The squirrels, believing they were digging for a lost nut, dug a small depression directly over the artifact before losing interest. Over a hundred years, the small depression grew into a ditch, that with rain, helped clear the mud above him.

When Liam, a simple hunter, suddenly had an urge to dig into the large depression in the earth and uncovered the golden tube, he wiped away the dirt and rinsed out the mud in a small stream that ran several hundred yards below. Seeing the sky centuries after his entrapment in the stone, Scrios rejoiced. He was so enthralled when the pig faced Liam gazed into the end of the tube, and Scrios felt that connection as he defiled the mind of his savior. It was so intense he almost convinced him to bludgeon himself to death... but he had learned patience and focus. Doing so would have only left him sitting at the edge of a stream for who knows how many more years. Instead, Liam became his steed. In his mind, Scrios encountered a language similar to one he knew during his reign as the Blue King. He took a perverse joy in learning, from Liam, that his name, bestowed by his mother's black heart, had not been totally forgotten, while he sat in the earth.

His name, Scrios, now had the meaning, destruction.

The locals in their guttural tongue had altered it a little to fit their primitive pallet, but there it was, "sgrios". Though his time as the "Blue King" had faded from history after 500 years, his name still resonated in their stories. Liam's pig face grew in a half-baked smile, emoting the pleasure his mind's passenger felt.

Chapter 1 - Jen

September 9th, 1979, NC State Campus, Raleigh, North Carolina

Jen, a 20-year-old college student in Raleigh, reluctantly left her night of studying behind to join her friends at Barry's, a bar on Hillsborough Street, for penny beer night. Meeting someone was the last thing on her mind. Her last "romance" had been a real prick that would not stop calling her on the dorm phone. Reflecting on her decision, she couldn't help but wonder why she had ever given him that number. Fed up with boys, Jen made a firm decision to recommit herself to her studies.

It took her approximately 15 minutes to walk from her high-rise dormitory, passing through the unique and constantly developing free expression tunnel; the colorful tunnel which served as a shortcut under the train tracks dividing the campus. Exiting the tunnel, she turned to the right and ascended past Mann Hall, making her way up to Hillsborough Street. This route skipped some of the depraved aspects of the walk, but you still had to face the attention of the older men loitering near the topless bar and Studio 1, the infamous porn theater, before finally arriving at Barry's.

It was there, one night at the beginning of spring semester, where she met a foreign student from Scotland by the name of Laoch. Even though he probably didn't need a line, she still remembered Laoch's. Amidst the loud driving music and energetic atmosphere of the dance bar, he approached, his voice booming in his thick Scottish brogue as he introduced himself, "Hi there, my name is Laoch, I'm cursed with the worst name in history, and now no one will dance with me. Would you... please... dispel this terrible witchcraft?" he said while offering his hand.

Tall and lean, he had sea-blue eyes and brownish red hair. With some people, acne scars like his, could ruin a face for life; with him, though, it gave him character and she could picture him as a boy living with that name. Before even stepping onto the small checkerboard dance floor, she sensed trouble, as her chest fluttered just being near him. People played darts on the left and foosball on the right, flanking the dance floor. She knew somehow, immediately; she was dancing with the love of her life.

Laoch, she would find, embodied the essence of a true gentleman. Not until the second actual date, did he even attempt to kiss her.

Whether fueled by beer or deliberately exaggerated, the thick brogue in his pickup line would haunt him for the rest of their days. The mere mention of Sean Connery would inevitably lead to endless teasing. In a theater in 1986, the movie Highlander had Jen in stitches. She burst into laughter when Connery, with a thick Scottish brogue, delivered the line, "I'm not Spanish, I'm Egyptian." Jen's howls of laughter filled the theater to such a degree, that they had no choice but to exit and seek solace in the lobby, leaving the other viewers in confusion.

She was aware of his feelings for her, yet their vastly different backgrounds posed a challenge. Their first meeting marked the beginning of a bond so strong that, as her mom put it, "they were attached at the hip".

It happened with no pressure. Their constant seeking of each other's presence resulted from their fondness for each other. The next summer, after her junior year, she eagerly joined him on a trip to experience, "His Scotland".

Atholl, the rural region in central Scotland where his family hailed from, was a place he held dear. Their house over there was massive. "Um, is that a castle?" Jen asked as they approached in a taxi.

With a laugh, he responded, "No, love. It's a manor house, although it does have very thick walls. We call it and the surrounding lands Wolfborn."

Surrounding the manor house was a small stone wall, which hinted at its history and the fortitude assuring those inside its solid walls. Multiple barns dotted the property, both inside and outside of the ancient stone wall, adding to the historical ambiance. Even though the house could accommodate 30 people, only eight individuals called it home.

As they arrived in the taxi from the airport in the late afternoon, Laoch's father, Laoch Kier Ferguson the III, and his wife Mimi warmly greeted them. According to his father, the Ferguson family claimed this area as their ancestral home long before recorded history.

Living with them was Mimi's father William, who, to Jen's surprise, was actually a descendant of minor royalty on his mother's side. He had been a celebrated celebrity and honored veteran of World War Two when he was young. The effects of dementia were clear in his anxious eyes, reducing him to a mere shell of his former self. A telltale sign was when you posed a question to him, when a momentary glimpse of self-doubt would flicker in his eyes, only to be masked quickly by his attempt to answer. Although he was usually quiet, when he spoke, his words were beautifully eloquent, captivating everyone with the stories of his youth.

Laoch's younger brother Kyle also lived in the house, destined to become a near replica of his brother, distinguished only by his flowing black locks. Kyle was going through the typical mid teen rebelliousness, with his messy hair and constant eye rolling. With his adolescent naivete, Kyle convinced himself that he was one of a kind, both in terms of fashion and enlightenment. This was a perception only shared by him and his friends. When he returned home from the private boarding school he attended, he would often immerse himself in his own world, tuning out the outside world with his spongy orange headphones and Sony Walkman.

Bynum, the family chef, also lived in the house, along with Nell, a nurse who assisted with William. Jen also met Donna, who diligently cleaned and managed the interior of the manor as if it belonged to her. Daniel was the last person Jen met. In his early thirties, Daniel, a cousin, contributed to the farming, livestock, and outdoor maintenance.

With the build of an NFL defensive end, Daniel appeared like he could effortlessly handle the animals while simultaneously mending a fence by driving posts with his fist. Despite his simian build, he possessed a graceful agility, especially when he was up high, whether working on a barn roof or pruning trees, exhibiting an unnatural sense of balance.

Chapter 2

June 3rd 1980 The Big House, Atholl, Scotland

Jen learned, as Laoch had forewarned, that his home was a functioning farm where everyone played a part. Although they had paid servants and helpers, they also considered them as part of the family.

Every hired hand had a long-standing family history of service, spanning multiple generations. Most times, their own families had grown up within the confines of these very walls. Bynum and Donna sat at the family table because everyone there considered them part of the family. As with any family, they all joined forces to tidy up the table, creating a harmonious symphony of clinking dishes and laughter. Their substantial land holding meant that many other extended family members in the vicinity played a role in ensuring that their existence remained sustainable. In fact, the area was bustling with extended family members. The family dinner was always a lively event, with the number of guests often reaching 20 or more, and fresh faces appearing almost every day. Lunch was a casual affair, with food laid out for everyone to help themselves or grab a pre-made sandwich.

Just like everyone else, the expectation was that Jen would lend a hand and assist with the daily tasks. Jen experienced a series of failures on her first day, from milking a cow to other manual farm duties, but she finally found her groove with feeding the chickens. On the second day, she struggled to get out of bed because of the intense muscle soreness reminiscent of her first skiing experience in high school. Despite her own discomfort, her solace came from knowing that her Laoch, or "Ceithir," as his family affectionately referred to him, was experiencing the same level of agony after his failed attempt to show off on the first day.

"After breakfast, take her to the stream... to the spot. And both of you soak for an hour," Laoch's mother Mimi said, in a commanding tone. So, once they finished breakfast, Jen and Laoch changed into their swimming attire and took a short five-minute walk from the house. The beautiful spot, near an "L" shaped turn in the small stream, provided a serene escape near to the house. It overlooked the expansive field and the rolling hills beyond.

Jen seemed impressed, at least until her foot first contacted the water. "No freaking way! That water is freezing!"

Laoch rolled his eyes, "Don't be such a wimp. It's not that bad... and in case you didn't know, this place, in these parts, has been known for its healing powers for ages." He pointed towards the carvings on the rocks across the stream as if they were proof of his claim. The ancient art, carved into the ancient stones, comprised intricate circles and knots. Aging and weathering had taken their toll on some petroglyphs, making them nearly invisible.

Demonstrating with bravado how simple it was, Laoch fearlessly stepped into the icy stream, displaying remarkable resilience as he tried to mask the pain. The only sign of his inner turmoil was the subtle tension in the muscles near his jaw, contrasting with his outward display of calmness. With a subtle tilt of her head, Jen responded to the situation, "fine." After cautiously maneuvering herself along the edge of a sizeable rock, she executed a cannonball into the water right next to him, causing him to discharge a high-pitched, girlish squeal.

As the splash rapidly approached his dry torso, he attempted to defend himself with his hands. Jumping in all at once, rather than the torture of gradual entry, was not totally without pain, but coming to the surface to see Laoch with his valiant bravery stripped bare by the splash was totally worth it. Once the initial burst of shock subsided, she adjusted, quickly becoming more comfortable with the water, as the temperature seemed to fade to a strong cool from a painful cold.

Later, with towels draped over their swimwear, they left the stream and started their walk back. It was at this point that Jen noticed a significant improvement in how she was feeling. Though she was hesitant to classify it as having "healing properties," she found that using the cold compress of the deep pools on her sore and swollen muscles acted as an effective remedy, resulting in a noticeable reduction in soreness.

It took her two days, but eventually she got the hang of the chores she was assisting with. On the second night, she took a seat in the main room and engaged in a pleasant conversation with William. There were moments when William strongly believed that Jen was actually Margaret, his deceased daughter, who had tragically lost her life to Polio many years ago. Initially, she took the time to correct him, but as she realized the twinges of pain on his face, she just let it go. She realized the correction might have triggered memories of the loss, causing him to re-experience the pain once more.

William appeared to be on the verge of falling asleep, muttering incomprehensibly, only to suddenly jolt awake and launch into a story that seemed to have no connection to anyone in the room. He experienced the poignant moment again in his thoughts, simultaneously taking part and recounting the events as if he were a narrator:

Tom walks into the room, and I ask him, "So, Tom, tell us about Tilly?"

"There's nothing to tell, really," Tom said dismissively, waving his hand.

"Jumping Jesus, you slept with her, didn't you?" I stood up from my bunk, yelling.

"What do you mean?" replied Tom.

"Tom, in case you haven't noticed, you have a distinct pattern. You find the girl of your dreams," using my fingers to count. "You pursue her to the detriment of everything else... school, work, friends... her other relationships. And you woo her away from any other distractions... and you take her out... and something happens."

"Sex!" Tim supplied helpfully.

"Immediately following, you break things off and soon..." William paused momentarily, taking a deep breath, "and just as if scripted, the phone on the wall suddenly starts ringing."

"Don't you bloody answer that!!!" Tom spoke at me.

I was gobsmacked. The intensity of my emotions caused my face to burn red and contort, almost as if it was on the verge of breaking, as I yelled at Tom. "You sir are a walking and somehow talking yeast infection." I picked up the phone and tried my best to sound composed. "Welcome to the den of sweaty men. This is Bill. How may I address your call? Em hmm ah one sec. Tom, it's for you."

Tom looked at me with all the friendliness of a rabid badger and I covered the receiver and held the phone away from him, "You be nice to her or I will hide you in the quad. I'm not bloody kidding. She is delightful, from a good family and way too fucking good for the likes of you already. Now be a man." I said, as I stabbed him in the chest with the phone.

Tom looked into my eyes and I think he could see that I was not kidding, and I think it scared him. I don't think he had ever heard me speak more seriously in his life. He stared into my eyes as he lifted the phone to his mouth and, with the change of a natural born evangelist, spoke with a chipper tone, "Tilly!! So sorry, I meant to call yesterday and got caught up in the lab... uh huh. Yes! That would be lovely... sure. How about we meet for coffee at Dregs in, say, 30 minutes? I just need to freshen up and I will be on my way... um hmm great! See you there. First one grabs a table... Bye now," and he gently hung up the phone and poled the room. "Better? Was that good enough to delay my destruction in the quad, Lord William?"

"I would have held you down, you troglodyte, so Bill could have hit you with the bloody edge." In his boisterous Edinburgh clatter, Tim, the towering Scot stated. "She is a bloody delight and way too good for you. If you let her down, you do it easy and don't piss about. And when you realized you peaked with her, don't come whining back about how you shoulda," Tim's ears and cheeks were flushed red.

"Well said Tim," I said. "We will put the beating on hold, but it is coming. I can feel it in my bones. Perhaps no one educated you on how to be a gentleman. You should be glad it isn't my father, Lord William, standing here... or he would hide me for warning you, before I decorated the bushes in the quad with your entrails. Now go drink coffee, you cretin... and be glad I love you like a brother... and not as a son... That was the day Tilly broke things off with Tom... at the coffee shop, I don't think Thomas ever got over that."

With the completion of his story, William's eyes cleared for a moment. He Grinned and said, "I understand that stories from elderly gentlemen may not interest young women like yourself, my dear Jen. Nevertheless, I am grateful for your attentiveness."

"Not at all. It was lovely."

A momentary smile graced William's face before his eyes became clouded again, his expression turning to one of sheer terror as tears welled up. "Tom... my beautiful Tom, no! It will be ok... we will get help. CORPSMAN!!! We need a CORPSMAN IMMEDIATELY!!!"

Nell, William's nurse, swiftly entered the room and soothed him. Jen felt helpless and was at the edge of tears herself when her Laoch wrapped his arms around her from behind.

William stared at Tom's blood covering his younger hands as they changed to those of an old man, as the blood vanished. He watched his fingers curl with age and his knuckles swell with arthritis, and he found he was back in the great room of Wolfborn.

William still smelled the blood, even though he knew it was gone. He still felt its coagulating stickiness between his fingers. The tears, balanced on the bottom of his eye, gave the room around him halos as he stood, and cleared his throat. He stiffened, looked at Nell, "I'm fine. Sorry I got caught up in the spirit there," and waved her off.

Adopting the disciplined stride of a military leader, he paced in front of the cold fireplace. The repetitive motion calmed him and soothed his racing heart. In his mind, he meticulously inspected the troops, visualizing their uniforms and assessing their readiness. Once he regained his composure, he returned to his seat and uttered the dreaded words that no one wanted to hear.

"Tom died in my hands, you see? A careless bloody round, fired in a battle that settled nothing. One second, he was there cracking a joke in the worst of situations, when I heard a sound like a bee fly from my left, as it passed me and suddenly Tom was silent. I thought it was part of his joke," as a self-conscious smile crossed his face through the fresh tears that rolled down his cheeks.

"He fell to the ground like a puppeteer's mistake. I barely caught him as he crumbled. There was a torrent of blood coming from under his lid. I lowered him and carefully remove his cap, which prompted his head to loll towards me. In a reflexive action, I held the remnants of his brain in his shattered skull, as I urgently called for help."

A minute passed in silence as William gazed at a scene unfolding in the distance, appearing lost in a different time and place.

Following the pause, he spoke again, stating, "Approximately one month after my arrival back in Britton, after Dunkirk, I coincidentally encountered Tilly at a Saturday market in London. I promptly inquired about her marital status, to which she responded with amusement, "Oh no, definitely not!" The question I asked next was overly presumptuous for a gentleman. I sought her opinion on the matter of my desire to court her. With a strange expression, she uttered, "I believe that would be quite grand." I took immediate action and as a result, we were married a half year later. It was a scandalous affair." William laughed.

74

Over the course of the following two hours, he spoke incessantly about Tilly and the light she brought to the world. He lauded her remarkable qualities and how she proved to be an outstanding mother. Just before retiring, he stared into the younger Laoch's eyes, "Ceithir? I like this one... this one is your Tilly. Don't cock it up."

As Jen prepared to retire to her room, a burning curiosity consumed her. Unable to contain herself any longer, she turned to Laoch and inquired, "What does Ceithir mean?" Laoch laughed. "The word means four," he clarified with a smile, "referring to me being 'the fourth Laoch' in Gaelic".

Chapter 3

June 9th, 1980, The Big House, Atholl, Scotland

On the sixth day in Scotland, a Saturday morning, they bid farewell to Wolfborn Manor, affectionately known as the "big house." Jen broke the silence as they drove away and asked, "What's the story behind the name Wolfborn?"

"It's a family thing," he replied. Our family once had a reputation for owning wolves. One of my cousins still does. In fact, he has about 20 wolves of different ages currently. The majority are rescues and rehabs from other countries, but a few are pets. Kier's expertise and bond with the animals is truly exceptional. Laoch explained that people once knew this entire area as 'dachaigh a' mhadaidh-allaidh,' which loosely translates to 'Home of the Wolves."

Jen turned towards him with a wry smile. "Ahhhh," she replied with a laugh, "Now I get why you picked NC State for your school."

"Pure coincidence!" Laoch's face lit up with a smile.

When their adventurous second week of traveling in Scotland ended, and they settled back into the manor for their last night. They enjoyed a fantastic dinner with his family, filled with laughter and delicious food, before retiring into their separate bedrooms.

The following morning, Laoch's parents kindly offered to drive them to the airport for their flight back to Raleigh, NC via good old JFK.

Chapter 4

May 16th, 1981, NC State University, Raleigh, North Carolina.

The next year, their senior year at NC State seemed to pass in the blink of an eye. The atmosphere at their graduation was electric as their families, who had never met before, came together to celebrate this momentous occasion. It was not entirely surprising, yet still disheartening, that William couldn't make the trip because of health concerns. As they posed for the ceremonial pictures in front of the bell tower after graduation, Jen couldn't believe that both their families had come together to be a part of the photo session. It didn't register in her mind until she turned around and saw Laoch on one knee, a ring in his outstretched hand. Everyone else was aware it would happen, and she had fallen for it. Jen almost said jokingly, "No way!" but tears welled up in her eyes and she could only manage a damp nod.

Chapter 5

September 12th, 1981, The Big House, Atholl, Scotland

On September 12th, 1981, Jen and Laoch exchanged vows in a forest bursting with fall colors at Wolfborn, a ceremony that turned out to be quite grand despite its humble original design to be much smaller. One of Jen's new family members, who owned a warehousing and shipping company in the area, presented her with a job opportunity where they were seeking an accountant for their business. Accepting the offer, her heart swelled with happiness at the sight of her husband's beaming smile. The chance to apply his soil science degree to his own family's farm thrilled Laoch.

So, Jen and Laoch moved into the "Big House," except this time they slept in the same room. An enormous suite comprising multiple rooms became their first actual home together.

Jen woke up early one morning two months later, feeling off. She thought back to the night's dinner and nothing had seemed out of the ordinary, but also nothing was sitting right now. Jen went to the bathroom, peed, and sat there for a few minutes. After a short while, she felt better.

When she returned to her bed, she took a sip of water. A sudden, queasy feeling washed over her, and her stomach lurched violently. Rushing back to the bathroom, she tried to open the door, only to have it hit her foot and swing back just as she dove for the toilet. The force of her head colliding with the solid oak door caused a burning sensation in her skull. The impact was enough to disrupt her aim, leading to a messy situation with the remains of last night's meal. Along with a vomit covered floor, she had a big bump above her right eye from a door that was much harder than her skull.

As she cleaned the floor, she heard Laoch outside as he asked if she was okay. "Yeah, I knocked my fricking head and puked on the floor. I think I'm catching a cold or something. Let me finish cleaning this and I will be out in a second." As she opened the door, she saw the illuminated room and him standing there. He looked at her with concern. "Are you okay, love?" he asked gently. She nodded, leaned into his chest, "yeah, let's go back to be..." as her eyes widened with panic and she turned to rush back to the bathroom for round two. This time, she made a clean entry. Once she finished vomiting the third time, she was prepared to go to sleep. As she exited the bathroom, Laoch greeted her with a hand towel containing ice, a glass of water, and a Wintergreen Lifesaver.

A few weeks went by smoothly, with no sign of Jen's usual monthly visitor. When she comprehended the timing, she gazed at herself in the mirror and uttered, "Well, shit." In a hushed manner, she visited a nearby small town and discovered a combined pharmacy/gas station/grocery store, all packed into a walk-in closet sized space.

Upon reaching the counter with the pregnancy test, a local, possibly a relative, exclaimed, "Oh, Jen! You think?"

Jen almost said, "It's not for me," but knew no one would believe her. After contemplating the situation, she ultimately decided to go with the phrase, "Hey, maybe I'm just being paranoid, but can we keep this between us?"

Kim, the attendant, replied with a cheerful tone, "Sure! Of Course! I hope you get the results you want sweetie!"

Jen left through the door, the bell ringing loudly as if passing judgment. As she walked to the car, she repeated under her breath, "shit shit shit shit SHIT!!"

The moment she arrived home, she immediately went to her suite and retreated to the bathroom where she eagerly tore open the Predictor box pregnancy kit. Inside, the kit appeared to be a child's home chemistry experiment, with its assortment of test tubes and vials filled with mysterious substances. Grateful for her knowledge from chemistry classes at State, she carefully followed the directions in the box and began the two hours wait.

For two hours, she battled with her thoughts, repeatedly convincing herself that each outcome was unavoidable. In one reality, she was just being silly. In the other, her heart raced with fear as she imagined Laoch's possible reactions. Would he be happy? Was this too quick? "I am 22 for Christ sakes... am I ready? What about my mom? She is 5000 miles away." Jen cried and giggled in equal measures. She ranged from excited to terrified and back. Checking her watch, she realized with a sinking feeling that she had to go through it all over again for another hour and a half.

At the end of two hours, after an epic battle to keep from looking early, it showed a clear positive.

When she stumbled upon her husband, he was in his lab, meticulously analyzing soil samples from different fields harvested last summer. Entering the room, she almost collided with Daniel, who seemed to fill the doorway like a goddamn mountain. Considering their height and weight difference, she wondered if he would have even registered her impact if they collided; her head failing to reach his chin.

In the room, Laoch looked up and flashed her that look that made her heart skip a beat. "What brings you out to the barn, love?" He asked. "I thought you were in town today for work."

"Nah, I took the papers I needed home. Was not feeling the best, so I figured I would do it from home and bring it back in the morning. I need to talk. Have a second?" Jen asked.

"For you, my sweet, I might even string together three whole seconds." He laughed. Jen hugged him and he embraced her.

She looked down at his stomach and asked, "Are you gaining weight?"

Laoch took a step back, patting his flat stomach with a wide smile, "How rude, you tart! That there, that is little Còig."

"No, no... This is Còig" as she pointed to her own stomach.

For about three seconds, or maybe it was years, Laoch had a confused look on his face, as it slowly registered. "Really? REALY!?!?!" as a huge grin grew across his face. He scooped her up in his arms, hugging her tightly and lifting her off the ground. However, he quickly released her and took a step back, as if he was afraid he might break her.

She laughed with tears streaming from her eyes, "You can hug me all you want. The baby will be fine!"

He grabbed her up again in a hug, switched the hold to carrying her like a bride on her wedding night and headed towards the door. "Let's go tell my parents; they will be delighted," when Jen interrupted him.

"Why don't we wait a short time, visit a doctor for a checkup, and make certain everything is fine first. We can tell them when we are 100% sure of things."

Laoch nodded and set her down gently, "Good idea, love. Let's make sure before we drop this bomb."

For the next three days, Jen had to kick Laoch to remind him to chisel the smile off his face. When the appointment came, the doctor confirmed the news and warmly congratulated them. Laoch had no way to know, but he felt sure it was a boy.

In the car on the way back to Wolfborn, Laoch pulled the car over. He spoke with a serious tone, "I don't want to frighten you, but babies are big things in my family. I mean BIG. You are also going to hear some history of Clan Ferguson that I have only hinted at. I don't want to weird you out or anything."

He paused, kissed her hand, "I wasn't lying when I said our family has a long history here, our familial existence on these lands predates most written records. I say MOST because my family maintained the oldest written records. The records date back to times before the Roman occupation, when the concepts of dated years were yet to be introduced. For instance, I know that my direct ancestors carved those carvings on the edge of the stream by the swimming spot. If we delve deep into the records, we could likely unearth the identities of those involved in etching them and gain a rough understanding of when they created each one. There are records of our land's defense against Roman incursions, and that is just a small part of the vast archive, which contains much older records than even that. The essence of what I'm trying to convey is that for thousands of years, my family believes it has inherited a significant responsibility. The earliest notes talk of the family's escape from what had to be Ireland. As Scots, that shame sits hard with us," he said with a smile.

He waved his hands in emphasis, but it became a shrug. "There are dire warnings in the archive, related to our family, based heavily on superstition... Our upbringing instilled in us the conviction that our family had a sacred duty, to confront a formidable darkness, and that we might be called upon to defend against it someday. Let me reiterate, this has no religious connection, even though our family is Catholic..."

Jen stopped him and asked with a hardened look of panic. "What the hell? Is this a joke? If this is a joke..."

Laoch stopped her. "This is not a joke and us having a child will bring out some odd discussions from my family, all related to the family responsibility I mentioned. That is why I'm bringing this up now."

"Wait, wait, wait. You said, written records?" she looked at him incredulously.

"Yes," he affirmed, staring into her eyes with the utmost sincerity.

She still could not believe what he was hearing, or that it was not a joke. "In what language? I mean, if it is Latin, that is post roman and the scribes were with the church."

Laoch nodded, "Much of the writings after Roman occupation and the church's missionaries are indeed in Latin, but the old stuff. That is even weirder. In the documents, it identifies who taught my ancient family a unique version of cuneiform. She was apparently from Greece or Persia? The documents say her name was Sanura. She scribed the first of the family's history from oral tradition. Sanura taught them how to read it and instructed them on how to write it. It was not a pure Cuneiform, because when I looked at pictures of Cuneiform tablets in the library in Raleigh, it read like gibberish to me. There are even some structural differences to some characters, but those of us that work in the archives have all learned it to varying degrees and taught it... and I will teach you if you want to learn." The look on his face as he evaluated her eyes was of mixed optimism and fear.

Seeing what he hoped was a positive reaction, he continued, "The main thing I want you to know though, Love, you are not required to believe ANY of this. But I ask you to keep family matters related to this completely private. We never discuss it in the presence of others, even your side of the family. Our family witnessed something evil and we believe we will eventually have to stand against it. We have all grown up understanding that whatever the evil is, it is probably more aware of us than we are aware of it. Whatever it is, it hates us because its 'magic' or whatever the hell it is, does not affect people in my family. I know this sounds crazy," he said as he rambled, "and I'm an open book, whenever you have questions... and I have no actual proof any of this stuff is really true. However, I believe it is, and that is the best way I can say it." Laoch said in a rushed stream of words, like he was trying to get them all out before a timer ended.

When he stopped, he cringed, like he was expecting a slap. The car was silent for a full minute before Jen spoke. "Ok, I need to process this... but if you are bullshitting me right now, I will hide you in the fucking quad and leave your entrails to decorate the bushes."

Laughing in relief, Laoch engaged the car into gear and continued the trip home. He knew, however, that the full impact of what he told her had not hit her yet. When she realized the timing of this discussion, he expected the betrayal she would feel. The ancient family rules, forbidding discussion of these secrets until a child joined the family, would offer him little protection when she inevitably grasped the entire significance. The rules had seemed so clear and reasonable until he had to actually use them in practice that day.

Chapter 6

That evening, they told everyone about the baby. The family's pending fresh addition brought great excitement to everyone. Jen toasted with the rest, but in her glass was apple juice. All present agreed that the baby talk would remain with the people in the room, obviously eventually including Jen's parents as well. That was the request, at least until the end of the first trimester, which was only about two weeks away. That was also the date of her next appointment and first sonogram.

There was a brief mention at a dinner a few nights later where Laoch's father mentioned some family things Jen needed to be brought up to date on. Laoch nodded, "Father, I have already told her the general gist of it and will work with her to help her understand the full scope."

His father looked Jen in the eyes. "How are you taking our family's strangeness, dear?" Jen still felt nervous talking to her father-in-law about this... this question had attracted the attention of everyone in the room as she replied.

"I find it challenging to grasp what he has shared with me, to be honest. It sounds like something out of a fantasy novel. To tell the truth, I thought he was joking when he started telling me. I am really looking forward though to learning and seeing the archives. Ceithir," she felt strange calling him that nickname, "Ceithir emphasized the importance of keeping this information confidential, and I've assured both him and you, that it is safe with me. I mean, they would probably isolate us in rooms with cushioned walls, wouldn't they?" An uncomfortable laugh punctuated Jen's conclusion, leaving a slightly awkward atmosphere in the room.

The patriarch of the family looked convinced, nodded, "Thank you Jen, we all know it is a lot to absorb and even harder to believe as we have all had our times in life where we either doubted the veracity or wished it was not true. In the archives, however, you will also come across the heart wrenching documents that vividly describe our ancestors' actions... some driven by disbelief, others convinced they, alone, could guarantee our family's survival. Their arrogance and ignorance cost thousands of lives, and their reckless mistakes endangered the entire family. There is no doubt in our minds our family has a purpose. That part is undeniable. The grand plan of that purpose, however, has always remained a mystery to us. We never received a rule book. So far, we really do not know what winning looks like, except for staying alive. There's no question in our minds that a creature by the name of Scrios is out there, somewhere." At the mention of its name, Laoch's mother Mimi crossed herself.

Chapter 7

December 5th, 1981, 5:01 AM The Big House, Atholl, Scotland

At 5:01 AM the next morning, Jen sprinted towards the bathroom door. Ceithir was chasing close, eager to hold her hair back. After 15 minutes, the room had found its correct orientation, and she felt better, at least from the nausea standpoint. "So, you truly believe this stuff about your family's destiny?" she questioned.

"I do. I mean, I grew up with it... I have seen the archives. Hey, can you clear your afternoon? I will take you and let you see it. You can start learning what you need to interpret the older documents." Laoch suggested, and Jen nodded her intent.

Jen cleared her afternoon and Laoch took her on a walk north from the house into the manicured forest of the family land. About ten minutes into the woods, Laoch lightly elbowed her and whispered, "Don't panic. We are being stalked by one of Kier's packs. It's a game they play." Just stay close to me and we will get you introduced."

After about 20 seconds, a large black wolf wandered onto the road ahead of them and paused. "That is Blackey, he is the leader. There are four more closing in on us right now as Blackey distracts us. As if on command, the woods exploded around them as four more wolves, two mostly black and two mostly brown, encircled them as Blackey closed from the front.

After a few seconds of the beasts showing aggressive posturing, Laoch used a commanding but gentle voice, "Blackey! Theres a good boy!" At the sound of his words, all the animals relaxed. Being released by Laoch from their duty, it was playtime and jumped on Laoch with a frisky exuberance. He sat on the ground as the wolves milled around him for scratches as he called Jen over to introduce her. The wolves watched her closely as she approached, with one of the younger beginning a low growl. Laoch looked at the young wolf, ready to call it down, when Blackey snarled and corrected it. Blackey walked over to her, tail wagging, and sniffed her hand and allowed her to scratch him. The other wolves visibly relaxed and went back for more affection from Laoch.

As if they all noticed a silent call, the animals all paused in mid play, looked to the south and took off into the underbrush as silently as they had run in it before. "Ok," Jen said.

Laoch laughed and shrugged, "I guess they had something else to do. Kier was probably calling them in for something." Laoch stood up, dusted himself off, and they resumed their walk.

"How did you know they were there?"

"Experience... Kier is a peculiar individual, and even as children, he displayed odd tendencies... I didn't hear them exactly. Everything else got quiet, and I had this situation happen to me a lot growing up," he said with a chuckle.

Jen looked at him with one eyebrow cocked, "but... Blackey?"

"Which part of weird do you want me to explain?"

The couple followed a narrow, winding path that led them deeper into a secluded pass through the hills. About 50 meters in to the hallway like pass, the valley suddenly opened up into a beautiful clearing, covered in natural heather and swaying grass.

At the far end of the field, a secluded old chapel, nestled against the base of a steep hill, its weathered stone walls blending into the landscape. While they walked, Laoch mentioned, "We constructed this chapel in the spring of 1412. The current chapel stands as a resilient replacement for the wooden one, which was tragically destroyed by an English army raid in 1308. Before that, there was a quaint stone and wood structure with a thatched roof standing in this same spot. Since approximately 970, it had served as a storage space for roots and vegetables... and so on. Roman troops destroyed the third building that stood here during one of Claudius's campaigns in 42 AD. The chapel, as you see it now, underwent a full renovation and update about six years ago."

As they approached the chapel's doors, she could see that someone had taken care of the small church, even though it had seen its better days. Stepping inside after opening the old metal banded oak door, she felt the weight of the building's history in the air.

A small, unpretentious raised stone altar adorned the front of the space, flanked by four neat rows of simple pews. Frescoes depicting the fourteen stations of the cross adorned the walls. On the left side of the altar, there stood a modest shrine dedicated to St. Michael. In worn gold leaf and stucco, he held a sword and triumphantly stood on the serpent's neck.

Although there was a thin layer of pollen and dust, the general upkeep was clear. "Ummmm, the renovation happened six years ago?" Jen inquired; her smile slightly mischievous.

He laughed as he kneeled at the shrine to St. Michael. "Maybe I used the wrong word with renovation. I intended to say... modernization. Way back before any human construction, a crack in a rock outcropping here revealed what we now call 'The Cathedral'. It's basically a cave." as he fished a plain white plastic card from his wallet and slid it along a crack behind the shrine of St. Michael. A faint beep and an audible clunk emanated from behind the main altar.

Laoch stood and approached the alter. He tugged on the stone supporting the dais. Smoothly and gradually, the altar, the stone beneath it, and the wall behind it all slid forward. "The trick is to get the momentum going, and it just glides."

"No fucking way!" Jen's hand flew to her mouth, as if she was trying to stuff the words back in, as she glanced at the crucifix beside her on the dais.

Laoch laughed as he guided her into a doorway that was exposed by the shifting altar. "You don't have to worry, my dear. There's no one here to scold you," Several feet inside the cavern, Laoch searched for and located a large lever switch, which, when pulled down, activated the electric lighting with a chunk sound.

With her mouth agape, Jen marveled at the thickness of the rock wall that had unexpectedly moved forward on hidden rollers. The stone brick of the back of the church transitioned into a thick, natural stone wall that rode on an inlaid railroad track. A thick, irregular gray foam lined the inside of the rock wall facing the chapel. "Sound proofing," Laoch said, pointing at it.

Laoch came back to her as soon as the lights fully illuminated the previously hidden area. "Excuse me love," he said while passing her in the narrow hallway. He took hold of two substantial metal handles and pulled, resulting in the wall retracting slowly. With a click, the wall returned to its initial position, and she noticed a sturdy metal mechanism anchoring it.

With a quick gesture, he directed her attention to a box affixed to the wall. "If you want it to open back up, that's the button you need to press to unlock. If power ever dies," Laoch pulled back the foam and showed her a large red lever, "just pull that and it will release the lock as well."

"What? No special key?"

He smiled at her, "Why? You are already in."

Guided by him, they walked down the natural hallway until they reached a stunning cave large enough for a basketball court, revealing modern hallways and doors in the distance. "You never told me I was marrying Batman! Seriously?" she said as she spun around, taking in the room.

Thousands of years of graffiti covered the walls. Jen came across a variety of content, including names, dates, and texts in languages she couldn't understand. It was possibly even scripture, she thought. The knots and symbols, reminiscent of the ones near their swimming spot, appeared to be the oldest markings. Recent graffiti in English appeared to be political statements condemning England. Someone wrote other inscriptions in Latin.

Laoch translated one set as a tally of food stores of grain and ale.

One organized place on the wall looked like someone had carefully chiseled a grid and inside the boxes, vertical lines and small pictures with horizontal and angled lines connecting to the verticals. Each symbol was in its own box.

"Holy shit, is that the cuneiform you mentioned? I remember seeing that in National Geographic magazines at my grandma's house!" Jen gasped as she took it in.

"Yes, this is some of it. There are a lot more samples in the archives. Sanura supposedly left this inscription here, but it's so far back in time that my mind can barely grasp its meaning. It's too deep a subject to talk about right now. However, I'm fairly certain the cuneiform style used here is "Early Dynastic," predominantly employed between roughly 2500 and 2000 BC, He told her, as she gave him a disbelieving look.

"I didn't say it was put there at that exact moment, but this cuneiform script style seemed to be the type she had learned. This is that modified version I told you about. These inscriptions, I can read, and they translate to a Pre-Gaelic language described by scholars as pre-Goidelic Celtic language. That one there, at the top, says the number one and 'breathnaígh súil' which means, eyes down."

"Wait, I have to learn this language that precedes Gaelic too?" Jen asked.

"We have books you can use, and most of us know it well enough to be a quick help, when needed."

Chapter 8

December 5th 1981 The Big House, Atholl, Scotland 11:15 AM

Jen studied the cuneiform for several minutes. It looked almost fresh. The moment Jen averted her eyes from the cuneiform, the mural on the far wall caught her attention and sent a chilling sensation throughout her body.

It was as if her instincts were trying to warn her; there was an underlying sense of wrongness that she couldn't ignore in the artwork. The artist skillfully captured the image of a small army advancing over a hill. A tall, slender figure led to the front of the army, and she couldn't help but feel unsettled by his presence.

He stood at full human size, with the army accompanying his image, flanking and trailing behind him. Unlike the soldiers behind him, he appeared unarmed. His color though... it was wrong and different from the soldiers he led. While the rest in the mural had appropriate skin tones, the artist depicted his skin as pale with a sickly blue tinge. She noticed a shimmer in his eyes, and as she approached, she observed they seemed to track her movements. As she drew closer, she observed the man's eyes, crafted from bluish crystal.

"Creepy, eh?" Laoch, creeping up on her ear, asked, causing her to jump in surprise.

Embarrassed and flushing red, "So not funny you asshat! What the hell or who the hell is that?"

Laoch pointed to the blue man, "That, my dear, is, or maybe was Scrios. We believe this place was used to train warriors to avoid eye contact during combat; unprotected by our family's unique abilities, his gaze could destroy their souls. The archives speak in depth of his dark powers, capable of captivating individuals and make them commit heinous acts. There are stories of Scrios making men murder their own families or inciting armies to fight against themselves, just by catching their eye. Thus, those rules that Sanura put on the walls. Pointing at the large cuneiform inscription on the wall, 1) Eyes down 2) The chest of your opponent does not mislead in battle. 3) If a friend turns on you in battle, he is now your enemy,"

Laoch paused for a moment before continuing, "There is a story in the archives that recounts the unfortunate fate of a family member who fell to Scrios' influence in the last head-to-head battle with him. Later research quickly deduced that what fell was the knickers of the child's mother behind a woodpile, with a lover who was not from our line. Since he was not carrying the blood as all thought he was, many people needlessly died in the battle. A survivor from Sanura's army, who they found barely alive after the clash, was the only account of a survivor who witnessed the tragedy. The fellow who led the assault went through life thinking he was immune to Scrios's powers. They trained him as the leader of the assault.

His lineage was unquestioned until the minute he met Scrios in battle, where the shocking revelation of his mother's infidelity unfolded." Laoch ended with a motion like he was washing his hands.

Jen looked at him pensively, "and when was this?"

"Oh, ages ago," Laoch said with a shrug, "the last time anyone ever reportedly saw the blue bastard in the flesh."

Imitating calm she asked, "Okay, and when was that?"

Laoch's voice wavered along with his confidence as he looked and saw the sharpened her eyes. "Oh, plus or minus about 500 BC," trying to make his voice sound flippant.

Chapter 9

Archives, Cathedral Room, Scotland

Laoch tried to catch Jen's shoulder as she raged back down the hall towards the stone door, determined to kick the stone wall out of her way with one blow. "You have got to be fucking kidding me. Your family hides who they are, hides the history they have seen, because they are afraid of a creature that has not been seen since 500, give or take, years before Jesus H. Christ-on-a-Cracker?" she said in red faced disbelief.

Laoch trailed close behind, "I know it sounds silly, but..."

Jen abruptly stopped and faced him. "Silly? No, this is not silly. Silly were those people a couple of years ago following Jim Jones down to Guyana and making that Kool-Aid for their kids. This makes those psychopaths look like intrepid pioneers!" She again turned to leave, but abruptly turned back to him. "Laoch... honey... you and this terrifies me. This feels more like a Scottish family version of the Stepford Wives. Please tell me something! Show me something that makes this make sense!"

"You just started looking, Jen. Give it some time. That is all I ask. The thing that sets it apart is not just our belief. I understand this may be difficult for you, but a few of us... including myself... I can feel him." Laoch said as he paused and squeezed his fist tight. "I can actually feel him when I dream at night. I've always sensed... his... I don't know... His presence? I have had nightmares about him since childhood, even before my parents revealed our family's history to me. How about we move to the back, and I can start showing you? In terms of recent occurrences, even though no one has laid eyes on him, there are events that exhibit certain resemblances to what he does." Laoch's voice lowered to a pleading whisper. "We would all love to find it is over and hope that one day it is."

Jen stopped as they moved towards the rear of the cathedral room and asked Laoch the question he dreaded. "So, as you described this as your 'family legacy', I'm struggling to understand why you let me walk blindly into it with our love, our marriage, and why you didn't tell me anything about it before you found out I was pregnant with our child? You don't have to answer me this second, because I do not want a bullshit answer. But when you have one, I deserve it." All Laoch could do was nod sincerely as he contemplated the lifelong rules his family had set for him.

Chapter 10

Archives, Cathedral Room, Scotland

Laoch guided Jen back through the cave, where ancient writings adorned the walls and the piercing gaze of the blue man's crystal eyes seemed to track her every move, until they reached the corridor on the left. "Is all this new construction?" Jen asked.

"Well, newish. There are new areas constructed in the last couple of years. This area here is hundreds of years old, but we updated it with modern air handlers and power for lighting. We even installed a terminal here for a new IBM System 34 computer in a nearby warehouse which does inventory work for the archive."

As they continued their walk past rows of shelving, he continued. "We have a system. I will teach you how to get to it. We hid it in a password protected area on the administration menu screens. To access our program, we ran a cable down here, connecting it to a terminal so we could interact with the system. The program is used to log all the materials, referencing locations and translations. It is in English and provides translations line by line and locations of the cited texts and the room, row, shelf and slot locations in the archive that we walked past coming back here. For instance," he opened the screen to show her. "If you see 'Athens', that is the old documents that Sanura most likely scribed herself on tin sheets... or a person she was teaching. The scribing continued in cuneiform for over a thousand years. These documents date back to approximately 500 BC," he stated, playfully grimacing at her, and continued. "These include a detailed written record of the oral traditions passed down over 500 years before that. To be frank, these give me the creeps. Family stories passed down through generations, from the time of their ancestors' departure from Ireland, intertwine with tales of a fierce battle against Scrios, a conflict that claimed lives from both armies and inflicted devastating losses upon our family."

He shifted in his seat to face her and continued, "The battle claimed the lives of many, including Sanura herself; searchers never found her body, nor the bodies of the others who died that day." Then changed the subject as he tried to build momentum.

With a new manufactured excitement in his voice, Laoch continued his tour. "If you see the word 'Rome', it is documents starting around 630 AD and they will mostly be in Latin. The quality of the scribing improved approximately 200 years later, thanks to the involvement of classically trained scribes, who were family members taught by Franciscan priests. Scribes during this period used primarily vellum, but some of the paper has survived as well. These scribes preserved the writings, as best as they could; but, in a cave, with the moisture, they also spent much of their time recopying older texts that had deteriorated. By the year 1640, the use of English became more prevalent daily, with some Gaelic mixed in. We have a section in the database called the London era, which details this period starting in 1640. Finally, around 1920, we started what we consider the modern era of documents. These, the latest delineation, are the 'Edinburgh' era documents."

He paused and took a deep breath and smiled with a growing confidence. "At the beginning of this era, my grandfather's family worked with my great grandfather to come up with this demarcation of the archive, as I described it to you today. My incredibly insightful great grandfather devised a storage and documentation method which was luckily easily adaptable to computers. Which was amazing considering it was before their invention. My great grandfather was an officer late 1800's, in charge of supplies and later owned a shipping company in Edinburgh. He was a very organized man. People still record new discoveries in paper volumes, before they add them to the database."

That is where Jen stopped him. For a moment, she looked like she was choking on a piece of food from last night's dinner that had refused to go down, when she said, "Laoch, this is an absolutely incredible place you have here, but a point of question for me. If you haven't laid eyes on this creature from the wall out there for 2500 years? How do you have anything 'new' to archive? What could you possibly have now that is new?"

Not anger, but a genuine discomfort caused Laoch's face to darken. "In part, it is that indescribable feeling I mentioned earlier; however, over the millennia, there have been significant events which have happened. Some, much more recent, that have caused us to look back not only in our own archives, but research public and private collections worldwide. One key to the recent, and when I say recent, I mean the last forty years, is William. You don't recognize him, but I bet your parents would if they thought enough about it. William is minor royalty, who at one point, at his peak of fame when he was young at the beginning of World War 2, was briefly famous worldwide. He was a hero who had the world in front of him."

Laoch adjusted his posture as a rest from speaking, "He was an Oxford grad, with honors, working thereafter as an apprentice to a well-known barrister and member of the House of Parliament in London. Later, a short, crazy man from the Austrian Alps, with a pension for brown shirts and Roman décor, started killing Jews and attacking his neighbors. It became clear to many that Britton was one of that crazy man's goals, so the young barrister William Atworth, in early 1938, became Lieutenant William Atworth of the 70th Infantry Brigade. By late 1939, he had shown clear leadership. He also had friends in higher royal circles. He displayed the outstanding decision making desired in leadership. During the early portion of the war, he rose quickly to a major's rank. His leadership style was in high demand and with every new appointment, the higher his profile among commanders and the higher his rank sailed. He experienced brutal combat during the Battle of France as part of the British Expeditionary Force. It was there that he lost his close friend, whom you know as Tom, from his story. Lieutenant Thomas Bainbridge, as you heard that night in his horrifying story, died in his arms in a skirmish in France." Jen nodded, engrossed in Laoch's story.

Laoch continued, "William received accommodation four times in those meat grinder locations near the Belgian border and the subsequent retreat to the evacuation at Dunkirk. Despite his troops losing 74% of his soldiers, to either death or injury, his leadership was exemplary. He received the honors, because the units on both sides of him experienced almost 100% casualties. There were few victories in that period of the war, but a victory William had, hurt the Germans deeply enough that even Hitler had taken notice."

Laoch leaned forward in his seat. "William and his boys had caught a German commando team, and its support staff, in a strategically poor location and swiftly dispatched them. The battle was quick, only prolonged by the refusal of the German commander to give up. Despite having no escape route, and his troops routed, this German officer executed a soldier as he attempted to raise a white flag." As Jen cringed in shock at his description.

"After the forgone conclusion of the conflict, one soldier presented now Lieutenant Colonel Atworth, with a small golden metal rod taken from the hands of the German commander. William showed little interest in it and was reportedly about to toss it back among the dead, but changed his mind at the last moment and kept it instead. His troops recovered important documents, plans, codes and communications among the bags carried by the support staff of the leader, a Captain Keller. Losing SS Captain Ludwig Friedrich Keller, enraged the normally stoic German people. Hitler attended his burial in a small Bavarian town outside of Munich in person and propaganda tapes made that day, canonized the memory of the young captain, as a model German."

"Ok" Jen interrupted. "I find this fascinating, but what evidence suggests a link between the Scrios creature and your family?"

Laoch walked over to the refrigerator in the corner with an air of confidence and asked her, "Would you like a bottle of pop while I try to put this all in perspective?"

With a playful grin, Jen suggested, "It would probably be better if you had some vodka to mix in with it."

Laoch smiled with newfound confidence, sensing traction with her. He retrieved them both a bottle of soda and popped the tops off using a section of the stone wall with many similar scratches to the one he just created. He sat back down and continued.

"William Atworth is a highly intelligent, well-planned, and cunning man. His brave efforts earned him a Knighthood and the rank of Brigadier in 1943. His rising prominence led the Royal Air Force to request his ground warfare expertise in a liaison role, commissioning him as an Air Commodore. He developed revolutionary air support strategies, the principles of which remain relevant even in modern warfare. Near the end of the war, in late 1944, following the invasion of Normandy, he shouldered immense responsibility and had little supervision. He was promoted to Air Vice-Marshal, and they gave him the responsibility of overseeing the Scandinavian theater. With each unprecedented victory against the Germans, his fame in military circles soared higher as he continued his remarkable ascent, leaving a trail of triumph in the eastward push of Allied forces. In the last days of the war, following Hitler's death and preceding the Nazi surrender by only a few days, William issued contradictory orders and allowed the bombing of several ships in Lübeck Bay, in the Baltic Sea. He claimed to have verified reports of extensive troop mobilizations aimed at turning the tide of Germany's downfall. The ships, however, were mostly inoperable and carried a tragic cargo. The Nazis crammed the ships' holds with Holocaust camp prisoners, transferred from death camps. On May 3rd, 1945, tragic orders caused the death of over seven thousand innocent lives. The devastating fire caused by the bombing of the SS Cap Arcona alone, claimed the lives of over four thousand people, making it the largest location of victims during that tragic incident."

As the shadows moved deep in his eyes, Laoch continued stone faced, reflecting on how these people died needlessly, just five days before Germany surrendered. They died from RAF bombing raids ordered by Air Vice-Marshal William Atworth.

"Jesus." Jen said.

Laoch continued and stated that the defendant, while charged, "believed the attack was justified by his intelligence on troop deployments. However, multiple verified sources provided William with information contrary to his assertion. These briefings showed that Scandinavian Holocaust victims were being loaded onto those ships. William disregarded them. He claimed his reports were thoroughly vetted and the attack he ordered was authorized, which was false. Because of his rank and reputation, no one challenged his decision before the bombs fell. None of William's claims received support from leadership, not even from his own chief of staff. William insisted he possessed telegraphs and communications that would clear his name; however, he could only produce blank pages. He contended madly that only he could see or decipher the information. If only they could read the papers like he could, everything would be clear, he insisted during a hearing. During his detainment, the military, in a search of his quarters, uncovered only service issued items in his possession. The lone exception to this was a golden or brass metal tube that had once been the property of the young German Captain Keller. William's subordinates testified in his classified court martial that he constantly carried a small scepter in his left hand, similar to how press photos depicted the deceased German SS Captain during the war. It was present in almost every press photograph of both men, during the time they each possessed the item. If you watch him, even today, when he paces, his left hand is curled as if he is still carrying something." Laoch paused and drank from his soda bottle.

He placed the nearly empty bottle on a table. "Following the war, the revelation of previously undisclosed records showed that Keller, despite his esteemed military record and impressive collection of battle gained medals, had single-handedly made the catastrophic decision that led to the slaughter of his soldiers. Anyone with any knowledge of the battlefield, which he certainly had as found in his own documents, would never have performed the actions he did that day, and it cost everyone under him their lives."

Shifting in his seat to lean forward again, Laoch was now speaking confidently. He looked into Jen's eyes. "William's stories following the bombing were so nonsensical that they eventually led to him being sent for psychiatric evaluation. According to the doctor, they found him suffering from extreme operational exhaustion and a psychological disconnect from reality. Following the initial reports of the Cap Arcona tragedy, a cover up ensued, attributing the disaster to a tragic wartime communication error and friendly fire, effectively silencing the truth. Officials, when asked later, failed to name who was in charge of the decisions on May 3rd, 1945. That information is Top Secret. The British Government and the RAF's pat response, was no response at all. They discuss in the media, when questioned, how the events were a tragedy. They dismiss the need for further investigation into the events as pointless. William spent three long years confined within the walls of Bethlem Royal Hospital in South London. Mostly forgotten by the media, he quietly retired from the RAF with a promotion to Air Marshal, receiving full military benefits for his time in the hospital and a full pension. His classified and sealed war related records remained top secret until recently. Friends in high places, you know, and this grace came from the highest place in England. Now those declassified files are simply gone."

In late 1948, they deemed William to not be a danger to himself or others and he moved home to live with his wife Tilly. The missing brass tube, discovered when his belongings were returned, led to the assumption that it was lost or stolen." Laoch concluded.

"Are you saying there's a connection between the golden tube and Scrios?" Jen asked.

"There has been extensive debate on that for the past forty years," Laoch replied. "Both my father and I believe there is a connection."

"That's pretty thin."

Laoch shrugged and began nodding. "By itself, yes, I am in total agreement. But through considerable research, we have found other examples of patterns that were similar to William and Herr Keller's tragedies. Our ancestors shared legends about encountering someone who wielded a similarly described, powerful artifact. Sanura, the woman I mentioned earlier, had a golden hollow scepter with a green gem, referred to as The Eye of Asclepius. No one ever discovered Sanura's body or most of the other casualties from the epic battle with Scrios. Witnesses described the battle area as devastated, like a massive storm had hit it. If the survivors' description of the damage took place in the present day, we would suspect either a meteor impact or a nuclear device caused the damage."

"The cataclysm," Laoch continued, "caused widespread devastation in all directions for miles from the battle site. From the center of the battle, the uprooted trees radiated out in every direction for miles. The accounts have similarities to the Tunguska event in Russia, but the trees near the epicenter were not in an upright position. They were absent, and the burning trees were visible at a distance to the assumed central point. According to the archives, the closer locals living in the vicinity, who ventured towards the heart of the epicenter, the more complete the devastation became. Near the middle, the scene was one of destruction, churned dirt, charred trees, and evidence the side of the mountain had collapsed and washed across the area. Perhaps this rod that was very similar in description to what William possessed had been hers? Maybe Scrios caused it to become corrupted somehow, and now it's being used by people or using people for its evil intentions."

"And maybe this is all a pile of shit," Jen replied with a kind smile, "my love, but you have sparked my interest."

Laoch smiled and put his hands up in surrender, "That is all I ask. I don't think the entire answer is here, but I think the keys to understanding it are in these archives somewhere."

Chapter 11

Atholl, Scotland

As the months went by, Jen's baby grew and the discomfort of the first trimester gradually subsided. Every weekend, and occasionally in the evenings, she made it a point to examine the archive collection. Holding the ancient artifact, crafted over two thousand years ago, in her hands, she felt a profound sense of respect, despite her doubts about its supposed significance.

In the presence of William, Jen's thoughts would frequently drift away, captivated by his words. His stories had a tendency to circle back and repeat themselves, and occasionally, his panics would echo with the same words she had heard before. His stories spilled out in a chaotic torrent, seemingly disconnected, as if caught in an unending cycle of narratives. However, as time went by, she detected a recurring theme. The late hours of the day were difficult for this kindly man, as thoughts of love, loss, and tragedy constantly plagued his mind.

During the morning hours, it was easy to overlook the fact that William was anything other than a regular older man. He could hold wonderful conversations, effortlessly answering questions about his childhood. He often delighted in recounting fantastic stories about the trips he took as a lad. These trip stories he told, of times with his mother's family, led to him occasionally dropping surnames that Jen recognized from the British tabloids and Sunday papers.

It surprised Jen to learn that William's current state was not the gradual deterioration she had pictured in her mind. Since the day he had come home from the war and even after his stay in Bethlem, this was the way he was. Something inside him had fractured, and the sheer loss of that unfulfilled promise must have been devastating for those who knew him. It surprised Jen to learn that William had moved to Wolfborn the year prior to her husband's birth, following the death of his wife, Tilly, from cancer.

Laoch's father's firm belief that the creature plaguing their bloodline caused the fracture of William's mind was the reason for his invitation to live with them. He admitted that his father's intention in bringing Mimi's father William here was not only to care for him but also to observe and study him. The disclosure of this secondary aim resulted in a time of disharmony between his father and mother. However, his father learned nothing of value during William's residency.

The elder Laoch did not fear that his father-in-law's living arrangement compromised their safety, because he had been around William most of his adult life, long before he suspected a diabolical cause to his neurosis. The acidic fact as he saw it... If there had been a danger, the compromise would have already cost all of them their lives.

William's life was good. He was functional to the extent that he regularly had breakfast or lunch with an old friend. Nell was a constant companion to him, and stated, "He seems like a normal bloke when his is out early in the day. No one would know what happens some evenings here. Him and Mr. Campbell just talk about old times and friends and family gone, and how blessed they are to still be vertical and among loved ones. Until a few years ago, they even played golf regularly. Now it is only occasionally and usually only nine holes when they go. Although with the winter settling in now, there won't be much of that."

Chapter 12

April 20th, 1982, The Big House, Atholl, Scotland

An extraordinary amount of snowfall characterized the winter of 1982 in Scotland, blanketing the landscape in a pristine white. Without the four-wheel-drive truck, they would have risked being stranded on their way back from the airport in Edinburgh after Jen's mother's week-long visit in mid-January.

It was nice to see her mother; however, the physical discomfort of Jen's second trimester detracted from her enjoyment of the visit. "The lamprey in my stomach is sucking the life out of me," Jen told her mother, and her mother's laughter filled the room. They had a pleasant time together, but after a week, both she and her mother were ready to say goodbye. The snow, which had stopped falling the previous night, lay deep and pristine as Laoch and Jen drove Jen's mom to the airport the following Sunday. The sky stretched above in a brilliant azure shade of blue, while the roads below were untouched, with untouched white paths, save for the occasional animal track.

All flights were on a temporary delay, as they cleared the runways and de-iced the planes, so they stopped for coffee and cookies at a bakery in Kirkliston, close to the airport. The recent storm hadn't closed the small independent bakery, which was a pleasant surprise.

When the time came for her to leave, they drove to the airport, helped her mother check her bag, and showered her with hugs and kisses as they said goodbye. They watched from the parking lot as the plane took off and they began the journey back to Wolfborn. On their return trip, they bought William coffee and pipe tobacco at a store. Jen sat in the passenger seat and observed the world as it climbed out from the heavy snows that seemed to refresh it. Perhaps the effects of the sugar or caffeine in the chocolate she had eaten influenced her optimistic perspective.

Chapter 13

April 13th, 1982, 9:15 AM The Big House, Atholl, Scotland

On Tuesday morning, Mr. Campbell joined them for breakfast. It was a "perfect day for golf!" Mr. Campbell joked, as the thunder rumbled outside. The winds and rain whistled as they assaulted the roof tiles.

William hit the table as the joke took him. He laughed with abandon, "Smashing, Tim, just smashing!"

Moments later, the name clicked. "Tim?" Jen said.

"Yes, dear?" Tim smiled.

"How did you meet William?" she asked.

In his deep voice and heavy Edinburgh accent, "Oh," he laughed, "I wasn't always a simple bar owner. No, once when I was a lad, a teacher had fingered me as brilliant!" Effortlessly, he switched to a high British accent. "I was an Oxford man mum, with old Bill here. We were roommates in Teddy Hall with our long-lost friend Tom; God rest his soul." Tim reverted to his normal accent. "Now I own and operate a pub with my oldest son. It's named, The Bishops Pulpit, or as some call it, Bishops Armpit or just Armpit. It is in Edinburgh, my dear."

William chimed in, "He likes to sound uneducated, but he never mentions the time that Niels bloody Bohr showed up at Oxford Union to discuss his... What was it?" William asked.

Tim buried his face in his hands. "His compound nucleus theory."

"Yes! Compound nucleus," William said with a guttural laugh. "In late 1935 Niels bloody Bohr is in town and Tim asks him these questions off the top of his head, and Bohr, at first impressed, quickly became agitated. There were only two people in the room that understood the discussion and one of them was this third-year kid." William laughed as he pointed at Tim. "He caught and captivated Bohr in a Union debate classic. For every point Bohr presented, Tim had a well thought out counter that questioned it... Bohr's face flushed and a speech issue he had became more prominent, as his frustration grew. Finally, Bohr had had enough, "Excuse me son," he said in his slight foreign accent, "but aren't you young to be questioning and disagreeing with me in this manner?" Tim looks at him piously and says, "Well, I read a lot, and my source is a bloody genius! He is here in the room with us if you want to challenge the veracity of my argument with him instead." Bohr scanned the room, "Sure... please present him so we may discuss this." Smiling an amiable smile, Tim snapped the trap shut, "The mirror is there over near the bar, Mr. Bohr. You said all of this between page 222 – 228 of your own book submission a couple of months ago." Bohr went red with fury

96

and embarrassment. Almost threateningly, Bohr asked him to stand up so he could address him as a man and to "stop hiding in the crowd". So, Tim did... and up and up he stood to his full height, towering over the crowd." William laughed a young man's laugh.

"And I weighed about 20 stones." Tim said, with his cheeks flushed.

"That's what, 250 or 260 pounds?" Jen asked.

"More! And like magic, cooler heads prevailed." Screamed Bill, still transformed momentarily into a young man.

"Actually, I was being a bit of an arse if I tell the truth," Tim admitted. "I kind of baited him, and he was a nice bloke who was very self-conscious about his inability to pronounce certain words."

Eventually, the breakfast had to end. Their treasured memory had become a new one for Jen and everyone else lucky enough to be in the room.

Chapter 14

April 29th, 1982, 9:15 AM The Big House, Atholl, Scotland

In late April, the cold weather finally released its icy grip. Despite the lingering frost in the mornings and the cool days, vibrant flowers had emerged. Jen sat outside, feeling the warmth of the sun on her growing belly, while the vibrant purplish blue, bluebell flower filled her with a deep sense of calm. It was quickly becoming her favorite flower. There was no mistaking her now. The gentle curve of her belly, a soft swell under her clothes, made it clear she was pregnant. When Laoch walked out to sit beside her on the bench, she leaned into him and smiled. "This is beautiful."

"It 'tis" he replied, but he could not articulate how the sight and smell of these flowers had always given him a level of discomfort. He wanted to like them, especially when Jen expressed her affection for them. He couldn't quite put his finger on it, other than the associations of their name to the creature. Something about them unsettled him. Reflecting on his father's similar sentiment, he wondered if it was something he had picked up from him. "Yes, beautiful my dear and the sun feels great!" he partially lied as she cuddled in to him.

Chapter 15

In a secluded back field, about a mile from the big house, Laoch diligently collected soil samples. Since the day was unusually warm for April, he made the choice to walk out to the field. With a small shovel in hand and a small backpack on his back, he strolled through the old family field. In order to rotate a new crop in, he had to conduct tests to determine the soil's contents, measure its alkalinity, and assess its overall condition.

Rows of impressive Fortingall Yew trees surrounded the field, creating a natural barrier. These trees, planted by his direct ancestor over 50 generations ago, served as a living testament to his family's history. In other parts of their lands, towering centuries old ash trees stood proudly. Among the purposefully planted trees were elm and chestnut, a few of which had survived a deadly outbreak which thinned their numbers two decades before. The burning of many infected chestnut trees by his father likely spared the rest. Despite the wild appearance of his family's lands, a keen observer would notice deliberate positioning. His family, unlike most modern society, had not forgotten many of their purposes. His love for these lands drove him to teach his family in the area about their worth and the need to protect them. As a child, he was repeatedly told by his father, "Whenever the wind blows, the trees wave to us."

Recently, he picked up much of the responsibilities his father once carried. He focused his university studies on acquiring modern tools to enhance his family's farming yields and safeguard their land for years to come.

As he filled a small bag with a soil sample, motion caught his eye in the woods. He casually looked and saw nothing but the forest, lined with that bluebell flower... or weed as he thought of it. So, he went back to securing the bag of dirt in his backpack.

The sound of a stick snapping in the same area once more grabbed his attention. He could have sworn he glimpsed a brown leather hat moving through the woods. The brief view of the hat resembling those worn by the flower power movement ten years previously, but he didn't see or hear anything more.

He called out loudly, "Is someone there? Show yourself!" he shouted in a voice artificially deep and was instantly thankful Jen wasn't there with him. He knew if she heard him, she would have mocked him for ages. There was no response, so he shrugged and pretended a calm that had already left him. The panic had stolen his normal voice and took it with it when it retreated to the suddenly empty spot in the pit of his chest.

As he bent intrepidly to gather the next sample of dirt, the sun above went behind a solitary cloud. He could see the field's weathered rows darken around him as a wave of shadow crossed. The hairs on his neck assured him he was not alone, even though his rational mind and Jen's voice in his head still mocked him.

The cloud's shadow baffled him, as it remained covering the entire field as if a spike anchored the cloud in the heavens. The darkness reminded him of an eclipse he had witnessed as a child. It seemed impossibly dark for a single ethereal cloud, like the one he saw above. He looked up and saw the unlikely cloud boiling and fighting the wind to stay in place. The easterly wind would try to push it, only for the western edge to boil up as the cloud dissipated to the east. Once more, he noticed something moving in the woods from the corner of his eye.

He looked to the edge of the field to his right and noticed the Bluebells there were withering like hair too close to a flame. The wilting of the plants created a ripple effect, spreading out from a central point like an expanding wave. As they withered, their once vibrant blue petals fell off the rapidly darkening stems, catching the wind that blew towards him. As he looked at the trees that had once greeted him with friendly waves during his childhood, he noticed their now sickly appearance.

The new buds on the trees dropped to the ground with a distinct click, eventually creating a sound reminiscent of sleet on the roof of the old barn. The temptation to leave tugged at Laoch's mind, but an inexplicable enchantment kept him rooted in place, his feet heavy as if encased in cement. He tried to turn away; he tried to leave, but his feet were stuck as if they had sprouted roots.

The unmistakable sound of tree limbs snapping reached his ears, growing louder and more intense with each passing moment. His eyes widened as he beheld the sight of trees waving violently, not under the influence of wind, but because of a massive and unknown impact.

As if blasted from the wood line, a man-like figure emerged, donning a leather cowl hat and overcoat that concealed his rugged attire made of what appeared to be a hemp fabric. Fury contorted its face as it menacingly approached Laoch. The speed with which he moved was inhuman, and his eyes... His eyes were a deep blue with light speckles that seemed to move and dance. The eyes imparted sadness while simultaneously screaming with a murderous hate. That was when he noticed its pale blue skin and lips were a light, air deprived purple. The terror hit Laoch fully as he knew the creature. Scrios, now only 30 feet away, impossibly jumped and eclipsed the cloud and sun above him and landed on his chest, knocking him to the ground with an audible whoosh; his feet straddling his prone body with his knees pressed into his upper chest. Laoch gasped for air from his destroyed chest. The creature grabbed Laoch's shirt and folded in close.

99

With the smell of stale pond water on his breath and insane confidence and sincerity, he said, "I will eat your fucking son!"

Laoch wet the bed as he woke up screaming.

As his eyes darted around the room in a panic, Jen gently tried to soothe him. Eventually, she pacified him, and his tense body relaxed. That's when her mind caught up and she realized she had also caught the echo of horrific screams coming from another area of the house.

Chapter 16

April 30th, 1982, 9:15 AM The Big House, Atholl, Scotland

When the panic vanished from her husband's eyes, it transformed into embarrassment as he fetched a leather-bound notebook from the bedside table and began writing. Curious, she questioned his activities, and he swiftly responded, "I need to write all I can remember about the dream in case there are any clues. I just need a minute or two." To himself, his response sounded like the feigned courage of a five-year-old facing his first ride alone on a school bus. He glanced back and met her eyes. "Sorry."

She saw a sadness and recognition in his eyes and that troubled her.

He threw the book onto the freshly stripped bed and directed her towards it after finishing and stared into her eyes. "Go ahead. Like I promised, no secrets here".

She picked up the thick book; she observed it was almost three-quarters full of entries. As she looked up at him, a redness appeared in the whites of her eyes, and tears welled up in the corners. With a cracking voice that twisted something in Laoch's heart, she asked, "These are all dreams?"

"Yes, love, and there are three more volumes you can find in the archives. There is a very full room there, with this type of information from the last 600 years."

"Do you mind... if I..." she pointed towards the book with her chin, as her voice failed her.

"Of course, like I said... no secrets."

She read his most recent entry, wiping tears from her eyes and near the end, her jaw locked into a set position and she closed the book. "He knows about our son?" she asked through clenched teeth, as a single tear coursed down her face, cruelly using her dimples and laugh lines to give it direction.

"No, we don't think so. See how I noted the time and date as close as I can to the second? We hope the dates and times might be significant. While multiple events sometimes align with specific dates or times, it is essential to avoid assuming that every negative occurrence is relevant just because of their correlation. We think something in the connection triggers the dream... at least that is our best guess. We have a nightmare that seems to encapsulate our worst fears at that moment. This is what I meant when I said I dream about him, or it, or whatever the hell this thing is." He caressed her hand, and could feel the tension in them.

"I have so many questions," Jen said, "but first let's go downstairs and see what the other commotion was."

"It will probably be similar. While this has happened before, synchronized nightmares are not something that happens often."

Laoch's father had indeed awakened from a start, but he insisted his memories of the dream had evaporated into the ether as soon as he had roused from sleep. Laoch, however, caught a look in his father's eye that made him question his sincerity. It was his father's third quick glance towards him that had solidified his suspicion.

Originally, Laoch had planned to conduct soil surveys in the back fields that day, but surprisingly, he postponed those activities and had breakfast with his bride instead. "That's a shame!" Jen chided with an evil smile. "The weather is warming up beautifully, with hardly any clouds in the sky."

With manufactured indignation as Laoch grabbed her up and twirled her around. "Shut yer pus ya blootered hen. I hope my baby son toe kicks you right in the bladder." They broke into smiles and laughter.

He gently set her down, and they headed towards the car, hand in hand. Laoch's mother Mimi, mock scolded them, as she shooed them out the door to their car, "Out both of you and don't come back till lunch time!"

Chapter 17

Dark and rich coffee awaited Jen and Laoch. It was black as night with the iron like bite of raw gun barrel metal. The food was a small spread of pastries with freshly churned and lightly salted butter. For the first ten minutes, however, they only drank coffee, as Laoch voiced frustration. "He broke the rules. He remembered the dream. I could see it in his eyes and I know mum could too."

"Why would he do that?"

"I dunno," Laoch paused. Jen noted his brogue was always much stronger when he was mad or scared, and this time it seemed to be a thick stew of both.

"My guess is that something actually frightened him... on an intellectual level. I think I need to get him alone and ask him directly." The decision made to confront his father seemed to calm him, and his smile returned.

With the concerns aired, the lightness returned to their conversation. The pastries were no match for the onslaught that occurred; even the ordered reinforcements from a second round quickly begged for quarter, but none was given.

Chapter 18

That afternoon, Laoch faced down his nightmare. Instead of walking to the field, though, he took the small green Gator Cart and Coulton, the intrepid tabby cat from his barn, rode shotgun with him.

When he got to the field, he tried not to think of the dream. With a wave, he acknowledged the trees and chuckled as they reciprocated the gesture. Walking into the field, he gathered samples and observed how closely the scene matched his dream.

He looked up and saw a small, lonely cloud drifting towards the afternoon sun and pointed an accusing finger at it, "No you fuckin' don't!" he commanded, and the cloud faded and broke as if his will had broken its ethereal spell. "Goddamn right!" he said to the world, and he finished gathering the samples.

He sprang back onto the Gator and drove back to his lab with Coulton, leisurely cleaning his genitals in the warm sun during the ride.

Chapter 19

That evening, the family sat around one of the last fires of the season in the great room while outside a large orange planter's moon rose over the highlands, marking the first day of May.

The usual banter was subdued when compared to the normal din. William had told a story or two and excused himself to bed. Mimi, too, had had a long day preparing flower beds and helping with planning for various other events in their little community.

The population of the great room soon reached three, counting the fading embers of the once roaring fire. Just two generations of Laoch remained, father and son. "Dad... what was the dream about?"

"I don't have any recollection, as I already stated this morning."

With a touch of disappointment affecting his tone, the son spoke. "Dah, you made me swear the same oath you have sworn... We agreed to notify each other whenever one of us had a dream, ensuring that we could record it and include it in the files and... I could see it in your eyes and I'm sure ma could too. Please, what was it?"

The father paused for nearly 20 seconds. "Well, it was different. It wasn't the blue man at all."

He waved one hand, rolling it in the air with determination, as if urging himself to move forward. "It was your great grandfather dead forty-five years now... warning me that things will change and that I needed to be strong. He said that events were in motion, and he warned I would lose people I love and he said, 'Sometimes the only comfort that pain brings is the knowledge that you are still alive', as if that helps somehow. When I asked the old man, still dressed in the last suit he wore, 'What Pappy? What is happening? What's in motion?' he was silent. He bowed his head, expressing a bit of annoyance, and looked over his shoulder towards the doorway just before he disappeared."

"Christ! That is a strange dream indeed."

The father shook his head. "That's just it Ceithir. I was not dreaming." He said, bringing his eyes up to meet his son's. "The yelling and clatter that others heard was not me. That was Daniel when he walked into my study, bringing me morning coffee before we were to go out to check the goats and do a pregnancy count. He heard me talking and came into the room. He thought I was talking to him. When he saw my grandfather look at him with a frustrated look, before he faded away. What you heard was Daniel, screaming as he dropped both of the cups of coffee."

Ceithir sat there, his mind racing as he struggled to think of anything that could elicit such a piercing scream from Daniel. "I asked him not to say anything to anyone about this," said his father.

Ceithir nodded his head. "I think I understand now."

The senior Laoch spoke with a wry smile, "No, but you will. I'm proud of Daniel... so big and strong. He is a good man. If it had been me screaming, my bellow would probably be a high soprano, as seeing Pappy just standing there made my bollocks climb up into me throat. Instead, Daniel's rise in octaves came out in my normal range for terror, so I claimed it like a sweethearts' pump in a crowded room. In reality, his yell allowed us both to save face."

Chapter 20

June 9th, 1982, 2:27 AM The Big House, Atholl, Scotland

The night had been long already. Jen would take a stroll through the halls every couple of hours, talking to her unborn son, pleading for him to get out of her belly. Lying on her back was uncomfortable and made her back hurt with burning nerve pain that shot like electricity down the outside of both legs. Lying on her side seemed to be little or no help and the baby was riding low today, forcing her to pee every hour.

As usual, Laoch had been there to massage the sore muscles in her back, but even that was having limited effect. And if he asked her one more time what he could do to help, she might put him in a hospital before she needed to be there.

About halfway down the long hallway outside their second-floor apartment, on the return of another of her laps, the gentle Braxton-Hicks contractions that had been her constant travel partner for the last 6 weeks, suddenly gave way to pain that buckled her and forced her to the wall for support. She stood there, leaning and biting her lip for what seemed like an eternity, but was probably only 10 to 15 seconds. Her stomach, as hard as a rock, slowly eased, and she stood back up, "Wow!" she said. With a nervous giggle, she walked back towards her apartment.

Laoch was sitting up and stretching when she entered. "I noticed you were not in bed and was coming to look for you... all, ok?" he asked.

"Yeah, I just had a big contraction in the hall and had to lean against the wall a sec." Jen replied.

Laoch glanced towards the 'go bags' he had lined up near the door and back at her with his eyebrows up. Jen laughed, "No. Not Ye..." as she winced and grabbed the chair back near her. The sudden and intense pain made her aware of the urgent need to use the bathroom, and she then realized her bladder had already emptied. However, somehow... illogically, she still had to pee. The awareness hit her like a slap. "Oh shit! My water broke!" Adrenaline flooded her system as she looked at Laoch.

Up in a flash, Laoch ran and grabbed the bags under his arms, and opened the front door to their suite. He started down the hall when he heard his bride. "Laoch honey? Pants?"

Sheepishly, he looked down at his blue striped boxers, and his shoulders slumped. "Yes, and probably should get you situated first too, before the bags, and before I drive off without you." They shared a nervous laugh as he went back into the room and pulled on his clothes.

As he walked her out to the car, he tapped on his parent's door and quickly alerted them to what was going on. Laoch's father stepped into the hallway, looking completely alert and presentable, except for his bare feet. He grabbed his son by the shoulders, scanned his eyes, "No bloody way I'm letting you drive. You would likely drive straight through the fields and forest thinking you were saving time with eyes like that."

Laoch gathered the bags after getting his wife in the boxy green Land Rover, and his father got the car warmed up. As soon as everyone was secure, they set off. The trip to the Royal Infirmary of Edinburgh was uneventful despite the need to get to the opposite side of town, but it was 04:00 in the morning, and traffic was almost nonexistent when they made it to the city.

Chapter 21

Infirmary of Edinburgh, Edinburgh, Scotland

Jen walked in to the hospital with Laoch as his father parked the car. As she walked in the door, a pleasant woman met her with a wheelchair and they immediately went to the back. 20 short minutes later, they were in a room and the night doctor was checking on her with a small army of nurses.

Laoch Kier Ferguson the Fifth, or "Còig" in Gaelic, meaning "Five", cried as he entered this world of pain at 7:47 AM GMT.

A cool, steady breeze from the northeast stacked the clouds on this early overcast day, like a crowd of curious onlookers, straining to see an accident scene. From the window in Jen's room, Ceithir's father peered at the conspiratorial clouds that seemed to converse in his thoughts. He watched as one cloud, shaped like an old woman, sobbed; shedding raindrops like tears, while proclaiming that his grandson's path would be brimful with pain. The other clouds seemed to swirl and nod, silently acknowledging this prophecy.

The elder Ferguson removed a handkerchief from his coat pocket and wiped the tears from his own eyes as he faked a yawn, turned, and did his best to join the celebration.

He looked at Jen. The new mother looked a strange mix of excited and haggard from the exertion. She caught his eye as he turned, and he executed his practiced smile at her. The smile drawn on his face as if by a child with a crayon failed to fool her as it did nothing to hide the sadness in his eyes.

Jen stared into his eyes for a long second, squinted slightly and tilted her head to the left gently, as if to ask if he was okay. The simple act of her, after all she had been through, worrying about him made him feel impotent for his inability to shield her from his worries. He found the courage, inspired by her strength, to nod and give a more convincing smile. Jen accepted it, but it would be a moment that she would remember the rest of her life.

Chapter 22

June 12th, 1982, 2:27 AM The Big House, Atholl, Scotland

With three generations of Laoch in the large house, the new baby picked up the name he would prefer the rest of his life. No, it was not Còig. Against tradition in the house, Jen nicknamed him Gus, and it stuck. The photographs of Gus's father taken when he was three months old were almost identical to Gus himself. His eyes, which were a deep shade of sea blue, were identical to those of his father, his grandfather, and supposedly his great grandfather before him. At six weeks old, reddish-brown tufts of hair had sprouted, adding a touch of color to his adorable little head.

Jen thought about giving up her job as an accountant and embracing the role of a stay-at-home mom. She soon discovered that her boss (and cousin by marriage) was completely fine with her bringing Gus to the office. With Gus sleeping much of the time, she had ample opportunities to delve into the family history she was eager to explore.

As she went about her workday, she made an interesting observation. The IBM terminal interface in the archives closely resembled the one she was using for accounting. Just on a whim, she navigated to the administration screen, where the hidden program was on the similar terminal in the archives. She found the archive software was on that system, too.

She quickly exited out and changed to accounting.

At lunch with her husband and baby, she directly asked if it used the same system; he nodded with a sardonic smile, "of course, love," then ate a crisp. After about four chews, he noticed she was just staring at him and even the surrounding birds seemed to have gotten the message and silenced their singing. "What?" he asked with an innocent smile.

"What?" she echoed, imitating his dull response. "I did not know it was on this system, too. How was I supposed to know?"

As if it were common knowledge, Laoch explained, "The old church is about a hundred yards down that hill love. This is the place I mentioned that had the computer system we used. I mean, you know this warehouse is family owned, right?"

A mix of embarrassment and anger accented her voice as she stared a hole in him. "You always drove me to work in the car, and it usually took about ten minutes to get here through the winding roads, so... No! I never made the connection."

He looked at her, bit his lower lip, and spoke in a soothing voice. "This is my fault. I grew up here. I should have helped you get a good mental layout. If that ride was the only way I ever got here, I wouldn't know either."

So, after lunch, he took her inside and showed her the hidden cable that led from the IBM System 34, under the elevated floor and eventually into a hole in the subfloor. "Instead of popping up at one of the other terminal places in the warehouse, it goes through an old air shaft, down and over to the room in the archives. It was not a simple task to do either. This wire is heavy and finicky to get working right. If it gets kinked, and that shaft is like spelunking a cave to navigate, it stops working. But as long as no one is in the room, you can do the same archive research stuff in your office if you want. Or do your accounting work down there, if there is a way to do that," he said, with a look on his face that showed the complete lack of knowledge of her day-to-day tasks.

Chapter 23

December 17th, 1982 The Big House, Scotland

When snow covered the ground once again and the Big House adorned with festive Christmas decorations, Gus, at six months old, began his journey of crawling and rolling for locomotion. He resembled an inchworm. Over the next month, as the squirming crawl led to pulling up and cruising around the edges of furniture, items on tables were no longer safe.

Chapter 24

February 8th, 1983 Raleigh, NC

As Gus approached eight months old, he developed the ability to cruise on the furniture, which he proudly demonstrated during the second Christmas celebration at Jen's parents' house in early February.

Gus's miraculous escapes from peril often involved him narrowly missing the edges of tables, legs of chairs, and corners of doorways. Now and again, Jen would hear a thump as his head contacted something solid. Instead of crying, Gus would often burst into uncontrollable fits of crazy giggling. Whenever he displayed his toughness, Jen's Scottish Clan members couldn't help but laugh along with him, finding immense joy in his actions.

Gus's first steps occurred on a chilly evening, on February 12th, 1983, just three days after their return from the States and visiting Jen's parents. Jen etched the date into her mind; it was a day filled with laughter and jubilant cheers as Gus and William proudly marched. It was adorable watching Gus try to imitate the march, with his playful antics bringing a smile to everyone's face.

As the day ended, a phone call from the states shattered Jen's world with the heartbreaking news of her parents' fatal car accident.

The next morning, Jen and Gus flew back to North Carolina. Laoch's parents mournfully accompanied them.

Chapter 25

February 14th, 6278 Mourning Dove Rd. Raleigh, NC

February 14th, 1983, marked the day when Valentine's Day lost its significance to Jen, leaving her feeling empty. On that day, she had back-to-back meetings with lawyers and morticians, and she cried a lot.

Jen made plans that matched the wishes her parents had expressed in a letter in their fireproof safe.

At first, the intention was to spend two weeks in Raleigh, attending to different tasks, and embark on the journey back to Scotland. The familiar sights and smells of the celebration they had left behind five days earlier greeted Jen the moment she stepped back into the house. The dry tree was still partially up, its branches brittle and needles falling off.

Cruel leftovers from the late Christmas dinner were still in the freezer. Carrying her sleeping son, Jen entered her parent's room and noticed a shopping list on her mom's dresser. Written on the back of the shopping list was a brief note from her father to her mom, expressing one of the many reasons he loved her. "I love you and the way your eyes light up when I see you across a room." Jen's vision blurred with tears as she broke into sobs.

For two consecutive days, she attempted to pack up her parent's belongings. They had to change their plans on the first day because it felt like a North Carolina summer in the middle of winter. As a result, they took Gus to Pullen Park and had fun riding the train and playing with him on the playground. Instead of working on the house on the second day, they watched a movie at a theater. They got some looks, bringing a baby to the movie, but no one brought a voice to their concerned look. Baby Gus slept the whole way through the movie. If he had made a noise, and others dared to say anything to her after this week? Well, just like her grandpa always said, they could "Go piss up a rope."

All subsequent attempts they made to pack up were equally futile. Jen's room remained unchanged from her high school and college days... well, except it was cleaner. At first, going into her parent's room felt odd, but finding solace in her mom's bed felt like a last hug. On the sixth day back, the funeral took place.

Chapter 26

February 20th, 1983, 11:00 AM St Raphael the Archangel Church, Raleigh, NC

When Jen arrived at the Catholic Church she grew up around, she gave Gus to Laoch and paused in shock at the number of people present. Yes, she had informed her friends through her mom's contact book, but somehow, she had reached out to more people than she initially thought. Abruptly, she remembered something her mom had said, and flipped through the address book in her mind. She had gotten in touch with Sandy, one of her mom's closest and dear friends. There was a memory of her mom advising her, "To make sure everyone knows you're getting married, consider putting your picture in the newspaper and paying for an announcement, or just let Sandy know, and she'll handle the rest."

The moment she walked in the door, Sandy was the first to greet her with a warm hug. Not one of those dainty brief hugs, either. This was a boob crusher. While Sandy had her in the vise, she whispered, "Your parents loved you very, very much. You were their prize. They were so proud of you and the adult you have become." Sandy pulled her in and she kissed her on both cheeks and let her move on to others as Jen focused on Gus's hand that held hers.

The service was nice, and it was helpful to reconnect with old friends who knew and loved her and her parents. While they followed the caskets out of St. Raphael's, the unmistakable silhouette of Daniel stood out in front of the stained-glass windows, his broad shoulders towering above the crowd, catching both Jen and Laoch's attention. To their surprise, Laoch's brother Kyle, William, and his nurse Nell, along with Bynum and Donna, who had made the trip, flanked Laoch's parents.

"I never knew Daniel even had a suit," Laoch whispered to Jen, as he hoped to elicit a smile. He hadn't seen one in a couple of days, and he missed them.

As they settled into the limousine, which would be third in line behind the two hearses, he added, "I've only ever seen him in blue jeans and a t-shirt during warm weather, and blue jeans with a flannel and coat during winter." As Jen smiled at him, he noticed a hint of sadness in her eyes, and a sense of shame occurred to him, as he realized. She, at that moment of terrible grief, was doing her best to console... him! Laoch's father and mother rode with them, and his father's eyes betrayed a deep sadness that extended beyond the loss of his daughter-in-law's parents.

Mimi asked to hold and take charge of the sleeping Gus during the ride. Jen was grateful and thanked her and her father-in-law for all their help. When Laoch looked at his dad, he noticed a mixture of shadows and sadness swirling in his eyes. "Dah, are you ok?" Laoch asked.

With a warm, practiced and possibly insincere smile, his father replied, "I'm fine."

Chapter 27

Oakwood Cemetery, Raleigh, North Carolina 12:30 PM

Upon arriving at Oakwood Cemetery, in the heart of Raleigh, his father's gaze darted around with a mix of fascination and unease. When they finally parked the car, a sudden pallor washed over his face. As his father's jaw muscles clenched and his eyes grew darker, Laoch was the only one who noticed the sudden ashen color of his face.

It was a look he recognized from his past... the same look as when his father found out a twelve-year-old boy, twice Kyle's size, with an adolescent beard, bullied him at school. The scrap left Kyle with a broken nose and a pair of black eyes as souvenirs. The other boy had weathered a small slap on the wrist from administration at the school and gained a perpetually smug smirk... which was allegedly forcefully wiped from his face days later. When his dad had THAT look, it meant trouble was brewing.

When the car door opened, Laoch was the first to exit, extending a hand to help Jen out. Outside the car, they watched as his parents got out of the limousine. As his father passed by him, Laoch whispered. "Dah?" and his father sharply responded, "Later!" as his eyes darted around like a fugitive trapped in a dead-end.

Laoch held his wife's hand and guided her towards the small tent prepared for the graveside service. As they made their way to the tent, the soft touch of tiny snowballs falling from the chilly February skies greeted them.

Taking a seat in the folding chairs of the first row, Laoch noticed Daniel's curious actions. Instead of heading straight from the car, Daniel had veered off in an arc, finally positioning himself under a tree a considerable distance away. In his uncomfortable suit and overcoat, he stood like a sentry, his eyes darting between the crowd and the cemetery. "Exactly like a sentry," he whispered under his breath.

Jen looked over at him, "Huh? Oh yeah, many of these are well over a century old." Laoch smiled and nodded blandly.

As the service completed, a queue formed, with Laoch's family leading the way and the others that were present following behind in a parade. Each person shared a handshake, or gave a comforting hug, while others offered a heartfelt kiss on the cheek to Jen while sharing their condolences.

Continuing their actions down the line, each turned their attention to Laoch and repeated the process. As Laoch's father hugged Jen, he glanced at Laoch. Leaving Jen's embrace, he offered his son his hand. Their handshake quickly developed into a heartfelt hug. For just a second, Laoch felt the strange pressure of his father's wallet in his coat, heavily brushing against his arm.

A few moments later; he questioned in his mind if it was a wallet. A visibly relaxed Daniel made his way over, after the line had diminished into a crowd of friends talking, while others made to exit to their cars. Daniel looked down at Jen and said the sincerest comforting words he could string together and gave her a small hug. She hugged him back, and he came to Laoch and offered condolences, "Sorry for all this, and your and Jen's loss". Laoch thanked Daniel for coming and, during their embrace, detected a similar protrusion, revealing it was not a wallet.

Laoch gracefully pulled Daniel aside during their hug, feigning a sad smile that hinted at a favor to come. When they reached the side of the tented area, he leaned in and whispered directly, "Are you carrying a gun?"

Daniel gave an awkward smile, as if there was a hidden joke between them, and leaned in closer and said, "Yeah, your father insisted. He said something didn't feel right."

Laoch locked eyes with him, his gaze intense as he whispered, "Ok, we will discuss this later, but how did you bring weapons on the plane?" Laoch asked.

In a low, bassoon like baritone, Daniel attempted a whisper. "We took the private plane... I mean, your dad's cousin provided us with his private plane. It was short notice,"

With a promissory stare, Laoch said, "Later... We'll talk about this later."

After he broke eye contact, he went back to his wife's side. She seemed to know something was amiss and was looking at him with her red eyes and a questioningly raised eyebrow. Gus shook his head to dismiss the concern he saw, but he knew it didn't fool her.

As the crowd dispersed and some headed for their homes, Jen, Laoch and his parents headed towards St. Raphael the Archangel Church, where parishioners had set up a memorial get together for her parents.

Chapter 28

St. Raphael the Archangel Church, Raleigh, North Carolina 2:00 PM

The memorial reception had a more intimate setting and took place in the same large fellowship hall area, where she had spent years of mornings and evenings growing up. On Sunday mornings, people used the hall's large accordion walls to separate the vast area into classrooms for CCD classes. The area at the end of the hall to her right, closest to the church, still had toys orderly stacked in the corner, as it obviously still served as the volunteer toddler and babysitting area during masses, Jen realized.

As Jen entered the church, memories of her childhood rushed back to her. She could see her childhood friends walking past her, recall the vibrant pictures she colored in Sunday school, and feel the rough texture of the wooden blocks shaped like a cross, with purple yarn braided between the nails. Awakening from her daydream, Jen found herself face to face with the parents of her childhood friends she grew up with. The image she kept of them in her mind, morphing and updating, aging them ten years or more when they introduced themselves. People introduced teenagers to her, whom she had babysat as infants, as the room seemed to swirl.

At that moment, the weight of the week finally washed across her like a wave. Her parents were gone. They were here a little over a week ago, vibrant and happy. The laughs and jokes from the last dinner with them were playing in her memory. The laughter was audible to her. In her mind, she watched them play with her son as Gus struggled for the balance and courage to take his precocious first steps. She had laughed with them that night and had adult conversations with them she never imagined having just a few short years ago.

There was no transition. There was no growing old for them and watching their grandson grow up and go to college. Her mom wouldn't wear some out-of-date blue dress to his wedding someday. Jen felt cheated, robbed of it all. The world had just become a colder and emptier place. A darker place too... "Wow, real dark," she thought as the tunnel vision she had just noticed faded to a dark gray.

She felt the sure grip of Laoch under her arm, and heard as he asked, "You alright Love?" in her husband's calm familiar voice. "Let's get you a seat and something to drink."

Interlude – The Searcher

The dark creature momentarily ceased its relentless frustration with its imprisonment and seemed to inhale the scent of suffering. A smell to it, equivalent to freshly baked pies wafting from a windowsill.

In this anguish, there was something different, yet strangely familiar. In its cage, in the recesses of its mind, recognition materialized and for the first time in a very long time. Scrios smiled in his prison. His suspicion, it appeared, was right. One of its searchers had found one of them, a member of the family, and dragged them from their hiding through pain. He could taste it and knew somehow its prey was not far away.

Chapter 29

St. Raphael the Archangel Church, Raleigh, North Carolina 4:00 PM

Laoch led Jen to a row of fold out tables lined with tan metal folding chairs. She had a flashback to her freshman year in high school, watching the boys in her confirmation class horse play before the lesson as they pretended to be professional wrestlers. In slow motion, they would imitate the way the wrestlers would swing these same types of chairs, playfully tapping the backs of their friends, who would collapse dramatically to the ground and flop around like a beached fish, while everyone laughed.

When she sat down, there was that instant familiarity in the cool metal on the backs of her legs and back. In an instant, Laoch materialized with a cup of water. This interrupted her thought midstream. He kissed her on the forehead and assuredly stated, "I'll be right back". Moments later, he was back beside her with a cup of black coffee from the large percolator on the table. "You had me worried there; I thought you were going down."

"I might have been," Jen confessed. "The world got all dark and suddenly you were there supporting me and talking and leading me to this seat."

When the get-together thinned, Jen and Laoch thanked as many people as they could, and returned to the cold, quiet home of her parents. Outside, on this gloomy day, the daylight had dwindled, and the shifting precipitation transformed from icy pellets to a freezing rain, leaving a glistening coating on the trees. Gradually, it transitioned into a delicate snowfall.

The weather in Raleigh that day turned out to differ from the forecast. Instead of just fog and a light chilly rain, there were even cooler temperatures, and a surprising amount of moisture with the system. To Jen, the weather that day seemed to follow her mood perfectly.

Chapter 30

6278 Mourning Dove Rd. Raleigh, North Carolina 7:23 PM

When they got back to the house, Jen was justifiably exhausted. Laoch leaned over the sleeping Gus in the travel crib and told Jen he wanted to get his parents to the hotel. Jen, exhausted from the emotional day, responded with a simple wave.

Laoch grabbed on of her last shreds of consciousness before she crashed to sleep. "Oh, Daniel mentioned he was having difficulty sleeping on the bed at the hotel. Would you care if he used the spare room here?"

"Of course not. If he would be more comfortable here, it's fine with me."

In the living-room, the small gathering waited for Laoch. The group comprised Daniel, Laoch's father and mother. "Is she alright Ceithir?" Mimi asked.

"As good as she can be, I guess, after a day like this."

Ceithir turned to the giant, Daniel, "I discussed with Jen, if you are having problems with that bed at the hotel, you are welcome to use the spare room here."

"Problems with the bed?" Mimi asked, as her husband put a calming hand on her arm. "You can hear him sleeping from three bloody rooms away..." Mimi trailed off with an "ohhh".

Daniel nodded, "I have my light bag in the coach," and he went outside to retrieve it.

Laoch looked at his father. "Dah, I would be glad to show you a better way back to your hotel and get you guys all settled. North Carolina winters are silly. Most likely this stuff won't freeze up, but if it does... you would be better off strapping on your skates."

His father nodded, "That would be grand." They stepped outside and dodged to let Daniel pass on his way back inside.

Daniel slowed his step and caught Laoch's eye. "They're safe," he whispered confidently and went into the house.

In the car, Laoch drove, while his father rode up front, and his mother in the back seat. "Dah, what is up with the guns?" he asked.

Mimi, in the back of the car, leaned forward in concern. "What?"

Her husband raised his hand, holding up his index finger. He looked at him. "Son, I don't know if your dreams have been different recently, but mine have been. Some more like that day when I saw my grandfather. It's ok, your mother knows about Pappy talking to me, and Daniel... seeing him."

"More how?" Ceithir asked, "What happened?"

"I have barely slept at all this week, lad. I had some bad dreams, but nothing that seemed related or that rated documenting... just bloody chaos."

Ceithir pulled the car over and looked at his father. "So, tell me."

His father adjusted in his seat uncomfortably. "Things changed for me the weeks before Gus was born. At first, I thought it was a mood, after I saw Pappy. I would walk down the hall or a flight of stairs and I would see him standing in the corner looking like he was weeping... but it wasn't exactly a normal view of him. It was like a poster of him, two dimensional. Sometimes he would reach towards me as if to grab my hand, with a hand that seemed to tear into the third dimension." His father paused. "I would say to him, "Pappy, what is the matter? What are you trying to tell me?", and he would fade away." The grandfather shook his head, wiping away a disobedient tear from his face that had rolled down seconds before, to his mid cheek. "I think he was just trying to give a general warning, but the dreams... the fucking dreams, lad. You know, in the archives, the years leading up to Sanura's battle, there is a part where they talked about the 'Tribulations of Aidan'. I think they meant these damn dreams. It mentions a mockery, describes a tumultuousness and his inability to rest. All of this was just before or when Cormic's debacle happened."

"Cormic?" Mimi asked from the back seat.

The older Laoch looked at his wife. "Cormic was supposed to be Aidan's son, a blood relative, but it proved out that fateful day all those years ago that he was not of our bloodline. By the description, Cormic was of similar proportions to Daniel and looked nothing like his father or uncles, but they did not know of genetics, just bloodlines, in those days. The unfortunate unfaithfulness of his mother and the bravado of a young warrior led to the loss of many lives to Scrios."

The elder Laoch sighed, "Anyway, before that, Aidan and others of the bloodline, to a lesser extent... and even reportedly Cormic. They all complained of tribulations. It would have been brilliant if they had provided more details about what that word meant to them."

The younger Laoch drummed his fingers on the steering wheel and bit his lip. "I think in the light of your descriptions, I might have overlooked something. It was nothing direct, like what you have been describing, but I have had dreams where I was being harassed or chased. However, I never saw what was doing it and I had just assumed it was just anxiety." Laoch admitted.

When Mimi spoke, Laoch and his father both turned towards her in shock. "Kyle woke up with a start late last night as well."

Laoch's father spoke decisively, "Let's get to the hotel. Now!" Laoch, without a further thought, dropped the car into gear and quickly made for the hotel.

Chapter 31

Ramada Inn, Raleigh, NC 8:07 PM

When they arrived at the hotel, they went to where their four rooms were located, knocked and enter the room Kyle was sharing with Daniel. "Pack up, quick!" his father ordered him. "And grab Daniel's gear too. All of it," he finished.

Kyle, who was lying on the bed with his Walkman earphone ajar, moved as directed. "Dah, is something the matter?" he asked.

"We will talk about it soon," his father assured him.

The room he encountered next was one of the adjoining rooms that Bynum and William shared. Laoch politely let them know to gather their stuff quickly, "five minutes, be ready." He then moved on to the other side of the adjoining rooms, where Nell and Donna were. He repeated the instructions and added, "Gather your stuff in the hall." From there, Laoch and his father moved on to his parent's room, where Mimi had almost completed the packing.

"What is the plan?" Ceithir asked his father.

"We are going to your house, lad. I don't like us scattered like this, and the house is our best bet."

"What am I going to tell Jen?" Ceithir asked with an innocent and weighty smile.

"If you like, I could mash that fire alarm over there on the wall, or we can just tell her it was going off, so we left the hotel, as there might have been a fire?" Laoch's father offered. "We can give William Jen's old room. Your mother and Donna can take the spare bedroom, and the rest of us can fight over couches and floor space... it will be fine." The fatherly tone he used let his son know that this was a settled conversation.

Settled at least until he got home and tried the story on Jen... Laoch grabbed his father's shoulder, meeting his eyes for a moment. "This is fine, Dah, but Jen gets the full truth, right from the start. I won't lie to her, not about this, plus, if I tried, she would know straight away."

His father stood statue still for a two count and stared him in the eyes, smiled and did one brief nod of his head, patted him on the shoulder, smiled again, and turned away.

Chapter 32

February 21ˢᵗ, 1983, 6278 Mourning Dove Rd. Raleigh, North Carolina

Jen was the first one up the next morning at 5:00 AM and when she left her room to make coffee, for about two seconds, she thought she had somehow traveled back in time to her freshman year of college, when her parents had left town... and an empty house.

Those conditions back in her college years were an invitation to a party. The house looked like the day after one of those parties. She could make out a person on each of the couches in the living room, at least two more on the floor and the feet of another sticking out of the dining room. She shook her head in disbelief, and prepared to clear her throat, when she heard as Laoch quietly said, "Honey? Shhhhh. There was an issue at the... shit. Come into the room a sec." So, she carefully back tracked to the room and quietly closed the door.

Jen looked at him with an incredulous look. "What is going on out there?"

"Oh, so last night I was... the hotel... dammit," Laoch started, "let me try again. I need to go back to where it all began. Wait, I have an idea! Grab your shoes and a coat, I'll change the baby and get Mimi to come sleep in here and keep an ear out for the 20-pound tyrant. You and I will go get an early breakfast and I will explain everything."

She looked at him with a conspiratorial smile. "One condition, the place better have excellent coffee."

With a slightly forced laugh that unsettled Jen Gus spoke. "We are in North Carolina, my sweet, not North Yorkshire. It will have coffee, but I cannot guarantee its veracity."

Deciding that they needed excellent coffee and food, they headed to downtown and went to Finch's Diner, like they had so many times in college. The food was great, and their wonderful coffee was hot and regularly refreshed.

Chapter 33

Finches Restaurant, 401 Peace Street, Raleigh, NC 5:45 AM

Noting that Laoch was thoroughly chewing each bite, just a little longer than his normal inhalation speed, she pushed forward the conversation. "You were saying at the house..."

"Oh, yeah. So let me get this all out... So yesterday at the graveside service, well after it..."

Trying to make him relax, she chided him, "Spit it out, Highlander."

He laughed. "Well, I went to hug dad afterwards, as we were going through the lines of people, and I felt something under his jacket. No... Before... it was before. I also noticed Daniel acting weird. When he left the car, he didn't come to the tent for the service." Laoch paused.

"I saw that too," Jen said, trying to help him, "and was wondering why myself."

"Yeah... so, after, when we were all hugging, he was near the end of the line. When Daniel hugged me, I felt the same bump on him under his jacket. It was not just a bloody wallet, so I walked him to the side and asked him if that was a gun and he said yes. So, my mind filled with questions on how, where, and mostly, why? It turns out my dad told him to carry one, and my dad had carried one as well. I couldn't make any sense of it, so I told him we would discuss this later, and... well, that was the reason I drove them back to the hotel."

Jen paused only a second, "Wait, is that why Daniel needed to sleep at our house? To protect us from something?"

With a wince, Laoch tilted his head from side to side and shrugged, using his body language to express a "maybe" gesture.

A note of urgency creeped into her voice. "Ok, what happened on the way back to the hotel that caused such a drastic change of plans?"

"Well, Dah talked about the dreams he had been having. He talked about how he had again seen Pappy, although I don't think Pappy spoke to him this time. Dah believes this resembles an event from the distant past recorded in the archives. He took a moment and gave her the CliffsNotes' version of the story of Aidan and Cormic. Laoch described to her his father's interpretation of the word *tribulations* and compared them to the dreams he was having recently. Then he told Jen how Mimi mentioned that Kyle had woken up poorly in the middle of the night with a night terror.

He paused and looked at her sheepishly. "Frankly, when she said that about Kyle's dreams, a wave of panic washed over all of us. From that point on, the decisions seemed to dictate their own path. Dah was afraid for our lives and thought we were too vulnerable spread out all-over town."

Gus looked down at the ground with a look that tasted like shame. "Dah took over like a general, and we were out of the hotel in 10 minutes. We crammed everyone and their belongings into two cars and moved here 30 minutes later. We tried to be quiet, and I was going to tell you last night, but that was the best sleep I had seen you have in weeks, love."

Jen reached across the table and held Laoch's hands. "Thank you, I can see that was hard and..." she trailed off.

"What love? You need the sky? I will fly up and snatch you a piece."

Tears welled in Jen's eyes. "Sanity, I need sanity. Your dad thought he needed guns at my parent's funeral... for some boogeyman that nobody has seen for over two thousand years! I have been trying to pack up my parent's life here and there is no sanity left here anymore. Laoch, honey, I need you. I need our baby, or should I say, our future brood of 22 children, that we've discussed so far." She said and smiled in a way that didn't reach her eyes.

Laoch eyes were stinging as well, and he listened. "I am up to 34 kids now," he replied with a calming smile.

Jen barked a laugh through the tears and, for the first time in over a week, a genuine, sweet smile appeared that melted Laoch's soul. "34, no problem... and that is up to you. If you want me to whistle like a train when we get old and it gets windy outside, I'll do it."

Jen took a deep, cleansing breath and continued. "I need this, and both of us desperately need to escape from this entire Scrios madness. I understand you feel unprotected when you're away from Wolfborn, but you successfully completed college here with no issues."

She squeezed both of his hands. "The house here will soon belong to us once we navigate through all the legal crap. Money may be tight, but we'll make it and work with what we've got. I am so sorry. I feel like shit putting this on you and pulling you from the family farm or even asking you to leave. I'm not saying they cannot be in our life. I would never do that because I really do, love their crazy asses, too. If they need your help during specific seasons, then go. I will back you and miss you while you are away. Sometimes, I might even come along with you. But I need to remove myself from the weight of importance that your family carries. I believe our son will also need that too. If Scrios is out there, I hope he stays away, leaving the burden of dealing with him or it to some other future generation. I am so sorry." As she finished speaking, a fresh tear bulged in the corner of her left eye.

Laoch was quiet. He sat and stared out the window towards the growing traffic on Peace Street. Several Pine State milk trucks drove by in a column, leaving the local creamery several blocks away, heading towards the western side of Raleigh. The first rays of the sun kissed the damp streets, with the sky a beautiful cobalt blue. Over this day of change, the sun rose, a day that Laoch feared might eventually come.

Laoch knew, though. Ever since he revealed the Cathedral and its archive to her... he knew. He expected and dreaded this day. He tried to trick himself into believing she would come around, and she put in the effort, a sincere effort. Laoch thought Jen might even somehow believe the story completely, but she didn't want it to be true.

She spoke, repeated herself, and only on the third repetition did he comprehend her words. With growing anxiety, she asked, "Are you alright?" as she squeezed his hand.

He looked up at her. "Yes," he said, surprising himself with the sincerity of his statement. "I will be, but I have to survive telling my dah first. Although he won't be pleased, he will still agree to it. He must. Last night's shit storm affected me as well. I was just as caught up in it as anyone else, and now I feel ridiculous. The combination of fatigue and stress exacerbated the situation. You are right. All was fine when I was here for school, and if you need this, that is what we will do."

The lasting memory she carried forward. The one that comforted her in her last moments of life, years later, was the memory of Laoch's beautiful and sad smiling eyes at this moment, with the sun showing brightly outside the window.

Jen nodded and smiled as tears of relief leaked down her face. She got up from the booth and came around to his side and hugged him. "Thank you!"

Chapter 34

Finches Restaurant, 401 Peace Street, Raleigh, NC 6:37 AM

Jen looked at him with a small look of rising panic, "I'll be right back, I have to hit the restroom" and she left. He sat there in the booth and took in the mostly empty room, absorbing the present before he confronted his father. The clanking sounds coming from the kitchen, the counter off to his left with the little white toadstool shaped stools lining the counter. He peered out the large, paned windows to his right and the view of the parking lot with its old drive-up awning. He noticed the other mostly empty booths in front of him, and something gave him a sense of unease. A feeling like he had missed something. A sense of foreboding and déjà vu flooded his mind. In the split second, while his eye was closed in a blink, an image flashed of an alternate version of that very room.

There were newspapers covering the windows, and the room looked disheveled and dark and completely silent. His eyes opened, and the room was as it was before the blink, hearing the familiar, "Order up!" from the kitchen. He shook his head, "Wow!" he thought. He glanced towards the counter and blinked. The counter for that same eternal slice of a time appeared dilapidated and painted with spray paint graffiti. Half of the stools were completely missing, and the remaining ones had their seat cushions stripped down to the rusty metal. There were parts of the tiled roof above the counter that drooped and appeared blackened because of leaks. When his eye opened, it was all normal and clean. Laoch again shook his head. He looked across the tables to where Jen had been sitting for breakfast. He tried not to blink, but he could not will himself not to.

In that blink, someone was sitting in the destroyed cafe, in the spot Jen had been sitting. They held a yellowing newspaper in their hands, as if reading it in front of them. The News and Observer newspaper had a large print headline which read, "Shuttle Explodes, Kills All 7 Aboard" accompanied by images of a rocket ship exploding and crashing into the sea.

Ragged leather work gloves covered the hands that held the paper, while a weathered leather hat peaked over the top. As the figure brought its hands closer together, the paper folded and revealed two eyes in a shade of sea blue, both fixed on him. Their eyes seemed almost identical to his own, the difference being the peculiar lights that appeared to swim within. Light from the sun outside illuminated newspaper that covered the window glass, showing a blue hue to the skin on his temple and the bridge of his nose, while long, red hair partially covered his ear.

When he opened his eyes from the blink, the creature was gone, and the room was again clean and undamaged. He saw Jen coming from the bathroom. She looked up at him and gave him a nervous smile. He quickly rose and dropped a

20-dollar bill on the table to cover their twelve-dollar tab and told the waitress, "Keep the change!" and stood to leave the restaurant.

Jen's eyebrows furrowed with concern as she observed his perspiring face. "Your sweating? Are you ok?" she asked.

He nodded nervously and held the door for her. As she walked by, another involuntary blink cursed him. The restaurant, from the door, looked abandon and quiet, except for his booth, where the newspaper now lay flat and the leering figure in a leather coat and cowl hat, grinned and watched him leave. The end of his blink was a seamless transition, with broken furniture magically renewed when his eyes opened.

Despite the blink ending, the creature persisted on the far side of the booth and kept sneering at him, even as the waitress, completely unaware of its presence, diligently cleared the table and expressed her gratitude towards him with a warm smile.

He quickly made for the car as his heart raced. Subsequent blinks did not repeat the effect, and he breathed a sigh of relief as he saw the now empty table through the window as he started the car.

Chapter 35

In the corner of Finch's Restaurant, Douglas Hanks sat transfixed on his coffee cup, his right hand caressing the odd metallic tube in his pocket that a political friend had asked him to hold at a fundraiser. When a woman came from the bathroom, the sleeve of her coat brushing his shoulder, the man waiting for her quickly rose and left money on the table and left the restaurant.

A moment later, Douglas shook as if just waking up, and reached for his coffee and tasted it, and spit it back in his cup. "Mam?" he called out with an annoyed tone, lifting a hand that displayed a slight tremor at the passing waitress. "My coffee is cold. Could I get another cup, please?" Despite his oblivious loss of almost 20 minutes staring at his now-cold coffee, the cold, tasteless mouthful of congealed eggs and soggy toast renewed his disappointment in his breakfast.

He rolled his eyes, a deep sigh escaping his lips, as he recalculated the tip, his frustration growing with the realization that the cold eggs and lukewarm coffee were not the start to the day he'd envisioned.

Chapter 36

February 21st, 1983, 6278 Mourning Dove Rd. Raleigh, North Carolina

The sight of his father smoking on the porch greeted Laoch and Jen, a blatant disregard for Mimi's aversion and a reminder of a habit he'd claimed to have quit years before. As they pulled into the driveway, he nodded once, extinguished his cigarette under his shoe, and made his way inside.

As they walked in, Laoch's father put on a smile that seemed strained and insincere. In an almost jolly sing-song voice, he asked, "Where the hell did you guys go?"

Jen's eyes locked with her father-in-law and she said, "We went for breakfast." With a quick gesture of his left hand, Ceithir silently signaled to his father to back off.

With a wide awake and cooing Gus in her arms, Mimi exited the bedroom. "He's got a fresh diape, and is having a wonderful morning."

Jen's face lit up with a smile as she spotted her boy, and she rushed over to him, planting a loving kiss on his cheek. "Can you watch him for five more minutes while I grab a quick shower?"

"Absolutely!" replied Mimi, "with pleasure!"

As she made her way towards the master bedroom at the end of the hall, a wave of steam engulfed the entire corridor as Daniel emerged from the bathroom, the second doorway on the right. After following him for a short distance, he abruptly broke off towards a side bedroom, while Jen continued to the end and entered her own room, already dreading the cold shower that she knew was now unavoidable.

In the living room, Laoch began a very difficult discussion with his father.

Chapter 37

After taking a tepid shower, Jen stepped out and noticed that a calm, but curt discussion was still ongoing in the living room. Despite not being able to decipher every word, she could still hear the deep resonance of her husband's voice echoing throughout the entire house. "It is our decision, dah. I know you don't like it, but there it is."

Although she couldn't fully comprehend what his father was saying, she could sense the desperate urgency in his rapid speech. If Laoch's voice was deep, the voice of Daniel carried as though it came from a deep well through to the master, as he said, "I will stay if you need me too."

123

Jen muttered, "ohhh hell no!" as Laoch replied with a more political version of the same response.

"Daniel, we need you at the Big House. We will be okay here, just like when we were in college." In a sudden moment of realization, Jen wished she had pretended to shower so she could quietly listen to the entire conversation.

As she emerged from the bedroom, a hush fell over the room. The return of Bynum and Donna broke the trance, their arms laden with groceries to feed the hoard. Following them in were William and Nell, returning from a morning walk as the house exploded with activity.

William was in mid-story about a tiger hunt trip he took in India, in the early 1900's, when he was fourteen. "... we diligently followed the trail of the beast for three days. Three individuals among the locals we employed to drive the beast from the tall cane fields lost their lives, while five others sustained injuries. When we finally cornered the creature, it turned and charged us. Bloody thing was running straight at me, and I froze. I have a distinct memory of being paralyzed, my mind racing with the thought, 'ah, this is the manner in which I meet my demise'. The distance between us became so minimal; I remember seeing my drop jawed face reflected in its enormous obsidian eyes. In these mortal conditions, time seems to stretch out, as if each second lasts an eternity. Suddenly, as if yanked by an invisible force, the enormous cat disappeared to my left, leaving behind only a whirlwind of hair and crimson fog where it was an instant before. It was so close that when I felt a sudden warmth in my pants, I was sure that it had disemboweled me like it had the porters. The next thing I heard was cheering as I stared blankly at the last place I had seen my reaper. Lord Curzon shook my shoulders with both hands and cheered, bringing me from the fugue. He applauded my bravery for standing my ground and declared my gun had clearly jammed. My brave stand, providing him with the decisive shot. Everyone just ignored the odor of my shame and talked of my bravery instead. Sometimes at night, during the war, that boy, reflected in the eyes of that beast, used to talk to me."

Chapter 38

Laoch's father and family returned to Scotland on the same plane as they did. After several days of packing, Laoch and Jen journeyed home with their little boy Gus. They landed back in Raleigh and began a life that no longer revolved around the fate of Laoch's family. Laoch deliberately broke every rule by not mentioning the morning breakfast at Finch's to his father. He knew that doing so would have exacerbated the situation. However, he wrote and dated a letter, which he placed in the fireproof box under the bed for safekeeping until he felt comfortable delivering it. He labeled the letter "To Father". The next year passed without incident. They made Jen's parent's house their own.

Laoch's father made a desperate plea to change their minds as they packed up at the Big House, knowing deep down that it was a futile endeavor.

As they sealed the shipping container, the weight of the previous day's discussion lingered, but he broke the silence by offering a heartfelt apology before they departed for the airport. "I'm truly sorry for letting my worries get the best of me. I know this is not likely to make a difference, but I wanted to be sure you know. If you change your mind, even if that is five minutes from now or five years. We will be here, this," he waved his hand at the property, "This is always a home for you, if you need it."

Chapter 39

6278 Mourning Dove Rd. Raleigh, North Carolina

The ensuing two years revealed the frequency of phone calls decreasing from almost daily to weekly. Eventually, even an entire month would go by without contact. The discussions on those calls focused solely on upcoming holidays and visits. There was no mention of Scrios or revelations of bad dreams.

Jen started a new job as an accountant at a computer chip manufacturing company in Raleigh. When she joined, she was the third employee, and the company had no permanent facilities. Deborah Smith, the company owner, and her husband Maxwell, or "Mack" as he liked to be called, were the first two employees. They received generous seed funding from a venture capital firm in London.

Despite feeling terribly unqualified, they appointed Jen to the position of chief accountant. She went as far as mentioning her concerns during the interview. With a smile, Mack pointed out that she was the only interviewee who had the courage to admit what they all were feeling. "None of us are qualified for our roles in this company, which is nothing more than a well-defined dream at this point. Fortunately, we have the support of a larger firm that believes in Deb and will provide us with the guidance to succeed. I want to handle the business side of things, and I'm counting on your help. This way, Deb can devote her energy to the chip designs she excels at."

Among Jen's concerns, the primary one was the cost of childcare and the related benefits. When Jen mentioned this to Mack, a smile spread across his face as he stood up and replied, "I'll be right back." A few moments later, he walked back into the room, his arms cradling a lanky little boy who was squirming with excitement. "Meet our son, Peter. We've been wrestling with the same questions, and we have some leeway in the budget. How about we hire some childcare staff and give them a big office for a playroom... and figure out a way for the company to foot the bill? As the accountant and third employee, I could use your help to figure out how to record that in our books," Mack said with a mischievous grin. "Oh, and until we have a full time HR person, I might need your help in finding and interviewing people for our critical needs."

Chapter 40

April 4th, 1983, 6278 Mourning Dove Rd. Raleigh, North Carolina

Upon arriving home, Jen discovered Laoch and shouted, "I've got a job!!!" When she described the job and the young company, it seemed almost too good to be true. They were both pleasantly surprised by the unexpectedly generous pay. They celebrated that night with takeout pizza and salad as they watched the national championship game on TV, with State completing the miracle run with a win over Houston.

After the game, they drove to campus and walked down the center of Hillsborough Street, which was flooded with fans. They alternated carrying Gus as they walked with the roaring crowd. Car speakers blasted Queen's "We are the Champions" as the crowd sang along and cheered.

Jen felt for the people who parked their cars along the primary thoroughfare, as thousands milled about, some walking right over the parked cars. The crowd was mostly well behaved, as people danced around and fed the enormous bonfire in the center of an open area, with chairs and couches from nearby campus buildings. Getting back to their car, they noticed red paint smeared all over them, concluding that they must have met someone with paint on their hands. Even Gus's clothes had paint stains.

The next day, Jen had to be at work for her first day at the new job. She was encouraged to bring Gus with her. Having Gus at work, just down the hall, under the supervision of a handpicked day care worker was a dream. Over time, they built out the office for kids and her worries about day care disappeared.

After work that night, Laoch, shifting the conversation slightly, asked, "Well, assuming everything goes well and everything seems favorable, how would you feel about me potentially returning to State for a master's degree... I mean, if the numbers make sense?" Jen leaped into his arms, planting a passionate kiss on his lips before they agreed to go out for a late dinner. Once again, Jen mentioned Finch's, but Laoch grinned and offered an alternative and said, "What if we check out Brother's Pizza by campus instead? We can see if it survived the bedlam. "Her exclamation of "ooooh yes!" settled the planning.

The next day, with Gus in one hand and a cup of coffee in the other, she walked towards the recently purchased 1976 Cutlass Salon parked in the front yard. Laoch mocked her the day before, when she brought it home because of the car's size. It was an enormous lane filling, four-door V-8 monster. It was dark green with a peeling tan vinyl hardtop. Upon her arrival home, Laoch stepped out of the front door and squinted through the front window to identify the driver.

The moment he spotted her, he erupted into laughter and collapsed onto the grass. "What in the living hell is that beast?" he howled.

"It is a $600 extra car with 28,000 original miles. It was owned by a little old lady... the mother of one of my dad's friends. She literally only drove it to the store and back a couple times a week." It silenced him. "Yeah," she said, in victory. Laoch surveyed the car now with a different eye, nodded as an appreciative smile grew on his face.

When she pulled out of the driveway the next morning, she spotted a new neighbor who had purchased the Ross's house. It took her by surprise when she realized it was her new boss Mack, walking towards his car, a shiny, newish Wagoneer. She stopped in front of the yard, rolled down the passenger side window, and teasingly warned, "You better hurry or you'll be even later than me!"

With a start, Mack looked up and said, "Wait, do you actually live in this area?"

"Yes, across the street and three houses down that way." Jen said, pointing with a laugh. "Alright, I'll see you at the office!" she waved as she pulled away.

The temporary office was in a small, rundown building in central Raleigh, near the intersection of Wake Forest Road and Six Forks. Aside from being shitty, it was prone to floods with every major thunderstorm or hurricane that came close enough to Raleigh to create a puddle. Luckily, their stay there was brief as the main office was being constructed in office space in the Research Triangle Park, also known as RTP.

Situated between Raleigh and Durham, close to the airport, RTP was mostly a rural area in and near Morrisville. IBM and Nortel had made tremendous investments in the area and many other companies were following. Right now, however, there were mom and pop farms next to the entrances to modern office buildings. Some were holdouts determined not to give in to the fast-growing crush of people moving to central North Carolina. The people were coming though, as if fired from a firehose from northern New York cities like Poughkeepsie and White Plains.

When Jen got to the office, she faced a sharp curve going from a "dumb terminal" to a PC, but it didn't take her too long to find her footing once she got into the accounting package. Occasionally she would think about Scotland and her life there, remembering the bad and the good. She still had moments of guilt from pulling her husband away from the family farm.

In the beginning, Laoch's parents funded his frequent trips for family support and soil analysis. However, these trips gradually decreased, substituted with soil shipments, along with remote work and sharing findings. The trips to Scotland were more dedicated to family holiday affairs. Over time, though, they too decreased in frequency.

Laoch's parents were pleasant when they visited the U.S. or when they visited Scotland, but there was a noticeable loss of intimacy. Their demeanor didn't show anger, but resembled a friendly greeting to someone on a passing boat.

Dinner conversations were no longer dominated by the blue man, but suspiciously, Laoch started accompanying his father on errands more often. Afterwards, he revealed to her all the details she wanted of the "secret" discussions. She tried not to take offense, but the cold shoulder and silent meals that replaced the dinner discussions felt like a slight, even though she knew it resulted from his family trying to respect her own desires.

With each passing year, Redwolf Solutions flourished. As a result, her availability to travel waned along with her desire to both take part in the family drama, and to feel like a fifth wheel at the dinner table. She didn't bother to burden Laoch with her feelings, and regretted the distance it created, as she also didn't bother to ask about family business.

Gus and Peter grew up more like brothers than friends. From the first time they played together as barely walking age toddlers, they were inseparable, and that relationship did nothing but grow tighter over the years as the company grew. The summers were always a whirlwind of excitement, with their birthdays falling in consecutive months.

Chapter 41

June 9th, 1987, 6278 Mourning Dove Rd. Raleigh, North Carolina

Gus's fifth birthday stood out as the clearest early memory he had, the only one where he could vividly recall his parents being together. The party took place on the back porch, with a long picnic table, with a vibrant red and white checker tablecloth covering it. The cake he had that year was not just any cake; it was an edible masterpiece. The birthday cake was a series of small cakes designed like train cars on an edible track, in a circle on the table. Paper cone hats and noisemakers were all the rage. Memory fragments of gifts and his parents socializing with Mack and Mrs. Smith while the children played flashed in Gus's mind. Even though there were at least six other kids present, Peter was all he really remembered being there. Later in life, he couldn't recall even one more name of the children present, when reflecting on it.

Chapter 42

November 25th, 1988, 10:45 AM Hwy 70, West of Goldsboro, North Carolina

With the warm November sun on her face and the thumping rhythm of R.E.M.'s "End of the World as We Know It," pounding through her car speakers, Genevieve "Jen" Ferguson was driving back from her Thanksgiving vacation at Atlantic Beach on highway 70. It was the day after Thanksgiving, when she realized she had completely forgotten to get the sales printouts necessary to work on the end of month statements. Her role as an accountant for a fast-growing computer chip manufacturing company was challenging, especially with updating the reports for the end of the month. It was impossible to do on vacation, especially when you left the very printouts you needed three hours away.

She'd left her husband and son relaxing at the beach house to make the long drive back to Raleigh. With everything she had to do at the office, maybe a little over six hours round trip.

Jen arrived at the office, grabbed her printouts from the dot matrix printer in the main computer room. As she tore the last report from the waist-high printer, the paper hung momentarily, and it sliced her finger. "Paper cuts are the worst!" she thought as she wrapped it with a band aid from the first aid kit. With the emergency addressed, she was back in the car. 106 FM was featuring a 'Rock Block' on the sunny Black Friday.

Since the house was just a short detour, she drove by to check on it; everything appeared fine, just as she expected.

While heading out of town, she spotted a sign showing an estate sale at the border of her neighborhood. She didn't know why she even gave it a second thought, but garage and estate sales were her weakness, and she thought, "oh what the hell," and turned at the sign.

Chapter 43

November 25th, 1988, 12:15 PM Killebrew Street, Raleigh, North Carolina

The house, which was new, almost made her reconsider, but there was something that compelled her to park and walk up the driveway. "I mean, what kind of good stuff could have built up in a new house?" Jen thought.

As she walked into the garage, she noticed a woman in her forties sitting there, with just a few tables set up. She had boxes of things behind her in the garage, all set for moving out. The woman sitting next to the merchandise seemed rather reserved. Greeting her with a smile, Jen surveyed the limited selection on the table and inquired, "Is this everything?" With a smile on her face, the woman looked up and cheerfully declared, "Oh, everything goes! I haven't unpacked most of it yet," she said. "These belongings were my soon to be ex-husband's..." A wry look crossed her face, as if she had just had that epiphany. "Well, I guess he is my ex now. I don't mean to speak badly of the dead, but you should have seen my face when I received the call about this stuff being willed to me. We went our separate ways nearly three years ago, and I had already taken all of my belongings. I am honestly just trying to get rid of all this shit. If you happen upon a box of crap you're interested in, I'll give it to you for a dollar. He accumulated knickknacks... They filled his shelves.

A plaque caught Jen's attention, featuring the words "Douglas Hanks Southeast U.S. Salesman of the year" and a picture of a man exchanging a handshake with an ancient woman. "That was him, probably the only thing in a skirt he didn't at least attempt to bang. Dougie was great at his work. I'll give him that, but... never marry a salesman. Well, I guess that's not fair," she muttered under her breath. "It's possible that a few of them are okay, I guess."

The former Mrs. Hanks scratched her head, weighing her words. "So, steer clear of those who wholeheartedly believe in their own bullshit. That fucker came home from a Vegas convention with a steaming case of the clap and insisted that I gave it to him." She said with a laugh. "Nuns get more action than I ever did during our marriage. I mean it, honey... Well, he's gone now. In reality, he had been gone for five years before I realized he had left."

Jen considered making up an awkward excuse for an exit when the conversation became too personal for someone she didn't know. It was obvious this lady had suffered a crappy relationship. Some of the stuff on the table was moderately interesting and most, not so much. "Look around if you want or grab a random box or five, if you are the adventuring type." They both laughed. Behind the former Mrs. Hanks, Jen stared at the towering wall of boxes in the garage, reaching almost to the ceiling. "Let me help you out," she offered. "Look at that box at the end. The Seagram's Seven box? That one is the best in the bunch. One buck takes it."

With anticipation, Jen walked to the end of the table and carefully popped the top open. Peering inside, she discovered a treasure trove of captivating items. The collection included arrowheads, small telescopes, and an assortment of other fascinating objects. She didn't feel right accepting all that for just a dollar, so she insisted on five dollars.

"I'm okay with just one," the woman chuckled, "but if you're offering five, I certainly won't say no. If you know anyone in the market for a house, send them my way. It goes on the market Monday, hopefully, and I'm selling it cheap."

Jen thanked the person and carefully loaded the box into the back of her large green car, finding the perfect spot in the cavernous trunk. Climbing back into the car, she continued her way to the beach.

Back on Highway 70, she took off, only slowing down for the well-known speed traps and crossing traffic of those leaving early from the beach. She noticed that most cars she saw were heading towards her and away from the beach, resulting in light traffic in her direction.

Chapter 44

November 25th, 1988, 3:30 PM Highway 70 East, Goldsboro, North Carolina

Jen waved to the county sheriff as she passed the speed trap in Goldsboro and sped up into the 55 zone that started 200 yards later. With a leap, the big green 1976 Cutlass Salon reached 63.

The car, dubbed "Green Piece" by their friends, Short for "Green Piece of Shit", was a force to be reckoned with. Green Piece dominated its lane and guzzled gas like a thirsty elephant, but oh, that 350... She could fly in a straight line, and the only thing she would see along Highway 70 East was endless straight stretches of road.

Here she was, a tired 28-year-old mother, sacrificing her day off to prepare for Monday. Her current behavior would appall her 20-year-old self, but that was a lifetime ago. Dancing at Barry's on Hillsboro Street and home by 1:00AM to cram for her statistics exam, or accounting, or whatever was coming up in less than twelve hours. Those were the days!

She got back to the beach house to find Gus and Laoch out playing on the beach with Peter and Mack, while Deb waited for her with a margarita, ready to pour on this unusually warm fall day. "Wait," she thought, retracting her recent conclusion, "No, these... these are the days."

Chapter 45

November 27th, 1988, 12:15 AM Atlantic Beach, North Carolina

The week at the beach ended way too quickly. With a touch of humor, Jen joked with her bosses, proposing the idea of a company holiday for tomorrow, or, with a mischievous grin, labeling the additional day off as an "executive meeting."

"The schedule is too tight," Deb said in a businesslike manner.

Mack glanced at her, playfully scolding, "You're such a buzzkill!" Laughter filled the room as they started the tradition of packing up and cleaning, as they had done in the previous two Thanksgivings.

Chapter 46

Sunday, November 27, 1988, Late Evening, Redwolf Solutions, RTP, NC

It was a long Sunday after Thanksgiving. The work that Jen put in late in the evenings at the beach had to be corrected on the computer for the November filings and that meant translating a lot of the mistakes she found into the ledger at the beach and manually making the adjustments. Since the in-house day care wasn't open, Gus stayed home with his dad. As the clock struck six, she had reached her limit. The neat arrangement of the account entries meant she could wrap them up by the next day.

As Jen walked to the car, numbers swirled in her mind. Nearly forty people, mostly developers, engineers, and testers, were now part of Redwolf, working under Deb's guidance and assisting with designs. Most of their budget and seed funding had gone into a small fabrication facility. The cost of building such a facility was so high that it made her dizzy. To ensure minimal vibration, the facility had to be built on bedrock.

The pockets Jen had access to must have been exceptionally deep, Jen thought. Although the initial results of their chip products showed promise, they did not yet offset the funds invested. The investors, who had committed to a long run investment, expected this, however. Momentum was already apparent, even this early, as some of Deb's ideas and patents had already noticeably swung the company's bottom line. Key to that was a chip technology patent licensed only to

Motorola for three years. There were three other patents getting similar interest, which had led to the hiring a young patent attorney named Philip Hooper.

Originally, Philip gained experience in criminal law, but he grew disillusioned with the justice system. He transitioned into real estate law and, unexpectedly, after helping a friend with a startup, found himself working in patents. In copyright and patents, he finally found work he loved.

Phil's addition brought along with it the need for a support staff and various new legal and accounting requirements. Business expansion led to Jen's promotion; next, she hired and trained a lead accountant to handle her previous responsibilities, freeing her for the more senior role.

Calling Laoch from her work, she agreed to grab pizza on her way back and promptly left toward the dependable green Oldsmobile. As she opened the building's door, the powerful wind outside snatched it, slamming it wide open.

Crossing the parking lot, she marveled at the leaves and sticks blowing past her feet in the strange warm wind, "Holy crap!" She was glad Gus was home with Laoch. The winds seemed determined to force her massive car into the opposite lane or off the road.

Although it wasn't on her way home, she made a detour to Amedeo's on Western Boulevard for a half sausage and onion, and half meatball and onion pizza. With the pizza in hand, she resumed her journey home.

Chapter 47

Sunday, November 27, 1988, 7:10 PM 6278 Mourning Dove Rd. Raleigh, NC

When she reached home, it was nearly ten minutes after seven. Laoch hurriedly went to assist her while she took her bag, and he collected the pizza. They struggled against the wind as they made their way to the front door.

Jen tried to censor herself while looking at Gus sitting on the couch. "Holy shhhh-crap, is it windy out there?"

"I came close to losing the pizza twice as I was bringing it inside." Laoch agreed as Gus ran over to hug his mother.

"I think she was going to say holy shit again, dad," Gus said with innocent sincerity.

"But we don't say that word if we can help it right, dear?" Jen said.

"Nope... we don't... but you do." Gus said as he went back to playing with his oversized Lego's.

Laoch snickered as he began devouring the pizza with the same intensity as a death row prisoner, enjoying his last meal, hoping to not fit in the electric chair.

Following dinner, Laoch brought Gus to his room, read him a book, and tucked him in. After 20 minutes, Laoch returned, and they recounted their day, discussing their problems and attentively listening to each other's adventures.

Once the deliberations were over, they attempted to enjoy the scary movies they had rented from Blockbuster. However, around forty-five minutes into the second film, a small, unexpected creature emerged from its tomb and entered the living room, crying.

Jen saw him first and paused the VCR, "What's the matter, baby? Come to mama." Gus ran across the room but made a B-Line for his dad. He collapsed into Laoch's lap as Jen smiled with a gush of pride.

Suddenly, Jen remembered the box in the back of the car. "Ooh, you got him? I have something in the car for tonight! It should be fun!"

Laoch nodded, "Got him."

With the wind picking up, Jen dashed to the car. Noticing intermittent flashes in the sky, she predicted an interesting November evening.

She combed through the back of Green-Piece; the nickname her friends had given the car during a night of drinking. She was the designated driver, as usual. That night, Mack had consumed a drink called the "Blue Whale" while they ate dinner and drank at Darryl's on Hillsboro Street.

When they left the restaurant, to head to the comedy club down the road, Mack had taken a folding knife and cut a slice in the belly and the back of the plastic blue sperm whale. The whale had come with the prophetic drink. He took the plastic whale and impaled it on the diamond shape hood ornament. Even before the bar incident, Jen and Gus's friends referred to the car as a piece of shit. Now it had a whale for a hood ornament... so the name Green-Piece, just made sense.

Behind all the remaining beach trip items, she discovered the Seagram's Seven box. She knocked stuff out of the way and slid the box to the edge of the trunk, picked it up and dashed back to the house.

As soon as she stepped inside, she noticed Gus lying on his dad's lap and shoulder, having calmed down quite a bit but still softly weeping. A quick glance at the clock showed the night had slid to morning and was almost midnight. Placing the box on the vintage trunk they used as a coffee table, Jen took a seat on the far side of the couch, beside her husband and son. Gus crawled over to her and gave her a hug when she sat down. He had grown so lanky in his first six years that he no longer looked like a baby; she thought with a flash of longing.

Abruptly, Gus sat up and looked at his dad as Laoch asked, "My boy, did you have a bad dream or something?" There was a brief pause as Gus turned his attention to his dad.

Gus spoke softly, relaying a heartfelt message, "Pappy wanted me to tell you I love you. He said I should do it now, and he told me after I did, I could go to sleep."

Despite his efforts to conceal his surprise, Laoch's skin turned noticeably pale, revealing his genuine emotions as he looked at Jen. "Pappy? Who do you mean, Pappy?" Laoch asked calmly.

"The old guy in my room. He said his name was Pappy, and he looked a lot like grandpa, except he had his green church clothes on," Gus said.

Imitating calm, Laoch asked, "Hmm, did he say anything else?"

"He just said that I have to be brave and strong... and that he was sorry." Gus responded. "When I blinked, he was gone. It scared me!" Tears welled in the corners of Gus's eyes and he pressed his face into his mother's shoulder. "I love you too, mama!" as he pressed his face into her thick sweater.

Jen did all she could do to retract her jaw from the floor. Minutes later, when Gus fell asleep on their lap, Laoch grabbed a pillow from the edge of the couch and made a bed on the floor at their feet. They put him there beside the steamer trunk table, as he twitched with dreams that they hoped were pleasant ones. They tucked the throw blanket around him and sat in silence for several minutes, just staring at him.

Outside, the first deep rumbles of thunder came closer and shook the entire world. "We will talk about this tomorrow. I just need time to process," she said, and Laoch nodded.

"Fucking weird though," he said with a forced smile that did nothing to mask the fear in his eyes.

Jen sat up on her seat and reached for the box she retrieved from the car. "Ok, let's change this mood. The other day, as I was driving back from the beach to retrieve the accounting stuff, I passed by an estate sale and made a stop." Laoch gave an over dramatic look of surprise and she replied, "I know, total shocker!" They both laughed, "This lady, was divorcing her husband when he died. She had inherited everything from him but wanted none of it. The ex-wife was basically giving his stuff away. She pointed out this box to me and said it had cool stuff. Well, it indeed had cool stuff, and she only wanted a dollar for it. I insisted on giving her five bucks and I feel like she really didn't want to take it, but she did... Anyway," Jen said, as she excitedly popped open the cardboard Seagram's Seven box.

With a swift motion, she reached into the container and carefully retrieved a professionally mounted collection of stone projectile points and blades that were crafted by Native Americans. She handed it over to Laoch, who eagerly accepted it with his greedy hands. "Oh my," he said, as he inspected it.

A deafening, cannon like report chased the sudden purple flash of lightning outside of the window, causing both to jump and the lights to flicker. "Holy Christ, that was close," Laoch called out, his heart pounded in his chest. Gus, amazingly to both, peacefully slept through the deafening sound of the closing artillery bombardment.

As Jen reached into the box, she marveled at the collection of expandable telescopes, their intricate design reminiscent of those used on old sailing ships. Among them, there was one that appeared smaller and completely made of brass, so she reached for it.

The storm raged outside and Laoch was still looking at the arrowhead collection. As Jen sat there, another loud clap of thunder reverberated through the house, causing her to jump in her seat. Simultaneously, a burst of lightning flashes outside turned the yard into a dazzling display of flickering lights resembling a disco scene from the 1970s. "Storms getting close," she heard as Laoch said somewhere in the distance. She considered her hands and saw the golden metal artifact she had mistaken for a spyglass. It had a raised area that resembled a highly weathered serpent coiled around it. Without thinking about it, feeling compelled in fact, she turned it to look in the end, as Laoch screamed, "Noooo!"

At first, Jen thought she heard a piercing scream, but the sound didn't belong to Laoch. It was something in her head that screamed; it was something in the artifact. From the artifact's green crystal, an agonized scream emitted that hurt her head. Memories that didn't belong to her flooded into her mind, as the roof and walls of their home crumbled around her and Laoch, plunging the world into darkness.

Chapter 48

Monday, November 28, 1988, 1:10 AM, 6278 Mourning Dove Rd. Raleigh, NC

The moment she laid her hand on the peculiar brass scope, the cold metal turned warm in an instant, and as she investigated the hole at the end, she discovered herself surrounded by the dark woods. Without moving a muscle, she stood frozen in place while her eyes acclimatized to the darkness of this inexplicable location.

After a short while, her eyes became more accustomed to the darkness of the night. Surrounding her were ancient trees from an untouched forest, mostly long needle pine with a few hardwoods. The leafless trees swayed in the gentle breeze on this cool, star filled night, as a half-moon cast its pale glow. It was clear from the saturated, soft ground covered with newly fallen leaves that there had been rain recently. She could see a small clearing about 30 to 40 feet ahead of her, revealing a primitive log house nestled among the trees. There was a trickle of smoke coming from a squat stone chimney.

The sound of an owl caught her attention, causing her to swiftly turn her head to the left. All she could see were ominous, deep shadows. Another owl's hoot softly passed through the forest, catching her attention from the other direction.

She quietly spun her head to the right. In the dark moon cast shadow, her eyes widened as she glimpsed movement, prompting her to focus all her energy on staying perfectly motionless, praying that her pounding heart wouldn't give her away. Out of the corner of her eye, she saw movement in the shadows on her left, and as she turned her head, the shapes transformed into humanlike figures.

As they passed into the moonlight of the clearing, the forms took on the unmistakable silhouette of indigenous American figures like they had come alive from ancient illustrations, as they moved with a mesmerizing silence towards the house. As they stood in the clearing, another figure slowly made his way towards them. He appeared clumsy compared to the five indigenous men, four of whom were equipping daggers and hatchets. The fifth held an old flintlock rifle he had been wearing on his back.

The last figure materialized at the edge of the clearing, his presence announced by the distinct sound of leaves and twigs being crushed beneath his feet. With obvious annoyance on his face, one of the five war party members looked back at the clumsy compatriot, his face lined with black paint and furrowed with disdain. The loud man must have given them some kind of sign as they all nodded and turned towards the house.

The five-man war party slipped into the house with the silence of a private thought, and moments later, muffled screams broke the silence of the night. There was a quick sound of a scuffle, which was punctuated with a sickening crunch and a stifled scream of a woman.

Within a few moments, the war party returned to the outside area. Two of the assassins, their arms covered to their elbows, drenched in a shiny black gore. They turned towards the noisy sixth member who had waited outside. As he gracefully entered the moonlit area, his fair complexion appeared to radiate, and he engaged in hushed conversation with the war party, his voice carrying a distinct British accent.

With a calm demeanor, he approached the porch and spoke in a deliberate, unhurried manner, as if addressing someone of lesser intelligence, before casting a glance into the doorway. After a few seconds, he stepped back out, his lips curling into a satisfied smile as he nodded his head. He faced the party again, presenting them with a small, dark bag that looked weighty in his hand.

He spoke with clarity, "Burn it." When he stepped back, they quickly disappeared into the building and reemerged moments later. Within a minute, light shone out from the doorway and the roofline had a lazy haze of smoke drifting from it. As the fire inside crackled and popped, the smoke escaped through the roof, creating a swirling dance of shadows and light.

After a few more minutes, the flames broke through the weaker areas of the structure, lighting up the small clearing. The war party departed as Jen watched the house exterior catch fire and now, to her horror, she could feel the heat from the fire, and the light was shocking in her eyes. With a whoosh, the fire fully engulfed the wood structure, the ground around it steaming fiercely. A pungent smell of burning wood choked the air.

The European man seemed to bask in the heat for a moment, sniffing deeply despite the thick choking smoke. He took several steps back, pushed away by the intense heat. Oddly, he was holding a small metal spyglass in his hand and was preparing to leave himself when he paused. A look of recognition crossed his face as his head tilted a fraction to the left. He slowly lifted his head and stared directly into Jen's eyes, and smiled. As to be heard over the fire's roar as he gave a slight bow, he spoke loudly, "I guess this is where you see me, huh?"

Chapter 49

Jen wakes up

As Jen regained consciousness in the hospital room, she noticed the invasive tubes in her arms and the sensation of something lodged in her throat, causing her to gag. As she choked, the blaring alarm on the wall behind her filled her ears, accompanied by the growing sound of squeaking footsteps down the hall outside. "Stay calm," a soothing voice whispered beside her, sounding uncannily like her mother. "Don't worry," the female voice said pacifyingly, "we'll remove it from you. Stay calm and remain still for just a moment."

Just as impatience settled in, she experienced a curious feeling in her throat, as if a never-ending tube was smoothly passing through. "Almost there... almost... there you go!" said the lady next to the bed as the end of the tube tickled the back of her throat, eliciting a gagging feeling. She turned her head slightly to see the nurse with the voice, but only saw her back as she was leaving the room.

With that damn tube out, Jen calmed and took an inventory. Her leg hurt the worst, followed by her head and right arm. "What the hell?" she thought. "Was I in a car wreck?" She tried to speak, but all that came out was a series of croaks. "Don't talk yet, let's get your throat a chance to find its feet," said a black lady nurse, with a hello kitty mask and beautiful, kind eyes.

In a flurry of activity, two doctors entered the room, with one attentively inspecting her bandages and the other explaining their tests in too much detail, both speaking to her in an annoyingly upbeat tone, as if she had just hit the one dollar, on the big wheel on The Price is Right.

While examining her eyes with a small flashlight, one doctor stated, "You're a very lucky lady." "You took quite a blow to the head, young lady," remarked the other doctor. The first doctor questioned, "Do you have any idea where you are?"

Having had about enough of Huey and Dumbass, she said, "Pretty sure this is not the massage parlor, and if it is, I want my goddamn money back!" she thought as a realization rose in her, "where is Gus?!" she asked in a panic. "Where is Laoch? LAOCH?!?" she called, as she could hear the heart monitor speed up.

"Sedate her!" the doctor to her left ordered.

"We are going to give you something to help you relax a little," Jen heard from the friendly doctor to her right, as the world quickly lost its edges, and a fuzzy sleep demanded her immediate attention.

Chapter 50

Jen wakes up again

Once again, Jen awoke in the hospital room. "Shit!" she thought. "I had hoped that part was a dream." A doctor was in the room with his back to her. Thankfully, there was nothing in her mouth and throat now. "Doctor?" she asked in a quiet and meek voice that sounded like a little girl.

Jen scolded herself. "What the hell was that voice?"

The gravelly voice of the doctor seemed to echo in the room. "I'll be right with you."

As her senses sharpened, she realized the room was rundown, with dingy ceiling tiles and a window that desperately needed washing. Looking out the window, there was a large, dead oak tree. A murder of crows weighed on the branches, squawking with their collective gaze on her. They seemed to judge her.

As she stared at them and in their heartless black eyes, from the corner of her vision, she could see the doctor was turning towards her. As he turned, the crows exploded into flight with a clatter. The combined sound of their caws, and the forceful flap of their wings, created a loud ruckus that reverberated through the windows and walls, shaking the bed.

As the doctor turned, a shadow fell over the room, obscuring the sunlight that had been streaming through the window. The doctor's voice, coarse and filled with disapproval, cut through the air as he uttered, "You have been a very naughty girl," his gaze fixed on the weathered clipboard in his hand... and it cost you your arms and legs you fucking bitch!!" the creature cackled as it completed its turn.

The doctor wore a heavy industrial apron, drenched in streams of vivid red gore that resembled paint splatters on waxed paper. His long gloves, reaching up to his biceps, also soaked in gore, dripped with the same viscous vital fluids as the clipboard. She noticed the doctor's face, covered in blood and sporting a savage grin, except for the clean patch of bluish skin near his eyes. His eyes, a deep-sea blue, had the familiarity of Laoch's, yet a sinister glimmer danced within them.

When she cast her eyes towards the closed door, she noticed two legs and arms, covered in blood, tossed aside as though they were nothing more than garbage. It was at that moment, with a sudden jolt of terror, that she realized her right arm, the arm she had been trying to lift to shield herself, was no longer there.

"Who are you? WHO ARE YOU!" Scrios paused awkwardly and continued. "Who are you... to challenge me?" the creature howled.

Despite the increasing momentum towards a justifiable panic, Jen paused. She tilted her head to the side, just a degree, and asked in a completely calm voice, "Is this the best you can do?"

Despite the abrupt disappearance of the dream, she couldn't shake off the lingering sound of a frustrated howl reverberating in her mind. As she opened her eyes, she immediately felt a sharp, genuine pain coursing through her body.

Positioned just inches away from her face, there was a dimly lit particle board with nail points jutting out at regular intervals. Her forehead throbbed with pain as she could feel blood dripping down her face, a result of something poking her above her right eye.

Behind her somewhere, there was an unexpected source of dim light, perhaps a flickering lamp. Something heavy, causing a sharp pain, pinned her legs down, causing a tingling sensation in her right foot. She could hear sirens coming closer and could hear heavy rain falling. She could feel the direct impact of heavy, cold raindrops on her wet right hand.

While Gus cried just a few feet away, she remained trapped and motionless, like a pinned butterfly in a shadow box.

She called out for Laoch but received no answer. She shouted over and over, with no result. Suddenly, a voice reached her ears. There was something off about Laoch, he sounded strange, and his accent was missing. "It's ok lady, we hear you. Don't move, we will get you out of there. How many people are in the house with you?"

Chapter 51

Monday, November 28, 1988, 3:00 AM, 6278 Mourning Dove Rd. Raleigh, NC

It took nearly 60 minutes to rescue Jen from the ruins of her inherited family home. The home she grew up in and had an awkward first kiss on the front porch at 15 with Billy Winsted, who lived two streets over, on a dare from her friends.

They moved her onto a gurney. Something was wrong with her right leg. Her ankle was swollen to the size of a grapefruit. A cut on her right arm was severe enough to require stitches. From the fire department truck's bright lights, she could see the rescuers searching through the remnants of her house. The weight of a colossal pine tree, with its root ball still attached, had hit the house like a wrecking ball.

It was peculiar because there were no pine trees in her yard, yet the violent storm had uprooted and hurled trees, sending them flying for hundreds of feet. A quarter mile away, the storm uprooted a house and placed it in the middle of the street, leaving it basically intact. There was a chorus of chainsaws, both working on her house and for miles around. One would stop and at least three others would carry the tune.

The rain had mostly subsided when they pulled Gus from the wreckage. She studied him and noticed that he appeared fine, except for the jagged gash on his arm that would likely require stitches. To satisfy her demand of not leaving without him and her husband, they brought Gus into the ambulance next to her.

When the rescuer handed Gus over to the EMT team in her ambulance, she asked him, "Can you hear my husband? Have you found him yet?" He looked at her and leaned in. "No may-em, not yet, but we will find him, I promise." He said with a thick southern drawl that turned 'mam' into two syllables.

When the rescuer departed, he quickly glanced at the EMT and intentionally held eye contact for an extra beat. He looked back to Jen intently, "May-em, they need to take you and your boy and get you patched up. I know you don't want to go, but that fellah of yours needs that arm patched up, so it does not get infected," and he leaned back in towards her.

He stared directly into her eyes, "I promise we will find your husband Leerock, and get him in the next ambulance. See that one right over there pulling up? We need this spot for it."

Jen nodded and looked him in the eye and pronounced Laoch's name phonetically and slowly for him. He attempted it again, and it was almost accurate. She acknowledged the EMT, who was busy securing the squirming Gus to a gurney beside her with a nod. Jen talked softly to Gus, and he calmed as the EMT did three curt knocks on the side wall of the ambulance yelling, "Let's go!" Moments later, the ambulance crawled out of the dark devastated North Raleigh neighborhood and headed for Rex Hospital.

She knew when they passed from the devastated areas as the streetlights lit the windows as they drove. Gus looked at his mother and saw the tears and concern and gave her a look that was 100% Laoch, "Me and you are going to be ok mama, I promise."

Part 3 – The Summer Reign

Interlude - The Avocado Refrigerator

Wednesday, November 8th, 1999, 11:42 AM, 6278 Mourning Dove Rd. Raleigh, NC

The autobiography, written in fourth grade, was stuck to the side of the refrigerator in the kitchen. Over the years, the vast life experiences of a nine-year-old became splattered with dots of drinks and food that had sprayed or dripped on it. Gus had a memory of a spot, a little off center, that he knew resulted from him triumphantly squashing a house fly one summer. The paper read:

April 4th, 1991

"My name is Laoch Kier Ferguson, the Fifth, but my friends call me Gus. My enemy's call me Laoch Kier Ferguson the Fifth.

I was born in the highlands of Scotland, but I'm not immortal. My family moved to the U.S. when I was a small child. I don't remember living in Scotland. When I was six, my mom, who is from the U.S. got injured badly and my dad, who was from Scotland, died when a tornado hit our house in Raleigh. My mom got better, but it took a long time. I think she is still sad and misses my dad. I don't remember much about him, but I wish I did because the stories, when my mom talks about him, are funny and he liked to laugh. My mom says I have his same blue eyes and laugh, and she can see a light shade of red in my brown hair like him. The only injury I got from the tornado was a scratch that went down the side of my arm and left me with a scar. I was very lucky. This summer I'm playing baseball and want to play football next fall. I am 51 inches tall, and I weigh 64 pounds. I am very fast, but not as fast as Brian or Bennett."

Scrawled at the top was the teacher's comment, "Very nice to meet you, Gus! Ms. Sigmund"

Though it may not have been reality shattering literature, that paper has remained on Gus's fridge since the day he brought it home from school. His mom proudly put it there. It didn't hold any value to him, except that it had always been there, acting as a constant presence, stuck to the side of the fridge where his mom had put it. That single fact alone made it important. Regardless of the refrigerator being replaced twice, the old red letter "S" magnet, the lone survivor from the alphabet magnets, remained firmly attaching the autobiography to the refrigerator.

A cold and blustery Tuesday, in his freshman year of college at Western Carolina University, Gus got a call at his residence in Harrell Dorm. As if November didn't suck enough, the RA came to his room, "You have a call in the main office downstairs". Even though finding it strange that he didn't get called in his room, he went downstairs to answer the call. Despite knowing his mother had his room's phone number, he expected to hear her voice. Instead, Peter's dad was on the line.

Later in life, he could recall almost every single moment from that day, as if it had just happened. After hitting pause on the Nintendo, he walked out of his dorm room and made his way towards the stairwell. Not wanting to waste any time, he skipped the sketchy dorm elevator and made his way down the stairs from the fourth floor. Gus remembered the worn off paint spots missing on the handrail in the staircase, making the railing have a pattern like a calico cat, from the multiple layers of different colored paint used over the years. The next thing he remembered was Peter's dad on the phone. His tone was serious. "Hey son, I have a car coming to pick you up. I don't want you to panic, but your mom is in the hospital. You need to pack a bag, and they will be there in 30 minutes. That is all we know right now."

The next few minutes were the only time he couldn't recall. His mind went blank. He remembered hearing Mack say other words just before he hung up the phone, but they didn't register. Hanging up the phone and moving like an automaton, he went up the stairs, grabbed a bag, quickly packed it with clothes and toiletries, and descended. The next thing he recalled was riding in a very nice black car to the tiny local airport on the hill above Cullowhee, NC, and getting on a small jet plane that was waiting just for him.

Peter's parents were loaded, and to a degree, thanks to their company's success, so was his mother. As he sat in the car for the five-minute ride to the airport, he remembered thinking, "this can't be good" and immediately, guiltily, tried to dismiss the thought. That thought though stuck with him for years when he blamed himself for having it, and it, for her dying. That thought had nothing to do with the brain tumor that killed her, but in his mind, his thinking, "this can't be good," had somehow inexplicably manifested the illness.

There were no last words in the hospital. His mom never said a final tearful goodbye like in the movies, "You go make the world wonderful" or "I love you and will miss you". There were just wires, tubes, hospital smells and beeps. The constant rhythm of the ventilator that assisted her breathing was his companion much of the time as he held vigil beside her bed. His mother's doctor had clarified that she had GBM, or Glioblastoma Multiform, and her condition was terminal. Her doctor didn't expect her to wake up, but he was determined to ensure she felt no pain. His mother had been suffering from migraines for years, but it wasn't until she arrived at the hospital in an ambulance that the doctors made this discovery on an MRI. They followed up with a scan with a new technology, a recently deployed PET/CT Scanner. The outlook was bleak.

Her migraines had been persistent since the storm that took Gus's father's life, and everyone always assumed the injuries she had sustained caused them. After they removed the ventilator, his mother's breaths became labored and sometimes punctuated by faint chirping sounds that escaped her lips, some like fragments of words trying to escape a dream. The next morning, she started moving her feet and arms almost like she was swimming; the nurses rushed in to clear the room, alarmed by her sudden actions.

From the hall, Gus watched as they administered the sedative, securing her arms and legs for her safety. One minute she was there and suddenly, she was gone. When Gus got home from the hospital and walked inside through the pouring rain that masked his tears, the first thing he saw when he walked in the door was the autobiography, stuck to the refrigerator by the red 'S' magnet.

So, the old childhood assignment stays there... with him. It defines home to Gus. The paper's importance, cemented simply by its longevity, where it lives on his refrigerator... It stays right fucking there.

Chapter 1 – Gus

Saturday, November 11th, 1999, 3:37 PM, Oakwood Cemetery Raleigh, NC

Rain fell like heavy tears mixing with Gus's as the 17-year-old stood in the cemetery reviewing the day's events in his mind. His mom's cousin, a rare visitor throughout his life, made an unexpected appearance. Prior to departing, she hugged him and reassured him that things would be okay... Whatever the hell that meant.

During the ceremony at the grave, Peter's parents had sat next to Gus. Peter's mother, Deb, held his hand. The priest, who was new to the church, spoke about his mom, mixing genuine praise with general compliments that could apply to anyone. It was obvious the priest didn't really know his mother. Hell, he called her Jennifer, and no one called her that.

In the funeral's aftermath, Gus stood in the rain for 30 minutes, or perhaps it was three hours. His eyes fixed on the gray coffin, covered with flowers. It rested on a metal scaffold perched above the hole. Beside it, the carefully crafted gravestones marking the final resting place of his grandparents. As much as he wished he could, he could not recall ever meeting them. He thought of all the people who loved him he never remembered meeting and felt frustratingly cheated. Still the crew on hand to bury his mother impatiently waited in the rain on the hill above, beside the medium-sized John Deere tractor.

Twenty feet from the workers stood an older man in an overcoat. He stood taller than Gus and had an enormous man in his fifties accompanying him. He stood patiently beside the older gentleman, holding a large black umbrella for them both. When Gus looked at them, the old man raised his hand as if to wave and paused.

Gus could feel the rain running down his back, as the heavy shower made sounds like fingers tapping on the canopy over the grave. His pants were getting heavy from the rain, which was gusting sideways, but he didn't care. He did not know what he was waiting for, when what he was waiting for arrived as a hand settled on his shoulder. Gus turned, and found Peter. Standing there, he wore a dark blue blazer with no protection from the rain. It was clear; he had just arrived. Ignoring the rain that was soaking his $3000 suit, Peter embraced him as Gus fell to pieces.

His mom's home, rebuilt when he was six, in the same spot that his father had died, became his in the will. There was a generous inheritance... a car. "A god dam 1984 Chrysler La Baron? Thanks ma!" She always had a thing for American gas guzzlers and never owned a new car in her life. He realized again that she was gone when he thought, "...and she never will own a new car."

On a rainy day like today, a year ago, Gus smashed the left front corner panel on it while driving too fast, and it hydroplaning in the rain. It seemed fitting that hunk-a-shit was now his.

Peter's parents came to console him. "You do not worry about anything. You are like a son to us and whatever you need, we have, and you are welcome to it."

The legal issues that most people must struggle with after a funeral were not a problem for Gus, Deb's lawyers and staff assured that.

In the end, Gus inherited a generous investment portfolio that included stock in the company his mother helped create. Being less than 18 years old presented a couple of issues, but with the friendship between his mother, Deb, and Mack, they had long ago planned for this type of tragedy. In her will, Jen set aside that he would get a stipend for school, along with a lump sum. When he was 25, he would receive the rest. In the interim, Mack was to oversee the funds and could issue cash releases upon request.

Chapter 2

Thursday, November 16th, 1999, 9:07 AM 6278 Mourning Dove Rd. Raleigh, NC

A week after the funeral, Gus still sat in his living room at home. He felt he was not ready for this new reality without his mother. He felt cheated, and the bitterness of it was welling in his throat. An imminent scream was growing there when his cell phone buzzed in his pocket, breaking his rumination. His favorite professor, Dr. Maxwell Schiller, was calling him.

Max was a remarkable individual, always ready with a smile and encouragement, or equally swift to deliver a kick in the ass whenever he detected a lack of effort or focus. If he had shown interest in statistics, Max could have been his advisor.

Max conveyed he had contacted Gus's professors, and they each gave him the freedom to do whatever he needed, including taking an incomplete and finishing the classes later, if needed. With school absence issues resolved, Max changed the conversation, "Now that we are done with that other bullshit, what do you need, son?"

Max was not only a friend while he was in college, but remained the friend who would kick Gus in the ass when he needed it. Let's just say, for several years while Gus was deployed, Max's virtual right leg was in great shape!

In the military, Gus would come to know firsthand the depths of human cruelty as he encountered the unspeakable acts perpetrated by people against their own countrymen. In his life, he would come face to face with the darkness that his mother had always kept hidden from him. During his mother's passing, he discovered the profound kindness of friends, whose unwavering love served as a source of resilience whenever he questioned his purpose in the world.

Chapter 3

Friday, November 17th, 1999, 10:00 AM, 6278 Mourning Dove Rd. Raleigh, NC

Nine days following his mother's death, a limousine appeared outside his house as he packed to return to school in the La Baron. There were only a few days before the Thanksgiving break, but he had a weekend full of work to do to catch up. Gus paused his packing, thinking that one of Peter's parents would emerge. Undoubtedly, it was Mack or Deb.

When the driver exited the vehicle, it turned out to be the massive man from the cemetery. Moving around to the back door, he caught the door that was partially open and opened it carefully. When he extended his hand to assist, the older man disregarded it and spryly stepped from the car.

A strange sensation came over Gus when he spotted the older man, his hair a blend of gray and auburn streaks. While taller than Gus by several inches, he possibly had an even greater height when he was younger. Making eye contact with the confused Gus, he nodded in acknowledgement and approached him, uttering the words in a thick Scottish accent, "Hello, son. Do you know who I am?"

The realization finally dawned, and he had little doubt who this was. So, Gus asked, "I think you are my grandfather, right?"

"I am. My purpose in coming here today, is to express my condolences for your mother's passing. I'm also sorry that you had to think to know who I am. Your mother and I didn't always see eye-to-eye, and I want to express my heartfelt apologies for any strife that may have resulted from our difficulties. I feel a deep sense of regret that we couldn't connect after your father passed. However, her dedication to keeping us in the loop was remarkable. She regularly sent us pictures and with email, she even sent videos of you. Hopefully, you recall some memory of visiting us during your earlier childhood. I am so sorry for yours and, frankly, our loss of your mother. She was a brilliant and lovely person. The rift between us, well, that was more my fault than hers. I will not bore you with the details and I am not here to intrude upon your life, but it would be grand if you ever wanted to visit the land where you were born, see your first home, and meet a family that knows and loves you. Again, I'm not here to abduct you." His smile was identical to the pictures Gus saw of his father and when he looked in the mirror. "We are here for you, if you ever have a need... for us."

His Grandfather handed Gus an envelope. "Inside, you'll find some money for college and our contact details for anytime you wish to communicate. Should you find yourself in the vicinity and simply wish to visit, I have furnished you with the address of the 'Big House'. No invite necessary. As soon as anyone sees you, they will know exactly who you are." With a sly smile, his grandfather paused for a moment. "If you are ever interested, there are family things we should discuss someday. I believe they are very important, and I hope when that day comes, you will too." He finished.

Gus looked at him and smiled wickedly. "So, you got stuck with this name, too? Bet you wish you could go back in time and kick number one in the ass for starting it." Gus laughed.

"Yes, the third... and I yell at him all the time," he said with a pallid smile that contradicted his eyes.

Gus's face squished in confusion. "Wait, he is still alive?" he asked.

"Oh no, he has been worm-food for 60 years, but he still won't shut the hell up." And he turned to walk back to the car.

"Wait gramps. Who is Goliath... your bodyguard there?" Gus asked.

The gigantic man laughed, "You are just like your dah. I am your cousin Daniel."

"You are my cousin? Man, if I had had your size, I would be playing college football right now." Gus laughed.

"I played football... oh, but not that American shite. That is just needless violence. Come to Scotland lad and I will introduce you to proper football, and if you need some needless violence, I'll take you out for a pint," he laughed, and they both spun to walk to their car.

As they got in, his grandfather lowered the window and yelled, "ALWAYS welcome," he emphasized.

Inside the envelope, he found a thick letter that contained a single page, filled with phone numbers and names that echoed in his memory from the stories his mother used to tell. Inside the paper list, there were 100 crisp 100-dollar bills, neatly stacked. Gus felt a wave of dizziness wash over him as he looked at it, and his immediate thought was the possibility of someone stepping out from the woods to rob him.

Chapter 4

Thursday, December 14th, 1999, 6:15 PM 6252 Mourning Dove Rd. Raleigh, NC

In the future, he spent his major holiday breaks with Peter and the Smith family. Their kindness went beyond what "treated him like a son" implies. Concern arose when Gus appeared at their house in a shiny new four-wheel-drive Toyota pickup truck, yet no one voiced their unease. Peter was brutal in a brotherly way, mocking him by making some Back to the Future references and calling him Marty the rest of the Christmas Holiday. For Christmas, Peter got 'Marty' a nice brand-new puffy orange winter vest, and they both laughed when Gus opened it until they cried.

Deb and Mack exchanged nervous laughter when 'Marty' jokingly posed, "What do you get someone who has it all, or the credit card to buy whatever they desire?" while handing Peter a gift wrapped in a shirt box. With a wary look, Peter examined the gift as if he half expected it to be a booby trap. As his parents

149

watched with trepidation, he carefully opened it, trying not to disturb its contents. Neatly folded in Peter's present box marked Spencer's Gifts was a 'Blow-up Betsy Doll', complete with negligee and a tire patch kit from K-mart. "I got you a girlfriend," he said, causing his father Mack to spew eggnog out of his nose like a fountain, while Deb blushed and tried to hide her smile with both hands and a napkin.

Chapter 5

Wednesday, January 12th, 2000, 9:30 AM, Harrell Dorm, Cullowhee, NC

Despite his occasional lack of effort or focus, Gus somehow won the newly endowed "Maxwell and Deborah Smith Scholarship" at Western Carolina University, for undergraduate studies. Funny thing was he did not recall applying for it, and the provost's letter congratulating him seemed a bit vanilla. The endowment by the Smiths included an enormous gift towards campus upgrades and redesign of the traffic flow in the part of campus near the bell tower at the center of the campus, where the construction was already under way.

The scholarship was generous. It covered room, board, tuition and provided a monthly stipend. It also included an internship at Deb's company, Redwolf Solutions, in the summers that shock... paid well.

Early in his sophomore year, he finally found some structure and direction in the ROTC program at his university. It was kind of weird at first, getting ordered around by some younger underclassmen, but the morning workouts reminded him of high school football and that time he tried out for the college team last year. What a goddamn nightmare that was! Best he could say is he survived the tryout, and now knew that he was never college football material.

The first two weeks of running for ROTC were the fiery hell he always remembered. That pain in his back, near his kidneys, was where his weakness tried to leave his body, or so he was told loudly by the little shit that he had to salute and call, "Sir", in his Army issue rape prevention goggles.

After morning workouts, the shower at Reid Gym was exceptional! All the hot water you could ever want to scour yourself with, until you were pink and tingly. After getting dressed, he debated whether to go to Dodson cafeteria on campus or hike an extra eighth of a mile to the Townhouse Restaurant for a more satisfying breakfast. The lady that owned that place had a reputation as a B I double-barreled itch to work for, but the food was consistently good, and she hired great people.

Looking back, her staffing with college students was probably demanding enough to make someone as saintly as Mother Theresa to speak like a longshoreman. Hell, Gus even worked there for a short stint during his freshman year as a line cook, so that time in the pit bought him special treatment on his orders from former coworkers. Extra cheese baby!!!! Before leaving for class, he would top off the coffee and get over to his 8:00 AM lecture. To maximize his free time, he always opted for a heavy morning schedule, which left him with ample opportunity to explore the area, catch up on sleep, or enjoy some quality Nintendo time with his buddies. Gus had a deep affection for the North Carolina Mountains. He enjoyed the dirt roads in his truck and having the mighty Tuckasegee River 200 yards from campus was a worthy distraction any day.

Chapter 6

Thursday, May 31ˢᵗ, 2001, 05:00, Charley Company, Fort Jackson. Columbia, S.C.

Following his first year of ROTC, he attended Basic Training. The structure of basic training just clicked for Gus among the mosquitoes and heat of central South Carolina. The click must have been loud, because the Colonel on campus seemed to have heard it. For the following fall semester, he assigned Gus the responsibility of overseeing morning workouts and encouraged him to challenge the men, which he successfully did.

Having that in his day helped distract him from other thoughts, okay... mom stuff. The primary way he maintained contact with the family in Scotland was through exchanging letters. Occasionally, they would call and have a chat. His grandfather repeatedly pleaded with him to come visit. However, after graduating in the spring of 2003, Gus found himself extremely busy, and back at the bottom of the totem pole as his active-duty commitment in Iraq began.

Chapter 7

Wednesday July 9ᵗʰ, 2003, 16:57 Baghdad, Iraq Green-Zone

In July 2003, he found himself in one of the hottest and sandiest locations on Earth. As a newly minted 2nd lieutenant, his primary goal was to avoid becoming a statistic in the aftermath of the Iraqi invasion. As his responsibilities consumed his thoughts, the connection with his father's family gradually faded away.

The moment he arrived; his captain wasted no time in grabbing him by the shirt and leading him away from the others. He informed Gus that he was taking over the roster spot of an idiot kid with a hero complex, who led his platoon into

151

a forbidden area and a terrorist sniper had punched his hero card and sent him home in a box with a flag draped over it.

He pleaded with Gus to just follow orders and avoid over thinking them. "Ask questions and always keep your goddam head down," he preached.

Gus completed two separate tours. In two years, he discharged approximately 200 rounds total under duress, but he believed none of them hit anything besides sand. At the conclusion of his second tour, he had reached his limit with the stress and escaped with no physical injuries, only mental scars.

Gus lost several good people he knew over those two years. One soldier died in an enemy mortar attack, and two others took their own lives because of the psychological toll of witnessing the enemy's atrocities against their own people.

The innocence in Gus's world shattered when he witnessed the locals engaging in savage acts against each other. Peter was always there for him, ready to listen and offer his perspective. While phone calls were a rarity, he found solace in exchanging emails, ensuring he disclosed nothing that might raise the top brass's eyebrows.

Email from Gus to Peter

Sent: Saturday 8/7/2004 16:57:23

To: PeterS@redwolfsolutions.com

From: Gus

Ok Peter, this just happened yesterday... no shit. The strangest story I have from my two tours. Me and a couple of the boys went to a fortune teller who was in the Green-zone. She was the mother of one guy who sells trinkets near the gates. He insisted she was "the real deal" over and over.

So yesterday afternoon we went. I mean, it was five bucks. We went into this smoky room with drapes hanging on the walls and the red tabletop. And we were all given a thick coffee. We drank it as we talked to her through her son the translator, and she tried to pick up on what would be right to tell us. So, she reads the first guy's cup and told him he lives under a shroud of danger.... "No fucking shit lady," said the 1st lieutenant in his Chicago staccato accent, "have you looked around?" and we all laughed.

The next guy, she says his wife at home misses him and he will have many children." He laughed because he wasn't married. "Strike two!!" howls the staccato 1st lieutenant from the first reading.

Next, the lady reaches for my cup. Picks it up and looks into it. Dude, suddenly everything goes quiet; I mean, we can't even hear the normal clamor of noise and traffic outside for a couple of seconds... Suddenly she screams and my cup she is holding cracks.

The lady backpedals from the table quicker than any of us thought she could move. So fast that two other people with us are looking for a gunman coming in the door or something.

Now to this point she has said everything in Arabic...and her son translated it... She looks at me and says in American English and in a much younger woman's voice. "You will face a great evil, seek your father's family in Atholl for help because you alone are not strong enough!" and she collapses.

We all make for the exit, appreciating the performance while the trinket salesman is trying to revive his mother and asking for help. At that point, we realize, he is not kidding, so we start trying to help. The first lieutenant from Chicago, who works as a medical assistant, said, "Bro, she is gone... like gone-gone." The son looks at us through tears and said, "I have never heard her speak English before."

Crazy shit!

My tour ends in the next couple of months. I will let you know when I am home. Tell Deb and Mack thanks for the care packages. The guys, and I love them.

Gus

"If there is no solution to a problem, cut off the end of the problem, shake shit out of the hole you made and fucking make a solution yourself, and shove the shit back in the hole."

^ Captain Sanders quote

153

Chapter 8

Monday November 8th, 2004, 14:00, Fort Bragg, NC

Gus left the Army with the rank of 1st lieutenant. They offered him an "accelerated path" to Captain if he reenlisted, but he had no interest in that. While in the sandbox, other groups offering him generous compensation to work for them in their private firms had approached him, but it would involve engaging in more perilous activities. No thanks.

After exchanging handshakes with people, some he admired, and some he despised, he wasted no time in climbing into the hired dark limousine Peter had arranged. Once settled, they cracked open a couple of cold beers.

The drive back to Raleigh up 421 took over an hour, but the familiarity of the route and the pleasant company made it fly by. "That is a hell of a tan you got there, soldier," Peter chided.

"I'm not a soldier anymore and if I take my shirt off, I look like a goddamn mutant panda bear," and they both laughed.

Peter looked at him and smiled. "It's great to have you back home. So, what do you want to do first?"

With a look of absolute sincerity, Gus said, "I really want a goddamn cheeseburger."

The Hardee's drive through was less than a quarter mile up the road, so the driver changed to the right lane. "Only one," Peter said. "Or it will spoil your dinner... ok my mom... She has a big surprise party waiting back at your place. So, act surprised, ok? I didn't want you showing up and whipping out your dick in the front yard to mark your territory with everyone looking out the window at your tiny penis. It would get awkward." Peter said with a smile.

"Wait, a goddamn second; did the mille-Peter just make a small dick joke? Gus asked. "Okay... okay, I'll act surprised and won't expose your mom to what a real man's dick looks like."

Chapter 9

Monday November 8th, 2004, 5:24 PM 6243 Mourning Dove Rd. Raleigh, NC

Memories of the three long years that had passed since Gus had last set foot inside the house overwhelmed him as they pulled up. The thought of entering his mother's room filled him with a sense of dread. He had gone through the effort of cleaning it, but he had left it untouched, just as she would have left it.

154

Peter's parents had taken care of the place, or more likely, had it taken care of, during his deployment and beforehand while he was finishing school. The tan fall grass yard was immaculate, with only a few leaves in the yard. Someone had recently painted the exterior of the house.

Peter looked at Gus with a conspiratorial wink and smile, "You ready for this? Remember, it is a surprise."

Gus took a deep breath. "Ok."

Peter assumed that Gus's hesitation was because of the party, but it was not on his mind at all as they exited the car. The house was dark as they approached. Gus estimated that around 20 people had recently walked across the grass, clear to him, from the obvious footprints. Unlike the dirt and sand, he had become familiar with, the ground here didn't speak to him as clearly, but it also didn't hide any dangerous surprises like IEDs. "Shit," he mentally kicked himself and thought, "I hope that kind of scrutiny goes away soon." Approaching the door, he absentmindedly let his hand gravitate towards the spot on his hip where he usually holstered his sidearm while on deployment, and he nonchalantly brushed off his blue jeans, expressing annoyance with a roll of his eyes.

Peter stood at the door, staring at him with a bewildered expression, as if he had sprouted a third ear on his forehead. "Are you ok?" he mouthed, and Gus nodded with a slightly embarrassed smile. As Gus made his way to the door, the distractions of his newfound awkwardness overwhelmed him, causing him to completely forget about the surprise party that awaited him in the darkness of his home.

Later, Peter would commend him on his exceptional acting skills, unaware that Gus's startled jump at the surprise had been completely genuine. In panic, Gus's mind had settled on three places to take cover, but his rational mind quickly transformed his shock into a wide smile.

As people came forward to embrace him, he bent at the waist, placing his right hand on his knee for support, and raised his left hand to signal "one second", all while he focused on regaining control over his breathing and heart rate.

He graciously accepted the warm hugs and firm handshakes from his friends and neighbors. 23, the number came to his mind. He didn't have to count, as in his mind he had mentally grouped them in a mental snapshot into groups of five with leftovers. He was eagerly expecting the survival adaptations to neatly fold themselves and find a shelf to sit on in his mind. "I need a beer," he said, and everyone laughed.

After several hours, the party thinned out. Soon it was just him, Peter, and Peter's parents. Lounging on the new living room furniture that had magically appeared while he was away, Mack, his father figure of the last decade plus, asked Gus, "So, what now?"

The question took Gus by surprise, leaving him momentarily speechless. For the past year, all he could think about was escaping the Army, and now, finally, that chapter was closed. "I honestly don't know," Gus replied. "Right now, I'm finishing up the plan I had," he shrugged. "Between the money from the military and inheritance, I'm ok for a while I guess, but you are right... I need to answer the 'what's next'. I honestly always braced myself, thinking that somehow, I would get dragged back into Army things somehow over there. Right now, I feel like I'm dreaming sitting here with you guys." Gus concluded as Deb chimed in.

"Well, your degree is a BSBA in Information Systems, right? If that still interests you, I can put you in touch with our veteran's outreach group from HR. The first six months you would be in training classes and assessments... if you would like that kind of thing?" She spoke.

"Wait, veterans outreach? How big is Redwolf now? It was like 200-ish when I was in college, right?" Gus asked.

Deb looked at him, "Yeah, it was that, give or take, but we have been fortunate. We don't just do chips anymore. Heck, even back when you were a kid, we were branching out and investing with partners. Some of those partners we purchased. Currently, we have offices in 27 states and four continents: North America, Europe, Asia and Australia. We have plans for an office in Buenos Aries and Rio in the next couple of years and already have sales efforts ongoing there with our sales analytics group. Think about it," she said. "We would..." she paused and attempted to drop the corporate CEO speak as her voice returned to her normal register, "I would love to have you there. Your mom helped to build what we have and setting the foundation that helped us grow. It would mean the world to me and we all love you and are so glad you are back safe." Deb finished with a genuine smile and tears in the corners of her eyes that he knew were for his mom.

Mack and Deb stood up and Deb said, "time for us old people to get home and get in bed and do old people's stuff."

"She means sex," Peter supplied as his mother looked at him with her mouth agape and the lightest of red flushing her cheeks.

Gus laughed and almost choked when he caught Mack behind Deb waggling his eyebrows over his glasses like an old Groucho Marx movie. "You are a beast!" she said to Peter, "and you better have those reports on my desk tomorrow morning!" she spoke with feigned indignation.

"I will have them on your desk by the crack of noon," Peter promised and received an evil eye in return. Mack walked over, opened the front door, and held it for his bride as she walked through, with him following behind. He made eye contact with Gus, winked, and silently gave a thumbs up before vanishing as the door shut. "They are totally going to go have sex," Peter concluded.

"Thanks for that image," Gus replied with a smirk. "Want another beer?" Gus asked as he rose and walked towards the kitchen.

"Sure! I mean, really, really gross old-people sex..." Peter started.

"Stop!!" yelled Gus. "This conversation is becoming more traumatic than my last two years." Peter took the bottle from him and rolled back into his seat kicking his feet in the air and laughed.

A couple hours later, Peter looked at his lifelong friend and, with sincerity not normal to him, "I'm so glad you are home. I was terrified when you were over there. I mean, I have other friends, but you make them seem like acquaintances. Thanks for listening to your commander and keeping that enormous orange-ish head of yours out of someone's gun sights."

The mention of his orange-tinged hair pinged something in Gus's brain and he said, "Oh shit!"

"What?"

"I need to make a phone call to my family in Scotland. I haven't contacted them since... well, since pre-deployment training." Gus said with a grimace.

"Well, they went how long without contacting you?" Peter responded. "Like your whole life, right until your mom passed?" Peter countered.

"It wasn't like that. I think my grandfather and mother had disagreements, and they stayed away to not offend her or something." Gus scoured the house for the paper that his grandfather had given him years ago. When he found it, of all places, it was stuck to the fridge, next to his autobiography. A black circular magnet had staked each corner of the paper to the avocado-colored refrigerator. "Sure," Gus thought, "they can replace all the tweed living room furniture with nice leather sofas and chairs, but the refrigerator is still avocado," and laughed at his own joke.

Gus picked up the new radio handset telephone in the kitchen and dialed the country code and phone number for the home he couldn't recall ever being in. The phone rang its strange international ring four straight times before Gus did the mental math. If it was 10:30 PM Eastern Standard Time, it was 3:30AM, and he reached for the hangup button.

Before his hand got there, he heard through the earpiece, "This better be good, or Christ our savior himself be inviting me to dinner," said the voice on the other side of the phone.

Gus cringed, "I am so sorry, this is Gus... Laoch Keir Ferguson the fifth. I'm so sorry..." Commotion on the other side of the line interrupted him. He heard what seemed like the sound of sheets and blankets moving against the phone, and he was certain he heard the phone hit the floor once.

"No, no, no, it is not a problem, lad. Are you okay? It's been so long since we... I feared you were still hiding in some foxhole or something..."

Gus interrupted his grandfather, cutting him off abruptly. "I'm fine. All is fine. Today, I was discharged from the Army. I had forgotten your address when I deployed, or I would have written you. It completely slipped my mind to call earlier. And when I remembered, I completely forgot the time difference. I'm so sorry. I just wanted to let you know I am fine and safe back home. Please, go back to sleep and we can talk tomorrow... maybe you can call me at your breakfast and pay me back?" He said with a laugh.

"I will. I will call you tomorrow. At this number?" his grandfather asked.

"This is the house phone, but I have a cell phone number, too. I will probably have that with me most of the time," and Gus gave him the number slowly.

"Do you need anything, lad? We can wire you money if you need?" his grandfather offered.

"No, no, I'm fine, and I think I got offered a new job tonight," Gus said. "Please, just go back to sleep and we can talk tomorrow."

"Ok goodnight my boy and thank you for the call, even if it is before the bloody roosters." His grandfather said with a smile Gus could feel through the phone and they both hung up.

"I didn't want to interrupt, but your phone call reminded me of something," Peter said. "Do you remember that fucked up email you sent me with the story of the old lady that read your coffee or something and died?"

"Yeah," Gus replied. "It almost made me shit my diaper."

"Do you know where your family is from in Scotland exactly? Like where they are located?" Peter asked.

"My mom told me they lived an hour from Edinburgh in the central highland region, northwest of Edinburgh."

Peter took a deep breath and let it out through his flapping lips. With a face twisted in concentration as he was trying to picture it. "It's real close, I think. I looked up Atholl, and apparently it is a region in Scotland and it's pretty close to where you are describing." Peter laughed, "And it is pretty appropriate," he concluded.

"How's that?" Gus said, walking right into the joke.

"It would make you an asshole from Atholl." Peter said, with a self-satisfied smirk playing on his lips.

"Funny... and freaky at the same time." Gus finished.

Peter rose from his seat. With a conscious effort to suppress the unsettling analogy about dead soldiers, he began picking up the discarded cans. He collected all cans within reach, and requested to Gus, "Toss me your empties."

Gus grabbed three cans and tossed them to him one at a time, "Dead soldier number one, two and three." Peter caught them and shook his head at his own over thinking.

Peter dumped them in the kitchen trash can. "Brother, you have to do something about this big, ugly-ass pickle refrigerator! I think it is the same color as that car your mom had when we were kids."

Gus smiled and thought, "It's been one damn day, and that guy can already read my mind again." Peter came out of the kitchen and Gus stood up.

Peter gave him a long hug, "Thanks again for coming home safe, but I have to get home and get some sleep."

Gus smiled and replied, "And you better get up early and get that report done for your mom, too."

Peter laughed, "I'm sure that thing is already done. Marcy probably has it spell checked, checked for accuracy, printed and waiting on my desk."

Gus took a step back and asked, "Wait a second. Who is Marcy?"

Peter laughed, "Marcy is my personal assistant... she was going to be here tonight, but she had a report to finish."

Gus stared at him for a long second, "I am pretty sure you are from Atholl, too."

They shook hands one last time and Peter was out the door.

Gus found himself alone in his mom's house, where a profound silence prevailed. Two weeks ago, 50 people would have bunked in a place this large. He headed towards his room, intentionally avoiding his mom's room, thinking, "nope, not tonight".

At the entrance of his room, he placed his two duffel bags and the rucksack he had slid across the hardwood floor. He took off his sneakers and removed all his clothes. Walking to the bathroom in the hall, he switched on the hot water. As he entered the shower, the room quickly filled with steam, and he washed away the remnants of the Army for the last time.

Chapter 10

Tuesday November 9th, 2004, 5:24 AM, 6243 Mourning Dove Rd. Raleigh, NC

At 05:00 the following day, Gus got out of bed and went for his usual five-mile run. With the sun rising in the east, he wrapped up his morning workout, fueled up with a satisfying breakfast, and took a hot shower. At exactly 07:30, he entered the garage, looking sharp in a white shirt, tie, and sports coat, and started his pickup truck. Noticing that Deb and Mack had kept the truck ready for him, he made a mental note to thank them. After 30 minutes, he arrived at the Research Triangle Park and easily located the building where his mom had worked. Driving into that parking lot felt strange, a bittersweet reminder of how much he missed her.

Stepping out of his car, he noticed Mack dropping off Deb in their Volvo sedan as they circled the loop. Mack waved enthusiastically and called out to Deb, who spun around in surprise to see him. "Hey there, handsome! Walk with me and let me get my stuff in my office, check my calendar to make sure I'm not missing anything, and we can talk as we go. I'm guessing by the tie that maybe you want to give this a shot?" Deb asked with a smile.

"I cannot think of anything else I would rather do, to be honest," Gus admitted. "As long as no one is shooting at me, I am great."

"Good, good. You didn't bring a resume with you, did ya?" Jen asked.

"Five copies, although outside of school and the military," Gus said, "it is pretty thin. I also brought several references.".

"Very nice, you are making my day easy... and don't discount the time you spent defending our country, dear. You also obviously mastered organization and self-starting. That alone tells me you will do well here." Deb said, as she sat to chat with him in the sitting area of her office.

Chapter 11

Deb introduced Gus to their HR director and handed them a copy of his resume. They went off and discussed open positions. Two hours later, after meeting with several managers, they made him a job offer on the spot, in a highly sped up hiring process. To Gus, his salary felt high, but pretty much anything was a boon after military pay. He signed up for the insurance plans and received an ID badge, complete with his name and photo.

He went to lunch that day with Peter, and at the restaurant, Peter introduced him to Marcy Kitchen, his assistant. Gus, as he often did around pretty women, stumbled over his words at the beginning. With a Cambridge education and an MBA from Duke University under her belt, Marcy was undeniably smart and well educated. Gus tried his best not to stare, but he couldn't help but notice how her brown hair framed her sky-blue eyes, and how her lovely British accent added to her charm.

Peter knew the look in Gus's eye and did everything he could to make the lunch awkward for him. First, he made them sit on the same side of the table, forcing Gus to make obvious his looks. Peter talked glowingly about him to Marcy and suggested she should give him a tour of the campus.

After lunch, Peter and Marcy dropped Gus off at his building, and as he watched them drive away, he committed himself to two goals. To kill Peter for his antics at lunch and to try not to be a total dork the next time he met Marcy.

The group that Gus worked for was a mostly autonomous group that Redwolf Solutions had gained through a corporate purchase. Only at the highest level did his management chain interact with Deb, and he received no special treatment.

After completing a two-week orientation training, they sent him to a demanding boot camp training course. From there, it was mandatory training. After the IRS training video, with the four people doing a pretend news cast, he found himself willing to do anything to make the orientation madness stop.

At the beginning of the boot camp, he would learn and hopefully certify at a basic level for Windows and Linux operating system administration. Next, he took a series of intensive, two-week training courses in various programming languages, culminating in training on Redwolf TRACS, a proprietary analytic product (Trending Research Analytic Control System).

The initial training goal was to equip him with vital knowledge to establish a base for further understanding. He quickly adapted to the new job. His coworkers were excellent, and their knowledge, along with their generosity with helping him adapt, left Gus feeling grateful. He surprised everyone by becoming productive almost two months earlier than expected, leading to a change in his workload.

Seven years later, he was running his own group and making double the money. During that same time period, Redwolf Solutions had doubled in size. When not working, Gus and Peter enjoyed going on regular trips together to engage in activities like hiking, gambling, or playing paintball.

On all of their trips, Marcy accompanied them and actively took part in activities, while also managing Peter's daily schedule, both professionally and personally. Gus held a private infatuation for Marcy, and she always was nice to him. However, he was pretty sure he had been friend zoned.

Despite being aware that Marcy was on the job, managing Peter's life when they traveled, Gus still highly valued her presence. He knew she received a high salary for managing and tolerating him. She was funny and suffered no insults without returning fire. She was more of a third musketeer than a third wheel. Despite the close bond and extensive knowledge of Peter, there was no romantic interest between the two, which didn't shock Gus with his intimate knowledge of Peter's difficult past relationships.

Their friendship and trust were clear. Hell, she knew his bank account numbers better than he did. Peter was a bachelor's bachelor. While he enjoyed the company of women, he had no interest in a long-term relationship. Marcy seemed far too busy for any romance and knew Peter for the dog he was. She obviously cared for Peter, loved him even, but these were not romantic feelings. It was more mother like or that of a big sister, and she adored the thrill and freedom of her job.

In the spring of 2012, Peter reminded Gus multiple times to leave his schedule open for his 30th birthday in June. The warning had an equal measure of ambiguity and ominousness, as every time he mentioned it, he waggled his eyebrows like his father did.

Gus remained in constant but distant contact with the family in Scotland throughout the years, mostly at Christmas, or to give or receive birthday wishes. Despite his grandfather's desperate longing for him to visit, Gus's busy lifestyle left him with no real personal ties aside from their blood relationship. The thought made him feel guilty, but he remembered his mother's old saying, "It is what it is."

Chapter 12

Gus and Peter and the "Perfect Plan" June 9, 2012, 2:00 PM Edinburgh, Scotland

"Thirty fucking years!" Gus thought as the bees buzzed in his head and he tried to shield his eyes from the light that seared his skull. "Fuck you, sun!" he mumbled. The sunlight streamed through the windows, hitting him full in the face and blinding his eyes.

"Thirty and I guess, maybe fourteen hours old? Maybe," Gus said after he checked his iPhone. "What the hell is that smell?" Gus thought as the recognition he didn't want to believe dawned on him, "Ugh, shit, that smell is me... not just my shirt, ME. Oh, Jesus... and what the hell is that taste in my mouth?" Gus thought. "Is that a cat's ass?" No, it had to be something worse. "Where the hell am I?" he asked the universe.

"Ok, so I'm in a room... like a rundown hotel room," he thought as he mentally took notes. Again, recognition based on flashes of memories tried to piece their way together. "Peter, My BEST fucking friend," he mumbled, but it was still so loud it hurt. Hell, even the echo of it from the wall across from him bruised his brain.

There was a shuffling sound, and he heard, "Prezz... Present," from the far corner of the room. Looking around in the dim light, he spotted Peter sitting against the wall, his body tilted and resting in a puddle that he was sure emitted that rancid odor... what it was? He didn't even want to contemplate.

Even the simple act of not contemplating was enough to make Gus's weak stomach churn. Thankfully, the door he opened revealed a bathroom with a high tank near the roof. Inside, a single light bulb hung with a pull-string from the center of the small room's ceiling. With the light swinging erratically, after he pulled the string, casting ever shifting shadows, Gus couldn't hold back the urge to empty not only his stomach but apparently also the stomachs of at least six other people.

There was fluid, food and chunks way too big to imagine their origin. "What the hell!" Gus said with a shudder after a giant chunk passed. Gus yelled at the toilet in a convulsive, nonproductive attempt to get more out. It produced nothing additional but made his mouth and eyes water.

After a few minutes, he flushed and returned to the room to see Peter attempting to stand while laughing at him. "Welcome to Scotland!!" Peter said with a grand wave that he tried to turn into a bow. Peter had taken Gus back to Scotland for his birthday.

The details of Gus's birthday were a blur as he anxiously glanced at his phone with a mere 1% battery. His eyes strained to open more, as he took in his surroundings, remembering how Peter had surprised him with a birthday dinner the night before his actual birthday, and that was how long ago? It turned into drinks, which turned into more drinks, which turned into an impromptu "perfect Peter plan".

Peter had taken out his black card and handed it to Marcy. "Book us a plane to Scotland," he said. Gus still kind of remembered him doing that, and thinking it was a joke. There was a quick drunken limo ride to each person's house to grab a bag, stuff it with some clothes and grab passports, and they were off to the international airport between Raleigh and Durham.

"Peter Cad Smith, you sir, are a motherfucker." He mumbled as he slid down the wall opposite of him in the room. "Let's recap. You are a miserable excuse for a life form. Your mother graduates in four years from Tufts and gets her master's degree and eventually her Doctorate from Stanford. You inherit her brains, but missed out somehow in the motivation department, I think."

Peter interrupted with a slight slur still in his speech, "That was probably my dad's genes."

Gus continued, "I'm not saying you're a waste of life or anything. Hell, you are my best friend in the world. I mean, I fucking love you like a brother, but if you ever dedicated yourself half as hard as you do when you try to destroy my liver, you could change the whole goddamn world. Instead, you are much more interested in women, parties and good times... pretty much in that order. Still, you are on the board of your mom's company and likely to fill her high heels. You're in charge (if you could call it that) of a division called 'Special Projects', in which you have only six employees." Gus paused for the grossest tasting burp of his life. "Ugh, oh God."

"Don't forget Marcy," Peter chimed from the far corner.

"Yes, you have your assistant, the lovely and beautiful Marcy," Gus continued, "and outside of your considerable salary, you complain of a limited budget." Gus paused a moment and breathed.

"Don't forget my black card and expense account," Peter said with a sickly smile.

"Yes, you have the black credit card and expense account and budget that are over ten times what I will make in the next decade... per year." Gus said, nodding painfully. "My question is. Peter, what exactly do you do?" Gus asked.

"If I told you all I did was work to protect you, I would have to kill you," Peter said with a laugh, like it was the funniest joke he had ever told, and the room got quiet for a moment.

"Back to Scotland..." Gus said. "So, it is June 9th, and a quick check of my iPhone says it is 14:30 and we both need a shower badly. That will require us to go to the public bath down the hall, I'm guessing, in this lovely old hotel. I will go first."

Gus hit the shower and let it get hot as he tried to piece together the night and... days before. He remembered being on the plane and the bottle of Blue Label that Peter broke out... and that is where things became foggy.

He remembered a blurry bar, and drinks poured, hearing himself as he said, "No WAY! No FUCKING Way!"

Peter grabbed the glass that Gus shunned and, with a boxer's stare, threw it back. Gus remembered Peter as he smiled and said, "It's nothing, just do it!"

At first, he refused, but eventually Gus relented... "What the hell was that drink? Why would I say no so vehemently?" he thought. Meh, the shower was ready, so he got in.

He scrubbed everything like his mommy and the Army always taught him to. After the shower was complete, Gus returned to the room feeling a lot better and passed "pecker-head" at the door. Gus thought about asking Peter a question, "Hey Peter?" but could not remember what it was he wanted to ask, "Oh never mind." With a shrug, Peter was off to the shower. To cover the wretched smell in the room, Gus sprayed enough aftershave and deodorant to coat the walls... Anything... to cut that smell.

Chapter 13

Saturday June 9, 2012, 3:30 PM Edinburgh, Scotland

After Peter got back from his shower and dressed, they headed out for breakfast... well, "late lunch". Peter mentioned something about the hair of the dog, as Gus spoke over him. "I still feel like I'm trying to get hairy dog parts out of my mouth." Gus said, and they both laughed gingerly.

Two doors down from the hotel, they found a place still serving lunch. Gus checked the menu, and he ask the guy tending bar/waiting tables if they have dry toast. The bartender laughed a full belly laugh and asked, "Do you want your coffee with a wee little sissy umbrella, too?"

Peter looked at Gus with a cold, long, daring stare... smiled, "I'll take today's tourist special and a Pint."

Gus winced when he heard it. The painful thoughts playing with his constitution, thinking, "ooh, shepherd's pie sounds way too heavy".

The barkeep smiled, slammed his ham-sized fist on the table, nodded, "There you go! One haggis coming right up!"

The toast came... and so did his coffee... with an umbrella and a dainty spoon with lots of cream and sugar. "So maybe it won't be too hard on your wee panties," said the barkeep with a condescending smirk. Peter's haggis came with the plate basically dropped in front of him like a challenge. It shook a bit like stiff Jello. His pint of dark, frothy stout arrived with a satisfying "thump", the creamy head slightly overflowing the glass.

Gus knew Peter and knew this was killing him, but with a clinical observation, the standup job he was doing, maintaining the character of stoic manliness, was impressive. "That haggis is very... haggissy today" Gus said, with and uncomfortable role in his voice as the smell drifted across the table to him.

When Peter turned to perform a confident nod to the barkeep, who was stepping back to return to his bar, Gus noticed a dead fly on the windowsill beside them. Without a second thought or hesitation, Gus snatched the fly by the wing and added it to Peter's enormous dish.

The front door of the bar swung open with a loud thump as the door slammed the wall. Simultaneously, the bell above the door emitted its unpleasantly loud and piercing ring. The noise was jarring, reminiscent of a hammer striking a bell to signal the beginning of a prize fight's first round.

From the door, a massive, sweaty Scotsman strided over to their table. In a booming voice, the large old man locked eyes with Gus and firmly demanded, "You had your fun, son. Now give it back," his hand outstretched.

Gus turned his gaze towards Peter, who spoke with conviction and said, "You really should," with honest looking uneasiness.

Gus struggled to recognize the man or comprehend his cryptic references. "What the hell are you guys talking about?" Gus Looked genuinely perplexed. He turned to Peter and asked, his brows furrowing in confusion.

With his hands, which were much larger and stronger than Gus's, the old man grabbed Gus's shirt. "Wait... WAIT," Peter said, with a sense of urgency in his voice, "Gus! Give him back the bishop's thumb."

As Gus stared at Peter, his eyes narrowed in expectation, as he eagerly awaited the punch line. "This might be the best joke Peter ever pulled," Gus thought, "because he somehow got people from the town to help him pull it off." Gus, clearly outmatched, was honestly dumb with the response, "I have no damn clue what you're talking about," Gus said to Peter.

"The bishop's thumb! Remember?!? The shot last night that has that old piece of jerky in it that looked like a finger?" Peter said.

"Nae, not a fenger," Gus's giant inquisitor cut in with a touch of irony. The latest lunch guest, who Gus in his mind, named, "Angry Angus," replied, "Jerky? That was the real deal, friend. That was Bishop Thomas' tadger taken in 1534 and passed down, a fixture in my family's bar 'The Bishops Pulpit' ever since... and I want it back... right FUCKIN' NOW."

Peter looked at Gus and laughed. "Remember? You pretended to swallow it last night?"

The unasked and forgotten question from the shower about the mysterious drink he had turned down the night before caused Gus's world to suddenly swim. He looked at Peter, and it was clear from his expression that he was not joking... a memory slowly emerged from the depths of Gus's mind.

The hazy memory... drinking the drink... drinking the drink... drinking the 'choke', (heavy swallow) drink. Laughter had filled the air, and he couldn't help but feel puzzled why everyone found it so funny. Ignoring the denominations, Peter slapped down a generous pile of British Pound notes.

"We knew it was time to run," he remembered. "We stumbled and hurriedly fled from the bar." His mind flashed back to this morning... the "what the hell was that chunk that just left my body" moment. Gus looked up at Peter in a panic.

Peter read his mind, and he saw a look of panicked understanding of what had happened to the Bishop's Tadger. Fork in hand, about to take a second small bite of the haggis, Peter saw the fly perched dead on the next fork full. Peter's tough guy facade completely crumbled as he turned his head and his stomach unleashed a tumultuous eruption, drenching Angry Angus from his left ear to his waist.

In Gus's head, as if all of this was in slow motion, his brain reached out for "What the hell is a tadger?" as Peter released an impressive stream that caught Angus in the left ear before trailing off to a fountain as his old friend belatedly covered his mouth.

Peter stared at the dripping Angry Angus, who had not bothered to dodge or wipe off the sick. With a comedic grin, Peter handed Angus his black credit card. "Let's work something out," he said.

At that exact moment, the door swung open, and Marcy's voice filled the room as she exclaimed, "There you guys are!" she said, taking in the scene. "What did I miss?" Marcy's said as she snorted her contagious laughter, which shattered the almost perfect silence of the absurd scene.

Chapter 14

Sunday June 10th, 2012, 10:00 AM Edinburgh Scotland

The airlines had scheduled their return flights for Monday, June 11th at noon. The flight time that seemed to defy the laws of physics as they would arrive in Raleigh two and a half hours, by the clock time, after they left. So, they would land in Raleigh about 2:30 PM.

Tomorrow's departure meant they had a day to burn and so Peter suggested they check out Gus's old homestead.

Gus knew he had been born nearby and racked his brain for anything his mother had told him. "My mom called it Wolfborn or the Big House."

Peter looked at him, "I'm going to ask something stupid, but did you ever take a picture of the letter your grandfather gave you on your fridge with your phone?"

The car got quiet for a couple of seconds. "Yes," said Gus meekly as he searched his pictures on the iPhone.

"You are an idiot, Gus." Peter said, and everyone in the rental car laughed.

With the address secured, they pulled up MapQuest and got directions and drove off into the gentle patter of raindrops and the ominous, darkening sky. The directions were flawed, but they brought them to the general vicinity. The conversation with the person at the small petrol station filled in the missing pieces of their route. As the car drove away, the person they had asked reached for the phone and dialed his uncle's number at Wolfborn and warned them to expect visitors.

In their rental car, they made their way across a small rain slick, wooden bridge that crossed a swollen brook running along the eastern side of the manor's property. As soon as they laid eyes on it, Marcy, in her lovely British accent, questioned, "Is that a bloody castle?"

Several eyes from in and around the house observed the approach of the rental car in the light rain as it slowly followed the gravel path towards the house.

When they reached the front of the manor, the house was busy with activity. An enormous man was unloading wet bags of topsoil from the back of a farm truck. Around the circular driveway, several men were busy trimming the damaged tree branches and completing other chores after the recent storm.

Except for Gus, no one in the car understood the significance of where the workers were, in front of the manor. Their precise placement reminded him of the memories he had been trying to forget since Iraq.

Their locations were almost identical to the interlocking fire formation they used in a fortified palace once occupied by Saddam Hussein. Some truly great mentors had drummed into his head in Young Officers' Course and in the field, the precise defensive positioning.

Despite his attempts to dismiss it as chance, the positioning of the truck and smaller carts, filled with soil and rock for the driveway unnerved him. The fire team, wearing mostly dry gardening coveralls and lacking rain gear, strategically used their maximum crossfire advantage.

Also concerning, these guys were skilled. Well, except for Daniel, who was standing by the tailgate of the big truck. All the gardeners possessed the sturdy and compact physique he commonly associated with the Special Forces soldiers, who confidently strolled through the camps in Iraq as if they were the owners.

Driving into the arc alarmed Gus to where he almost told Peter to just turn around... if he hadn't recognized Daniel and hadn't just noticed his grandfather standing near the large front door, he would have. When the car stopped, Gus stepped out first onto the wet pebbles of the driveway, and his grandfather brought both hands up and smiled. "Gus!"

Gus noted the slight gesture his grandfather made with his palms facing downwards, which led to the gardeners visibly easing their tension. One at the far left of the building that Gus had not noticed came around the corner as he spun his hat back around to forward facing.

"Sorry to surprise you, grandfather, but we were in town unexpectedly." He said as he glanced towards Peter.

"Wonderful!" said his grandfather.

As Gus prepared to introduce his friends, a large hand slapped him on the back hard enough to clear his throat, as if he had been choking. "Good to see you again Gus!" said Daniel with a voice that seemed to come from the bottom of a well. Gus laughed and shook his hand. "Grandfather, Daniel... This is Marcy and her sidekick..." he started.

"Peter, right?" said an excited Daniel.

"Uh yeah, I am Peter," he looked at Gus slightly shocked.

169

Gus caught the end of his grandfather's icy stare, which could freeze water, before his kind smile returned. Wearing an expression reminiscent of someone who had just let out a fart in the queen's presence, Daniel excused himself and proclaimed, "Back to work! See you all when I get this stuff put away." Daniel seemed to castigate himself as he walked away.

"You're all welcome here. Please come in!" the family patriarch said. "Out of this gloom and rain and dry off some near the fire." He led the way to a great hall with a large burning hearth. "We rarely do a fire this time of the year, but a cool gloomy day like this..." as he waved at the weather.

An ancient man sat in the room already, reading the paper. He wore a well-tailored suit and a remembrance poppy pin on his lapel. Gus's father addressed the crowd and said, "Allow me to introduce Sir William, ladies and gentlemen."

With some effort, the old man rose to his feet and politely asked for, "Please. Just Bill."

"No, no" said Gus, as he pleaded for Bill not to stand.

"Pshhh. The day I cannot rise for family, friends or a beautiful woman, it will be because I hit my head on the lid of the coffin." He said with a smile. Upon turning, Bill's gaze fell upon the visitors. "Well, it appears that all three apply here," William said with delight. He looked at Gus. "My boy, you look like a perfect mix between your father and mother. I remember you following the edges of this very furniture before you had the balance to walk and being a bloody terror on the run two days later. We had to remove all the dangerous stuff in reach, because you tried to climb everything." William smiled. "Sit, sit, let's shoot some air, as the young crowd says."

"I think he meant shoot the breeze," clarified Daniel, walking in the room, no longer in coveralls, "plus if Bill shoots some air, you would be best to evacuate the entire bloody county," he added with a belly laugh that made everyone relax.

Two women walked into the room, one carrying a tray of cookies and the other pushing a cart with a tea set and an excessive number of cups. "This is Nell who works with William and Donna with the biscuits, who runs this place and keeps us all fat," said Gus's grandfather. "After we ruin your lunch, you are more than welcome to join us in pushing around a lovely meal on your plate in only about an hour. Don't worry, there is always enough."

"Oh, really... we just came by because we were close. I didn't mean for us to impose," said Gus.

"Nonsense. Plus, it will take at least that long to show you around the place and maybe a quick drive around the lands... I can show you the lab facility your father built to improve our crop yields. Your father was, and I'm not just saying this because he was my son... He was a lovely man, and your mother was an amazing woman also, but the differences your father introduced here with our processes, changed the trajectory of our farm to this day." The grandfather said, obviously not wanting to get into the differences he had with Gus's mother.

"We would be glad to." Gus said, after seeing the nods from his friends.

Chapter 15

Sunday 2:30 PM June 10th, 2012, The Big House, Atholl, Scotland

Laoch the third, Gus's grandfather, walked them through the house and showed them the living quarters, including his first home, relating stories to his childhood. He took them to the ancient barns inside the wall and showed them the livestock of a self-sustaining farm and discussed their use of refuse and manure to fertilize their fields in the early spring.

Laoch, Gus's grandfather, discussed the age of the house, with the original area being the great hall where the fireplace was. "At first, everyone lived in that one room, built in 1426," as he discussed how it was the first fully stone home in the area, and how additions over the next 50 years, brought the house to its current form. "I mean, minus the electricity and the conversions of the privies to running water bathrooms and such," He even showed them an entrance to a wine cellar hidden in a stone wall that they referred to as a "priest's hole" entrance. "In the dark days of conflict, the women and children used it as a hideaway."

With the house and barns local to the house all viewed, they made a quick trip in an older Land Rover about five minutes down the road to another barn. They had converted much of the inside into a modern laboratory, and several people were working in there. "Your father started this, Gus. By bringing science to our little farm, he transformed it completely. Our techniques were decent, but his effort catapulted us from the Stone Age to modern farming. He never stopped teaching us, even after your grandparents' tragic accident and your move back to the United States. When he passed away, we established a scholarship in his name and partnered with his alma mater. The dealings with the university are why we were in town originally when your mother passed. We had meetings with North Carolina State, and were visiting with administrators there, when we heard the terrible news. The day of her interment, we met Peter's father and mother when they introduced themselves at the funeral. They mentioned how close you two were."

As they walked to the car to head back for lunch, Gus's grandfather pulled him to the side. "Please, someday soon I need you to come back... or I can come there I guess, but here might be better. I need to sit down with you and talk about something very important. It is a kind of inheritance thing... but it is much more complicated than that. Frankly, it is part of what drove the wedge between your mum and I. She wanted you to have none of the responsibility it carries. The problem is, I don't think our wishes are always a limiting factor in the order of things. I just need to tell you about it and let you decide for yourself."

Gus responded. "I'm not like the secret heir to the Scottish Crown, right?" Gus laughed.

"No, but you are heir to your father's legacy as a smartass, and he got that from yours truly," he said with a smile.

"I promise, I will set aside a week of vacation and visit and meet the rest of the family," Gus promised.

"Good!" Laoch said, "because Mimi is going to be pissed that she missed seeing you. She is off on a trip this week, ironically, in America, New York City."

Gus's face took on a serious look. "One question back, and you don't have to be specific. Is whatever you need to talk to me about related to the ex-spec-ops guys you have posing as gardeners?" Gus asked, staring his grandfather in the eyes to see their reaction.

Laoch didn't even attempt to deny it. "Oh, you saw those. Let's just make this tidy and say yes... and if you haven't mentioned them to anyone else, please use discretion, as I do not want that known."

Chapter 16

The tour group arrived back at the house to find a covered delivery truck parked in the drive. "Oh, Tim is here, I am guessing with his son," Gus's grandfather said, "as I doubt, he drives anymore. He is one of Sir William's friends from college."

"Wait, a friend from college is still alive?" asked Marcy. "Didn't someone say he was near 100 years old?"

"Indeed," Gus's grandfather Laughed, "but Tim is too ornery to die a normal death too, apparently."

When they entered, they could hear William laughing and pounding on the table, as he asked incredulously, "He did what?" followed by more pounding.

Gus heard an oddly familiar voice as it said, "Apparently, the American tosser swallowed the bishop's tadger with the drink. For the life of me, I thought they were kidding, and he was trying to steal it," as more laughter burst from the room.

"Stop, please stop. I'm about to piss my knickers, or throw up, or probably both." Came the hysterical voice of Nell.

Gus's head lolled back on his shoulders, and he wanted to run for the car, or find a large rock he could hide under. When from beside him came a snort. When he looked over, Peter had his hand over his mouth as he tried to suppress the laugh and tears that formed in his eyes. "Shiiiiiiit" Gus said, while his grandfather looked around at the group in total confusion.

Gus felt like he was walking the plank as he took the five steps into view of the formal dining room, where the laughs had originated from. There, holding court, 'Angry Angus', or Rory, apparently his real name, told an all too familiar story which was interrupted by their entrance. "Holy Shite! It's you!" Rory said, as he poked his large sausage like accusatory finger at Gus.

Bill looked up and laughed a laugh that continued into an almost silence, just a carrying whistle of the last drops of air leaving the old man's chest. He finally, thankfully, took a deep recovery breath.

"No Gus, say it isn't true... You swallowed the poor bishop's tadger?" Bill screamed as tears streamed down his face. All Gus could do was blow air out of his mouth, scratch his eyebrow with his thumb and give a simple single nod, and the room exploded in laughter, with everyone crying tears, except Gus and Rory.

When Donna entered the room, pushing the large, wheeled serving cart, and the room tentatively settled. On top was a basket with freshly cooked bread, some fruit and a large, covered earthenware baking pot. Daniel grabbed the potholders and lifted the pot to the middle of the large table. Gus saw a strange glimmer in Donna's eye, but did not know what to make of it. Not until she lifted the cover of the pot and inside was... bangers and mash.

Like schoolboys, Bill and Tim howled so high that people were concerned they would both stroke out. The laughter in the room was so loud they couldn't hear Gus's head thump on the table as he said, "Kill me now".

A red-faced Nell excused herself and left the room, walking stiff legged, and was back in a new outfit minutes later, before the laughter had stopped.

When it slowed, Gus, also red-faced and laughed along and finally asked what he had asked himself all day, "What the hell is a tadger?" and the room erupted again in laughter.

When it calmed, Rory stared at him, "It's a boabie... "he said, seeing no recognition in Gus' eyes. "Gah... the bishop's love tackle," he tried again.

173

"Wait," said Peter, as he smiled in recognition.

"Not another damn word Peter." Gus interrupted, "or I will bury you here on family land and Daniel will help me."

Peter looked at Daniel, who was wiping a tear from his eye. He met his gaze. Daniel shrugged and nodded in agreement.

Exhausted with laughter and sore muscles that all would certainly feel for days, Tim looked earnestly at Rory, "Son... just get a piece of jerky. No one will know the difference and it will be fine."

Chapter 17

After lunch, with the winds beginning to howl outside, they all shook hands. Daniel approached Gus, "Sorry we didn't have the chance this time to take you to a real football match or much time to talk. Come back soon lad, please."

William stood up with military precision, transforming, and suddenly, just Bill was there again. He shook hands and when he got to Marcy, he had his only real mix up of the day, "Jen dear, it was a delight to see you again. I love what you have done with your hair," and kissed her on the cheek. Marcy glanced at Gus, and back to Bill, "It was wonderful seeing you, too."

The moment they opened the front door, a fierce gust of wind rushed in, threatening to turn the sturdy, steel banded front door into a dangerous swinging object. With impressive speed and agility, Daniel caught the swinging door just in time, averting a dangerous situation. As they looked towards the east, they noticed a billowing gray curtain slowly engulfing the grassy fields, creating an illusion as if the world was vanishing. "Oh dear, best get to your car before that squall gets here," said Gus's grandfather, and they ran for the car. Tim and Rory decided waiting out the storm in the big house seemed a better option.

As Peter drove along the rocky road towards the bridge on the east side of the estate, the squall suddenly unleashed its fury upon the car, engulfing it like a crashing wave. The winds at the front of the squall roared and violently rattled the car, while the raindrops bombarded the back and side windows. After crossing the bridge, they followed the flooded back roads until they reached the major thoroughfare and resumed their journey back to the fancy hotel Peter had arranged for their last night. "What should we do for dinner tonight?" asked Peter.

Everyone just kind of shrugged. "I have an idea," said Peter, "maybe we should have Gus take a poll... again," as Marcy gently slapped the back of Peter's head.

Chapter 18

June 11th, 2018, 8:22 AM Prestonfield House, Edinburgh Scotland. The Churchill Suite.

"Fuck my life!" Gus screamed. "Peter, I have to be back in NC by tomorrow morning at 9:00AM at the latest for work. Some of us have to work to cover our mortgages."

Peter laughed. "Dude, I cannot control the weather. They have grounded all flights across Great Britain... and you inherited your house, and you don't have a mortgage," Peter replied.

"Peter, you sound like a douchebag calling it Great Britain. It's fucking England," Gus stated.

"Marcy!?!" Peter said over his shoulder and snapped his fingers, "Marcy dear, you are from here... Is it England or Great Britton?"

"It's Great Britton, sir," Marcy dutifully called back as she packed Peter's baggage.

"She is your assistant," Gus complained. "You pay HER mortgage. Of course, she is going to agree with you," Gus joked.

"Marcy? I order you to tell me the God's truth. England or Great Britton?" Peter said, as he applied toothpaste to the toothbrush and brushed his teeth.

"Well..." she paused, "it's England."

"You bibph!" Peter said as he paused the brushing of his teeth. Marcy laughed and shot Peter a single middle finger in solute, and continued packing.

"You're rich, Peter, not royalty." Marcy laughed. "Royalty calls it Great Britton. The Queen, yeah, she would agree with you, but you would not agree with you, if we were sitting at the Carnegie Deli."

"Marcy, you're so fired!"

"Yeah, yeah, yeah..." Marcy said, "you don't even know where your wallet or car keys are. Without me, you'd be lost.

"Shit. You're right," Peter wiped his face with the towel, "so you keep your job for one more day!"

"Peter, we have to get back... seriously," Gus said.

"Sorry bud, but Mother Nature does not take credit cards. I checked. This storm is a doozy," Peter said as he grabbed the TV remote.

When Peter increased the volume, at least the TV obeyed his commands.

"...BBC One. When the wind is out of the east, 'tis never good for man or beast. And out of the east this one comes, and it is no joke. Gale warnings are up for all of Britton and small craft advisories extend well inland along the bays and all waterways. All airports are closed as of 4:00 AM GMT. Stockholm is closing in two hours and Northern France, from Brittany to Normandy, are looking at severe effects from this storm and are instituting mandatory evacuations of low-lying areas along the Channel and inland waterways. The Netherlands is due to announce emergency plans later today... You're watching BBC One..."

"See There? You are missing work, asshole!" Peter laughed.

"I have to call work... shit, shit, SHIT!" Gus stated.

"Chris!" Gus said into the phone. "Um. Major problem. You know Saturday was my birthday... yeah... Well, my friend surprised me with a party, and we ended up in Scotland of all places... Yeah... Yes! The storm, and I'm stuck here with my laptop sitting on my desk three thousand miles away. I did not know he was taking me here... yeah... I am so fricking sorry. Yeah, no way I'm making the meeting tomorrow. I can call in, but I have little to show... uh-huh... yeah... yeah, I can call her... Yeah! I can wing it some and I will get the info out when I get back... Man, I'm SO sorry. Yeah... yeah... thanks Chris... 30... yeah, thanks. Chris, thanks man, I truly appreciate it."

Gus collapsed into the chair. "He wants me to sit in on a call today... and afterwards, I am good for the rest of the week."

"Hell yeah!" Peter said excitedly. "Paris! No, no, Santorini!!"

"No! Weatherrrrr? And when it clears, I have to get back and prep for a meeting I am missing today." Gus exclaimed.

"You're not missing it; you are sitting in on it?" Peter retaliated.

"I am sitting in on a meeting and trying to buy time by dazzling them, hopefully with bullshit today. Somehow, I still need to make it work next week!"

"It's Monday!" Peter said calmly. "I'll have you back by Friday night!"

"Peter! I can't..." Gus said. "I have to get this stuff done, and it is going to take me time to create the presentation. Probably four days, at least. I don't even have my damn laptop."

Peter raised his right hand and pointed to the pretty lady across the room and Marcy said, "Shit... on it... Windows or Mac?" she asked, "Office? What else do you need?"

"Peter! Marcy!" complained Gus, "I can't!"

Marcy laughed, "Gus, maybe you haven't met him before... this is Peter... he is a Grade-A asshole, and he is rich."

"Shit... Windows," Gus said. "Oh, and Marcy? Make it hurt."

"Pffft!" Peter let escape his mouth dismissively.

"Now time for breakfast!" Peter said. "Plus, if they fire you, I'll hire you in my division and pay you twice what they do."

"For what? Your group doesn't do what I do, and I like my job. Oh, and I doubt your mom would let you." Gus replied.

"I still don't have a dancing monkey... you wear a 36 long, right?" Peter asked, as Gus rolled his eyes and gave up.

The storm now named "Sebastian," by BBC One, raged until mid-day Wednesday. Peter... well, Marcy, true to Peter's word, got him a sweet laptop. "This thing has more RAM than some servers in the production environments," Gus exclaimed. "Dual SSD drives?" and laughed when he saw it had an 8 Core processor and a custom video card with multiple GPUs. He swore he heard Peter's credit card whimpering in the corner.

Chapter 19

Thursday morning June 14th, 2012, 6:00 AM Still at that opulent fricking hotel

"I'm in the shower," Gus said.

Marcy called back, "Best get a move on, wheels up in an hour and 15 minutes."

Gus thought to himself, "I know, and thank God it is towards home and not somewhere else to get stuck."

The news played on the television when Gus got out of the shower.

".. damage from the rare early summer cyclone Sebastian" The TV blared.

"Why the hell did they name it after a butler?" Gus laughed to himself. Marcy overheard him somehow and laughed from the other room. God, he loved her laugh.

The TV continued,

"...damage is expected to be in the billions of pounds across England. We bring in geologist Dr. Roger Pilfrey from the University of London to discuss an unusual tremor that rumbled through central Scotland during the storm. Dr.

Pilfrey, an earthquake during a terrible storm? What did you think when it happened? I understand you were actually in the office and saw the reports of it live? Yes! It was quite exciting, but these happen more often than many think. Not that it is common, but it is not out of the norm. It is, however, a bit more rare or special to witness it here in our backyard. There are multiple examples of this happening in the Americas and the Caribbean, but quakes are not as common here and certainly storms like this are maybe once in a lifetime. Dr. Pilfrey... Please call me Roger... Oh quite... Roger. I understand there are also reports of a large landslide in the same area... related? Well, I would imagine so. I mean proximity and timing would seem to indicate so. However, more exciting are reports of the landslide unearthing a possible undiscovered archeological site. I am meeting a good friend and archeologist, Doctor Sebastian Blane, to investigate the area. Wait, the Archeologist has the name Sebastian also? I know it is quite the crazy coincidence. I mean, if true, this archaeological site was literally tailor made for him. We look forward, once the flood waters subside, and maybe the mud dries out a little, getting up there to see the effects. I look forward personally to watching my good friend Dr. Blane geek out if there indeed is, what some are reporting. Word is it is a previously unknown megalithic site which is exciting..."

Abruptly, Marcy turned off the TV and Gus notice her staring at him. "Wheels up in one hour... you ARE in a hurry, right?" His spell of fascination broken, he smiled at Marcy and got about to the business of buttoning his shirt.

"Peter!" Gus called. "Did you catch that on the television? The Dr. of Geology from London referred to here as England! And he is even smarter than me."

Chapter 20

Leuchars Airport. Scotland 7:00 AM

They met a private jet at Leuchars Airport, a small airport and former RAF facility dating back to the early 1900s. Money indeed has its privileges, and Peter demonstrably had both in spades.

On the plane, their pilot, a supremely confident individual named Nigel, was busy doing preflight checks. The flight crew made sure we were comfortable. Marcy and Peter had pastries and mimosas, and Gus had coffee. "Coffee with lots of cream and sweetener... the way God intended," Gus declared.

Peter opted for coffee later too, but since our flight path was going to take us over Ireland, he opted for the Irish version... "extra Irish." His second cup, he passed on the coffee all together and just had the Irish. Marcy thanked the crew for her mimosa and had a cheese Danish.

Fifteen minutes into the flight, Gus closed his eyes. Peter's voice faded into the sound of the jet engines.

Gus dreamed of the sea. He dreamed of a farm on the windy coast of the sea. A boy came to him crying, dressed in rags, with a terrible wound in his stomach. Blood poured from the wound, and he was speaking the same gibberish over and over, "Thig Sgriosadh, agus thig e air do shonsa..." The closer he got, the louder he shouted. Gus woke up as the plane passed a turbulent spot.

Marcy, seated next to him, grabbed his arm, "it's just turbulence," she whispered. Gus nodded. Despite his nervous blood pumping, her hand felt warm, and she really had a genuine and kind smile.

Sleep would not return soon, and honestly, he had no desire for it after encountering that freaky child. Therefore, he opted to find out what was playing on the television. "I mean, when in Rome." he thought.

He checked the CNN feed and saw the storm was still everyone's focus. And just like that, he reappeared. Dr. Pilfrey, slogging through the muddy turned soil with a new look. He shed his suit and scholarly appearance, transforming into an intrepid adventurer clad in coveralls and sturdy boots. Yep, and there was Dr. Sebastian Blane... "I guess being first and muddy was better than being warm, dry and last." Gus thought.

He watched them hike for a while, all while the hosts of the show constantly regurgitated the same words describing their journey.

Gus flipped around channels until he stumbled across a rebroadcast of the Boston Red Socks versus Marlins baseball game from the night before. He watched David Ortiz crush another home run as Boston won 10-2 to win the road series 2-1.

They landed at Raleigh Durham International at 12:45 in the afternoon, and Gus was home by 1:30 with his new laptop in tow. Peter called it his birthday present... like the last week was not enough.

Friday, Gus drove to his office in the RTP. Once he reached the campus, he proceeded past the security gate. With the low attendance that day, he had the chance to catch up on work. Chris swung by his office and chuckled at the disheveled Friday look Gus had. "Dude, you're back! How did it go?" Chris asked.

"Doing great. A bit tired but glad to be back. Thanks for covering for me. That was a crazy week." Gus said as Chris got an excited look on his face.

"I watched the stuff on the storm last night. It just blew up and smashed all of Great Britain," Chris said, and Gus almost snorted a laugh. "Those stones!" He continued, "Did you see the stones that they found after the storm? They were part of a really old Celtic circle, they think. But what was genuinely weird is that the stones were all laid down on their face like something had pushed them over. At least that's what they said. Water had washed out the dirt at the bottom of one stone, revealing Celtic carvings near what used to be the top. In the middle, below the Celtic stuff, there was another language. The anthropologist guy appeared on every channel, saying that it appeared to be Cuneiform... both on the SAME rock!"

Chris left his office, and Gus took a couple of minutes to check it out online. It really was crazy, but also extremely interesting. Another geologist discussed the stones' backs, apparent exposure to intense heat. The heat was so intense that it melted the stone's surface, and a force so strong that it etched the malleable stone.

People speculated about legends of an ancient cataclysm in the area, finding it odd that the stone circle was the center of the most catastrophic damage. Immediately after the event, researchers speculated that the weakened hillside above must have given way and buried the site with a landslide.

The news dubbed what happened there, the Fincastle Incident, after the area where the stone ring is located. The name stuck. "It is fitting," said the evening news anchor in summary when discussing the developments, "that the site is an area so rich in history and bound in superstition. Local oral tradition tells of a fearsome tyrant, his name lost to time, who faced the wrath of the gods in the region. Gods, who were swift in their justice."

The story featured an interview with one local. "The Gods of old did not mess about," said one Scott, interviewed in front of a small crowd. He even claimed the bastard king was probably an Irishman, and everyone present laughed and nodded.

Observations made during the subsequent month led to a revised comprehension of this and other events. First, the entire area for miles around centered on the stone ring had experienced some kind of catastrophe they believe between 1500 and 1000 BC. Second, the area of this ancient event was surprisingly close to his grandfather's estate. Third, Gus finally asked Marcy on a date, and she said yes.

Chapter 21

Thursday, June 28th, 2012, 5:02 PM Redwolf Solutions Headquarters, RTP, NC

Gus's iPhone rang at precisely 5:02 PM. The ringtone "Yakety Sax" let him know immediately it was Peter. Peter hated that ringtone, and that was what made it so funny to Gus. Peter despised Benny Hill, and that again just made it even better.

"Laoch Kier Ferguson!" boomed the voice through the phone. "What is this I hear about you distracting my assistant?"

Gus knew this was coming eventually and tonight was the night they had settled upon to meet up.

"She is very busy... No, seriously," as his voice changed to its normal tone. "It's about damn time. I seriously thought I was going to have to maroon you two on an island somewhere and force you guys to spend time together. The damn googly eyes were getting annoying."

"Was I that obvious?"

"Dude... your constants search for witty, sweet banter was almost enough to make me take a diabetes check. I seriously thought I was going to have to come up with a reason you two needed to work together on something." Peter laughed. "She is totally into you too, with the 'so what are you and Gus up to this week?' and so forth. Just tell me you are taking her someplace nice and, for Christ's sake, please tell me you are not wearing a blue oxford shirt and tie... she fucking hates those."

Gus reactively looked down at his blue oxford shirt and thought, "oh shit," and glanced out and down the hall as Peter tried to blend in with the Ficus tree in the hall's corner. Gus hung up the phone and called out, "Peter, you are an asshole!"

"You know it and you love it," he said as he strode down the hall and into his office.

"I just wanted to stop in and wish you well. Marcy is a catch and you two could be perfect together... Oh, and she is really into clown cosplay... like REALLY dirty, nasty sexy clowns." Peter said, as he hugged his lifelong friend. "Are you good? Need any pointers?"

"Honestly, I think I'm good. All I really have to do is, not be you.".

"Ouch!" Peter said with a mock hurt look that spread into that same smile Peter had given him after some bully named Walter had tried to beat up Gus after school in 3rd grade.

Walter was a genetically enhanced fourth grader, twice the size of every kid in the school and was a terror on the playground as well as walks home after school. In the future, Walter would play offensive tackle at Georgia, but that day after school was on his schedule as, "kick the shit out of Gus day," and Walter was a slave to his appointment book.

He apparently had already checked the box beside this appointment. Effortlessly, he pulled Gus's backpack off and flipped it over his shoulder into the bushes like discarded wings from a fly. Gus stood there deflated with the sense of inevitability to the coming pain and embarrassment.

He knew that all Walter really wanted was Gus to cry. He seemed to get his jollies from that, a trait that would serve him well in the South Eastern Conference in football. The crowd of witnesses had already gathered as Walter shoved his shoulders and Gus skipped across the rocky dirt on the backside of his Tough Skins jeans.

Gus bounced back up off the ground, because even in the face of a complete failure... he was a gamer. Walter seemed to contemplate the method of extracting the tears. Would it be the classic head butt? His patented super move, or the dreaded atomic wedgie? The idea of the wedgie unveiling his Power Ranger underwear, which his mom had prepared for him that morning, caused Gus to nearly panic.

He weighed his chances if he tried to flee in a panic, but Walter was also faster... another trait the coaches would drool over. As Mongo stepped forward, apparently settled on option one, the head butt, Gus almost relaxed mentally. This time, when Walter grabbed his shoulders, he reared back like a professional wrestler on Saturday at noon and brought down the hammer. There was no forethought as Gus shrugged his shoulders. The act lowered him an inch or two; he slid his head forward as his body tensed, preparing for the inevitable impact. The tensing of his legs raised him back up those same one to two inches as the impact landed, sending a burning sensation through Gus's entire head, but it differed from normal.

A sickening crunch announced a tidal change in the world that day as the 54-pound Gus's head had moved forward just enough to slip past the mallet shaped forehead, crushing the giant's nose and removing all four of his front teeth.

Dazed and still with a head full of bees, Gus stood there as Walter dropped to his knees, his mouth and nose a horror, and cried for his mommy. Peter grabbed

Gus's shoulders, spun to look him in the face, and there it was, that same smile he was looking at right now.

Chapter 22

Friday, June 29th, 2012, 5:02 PM 1503 Craig Street, Raleigh, NC

The date differed from anything either of them had ever experienced. Gus was just Gus and Marcy was just Marcy. The expected nerves that Gus prepared for never emerged. Also absent, was Gus's widely noticed and famous inability to speak in the presence of a beautiful woman.

They discussed Marcy's childhood in England and laughed about how her MBA had led her to the glamorous life as Peter's assistant. That she truly liked Peter didn't surprise him, although she felt a touch of sadness for him. She felt he was a man of great potential, a potential he might live up to someday, but now contented with the work he did, even though he was capable of so much more.

The topic changed to Gus and how he too was from the islands, and Gus admitted to his dual citizenship as they laughed. This led to a conversation about the birthday trip. It prompted Gus to discuss the observations he made of the gardeners outside his grandfather's house and the related knowledge from his military days. In addition, they discussed the peculiar conversation he had with his grandfather and analyzed the interpretations of his statements. The topic again drifted to their arrival at Gus's grandfather's estate. It was something that they had both caught, individually, as strange that day.

Daniel somehow knew Peter without an introduction. Gus shared with Marcy about the icy stare from his grandfather towards Daniel after he mentioned Peter's name. She had caught it too. Something was there, and her agreement allowed Gus to feel emboldened to pursue it later with his grandfather.

They had met Peter's parents in Raleigh during a scholarship event, which was organized in his dad's honor? The event surprised him because he knew nothing about it, and neither his grandparents nor Deb and Mack had invited him.

The date ended after they had talked late into the evening. Hours had flown by and despite it being his first proper date with her, he felt like he had known her much longer. Longer even that the time since his first meeting her years ago. At one level, the step from friend to something else terrified him, because in doing so, he was taking a chance. Once you take that step or even try to, there is no going back. You are taking the real chance of losing something and wagering it for the possibility of something amazingly better. In his experience, the failure of the relationship step meant awkward handshakes and greetings in the future.

They left the coffee shop where they had ended up after a walk around downtown, hours before. They were the last ones in the shop. The workers had finished the cleanup of the surrounding store, with both oblivious to their toils. Their clue to the exasperation of the workers staring at them was the sudden darkness as the lights turned off in the back kitchen area. Gus fished in his wallet and left a 20-dollar bill on the only dirty table left, and they exited the shop.

When they got back to Marcy's place, she kissed Gus on each cheek, flushed slightly, "goodnight handsome."

Gus stood there and watched her walk the short cement path to her small two-story house and climb the five stairs to her door. She spun around and smiled at him, and nodded. He smiled at her, and he said, "Good night, sweet lady!"

Neither of them slept that night as their minds rushed too fast to allow sleep to gain purchase.

Chapter 23

The two were inseparable from that day forward, and over the next several years, they would often go on drives together and just talk as they drove around the area. There was rarely a defined destination. The drives were their way to decompress or bitch about something that they just wanted heard. Most of the time, neither needed a solution. The solution was getting the frustration off their chests. And like the first date, Thursday nights were their designated nights.

One Thursday night in early September 2014, work was keeping him a little late. Marcy waited for him at his house in the living room. When Gus got there, he said, "Give me five minutes... I need a quick shower."

When he was done, he came from the back bedroom carrying his socks and shoes. Marcy looked at him. "I'm just going to say it,"

"Okay"

"Why do you still sleep in the little bedroom in the back?"

"Well... I don't know... The main bedroom is my mom's room, I guess." He said weakly as his voiced rose at the end, almost sounding like a question.

"I like this house a lot more than my house," Marcy said, "and if this relationship is going in the direction that I hope... We need to fix that... I know you loved her, but I am not sleeping in that single bed in your room with you, and we won't have that old NFL football helmet bedspread, either."

Gus breathed out almost like a weight had dropped off his back. "You busy this weekend?".

"Nope!"

"Good, I think it is time for me to move to the big boy room. Wanna help me clean it out?"

"Do I get to wear some coveralls with my name on a patch?" she said, patting herself on the left side of her chest.

Following the date with Marcy, he stretched out on his mother's bed for the last time alone that night. In his mind, he visualized her being there and spoke to her, just as he had done countless times since her passing.

While describing Marcy, he could picture her eyes filling with tears of joy. He listened to her silence, but in his head, he could hear her voice, filled with joy, because he knew she would always want the best for him. He apologized for what they were getting ready to do to her room and she laughed, "It's about time!"

For the first time since she died, over a decade before, he fell asleep in her bed. In contrast to the great night of reminiscing, Gus experienced dreams filled with vivid images of that little boy he had seen in his dreams on the plane. The sickly boy yelled at him, "Thig Sgriosadh, agus thig e air do shonsa", but he felt he somehow understood what the words meant, "Destruction comes, and he comes for you!" He looked at the boy standing before him. A harsh landscape stretched before him, rocky ground dotted with patches of green grass, and a turbulent sea with dark gray waves crashing behind him. The child's eyes flickered with an unsettling energy, and a lack of oxygen tinged his lips with a purple hue. The child's rain-soaked red hair blew to the left as a powerful gust of wind passed by, while he noticed the child's eyes actually stared through him, not at him.

When he looked back over his shoulder, he noticed a tired older woman standing forty feet away in front of a hut made of wood and stone, topped with a dense thatched roof. When she locked eyes with the child, time seemed to freeze around them. Gus smelled a pungent odor and a hint of ozone, while glancing between the boy and the old woman, as a mysteriously deep voice emerged from the boy. It said, "Your husband is with Mags, the whore... She's young and attractive, while you're just an old, deflated bag. The only way to inflict the same pain on him is by snatching his children away, leaving him as alone as he's left you. You wore out unworthy husk."

It felt like the world was flashing between stormy darkness and radiant sunlight, until finally settling on a clear day. The sickly-looking boy, now holding hands with an older man, slowly approached the old woman. The old man's walk was unusual; a stiff, hinged gait, as if his hips were fused to his pelvis. The man and the older woman were engaged in an argument. The old woman stared at the man, "If you want to find him, best do it before I do!" and tears flowed as she cried and went back inside her hut.

Gus watched as the man looked ready to say something and instead rolled his eyes sarcastically and mumbled something. The man and the boy turned to go back in the direction they had come. As they walked away, the boy looked over his shoulder as if studying the area where Gus stood, with a look of confused interest.

Gus woke up with a start. He walked to the kitchen and poured water from an old glass orange juice jug that had been in the fridge for ice water since before he could remember. He closed the door and saw his autobiography on the door and flicked the old page before he took a deep draught from the glass. In his mind he heard his mom's words as she called the big drinks of water he did "Ent draughts", ever since she had read the Tolkien series to him when he was younger.

The memories made him smile and washed away the nightmares sting. However, the rest of the night would be tumultuous with dreams.

Chapter 24

Saturday, September 8, 2014, 6243 Mourning Dove Rd. Raleigh, NC

Saturday morning, after a quick drive around looking for local yard sales and breakfast at the Farmer's Market Restaurant, Gus and Marcy set to work with liquor boxes from the ABC store and a large box of contractor trash bags from the hardware store.

There was little space left in Gus's mom's walk-in closet. Inside was a mixture of family treasures and family trash. It was not untidy. It was more like no one needed Jane Fonda workout VHS tapes anymore, as possibly the only working VHS player within 10 miles was in a box directly below the workout tapes. The box was marked, "Still Works!!!" in his mother's script.

Eight contractor bags later, with three to be donated and five with trash, it was 4:30PM. They had filled twelve of the 15 boxes from the ABC store and labeled them. They also discovered a thousand pictures and some rolls of 35mm film that were undeveloped. Gus saved two full boxes of books his father used in college at State, with each one highly underlined and marked with sticky-note bookmarks on important areas.

The phone rang, and of course, it was Peter. "Hey guys! You want to come over and watch a game or a movie or something? I'll buy the pizza!" He offered.

"Sorry Peter," Gus said into the phone, which he had switched to speaker. "We are up to our elbows in my mom's stuff. It's time to reclaim her room finally."

"Oh shit, Gus, you should have told me. I would have been glad to help."

"I know, just so much stuff I had to go through, ya know. Not sure another pair of hands would have helped much. I could, though, use your truck next week to get stuff to the dump and to the donation center."

"Absolutely no problem, man." Peter responded. "How about this? I will grab some pizza and stuff from Amedeo's and bring it by?" Peter offered.

Marcy shrugged and nodded. "Sounds great man," Gus said.

"Anything special you guys want?"

"I would love a salad with grilled chicken," Marcy said. "With extra blue cheese dressing."

"Done!" Peter replied. "I'll be there by seven. Later!" Peter finished and hung up the phone.

The condition of his mom's room was now a complete disaster compared to how it looked initially. Gus used hand signals to call a timeout. "What do you say we take a break, drink some water and chill out for a few minutes?" Marcy nodded her agreement.

They both went to the kitchen and washed their hands in the sink. Gus grabbed two cups and the glass water jug from the refrigerator. Marcy noticed the autobiography on the fridge and carefully read it as Gus closed his eyes.

She didn't do the "Oh that is the cutest thing ever" or the long "Awwwwwwwwww", she just read it. When she was done. She took the glasses from Gus's hands and put them on the counter, and she took the jug of water and did the same. She wrapped her arms around him and just hugged him for an extra-long moment and kissed him on the cheek. When complete, she handed him the jug and took the glasses herself to the living room.

They flipped on the TV; the weather was on, on the local station. They were discussing the hurricane season and a tropical wave that showed a 60% chance of development in the Atlantic. The area of development was not one that usually affected the eastern seaboard, being almost 25 degrees north, but it was still worthy of mention.

The discussion of hurricane season led to follow-ups of other major storms over the years, including Super Storm Sebastian, that had caused 22 billion dollars of damage in Europe several years before.

That follow-up sparked Gus to search on his phone for whatever happened after they flew back. Details were sparse on most major news sites, but he found YouTube videos from Dr. Pilfrey and Blane and cast them to the TV.

The first video focused on the stones from the circle. It described their makeup and their size before getting into their splayed orientation. It moved on to possible and improbable theories of how they became laid flat and described as being arranged like "petals of a daisy".

They displayed drone footage of the mostly excavated stones from above. One overly nerdy guest on the video made a guess at the Newton force that would have been required to topple the stones. The guest also mentioned that the same force had thrown all the stones from their foundations and slid them up to three meters away.

In a recently uploaded video titled "Exciting Discoveries at the Fincastle Incident's Circle," The video showed Dr. Blane standing on a platform with tears in his eyes. Behind him, a group of young adults were hugging, shaking hands, and giving high fives. "Ladies and gentlemen, it is an extraordinary day at the site. Frankly, it is beyond my comprehension." Dr. Blane paused for a moment, holding his hand up, overcome with emotion as a male voice off camera yelled, "We love you, Sebastian!"

Dr. Blane looked up and nodded to a person off camera and composed himself. "We can edit this later... The site here has been unbelievable, as we talked of in previous videos. The megalithic stones themselves will remain a topic of discussion for eternity. Whatever leveled them had terrific force and heat. Heat enough to liquefy some of the stone. Celtic designs were present on the other side of multiple stones, and below them, there was cuneiform style writing, etched at a similar time... within 200 years, at least. The cuneiform translates to be a prayer of apology, hinting at some action that would desecrate the circle. Now to today, one of my brilliant students, Thomas... Thomas, where are you? Thomas, yes... come here, boy. This lad in his brilliance, Thomas Chambers, suggested what I guess should have seemed more obvious than it was. He suggested we use metal detectors and other ground penetrating devices to pinpoint hot-zone locations with the best chance of finding artifacts. Our focus was on mapping the underground structure of the site, but Thomas introduced a rational thought we had all overlooked." Sebastian said as he took a deep, dramatic breath.

"Today," he continued, "in the third hot spot we worked, we found an item that boggles the mind. We found a perfectly preserved sword. More importantly, this sword also is not a design found anywhere for thousands of miles." Dr. Blane continued, as he led the camera to a sturdy plastic table under a portable shelter. On a white sheet sat a perfect and even shiny, golden metal short sword. "Isn't she beautiful? It somehow has no corrosion at all. The only thing it possibly is missing would be any material such as leather, but we see no real incompleteness that would require it. It is an anomaly in equal to opening the Great Pyramid of Giza and finding an ancient working ice cream machine. We don't know, one, how this got here, two, where it came from and three, its composition; as it appears to be gold, but its hardness is fantastic, and its edge is immensely sharp and unblemished. We frankly would have classified it as a funeral gift, but we cannot imagine anyone placing it here when the catastrophic event happened. It is being sent to the lab for future testing. The team decided it should have a name, and they picked a name for it. They insisted upon calling it the Blane Blade, and I am so honored. In the next part of the video, we will show you the unearthing of this wonderful blade after the tech boys do their magic. I am off with the lads to the pub and, as you see, before we made this video, we contacted the authorities to have the entire site, which now makes up just less than 650 hectares cordoned off by security forces. We have worked and will work closely with our friend from the Council for British Archeology and will keep you up to date with other findings from this amazing... amazing site."

They went back and watched the older videos too, but nothing was as cool as the one with the sword.

Peter arrived right at seven with the pizza, salad, and beer, and they played the videos for him, leaving him amazed as well. While they were watching for the second time, Gus shared the video with his boss Chris, who replied five minutes later with, "Dude!!!".

"How close was that place to where we met your family?" Peter asked as he shoved the meatball and mushroom pizza towards his mouth.

"Not far," as Gus pulled up the mapping feature of his phone and showed it to him. "It looks like about forty miles plus or minus?"

Peter hung out at the house as they discussed college football, and remember they were missing the State game. They began streaming the game against Presbyterian to the TV at halftime.

While watching the game, they discussed the weather and, eventually, the topic of Marcy. They talked about how she had moved out of her home she shared with several roommates a few hours ago, to "Live in Sin" as Peter had said while he clutched his imaginary pearls. No one in the room doubted the trajectory Gus and Marcy were on, and Peter was ecstatic for them both.

Chapter 25

During the four-year anniversary cookout of their co-habitation, Marcy, Gus, and Peter gathered to watch another NC State football game in the redecorated house. The last four years had been great for the couple.

Tonight, they had cooked steaks on the grill and turned on the football game. Marcy still was not much of a football fan, as she had grown up with much more elegant sports... in her opinion.

"Anyone need a drink?" Marcy asked as she got up off the couch.

"I'll take another beer, Peter said, "Oh, and could you check the steaks and make sure nothing is burning?" he asked.

"On it," Marcy replied, as she stepped out through the kitchen door to the back porch.

As the door closed to the porch, Peter snapped his head at Gus. "Dude, what is up with you?"

"What?" Gus asked.

"Are you ever going to ask this poor lady the question?"

"Has she said something to you?" Gus asked in a minor panic.

"No, but does she need to?" Peter said. "Is that your measure? You guys have been living together for four freaking years now!"

Gus paused and blinked his eyes hard at the incredulity of Peter's statement. The sound of the back door opening again broke the silence as Marcy was coming back in the door.

"Hey Marcy," Peter said, "Did you flip them?"

"Did you ask me to flip the steaks?" came the sarcastic response.

"Please? If you would? My watch just went off. That is why I was asking." Peter said sweetly.

Both Peter and Gus heard the door open and close again.

"Sorry, did you just chastise me for my imaginary lack of the ability to commit?" Gus asked.

"Holy shit," Peter said, "Did I?"

"I mean," Gus said, "you started dating a woman, excused yourself to the restroom, and ended things with her before you even wiped your ass."

"Ok... all of that is true." Peter said, "but you are better than me. That's right, big boy, talk your way out of that before Marcy comes back in."

"Dammit," Gus said. "How about I will take it under advisement?"

"Good. I'm not getting any younger and I will need to look good in those pictures on your wall for the next 60 years."

Marcy came back in the door, grabbed the beer for Peter, and walked back into the living room. She paused in the doorway, "What? Is there something up?"

"Um, no," said Gus with a look of innocence.

"Okay," Marcy said, "because the room smells like estrogen... you guys sure you are, ok?

An hour later, they had finished their steaks and scalloped potatoes. The state game was a blowout. The Pack was crushing Georgia State.

Peter yawned. "Guys, I am whipped."

Peter was already getting up to leave when his phone rang. "Oh, look... it's our boss!" as he punched the green button on his phone.

"Hello Ma... Wait, wait what?!? Slow down," the alarm clear in his voice, and Gus and Marcy looked on with trepidation. "Mom! MOM!! Put him on the phone." He cupped his hand over the phone. "My dad. Something happened at a traffic stop, they are saying..." he lifted his hand off the phone. "Yes, Captain Johnson... I heard her say... What the ever-loving fuck!" Peter exclaimed as he sat down to the ground, missing the sofa as water and madness pooled in his eyes.

Suddenly, a business-like mask fell over Peter's face, which alarmed both Marcy and Gus. They watched him as his eyes hardened and listened to the, "Wawa wawawa wa wawa" sounds that were carried across the room.

The sound reminded Gus of a Peanuts cartoon special when the adults were talking. A realization he chastised himself silently for, for even letting it creep into his mind at a time like this. "I'll be there in 15 minutes," Peter punched the hang-up button like he was trying to crack the screen.

"Holy shit... my dad is on the way to WakeMed Hospital. The police said he resisted during a traffic stop, and the cop shot him in self-defense... I should go,"

"I'm driving you," Gus replied.

"I'm coming too," said Marcy as she grabbed her coat.

Chapter 26

When they arrived at WakeMed Hospital in northern Raleigh, Gus dropped Peter and Marcy at the emergency room door and went to find a parking spot. Not finding anything, he parked the four-wheel-drive pickup on a grassy median, similar to the other vehicles he saw at the busy hospital that night. He rushed inside and saw Marcy standing with her hand on Peter's back; Peter was doubled over, hands on his knees.

Standing there, the doctor, dressed in a surgical gown and hat, had a comforting hand on Peter's back as well. Several feet away, Peter's mother, Deb, sat in a chair, her head buried in her hands. Sitting next to her was a State Highway Patrolman, his uniform neatly pressed and badge reflecting the emergency rooms lighting. Gus went to Peter first. As he arrived, Peter turned to Gus with stricken eyes and collapsed onto Gus's shoulder, unable to utter a meaningful syllable. The doctor stood behind him for an awkward minute, and Marcy turned and thanked him with a grace, even in this terrible time; charmingly releasing the surgeon, performing the worst part of his job to leave.

When Peter could, he quietly told Gus what the doctor had said: "He was shot in the left side of his head and is brain dead. They want me to... to get my mother to... to okay them to remove life support. They said he is an organ donor." Over Peter's shoulder, he could see the older patrolman stand up from the seat beside Deb. He seemed to wait for Peter. Gus gave him the "one minute" sign, and the officer nodded his understanding.

After several minutes, the officer, Peter, Gus, Marcy, and Peter's mother gathered in a borrowed consultation room. On their way to the small conference room, they spotted a news van driving past the windows facing the parking area. Also, they observed the Raleigh police and Sherriff deputies taking their positions near the entry.

Around a smaller wooden table, they sat in a small, sparsely appointed room designed for a maximum of four people. They had squeezed a fifth chair into the room. The State Patrol officer had the last name Dempsey on the left side of his gray uniformed chest, emblazoned on a copper toned metal plate. "Hello, I'm Lieutenant Colonel Michael Dempsey with the North Carolina State Highway Patrol." he said as he handed out business cards to all present.

Officer Dempsey was a kind faced black man, who would make most rooms seem small. He stood about six foot four and had a well put together appearance, even though his graying hair would suggest he was in his fifties. The smile lines around his eyes and mouth appeared out of place as he performed the grim task assigned to him today.

"I am here for you all in this time of need. I want you to ask me anything. My knowledge is very limited, but I'll try my best to explain what I know. This explanation will only include the information I have confirmed so far. Everything we will discuss; we are still working to corroborate. I will refrain from discussing some things for legal reasons. Please understand that I don't intend to be guarded when I do that. I simply do not want to say something that I will have to correct with you later. Everything I must tell you is still under investigation, and I request you to keep confidential and avoid sharing it with the media. You might have observed them circling around like crows. Expect to be asked questions as you leave the hospital and possibly before you reach your home. If you want, I can work with the local police to ensure they stay away from your property and ideally stay on the other side of the road. We cannot stop you from discussing anything, but we ask..."

Officer Dempsey paused as three sharp knocks broke through the conversation. Gus looked at Marcy with the questioning look, only to have her give him a confident wink.

Officer Dempsey opened the door, and a sixth person squeezed into the room. "Hi," said the new person who everyone minus the officer recognized. "I'm Philip Hooper, legal counsel for... well, frankly, for everyone in this room. I work for Deb as my firm provides the corporate counsel for Redwolf Solutions, and I am the personal legal advisor to... everyone else here," the lawyer concluded, while waving his hands toward his tribe in the room.

"I've been providing general guidance and offering support where needed," the officer said, "respecting privacy and asking the same questions I would ask of you. Please allow us the opportunity to gather all the pertinent facts to the best of our ability before addressing the media. If they need privacy at the home, or getting to their cars here today, we can help." The officer said as Philip nodded with a professionally content look.

The trooper took a deep breath, "So, here is what we know currently. While driving westbound on Spring Forest Road, the policeman stopped Maxwell Alexander Smith for an unknown moving violation. The stop happened in Raleigh, on the 2800 block, just short of Departure Drive. At 19:28, the officer radioed in to report that he had pulled over Mr. Smith's car. After collecting the driver's identification and registration, the officer retreated to his car to input the information into the computer.

At approximately 19:33, the dispatcher heard what sounded like the second part of a discussion on the radio, and the officer did not seem to respond directly to her. The officer appeared to think Mr. Smith's car was flagged as stolen on his system. The dispatcher informed Trooper Stanley Corr that the car was not stolen, but he didn't acknowledge receiving the message.

Because of a sharp drop in the road at that location, it's possible the signal was weak, or the officer heard crosstalk from a neighboring area, although both are unlikely. The officer exited his vehicle and approached Mr. Smith's car, while the dispatcher coordinated backup to the scene for better communication with Officer Corr. Before the backup arrived, the officer reported seeing a gun," Officer Dempsey said as Peter interrupted.

"That is complete bullshit!" Peter said as Philip put his hand on his arm and signaled the officer to move forward, while he took notes on a legal pad.

The officer continued, "...and shots were heard over the trooper's open microphone, which nearby residents reported to 911 shortly thereafter. The officer was wearing a body cam; however, that footage has yet to be reviewed. Internal Affairs has opened a standard investigation, and Officer Corr has had his gun taken as evidence. Following a psychological evaluation and a mandatory one-week leave, he will be assigned to desk duty, pending the investigation's results. Officer Corr confirmed discharging his weapon three times in self-defense, missing his target twice, with one shot that unfortunately, mortally wounded Mr. Smith. That is all we know currently. I am so sorry for your loss," Officer Dempsey concluded.

The legal counsel Philip asked the only questions, "You said in self-defense, was the officer fired upon? Was there a second firearm recovered at the scene? Can we get a gunshot residue test run on the victim, Mr. Smith's hands?" asked the lawyer in rapid fire, and the officer nodded after an almost unpronounced wince when Mr. Smith referred to Mack as the victim. "Those have been requested, and I will get you your answers as soon as I have them," promised Officer Dempsey.

Chapter 27

Sunday, September 9th, 2018, 1:13 AM 6243 Mourning Dove Rd. Raleigh, NC

The night after Mack's death, Marcy woke Gus up repeatedly as he thrashed, jerked, and whimpered in his sleep. Whenever he woke up, he would insist that his dreams were hazy or forgotten, but he was hiding the truth from her.

The haunting presence of the little boy lingered in his memories, refusing to fade away. In his dream, the boy felt a sense of deep satisfaction as his father gazed down at his mother's broken body on the rocky shoreline beneath the cliff, where she had leapt. With each wave, the tide swept over the rocks, washing away the blood and eventually causing her body to vanish in a frothy surge. It was the dream before this one, which had explained her fatal leap.

In the dream before, the boy's mother had looked into the child's eyes with an adoring sadness. He could feel that she wanted to love him. He could also feel somehow that she lacked the capacity. She tried to see and feel the emotion that she had wished away, because she missed it. It was his mother, so the boy let her really see him. As she looked at him, he maintained eye contact. Unlike his sister, he could keep her from seeing his true nature. He didn't know how he knew he could keep her out if he wanted, or why it worked that way with her. It just did.

The boy smiled as the terror of realization crossed his mother's face. She recoiled onto her back from her squatted position, and crab walked across the dirt floor to get away from him. "What's the matter mommy, don't you love me?" he said. She heard the innocent child's voice through her ears and the darker, menacing voice he projected into her mind, synchronized with it.

She screamed and ran past his father, who was walking in the same doorway. The man looked at the boy quizzically, and back at his wife as she ran down the hill towards the ocean. He pivoted to follow her in a limping gate, calling to her back, using the name Srene.

When the older man caught up with her, the boy had followed him and witnessed as Gus did; when Srene looked back at her husband, and her focus shifted beyond her husband to her son. Gus stood there, a ghost in the middle of the scene as it played out for him. He looked at the woman, standing at the crag of an enormous drop to the loud surf below as her husband pleaded to her with tears flowing down his cheeks.

When Gus blinked, his perspective changed. Suddenly, he perceived her as though he were in the same place as the strange boy. In an instant, his vision shifted, and he beheld her as a vulnerable young teen, trembling in fear. Subsequently, he observed her assuming the role of a mother, clutching a succession of deceased children as she aged, a second boy and later a third, who was slightly older. Abruptly, Gus saw her resolve again as the terrified mother at the top of the cliff.

She glanced once more towards the man and the boy in succession. A look of resignation spread across her face as she turned towards the cliff. The man roared, "No, no, no, no, NO!" She leaned towards the abyss, slipping from the world and was gone. The boy's back arched in ecstasy as he inhaled the air as if

195

it carried something sweet on the wind. For a moment, a pinkish hue came to his normally pale blue skin.

Chapter 28

Sunday, September 9th, 2018, 3:07 AM 6243 Mourning Dove Rd. Raleigh, NC

At 3:07 AM, Gus woke up with a start. Marcy reached over and stroked his back, awakening just enough to notice his distress, and attempted to calm him with her touch. Gus shook his head to clear the dream and swung his feet to the side of the bed. It still felt weird when he woke up in his mother's room. Although, since Marcy had moved in, it had lost a little of its strangeness. He stood up and walked to the kitchen for some water.

He stood in the kitchen, contemplating what had happened just a few hours before to Peter and Deb, and hoped they could find some good sleep even if he couldn't. It wasn't the first time he had a troublesome night sleeping. He remembered a book about dreams he had read in college as a grin grew across his face. "What a complete pile of shit that was," and laughed quietly.

As the water in his coffee cup dwindled, he prepared himself for try number 27 at getting a good night's sleep, reading the side of the old cup gifted to him by PFC Jasper Knox on his birthday in basic training. It read:

"We don't rise to the level of our expectations; we fall to the level of our training."–Archilochus

The image played through his mind of the man that yelled that quote at least once a day during Basic Training. "Oh, bite me Archilochus and you too Drill Sergeant Bigham!" He obeyed the sergeant, as if it were an ancient echo of a command. He crept quietly to his room and slid on his shorts and a gray hoodie over his t-shirt. He retrieved his running shoes and quietly put them on. When he was ready, he walked to Marcy's side of the bed and gently shook her shoulder. "Hey, I'm going for a run. I'll be back soon, and we can go get some breakfast."

She stirred just enough that her wild hair emerged from the pile of pillows and comforter. "Okay, go be stupid while I sleep, dear."

He kissed her on the cheek and quietly left the house, pushed his ear pods in each ear and stretched in his old military routine while Rush's Tom Sawyer got his blood moving. It was a still and sticky 67 degrees on this foggy Friday morning. He pulled out his phone and dropped an email to his boss, Chris, while he stretched his legs.

"Hey Chris, sorry for the late notice; I'm taking a personal day on Monday at least. When you awaken this morning, you are going to find out on the news that our CEO's husband, Mack, was killed by a policeman last night during a traffic stop. I spent time with the family, since they are family to me. I will make sure all of my stuff has coverage, but I was expecting a slow day on Monday. Thanks! Gus."

Gus clicked send and heard the whoosh of the message sending. He let the next song from his mother's playlist, R.E.M.'s Stand, take him as he bounced a little in place. He turned and started down the road to his five-mile route, while starting the timer on his dad's old diver styled watch.

Despite not getting enough sleep, the run seemed to go by more effortlessly than on other days. The third, long hill that some days made him want to stop and do pushups to cover for its grind, flew past. His complicated thoughts prevented him from noticing his exertion. As he rounded the last corner that led the half mile towards his house, he felt so good that he almost took a diversion for an extra mile before shaking the idea out of his head.

As he reached the "Left Turn Only" sign that he used as a finish line, he stopped the timer on his watch. He had beaten his best time by nearly one and a half minutes. "Wow," he thought as he checked his watch, while slowly cutting through the wooded grass area at the side of his property.

He looked up and saw a North Carolina Highway Patrol cruiser parked on the road in front of his house and popped out his earbuds. He could hear the cruiser ticking as the heat was dissipating from the engine.

Gus knew, as it was still dark, the poor appearance it would be, if he just said, "Hello!" from his concealed, dark location. So he slid back out towards the road a little. He watched the trooper backlit by the motion light over the garage as he approached the house, and as he fiddled with something in his hand.

As the trooper reached the front of his home, the porch motion light turned on, as the garage light had moments before, alerting Gus to the officer's location. The once shadowy outline that walked in front of the lit driveway turned diagonally across his grass and became lit from the front.

"Dick bag!" thought Gus, "Who just walks across someone's grass?"

That thought had tied up his thoughts for just a moment, before it moved on to the object in the officer's hand. He looked at his hands just as the cop slid the clip back into the pistol he was carrying in his right hand.

When Gus saw that, an alarm sounded in his head, and his neck tingled like the days in Iraq during the Gulf War when his superiors ordered his men into an unsecure location. Gus didn't hesitate. He didn't even think as he borrowed the shade of a tree and approached the house, closing the distance to the threat in a squat run. The officer started up the front stairs and racked the slide on his pistol, loading a round into the chamber.

The trooper calmly, like it was just another day, pressed the glowing blue light on his doorbell camera. Gus knew this guaranteed he was now on video from two angles. One from the camera in plain view under the corner of the porch area and from the camera built into the doorbell itself.

He heard the doorbell ring; he heard the muffled shuffle of Marcy's feet as Gus closed the distance to the front door, behind the cover of the ancient oak. This tree was the only tree in the yard that survived the tornado so long ago. It was near the front stairs. As he heard the bolt lock move, the officer raised his gun, and Gus ran out of strategic moves. With pure adrenalin, he just reacted, speed and instinct.

He Grabbed the banister and pulled hard to aid his dive towards the trooper. Aided by the rush of adrenalin, he exploded forward from the shadows and threw himself like a projectile. As he collided with the officer, Gus used his right hand to control the hand with the pistol, pushing it up, which continued its rising motion, and knocked the officer to the side just as the door cracked open.

The deafening gun report from the trooper's gun was like a cannon in the quiet morning. Gus drove the off-balance officer into the brick wall edifice to the left of the door, hitting it hard and feeling as much as hearing a satisfying, yet sickening, crunch as the officer's face planted into the wall and twisted. A second shot ripped the wooden porch between both of their feet as the gun dropped from the officer's now limp hand.

Gus, now straddling the gunman, pulled his hand back with the murderous intent to "absolutely pound this motherfucker", however, he noticed the blank stare in his eye and the odd angle and twist of his neck and stayed his fist.

He let go of the officer's tie and recoiled as his mind immediately switched to Marcy. He jumped up and saw her as she peeked out of the door with a stunned look on her face. The first 9mm shot had buried itself in the heavy oak door about four inches above where her head would have been.

Moments later, after embracing Marcy, Gus brought out his phone and, shaking with adrenalin, dialed 9 1 1. For a moment, questioned this decision as the operator picked up. He calmed himself.

"We need help. A person dressed as a State Patrolman just tried to kill my girlfriend. I stopped him, but I think I killed him... yeah, I definitely killed him."

Gus said as he looked at the body on his porch. Light from the porch glinted off a metallic nameplate on his chest that read, "Corr."

Chapter 29

4:28 AM

The first cruiser arrived, sliding to a stop near the State Trooper's car. It was a Wake County Sheriff's deputy, running with just his lights on. Marcy and Gus stood together on the porch, carefully avoiding the trooper's body and the gun lying on the ground, just out of reach of the corpse. As the deputy waited, the sound of a siren grew louder and another car pulled up, its lights illuminating the scene. As the commotion grew, lights turned on in the neighbor's houses one by one. It's funny, Gus thought. Not 15 minutes ago, two gunshots had echoed into the night like a cannon, and no one stirred. But if even one siren chirps, people immediately jump out of bed to capture their own reactions on social media. The second vehicle to arrive was a Raleigh police officer. The officer exited his blue and silver car, shook hands with the deputy, and the two cautiously approached the house. Gus and Marcy waited on the porch, being careful to both show their hands and to remain completely in the view of their camera.

The first officer to speak was the Raleigh police officer. He asked, "Can you show me your hands and lift your shirt and show me your waistline?" Gus and Marcy complied, and the officer visually relaxed. Gus spoke to the officers and explained the broad strokes of what he witnessed, as other officers, who now filled the street, listened and took notes. Several others cordoned off the area, as they had called for a forensic team.

From their porches, the neighbors watched the drama unfold. The media marked the third group to reach the scene. The police established a line to ensure everyone stayed back. Under bright lights, beyond the police tape, the neighborhood expert gave a witness statement to the first television reporters on the scene, as a man in casual clothes approached Gus and Marcy near the front porch.

"Hello, I am Officer Norman Bradbury. Do you mind if we go inside and discuss what happened this morning and get out of these good people's way?"

"Absolutely," Gus said, as he led them through the garage, past the kitchen, and to the dining room table. Taking their seats, memories flooded back for Gus as he remembered his mom selecting that table months after his father's death in the tornado.

"Hello, as I stated outside, I am Officer Bradbury, this is my assistant, Officer Thomas Parker, and we are here to take your detailed statement. This is not an arrest or anything and you are free at any time to stop this conversation. I want to disclose upfront. While I wasn't close with officer Corr, I recognize him from previous encounters. I don't know about his marital status or if he has children. I noticed you have one of those fancy video doorbells. Do you know if it captured this encounter?" he asked.

"My laptop is right over there on the coffee table; we can look together if you would like." Marcy said.

Gus nodded and spoke up. "But first, our lawyer Philip Hooper should be here any minute, and rather than have to do this all over again, can we wait for him?" Both officers gave a brisk nod as they placed their hats on the kitchen table.

Officer Parker stood and walked to retrieve the laptop, squeezing the microphone hooked to his left shoulder. "Dispatch, inform everyone that Philip Hooper, the homeowner's lawyer, will be, or perhaps already is, waiting at the line outside. When he arrives, please have him escorted in through the garage," he said as he picked up the laptop.

The officer returned with the laptop, as Gus added, "We should also have a secondary angle from the other camera on the porch... we got it for porch pirate issues in the neighborhood and it is a 4k camera."

Officer Parks placed the laptop on the table and Marcy logged in and pulled up the website first for the front porch camera and, in a second tab, the doorbell camera. "Give me an email address and I will send you all of today's videos for both cameras once Philip okays it," Marcy said.

Officer Bradbury slid her his business card. He also gave her a second email address and a case number as he worked on his own phone for a moment. "Put the case number in the subject area and it will add the videos directly to the case as well."

They prepared to watch the video on the large flat screen TV as there was a knock at the garage doorway. Gus looked up to see the dower face of Lieutenant Colonel Michael Dempsey of the North Carolina Highway Patrol and Philip Hooper, their attorney. "Hi, mind if we join you?" Philip asked tiredly.

All present nodded their approval. "We are just about to watch the video footage from the doorbell and front porch cameras, if that is okay with you, Mr. Hooper," replied Officer Bradbury.

Philip nodded and took a seat.

To Gus, Philip looked as though he had just rolled out of bed. He was wearing sneakers, sweatpants and his t-shirt was inside out and backwards. He had the worst case of bedhead ever, paired with his thick glasses, which brought his entire ensemble together and gave him the appearance of an escaped asylum patient. The only thing he lacked, thought Gus, was bunny slippers.

Chapter 30

5:15 AM

First, they watched the front porch video. It started at the first sign of change, when the garage lights had triggered the recording. Under the roof of the porch, they could see walking feet appear in the strange dark IR green view of the world. As the view reached the walker's waist, you could see both hands in front of him as he fiddled with his sidearm and shoved a clip into his gun with his palm. "Jesus Christ," escaped Officer Bradbury's mouth.

Behind and to the left of the screen, Gus's eyes glowed white in the IR as he closed in the shadow of a tree. In an instant, the screen flashed and transitioned into a color image as the porch light flickered on, and the officer ascended the front stairs.

The trooper reached out with his left hand to ring the doorbell with the gun in his right hand, holding his sidearm slightly behind his thigh. Setting his feet like a shooter at the range, leaning slightly onto his front foot, he waited. In the dim light, glimpses of Gus's elbow kept appearing as he maneuvered among the tree's shadow. They could see that Gus had paused in a shadow before he proceeded slower and more deliberately. "I was afraid he would hear me," Gus said. "I could hear Marcy walking, and I knew where she was by the creaks of the floor, so I quietly crept closer here." There was a flash of movement as the trooper lifted his gun at the door and Gus threw himself out from behind the tree, catapulting himself over the stairs with the use of the banister.

In a split second, Gus's right hand closed around the trooper's wrist, forcefully lifting it up as he lunged at him from the blindside, the impact like a football linebacker. With a burst of momentum, the trooper's upper body surged ahead, while his feet remained firmly planted. The gun's discharge created a "Bang". In a swift motion, Gus's right hand grappled with the trooper's right hand, overpowering it and forcing it down.

Simultaneously, the officer reached out to grab onto the wall with his left hand, but misjudgment caused his fingers to slip through the air. When the trooper's head contacted the wall, it appeared to cling momentarily while the rest of his body forcefully collided and moved forward. The gun fired again, pointing downwards, miraculously avoiding Gus's and the trooper's feet, but leaving a groove on the porch boards.

The image captured Gus preparing to punch the immobile and helpless trooper, only to realize he was beyond unconscious. Gus in the video recoiled in horror as he recognized the mortal nature of his injury, while the Gus watching the scene on video turned his head away.

In the video, as Gus stood up, a shocked and dazed Marcy stuck her head out of the doorway and cupped her hand over her mouth.

Nothing appeared different when they changed to the doorbell cam except the fisheye perspective. Trooper Dempsey remained silent, observing, displaying no emotions on his face. "Can I get a glass of water, please?" he asked.

"Oh, sure!" replied Marcy as she got up to get one.

"I simply don't get it," Trooper Dempsey admitted. "I don't know what he was doing out this morning. I had placed him on seven days' mandatory leave last night. Last night, Trooper Corr expressed how horrified he was and was debating resignation... It just makes zero sense. I must get in touch with his Internal Affairs assigned agent... we are going to get to the bottom of this," Trooper Dempsey promised as Marcy returned with the water.

He downed the glass and returned it to Marcy. "Thank you. Mam, I am so sorry you had to go through this, and I promise you, I will understand what happened here."

Chapter 31

5:48 AM

Outside, the news crews witnessed an impromptu announcement from usually unflappable Trooper Dempsey, who made statements and costly admissions that would cause his retirement later that year.

"The incident this morning is a tragic end to the last 24 hours. We won't speculate, but all evidence so far collected points towards the homeowner defending against an attack from a decorated fellow trooper. It saddens me to say that, because it hurts our brotherhood. We will investigate motives for today and last night. We hope to have a full or at least a better understanding of the events over the last 24 hours. As both events involved the same trooper, we believe the chances of further violence to be remote. Nonetheless, we will partner with fellow members of the police brotherhood to offer around the clock protection to both families until we fully comprehend the events and their underlying cause. There will be no other statements made on this issue until we have had time to examine all the circumstances. We ask that you please give this family and the

Smith family their privacy in this troubling time." Trooper Dempsey put his hat back on his head and walked to his waiting car, and left the scene, while ignoring all further questions.

Chapter 32

Monday, September 10th, 2018, 5:00 PM Marriott, Raleigh, NC

With Gus and Marcy's house considered a crime scene for several days, after a night crashing at Peter's, they sought refuge at the Marriott hotel near Crabtree Mall. To assist with funeral plans for the only real father figure he had known, Gus took the entire week off.

Once investigators cleared the house, Gus spent a couple of hours finding a contractor to replace the front door and damaged porch board. In addition, he asked for the front porch to be stained to blend in with the new board. The house would not be fully complete for several weeks.

"Mack's funeral is in two days." Marcy stated. "We are going to need better clothes than these."

Gus nodded, "Yeah, we will need to swing by the place... I can do it if you want me to."

Marcy laughed, "No, I'll go or else you will have me looking like either a cheerleader or an old maid, but let's go in through the motor house... umm garage. Okay?"

When they arrived back at the house, the yellow tape was still in place and the house seemed still. Gus pushed the button on the visor of his car and the garage door obeyed. Once inside, they made their way to their bedroom, and Marcy spread out several dresses on the bed. "Alright Mr. Man, which one of these do you like the best?"

With a cocked eyebrow, Gus thought to himself, "Hmmmm, which one looks more like what a cheerleader would wear?" While knowing he better not make that joke aloud. "I like this one... It is more cheerleader like," as she punched him in the shoulder. "What? The other makes you look like an old spinster and that third one over there says, 'I live alone and have lots of cats... lots and lots of cats," he laughed.

"The joke was, old maid, you twat!" Marcy said, as he tackled her onto the bed.

"We are going to ruin the dresses!"

"Screw the dresses. They all suck anyway." Gus kissed her. "Besides, I know you still have the one you want in the closet."

Like a runaway train, Gus skipped the tracks of the conversation. "Hey, I have a crap ton of vacation timed banked. I think we get away for a week after the funeral," Gus suggested. "The house is going to be a minor construction zone for a while, even after the police tape comes down."

Marcy gave him a skeptical look. "What about Peter? Is this really a good time?"

"We can talk with him before we decide, and if he wants, he can go, too. All I know is, after the last couple of days, I need a break from here." Gus said as Marcy nodded her tentative approval.

Chapter 33

Wednesday, September 12th, 2018, 2:00 PM Oakwood Cemetery, Raleigh, NC

Mack's funeral was a somber affair. It was in the same cemetery as Gus's mothers, but on the other side of a large hill. They had driven past the often-visited spot on the way in. Gus could not shake that itch he had on his neck, like when he was in the sandbox in the army.

He spent much of the service surveying the sightlines as he told himself it was just the trauma of the last few days. In the distance, at the top of the next hill, away from the ceremony, he saw an older woman in her fifties. The woman, dressed in a veil and dark funeral clothes, was staring right at him when he saw her.

He felt a shiver run down his back as he stared at her. He nudged Marcy and subtly pointed towards the woman with his chin, "Old lady on the hill staring," he whispered.

Marcy found the older woman just in time for her to salute them with a defiant middle finger. "What the," she whispered.

She was carrying what appeared to be a metal spyglass in her hand, although neither Gus nor Marcy ever saw her use it. She just slapped it into her other gloved hand like a London Bobby, with his truncheon, as she stared at them menacingly for another moment. When another person appeared on the hill behind her, her face instantly softened as she turned to the man and seemed to collapse, grief stricken into his arms. The portly man led her away down the hill.

The tone of the funeral was so solemn, they felt dropping their plans to travel was just proper, so they spent some more time at the Marriott in town.

Chapter 34

5:16 PM

Back at the hotel, and minimal internet searching later. They mostly figured out who the grief-stricken woman was. They found a funeral announcement for the NC State Trooper, Officer Corr had taken place a half hour before in the same cemetery. Tilting her iPad and pressing her face close, she and called to Gus, who was making loud noises behind the cracked bathroom door of their hotel room. "That must have been his mother or his wife."

"Jumping Jesus! Close the door before the fire alarm goes off and... use the spray... and wash your hands with soap... AND water!" Marcy said as she probed the fixed external window in their suite for any kind of air flow. Eventually, she just parked her head in front of the window air conditioner in search of clean air.

Gus left the bathroom with an innocent look on his face, only to be met with a withering stare. "You better close that door and leave the fan on!" Marcy started as there was a knock on the door.

"Hello lovebirds," called Peter from the far side, and Gus opened the door. "Holy Christ!" Peter said as he jumped back into the hall.

"I told her she should have flushed twice... it's a long way to Chapel Hill," Gus said as Marcy stared from her safe zone near the vent.

"Don't you dare blame that filth on me, you creep!" she said.

"I'll just pass out near the elevator. When you guys are ready to go eat, come revive me." Peter said, as Marcy ran past him as if shot from a catapult.

Gus shrugged and slowly slid on his shoes and strolled to the elevator as the hotel-room door clicked closed behind him.

"Where to?" asked Peter.

"I say we go downtown. Maybe get a steak or something. I'm about on empty," Gus suggested, as the elevator door opened.

"I would think so," said Marcy.

Chapter 35

Monday, September 17th, 2018, 4:00 PM, Gus and Marcy's home, 6278 Mourning Dove Rd. Raleigh, NC

After a week of media silence, Gus, Marcy, Peter, and Deb received an invitation to an internal meeting. Shockingly, there was very little new information collected. In the statement by Officer Corr's wife, she stated he seemed normal until the night of the shooting of Peter's father. When he came home that night, he told her the story of what he had seen with Peter's father pulling a gun from the central console of the car and shooting at him as he drew and returned fire.

Lieutenant Colonel Dempsey said he would show them the body cam video if they absolutely demanded, but he would prefer they believe him that Peter's father did no such thing. "The shooting was almost immediate, and unexplainable. The Trooper had asked for Mr. Smith's license and registration and informed him he had been speeding. Dash camera footage also does not support that speeding claim. When he went back in his patrol car, he had what we describe as a 'curious conversation'. In the video from his body camera, we can hear both the trooper and the dispatch. He confirms something with dispatch that dispatch never said, inferring the car as being stolen and confirmed the driver of the vehicle being armed and dangerous. The dispatcher attempts to correct the trooper's misunderstanding, but he doesn't respond to her after that. Officer Corr walks calmly to the car, holding the license and registration. Gives them to Mr. Smith and tells him to have a good night. As Mr. Smith prepares to put away his information, the Trooper, pulls out his sidearm and shoots Mr. Smith in the side of his head. Immediately after, he shoots twice more into the car before dropping to the ground for a moment and calling for backup and declaring 'Shots fired'. On the dashcam, the officer appears genuinely distressed as he hits the ground. When he stood back up, he was checking his ballistic vest for damage and placed both hands on his knees, like he was trying to catch his breath for a couple of seconds. He grabbed his mic and reports that the suspect was down, and requests EMS, referring to the shooting as self-defense." Trooper Dempsey finished.

"He had to know he was on camera, right?" asked Mrs. Smith incredulously.

"He did," responded the Lieutenant Colonel, nodding.

"How was HE not detained?" asked their lawyer Philip, as all in the room nodded.

"The body cam and car cam were due to be reviewed the next morning, and the officer seemed to be shaken, but seemed rational that night, after the shooting," the Trooper stated. "And before you ask, the weapon he used at Mr. Ferguson's house was his own personal property."

"No one... NO one saw this coming," the trooper reiterated. "We have asked for a full autopsy of Trooper Corr to see if he was under the influence or had a health or other impairment that might shed light on his irrational actions. Before his interment, investigators collected a complete set of tests and samples. Our investigation will include a full review of his financial dealings and a safety check on his relatives. We are reviewing his actions for the last several weeks; we are requesting anyone who had interactions with him, even if they seemed normal, to discuss them with us. I know there is nothing I can do for anyone in this room at this time except give my sincere condolences and apology." Lieutenant Colonel Dempsey concluded.

Chapter 36

Tuesday September 18th, 2018, 6:15 PM 6278 Mourning Dove Rd. Raleigh, NC

When they returned to their home from the hotel life, Marcy noticed the new door and fresh look of the porch and smiled at Gus. With a whimsically pinched face, she asked, "Now, maybe we can replace your mom's bed?"

"But I love that bed!" as Gus feigned, hurt look. "Ok, ok... I get it. It is kind of creepy. We can go look after lunch."

Six days later, the 24th, the new bed came, so Gus and Marcy got the old bed out of the way. They stripped the old mattress and stood it up. They propped it against the wall and removed the dual box springs from the frame. The usual dust bunnies greeted them under the bed, their fluffy forms a testament to the lack of recent full cleaning. The whirring of the shop vac, however, quickly dispatched them, leaving the room feeling fresher.

They kept the bed frame, because they liked the shelf space at the head of the bed; however, Marcy really wanted to change the bed's location. Gus didn't care where it was. When they pulled the frame away from the wall, they heard a clunk sound. "What the hell was that? Did we break something?" Gus asked as Marcy walked to the location near the wall at the head of the bed, where the sound emanated from.

"Oh, it is just some old book... No, wait, it looks like a diary or something," Marcy said, as she looked at the book and pulled a stamped envelope with a long letter in it from inside the cover. "It looks like it says it is from your Ma... oh wait, it might be your dad, maybe? It looks like it was to be sent to Scotland, but never reached the mailbox," Marcy said, as Gus rounded the bed frame to look.

They took the book and the letter and retreated to the kitchen and sat at the table. The letter was in a water damaged envelope from Gus's father and dated February 18th, 1983:

February 18th, 1983

Father,

I am writing to you to tell you I had an incident. The best I can describe it; it was a waking dream. I know I should have told you immediately, and right now your eye is probably doing that twitch thing it does, like when I ran the tractor through the barn wall.

It happened the morning after the funeral, and the panic, where everyone camped at Jen's parent's home. In the morning, Jen and I went to breakfast. The meal went fine; however, before we left, when Jen went to the loo, I experienced something that frankly scared the shite out of me. I know I should have told you, but I just could not, for some reason.

At 06:38 Jen went to the loo. While she was in there, I experienced a waking dream. Each time I blinked, the room I was in at Finches Diner seemed to change and age as if the room became decrepit in the time my eyes were closed. That small instant seemed to linger for full seconds as I could look around the now abandon diner, where windows were a moment before. Now they appeared covered in a layer of old, moldering newspaper. Many of the tables and chairs appeared to be broken or completely gone. When I would open my eyes, I would see the room restored and our now empty breakfast plates in front of me.

I dreaded each blink. When I looked up from the plates and blinked, there was someone in the seat across from me, reading a newspaper in this shattered ruin of a restaurant. All I could see was the paper with a headline discussing something about a "space shuttle exploding." His gloved hands that held the paper, held it so high that all I could see was the top of his leather hat.

As I looked at the hat, it lowered the paper just a little, so I could see his blue tortured eyes and the sickly skin around them.

When that blink ended, Jen was leaving the restroom. So, I quickly paid the bill and left. When I was at the door, as I held it for Jen, something forced me to blink one last terrible time and I could see him sitting in the shattered ruin of the diner with the paper fully down, grinning at me with dead blue eyes, like a demon from hells gate.

Father, that last blink... even when I opened my eyes, I could still see him sitting there, a stain among the pristine surroundings.

I'm sorry, *but to tell you that day as I should have, when we arrived back home, felt impossible. I had just agreed and promised Jen that we could stay in North Carolina moments before this terror... and I was, regarding this responsibility, acting like a coward. I'm so sorry, father, for failing you and the family.*

-IV-

A sketch of the diner, marred by water damage with the ink bleeding into a hazy mess, appeared on the second page of the letter.

Flipping through the book, they saw that someone had written the earlier entries in a meticulous hand, while someone else had scrawled the later ones in a rushed, familiar script. The writing of the entries at the front of the book matched the script of the letter, which meant it was in Gus's father's handwriting.

Also, noticeably different were the notation methods used and the subject. Gus's father had written, "Possibly Pertinent Dreams Volume VII" inside the cover of the book, and beneath that in neatly printed words "Laoch Kier Ferguson IV".

Each entry represented a dream and an accompanying date and a time. Despite the neat handwriting, grammatical errors, and the incorrect use of homophones, which echoed the same mistakes which had plagued Gus throughout his life. The entries described dreams. Each story was seemingly unrelated, except for their sinister feel and the appearance of a common nemesis. There was always the presence of a dark figure with blue eyes and light blue skin. Sometimes his father described the eyes of the creature as having a strange play of lights in them.

There was also a word that made them both look at each other in confusion, the word "Scrios" always written with a capital 'S' like a formal word. Like Scrios was a name.

The twelfth entry made Gus close the book as he read it, while Marcy was still hovering over the end of the eleventh entry. She almost dropped the book as he withdrew his hands that helped her support it.

This dream, dated June 9th, 1985, was Gus's third birthday. It described a small and emaciated boy standing with his back to a boiling sea and rain pouring as the wind blew his red hair like a flag in a storm. The boy spoke loudly through the storm, "Thig Sgriosadh, agus thig e air do shonsa". The story went on, but he slammed the book closed as Marcy snatched her right hand out of the rapidly closing book.

"Whoa, are you ok?"

"No, I don't think I am." Gus replied.

"What is the matter, baby?" Marcy asked.

"That next story... I had that dream... well, parts of it twice."

"What? No, seriously..." she said with a sideways stare. "Ok, I will read it and you tell me about your dream."

So, Gus started telling her the story as Marcy read from the book.

"This child seems to yell at me in some foreign language. These were the words, "Thig Sgriosadh, agus thig e air do shonsa", and I notice he is not looking at me, he is looking through me. When I spin around to see what he is looking at, I see the same boy. Except it's not pouring rain anymore. Instantly, it is a partly cloudy day and he and his father or uncle are walking down the path yelling at someone. Suddenly, I can understand the echo of what the boy was yelling. What the boy was yelling was 'Destruction comes. And he is coming for... you!!'"

Gus paused as the color was draining from Marcy's face. He continued, "The man is arguing with an older woman, when suddenly everything freezes except the boy. The boy utters something in a voice way too low for his tiny vocal cords, telling the woman she is worthless, and her husband has run off with a younger woman and that she is just a dried-up old bag," he said as Marcy slammed the book.

"What the hell?" she said. "It was not word for word, but it was way too close not to be identical." Marcy looking shaken.

Two dreams later, on November 7th, 1986, in the book was another featuring the small boy. He was standing in front of the same thatched hut as he watched the dark smoke billow from the inferno that had been her home. As his father tried to enter to help those inside, being pushed back as the wet blanket he carried steamed from the heat; the boy smiled thinly and seemed to breathe deeply, gorging on the horror of the crowd and the woman's loss.

Somehow the boy knew that her three daughters were in the hut and that they were dead... murdered gruesomely, before the fire started, by their mother's hand.

At the end of the entry written after the dream's conclusion, was a single question, "The boy must be Scrios?"

The whole thing was way too much for them both to process, so they called Peter and told him to come over.

As they waited for him to get there, they noted that the other writing hand in the book was from Gus's mother, Jen.

Chapter 37

8:21 PM Mourning Dove Rd. Raleigh, NC

Peter listened to their story about the book and the ties to Gus's dream with laser like concentration blended with trepidation. They thought they were losing Peter's interest when he pulled out his iPhone and began clicking intently. Gus trailed off and Peter said, "No, continue. I'm listening. I'm just trying to find something important to this." So, Gus continued.

A minute later, as Gus got near the conclusion, Peter interrupted him. "I need to show you something," and showed him the email that Gus had sent him about the incident in Iraq with the fortuneteller. "Read that aloud for Marcy."

So, Gus did:

Email from Gus to Peter

Sent: Saturday 8/7/2004 16:57:23

To: PeterS@redwolfsolutions.com

From: Gus

Ok Peter, this just happened yesterday... no shit. The strangest story I have from my two tours. Me and a couple of the boys went to a fortune teller who was in the Green-zone. She was the mother of one guy who sells trinkets near the gates. He insisted she was "the real deal" over and over.

So yesterday afternoon we went. I mean, it was five bucks. We went into this smoky room with drapes hanging on the walls and the red tabletop. And we were all given a thick coffee. We drank it as we talked to her through her son the translator, and she tried to pick up on what would be right to tell us. So, she reads the first guy's cup and told him he lives under a shroud of danger.... "No fucking shit lady," said the 1st lieutenant in his Chicago staccato accent, "have you looked around?" and we all laughed.

The next guy, she says his wife at home misses him and he will have many children." He laughed because he wasn't married. "Strike two!!" howls the staccato 1st lieutenant from the first reading.

Next, the lady reaches for my cup. Picks it up and looks into it. Dude, suddenly everything goes quiet; I mean, we can't even hear the normal clamor of noise and traffic outside for a couple of seconds... Suddenly she screams and my cup she is holding cracks.

The lady backpedals from the table quicker than any of us thought she could move. So fast that two other people with us are looking for a gunman coming in the door or something.

Now to this point she has said everything in Arabic...and her son translated it... She looks at me and says in American English and in a much younger woman's voice. "You will face a great evil, seek your father's family in Atholl for help because you alone are not strong enough!" and she collapses.

We all make for the exit, appreciating the performance while the trinket salesman is trying to revive his mother and asking for help. At that point, we realize, he is not kidding, so we start trying to help. The first lieutenant from Chicago, who works as a medical assistant, said, "Bro, she is gone... like gone-gone." The son looks at us through tears and said, "I have never heard her speak English before."

Crazy shit!

My tour ends in the next couple of months. I will let you know when I am home. Tell Deb and Mack thanks for the care packages. The guys, and I love them.

Gus

"If there is no solution to a problem, cut off the end of the problem, shake shit out of the hole you made and fucking make a solution yourself, and shove the shit back in the hole."

^ Captain Sanders quote

Marcy sat there stunned as Gus said, "Ok, I will call Scotland in the morning, but I need to look at the other entries. My mom wrote a lot of stuff in this book, too.

The Chronicle

Jen's note

Jen's first note in the book was strange and dated a month after the tornado that killed Gus's father. Their subjects were not from dreams or the recounting of them. That immediately created a stark contrast.

December 29, 1988

Laoch,

I don't know how to start this. I know we had our differences and the stories I was told and read about the family seemed the things of fantasy to me. This is the last of my Laoch's journals. I found it in the salvaged things rescue workers and friends pulled from the remains of our home after the tornado that hit that terrible morning and took my love away. This is going to take longer than it should to make it to you, as I want to include my experiences that night.

I know this will anger you upon receipt because of the delay, but hopefully, my complete recollection will somewhat ease your anger, as it relates to yours, my late husbands, and even our son's dreams.

My skepticism is over, and I am sorry.

--

On November 25th, 1988, I had traveled home from the beach to pick up some printouts for month-end closing for work. I picked up my printouts and stopped by the house just to make sure everything was ok. It was, so I departed back to the beach. As I left the neighborhood, I saw a neighbor was having an estate sale. So, I stopped and looked.

The sale itself was unique as everything in the house was for sale for cheap. The woman running the sale indicated that the house and the belongings were the property of her estranged husband, and he had left everything to her. She "just wanted it gone". I looked and found nothing, as most of the sale was still in boxes and something about it, and she seemed off. I thanked her and started to leave when she pointed me towards a box with some cool stuff and said, "You can have it all for a buck". I felt sorry for her, so I took it but insisted on paying her $5. She was happy and I was happy.

The box stayed in my car until November 27, 1988. I had honestly forgotten about it. We were having a late-night movie and pizza night when I remembered it was in the back of the car. Gus had just woken up crying and Laoch was holding him while I ran out into the gathering storm and retrieved the box.

When I came back inside, Gus was telling Laoch about a bad dream he had, where someone named 'Pappy' was talking to him. Pappy apparently told Gus he was sorry for scaring him, but that he needed to be strong. I thought it was strange, but it didn't dawn on me the similarities of what happened those years ago at the big house. A few minutes later, he was back asleep on Laoch's lap, and we set him on the floor, wrapped up in a blanket, to sleep with us in the living room.

I opened the box from the sale and started giving Laoch some things in it. As he examined a few, I produced what I thought was a metallic spyglass-like item. As I touched it, I had a dream I was in the wilderness. It was a long time ago, two or maybe three hundred years ago, and the location felt like the area I'm in right now, North Carolina or at least in the Southeastern United States. An Indian war party was sneaking up on a house in a small clearing. The party had what appeared to be a European man with them. The party at his command went in and killed the occupants and received some kind of payment from him after they set the house on fire. I had just been standing there and somehow no one had seen me. Except, as the European man prepared to leave the area, he seemed to sense me and turned to look directly at me. He said, "I guess this is when you see me," and I woke up from this daydream, still holding the metal object.

To describe it, it seemed to be made of gold. It had a weathered serpent that seemed to coil around its length, maybe four times. I can't explain why I turned to examine the open end, but I did. As I did, Laoch screamed "No!" Immediately after, the tornado ripped through the house, the roar of the wind and the screech of wood shredding filled my ears.

I told the rescuers that I lost consciousness and woke up right before they saved me, but that was not entirely true. When I was captured by the tube, I saw many terrible things. They were not stories but came to me as memories and as if I had done them or witnessed them. The memories were of other individuals. I believe for a short time as the storm hit, I had somehow absorbed or partially absorbed the memories of that creature, strangers and maybe some of your family members.

Things you need to know:

Scrios hates the family, and he seemed certain I was one of you.

Scrios knows nothing of the exact location of the family's home. He suspects Scotland, and he has people searching. Here are the names of people he has used and influences. Some are deceased.

Allen Pinkerton – Deceased in the 1884

John Milbrow – Deceased 1928

214

Kenneth Riedling in his 70's living in Chicago Illinois. Address is in the rear cover of the book.

Marcus Peige. London, England. Peige Partners Inc. (active)

- The client he is working for is a politician in the North Carolina Senate. Harold Emerson Scandling, a Democrat from Mecklenburg County... Charlotte, NC

- Mr. Scandling thinks he owns and controls the artifact that somehow contains this creature.

Scrios has destroyed more people through his coercion than anyone could think possible.

One of those people is indeed William Atworth.

The creature feeds off pain and misery, as previously reported. To it, everyone is perceived to have a unique taste... as identifiable as the difference between honey and chocolate, for a comparison.

He manipulates the memories and minds of people to give them new understandings with disastrous results.

He did not see Gus and knows nothing of him.

He recognized Laoch, however. I was a surprise to him somehow, and he screamed in pain when I looked into the crystal.

After the storm, a thorough search for lost belongings revealed countless objects, yet the serpent rod was nowhere to be seen.

Someone purposely gave me that artifact. The creature suspected our family, and the week before the Estate Sale, Rep. Harold Scandling gave the artifact to Emily Hanks to hold.

She murdered her ex-husband, Douglas, who suffered with Parkinson's, an hour later. Emily disposed of his body with the help of a rented wood chipper. She later drove the wood chipper to Jordan Lake at 2:30 AM, near the Pea Ridge Rd. Entrance; and used an old road that disappeared into the lake there to submerge the chipper in the water. She later reported the rental stolen. It's probably still there.

She had knowledge, and I don't know how, that I would stop there for the estate sale. I cannot figure out how, and that fact still haunts me. Her only goal was that I took that box.

Several months after our encounter, she died from a cocaine overdose, when the disappearance of her husband brought inquisitive police to her door. She was the only suspect in his disappearance, but the police have since marked the case inactive.

There are so many memories I had pushed into my head, as the creature screamed the name 'Lil... his sister's name. I will attempt to write them here before I send you the book. I will also try to provide a context for whose memory they were and somehow, when they were.

The memories are not like files on a computer; they are just there in my head, like a lingering dream or an old memory of my own, except somehow more vivid? However, sometimes there are memories from several people of the same incident. Seeing the same thing in my head from different perspectives gives me vertigo and triggered migraine headaches worse than any I can remember. Older memories seemed to be more general with dates... perhaps they can be cross-referenced in the archives?

First, I will focus on Srene and Dearn, Lil's parents, their meeting and the tragedy of their lives that led to the birth of that creature. Maybe it will help you somehow?

Since the storm, I too have had terrible dreams that started when I was in the hospital. I have documented them near the end of this book. I'm not sure if they are from the trauma of that night or something different. But after each one I seem to have migraine headaches. I don't recall Laoch having issues like that, so I'm guessing they are from the damage of the storm.

Entry 1 - Srene

The first memory of Srene's childhood came to me in a strange context. It was from her last moments... of her taking an inventory of her life just before she ended it.

I don't know how I know, but it was the year 1143 BC in the Hibernian Wilderness of what in modern-day would-be Ireland's western shore. I could see her in flashes many times staring out at the ocean and she loved blue. Srene was the mother of the creature and she named Scrios.

Srene was standing at the edge of a jagged cliff overlooking the ocean crying... well, more than crying. She was guilt-ridden and contemplating the jump to the cool blue waters that were violently impacting the boulder lined seashore below. When I think about it, I can hear the thunder of the waves. She wondered if she would feel the pain or if life would simply just end? Reflecting on her past, she deliberated over her decision.

She understood what Scrios was, as he had allowed her to see his true form. She blamed herself for his very existence. Scrios had given her some of his memories, exposing his real self to her. This revelation he gave her confirmed her fears and, instead of pride, she had rejected him. Ironically, this rejection caused Scrios a moment of pain that puzzles him to this day.

As Srene stared at the water below, she remembered how she had watched her parent's death because of starvation, when she was only ten summers old. She remembered how they refused food so she could eat. How sickness had taken them in the bitter cold winter. She had no brothers or sisters, so this had left her totally alone.

Her days living with her parents were hard, as they scratched food from the windblown shoreline covered with rocks and boulders. "If only rocks were edible, every day would be a feast," her father said, as they attempted to grow or gather anything edible. Him saying that would be the only lasting memory of her father, and the only way she could invoke his kind, smiling face in her memory. She knew him only as father.

The morning her mother died, she had been tasked with retrieving water and gathering herbs to flavor it. The sun in the blue skies, warmed her face as she walked to the stream with the wooden pail her father had made years before. As she walked, she chanced to think of a different life where edible roots hung from the roof in abundance and more goats than she had fingers were in the fenced area around the home. Srene dreamed of a life where her biggest concerns would be, how to keep the goats in the yard; and how to not get too fat that she would never find a man. She may have lingered in her dreams too long. Was her mother dying her fault? She blamed herself for this eventually, too.

When she got back in view of the grass covered, old wooden structure that was her home, which was barely bigger than an average modern second bedroom; she had crossed the last hill and saw heavier than normal smoke coming from the fireplace. "Someone was burning too much wood and father would be angry," she thought as she hastened her step.

When she walked in the doorway, her aunt and uncle were there. Father was pacing at the far side of the room, while her mother stared forever into space with a look of ghastly surprise. Her aunt was respectfully sewing her into an old blanket with a long bone needle and a strip of fabric cut from the blanket she laid on. Her uncle was adding more wood to the raging fire, loudly complaining about how cold it was in their home. He failed to realize or didn't care how much effort it took for her to drag the wood she had gathered. He was burning a week's worth of wood in a single day. The economy of it was oblivious to him, as his four sons gathered the wood for his fire.

Her aunt had brought a jar of stew she called "leftovers" from their previous night's meal. They pushed the pot near the fire to warm it. Their leftovers were more in quantity than she could recall seeing at any meal.

On the top of the stew was a thick layer of fat, promising the meat it contained. There were roots of the colors she dreamed of as she walked for water. The stew also contained some kind of leafy vegetable she was unfamiliar with. The meat it contained was goat. There were fresh pieces that all tasted lovely, even tongue, which was her favorite part.

Her father initially declined the gifted food, but her uncle took him to the side and talked to him quietly. She heard only the part where he said, "If you don't eat something, brother, your spine is going to fall through your asshole." They talked for a while longer, and she watched in amazement when her stern father, who seemed to be carved by the weather like the large stones outside, hugged her uncle and tears rolled down his face.

Her father grabbed a bowl and a small portion from the jar that now sat farther from the fire and ate it. After the feast, Srene again passed her mother, now sewn into the blanket as she went to fetch more water.

Outside, the clouds masked the sun. As she walked the familiar trail for more water, she saw her father and uncle clearing stones near the gully that overlooked a view of the sea. Clearing the rocks on the surface was the simple part, she thought, while remembering the efforts to remove buried stones.

When Srene returned with the water, her father and uncle carried her mother in her blanket across the rocky clearing towards the space they had prepared. It wasn't as deep as they wanted, but there were enough rocks to create quite a pile to deter the scavengers.

When they set her in the shallow ditch they had scratched, they placed the first smaller stones as tightly as they could. They packed them with as much soil as they could find and moved on to larger stones until the pile was nearly at her father's waist.

Srene's mother exited the world with what she carried into it; her only addition was an old, tattered blanket.

The blanket that was used for her mother's tomb represented much more of a loss, though. Not only had they lost a blanket, the key to staying warm on a cold winter night, they also lost their mother, who was a key source of that heat.

They, more importantly, lost the skills their mother possessed. She had been the keeper of the knowledge of how to make more blankets. Her mother was also the luckiest amongst them in finding the few, well-hidden root vegetables and other edible plants among the rocky barren landscape.

Her aunt and uncle left the jar of leftovers, and they ate as much as they could before the third day, when the smell had turned rancid. Mother would have saved the grease; other men would have saved the rancid meat for fishing. Father was no fisherman, as he feared the sea, having almost drowned as a boy.

He could have traded the old meat for fish if he had thought about it before he poured the last contents onto the fire.

Srene's consciousness shifted back once again to her present time at the top of the cliff as she thought hard about that moment. "Father was a fool and fools make their own luck. Later, they claim themselves a victim," she concluded while staring at the water she was longing to leap into, as her mind wondered back into memories.

Two weeks after her mother passed, the newly motherless Srene awoke to comforting warmth in the bed. She rolled over to see her father sweating with fever. Her warmth quickly changed to horror as she realized the similarities to her mother's condition only weeks before. What they gathered and cooked recently, he had taken token pieces and ends that were bitter and chewed them as if they were exactly the parts he wanted. He would act amazed, as they had completely sated his hunger. His stomach at night betrayed his lies, as it grumbled for something to work on.

She visited her mother's grave daily, watering the stones with her tears that mixed in with the rain that regularly joined her at the tomb. Sometimes her father came too. He regularly commented on the rain, "Oh dear, you are just like your dear mum. You bring the storms with you." He said as he hugged her shoulder.

A week after he began sweating with fever, he too was gone. He had told her for several days, "If my time comes, go to your aunt and uncle and tell them. When it happened, she did as she was told and walked the half hour to their home.

In comparison, the relatives' home was enormous. They had three rooms as large as her entire house. The walls, constructed with stone at the base, packed with mud and constructed above with wood all the way to the roof.

Windows shuttered for winter, dotted two of the eastern facing walls. She saw her aunt in the yard gathering round brown rocks that she suspected were eggs from chickens that ran in the yard; she knew what they were, but did not remember ever eating one.

Her aunt and uncle walked with Srene back to her home. Her aunt supported her with an arm wrapped around her waist as they walked. She warmly promised Srene that things would be alright and told her how she always wanted a daughter. During the walk, she outlined the chores she expected Srene to help with.

When they arrived at the only home she had ever known, her aunt and uncle told her to grab anything she wanted to bring, but not too much of the clothes as they may carry the curse of whatever consumed her parents. She gathered a few keepsakes, including a simple rock on a string. A natural hole in the rock allowed someone to thread a twisted fiber string through it. It had been her mother's.

She also gathered a stone knife her father used every day of his life. In her memories, she saw him taking care of the handle, which included one time he fixed a broken part. His fix had been rudimentary compared to the original makers, but it had been functional enough to last.

After she had retrieved those things, her aunt and uncle looked for anything left that had a use. They decided that only the jar used to bring the food to them, several weeks before, would be worth carrying home.

Her uncle tore thatching from the walls. He dragged the heavily weaved grass matt that still held her father to the middle of the single room. Srene looked at her father. He had been so large, she remembered, and now his stiff body looked tiny and frail, through her tears that lensed the room.

Her aunt and uncle pulled every flammable thing from the walls and floor and stacked it on him. When that was complete, the uncle used a stick to sweep hot coals from the fire pit onto a flat rock and carried it to a cleared spot on the bed. He poured the coals there on the grass mattress and blew on them several times until a flame appeared. The uncle took his stick, and a torn piece of blanket and made a torch. He lit the rag in the small growing mattress fire and walked to the back of the room, where he began lighting likely flammable areas as he worked his way back to the front door. As she and her aunt watched from outside, the room grew bright behind him, as he exited and closed the door.

As the fire grew, the whole place began to crackle and pop. The grass covered roof steamed and soon all the walls burst into flames. At nearly the same time, the heat from the blaze forced them to move away.

After five minutes, with the heat so intense they had to step back even further, the roof collapsed, pushing an enormous gust of heat and ash towards them which almost engulfed them, before rising to the sky.

Her aunt recognized the rotten smell emanating from the fire and it turned her stomach. She was thankful that Srene had very little experience with that smell and all it implied.

Later, with the fire burning itself out, they turned and began the walk home.

Upon arrival at her new home, Srene slept alone in a bed for the first time. It had an actual wooden frame and a heavy blanket that held piled grass in place. In a corner of one of the three rooms, a makeshift blanket wall gave her a bit of privacy from her four new brothers while she changed.

In the two years that followed, with regular good nutrition, Srene grew from a spindly petite girl and blossomed into a beautiful young woman.

With her growing health, her aunt, who worked beside her daily, seemed to become more distant and shorter on patience when she made simple mistakes. Her uncle was quick to correct her aunt when she was cruel, often putting an arm around Srene and telling her it would be alright. Her uncle's leering stares made Srene uncomfortable. His defense of Srene did nothing to stop the growing hateful looks her aunt gave her. Srene could not understand what she had done to make her so mad.

One day when she was collecting water, a chore she still loved, as it let her get away to her own dreams as she walked, she met someone. While filling her buckets, she met a boy who was also at the pool, fed by a small spring which wept into an artificial basin.

She had passed him on the path before and nodded a greeting to him, but they had never talked. This time, they both carried two buckets. As usual, she had taken a drink preparing for the long walk home when he entered the small clearing.

He nodded to her, and she nodded back in their continued mute conversation. To her surprise, he spoke, "The whole way here, it was nothing but fog and somehow you find the only place where the sun shines. How is that?" he said with a smile.

"It was shining like that when I got here," she said, confused, as it had been sunny most of her trip after leaving the house.

She grabbed her buckets and stood to leave, and he gathered his courage. "If you are just going to leave, can I at least know your name so when we meet, I can greet you properly? My name is Dearn."

With a blush of red that highlighted her dark blue eyes, she responded, "My name is Srene." She responded and quickly turned to leave. The bucket in her left hand caught on a branch and spilled half of its contents on her foot, forcing her to refill it.

Her awkward giggling of embarrassment dominated when Dearn raised his hand to stop her and poured water from his bucket into hers to aid her on her way. She was aware of his eyes, glancing back to see them as they followed her until she disappeared along the path.

Entry 2 - Dearn

In the next entry, Jen wrote from the early memories of Dearn. When Srene left the clearing and disappeared, Dearn collapsed, sitting upon the small rock wall of the pool, and shook his head. He dared not think of this young woman, but he could not stop himself.

After a moment, he distracted himself by filling the buckets and started his own trek back to his home. He noticed an emptiness in the pit of his chest that he had never known before. The pit contained pain, joy, uncertainty and longing, all in equal measures, and he feared it might never go away.

From that day forward, for weeks, he tried to determine her schedule, so he could chance meeting her as often as possible. He often would linger too long at the spring, which would translate to a lashing from his father for his apparent laziness.

His cousin Merl was the only one who knew the truth about his slow trips for water. He lived close by and would always chide him about how he was going to get a beating for some lass again. One day, Merl came with Dearn for water and met Srene. He immediately knew why Dearn would risk his father's rage. "She is lovely," he said. "I think I understand your recklessness now."

About two months after their first discussion, Srene and Dearn met at the agreed upon time. Each had structured the timing of their chores to be there, although occasionally Srene was a bit late. When she arrived late on the partly cloudy spring day that was prominent in Dearn's memories, a cloud eclipsed the sun as she entered the clearing for the spring.

Dearn's first thought was that she must have fallen down a hillside and skipped off every stone. Battered and swollen, her beautiful face was a mess. "What in the gods has happened Srene? Are you ok?" he said as he dropped his buckets and ran to her.

A stiff breeze rustled the young leaves in the trees as she poured her misery into his world. She told of her uncle and an unwanted visit in the night, the silent violence he forced upon her and the beating she had taken at the hands of her aunt when she went to her for help. "My aunt kept hitting me and screaming that I was not taking her man away. She called me a creature of darkness."

The first time Dearn ever touched her was to hug and comfort her in this moment. Before that, the thought of touching her seemed impossible, like touching the moon in the sky. In that instant, Dearn raged with hate and knew that he must protect her. He swore this to himself as he held her and covered her, while a quick moving shower passed, drenching them. Soon, as they talked huddled under his covering, the sun reemerged.

The thought of her going back to that place was impossible for him, but the type of plans they discussed required preparation. He swore to her he would gather supplies that night and meet here early in the next morning at sunrise and they would leave to make a life of their own... if she would have him. She would. Srene, just past her 13th year and Dearn, only two years older, would be alone in the brutal world.

Entry 3 - Srene

Srene had memories of when she returned home that day. She returned to her home for one more night, carrying the water as expected and not daring to mention the naïve plans to any of her new family. She quietly gathered her meager belongings, including her father's knife.

Early the next morning, she folded them up in a heavy fabric blanket she used on her bed and tied them with a strap. Before her uncle stirred, she quietly stepped out into the low hanging fog, towards the area they used for a latrine, and disappeared over a hill. She was gone before the sun lit the morning sky. She worried a bit about running into wolves, but she worried more about being caught trying to leave.

In the morning, her aunt went behind the curtained off area to rouse Srene and found her gone and made a simple contented shrug. Her uncle was mad at Srene's disappearance, but the look he received from his wife, as she cut meat from their stores, made him decide to never mention it again.

The sun lit the sky near the spring and Srene waited in the chilly morning air. The brightening orb crept up and over the hills to the east and as she felt the heat from it rise, she felt a panic rise in her chest that Dearn would not come.

Later, she saw him walking on the path, carrying a large bundle. Merl was with him. Merl carried a large bag and Srene looked at him with confusion. "Are you coming too?" she asked.

"Oh no, I'm just helping him carry some things to here," Merl said. He indicated towards the bag with his eyes, "This is dried meat and some roots... and it's very heavy. My father gave it to him... and to you."

Merl set the large bundle on the ground and pointed to the pack that Dearn was setting down. "He also gave you some of his old basic tools you will need. In the bundle are some skins to cover with at night until you get something built."

Dearn turned and hugged his cousin, thanking him. Merl prepared to leave when Srene hugged him awkwardly, too. Merl wished them many children, and he departed back the way he had come.

Srene and Dearn looked at each other and broke into a nervous laugh. They reorganized the piles and set about repacking the loads so they could carry everything.

Dearn seemed intent on carrying it all. Srene looked at him with a skeptical eye, "I need to carry my share, or you will hurt yourself. That cannot happen." Dearn nodded, defeated, and they started separating and packing again.

Entry 4 - Dearn

Dearn trembled with fury the night after the meeting at the spring and wanted revenge for the terrible things Srene's uncle had done. His cheeks burned at the thought of her aunt's cruelty. It took some reasoning from Merl during the walk to the meeting place the next morning and from Srene after, to convince him to walk away. He was never able to leave behind the pain of that day. He felt ashamed for never doing what he felt needed to be done.

He and Srene departed together early that morning and never returned. It was early spring, and they walked for days to get away from her family, seeking unclaimed land that looked promising to their naïve eyes.

Srene, with the wisdom time gives later in life, concluded that because of her aunt's resentment, there was likely no one who looked for her when she left.

They settled into a rock-strewn field near the top of a hill that overlooked the ocean to the west. While beautiful on the sunny day when they found it, the prevailing straight winds off the ocean would cause them many chilly nights. It was the location that they would call home for the rest of their lives. Life there was hard. The weather that blew off the cold ocean was cruel.

Through the years, they fought to have a garden, constantly clearing a small area of rocks to plant a small plot. In it, they would replant roots they had foraged for, and the remaining supply Merl had given them. Early mistakes cost them. The perpetual wind from the ocean would blow away the loose soil they created. Before they figured out how to stop that, the only thing that seemed to grow with regularity were new stones that rose from the ground.

The second planting, they used larger rocks to create a shadow from the wind. This approach helped. Srene used the skills that she learned while living with her aunt and uncle after her parents died. Her parents were not nearly as knowledgeable about how to grow food. The learned skills from her aunt also included a much better understanding of how to tan small hides and sew. Still, starting with nothing was harder than ever expected. If not for the generosity of Merl's father, they would not have survived.

The darkness of Srene's brief childhood stretched behind her like her shadow in the cold winter sun.

Dearn noted the place where they called home seemed unnaturally prone to low clouds and a misty rain. Srene's outlook on the world seemed to be determined by the weather. When it was cloudy, she would be sad or short-tempered. Srene loved the sun and Dearn loved how it brought out her smile. He would joke with her on gloomy days that if she would just smile, the sun would come out.

Originally living heavily off the food that others gave them; they slowly established enough renewable crops to survive. They gained a few goats from neighbors through the barter of hard labor, helping them to clear their land of stones.

Entry 5 - Srene

At home, each day they cleared rocks, stacking them in walls to build a pen for the goats. They stacked additional rocks to make a lower wall for a more substantial living space. This effort paid off with a small sense of stability. Stability led to a family of their own, but this early joy quickly crashed into misery.

The later years of her life were more punishing to Srene than the ones before. Nothing causes a mother more pain than burying a child, and Srene would be a constant traveler on that horrible road. Each time, it stole more of her. She replaced those spots with hate. Hate for the world and a powerless, frustrated desire for retribution.

Srene stood on the cliff, remembering the trials. She thought of her eldest son Yurl, who died when he was five from a fever and for that, she blamed and cursed the Gods for their cruelty. When she buried him, her heart grew bitter, and she knew she had buried a part of herself with him. She remembered kissing his pale, cold forehead.

Her youngest, Todd, died in his adolescence. Grier, a local warlord, horridly maimed Todd as an example after a revolt. Todd died a slow, gruesome death from those injuries.

Entry 6 - Dearn

The rebellion was over in minutes as Todd watched from a hedge. Seeing one of Dearn's group mortally wounded in the opening seconds, they quickly realized surrender was their only choice. In truth, the people that Dearn was in league with hoped that a bloodless show of unity would force Grier to relent. It did not work out that way.

Grier was a spiteful man, who also saw himself as practical. Rather than killing them all, he indentured them for their petulance. He imposed a penalty so severe that payment threatened a family's chances of surviving the harsh winter. But that was just the start.

He punished each participant corporally. Though not meant to be fatal, the punishment was brutal, meant to leave a lasting impression, and a few unfortunately succumbed to its harshness. The ones who died found no pity from Grier. "So is life," he shrugged and pointed to the next of the condemned. He wanted each to carry his scar for the rest of their lives as a warning to others who might oppose him.

Grier clarified while staring at Dearn, he decried that "anyone who had helped in any way, were to face the same punishment" as the surviving rabble. "Those who provided, sticks or stone" he said, "shall face the mallet... even him," he said, pointing at the spindly boy, Todd, who was shocked to be noticed in the bushes.

Dearn faced the mallet first and had awakened briefly to witness the punishment of his son. Even though his mind tried not to remember, Scrios reveled in the pain's taste the memory evoked. Todd cruelly lived through the slam of the wide wooden hammer and remained conscious for every minute of the rest of his life. After immediately vomiting, he began screaming at a pitch that shredded his throat, with his hands scrambling for purchase in the air around him and finding nothing. "Take him far away" Grier ordered. "I cannot keep hearing that... take him to his home and dump him there!"

Srene found them on the ground outside of their home. Dearn was back and forth between moans of consciousness and stillness, but Todd was screaming in delirium. His eyes were wild, like a beast on fire.

She dragged Dearn inside and got him to the blanket covered pile of braided hay they used for a bed.

"Love," Dearn squeezed out through clenched teeth, "are you alright?"

She cut her eyes at him, stunning him with a feral look, with panic in her blood-red eyes. She said nothing, and it said everything. The impotent anger was crushing to Dearn's soul.

Srene went outside to soothe and bring her sweet son inside. However, there was no soothing this pain.

For the women, the punishment was possibly more nightmarish. Dearn wore the shame of it every night when his wife cried out in her sleep.

As Dearn lay helpless on the bed in agony, again unable to retaliate against those who hurt Srene. Srene's thoughts broadened to Lil, their daughter, who Dearn and Srene hid in the house for years. She was a beautiful child and neither parent could bear the thought of her fate if Grier's men discovered her.

From not long after she could walk, they only allowed her outside at night, and only if she remained quiet. Her blue eyes and fiery hair foretold the beauty she would become as she danced beneath the moon and stars.

As practiced, she hid in a hole beneath the hay bin, where she kept a small parcel of food and an earthen jar of water. She was told to hide the day Dearn and others challenged Grier as a precaution that should have served as an omen.

They had vastly underestimated the warlord. They were herdsman and farmers and knew nothing of battle. Dearn had promised her and had honestly thought that if they showed up in enough numbers, Grier would relent and come to a deal with them. How unbelievably naïve they had been, she thought as a tear formed in her eye.

Worse were the thoughts of Grier's men and what they would have done to Lil if they had found her.

She was well practiced by that time and knew to keep still and quiet. Years of hiding her existence as a family secret is all that saved her, as others belatedly tried also to hide their daughters after the failed revolt. However, the community knew their daughters, and this doomed them.

Neighbors, who had seen her third child Lil, remembered the beautiful red hair and blue-eyed toddler. Her neighbors thought of her disappearance, years before, as another tragedy that had befallen the cursed family at the top of the hill, and Srene allowed them to believe that. That deception saved Lil.

Grier and his men made the women and even girls in the rebel families live with the humiliation of them knowing them in the most intimate ways. Srene hated and blamed herself for not having the courage to fight them off or resist until they killed her.

The atrocious experience was almost unbearable, but Srene clung to the knowledge that their daughter was safe, a tiny comfort amidst the pain.

Srene's older son Pal was away tending to the flock in the hills and missed the affiliation to the crimes and the punishment, but he was soon to follow his own deadly path at the hands of Grier.

Lil hid for almost two days in the hole before her mother uncovered her. Her mother was unrecognizable. Lil looked at her mother as if she was a creature from the abyss coming to steal her, like some stories she had been told around the fire at night.

Despite attempts to clean, the blood and dirt still matted Srene's hair, and her eyes had blood red sclera, with dark circles around them radiating from her broken nose. The punch that broke her nose sent her into a dazed darkness and silenced her resistance. Her once beautiful sash was torn and later that night, would burn in the fire as Srene sat naked scrubbing herself for hours with water from a bucket, while Dearn moaned in the corner like a specter. Srene had reflected, "Some stains cannot be washed away."

"Todd lingered for two days and died from a massive infection. I could hear his sounds in her memories," wrote Jen. "His constant screaming sounded more like a hoarse cough by that point, tearing through the boy's shattered throat."

The strike of the heavy mallet had been slightly off center, as seen by the dark purple bruise that showed the mallet's head's outline. It had crushed flesh and splintered bone. Shattered sharp bone had pierced his colon and skin in several places. Even if a miracle had happened, allowing him to live, he could never have walked again.

"There is a mixed memory here of Grier himself," wrote Jen. Even he secretly felt haunted by the sickening crunch and the scream that rose from the boy after the mallet fell. His screams climbed to the registers beyond that any young girl could make to the heights of a whistle before it ravaged his throat. The ruined throat that would never deliver a conscious word again. Grier woke up some nights in a sweat hearing that sound.

Todd's temperature became so high, he felt like coals from a fire smoldered beneath his skin and the area below his bellybutton was purple and distended. From his penis oozed a watery brown blood and pus mixture that smelled of rotting flesh. The decision Srene had to make was one no mother should ever face, the agony of choosing between her child's peace and her own. She carried the heavy burden of her choice, knowing she had failed to give her child the comfort he needed.

Todd died in the afternoon of the second full day as the rain poured outside. The storm discharged rain in heavy droplets. It had rained the morning after Srene found Dearn and Todd in front of their home. For three straight days, the rain continued in a deluge and thunder rumbled with flashes lighting the night. It appeared, even the Gods, were grieving.

The flashes from the lightning forced Srene to see her dead son bound in blankets and rope, as the smell of rot and feces carried by the drafts reached out like hands. The cruel lightning flashed from different directions, creating the illusion that her son was moving despite his body being cold. Srene was awake for it all, sitting on the ground with her arms wrapped around her knees, mourning her own existence as much as the death of her second son.

The hatred in Srene had almost a physical form in her mind during this crisis. All present when Todd died carried the guilt of being glad there was no more screaming... although they all heard it forever in their minds. The trauma of this event destroyed Srene, as she blamed Dearn for it all. Without him, she no longer had a refuge from her hate and despair. Darkness grew like a cancer inside her.

Every time she looked at the tied blanket containing Todd, she cried and apologized for her weakness and inability to end his pain. Srene's consciousness eventually collapsed from pure exhaustion and the rain let up less than an hour later.

A neighbor named Denmore, who was dealing with his own demons, leaned over Dearn and wept an apology that Dearn could never accept. Dearn gritted his teeth in pain and anger, unable to answer him. Denmore assisted by burying their son for them.

Dearn knew he was one of Grier's men. That horrible night haunted him and filled him with anguish and guilt for their actions and his own cowardice. Dearn never told Srene Denmore had been there supporting Grier, or that he had admitted to watching the punishments being carried out, helpless and horrified.

Denmore would never have a non-tremulous night sleep again. He knew his actions and inactions had damned him.

"The creature Scrios, years later," Jen wrote in the margin, *"used the memories of how he had vomited in cowardly disgust afterwards, to drive him to kill his own family, thinking it was his only path to redemption."*

Dearn's limp and mutilated penis, were a constant everyday reminder of that night. Worse though, was Srene's crying and twitching in her sleep, which made him feel like less of a man than the effects of the mallet.

Months after the mallet incident, Dearn attempted to create intimacy with his wife, hoping it would help her feel wanted. As his wife, Srene tried to submit to an intimacy she no longer felt. Shame manifested almost physically, joining their awkward embrace as another lover, demanding their full attention. The blackness of Srene's hate intensified.

When several years later, after the battle, Grier dropped his punishments related to the revolt that demanded a share of Dearn's livestock as continued punishment, it seemed like good fortune had finally shined upon them. Before that, each summer "that fucker" as Dearn referred to him in a subdued voice, after checking all sightlines... would collect and feast on tributes with his supporters.

They feasted and laughed all summer on the animals of those families who lost the battle. All the while, the defeated walked with a permanent limp and their wives and daughters slept through a tempest of horror every night in their dreams.

When the terms to the end of Dearn's tribute payments were told to him, Dearn's blood boiled. Grier was taking his only living son, Pal. The son who had carried the load his father no longer could in the fields. Grier said, "Good news, friend. I have forgiven your attacks on me. I will no longer take first privilege on your livestock and stores. You grow and you can keep, and I might even trade with you in the future." Grier said with the smile of a butcher. "I am converting your debt to the servitude of your son... Pal is his name?" he asked, as he checked with one of his men, who nodded confirming the name.

"Pal will pay your debt through service," Grier said. "He will work in my fields and tend to my animals. If called to, he will join me in defense of what is mine."

Pal, who had grown into a strapping young man, balled his fists as his face reddened. He was preparing to yell something foul when Dearn stepped in front of him and grabbed his chin, dragging his face downward to meet his eye. "Don't!" he said. "He is doing this to hurt me, hurt your mother, and he would like nothing more than a reason to kill you. Don't give it to him. Go. Work for him. I will manage and we will miss you terribly, but go and thrive if you can. Live! Live my son... Live." He said with a voice slowing and imparting calm.

Pal's eyes burned with hatred the day that Grier demanded his service in the final settlement of his father and brother's offenses, but he nodded and walked away with them.

He worked in Grier's fields, but less than two months later, he was handed a barely functional spear and ordered to charge his own former neighbor's house. The neighbor had resisted Grier's absurd tribute demands, claiming it would surely lead them to starvation, since he demanded their last female goat. Grier smiled and simply shrugged.

The neighbor's wife stabbed Pal in the stomach as he appeared in the doorway. Just before, he attempted a quiet call, announcing, "It's me Pal..." The tine of the crude pitchfork she used to shovel the dung was her weapon. Her husband saw it was Pal coming towards his wife and tried to warn her. She didn't recognize Pal, as all she saw was an enormous man rushing into her house with a spear.

She looked up to curse the intruder, knowing this decision to stand would be her last. Pal winced as the fork pierced him; the left tine had fully embedded itself slightly above and to the right of his navel, the middle tine raking his narrow waist.

Seeing who it was, she dropped to her knees and offered no resistance as Grier stepped forward with his stone headed mace and split her skull with one thunderous swing.

The neighbor's husband died over the winter from starvation and the devastation of his life. Grier took their child of six years as last payment, along with all his remaining livestock and stores. In a memory that was entirely from Scrios about the incident that killed Pal, Scrios noted, "That son, a boy named Vagish, nearly 20 summers later would avenge his mother's death, killing Grier after a simple suggestion from the creature."

Grier inspected Pal's wound and shook his head, "I release you. You can go die at home," he said.

Death would not be swift for her second-born son, Pal, either. He suffered for days as he rotted from the inside out. Srene knew immediately when she saw the tool covered in animal feces that impaled him. Everyone there knew that a torturous, slow death waited to steal him, too.

Pal died six days later. Srene regularly would go outside and cry, trying to hide her shame and misery from Dearn and Lil. Pal's death consumed Srene. All her boys had died.

Entry 8 - Srene

Srene welcomed the change when it happened. She hated the sweats that would hit her amid the coldest and darkest nights. While others huddled under blankets, Srene sought to unburden almost all her clothing in search of relief.

That is when she started doing her "walks". This mostly comprised going out by the sheep and goats and sitting on the flat cool rock and letting the wind off the sea cool her. Sometimes she sat for hours and watched the Sun wake up.

Mostly, she would sit and think. Think of her life with Dearn, wail at the faces of her children she saw in her memories and curse herself for the guilt of other's horrible actions. She would sit there and dream of curses for the world that had tortured her so.

Srene would cry for her dead boys and dream of a world for Lil. She knew Lil had to survive, and that would mean getting her away from this wretched place. With her beauty, she could never be safe here, and it was cruel to keep her inside. Her skin was as white as a fish's belly, as she only remembered seeing the sunlight through an open window or door.

Lil had become skilled at cooking and with the needle. She made wonderful clothes with the scraps her father had bartered for, but they were impractical for working and would draw far too much attention if she ventured outside.

They discussed plans to move her to a relative's home. Perhaps Merl, the cousin Dearn was close to as a child, if he would take her. The specter of Srene's encounter with her uncle haunted her and Dearn knew it. Even though it was unsaid, Dearn placed his forehead on Srene's, "Merl is not your uncle."

They had been playmates and dreamed of travels to anywhere but where they lived, but there within a 30-mile circle, is where they would stay their entire lives. As Dearn and Merl reached maturity, they had less time for childish things, and each took on the mantel of adult responsibility. Soon after, Dearn left with Lil. Over the ensuing years, they had only chanced upon each other rarely for prolonged visits, in the high summer fields with their flocks.

They would camp together for a night when they happened upon one and other and discuss old times. Both were glad the other was still alive. The first encounter was years before the battle with Grier and the tragedies of his children. They found they had each settled about a half day's walk from each other.

232

Even though just a short half day walk away, rare chance encounters since, were nothing more than a pleasant smile and a greeting with a promise to get together someday.

Over the next two years, Dearn made a greater effort to visit Merl, while bringing the goats down from the summer lands, to see if the boy he loved as a brother had grown into the man he hoped him to be.

During those years, Srene's sorrow over her life soured in her heart until it became a deep hate of the world itself.

Entry 9 - Dearn

Merl's community, like many others, had issues with a local would-be tyrant, but had assembled quite a defense. Stone was plentiful and multiple families had pulled together to form his community. They had together built several strong stone buildings between their farms, around a shared year-round spring and a small but sturdy wall with a trench for defense.

Merl was notorious in his community, because during a spring many years before, a wolf pack had come to the area. It had killed livestock and even a person working in their field. Merl and a hunting party tracked down and killed a mother wolf, separated from the pack, capturing her four pups.

The pack moved on to look for easier prey, and the attacks in their lands stopped. People honored Merl as a celebrity of sorts.

He took and raised the pups, despite the skepticism of his friends. Over the years, the wolves had multiplied to their current number of 13. The wolves tolerated only the people who Merl tolerated. Despite the stone building, the wall, and the silly trench, it was the threat of a bite that truly kept the bandit neighbors at bay.

Dearn, over a visit, confided in his cousin the existence of Lil, the troubles and their need he had. "Family is family," Merl told him, and he promised to keep her safe. He offered to take her in as an orphan to further hide her identity and let her earn her keep in the house, but it would cost him four female sheep. He instead settled on two female goats and one pregnant female sheep.

Late that summer, near the same time as her birth, at the end of her 13th year, Lil traveled with her father to Merl's home. They left in the early morning, with nothing but the nearly full moon to light their way. Upon arriving, her father introduced Lil to her uncle Merl. Through her eyes, Merl was a stern giant, almost a head taller than her father, like Todd had been. Merl's wife Garran and adult son Kegan were awake to welcome the foundling girl dressed in the blanket, tied to act as a hood. Before she left, her mother gave her the simple stone necklace she had taken with her so many years ago.

Lil was a natural with the wolves and the pups, who soon accepted her even without Merl's presence. From a security standpoint, Merl found the situation unsettling, yet it appeared to be limited only to her. They snarled impressively at anyone else. Lil had found her job. She became the keeper of the wolves.

Entry 10 - The Deal - Srene

Two summers after Pal died, despite her own childhood experiences, Srene was glad her daughter was now going to a safer place, but the absence of Lil's light brought Srene back to the darker place in her brooding. The memories of the demons of her early life haunted her.

Now, she remembered only sadness in her past and saw no future beyond a lonely existence punctuated by her own and Dearn's death. While she sat there that cool summer night waiting for her husband to return alone, a dark fire lit inside her and consumed her soul.

She dreamed of impossible retribution, not just for the likes of Grier, but for the whole damned world. She uttered a curse so foul; it was heard in worlds beyond this one. Creatures of complete darkness in distant corners of the universe turned their heads and took notice of these words of desecration.

In them, she offered all of herself. Her wish carried so much cruel sincerity, her hate was so pure, and her sorrow was so complete, that something impossibly dark, folded its enormous wings and nodded its many tentacled head, silently accepting the exchange.

In the trance that Srene had put herself in, repeating her dreams of annihilation, strange images flashed through her consciousness. Despite her inability to understand the images' meaning, Srene gained a certainty that something had accepted her offer, though the terms of this pact remained a mystery to her.

Over the next year, without the aid of Dearn, somehow her long dead womb fluttered. This was not possible as Dearn had lost the ability and much of the desire from the cruel punishment years before, but she knew the familiar feeling in her womb.

As it grew, she felt cold sharp pains that left her with fevers that would sometimes last for days. A parthenogenesis had occurred. A withered egg from her dormant ovary broke loose; somehow the cursed egg split and formed an embryo which even more unlikely found purchase to her barren womb.

234

Future scientists might hypothesize, calculate, and witness this type of event under perfect conditions thousands of years in the future, but it is almost unheard of in complex organisms like humans. Those conceptions would rarely occur naturally and were even difficult to produce when intentionally attempted in labs, but this one... this one was unique. This was an impossible child... of darkness.

The sickly child slowly grew in her womb. It should have never survived, and it would have died, but Srene's hate and utter despair nourished it. The sickly and wrong fetus found sustenance in its mother's sorrow. Minus the creature's unnatural ability to find this as nourishment, the frail body it inhabited, would have withered and died.

As Srene's certainty of the baby's existence grew, the guilt and terror to tell Dearn intensified. When she told him, it created distrust between the couple. "You're WHAT?" Dearn had said.

"With child you oaf," Srene said, hoping to make light of it.

The insurrection's punishment injured him, though not completely crippling him. Since the punishment, making love was impossible because of the damage he had sustained. He could not remember the last time they had even attempted it.

While Srene insisted there had been no other, it took months for Dearn to deal with the feelings of betrayal and fool himself that this child was possible.

She was so small, even as she approached what had to be full term, that her bump could almost be mistaken for poorly carried extra weight. But these were not the years of plenty and few people carried fat. Minus the bump, Srene appeared as malnourished as she was.

Through the anger and mistrust, the baby's existence created in their marriage; the creature she carried continued to grow stronger. Srene confided in a neighbor who helped as a midwife for her approaching need.

The neighbor had looked at her twice in a wry, disbelieving way when Srene asked. This would be the first and only child born by the families that had taken part in the poorly planned and executed revolt. The midwife's skepticism was further enhanced because of Srene's petite size. Also adding doubt, she was the oldest woman she had seen with a child by at least five years.

Neighbors talked as neighbors would talk, and Srene quietly brooded as stares belied the stories spreading through the community.

One of the final righteous thoughts Srene had in this world was shortly after her new son slipped into this world, slimy and covered in blood and afterbirth on a cold winter solstice night. This steaming worm of a child shocked the midwife.

235

The smell of the birth was that of decay. As she held Srene's still child, the mother leaned forward and grabbed the baby. Still covered in ichor and her lifeblood, after a painful breech birth, where blood discharge still trickled from her loins, hitting the floor with the sound of a summer shower, the child's name came to Srene.

As an unnatural paleness whitened Srene's skin and darkened her vision, there was a heaviness threatening to pull the still child from her weakening arms. With the midwife whimpering as she looked at the baby's pale blue skin and purple lips, she was certain the child was dead. She had once seen a neighbor dead after drowning in a large storm and this was the same pallor the child had.

Abruptly, the baby, without a visible inhale, suddenly cried out in a high-pitched, avian screech. The midwife shrieked and recoiled from the mother and unnatural baby, falling backwards off the stool she sat on, with her feet rolling up to the sky as she squealed.

Time ticked on. The baby continued to cry, and the mother's gaze faltered as the child's bluish skin failed to regain a healthy pink hue. As Dearn crashed into the room, unable to further ignore the commotion, Srene cracked a weak smile at her beautiful baby boy and gave it a name.

No one would forget this child's name. Srene's blank, widening pupils could only see the beautiful flower from her childhood musings as she stared at her son. The bluish hue of the child destined for a cruel greatness and unprecedented longevity, evoked the picture in Srene's exhausted mind of a beautiful early spring flower. As a tear rolled from her eye, she said, "His name is Sgriosadh," and the darkness enclosed around her as Dearn caught the child from her faltering arms.

The word Sgriosadh, the name of the local blue spring flower, would change, as no one would associate Sgriosadh with a flower or anything beautiful in the future. Later, in modern English, this lovely spring bloom would be called a Blue Bell. The creature its mother named Sgriosadh that day, in that ancient language, would live a life that would change the meaning of the word.

"His name, when I Googled it, is an ancient word that means destruction," Jen wrote in the side column. "Over time, its pronunciation changed to simply Scrios in modern Gaelic.

Entry 11 - Dearn

There was also a memory from Dearn, Jen wrote in the journal; it was sometime around 1143 BC estimated and it was his memory of the birth of Scrios. In Dearn and Srene's home on the northwest shore of what is now known as Ireland.

Five-months after the first recognized flutter, Srene's clarion screaming started at sundown of the winter solstice. As the full moon rose, the screams chased away the feeble sun's warmth. The labor lasted until the moon was almost directly overhead, when Dearn heard an almost inhuman screech followed by the collapse of furniture.

Dearn crashed into the room to find the midwife toppled to the floor behind the tipped stool with a terrified look on her face. His wife was holding a tiny corpse-like child. His first thought was, "this miracle child is dead". The strange child screeched again. Dearn barely made it to his wife in time to brace her arms as her strength faltered. He didn't argue the name, even if naming him after a flower seemed feminine, as he realized he was likely losing both that day.

This small, sickly bluish child born of hate she had named Scrios, was there, wrapped in the blanket made from fox hide. Its appearance appalled the midwife as she warded herself from it. The baby's purplish-blue lips and moon-pale skin, radiating a bluish sheen, made it look as if he had drowned.

Sarah, the midwife and neighbor, who helped with the birth, felt violated when the child turned its head and seemed to stare into her. The child's gaze caused her throat to constrict, choking her. She had been the midwife for several births prior, one breach where both the mother and child had died, but she had never experienced fear like this night, looking at that child. She would never volunteer to midwife again and would decline when asked.

The sporadic screech cries from the baby lasted until the moon receded into the icy sea to the West. No animals moved or made a sound that night except for the wild wolves in the distance, whose sorrowful howls seemed in revulsion to the newborn monster's existence.

Entry 12 - Dearn

Scrios and his wife both made it through the winter, which surprised Dearn. He worried terribly that Srene's fever, while nursing, meant they'd both die before spring. Dearn was prepared for the nightmare likelihood of the Gods taking both, but the Gods had no sway here, as the monster had already awakened to its destiny.

Srene was strong, and she rallied several times from mortal sickness. Scrios, ironically, seemed to gain weight like a parasite during the time of his mother's worst illness. The spring came, and the spring sunlight revealed that Dearn and Srene had both visibly aged.

Gray now dominated the new facial hair growth of Dearn, showing a clear transition from the youthful beard he had in the fall. Srene had lost a lot of weight that she could not afford to lose, and her skin had taken on a gray and wrinkled complexion. Her compact form was now almost childlike. Her skin hung from her bones and a dark shadow lined the bottom of each wrinkled eye. Dearn had accepted the certainty of the way he feared the winter would end. Now, her body felt weightless, like dry grass when he hugged her.

He had spent winter days tending to the flock as best he could, however, prioritizing the care of his wife and child.

Sarah, the neighbor midwife, who had helped deliver the baby, always seemed to be too busy to talk and unable or perhaps unwilling to visit.

Dearn found his new son's ways differed from all his previous children. While he may have spent more time with Scrios than the rest, the child showed improved behavior, crying infrequently after that first night. During Dearn's worst moods, his child's small, subtle smile and bright, dancing eyes, like lights in cold, dark, turbulent blue waters, caught his attention more than once.

In mid spring, to the surprise of his recovering mother, at about five months old, Scrios, the blue child, sat up in one attempt and balanced. At eight months, he muttered his first word, "brón" (Sadness) he said, and smiled.

Both parents changed their memory of having heard him say, "mham" for Mom. That became the story they told themselves until it was true. At a year old, Scrios walked with a purpose and ran free.

At two, the quiet blue child went with father to tend the animals. His father carried him, and he could taste Dearn's concern for the family, the flock and the crops. The animals in the pens, with their skittish movements and panicked gazes, clearly showed Dearn their fear upon his arrival. He quickly scanned the field and the surrounding hillside, searching for any sign of a lurking predator. Satisfied there was no threat, he relaxed, but the animals did not. The animals kept their distance from Scrios and because he carried it, its father. Millions of years had taught these animals what a predator was. As Scrios could sense his father's anxieties, the animals could sense the malevolence in the tiny creature the father had brought with him that day.

Scrios found he could sense the animals, too. He knew better than his father, that the large ram alpha of the herd was balancing the odds of attacking the blue creature that it believed threatened its flock. Scrios met eyes with the ram and conveyed upon it that his flock was not his food. The ram, unnerved by the communication, slid back into the herd and put other animals in his sight lines. It then led the flock to the farthest side of their pen.

When his father placed him in the grass while he worked, he sat patiently, quietly observing. None of the animals turned their backs on Scrios, but all averted their eyes, and none dared come close.

Rumors spread among the neighbors about the strange boy and his slight blue hue. It was the oddity of his appearance that began the isolation of the family. Sarah, the neighbor and midwife of Scrios's birth, cackled to the community of her fears of the cursed blue child. "The blue beast changed everything," she said, explaining every misfortune. Word of this betrayal eventually fell on the ears of Srene, who quietly brooded in anger, and therefore garnered the attention of Scrios, who assessed the neighbor as a risk.

Scrios marked the woman as a threat and quietly weighed his options. Although he involuntarily nodded in agreement when he quietly evaluated her accusations. She was not entirely wrong; he quietly conceded with a smile.

Jen wrote in the margin with a different pen, her handwriting with an obvious unsteadiness when compared to the other text she had written at a different time. She underlined this point, and wrote, "He knew! Before his parents knew, he was self-aware. He knew he was different! He knew he was a monster!"

That summer, blight infested much of the root crops of all their closer neighbors. In midsummer, the weather was much cooler and damper than most years. Instead of the welcomed sun of summer, there were rainy days that gave way to a dank fog. Early stored crops moldered in their storage.

Some local families starved in the harsh winter that followed from the fouled harvest. Dearn's crops, however, were remarkably healthy. For once, comparatively to previous years, and their neighbors, they ate well. Their neighbors shunned them when they tried to share or barter.

In a dramatic turnaround from the previous year, the following summer was a sweltering scorcher, with days of unbroken sunshine. The night of the midsummer lunar eclipse was clear and unnaturally quiet.

However, the next morning, someone found eight of Sarah's, the former midwife's sheep, dead. Their wide eyes intimated how they had died in panic. Their lifeless bodies, mangled and disfigured, showing clear signs of being beaten and stomped.

The largest ram's eyes seemed wild. Its horns and hooves had blood on them, and it was acting so strange that Sarah's husband Felim put it down and burned its body with the other dead sheep, fearing a blight. The animals' destruction by Felim squandered irreplaceable food resources.

No one saw the small, naked, skinny figure walk across the enormous field to Sarah's flock the night before. No one heard the silent bargaining being done that led to the ram turning on some members of its flock. At first, before the ram's guilt was plain, the gathered people feared it had to be wolves; however, there were no sounds other than thrashing sounds and screeches like a baby's scream. There were also few external wounds, mostly crushed chests and damage to the heads of the dead animals and their murderer. The only tracks found were from hoofed animals, and the bodies showed no signs of scavenging.

Sarah knew though... oh, she knew. She could feel it in her bones, and she stirred the stew about how the cursed blue child had made this happen.

The following winter was hard. Several more people in the area succumbed to famine or disease. Nourished by the neighbor's despair, his father's fears and mother's sadness, Scrios grew long and vine like through the winter.

In the spring, other families nearby, who used to be helpful, kept to themselves in fear that Sarah might be right in her accusations. Two families used the good foraging season of late spring to abandon the area.

In the midsummer, when Dearn returned from the highlands, a new rock wall appeared bisecting his shared meadow with Sarah and Felim. Seeing this when he arrived with his heard, the stacked stones caused him to pause and grind his teeth. The wall separated the large upper pasture from the smaller, lower part of the hill and Sarah's home.

That was the last humiliation, and Dearn could not abide it. He knew of her crow like behavior in the community and had tried to ignore it. He knew Felim pretended to never see his wife's behavior when they talked. Three days prior, while camping amidst the peaks with Felim, the new wall plans remained unmentioned.

Against Srene's wishes, he grabbed his last and only son and went to confront his newly walled off neighbor's wife.

Sarah was in the yard, bringing in wood for the fire when she saw Dearn approaching, carrying the cursed blue child. She knew the reason he was coming by his determined walk. In her mind, Sarah and her three daughters had left him a larger than fair share size of the pasture. She did not want his animals mixing with theirs because... well, because she knew good and damn well why.

Sarah and her daughters had taken on stacking the pasture rocks and anything else they could find to make the new wall. It had taken ten long summer days of backbreaking toil for them to build. She intentionally chose the day Dearn left with his flock as the day to start the wall.

As Dearn reached talking distance, he placed Scrios on the ground and held his hand as he continued to walk closer. Sarah, who had been outwardly ignoring his approach, stiffened. "Sarah, is your man about?" Dearn said with a practiced calm he had tried to refine during the walk over. The grumble he wanted to hide made its way into his voice, anyway.

Sarah looked at Dearn's blue spawn and hissed, "Felim is away and won't be back until the morrow at least". As she looked at the boy and caught the stare of his dark, dead ocean blue eyes, she became off balance for a heartbeat, and a certainty came to her.

Suddenly she knew... her husband was not just away; he was away with that filthy whore, Mags, who was his friend during childhood. She flushed red with immediate intense anger and snapped at Dearn, "If you want to find him, best do it before I do!" She turned and stormed inside her home with tears welling in her eyes.

Dearn stared at the outside of the cottage, words filling his mouth, but with no one to speak them to. Feeling emotionally constipated and confused by her sudden emotional outburst, he made his way home, muttering all the words he should have said.

The next morning, Dearn awoke with a start, seeing his son standing quietly at the end of his bed, staring at him. "Don't spook me like that, lad!" he boomed.

He could not be sure, but Scrios looked older and taller today. Now that his father was awake, he asked clearly, "Can I come with you to do chores today?"

The clarity of his request and eagerness surprised his father. Dearn didn't even notice that Scrios' lips didn't move when he said it. "Yes," his father said even before he thought it through, and he got them both some jerky and goat's milk for breakfast.

He likewise didn't notice that Scrios barely ate and only politely sipped the milk from the crude cup. Scrios already felt full before they ate. They finished getting dressed and headed outside.

Upon exiting the home, Dearn said, "Is that smoke?" While smoke was not unusual, it seemed heavier than a normal fire and carried a foul stench. With a panic, he noticed that over the hedge wall that Sarah's house down the hill was smoking heavily. The smoke was so thick that it was coming through the

241

thatching on the roof, looking like wet hair on a chilly day. Smoke poured from her windows.

With recognition of the peril and forgetting the troubles of the day before, Dearn broke into as close to a run as his damaged, arthritic body could manage. Running to help, Dearn noticed the heavy, dew-soaked blanket, smelling faintly of earth, that had been carelessly left outside; he snatched it up.

Scrios trotted behind him, but without the same sense of urgency as his father. As Dearn came down the hill, he could see smoke now pouring through the thatching of the roof, like a tinder bundle about to burst to light.

As he got closer, he saw a figure standing out front. It was Sarah; she was safe, so he slowed his loping run. She was just standing there, staring at him as he trotted towards her... no staring through him. Did she see him? "Sarah?" He called out. She did not reply. "What's going on?" Dearn asked with a voice an octave higher than his normal voice. Her eyes were dark, and a dark shine covered her hands and the front of her clothes. When he was about 25 yards from her, she dutifully turned and calmly walked into the house, as the roof burst to flame with an audible, "whump!"

Dearn screamed, "NO!" and broke again into a sprint. With his mind set to get her back out of there, he tried to increase his speed, but as he got closer, the heat of the fire stole the air from his lungs.

The fire was immediately so hot that the damp blanket he carried instantly steamed when he tried again to get close. The flames jetted out of the doorway, searing his open skin and curling the hair on his head and arms as it drove him back.

Other neighbors showed up, and all helplessly agreed nothing could be done. Several of the neighbors hoped aloud that no one was in the home, but Dearn confirmed, "Sarah is in there... she just walked right in," he said, making a walking gesture with his fingers on his upward facing palm.

The faces of his neighbor's tortured looks became scorched into Dearn's memory. Their concern and loss were clear.

They looked at Dearn and next at Scrios with silent accusation. Dearn looked at his son and noticed Scrios's expression appeared almost bored with the traumatic scene. Dearn excused it, thinking that a five-year-old couldn't be expected to understand what had just happened. But the look on his son's face still unnerved him.

The thick thatched roof burned quickly, and soon the main heat of the fire was gone. Working together, the neighbors pulled apart the burning wooden timbers that remained of the walls and were horrified to see the remains of Sarah sitting upright in the middle of the room. Her hair was gone, and head burned to the bone of her burst skull. Burned skin and cooked muscle dripped from her arms and torso, while the rancid smell of the sizzling, charred meat and fat poisoned the air.

Her three daughters lay on the ground on their stomach with their clothing burned away from their backs. They too, smoldering, with the backs of their bodies scorched and cracking. The line of bodies lay with remnants of their clothes visible beneath them. Scorched leather cordage bound their baked hands behind their backs.

Mercilessly to all gathered, the fire had burned not only hot but fast, ensuring the most gruesome of scenes possible. The heat had scorched the backs of her daughters to the bone in some places and broiled the flesh beneath. The directional heat somehow preserved most of the clothing on their stomachs, which revealed the telltale signs that their mother had cut her three daughters' throats after she bound them on the ground.

Felim, her husband, arrived home later that day. People tried to stop him, to warn him as a panic rose in his heart. He ran to his home, abandoning his flock. When he arrived at the front of his still smoldering home, he collapsed to his knees in anguish.

Scrios feasted that day. The child smiled inwardly as he relived the day in his mind; he hadn't even known he was hungry, but the taste as he consumed the emotion of Felim was orgasmic. He had gorged for the first time.

Entry 13 – Scrios meets Lil

As fall showed its signs, Dearn decided it was time to introduce Scrios to his sister. He was not supposed to know she existed, but his father's thoughts came easily to him. Dearn made plans with Merl to visit for a harvest meal. Scrios wondered mildly if his sister were like him and immediately dismissed the notion.

The day of the visit, the family took the long walk to Merl's. When crossing the last hill and the stone buildings coming into view, a sense of irrational foreboding came over Scrios. It surprised him. This was a new feeling, and he examined the panic almost clinically.

The uneasiness gave way to strong discomfort the closer they got to their destination. Something in his stomach was turning and there was an ache in his chest. As they approached the house, a chorus of howls greeted them.

243

Dearn smiled as he heard the wolves and he turned and spoke to his family, "It's okay, they belong to Merl's family," he began, but when he turned back to the house, he saw several people wrestling a large wolf into a doorway that seemed intent on not being caged. A smaller figure stepped out of an archway and stroked the neck of the enormous beast. The creature seemed to relax, allowing itself to be led back into the archway and a heavy banded door shut behind it.

With the situation handled, they proceeded forward. As they came close, the large door opened briefly, allowing a loud growl to escape, as a flash of red hair cleared the portal. When she emerged, Lil's blue eyes smiling as much as her mouth, stunned her parents... as they became aware of her large pregnant stomach. She shrugged, smiled again and grabbed the hand of Merl's son, Kegan, and came forward.

Scrios peaked from behind his mother to see a large man walking with a woman with red hair coming closer. "This must be my sister," he thought, as she vaguely matched the images her mother remembered. When their eyes met briefly, Scrios yelped as a sharp pain pierced his brain, and he slumped to the ground.

Though awake, a wave of panic washed over him; his mind was racing as he tried to make sense of what just happened. A high-pitched ringing resonated in his ears. Her presence terrified and confused him, and he did not know why.

It was not what he saw in her eyes. It was what he didn't see. Lil's inner self and motivation was blind to him and that terrified him. Her effortless and unconscious rebuke of his attempted invasion caused him actual physical pain.

Moments later, Scrios pretended to wake up on the ground, feigning more confusion than he felt. His father hovered over him, and asked, "Son, are you okay?"

Scrios squinted as if the light of day was too bright, "I think so," he said.

"What was that?" His mother asked.

Scrios explained, "I had a spinning feeling and fell". To his continued terror, he could not read his father's motivations now, either or anyone else, for that matter. It was as if he had lost his most important sense.

Scrios's heart pounded in his chest, and he knew he had to avoid making eye contact with them, no matter what. Maybe the rules here were different and they could see his true self? He could not take that chance. It was a hard habit to avoid, as he felt lost and blind without his usual senses. It terrified him that maybe they could now see his motivations and maybe alter them like he did to others.

Lil and her new family saw the young boy of five or six and some immediately noticed the faint sheen of blue in his skin. Merl had seen that look somewhere, but he could not place it. One day in the future, in a land to the east, he would associate Scrios' color with when he came across his beloved bride, collapsed and cold in the field after she was late returning for midday meal. The thought would plague him throughout the burial and beyond through his life after. Merl would not be the last to associate death with Scrios's pallid appearance.

Scrios imitated normality through the meal. When directly questioned, he responded politely, "Yes, it is nice to meet my sister and Kegan," a smile graced his lips as he acknowledged the expected greeting. He felt fear for a good reason, but did well at presenting the guise of normality, pulling on memories that he knew were not his own.

He used the memories of the now dead neighbor, Sarah, as his guide to acting normal. Scrios could not sense Lil except through his eyes and ears, and it made him feel as if he was being physically restrained.

She was unreadable to him, and with her this close, others were at best, faint garbled echoes when he chanced to meet their eyes. And when Scrios caught their eye, their reaction to him was strange. They looked offended, impatient or perhaps like someone would look if they just found a forgotten fish, left to rot in a basket beside their bed for a week.

Finally, with the meal over and discussions complete, they exchanged pleasantries and prepared to leave. Mother hugged his sister; next father hugged her. He stood near the door, hoping to leave and return to his home. He had to get away from this place!

A shadow crossed him, and he looked up to see his sister stepping towards him. She bent at the waist to be at eye level with him, but he refused to meet eyes. "It was nice meeting you, Scrios. Perhaps next summer you can come and meet your nephew or niece and spend a day here?"

Scrios was silent and tried to remain distant. When his mother said, "embrace your sister lad, give her a hug." Scrios's eyes flashed in terror as a long moment passed. His sister leaned in awkwardly and reached to hug her brother.

As Lil embraced her brother, the faint crackle of fairy fire, imperceptible to others, sparked between their skin, a detail she'd recall later.

Tamorn, the alpha, let out a gut-wrenching howl from his distant cage, a sound like tearing fabric that ripped through the quiet, momentarily distracting her. Sudden clarity washed over her, and she realized... Time seemed to stop for her as all in the room froze in place, and a terrible knowledge entered her like a foul wind when she looked into his eyes.

Suddenly, she knew Scrios. He was the creature of a child's bad dream. He was wrong, foul and somehow young and ancient at the same time. She felt the terrible things he cherished, as if a creature such as him could feel love. She knew the horrible acts he could commit and witnessed what he felt when he fed in the way only he could.

He was the corrupter of things pure, the source of deceit, the bellows of the flame of self-doubt and the violator of minds... and something about Lil, he feared like nothing else on this earth. He feared her.

This also came with the certainty and promise that he would cause her death someday if he could. She pushed back from him and looked into his eyes again, even as he tried to avoid her. She grabbed his chin to steady his face and demanded his attention, and with a quiver in her voice, whispered, "is this true?"

A shaky notation, highlighting the paragraph, appeared in the margin. *"This was almost identical to my experience with the golden cylinder the night of the tornado. If not for the house coming apart, I think there would have been much more memories, but the roof collapsed somewhere in this... transfer?"*

His sister's grip on his face was like a vise, her eyes, two hollow pits, boring into his soul as she forced him to look at her, the chilling emptiness washing over him. She whispered, confirming her new knowledge of him, "is this true?" The strength in him from a recent gorge surged for just a moment, enough strength for the monster in him to force a confident, knowing and corrupt smile as he tried not to vomit with the humiliation.

As the pair separated and mother and father smiled, totally having missed the interaction. Only Kegan noticed something was off, giving Lil a quizzical look as their eyes met. In their silent conversation that their love and familiarity had born, he knew something was very, very, wrong.

They had shared an embrace as sister and brother and separated as adversaries in a battle neither fully comprehended yet. Mortal enemies... and there would be no visit next summer.

When Lil's family and the monster receded beyond the distant hill and fell out of sight, Lil excused herself to the latrine. She vomited in the hole, and it was not from the with child sickness. This was different. The pregnancy sickness had passed months ago. No, this was disgust for that vile thing, wearing the skin of her brother.

She stayed to herself for a while and visited the pack in their den. Tamorn greeted her like she had been gone for a month; with the animalistic concern it shared with no one other than her. She sat with the pack for a while and cried tears of anger as she processed the day. Kegan entered, knowing he would find her here. Tamorn stood ready to challenge, quickly relaxing its body as he recognized Kegan's familiar musky scent and broad frame. As the Alpha relaxed, so did the pack.

With distance, Scrios's fear and feeling of impotence subsided. On the walk home, they passed a traveler walking in the other direction. The man carried an instrument across his back. Scrios caught the musician's eye for just a moment and ruined him.

A fleeting glimpse convinced the musician of his inadequacy; convinced that he was terrible and the audience shared the sentiment, he decided to quit performing. When his love for music faded, so did his passion for life, and he died that year. Scrios smiled contently as the traveler continued past, feeding on the anxious loss of the traveler's ambition and knowing the end that awaited him.

Entry 14 – Scrios

Through the long centuries, Scrios's comprehension of his own being grew, yet the agonizing consequences of his procrastination concerning his sister's destiny haunted him, a choice that now appeared irrevocably disastrous. As she was the other last living of his mother, as sure as he was about the location of his thumb, he knew that his mother's blood must be the source of his weakness. "Life would have been so much simpler," he reflected, "if only he hadn't given Lil the chance to spore."

At eleven years old, the emancipated Scrios led Grier and his men to attack Merl's compound. This was years after meeting his sister. His intent was to slaughter everyone in the stone houses. He stayed far back as the brief battle raged with trepidation of the forces that blinded him during his previous visit. When it was over, only a single person who inhabited the dilapidated houses was alive. His warriors shivered when the sickly, almost teenage boy that walked in after the battle stared into the flickering eyes of the dying woman on the ground. Scrios saw how her family had come across the abandon houses two years ago. They had thought maybe the builders had died of disease until they noticed that almost every belonging of value was absent.

However, he frustratingly did not find his sister or anyone he recognized in and among the dead.

Scrios's failure to take initiative would now haunt him into eternity. Scrios quietly counted on his fingers, calculating the scope of his error. "There was a pregnant Lil he met, so two or perhaps three more children by now," the boy like version of himself thought.

"Where now, the number after 500 more winters?" The Blue King thought and kicked a stone in the dirt at his feet in self-disgust. The sour memory led Scrios's mind to meander back again to his earlier years.

Scrios knew they escaped somewhere and throughout the centuries, he had several chance encounters with descendants of his sister.

He'd never been so near defeat as he was during one of their first attacks. His mistake had been thinking the people he made loyal to him through manipulation would naturally defend him when a relative came near and his powers failed.

The men he commanded stood there incomprehensibly until he verbally ordered them to defend. As if startled, they defended themselves, but their concern was not for him. He found it disturbing that they lacked the common sense of even the ram he had negotiated with as a small boy.

The descendant of Lil had made an equally naïve assumption, thinking that his presence alone would win the fight. Scrios experienced the ringing in his head that made him scream all those years ago, but that ringing had scared him more than it hurt. The helplessness that he felt as a boy, he justified, was simply because he was a boy. That desire to kill this abomination of his sister's descendants was there, but he also needed to understand his weakness, and this was an opportunity for that, he surmised.

Scrios gambled the uninvited, almost childishly brash person who invaded his home considered him weak. True, Scrios was slender like a sapling, but his wiry limbs were fast, and he had more lifetimes at this point to become an expert with the light and narrow sword he carried than this foolish boy had years of living. Even without his powers, he was quick and possessed none of the delay of action someone burdened with a conscience does. That is why, when the one named Sean came and his men did almost nothing in reaction, Scrios, recognizing his peril, fled.

Scrios had to know what he was facing. As he fled the main building, he expected a small army had likely overrun his stronghold while he was powerless, but found no other soldiers. So, the sword could stay at his side. Confused yet excited, he used the opening his defenders purchased to create distance with the assassin.

He felt a pressing need to determine the extent of his sister's bloodline's influence on her children; to discover the true limits of the strange effects it had. He would use the ringing in his head as future colliers would use a canary. He considered retrieving his horse, but the path back led dangerously close to where his attacker still might be lurking. So, he simply ran towards the wooded area ahead of him, swerving past an outbuilding to break the sightlines. When he reached the woods, which he had been silently cursing as he ran for being so damned far, the ringing ceased.

For a moment he wondered, "Is it the woods?" The ringing returning to his ears, answering his question like a sharp rebuke, as Sean paused beside the outbuilding he had run past moments before.

A wave of frustration washed over Sean as he scanned the empty landscape, the sun beating down on his neck. Scrios took two steps back, and the ringing ceased as if muffled by a blanket. He stepped forward, and it returned. He marked the spot on the ground with his foot kicking at the rocky soil and noted the location of the would-be assassin, Sean.

Sean stood growling in anger at the edge of the small barn, scanning the distance and seeing nothing. "He fucking dashed," he said to a crow perched like a witness on the fence post to his right. Uneasily from its perch, the crow sized him up.

Sean glanced over his shoulder, prepared to go look in a different direction, when he heard a loud pop of a branch in the woods ahead of him, like a clumsy stag during a hunt. There, nearly 200 feet in front of him, he saw movement in the trees and glanced at a leather cowl as it retreated deeper into the woods. With renewed energy, Sean ran towards the woods with a howl of a lone alpha wolf separated from its hunting pack.

Scrios watched the human standing near the outbuilding, "not quite a man yet, but close," he thought. He watched in fascination as he seemed to talk to a large blackbird sitting on a post 30 feet away. As he gave up the hunt and took the first step to walk away, Scrios grabbed an old dry stick and broke it over his thigh. Upon seeing the man child look his way, he ran. In his effort to be noticed, he waved his arms while he ran away.

As he ran into the woods, a howl rose behind him and Scrios smiled as he dashed. Now, though, he ran with a lead and a purpose in the dark woods. In a dry creek bed, he disappeared like smoke on a breezy day.

Careful to use as many large stones as possible, he ran along the creek and climbed the side quietly. He used his pursuers smashing in the woods and frustrated screams to locate him and his progress. As he heard insults and challenges, he continued to make his way quietly, only pausing when his pursuer listened for a clue to his location. After a few moments, the childish tantrum resumed as Scrios concealed a laugh. Knowing he had passed the creek, Scrios returned to his stronghold, unencumbered by his pursuer's suppressive effects.

When he arrived at his home, he gathered members of his idiot army and sent them to collect the boy. He imposed upon them the same understanding. They could hurt him, but under no circumstances could they kill him. If that meant they died trying, that was fine. If stabbed, they were to walk into the blade and hold it so others could capture and restrain the man. When captured, they were to restrain and bind him and build a fire. When the fire was hot, they were to heat a blade until it glowed and remove his thumbs and burn the wounds to staunch the bleeding. He gave them a specific understanding of how to tie and restrain his limbs in a supine position, poisoning their minds with images of his desires and making them see it as a caring act of compassion.

After they achieved this goal, they were to dispatch one of their remaining numbers to let him know where he could find the thumbless one called Sean, as the remaining living, guarded. As an afterthought, he wanted the thumbs delivered to him.

For a boy at the edge of adulthood, this Sean proved brave even when he embraced the end of his own song. Reluctantly, Sean revealed he had arrived by boat from an unfamiliar eastern land after Scrios shattered both of his lower legs, and gorged on the agony it created.

As Sean called to his mother in tears and apologized to his father for not listening, Scrios piously waited. The trip across the sea from the land to the east was about all the useful information he gathered. It was enough.

His sister's disappearance, shrouded in a hundred years of silence, led him to suspect she'd gone there. If they hadn't, he certainly would have known.

Nature ate at Sean's mutilated body, lashed to the same fence post where he had conversed with the crow three days before.

Scrios wondered if he would feel any different killing someone from his own family, and he did. It felt right.

The traveling story tellers sang variations on his song for hundreds of years.

There had been a different attempt, centuries later. By that time, people recognized Scrios as the king of a large area. This fanatic was no relative. Just a scout sent to spy on his kingdom. "He thought he could just stroll into Scrios's hall unnoticed?" Scrios mused.

It had been several hundred years since Sean had come. A story carried by the singers before his court talked of an exotic band of warriors that had traveled to the island in the east with a noble purpose. The king met with the storytellers personally, and they knew nothing beyond the poems they heard. He heard other stories in their memories. Songs they had witnessed and maybe forgotten. In his mind, he heard poems about great Hellenic warriors killing one-eyed giants and serpents. He heard stories of warriors with the favor of the Gods, who fought in their stead. He wondered if these gods were like him.

The exotic warriors in the story were from a land referred to as Hellas. If serving gods was their lot in life, why shouldn't they serve him?

He searched the memories from the thousands of people over the centuries he collected, and there were very few other references to Hellas. One old beggar had once worked on boats and encountered a trader that had used the word Hellas. They had purchased oil and wine, supposedly from the mythical land to the far south. One of his guards, a century prior, asserted his sword was of a Hellenic design and artistry, though he'd only learned the term during an overpriced trade.

Disguised as a merchant, a spy infiltrated the region and, after roughly a week, neared the target's medium sized stone and timber stronghold, a six-day journey south. A mostly completed stone wall, wide and taller than a man, surrounded the keep and storage areas.

The squalor conditions of the land the Blue King controlled shocked the scout, and it only became worse as the closer one came to the seat of his kingdom. Amidst the squaller, the king's keep stood out as a shining spot.

The spy's careless actions and appearance led to his capture. He had goods to trade in a land stripped of its wealth. The fresh clothes he wore were clean and unmended compared to everyone else he passed on the streets. Despite his travels, his horse looked healthy and was the most likely source of fresh food for 50 miles.

Before his capture, blank stares and hollow looks condemned him. He became self-aware, even before they apprehended him, of how he stood out. He was a flower blooming in a dung heap. No matter of changing appearance would suffice, as he looked too healthy.

In his last moments of freedom, he had run in the night, but he didn't make it far. He became aware in the dark streets, as he dodged the occasional spill of firelight, that he was not alone. From his left, in an open, lit doorway, he heard a voice say, "Well, hello."

That was the point his mind and desires ceased to be his own, when he met the eyes of a sickly blue-eyed man who stood in the doorway smiling.

Oh, what a trove this one was. Ralf, the spy, knew of the army from a far-off land led by a woman. She never said her name to Ralf. He had not been privy to too much conversation, as he had met them in a camp in a high walled valley. She wanted him for his hunting prowess and stealth, which she said he had a reputation for. She had also heard of Ralf's bravery, a trait that he was dubious of, when he thought about it later.

They employed him to gather information on a king on the island to the west. Learn what he could of the king's intentions and look for signs the king was building an army or planning to invade their land.

"Be careful," they warned, "the king's spies infest the land, and his wrath is swift and terrible; his cruelty is renowned." The promise of a life of untold luxury, filled with the bounty of countless animals, they offered in return. Enough to feed him and his family richly and clothe them warmly.

Scrios looked through the eyes of Ralf in his memories, looking at the land that surrounded them. A high walled valley, with a raised center with a structure on it, perhaps a ruin as it was hard to see at this distance with bushes and trees that hampered his views. He saw the mass of people camped in the valley. Scrios estimated campfires for 50 to 70 people. A woman with dark skin and long black kinky, curled hair, who seemed to ooze confidence, spoke to him, casting a brief smile that had instantly excited Ralf.

She was young and beautiful, with a sword on her hip. Flanking her were two other men. One with a darker olive complexion, and black curly hair. The other, much older than she, who stood and looked at him sternly. Neither of the two guards seemed to comprehend the conversation.

"The exotic army," Scrios thought. "My army... the army of a God!" he said aloud as the desire overwhelmed him.

Scrios mentally followed the path of the spy from his memories. He found where the spy crossed the sea from and where he landed. Everything he saw, Scrios knew. Banishing the spy home, he cursed him with endless sleeplessness; his only goals were to report back to his handlers and to tell everyone along his path a single message.

When he was hungry, he was to eat like a feral dog and when he was thirsty, drink from puddles or whatever he found first. No other words were important enough for him to speak. The message to everyone he met was, "The Blue King comes!"

The next morning, Scrios issued orders to 15 men from his keep. He had them gather supplies and the weapons they were comfortable with. They mounted horses and left.

After a family of fishermen at the coast, where Ralph had crossed, met eyes with Scrios, they begged the king to allow them to take him and his men to the distant shore to the east. They were also kind enough to give their fish stew to his men, as well as the dried fish on their racks.

They arrived at the far coast quickly because of a favorable breeze that pushed them across the expanse of water as if the land they left no longer wanted them.

Their first challenge was when three men appeared on a road near the shore, while a fourth person, possibly a child, quickly rode away to the east. "Gentlemen!!" called Scrios with the smile of a butcher addressing condemned livestock. The men who had stopped hundreds of yards away appeared intimidated.

The words reached the three men ahead as a gust of wind spun the sandy dust off the road in front of them, making the horses draw back momentarily. The men on horses looked closely at the armed band of soldiers they had watched exit the small boats and don their armor. "They are welcoming their new king!" Scrios said, pointing with his chin as the surrounding men laughed.

Two of the three men standing ahead on the worn path looked at their leader as if confused by his inactivity. The leader sat forward on the horse, clearing his throat to reply when he thought better of it and instead, he listened to the ache in the pit of his chest. An ember of intuition that had kept his ancestors alive on the savannahs of Africa, millions of years before, was screaming to him to stay in the tree and remain perfectly still or timelier... to flee.

This was the same feeling that his ancestor listened to, when others of his species lacking the intuition became food of one of the many predators; all while that ancient relative passed its wary, lifesaving genes on to his progeny.

In a moment of his own mortal recognition, he noticed his ache was the same ache that his unsettled horse was feeling. The cramping muscles from constantly applying pressure with his left leg to keep the beast with the flared nostrils he rode, from spinning in panic, reinforced his feeling.

He commanded his companions, "This does not feel right, and the smiling man down there is definitely not right. Leave and take a circuitous route to your home."

Scrios watched as the men turned and proceeded back up the road at a gallop. "Hmm, I guess I am walking for a while," he said with a shrug to his band of men.

Scrios knew he had many names over the centuries; he was called "The Bringer of Pain" by some. Others called him King Scrios, the Blue King or just Scrios. His pattern of brutality was all too familiar to those who survived him.

Most recently, in this new land across the water, after only a week, they had named him the "Eater of Babies" and he liked that. He had to admit, when prepared right, they were quite tasty, as they had been that day in the field as he watched the leaders of that rabble army hang themselves at his suggestion.

Leftovers from other skirmishes and families of farmers, fearing the stories they'd heard, composed the army that faced him that day. He smiled as he reminisced about the memories he had collected from the riders, who had come with the intent to "end the scourge".

This motley group was not the army he sought. This was not the exotic army he coveted, the one fit for a god; but they had heard the rumors of the exotic group destined to be his.

The rabble army attack had been exciting to Scrios, with so many riders coming at him at once, in an arc. This was so much more fulfilling than watching an army of rubes fighting for him. The confidence it brought when he could invade their minds so quickly and have them do his bidding was intoxicating.

The first rider he dominated feared for his daughter. He could see her through his eyes as she cried when he left. He had promised her he would be back and would take her to the stream to play when the weather warmed. She was the key to him.

The new memory Scrios provided was that same trip to the stream, but changed to where he pushed her face into the sandy bottom until her legs stopped kicking. He knew it was the best thing he could do for her. His guilt for murdering her hung upon him like the wet tunic he wore after he drowned her, and the only release from that guilt was in the limbs of the tree he saw ahead of him, under the accusing eyes of the crows.

After finding each of their weaknesses and prying them open; giving them a new understanding was easy. Pointing them to their salvation in the tree was glorious. The utter sorrow that consumed them had the sweet smell of mother's

254

milk to him. He had expected that it would take longer before he could have his feast. That somehow, they would resist him, and he knew he was taking foolish chances, knowing his sister's descendants were in this land somewhere.

He had wondered with a laugh during the charge if someone would get close enough to attack him? They did not.

He made the chargers disrobe on this frigid day; they took anything that could work as a rope and used it to hang the first few of the riders. Next, they fashioned rope out of their clothing. While they did that, he ate and drank, sitting in a farmhouse chair his men brought to him. He ate his meal and drank the wine seated at a table, also provided by his troops as he watched the show.

When they ran out of materials for ropes, only a handful remained, shivering in the icy wind. Submissively, they lined up for their army's similarly naked leader, and he cut them down with his sword, one by one. When he was done, Scrios sent the leader, naked, covered in the gore that had sprayed from the necks of his men, back on his horse to the rest of his quiet army.

None of the ones swinging in the tree or the ones slaughtered by their leader knew anything except rumors of the exotic army that the storytellers had talked about, and that frustrated Scrios. Still, however, somewhere his army was being built, so he would continue to follow the path he wrenched from the spy.

He felt fortune had swung his way. He could feel that he was finally on the path Lil had taken centuries ago, and if he had to kill every mongrel on this new land to clean up after that whore, well, that is what he would do. As a bonus, he would get the army he deserved.

Tales of the strange encounter with the riders spread along the rocky coast, carried on the salty wind to the ears of the fishermen, and inland along bustling trade routes.

A lone man, arriving two days prior in a small boat, had warned them about the approaching Blue King, yet they dismissed him as crazy. He, repeating the warning with a parched tortured throat, "The Blue King comes" in answer to every question, as he tracked off to the east and north, repeating his warning. So, the south looked the prudent direction of travel.

Many dismissed the crazed man, who repeated the same warning over and over. Most were just glad he had moved on in his path. However, they had heard of a Blue King. In recent years, there had been many that had abandoned the island to the west with stories that scared the children around the fire.

The stories of a cruel and ageless king who some insisted was a creature or demon that could haunt their dreams and found delight in the torment and death of his own subjects. Stories said the lucky ones in his kingdom were the ones who were dead, and free from his influence.

In the following weeks, an increasingly large army gathered to oppose the small group led by the frail blue man who'd arrived on the shore weeks earlier with less than a score of followers. The walking corpse, as some survivors described him, and his men waded through each battle with ease. Strange stories emanated of men turning on their brother or impaling themselves on their own weapons.

Some survivors who joined his army, mid battle, became part of his growing entourage of protectors. Some onlookers, who got too close, testified that he wore a braided hair necklace with two dried human thumbs strung on it.

There were stories of farmers that filled the ranks of the resisting armies with any sharp implement they could find. Many of whom returned home from battle broken and crazed. They had burned their own homes, sometimes with the families still inside screaming, as the soldier apologized outside.

Death and despair invariably marked the Blue King's path northeastwards along the trade road, following his deranged harbinger. In the woods in the distance and from the tops of hills, unseen scouts tracked his progress from a distance, being careful to go unnoticed by either side in the conflict. They noticed flocks of carrion birds choked the skies in his wake, assumingly feeding on the bodies of the fallen, that marked the progress on his journey north.

Entry 16 – The Battle - Jen

There are so many memories of his time before and after the encounter that trapped him in the artifact. My Laoch had tried to tell me him being trapped in this way was a possibility. I'm trying to focus on the meaningful memories... the ones that might help defeat it... but I'm terrified that I may miss something that is important.

Scrios's memory of that battle is telling. His machinations in the days before the battle cast light on this monster.

The creature figured out days before that it was being drawn to the broad valley by someone's plan. Ralf's memories showed the steep walls of the valley. A higher area he saw in the stolen memories from the spy, intrigued him. Scrios knew they were plotting to kill him. Someone always tried to kill him; the lack of attempts would be an insult. That was what made life so enjoyable for him.

Previously, in his homeland, peasant revolts were the source of delight. It was almost like a sport with a splendid feast as spouses watched their loved ones turn on each other. Larger assaults from distant and valiant leaders met similar predictable ends.

This trip, however, promised a foreign flavor in a new land and the final rebuke of his sister. The spy knew of a contingent from the lands far to the south. They came from a land of heroes and magic. They had come at their own cost, when they heard a legend of a fiend that cursed these islands; because that is what heroes do. They had come clad in strange clothes and brandishing weapons made in the distant lands. These weapons, a glimmering iron, that was said to cut other swords into pieces in battle.

The enticement of usurping these new soldiers for his personal use was too great. Also, the threat of someone coming from that far away and being from Lil's blood, was as close to zero as he could imagine.

The instant before his entrapment in the stone was shocking. Unlike the blood relatives of his mother, Sanura, the ancient bitch, as he thought of her, had no familial relationship with him. With a blood relative, Scrios was powerless and his unique sense was blind. But that was not the case with Sanura. Something else was at work. Something that was new to him.

Every time he tried to connect to Sanura that fateful day, he sensed her weakness to him, only to have his connection frustratingly rebuked immediately. This differed totally from dealing with a relative. With them, he would feel a scream go through his consciousness. It was a panic feeling that clamped down on his chest.

As she closed across the battlefield, like a farmer reaping hay, he saw her heal almost instantaneously. With the frenetic pace of the battle, Scrios could feel a growing weakness in Sanura's defense to his control. During one of those cracks, it realized the golden artifact she carried, and its importance to her. Instantly, he knew he wanted it. When she was close to getting to him, he suggested he hand her the item and, shockingly; she reached it out to him.

When he touched it, something catastrophic happened. It was catastrophic on a grand scale. An enormous explosion of sorts, Jen wrote.

Just before the explosion, Scrios or his essence became trapped in the stone. He could witness the explosion and aftereffects. The result left him buried with the artifact that contained him, and his physical form destroyed.

Entry 17 –Trapped and Buried

Hours became days and days, months with him alone in his prison with only his vivid memories and the memories of those he stole to pass the time. Years came and went and the prisoner sat in the stone. He felt certain that his destiny was to be here for all eternity as some kind of punishment. As time healed the scar on the land above him, he felt something he had never felt before as he starved. In his desperation, his senses sharpened.

He found he could sense animals when they came close. On an even more rare occasion, he felt a human wander past. Their concerns about daily survival trickled precious drops of nourishment. His senses honed further as desperate hunger grew inside him. He was certain he was dying when a realization hit him. "Maybe, for beings like me, this is what death looks like?" he thought.

Over hundreds of years, he became even more in tune with the despair of people as they walked above him. He reached a point, even though their travel coming near enough to him to make such an observation possible was rare, that he could delineate which person walked past. If he had felt them before, he knew it when they wandered by again.

Those tiny morsels sustained him, like morning dew watered a cactus.

As his sharpened senses, honed by the gnawing pain of starvation, pierced the fog of his misery, a wave of unexpected abundance washed over him, momentarily interrupting his agony. The tidal wave of suffering, so alone in the surrounding sensory vacuum, had direction to it, and he knew it came a great distance from the southeast. As it passed like a dry streambed, momentarily flooded by a distant thunderstorm, he drank from it, gulping it and almost choking. As quickly as it had come, it passed.

His refreshment did not ease his hunger. Somewhere something significant had happened, because as the flood of pain passed him, images flashed in his mind of pain and battle, much like when he entered his meditative dream state.

The great suffering thousands of miles to the south and east, he pictured in his head, had created a wave much like a rock thrown into a still pond. He could estimate direction and distance based on the signal's strength and attenuation. He did not know the cause, but he knew if he got out of this hole and out of this trap, he needed to go that direction someday. Since even from this distance, he could tell the disruption which caused the wave was immense, as its faintest ripple had nourished him. The abundance and possibilities for his birthright had to be in that direction.

As animals and people continued to wonder near through the decades, he figured out he could influence them some. No, he could not outright give them a purpose as when he had met their eyes. Nor could he give them a new understanding of their life, but he found he could distract them or even garner their attention. He could make them think thoughts like, "What's that?" or, "Ooh, shiny!" directing them to the area above him. To a lesser level, he found he could also influence the furry rodents that lived in the trees the same way and encourage them to dig for nuts above him. Occasionally, they would dig in the land directly above him when he gave them the proper motivation. However, like the humans, they would lose interest as soon as he became exhausted. The exertion of focusing on them caused his strength to diminish quickly because of his malnourishment. He had plenty of time to perfect this new skill.

Sometimes years and other times decades would pass without a human wanderer, but slowly a depression grew in the ground over the buried artifact which contained him.

The stone that trapped the essence of Scrios, while not ideal, had its minor advantages. He no longer had a body that required its own sustenance. Scrios disliked feeding in a traditional sense and only partook in food, because it was necessary. His time in his prison clarified that this was no longer a limitation. However, the suffering he experience in the ground, trapped, was more painful than anything he had experienced.

He sat buried in the ground for longer than he had lived as a man. That was, until one day, a simple man wandered close. Scrios could sense he was searching for something in the foliage above, and this provided him with an opportunity. Concentrating, Scrios could get the simpleton to dig two feet down before he again lost interest and left. That had been a hundred years of progress in one day and when he left, Scrios shuddered in frustration.

However, the next day, he stumbled back... and the day after he returned once more. On the fifth day of digging, Liam plucked a golden tube that contained a dark green crystal from the dirt. He almost tossed it away before he brushed the dirt from it and gave it a look. He smacked it against his palm to knock the encased dirt from the inside; eventually deciding a tree would work better.

By the time Liam unearthed Scrios, the valley had transformed. Now ancient trees grew around the spot where he had fallen, and the lack of sightlines made it almost unrecognizable. Liam, after clearing the debris, examined the tube and saw a curious green stone.

After half a millennium of darkness, seeing again was disorienting to Scrios. Especially dizzying was being able to see all directions at once.

When Liam peered into the tube, Scrios felt a familiar feeling of connection to the man's simple mind. Liam did not remember standing still, looking into the tube for more than a split second, but he had stood there motionless for almost an hour while Scrios leisurely probed the man's mind.

Over time, Scrios understood that once someone viewed the gem that was his prison, he could influence them while they carried the artifact as he had in his corporal form, when they met eyes.

He suggested Liam pick up a fist sized rock and hit himself with it in the forehead. Liam did it with gusto, dropping to a knee as darkness filled his vision.

Scrios saw no sign of healing in the daft man, like what had happened with Sanura, so he concluded something else was the key to that ability.

Beyond the enjoyment of dominating the mind of an individual, the violation it committed to them was what he had missed the most. He learned to leave behind impressions that could control or even trigger certain actions.

From his centuries buried in the soil and the lessons learned there, he frequently used the ability of garnering attention, to compel individuals holding the golden artifact encapsulating his prison, to look into the end and meet his eye.

Upon receiving the object, Scrios induced them to look into his eye. They would only remember doing it if Scrios allowed them to. It wasn't forgetting exactly, because if a person asked "hey, did you just look into that?" the person said, "Yes I did" and remember doing so, but without actually remember the experience itself.

The most ironic aspect to Scrios's existence in the stone was the belief by the person possessing the baton shaped artifact which contained him, that they had ownership of it. When, if he allowed them to remember the reality of the experience, the debasement and outright rape of their very consciousness, Scrios wagered, they would likely feel differently.

They were a possession of Scrios in every meaning. After he took possession of them, he found he could communicate his desires of them soon, without their even touching him.

Over time, it grew from inches to feet and feet to yards. He did not at all understand the mechanism that caused this effect and wrote it off to being an aspect of his new self. He saw the correlation between this and how he influenced the forest animals and the wanderers, who eventually dug him from his tomb.

As before, when someone looked into the crystal, his eye, instantly, Scrios would know the viewers' language and any languages they knew. The rush of that when it first happened so many years ago was like a ripple across his consciousness.

It was still a rush, thousands of years later, but it was rare that he would get full new languages now, as he had encountered so many people.

Sometimes it was only a new dialect or an unfamiliar word or usage. There was always the rush of fresh memories. Memories that were more complete than the host could recall themselves. Rushing in with the memories was the understanding of their fears and aspirations. Their intimate thoughts, he could rip from his victim.

In a manner, he grew to like this "life" in the crystal at some level, even though his entrapment here was hardly his choice. From the inside of the stone, the world appeared as if through prisms that allowed him to see in all directions at once, but more. He could also see the world as his host saw and heard it. At first, it was dizzying.

His golden tube did not impede his awareness of the surroundings, yet concealed his imprisonment from view. Perhaps, he thought, it even protected the delicate crystal that contained him.

Jen wrote in the margin, "Scrios sewed deceit for thousands of years while trapped in the stone. One of the older significant memories he had, that are complete in my mind, is entry 27." Jen's handwriting seemed to show further signs of deterioration of control in the small sidebar message.

Chapter 38

Wednesday, September 19th, 2018, 1:00 AM, Gus and Marcy's home. 6278 Mourning Dove Rd. Raleigh, NC

Marcy had read aloud the entries as Gus and Peter sat entranced. No one knew how long they had been sitting listening to Marcy read. All they knew was that it was now late. "These damn entries go on and on," as she flipped through the book. "What the hell did your parents stumble onto?"

Gus shrugged as Peter sat awkwardly quiet. Gus looked at him, expecting something totally off-color to fly from his mouth and make this strange moment somehow funny, but Peter sat there. "What Peter?" Gus asked.

"I'm trying to piece something together. Give me a minute."

Before Peter could talk, Marcy had an epiphany, and flipped through the book to the later entry Jen mentioned.

"Holy shit! Shit, shit, shit. There are so many things here. This one involves ancient Rome..." and she read it aloud.

Entry Twenty-Seven - Arminius

1 - September, 9 AD Teutoburg Forest, Lower Saxony

Arminius stood overlooking a clearing. The air smelled like a rancid mixture of copper, sweat, upturned dirt, and feces. He had planned and plotted, surviving since he was a small boy by caring for their animals. "Shoveling shit and sleeping in the stables," he thought.

Eventually, the people of Rome mostly forgot who he was, and he lost his notoriety. Romans eventually thought he was one of them. Sure, he looked different from the average Roman, but this was the center of the world, and it had people there from everywhere.

After serving valiantly in the army, Rome declared him a citizen.

He used them; he took what they would give him and played the good soldier. Arminius learned their ways, culture, and their strategies. He distinguished himself on the battlefield. The whole time plotting and praying to the gods of old for this day. Victory was sweet, but not exactly like he expected. He was responsible for killing thousands of people, some who thought he was their friend, and that still stung and stained his soul. It surprised Arminius to feel tears running down his face.

He knew their families, their children... hell, he even killed the son of a loyal friend that day with the son's own sword. Watched as the fear in his eyes turn to a horrified look of betrayal and faded to a blank stare as his ancestors greeted him.

At the last moment, Darius had called for his mother. "They all call for their mothers," he said, shaking his head.

He issued orders to the Roman troops even as he betrayed them. He murdered them, as they obeyed him in the swirling confusion. It started as a typical march to squash an uprising and ended as a massacre of three legions and their support staff. The path, between swamp and bluff, held nearly 20,000 dead and dying men and boys; the Germanic tribes, awaiting retribution, had hidden above and descended together in the slaughter.

Arminius's father, a Germanic king, had told him and his brother before he gave them up to Rome as a token of subservience. In his last moment with them, the father said, "Remember who you are! What they did to your people! Learn their ways and you will know their weakness. NEVER forget who you are! Never forget what they have done here today!"

Many years later, this was the message he remembered on Varus's vast patio in Tibur on the hills outside of Rome. Following the celebration where Caesar

Augustus promoted Arminius to a similar rank, he and the general, his mentor, sat drinking late into the night; the rich aroma of wine filled the air, mingling with the lingering scent of roasted meats.

The duplicitous memory of Arminius's childhood soured him. His younger self peered at him from the bottom of his goblet with a look of disgust.

2 - Fall, 20 BC

Rome

Arminius and his brother were prizes, carried to Rome in an open cage like animals and fed scraps and water from streams. Upon arrival, Roman authorities paraded them, along with the other treasures and tributes stolen from his homeland, through the city.

The severed head of his uncle Umfried, pickled in mead, tossed unceremoniously on the steps as the crowds cheered. For just an instant, Arminius remembered his uncle correcting his hand position on a spear. "No, no, thumb down, or you will lose it." The memory of the training evaporated as a thrown rock hit the cage's bar and careened to his head, causing his entire skull to burn.

Insults and rocks rained down on him and his brother as the parade meandered through the city's crowded streets. They were spit upon and far worse at the hands of their handlers.

They survived the first month, which did not feel guaranteed, and the years that followed were a struggle. Arminius and his brother earned the trust of their keepers. As their fame waned, their keepers eventually abandoned them to the streets, leaving them to fend for themselves during a time of famine.

Fighting Arminius could do. He had done that since he was a child. With his early notoriety, he was in fights almost daily, and it required him to be very good, because he had to survive the fight but not look like he won.

If he had clearly won, they would put him in the pit, and he would be dead within days. But if he lost, his attacker would have his own little parade with the friends that watched. Losing was politically correct, but knowing you caused enough damage to not make it attractive to try again was an art form. Losing gracefully and retaliating mildly would earn him some mockery, but throttling a citizen's son would land him in the pit. That is where winning would get him.

On the streets, they stole food to survive and took lashes when caught. One night, he and his brother found a stable to sleep in, only to be discovered by the stable master the following morning. The stable master too was from Germania;

he allowed them to stay and sleep there if they worked. In compensation, they received a first pass on the leftover food before it went to the pigs.

Eventually, they mastered handling the stock, and the property owner even compensated them for their efforts. After a battle 15 years earlier, someone enslaved the stable keeper and brought him here as well. He instilled in them a work ethic and helped them understand how to live here among their conquerors.

Arminius grew into a large young man, even when compared with others from his region. When he stood, most average Romans failed to reach his chin. When they called the owner of the stable and the attached large house to service, they also called his staff. While his brother maintained the horses for his master, Arminius, at 16, joined the legion as a spearman.

Two years later, and thousands of miles away, he was on a long walk to the other side of the world as reinforcement to Legio X "Fretensis". He walked to a land hotter than Rome; to a dry place where small bitter bushes imitated the plants of his second home.

Arminius distinguished himself in battle in a campaign in Syria when, as a lowly peditatus, nearly the lowest rank and file in the Roman Legion. In a combination of luck and opportunity, he made a choice that could have ended poorly for him, but when he did it, he did it to save lives, not to undermine authority.

Their third battle, about two years after he joined, had gone terribly wrong. The flank collapsed near him and the archers were about to be overrun. In his fateful decision, he broke ranks. He had his reasons and consciously accepted any reprimand this choice carried. He surveyed the battlefield with his father's eye, hearing him speak in his head, and knew that no reinforcements had been called or deployed. It was about to be too late.

He grabbed four men and told them to follow, and with the command in his voice, they did so without question. This kind of protocol break could have had him either put to death, lashed, or at the least given latrine duty for the next six months. The five spearmen slowed the flanks' collapse and allowed for tardy forces to adjust and eventually push back the break. It turned the tide of what could have been a disaster. Minus this delay, purchased in blood, it was conceivable the enemy incursion could have eliminated the archers or even reached the officer's guard.

A fast-rising officer with the name Publius Quinctilius Varus saw the five soldiers break ranks and at first flashed with anger. He, however, saw what they did. After the battle, he called Arminius to his tent and discussed the action.

After introductions Varus said, "Hello son, I'm looking to understand why you abandoned your post. I saw your performance today, and I want to know what you saw and what you thought would justify your actions."

Arminius stiffened and prepared to bargain for his life. "Sir, I saw a movement to the left that hid in the lines. The ones in the front were engaging but more occupying us than truly trying to attack." The others were moving low behind the ranks. I looked left and saw the leading edge starting forward and they had a clear path to the archers. If we lose them, we lose all, so I alone decided and will accept any punishment. I told the others to come, and they did, but it was my fault." Arminius finished and bowed his head.

Varus's stiff demeanor softened. "You may very well have saved our day... and many lives. I know who you are and where you come from. I remember when they brought you to Rome. They did not treat you well, I am sure. Your actions today, while militarily wrong, define you as a Roman, and I want people who think like you and react like you in my guard." Varus said. The reply shocked Arminius, but he controlled his expression and saluted.

Two days later, they presented Arminius with a red sash, signifying his elevated status, and moved him to quarters with softer beds and better food. His training intensified, and they ordered him to work daily with a scholar documenting the campaign until he could read and write. His superiors ordered him to remove "failure" from his vocabulary, and he began receiving more in-depth instruction on the meaning and use of the signal banners in controlling the field.

Although Varus was kind to Arminius, he was a man whose cruelty to his enemy was unmatched. Arminius witnessed and assisted with fulfilling Varus's orders to crucify thousands of followers of David, who had resisted Rome.

The years that followed would add to Arminius's glory. His battle prowess became legendary among the Legion. His commitment to Rome was unquestioned. He would ascend to Varus's Tribunus Laticlavus after he lost his previous one to herpes. His previous second in command didn't die from the disease, but Varus was so repulsed by the sores he sent him home. Arminius, son of a conquered king, received a prestigious position typically held by the elite, as Varus's friend, the future Caesar Tiberius, confirmed Arminius's genuine high social standing. This recognition of social standing alone allowed Arminius to rise to the rank of Tribunus Laticlavus.

Afterwards, he attended weddings and birth celebrations in palaces with senators and members of Caesar Augustus's family. Augustus would honor Arminius personally and give him a general's rank of Legatus legionis, referring to Arminius as a pillar of Rome as he awarded him the Civic crown.

3 - Mid June, 7 AD

Tibur Hills east of Rome in the Hillside Villa of Marcus Caelius Varus,

Despite the conditions that brought him there, Arminius had grown to love Rome and saw it as his home. He recalled his childhood, a garden where the seeds of his discontent easily could have grown. He had risen above his beginning.

It was a late evening; just he and General Varus the night after Arminius himself became a general. They sat and drank wine, toasting his new rank. They were reminiscing on a balcony overlooking the hills of Rome. Fires burned in the distance and the smell of Rome was all around them, even in this remote location.

One minute he was the committed newly minted Roman General, discussing coming campaigns with his mentor and friend, when Varus said he wanted to show him something. Varus offered the golden rod like artifact to Arminius, which seemed to be in his mentor's hand almost every waking moment. He could not remember ever being asked to hold it before, although he had.

"Many wonder at the source of my decisiveness, and if I was truthful," Varus said. "I would admit my certainty comes from this simple relic."

The odd, ancient rod appeared to be made of gold and had a coiled serpent wrapped around it in raised relief. "Alexander of Macedonia carried it in all of his campaigns," Varus lied.

Its age was apparent because of the wear on the metal, and it oddly was hollow and lighter than Arminius had expected. "There was a time before that, where it was called Eye of Asclepius... they say the Titans forged it." Varus added in another difficult to support summary.

A compulsion overwhelmed him; to investigate the hollow end. He glimpsed a faint glimmer of what looked like a gem, hidden or placed deep within the tube for protection. While it appeared to be gold, it had neither the weight nor the soft feel. He decided it must be bronze or some alloy.

He didn't remember the moment of terror when the stone saw him and the stone saw into him. It lived in him, invaded him, and gave him a purpose that matched its need. After a few moments of contemplation and turning the artifact around in his hands, Arminius gave it back to his old friend, but he didn't feel the same affinity with him he did moments before.

The wine did little to mask the rising bile in his throat as he finally saw Varus for the man he really was, a sight that filled him with disgust.

When Arminius bowed to leave, Varus walked him to the gate. Arminius thanked him and his mentor embraced him before he ducked past the guards and went home.

Varus saw the manicured version of what the stone saw in Arminius, assuring him of Arminius's loyalty, and Varus smiled. Scrios, however, did not let him know the cascade he had put in place. Scrios knew a feast of sorrow was coming, and he rejoiced in anticipation as it baked.

4 - September, 9 AD

Teutoburg Forest, Lower Saxony

A tear welled in his eye as he looked at the Roman dead on this field in Germania, killed at his orders. Arminius trudged through the field where he became a criminal and a traitor to Rome. "I was actually proud when they called me citizen... proud," he said to himself, shaking his head, unable to shake the duplicitousness of his own thoughts.

He remembered that night of drinking on the porch in Tibur. He remembered seeing the opulence around him and flashing to his childhood and seeing through fresh eyes the disparity between his two lives. That night, a fire of resentment he didn't know he still possessed ignited within him. A change of heart that would lead to treason and both make him a legend in the land of his childhood, and a fugitive for the rest of his days from Rome. As he walked the road littered with dead Romans, his past washed through his memories.

He had walked into the party a proud, newly minted general with a glorious past and a promising future. He walked out a treacherous traitor bent on the destruction of Rome. Not only that, but that night, in his mind had appeared a fully laid out plan for this deceit.

The plan had somehow even included contacts and things he could say to communicate his intent without a full admission of his sedition should someone suspect his plans. Arminius never questioned why or how he knew these new things. They were like old memories to him, and he remembered planning them... when he thought about it. He even remembered talking about it in his dreams to a skinny old man with bluish skin and eyes that unsettled him, as they sat near a warm fire and drew out plans in the sand. He didn't remember when the dreams had happened, but it had, and this person of his dreams had offered sage advice and seemed to understand him completely. The blue man understood why he had to betray Rome and encouraged him to do what he must do to avenge his people and make his father proud.

Arminius devised a flawless and simple plan. He would lure his friend's troops into a deadly trap, attacking the vulnerable columns as they marched through the dense forest. Their ranks there would thin and spread out. The forest would limit communication. He even knew the perfect place, although he never remembered being there. The blue man laughed with a cackle, "Banners don't work in the woods!"

They needed to raise an army far exceeding the three legions advancing that day; a massive, coordinated assault from every direction was crucial to prevent the enemy from regrouping. Klaxons fashioned from oxen horns would coordinate the attack. Each group had one at least who could make the noise from the instrument. The signal for attack meant no retreat. The only path to living was to win.

Arminius predicted to his coconspirators at a clandestine meeting, "When the attack starts, the officers will stay with the fight, thinking it is another Barbarian raid. However, when it becomes apparent that they are in trouble, the officers will rally their personal guard, and anyone else near, to get them clear of the melee. They will try to dispatch messengers, so we need several teams of your fastest horses to track them down should they escape the fight. Don't let the archers have time to notch their bows. If the bowmen become ready, it may shift the battle," Arminius warned as he ironically thought of that battle so long ago, where he had caught his mentor's eye.

The Germanic tribes launched their attack from the high land, from dug in, hidden locations above the small forest road. The boggy swamp on the low side of the road formed a natural barrier to any retreat.

Quickly, Arminius knew, "the guard will move General Varus and the other surviving officers forward and find a defensible clearing. The general will order them to assemble a defense there," he said. Arminius had made that fateful prediction with absolute certainty that dared any of the assembled leaders of his assault to question him.

Amazed by Arminius's knowledge of the area and the clearing, one attending member, who had traveled that road since childhood, nodded, assuring the others of the clearing's precise location as described.

So, before the battle, the small clearing was prepared and would look like a gift from Mars himself. There, the last trap would close. He tasked the seven thousand men, hidden amongst the dense trees near the clearing, to wait for the officers to settle before launching a surprise attack, aiming to eliminate the remaining officers and their support.

Teutoburg Forest, as the blue man had mentioned in his dream, with the swamp on one side and high ground on the other, was the perfect place for his father's retribution.

Rome recalled eight of the eleven legions assigned to Germania and sent them to the Balkans to crush other uprisings. Somehow, Arminius seemed to know this was going to happen and when his predictions had come true, it helped to unite the many tribes that made up his army.

5 – September, 9 AD

Teutoburg Forest, Lower Saxony

Publius Quinctilius Varus remembered the first time he looked through the hollow scepter that was given to him, or at least he thought he did. Like many others through the centuries, he studied the tube; the creature inside the stone weighed and measured his potential. Because the stone did not want him to recall the intrusive examination of his deepest fears, motivations, and thoughts, he could not remember the first time he had ever truly studied the artifact.

Varus spoke often of his good fortune and certainty of victories. When Arminius told Varus about the barbarian uprisings 50 miles northeast of their camp, Varus smiled and ordered his commanders to prepare for a morning departure, moving with his characteristic certainty. The General's legendary brutality was the only trait that exceeded the General's famed decisiveness.

In battle, Arminius had found it unnerving, the insight General Varus seemed to have of the enemy, and how to defeat them. His peers and underlings agreed his ability to assess and make the right move decisively was legendary. His arrogance from the insights of Scrios had served him well, but he never understood that Scrios only acted in his own interest. These people represented food to the creature, and that food only came with destruction and ruin. That was where Scrios's loyalty always dwelled.

The general's cruelty, inspired by the creature, earned him no quarter that day and as word of his demise spread to the corners of the Roman Empire, while his friends mourned, few who faced him on a battlefield and lived, spared a tear for him. Emperor Augustus, upon learning of the slaughter in a tantrum, allegedly screamed "Quintili Vare, legiones redde!", demanding the dead general to "return his legions"!

In the center of the clearing 30 Centurion lay scattered in rough circle, Arminius' friend Erastus the Praefectus Castorum, third in command of the 19th Legion, among them, had died poorly, laid in a puddle of his own gore.

269

Sitting in a small space among his fallen protectors, with an arrow down through the base of his neck, with the point protruding below his right armpit, General Varus sat struggling to breathe. He stared at the tubular hollow artifact, somehow remaining in his useless right hand. He looked at the tube with a look of absolute disbelief and like he was expecting it to provide him an explanation.

As Arminius approached, he saw the scepter that Varus held and memory images flashed through his mind of multiple times seeing him carrying it in theaters of war, all over the known world. He had retrieved it for him once. Its odd weight and balance made him wonder why anyone would bother with something so trivial in their hand during battle.

He arrived back in the moment. General Publius Quinctilius Varus, his friend, mentor and the confidant of Caesar Augustus himself, the leader of the three legions, whose blood would nourish the trees and grass of this damned place eternally, sat dying.

The general met eyes and silently mouthed the question, "friend?" with a wry, knowing smile. A frothy dark blood trickled from the corner of the general's mouth; the depth of Arminius's betrayal was painful in his eyes.

Stepping toward his friend, Arminius raised his mentor's chin, then covered his eyes while plunging a dagger taken from Verus's own belt into his friend's left armpit. He slid it along the top of the armor plate, found the spot between two ribs, and thrust it through the sinew to hasten the general's death. Arminius felt the dagger brush the bone and crunch through the grizzle between his ribs and find the heart. Hearing his mentor's almost childish whimper, he felt a lump in his throat and tears welling up.

Arminius thought of Varus's wife Vipsania, who had hugged him for the last time when he had left Rome for Germania. He had had many meals with General Varus and his family. As he held the corpse, a profound struggle consumed him; the insidious nature of his own deceit warred with the deep friendship he had shared with Varus. If his intent was simply to have his friend killed, the opportunities were plentiful; a thousand ways in faraway countries or in the vast, unsuspecting city of Rome itself.

Years earlier, Arminius, having served with distinction in Judea and earned both Varus's favor and Roman citizenship, when he returned from his first campaign. More recently, Vipsania and others had wished him well personally as he departed to help tame his childhood homeland in Germania, never suspecting he had plotted against Rome.

Arminius held the general's body as his life dripped to the dirt below. As Varus's eyes lost their light, he found himself unable to look at him. Rome trusted him fully, believing his lineage would be invaluable to the cause of taming Germania for Rome. When Publius Quinctilius Varus had suggested Arminius to rule Germania after they conquered it, Caezar Augustus saw the poetry in the suggestion and agreed.

It turned out Varus's faith in Arminius was only worth the piece of silver left in his mouth for the boatman. Arminius would place the coin into his severed head, impaled on a spear, from his own pocket.

As the carrion birds circled, Arminius shed his Roman skin for the first time since he was a boy. They took the weaponry from the dead Romans. They knew they would need the quality weapons to defend their now sovereign land. The tribes shared the legions' food. They consigned much of the rest to the forest or swamp to rot with the abused bodies.

Arminius took only one item. It was the small golden scepter he always saw General Varus caressing as he contemplated decisions. As Arminius had shed his Roman armor, he shed his Roman name. The Germanic tribes had a new name for their hero. They called him Hermann, which translated the Man of War.

Hermann noticed the hole in the item and peered into it. He found nothing but blurry darkness. There was no enlightenment, and he failed to understand the general's infatuation with the item. He presented it to his brother's son.

"That is all that is in my head related to this," Jen wrote at the bottom of the entry. "I also found this picture, when I did some research on the general's name," wrote Jen in the space beside the picture, which she apparently cut from an old book. "Look at his hand."

160.

De Rechtspleegingen in de leegerplaats van Varus.

Varus receiving German leaders. The right-hand passage in the encampment of Varus'. The Trial in Varus' camp from Peace Palace Library from the collections of studies in international law in The Hague, Netherlands.

272

Chapter 39

Marcy finished the passage and closed the book, "Well, that was crazy, but did you get the description of the artifact?" she asked awkwardly.

Gus shook his head, "My mother mentioned none of this to me. She mentioned that my family in Scotland was a bit strange... and I know from vague mentions from my grandfather that she and he, did not see eye to eye on something." Gus looked at Peter who seemed like he was biting down on something. "What?"

Peter took a deep breath. "So, I'm rolling things through my head. It started with me, on that birthday trip to Scotland, and that giant ass dude at the farm who knew me by name."

"Yeah!" replied Gus. "That struck me as weird at the time too... even weirder was the look I caught my grandfather giving... Daniel... that was his name. It was a pissed off look. Daniel quickly excused himself right after that burning stare."

Marcy shifted uncomfortably, "Your mom, at the beginning of her section of the book, it felt like she was confirming a warning that your grandfather had given her."

Gus scrunched his face. "Maybe... there was also something else weird that happened that day in Scotland that I don't think you guys realized. I even confirmed it with my grandfather. He had some serious security at the farm, and I'm not sure I saw all the security he had."

Marcy laughed. "You mean other than Daniel?"

"Daniel was not even part of it. My grandfather asked me not to mention it to anyone, but this freaking book has me kind of spooked. He had some well-trained ex-military dudes posing as his groundskeepers. When we drove in, my neck was tingling like when I was back in the desert again. As we pulled up, something bothered me almost to the point of panic. The groundskeepers were setup in a very specific crossfire formation I studied in Officer School... Heck, I even helped set it up at one of Sadam's old palaces, when we used it for a hotel. As soon as my grandfather gave them a palm down, they packed up their important grounds keeping stuff and put their tools away." Gus explained.

"And your grand pappy admitted that?" Marcy asked, as Gus's eyes seemed to lose focus for a moment.

"What?" Marcy asked.

"Sorry... When you said Pappy, I had a memory of when I was a kid. I always thought it was just a dream, and I didn't even remember when it happened. I woke up in my bed and there was an old man standing there in his Sunday suit. It was dark in my room, but I could see him standing in the light from a streetlight outside or something. When I saw him, I jumped a little with surprise."

"He was an older man," Gus continued, "with very sad eyes. At first his mouth was moving, but no sound was coming out, causing a look of frustration to cross his face as he seemed to concentrate harder. When he tried speaking again, I could hear him. He looked at me and said in a strange accent, "It's ok son, I am Pappy. I'm very sorry, my boy, but I need you to be brave and strong for your mum."

I said, "okay."

Gus continued to speak as a tear formed in his eye. "I want you to go out there," and he pointed to my door. "You go out there now and tell your daddy that you love him, and you can go back to sleep. I'm so sorry, sweet boy. When I blinked, there was a small crackling sound and Pappy was gone, and I remember it scared the crap out of me. So, I got up out of bed crying, and I went out to tell my dad." Gus said, shaking his head. "I always thought that was a dream. That was what my mother was describing in that first part there."

They all sat quietly for a full minute. Finally filling the quiet, Peter said, "Backing up a bit. Daniel knew who I was by looking at me. I wrote that off too. Except I kind of recognized him also and I couldn't place it for the longest time. That is when I realized. One day at the office I had a memory of him when I was young... I don't know, maybe six or seven years old. He was with an older man, talking to my father in his office and he smiled at me, and I remember him telling me his name was Daniel. The older man with him seemed angry with him for that, and Daniel got quiet." Peter paused and spoke again. "When I asked my dad about Daniel after our trip, my father insisted it was someone else, but he looked uncomfortable when he said it. Old Mack was a terrible liar," he concluded as quiet again displaced the conversation.

"Well," said Gus authoritatively, "my grandfather admitted to me he met your parents."

Peter took over, "Yeah, but that conversation he described, though, would have been years later and Daniel sure acted like we had met before... and I think I would have remembered meeting a giant like him."

Gus looked at the crew. "Guys, this has me weirded out. I think in the morning we talk about this some more over breakfast and come up with a plan.

Peter, it's late and something about this I really dislike. Do you want to take the spare room tonight?" Gus said as Marcy looked on pleadingly.

Peter read the room and nodded, "I have my go bag in the car with extra work clothes."

Marcy laughed, "You mean your 'non-commitment bag' for if you meet someone in a bar!"

They all laughed as Peter got up and walked to the door, shaking his head. Upon opening the door, he looked back at Marcy, and called to her. When she looked at him, he flipped his middle finger at her and went out to retrieve his bag... leaving his finger dangling in the crack until the door closed.

Chapter 40

Wednesday, September 19th, 2018, 7:15 AM Gus and Marcy's home. 6278 Mourning Dove Rd. Raleigh, NC

In the morning, Gus woke up first with the low sun streaming in the windows through the trees. His night's sleep had been tremulous, but when he got the coffee started, he could feel his awareness increase with the smell of the grounds as he measured them from the grinder. A few minutes later, Marcy walked into the kitchen, stretching in her feline way. She walked over behind Gus and wrapped her arms around his waist. "Good morning, love."

Gus grabbed her hands and separated them and slowly turned as he spun her like a slow tango dancer into a long embrace and kissed.

"Get a room!" Peter said, as he wandered into the kitchen.

Marcy didn't break the kiss, but did signal Peter that he was still number one in her book.

Peter looked at the coffee longingly as the pot was filling past the halfway point. He nodded approvingly and walked past it and over to the refrigerator. Opening the door, he picked up the egg carton and weighed it in his hands. He squinted towards the back of the refrigerator and smiled. Pulling the unopened carton of eggs from the back and a pack of bacon from the fridge, he looked up. "Ok lovebirds. I'm taking egg orders. How do you want them?"

Marcy excitedly answered, "Two eggs scrambled with cheese! And I will get the bread ready for toast!"

Peter pretended to write in the palm of his hand, "and you sir?"

"Um, I'll take three eggs over hard with a little extra pepper." Peter nodded and finished his notes in his palm with his imaginary pen.

Fifteen minutes later, they were all seated around the dining room table. A pile of toast sat in the middle of the table. Butter and strawberry preserves completed the center piece along with the jug of orange juice. Because every meal is an occasion for Peter, he broke out the Mikasa plates from the top shelf above the drinking cups. Peter set each plate with three strips of perfectly cooked bacon and the eggs to order. He also made a small area of fresh fruit for decoration as they sat and ate a family breakfast.

It was like there was a silent agreement. No one brought up the heaviness of last night's reading or conversation. It was as if they all knew somehow that peace was leaving their lives. This breakfast, though, was their time. They sat and sipped on the recently refilled coffee as Peter cleared the plates after they had finished eating.

In the blink of an eye, the breakfast ambiance shifted, as if the sun had momentarily vanished behind a cloud, and everyone's attention sharpened.

Gus spoke first. "So, it is near lunch time in Scotland, and I think it is high time we get some answers." Peter and Marcy both seemed resigned to the decision as well, and answered with a simple nod.

Gus picked up his iPhone and dialed 01144 and his grandfather's "Big House" number.

Nell's cheery voice answered the phone. "Hello? May I ask who is calling?"

Gus smiled cautiously, "Hello Nell? This is Gus. Is my grandfather around?"

"Gus!! Wonderful to hear your voice! Yes, he is in the other room and probably walking this way right now as loud as I am," she said. Touching the screen, Gus placed the phone in speaker mode, and they could all hear a muffled shuffling sound.

"Gus?" came his grandfather's voice, sounding older than the last time they talked. "How are you, boy?" rumbled the voice, a little clearer now.

"I am well, grandfather, I think we need to talk."

"Okay, what's on your mind, son?"

"Well, yesterday, we were rearranging the bed, and we found an old book. It looked like a diary or something from my dad," Gus said, and his grandfather stopped him.

"Son, I am going to ask you to do something right now and it is going to make no sense at all, but I'm asking you to just do it and not ask why until it is done. I will wait right here. I want you to go to a store, any store, and buy a disposable phone and call me from that. Bring the book with you. Please, no more questions or statements until we speak again. I will wait right here, and I will answer as completely as I can, when you call back," the grandfather swore.

"Okay, grandfather, I will. Talk to you soon," he finished with a confused look to Marcy and Peter.

Chapter 41

8:15 AM

A quick shower later, all three were out the door and headed to a Wal-Mart. 20 minutes later, they had a phone with a one-month chip installed. A few minutes after they initialized it, they dialed Scotland.

Gus's grandfather answered the phone on the first ring. "Hello?"

"Hello, this is Gus."

"Are you alone?" asked his grandfather.

"No, Marcy and Peter are here with me. They were there when we found the book and we looked through it last night together." He replied.

"Ok, I'm assuming your father made some entries in the book, like a diary?" he asked.

"Yes, but there is a lot more there, too. There is a letter that he was going to send to you, but never made it to the box, and my mother wrote a gigantic section, well, most of the book. It's hard to explain."

Five seconds of silence followed after Gus stopped talking.

When his grandfather asked, "Are you safe right now, son? Any strange happenings?"

Gus looked at the phone and glanced at his family in the car with him. "Well, a bit of craziness has happened recently with Mack, Peter's father. A police officer murdered him." Later that night, the officer came to our house... well, he had bad intentions, and to keep the story short, I killed him in self-defense. That was a couple of weeks ago, though, and nothing other than that."

Gus again was met with a prolonged silence.

"I don' want to overreact and spook you here, but I'm highly concerned." His grandfather said. "I am guessing the stuff from your father was some kind of diary of dreams. Any idea what the note from your father was?"

"Yes," Gus replied, "my dad's entries seem to be a diary of some sort where he discusses nightmares. The letter looked to be damaged also, probably from the same storm that damaged the book and took him away. The note was some kind of apology to you. It related a story of some kind of strange vision he had while out at breakfast with my mother. It was strange. His apology was that he didn't tell you that morning. By the date, it was really close to the time my mom's parents died in a car accident."

"Okay... what about your mom's notes?" his grandfather said, with a hint of emotion in his voice. "Ermm, wait just a second, son."

They could hear his grandfather cover the phone and speak to someone in the background. Despite the muffled conversation, they glanced at each other, sensing the urgency in the voice. "I'm back, sorry. Your mum's notes?"

"Her first entry contained an apology... to you. Later, the entries got strange. She mentioned looking into some telescope she got at an estate sale. It mentioned some creature and how she had somehow taken..." Gus paused momentarily. "Okay, this is sounding even stranger trying to say it... That she had somehow taken he... or its... memories as the tornado struck... as she looked it in the eye?"

He was immediately cut off by his grandfather. "You have the book with you now?" he asked.

"Yes." Gus responded.

"Do you have your travel documents... eerm, passport?" he asked.

"No, but they are at home in the safe... why?" Gus replied.

"Again, this is going to sound senseless. Can you... all of you, call in to work sick to your managers? I need you all here. Really, I meant to do this long ago, but I need to give you the lay of the ground you are already walking in. I'm not flippant when I say I feel your very lives are in danger. If I am right... Peter?"

"Yes?" Peter replied, leaning forward over the back seat with an awkward mix of surprise and confusion on his face.

"I can explain this later and will, but call your mom on this phone as soon as we disconnect. Say these words to her, "Destruction, Plan Three," and next I want all of you to get your passports and take U.S. Highway 1 south from Raleigh towards Sanford. Don't worry about packing; we can get you clothes here. About halfway to the town called Sanford, look for the Raleigh Executive Jetport signs and go there. I want you to take two separate exits before you get there and get back on the highway. Note if any vehicles do the same behind you. If any do, call me here. Let's see, it is what, 9:00 AM your time? Be at the Jetport by 2:00 PM, sooner, if possible," he finished.

"Wait" said Gus, "We can't just..." he began, but his grandfather interrupted him.

"Sorry son, you must, and if we are lucky, this will just be a week where you catch up to date on things... the very things I tried to get you to come and visit for... This relates to the same things it sounds like your mum has written about. When Peter contacts Deborah, all will be fine at work... for all of you. Now son, promise me you will, and Peter, and Marcy, please... come. A week for sure and more if YOU decide YOU need or want to," the grandfather finished, and another long silence waited for a reply.

Gus looked at the people in the car. All seemed cautious and rightfully on edge, but each eventually nodded in agreement. "We will be there, grandfather."

Chapter 42

9:52 AM

The same feeling of tension flooded Gus's body. It was identical to when deployed with the Army in a war zone over a decade ago. The moment he exited the car at his home, he had an expectation of sand and pebbles under his feet. When they got inside, Gus changed into new clothes. Sliding on his socks and sneakers, he walked through the kitchen to the safe and retrieved the passports.

As he ran through his mental checklist, he double checked the packed travel bag for any missing items. He also checked Marcy's bag, knowing she had likely done the same for him. When he entered the kitchen, the aroma of freshly brewed coffee surrounded him, and he saw Peter huddled over a steaming cup. "One for the road?" Gus asked Peter.

"Yeah, trying to settle my nerves. Want a cup?" Peter replied.

Marcy spoke with a pinched face. "Me too! Something was rolling through my mind since we spoke with your grandfather. I couldn't quite figure out what it was. About ten minutes ago, however, I think I finally figured it out. Your grandfather said, "Talk to Peter's mum and everything will be fine for all of you at work." Like how the hell would he know that?" she asked.

Peter, looking pained, offered, "Well, they know each other from working together on Gus's dad's scholarship, right?"

Gus chimed in, "Yeah, but it is still a good question. How did he know that Peter talking to Deb would make everything fine?"

Peter, with a distant gaze, stared into his coffee cup as if searching for answers, and broke the silence by saying, "It's early, but mom should be done with her early status meeting by now." He plopped the burner phone on the table and selected his mother's contact and turned on the speaker.

The phone rang twice, and Deb answered with a slightly panicked edge in her voice, "Hello? Peter? Everything okay?"

Peter hesitated a count, "Hey mom, I'm sitting here with Gus and Marcy. We had a strange night." He took a few seconds and told her broadly about the book that was found, with Jen's chronicles, and lightly went into some background. Deb's noticeable silence hung in the air as he recounted the previous night's events. Next, Peter moved on to the call with Gus's grandfather in Scotland. "In short, Gus's grandfather was spooked worse than we were. He wants us to fly there today. He said to tell you "Destruction, Plan Three". He is..." when Deb cut him off.

"Hey, all of you, meet me at the office. We should not be talking about this on an open line. Sorry to cut you off, but see you all in my office in 30 minutes, or as soon as you can get here... okay?"

The silence around the table was complete for a full three seconds, when Gus managed, "Okay we will see you there," and they heard an audible click as Deb cut their connection.

"What the absolute hell was that?" Marcy said. Gus and Peter shook their heads, looking at the phone as if it was about to sprout legs and walk away.

Five minutes later, they hastily checked their bags one last time and loaded them into Peter's truck. With a sense of paranoia lingering in the air, they fled the home.

Chapter 43

10:43 AM, Redwolf Solution's Main Campus, Building A, RTP, NC

The journey took 35 minutes, and they were relieved when they finally arrived at the gate to the company. The usually open gate, once entered with a friendly wave to the security guard, had undergone a noticeable transformation. With the gate lowered, they carefully examined the identification cards of each person in the truck.

Moments later, they pulled into a parking space near the executive headquarters where Peter's mom awaited in her expansive office. When they walked in, there was coffee and cakes in the center of the medium size conference table. Deb hugged and greeted each of them and closed the door. It was noticeably darker than normal in her office, with the privacy shades drawn.

They awkwardly sat down, fidgeting with their hands, and exchanged nervous small talk for a minute or two. Peter's words broke the suspense. "Mom, we have been chatting about this the whole way over and trying to figure out something Gus's grandfather said. He basically implied that if I talked to you, you would make everything ok with us leaving town without notice."

Deb nodded her head, "Yeah, I imagine that does sound strange. I can also tell you that the explanation is complex. I will do my best to help. Since you are all employed here, this is internal information. Thirty-five years ago, this company was just me and Mack. We were in debt to our ears trying to launch this company. I was renting development space, and we were struggling to sell my chip designs. We had tried to find financing. We had tried venture capital. Many people shook our hands and talked about how impressed they were, but no one would budget financing for us. I was about to take a developer roll at Motorola. We received a call from a firm we didn't remember meeting. They wanted to fully fund us and were offering terms that no one else would come close to. Peter was eight months old when they flew us all to London. In a conference room the next day, a tall stern Scotsman walked in the door. That was the day I met your grandfather." Deb said, as she looked at Gus.

Gus shook his head. "Investment firm? My family over there are farmers."

"They offered us twenty million in seed funding over the first five years. The offer was generous, shockingly generous. Financially, Mack and I would keep 67% ownership of the company. A trust held the remaining 33%, intending to unveil the beneficiary's name at a later, undisclosed date. There were very few stipulations, but one of them was strange, to say the least. The stipulation was that we were to hire an accountant that they would specify. He assured us that this person was genuine and good at their job, but that they could never be told about this agreement clause."

"That was my mother?" Gus interrupted, and Deb nodded and continued.

"Yes. But honestly, we would have hired her, anyway. She really was great and exactly what we needed... a God send. I see the look on your face, Gus, and I have known you since I changed your shitty diapers. Everything about our friendship with your mother was genuine. There was no clause for us to be friends. There was not anything that stated she had to stay employed at Redwolf. We just had to give her a shot. When she died, your grandfather hand-delivered to us a large envelope after the funeral. In it was the declaration that you, whenever you desired, could claim the other 33% as the third partner. The only stipulation your grandfather specified was that he would decide when you were to be told, and he told me this morning I could notify you. He said he would have all the final paperwork ready for your signature when you got there. We have the option to keep this information discreet or make it widely known, according to your wishes. However, your grandfather is very concerned about something. I am certain I don't understand what, as he said, he was intentionally keeping me in the dark for my safety. The security you see outside was all at his request and, frankly, he supplied the guards you might have met today. What the hell did you guys get yourself into? God, I hope it is not something illegal. Peter gave me the security phrase today to notify me that Gus's grandfather felt your personal safety was in jeopardy. That I was to do anything needed to help you guys get safely away from here."

"Ma?" Peter asked."

"Yes, dear?"

"This doesn't mean that Gus is..." Peter paused, "like... richer than me, right?"

"He is much richer honey, all that money you have blown through. That was mine too, baby." Deb smiled.

Peter looked at Gus, "Being rich was my thing, you bastard!" and laughed.

Gus looked at Deb, "In our next board meeting, we need to discuss Peter's expense account."

"Agreed!" said Deb.

"Hey!" Peter protested.

Chapter 44

11:33 AM

When the meeting was over, they all hugged Deb. She looked at Gus, "Hey, talking to your grandfather this morning really spooked me. He expressed significant worry for your group and instructed me to remind you of a protocol you'd discussed this morning, adding that I should not ask about the protocol's specifics and that I should stop you if you tried to share details. He said it was safer for all involved or... something."

"I'm not sure if any of us understand what he is worried about, but last night was crazy." Gus said. "I'm not sure if what my mom wrote about was fiction, truth, or early signs of the brain tumor that killed her. However, I have never seen my grandfather respond like that."

"With all that in mind, whatever the plan is, be safe and find a way that your grandfather approves of to let me know you are safe." Deb said, catching the eye of each of them.

"Mom," Peter said, "we will have some irises sent to you at the office when we are safe."

"Thanks dear."

"Totally on my new expanded expense account," Peter finished with a large, loving smile.

Chapter 45

12:37 PM Raleigh Executive Jet Port, 700 Rod Sullivan Rd. Sanford, NC

When they left Redwolf, they had two options for their route from the Research Triangle Park: either take Highway 55 or use Interstate 40 to get to U.S.-1. By flipping a coin, they chose the I-40 route. There were no stoplights along this path, making it a sensible choice. Contrarily, if there were more vehicles, it would provide additional cover for anyone attempting to tail them, Gus thought, and immediately hated that his mind had fallen back into that mode again.

As Gus's grandfather had suggested, they took several exit ramps along the way, which offered the ability to get right back on the designated path. They satisfied themselves that no one was following them.

When they arrived at the Raleigh Executive Jetport, they parked and entered the two-story building through the sliding automatic doors. Inside, seated on a plaid backed couch, sat the giant form of Gus's cousin Daniel, reading a magazine. As the door opened, he looked towards them and stood with a wide toothy grin. "Good to see you Gus... Peter annnd, Marcy, right?"

"Yes," Marcy smiled.

"Great. You guys got here just in time to catch our first filed plan window. I think we shouldn't doddle," Daniel said, and without sitting, he passed the enormous fireplace with a propeller mounted above and walked straight out to the plane that waited for them. Eight minutes later, they were in the air, flying north.

When they reached a stable altitude, Peter walked around the G6 looking at with admiration and the excitement of a 10-year-old. "Do you know how much these things cost? Peter asked. "Like 70 million. 70."

"That seems like a lot of money for a plane," Gus said.

"...and it has nothing showing it as a rental. No brochures, no advertising. Nothing. Someone is lo-ho-ho-ded!" Peter said. "Your grandpops must have some seriously rich friends or someone rich by the balls. What did you say he did for a living?"

"They own a farm," Gus expressed with a shrug. "As far as I know, that is really about it. It is a big farm like we saw last year. I mean, they are pretty much self-sufficient plus forestry land and God knows what else."

"Gus. Do you know how much it would be to charter this flight... if whomever didn't own the plane? I mean, that flight I chartered a couple of years ago. That was the closest I ever got to my mom firing me. As it is, I paid for it out of my savings and still owe some. Mom insisted on it as a lesson."

"No!" Gus protested. "Jesus Christ, Peter, I didn't know you did that. How much was it?"

"Let's just say it was a little shy of two hundred." Peter held up both hands to hold back reactions. "I was drunker than I thought."

"Two hundred... THOUSAND! Holy shit Peter! We could have waited for a regular airline flight. I knew it was expensive, but... I had no goddamn idea." Gus said. "My first act as a partner should be to fire you! I will hire you back as my piss boy."

The flight touched down at Edinburgh International after seven and a half hours. Upon clearing customs, Gus's grandfather warmly greeted them with a smile and handshake. "We'll talk about everything once we reach the farm and after everyone has settled in, grabbed some food, and maybe even gotten some rest," he stated. The journey back to the Big House was unremarkable, and the old family Range Rover was strangely quiet.

Chapter 46

Thursday, September 20th, 2018, 2:09 AM Atholl, Scotland

Leaving Edinburgh, the Range Rover went north on the M90 and around Perth and moved on to the A9 for another 20 minutes. From there, a turn to the left on an old back road, which led to another back road, and eventually, an unmarked and overgrown turnoff to an unremarkable rocky and rutted dirt road. Quickly after the turnoff, the road became much more manicured and pleasant.

As the Range Rover crossed the bumpy bridge over the stream at the edge of the property, Gus woke up, not even aware that he had nodded off. Marcy was awake beside him, "There you are! Welcome back to the world!" In the far back row, Peter still slept with his mouth wide open, as if he were catching rain drops, while sawing wood with a nasal snore.

In the front seat, Daniel filled the left side of the car, curled up in the seat like an enormous squirrel. For a moment, Gus panicked, before remembering the driver, his grandfather, was on the right side of the car.

When the car pulled into the circle at the front of the house. Thick stone walled, raised gardens and a fake heavy stone well, had hardened the crossfire positions the "gardeners" took during his last visit. Gus also noted what he expected was an occupied, over-watch position on the roof of the old stone barn. It was an ancient looking large cupola that had most certainly not been there on their last visit.

The SUV came to a stop, and the front doors opened to the house. "That is Nell's assistant Ned. He is also your cousin." Gus's grandfather informed. "He will help get the stuff to your rooms. Gus, you and Marcy will be in your old suite. Peter, Daniel will show you to your room."

"Sounds great!" said Peter as he exited, grabbed his bag, and followed Daniel through the door.

Gus grabbed his own bag and Ned grabbed Marcy's for her. When they entered, the smell of food hit Gus in the face. A lovely shepherd's pie and an assortment of fruit and rolls were on the table. It was just past 2:00AM local time. As they ate, they caught up on the last several years, plus a few months since a similar group gathered around this table. Peter, as usual, lightened the mood and entertained the local family with the exploits of Gus and how he finally got the guts to ask Marcy out on a date.

"About bloody time," said Donna, Lord William's assistant. "It was so obvious last time you were here, always glancing her way with puppy dog eyes and mortified after swallowing the poor bish..."

"Enough!" interrupted Gus's grandfather with a laugh. Gus thanked him with his eyes.

"Anyhoo, I thought I was going to have to bloody ask her out for him," Donna finished with a chuckle.

After a few minutes. Donna excused herself to go to bed. She took time exiting the room to hug and greet all of them. When she stopped at Gus, her hug lingered an extra moment longer. "My. You do look so much like your father, but with your mom's smile lines around the eyes."

Other of the local contingent headed off to bed. Soon, Gus, Marcy, Peter, Daniel, and Gus's grandfather, who insisted on being called Laoch, were the only ones left around the table.

Gus looked at his grandfather and asked, "I think we are all good to talk if you are. It's early evening to us, and we somehow napped most of the drive here."

"Some of us did," Marcy added.

"Well, I sleep little these days, anyway," Laoch admitted. "So, I might as well not sleep here at the table. Who has your mother's book?"

Marcy jumped up, went to her bag, and retrieved the book that she had wrapped in a heavy cotton cloth. She handed the book to Laoch, with the letter sticking out as if it were a bookmark. Laoch removed the letter first, put on his reading glasses, and through teary eyes, read the note from his son. Several times during the reading, Laoch said, "No. No, no, no son," and winced in anguish.

After Gus's grandfather finished reading the note, he cleared his throat, "Over the next week and probably beyond, you will hear me stress the importance of sharing information," as he shook his head. He moved on to the book and Marcy pointed to the marker where she marked Jen's first accounts in the book. Laoch read the first several pages of her testimony and again shook his head.

"How about this?" Laoch said. "I will read this tonight and try to wrap my head around it. Tomorrow after breakfast, we will go someplace and sit. I will answer every question you have, or at least try. I just need some time to absorb this."

They all agreed. They stood and gathered their bags. Laoch stepped over to Peter. "Your father was a wonderful person and always made me laugh. I am deeply sorry for your loss."

"Thank you. I'm looking forward to understanding your relationship with him better. I feel like I'm missing something special that you had with him and my mother."

"Indeed, you are, and I will be glad to tell you everything."

Chapter 47

Thursday, September 20th, 2018, 8:17 AM The Big House, Scotland

There is a short-lived benefit to flying east from the United States to Europe. When you get there in the evening, it still feels early to you. All of that comes back the next morning when you try to get up for breakfast. The morning sun ran across Gus's face with the gentleness of an avalanche. All the travelers felt the time change. They all knew it was best to just get up and start your body's change to the new time zone, but it was never pleasant. Gus could see it in

Marcy's eyes, and when they saw Peter in the hallway, it became comical as they all laughed at each other and nodded.

The smell and promise of coffee led them down the stairs and carried them to the dining room. Fresh and pressed was Lord William, who dropped all regal capacity at the sight of Gus and his friends. "Ah, Gus, my boy, wonderful to see you. Marcy, you look beautiful as always and Peter, it is great to see you as well." He rose and hugged Gus, Marcy, and followed with a firm handshake with Peter. William stood awkwardly by his chair as Gus helped Marcy with her chair. Peter almost sat until he noticed Peter and Laoch both standing and waiting. Once Marcy took her seat, everyone else took their seats.

After they finished breakfast, they all helped clear the table of everything but the coffee service before settling in to talk. William lingered at the table, but Laoch waved his hand. "He has heard all of this stuff before."

When Laoch put the book of Jen's testaments on the table, William sat stiff in his chair and stared at the book in terror. His eyes welled with tears.

Laoch looked at him with fascination mixed with fear as William spoke.

"Don't you see it?" He said with a plea, "His echoes fill the book. Get everything you need from it, and when you are done with it, burn it... salt it and burn it. Burn it!" William said, with enough fire in his eyes to cause the book to ignite, if that had been possible.

Laoch took the book off the table and placed it beside his chair. As soon as the table blocked his view, William spoke again with a staggering calmness after his recent outburst. "Would someone be so kind as to pour this old man a spot more of coffee?"

With no outward reaction, Marcy pulled off a decorative scarf she had on and handed it to Laoch, who took it, reached down and wrapped the book up in it.

Chapter 48

Several thousand miles away, a frustrated monster trapped in its crystalline prison had a sensation like a favorite smell from its childhood. Its attention shifted to the northeast for a moment, far in the distance, and to itself, it said, "William? I thought you long departed this world." As if a switch had turned off, the sensation was gone again.

Chapter 49

Thursday, September 20th, 2018, 9:05 AM The Big House, Scotland

William's piercing remark caused an abrupt halt in the conversation around the table for nearly a minute. All eyes turned to him as he sarcastically quipped, "Some conversationalists you lot are. I think I will take my paper and go read it in the study." Rising to his feet, he poured more coffee, tucked the paper under his arm, grasped his cane, and exited the room.

Four sets of eyes followed him as he left the room, and Peter whispered, "What the fuck was that? Excuse my French in your house, sir."

"I have no putain idea. Excuse my French." Laoch exclaimed with wide eyes. "I have never seen such a reaction out of him, to be honest."

Laoch immediately grabbed his phone out of his pocket and sent a message. Moments later, Nell shuffled out of the kitchen. "I will go sit with him."

With the crisis contained, Laoch's face hardened some. "I took the time last night to read my son's and your mother's chronicles. I imagine right now, if I had read them without context, I would think she was a loon." And the three around the table nodded. "What you just saw with William, that is part of the reality I am going to introduce you to this week. You are going to find some of it difficult to believe and, frankly, a good deal of it is indeed conjecture. Gus, your mother, was a skeptic, and I expect all of you will be... at least at first. Hopefully, I can convince you, or at least make you question and take precautions. If I can't convince you, maybe Jen can, when you read what she wrote again, after I run out of words. She only became a believer later, after your father, my son, died. I also do not for one minute believe it was a total coincidence that it all happened that night. The artifact, and even the storm and, to some degree, his death... This was another battle in the war my family has fought for thousands of years. Another in the list of tragic deaths this creature has caused our family. Peter's father as well, I suspect." Laoch paused and composed himself.

"I'm not sure I get what you mean," Gus exclaimed.

"Well, based on your mother's witness, your father's letter to me, and yes, again conjecture," Laoch said as he stared into his eyes. "I think you, we... are being stalked by this beast."

"Ok, that is crazy!" Peter said. "A North Carolina State Trooper that had apparently lost grip on reality killed my dad."

Laoch leaned forward with an intense look in his eyes. "The same nutty state trooper that showed up the next morning at Gus's house in the early morning to kill whoever was there?" Laoch retorted. "Gus, your mum provided, in her original writing in the book, corroborating evidence of a suspicion we have had over two millennia. Your mother mentions a golden or brass tube she mistook for an ornate spyglass, in her earliest writing in the book. I think I know what that tube is. In the family archives, there is the description of a scepter that the family scribes believed to have mystic origins. A Greek woman warrior brought the artifact with her when she came here. Her name was Sanura. Some writings from that time in Greece described her as a Demi-god. Those stories carried by travelers and minstrels spread from farm to farm and town to town. A member of my family journeyed to Greece to find her, based on songs from those traveling story tellers. She carried something like what your mother described. Amidst the chaos of a cataclysmic battle, the fabled scepter, renowned for its miraculous healing properties under Sanura's command, vanished along with her and the warring factions. No one has seen Scrios in body, except in nightmares, since that event."

Gus, Peter and Marcy exchanged skeptical glances as Gus's grandfather seemed lost in thought. "She must have somehow entrapped the creature in the scepter." Laoch said, again ruminating.

"This is great and all," Gus questioned, "but how does this all relate to us? I mean, we read my mom's stories or whatever you called them... my dad's too."

"They were fucking weird Scoob!" Peter added, mimicking Shaggy's voice from Scooby-Doo.

"Right!" Laoch said. "I probably sound like a lunatic. I need to take you to the archive. Gus? Your mum called it the Bat Cave." Laoch rose as he swallowed the last of his coffee. "Everyone, grab your cups, and let's clear the table and we will go."

Chapter 50

Thursday, September 20th, 2018, 9:25 AM The Big House, Scotland

The group walked outside of the big house and over near the large barn and commandeered a pair of gator carts. "I assume at least one of you can drive one of these, right?" Laoch asked.

"If it is anything like a golf cart, I will be fine," Peter said, as Marcy hopped in the driver's seat. "Hey!" Peter exclaimed.

"I have seen you drive a golf cart... remember?" Marcy said.

"That was once, and who knew they were top heavy?"

"You tried to jump a sand trap at Pinehurst #2," Marcy claimed.

Well, who knew they were so slow? And, it was on a bet by your boyfriend!"

Laoch glanced back and forth at Peter, and at Gus, with his near eyebrow raising at each glance. "Marcy drives," he declared.

They drove the forested path, and through a tight valley that opened into a meadow surrounded by a bowl of hills. At the far side of the meadow was an ancient looking small chapel which backed up to a steep wall of the hill. "How lovely!" exclaimed Marcy.

They pulled up to it and got out of the carts. "Let's go inside" said Gus's grandfather.

Stepping into the small chapel, they walked past several pews and up to a small side chapel on the left wall. "Is that St. Michael?" asked Gus.

"Indeed," said his grandfather as he pulled a plain white plastic card from his wallet and reached under the small altar. A heavy clunk, like metal on stone, startled them both.

The older man moved to investigate the sound behind the altar while Peter, ignoring the noise, stepped onto the pedestal to marvel at the ancient carvings of the altar. "Down off the pedestal please," Laoch said to Peter, and he complied quickly, as if shunned. When it was clear, Laoch pulled on the large old pedestal, and it slowly slid forward with an attached piece of the stone wall. As they walked behind, they could see the modified train tracks the pedestal rode on.

"Nice," Marcy said. "The Bat Cave... I get it."

They walked down a rough natural cave hallway, hearing a slight commotion of talk ahead of them. The hallway opened into an enormous natural room, with multiple desk and cubicles setup. Directly to the left was a large modern conference room table with video conferencing capability. "This, good people, is what we call the cathedral room." Laoch said.

"It's Fu... uh, enormous," Gus said, looking up at the amazingly high natural ceiling.

"What the hell is that?" Marcy said, as Gus looked at her to see what direction she was looking. He followed her gaze to the right-side wall, where an ancient mosaic featuring a sickly blue colored man stared at him. Behind the walking corpse, an army of soldiers followed. He could see them in his peripheral, but the gaze of the central figure locked his eyes. Gus's heart sped up, and he felt a pang of fear that made him want to leave the room. On the wall was a creature of his childhood nightmares. He had never spoken a word about the creature to anyone. He even kept these dreams from his mother, yet somehow there on the wall, was a depiction that was so close to his memory. That the cheek bones being a little too sharp and the chin too long, barely registered as a complaint in his mind.

"That is him," Gus said, "isn't it? Scrios?"

"Ding!" Laoch said. "Gus wins the prize."

While others talked, Gus stood there mesmerized, not even hearing the continued explanation until he felt a hand on his shoulder and jumped. "Are you okay?" Peter asked.

Gus felt a wave of self-consciousness as he realized that the entire room, even strangers, had their eyes fixed on him. Strangely, the cool breeze blowing from the air handlers behind and to the side of him highlighted cool streaks on his face. He reached up and wiped away tears he didn't notice had fallen.

"I knew him," Gus pointed with his chin, "as Death. He haunted my dreams as a child. He said he ate little boys like me. The night my father died; a different older man came to my dreams. He said his name was Pappy. He told me not to fear it. Pappy told me that this creature had no hold over me and it was only here because it feared me. I don't think I ever believed him. One day, the day my dad died." Tears welled up in Gus's eyes again.

"I never remembered any of this before the other day." Gus's voice deteriorated to croaking, emotion choked voice, "Pappy came to me when I was awake... and told me to be brave." biting off his words in apparent anger. "Pappy said, be brave..." He waved his hand flippantly. "Go out there... and give your father a hug and tell him you love him," Gus said as angry tears flowed down his face, forming rivulet's. "He fucking knew what was going to happen, and he told me to go hug him? Because he was taking him away?"

Marcy wrapped a supportive arm around his waist.

"Pappy didn't take him away," Laoch said. "It was the storm, it was the creature," he said, as Gus's head snapped towards him like a challenge.

"He said to go hug him... he knew what was happening," Gus said, with his eyes burning with intensity.

"Aye lad, he did. That was indeed Pappy, you saw. I have seen him too. He came to me the day you were born. He wasn't specific, but I think he was warning me of today... and I'm so very sorry." Laoch said. "Was he wearing that garish old three-piece suit still?" Laoch offered with a soft, gentle smile.

The tension in Gus's shoulders seemed to release, and Gus sat down on the floor as if deflating. "What the hell is happening?"

"Pappy is what I have called a harbinger. I am not sure if other relatives filled that role in the past. He says things when they are important. He must think you are pretty damn important. Also, interestingly, others can see him when he visits. Just ask Daniel. When I saw him for the first time... well, the first time since the day he was interned, Daniel saw him too and shrieked like a wee girl when he walked in and saw him. Probably shit himself too, but if he did, he wasn't alone in that endeavor. Take a couple minutes lad, I'll get you some water. There is no timeline here."

Chapter 51

Thursday, September 20th, 2018, 10:00 AM The Archives, Scotland

After a few minutes, Gus's normal demeanor returned. His grandfather, sensing the change in the room, began introducing the other people standing around the cave. "These gentlemen and this lady, Sonya, great to see you... are part of the analytics and research team we have." Sonya, a petite black woman from Yorkshire, shook hands with the party and exchanged pleasantries.

"This, is..." but before Laoch could finish, Gus cut him off.

"This is Thomas Finch, He was an intern on my team several years ago and left," Gus said with a quizzical look on his face.

"Well, the cats out of the bag... to come here, yes," Thomas shrugged.

"Thomas leads up this group of researchers." Laoch said. "He has been invaluable with authenticating pieces from the archive and improving the database, as well as helping gather massive amounts of data and turn it into... err um."

"Insights." Thomas finished for him.

"Yes! Thank you, Thomas. He does lots of technical mumbo jumbo I will never fully understand. He is also the one working to add the book you provided to the archives and verify the stories where they duplicate information already known or add depth." Laoch said with a smile. "He also has a team tasked with finding out information on the people your mum listed, the private investigators and such."

Laoch went around the room introducing the team, and as most of the workers returned to their desks, Laoch led the party to the large conference table near the front of the cavern. As they sat down, Laoch called to Thomas, "Thomas, could you have someone grab me a sample from the archive of the different eras of the chronicles?" Thomas flashed a thumbs up and headed out the left doorway at the back of the enormous cathedral room.

As they sat around the table and made themselves comfortable. Gus's grandfather worked at a keyboard on the laptop computer on the table with the pointer finger on each hand. The large flat screen television came to life. He looked up at his grandson and his friends and spoke. "I think the best thing I can do right now is answer questions you might have as best as I can. It has already been quite the morning, and it is only... a quarter past ten."

"So, let me start this off I guess," said Gus. "This past couple of days have been a whirlwind. Hell, the last month. I see that... that thing on the wall. I cannot speak for the rest of these guys, but its presence on that wall, when I have told no one about my tormentor from my dreams, has my attention. Setting that fucker aside for a moment. The reason I came here originally, besides the book, was to get an understanding about your relationship with Peter's parents. You should know, Peter and his mom and dad are family to me. Not like family... family. From our phone call, when you told us to come to Scotland, you seemed much closer relationship with Deb than any of us knew. You even seemed to know how she would react to us calling and telling her we all were disappearing for a week. We went to her office that morning. Was that yesterday?" Gus paused and looked towards Marcy for a sign that he was right and received a nod.

His grandfather leaned forward in his seat as if to speak, and Gus raised his hand in a "stop," signal. "Sorry, let me try to get this out... Deb dumps on me, after apparently clearing it WITH YOU, that I'm some kind of double, extra top-secret partner in the company that hired me after I left the army. I'm guessing I inherited that from my mother... who I assume never knew this connection between Deb and you, either. Years ago, you told me you and my mom were at odds, and that you had kept your distance because of that disagreement." Gus leaned forward, and his eyes seemed to burn with intent. "Who knows that you were the investor that allowed Redwolf Solutions to become a company? Did my dad know? I implied the question to Deb, and she denied it played a part in her keeping my mom, but also said it was part of the agreement that they had to hire her. But you can't really fire a partner, right? Peter is my brother. We share no DNA..."

Peter chimed in. "That we know of, but I am open to that possibility if it makes me also a partner."

Gus snapped his fingers at Peter. "Shut it, Peter, not the time," as his eyes took a laser focus on his grandfather. "Has my entire life been some kind of orchestration? For example, did I earn the grades I received in school? After basic, they made me the leader of my ROTC unit. Did you have a hand in that too? The first thing I need to know is, what about my life is real and not manipulated?"

A moment passed as Gus stared into his grandfather's eyes. Laoch answered calmly. "I promised you all cards are on the table, and I meant it. Let me know if I miss anything and I will gladly explain it. That goes for today or any time you ask. If we are in a secure location where I can answer, I will. The reason I had you come here is for that security of communication. When you leave here, I have a phone for you that is secure. This property and all family holdings, the big house, etc. are all secure. The people here are each vetted and many of them are even your relatives. There are passive and active assets at work to ensure your security here. Embarrassingly, you noticed some of that during your first visit, and the review of that clumsy display resulted in the lead person on that detail losing their job. Hopefully, they have been less obvious this time."

"You mean like the over-watch position on top of the old barn disguised as a cupola?" Gus said, as his grandfather's cheeks flushed red. "In all honesty? If I had never been here before, I would never have noticed, so that was a great job making it look like it had always been there."

"Thanks," Laoch said, as his face relaxed. "Anyway, your life has been your own. Your parents noticed the security detail we had paid for. Your dad had eyes like you, apparently. During a trip here to help on the farm, he ordered me to, and I quote, 'stop the bullshit,' and we did. He knew that help was a phone call away, and I want you to know that as well. I offer you protection if you want or need it after you leave here," as he waved the offer away with his hand. "I know... you are just like your father."

Laoch shifted in his seat a little, and continued, "The investment in the company that became Redwolf Solutions was genuine. Peter's mother is a bona fide genius. The return on that investment has been even better than ever predicted. We invested in her, because others were taking advantage of her intellect and trying to monopolize her talent. She was under research by our investment team for a year before your parents returned to the states. I won't lie to you and say that when you and your parents returned, the timeline of our investment didn't speed up, because it did. It was a financial decision to help your parents to get Jen a job in the Raleigh area quickly because the economy was tight. However, as Deb told you, there was no requirement that your mom stayed employed there. Hell, if she had found out, I have no doubt she would have quit. They gave us their assurance that her financial offer would be commensurate with her value in the marketplace. Everything she did to advance her career, was her. Your mother was a special and gifted person. We knew Deb would see that too, based on her efforts here. We also had zero-doubt that your mother would never be party to malfeasance, so her employment there was also protecting our investment." Laoch reached for the pitcher of water in the middle of the table and poured a glassful for himself.

"Your mother never owned the portion of the company you're entitled to. Her equity in the company, which you inherited from her, was from the public pool of common stock that Peter's parents created out of their own portion of ownership."

Gus's demeanor noticeably relaxed. "Okay," he said nodding, "thank you for that. Now, you said that you and my mother were at odds"

Laoch nodded. "Indeed."

"About what?"

Laoch smiled lightly and spoke. "There were hints in her note to me at the beginning of what she wrote. I always suspected that she didn't fully believe in that blue fucker," Laoch pointed to the mural on the wall. "In her defense, it's not an easy sell to say. My family, for thousands of years, has been trying to protect the world from a monster that no one has seen for two and a half thousand years. I have no real physical proof of its existence, but our family lives a quiet life, out of the public eye, with most choosing to stay on our family lands... The same twelve thousand acres we have possessed and defended since records began. People tend to look at you funny."

"That, plus a banjo, and a move to rural Arkansas and you have the makings of a decent horror movie." Peter injected and jumped back when a loud thud emanated from under the table beside Marcy. "Ow, that frickin' hurt!" Peter met the daggers coming from Marcy's eyes for a split second before looking away with disinterest.

"We, sitting at this table," Laoch emphasized with his finger poking the tabletop, "are breaking thousands of years of tradition. Some of that tradition is what first angered your mother." He stared into Gus's eyes. "And honestly, I understand why the tradition existed so long and I also understand why Jen was so angered by it. You see, she was not told about this place or the family secret until long after she married your father. Tradition dictated that it didn't happen until she was pregnant... with you, Gus."

"That's fucked up," Marcy said, as Peter and Gus nodded in agreement.

"Aye, to say she was angry, as I heard from your father, is a vast understatement. After a few weeks, I convinced myself that everything was going to be fine. Your mum was even taking part in the research in the archives... despite having an enormous amount of skepticism.

295

Laoch looked down at the table, gathered himself, and looked back up at his guests. "I was a pig-headed bastard. See, I had grown up with the belief. With the creature being a reality as unquestionable as the water in that pitcher." As he waved his hand at the water in the middle of the table.

Marcy's voice was tense. "She wasn't giving in; she was bloody trapped."

Laoch nodded his head solemnly. "Yes. I see that now. I think I might have at that time, too. But it was the way it was. It was all I knew. The way it had been for generations. I concede. It was wrong and as you see here today; I have changed it. That tradition is ended."

Shifting the conversation after granting the point, Laoch pointed at his head. "You see, like you Gus, I had dreams. Before I ever saw this room, I had seen him." Laoch pointed to the far cave wall. "Right now, Gus, you are making the same mistake I did 30 years ago. You believe that Peter and Marcy have the same certainty as you do right now? I'm telling you, warning you, in front of them, that they don't believe what you do, the way you do. Marcy, Peter, I'm not saying that to be mean." He looked at each of them. "If you're feeling skeptical, that's completely fine. It's bloody natural. I appreciate your skepticism, and I encourage you to express it freely whenever you have a question. What I failed to realize was that Jen's lack of pushback didn't mean she had accepted our truth. I wanted to believe that our persuasion had worked, and she now regarded the existence of the creature as an indisputable truth, just as I do. However, without concrete evidence, any rational individual experiences doubt, and I failed to account for that. Doubt made me feel weak, and I responded with hostility. I caused her to distance herself. Rather than embracing her doubt and offering an explanation, I responded with bluster." He paused and took a long drink from the cup and refilled it.

Laoch, set the glass down and continued. "Gus, just after you and your parents came back from visiting them in North Carolina, Jen's parents tragically lost their lives in a car accident caused by a drunk driver. We all immediately flew to the states to support her. I'll explain more later, but I was having a storm of terrible and vivid dreams every night. I spoke to your father about it many times and I even more strongly believe now that these dreams were a sign that Scrios was threatening us. Many of the archives talk of *tribulations* and poor sleep when he was near. The problem is, his proximity may not always cause the nightmares. It could be general anxiety or eating or drinking a beverage too late. Determining which dreams he causes is difficult, or even impossible. Sometimes there seem to be tribulations during or before important events. Like the days when your mother was pregnant with you. Those could have just been my anxiety... except for when I saw Pappy. A few times, he would try to say things to me. Others, he looked frustrated because he would move his mouth and no sound would emanate, or he would look two dimensional, like a poster." Laoch said, shaking his head and blinking his eyes.

"Anyway, in Raleigh, I was having terrible dreams. I was tired. After the funeral, your father drove us back to the hotel because he wanted to know why Daniel and I were carrying firearms at Jen's internment. We compared notes and your father admitted a dream... anyway conjecture got out of hand. We checked out of the hotel and took over your mom and dad's house like pirates on shore leave at a whorehouse. There were people sleeping everywhere: beds, couches, chairs and even the floor. Apparently, your mum woke up, and your father caught her before she roused all of us. He took her to breakfast. That is the setting for the note in the chronicle that I only received yesterday, when you brought the book. Between my dreams and your fathers waken experience, I feel strongly the creature was very close indeed. All these years later, it casts the question in my mind if the accident that killed Jen's parents was indeed an accident or another incident in the war with this evil."

"What about the book and the letter?" Peter asked.

"They are being added to the archive, but first we are fully vetting them, as I mentioned earlier. Jen had some amazing observations, and her experience was unique for a non-family member. I have never heard of anyone Scrios failed to dominate that was not a blood relative. We are digging into your mom's family tree to see if there is a link to more of our family line, a lost branch perhaps. We are also working to gather your mother's full medical history, with scans and such to add to the database in case something else was the cause. Maybe her condition made her immune? I simply don't know. We are also tracking down information on the different private investigators your mother listed, both dead and the last one, who is still active. We are worried because he is working for someone who operates out of Charlotte, and that is a bit too close for comfort. Besides his own influence, he has powerful friends and customers that include a senator out of the Midwest, with presidential aspirations. Now is when having the resources we do, is beneficial. We will be cautious and never have a path back to here or any of us."

Laoch stood up. "Let's take a quick break. Bathrooms are through the right doorway, take a right. You will walk right past a small kitchen, and we will meet back up in there in, let's say, ten minutes. I can take you on a small tour, and also show you how to get out of here if you ever need to." As Laoch was giving instructions, Thomas walked up with a recycled cardboard Amazon box. Laoch popped the top and took a peeked in at the contents and thanked Thomas with a smile. "When the tour was over, I will show you what is in the box," he spoke.

Peter, performing his best Brad Pitt imitation, asked with a whine, "What's in the box?"

"You have been around him since you were both babies... was he dropped on his head?" Laoch asked Gus.

Chapter 52

Thursday, September 20th, 2018, 11:00 AM The Archives, Scotland

Laoch led his grandson and friends into the rear of the facility. He started with the oldest archives. Thick glass walls surrounded the room, and entry was possible through an airlock made of a transparent material. Inside the lock, along the stone wall to the right, were white body suits on hooks and lockers. "To access this, the oldest archive, you go through the lock. When you enter, the body suits you see on the right go over your clothes. In the lockers, there are footies to go over your shoes, and various types and sizes of gloves. There are masks, but they are not required. They are there to protect the artifacts, not you. We ask that you wear a hat that is provided as well and pull back any hair under it. We do this more or less to keep as much dust and particulates out of these rooms. You also find that we keep the humidity in these rooms dramatically lower than the cave's natural level. As you will see in subsequent rooms, where there is parchment and other media that break down. Time is a cruel bitch."

With a grand wave of his hand, Laoch pointed to square holes in the rock walls. "The cubbyholes you see, both new shelving and those carved into the walls, contain our oldest chronicles, which date from approximately 500 BC. However, Sanura, the very important visitor from Greece I mentioned, was the one who scribed the writing on them. Yesterday, we discussed how she came here at the request of one of my ancestors. While she was here, she converted our oral tradition to written documents and taught members of my family how to read and write them themselves. Ironically, since she was from an even more ancient time, at least in legend, the writing style she taught and used is a customized version of cuneiform. We didn't know that she had altered it for us until your father," he looked at Gus, "came on one of his trips with a pile of research he had done at the university."

Something about cuneiform writing resonated in Gus's head, but he could not remember why. "This writing," Gus asked, "was it done on stone tablets, like you see on the TV?"

Laoch put his hands up like he was comparing the weight of two items. "Yes, and no. In the cathedral room, there is a wall you probably haven't noticed yet. There is a large inscription on the wall opposite of the mural of Scrios. I will show you that when we go back. Sanura carved those inscriptions into the stone wall herself. What she carved there were training instructions for troops preparing to fight Scrios, warning them not to look the beast in his eyes. The mural, according to the archives, was a training aid for them, where they practiced sparring. They had to do so without raising their heads and even glancing at the creature on the wall. I know you have seen the things Jen had written about Sanura, so let me know when I am just repeating what you know, rather than giving you the context to understand it."

Laoch adjusted his stance in the hallway and emphasized his words with his hands. "Jen filled her writing with intricacies, using a type of shorthand that assumed the reader's familiarity with the same background knowledge she had gained. So, bear that in mind, and when you read her writings again, hopefully I will have filled in some gaps of knowledge for you."

Laoch shook his head, chastising himself. "Sorry. Getting back to the tour... what you find here in room one. You will find the writing in this room recorded on tin sheets. Why tin sheet, you ask? Well, the metal worker she brought with her found rich deposits on the property and he knew how to extract it. It is durable, doesn't rust and frankly, we wouldn't need all these air locks and stuff if they had stuck with it. But as with everything, the younger generations always know more and better ways." Laoch smiled whimsically.

"I will have a sample for you to look at when we get back to the table... as well as lunch" Laoch looked at Peter. "It is what is in the booooxxx!" he said as Scottish, old man Brad Pitt.

Moving down the ancient chiseled out stone hallway, they arrived at another room. Either white dry walled construction or clear glass walls that showed externally lit stone made the walls to this room. "The previous room is called the Athens Room, as it contained all tintype, cuneiform documentation, time wise logically from 1200BC until they switched to parchment in or around 630 AD. This, the second room, we refer to as the Rome Room. It contains parchment, vellum and hundreds of thousands of fragments of both. All writing here is in Latin. Latin was the language of the Catholic priests. Several of our ancestors became priests and learned the art of scribing. They brought the practice home and taught it to others. We hermetically sealed much of their writing for its protection. There is also an active recovery room in the back, where you can see the back of Talia Levin, I believe, who is working to restore and preserve documents. Talia, who we stole from the Israel Antiquities Authority (IAA) nine years ago. She is an expert in ancient parchment recovery and preservation. I was kidding when I described it as stolen, as if she had been pilfered. Through a subsidiary, we reached out to the IAA directly. We have heavily funded their efforts and they, in return, have been extremely helpful in our efforts both in this and through established connections, enhancing our security protocols and surveillance. No one keeps secrets better than the Israelis."

Gus shook his head. "I won't ask."

"Good. We understand each other." His grandfather winked and smiled. "Moving on, next is the London Room. London chronicles are again on parchment and vellum. Again, there is a staffed room for preservation and recovery. This group, partially funded by the British government, also works for the Crown aiding in public museums and we have many leaders in the field helping us. Most are now considered adjunct or partially retired, despite some being rather young for that designation. The language documented here is primarily English and Gaelic, although some older transitional documents are still in Latin. Moving on." He continued down the hall to a newer room on the opposite side of the hall.

The fourth room, although it appeared mostly empty, was enormous. If not for the airlock entry, someone might have mistaken the array of wooden tables for a cafeteria or a sitting area in an enormous library. There were no white suits for entry, just the airlock. "This is the Edinburgh Room. In it is everything starting in about 1920, to the present."

Peter shrugged. "Looks kinda empty,"

Laoch smiled. "Oh, I assure you it is not. Directly to the left is the artifact area, where you'll discover a collection of physical objects that serve as tangible records of significant items in the collection. These items span three millennia. The tables in this space offer versatility and accommodate both independent research and team meetings. The isolated network exclusive to this facility allows users to view easily on demand the inventory of every room. In addition, I will provide you with credentials and a secure device that allows you to request reports. We will send these reports to you using certified and encrypted sources. We used different light frequencies to scan or photograph every document and artifact to preserve every detail. Let's go inside." He pressed a large button glowing green beside the door.

The doorway split in the middle, separating with a lightning bolt shaped, self-reinforcing design, and retreated into the hole at each side of the door. They all entered the lock, and the outside door closed. The sound of air handlers kicking in alerted them that the floor was just a large, grated vent. From the roof, a series of three puffs of air, just enough to move their hair, pulsed. A flow of air sufficient to completely replace the air in the small airlock followed. Once the air exchange completed, the barrier around the door glowed green and the interior door opened, allowing them to enter.

"Ok, what the heck was all that?" Gus asked.

Laoch explained as he picked up a tablet computer from one of the multiple charging cradles and logged in, and stepped over to the group. "Similar to some airports, but this may be a bit more thorough. You will be glad to know that no one is armed, except for Peter, who has a small penknife on his keyring. I am sure glad you didn't take that on a commercial flight. No one currently has a communicable disease of note. At least not one that is airborne," as everyone stopped to look at Peter, who was scratching his crotch.

"Hey, they got bunched up." Peter exclaimed with a wounded look.

Laoch shook his head as others laughed and returned to the tablet. "There were no signs of recent exposure to explosives or accelerants. There is a maintenance reminder to replace filters as grass pollens are showing as high, coming from outside, and mold spores are at a manageable level. Radiation levels are normal." Laoch finished and the surrounding group stared slack jawed.

"Radiation levels?" Marcy asked.

"Mostly for radon gas, as uranium breaks down in the surrounding rock," Laoch stated.

Marcy relaxed visibly. "Oh, ok... I was thinking... you know."

With a cryptic smile, Gus's grandfather said, "Oh yeah, we are all set for that, too. Hope we never need it, but our radiation detectors are military grade. We have safer shielded areas. Plus, we have a spring fed cistern, multiple power sources and food reserves. If we didn't take a direct or near direct hit, you could probably live long enough to starve down here.".

"Lovely," replied Marcy.

Laoch walked towards and through the artifact room. "Anyhow, follow me." They walked past museum quality artifacts. Preserved leather armor with an overlapping leather sheets from top to bottom, to cover a torso, sat in a clear walled box with independent climate controls. There were swords from multiple ages, muskets, and even a small cannon. On a manikin near the door they walked towards was a perfectly preserved and highly decorated World War 2 British officer's uniform. At the bottom was a small plaque that said Lord William Atworth.

Amid the many ribbons, one caught Marcy's eye. "Excuse me... that medal in the center of its chest, below the collar, with the gold-ish metallic star like background? Is that from the William we met?"

"Ah yes, that is William," Laoch said. "That is the Royal Victorian Order Knight Grand Cross, presented to him during World War 2 by George the VI."

"I notice you call him Lord?"

"Yes, he inherited that title from his father, the knighthood he earned in blood."

With that, Laoch removed the card from his wallet and scanned it. Next, he punched in a code that popped up on his phone. Last, he entered a second code from memory. "This room contains everything that makes this place tick." The normal wooden door made a deep sounding 'chunk' sound. From the wall came a mechanical click, soft but loud enough to be heard over the air handlers that ticked inside the walls. Instead of opening, the door receded itself about eight inches and swung heavily out of the way.

As they entered the room, Gus noticed the wall was exceptionally thick. More than a foot of what appeared to be layered and reinforced steel and other polymer layers. The seemingly wooden door they had approached was a facade that disguised a door that more resembled a heavy vault like one would see at a bank.

Gus had casually observed the buzzing sound of computer fans and the raised floor of a server room, as the construction of the wall and door diverted his attention. He felt an elbow prod him and he looked at Peter, who was standing there with a look of surprise. The secure server room was larger than any of them would have thought. There were four rows of state-of-the-art computer racks.

"Whoa," Gus said. "I didn't expect that in here."

"Me either," Peter said. "That is some pretty state-of-the-art shit! What are we looking at?"

Laoch smiled and shrugged. "I am not the super tech person here in the room. However, the basics, the front three rows are the systems only accessible by the internal network, which is physically separated from the fourth row, which has external connectivity and extends cellular service down here. The large internal system is the primary research, database, analytical system and rudimentary artificial intelligence dedicated to help find meaningful connections in the data. There is a sneaker net import of data from key external sources that the geeks clean up and import to the Big Data Farm section of the internal system. Twice daily, analytics software analyzes the imported data for keywords and patterns security reports. There is storage of all research, for all the rooms, and their inventories. The internal systems also handle control of the security and environmental system." Laoch said as Peter raised his hand.

Laoch nodded at Peter to ask his question. "I saw how we came in. How the hell did you get all this shit down here?"

"Ah, right over here." Walking around the back wall, he led them to an industrial elevator. It too had enormous doors on the front of it that provided access to it. "Directly above us, one hundred and forty-seven feet, is a warehouse that has been there since 1974. Jen, Gus's mother, worked in that warehouse when they lived here. They built the lift in the rear corner of the warehouse and disguised it as a separate room about 14 years ago. The elevator's construction alone exceeded the cost of the computers and the entire server room combined."

Laoch lightly clapped his hands and held them palm up at his side. "What do you say if we go back to the conference table and eat?" Checking his watch, "food should be about ready. After we eat, we can discuss more, and I can try to bring you more up to date?"

Chapter 53

Thursday, September 20th, 2018, 1:17 PM The Archives, Scotland

When lunch was over, Laoch picked up the box from beside his chair. The first item he pulled out of it was a roughly rectangular tin sheet. Straight lines marked the sheet, separating sections that looked almost like chicken footprints to Gus. "This," Laoch said, is a "tintype from the Athens Room as we have grown to call them. There are over 30 thousand of these stored in the first room. We tagged them in the upper corner with a serial number, row, shelf, and bin location. That is how you find them if you need them. The serial number dictates the storage sequence in each bin. If you take them out, take the time to put them back correctly. If you don't, you are signing yourself up for the yearly inventory, and I will bloody fly you here for it." He smiled directly at Peter.

"Rude!" Peter mumbled, as Marcy snorted a laugh.

Laoch continued, "Interestingly, as I mentioned earlier, this is not any traditional cuneiform found anywhere else in the world. There are special characters that Sanura must have made up which are distinctly used by us in the family, and the translation here is directly to an ancient language that predated Gaelic. I see the look on your faces. We have translated each inscription into English; the tablets display their image and multiple translations. If you discover a variation in meaning, you can submit those to the CCB for approval. That's the Change Control Board. There is a button on the interface. From that one button, you can take private notes tied to your account, which you can choose to share if you think they are meaningful. You can submit your notes for internal publishing or as a support for your submission to the CCB." Laoch looked at the plate in his hand. "Ah yes, I remember this one. Lil, the only surviving sibling and sister of the beast, Scrios, was the first to see him for what he was. This one's tricky to

303

read because of its rhythmic, song-like structure. This was some of the oral history that Sanura scribed herself. The meaning of it, first in the proto-Gaelic language.

Laoch bounced his head in a rhythmic bounce, and the foreign guttural language flowed for about 30 seconds. He stopped and translated it into English. *"When she touched his shoulder, it flashed with fairy fire. The creature lifted its eyes, and they met. Its lifetime of memories displayed in its eyes. The manor, impossible for her to forget. Evil thought, monstrous deeds. Its black heart had conceived. Scrios's intentions were far worse. For stripped barren was he. His thoughts and intentions for her to know and see."*

"Jesus Christ," Gus expressed. "That is dark as shit."

"Indeed. There are several times where family of blood relation met eyes with the beast and lived long enough to record it... The last one was your mum, Gus."

"What do you mean? Are you now claiming my mother is a relative? Gus asked.

"That is still just a working hypothesis. We have sent some of your DNA to be tested as it carries your mother's RNA and should be traceable to Lil if true. Hell, Genghis Khan apparently has one descendant in every two hundred people in the world. Strange things happen."

Reaching into the box again, Laoch brought out a beautiful page of flowing script with a dragon-like creature at the bottom and an illustration of the Archangel Michael, impaling it with a spear. Protective plastic encased the page, protecting it from the environment and maintaining its flat appearance. "This is from the Rome Room. By all appearances, it looks like a page from the Bible. It is not. This passed for a children's book back in the dark ages... kind of 'Grimm Tale', if you will. It is in Latin, as you might expect. It is the story of a relative who went off to slay the beast Scrios. This relative thought he was the embodiment of the Archangel Michael. This is just the front and back of a single page, mind you. Sirus, the relative, embarked on a quest, believing God had ordained him to kill Scrios, as Michael slew the serpent. Things went poorly and the beast," Laoch flipped the page over, "traced his steps back to where he lived with his family. Most likely through torture. Where he cooked and ate Sirus's children in front of their mother. The creature forced the newly armless and legless Sirus and his wife to watch." Laoch paused, the build in his voice that had reached a veritable shout, and complete silence had filled the room.

The moment captivated even nearby eavesdropping workers, shocking them into silence. Laoch continued, "Kindly, the next page is not present in this room.

It depicts what his army did to his wife... until she died days or weeks later, while Scrios's minstrels played music and everyone had a grand time."

Marcy chokingly excused herself, and ran for the bathroom, retching on the open right side passage doorway as she passed.

Gus stared daggers at his grandfather. "Was that necessary?" with the anger rumbling in his voice barely contained.

"It was. Each of you needs to fully understand the creature that is out there. It doesn't give a shit about your cross. It is not afraid of sunlight. Silver? Scrios will fucking laugh at you. Its only weakness... flows in your veins, Gus. If given half the chance, he will turn your friends against you and use them to ruin you as he languishes in their misery!" Laoch stood up from the table. "Come here and look he said." Leading them 20 feet into the middle of the cathedral room, where he pointed at the inscriptions on the wall opposite the mural.

Marcy reentered the room but stayed back near the doorway.

"There!" he said. Sanura carved that there, and they used it as a training mantra. It says:

One: Eyes down

Two: The chest of your opponent does not mislead in battle.

Three: If a friend turns on you in battle, he is now your enemy.

It doesn't say, if you face this beast, ask it politely for a time out, because you are now in a stressed state and need to go find a fucking safe space!"

Laoch stopped, looked down, shook his head, visibly deflated, "I'm sorry. You are right, that was probably too early for that kind of thing. However, you are going to find entries in the archive that make that look like child's play." He turned and started leading them back towards the table.

As they walked, Peter bumped shoulders with Gus as Marcy grabbed his other hand. "Okay, I thought that page from the Middle Ages version of the Hostile movie was messed up, but the safe space line was pretty damn epic!" he whispered.

Gus shook off Peter's comment, and he faced Marcy. "Are you ok?"

Marcy wore an embarrassed look. "Yeah. That whole horrible page freaked me the hell out. Suddenly, out of nowhere, I felt lunch coming up and ran for it."

They returned to the table, and Laoch pulled two more items from the box. The first was yet another piece of parchment. "This is a parchment with the recording of dreams from an ancient relative. Gus, you may find these interesting

305

for comparison if you have had anything more significant. I won't go deep into this one, just safe to say... it's not pleasant."

Laoch took a breath and reached into the box again. "The next artifact is from the Edinburgh Room. Your mother's writings all but confirm that William, whose memories and stories are presented here, was used by the creature. In it, if you choose to look, you will find his military record in its entirety. His letters to home, and official letters during the war. The amazing record that had him knighted. The documentation of the horrific event that had him on the verge of court martial before he was institutionalized. Further, you will find his medical records in their complete representation. These exist nowhere else, as the Crown ordered their destruction. Their existence here is highly illegal and probably treasonous. These are better viewed on the tablet where you can see links to research and previous conclusions.

"Last," Laoch reached into the box and produced metallic points and a knife. "These don't belong here. By that I mean they don't belong in this country. These are arrowheads and a knife made of iron steel. The points are over two thousand years old, and metallurgy confirms that they and the knife are from Greece. Several prominent regions there forged them. We also have others of the same age, and design, locally forged here... from about six hundred yards in that direction." Laoch said, pointing towards the wall. "They are not trade items that were delivered here or bartered for over the past millennia, as we have several thousand of them in our Edinburgh archive room. In an ancient, sealed room, we discovered some points that are still fastened to the wooden arrow shaft."

Laoch relaxed, and from the box, produced three white cards. "Take these. One of the kind people here will help you set up your pin codes which are connected to these phones." He handed each of them identical phones.

Peter was the first to notice a piece on the back that slid and twisted up. He looked at it with a confused look, pointed at it, glancing at Laoch.

Laoch smiled. "Well, they are special." Speaking slowly and deliberately, he said, "That is a Tel... e... phone," emphasizing each syllable. "No seriously. You will pair those with your card. It does both cellular and eventually a satellite connected phone, although that part, when it works, will only be outdoors. Through a partnership with Redwolf, us, and a certain South African billionaire, it will also work as a satellite internet router. We expect that part will be dreadfully slow at first, but next year he plans to send up low orbit satellites that future versions of this phone will use. That fold out piece for now, unfortunately, is decoration. The phones also have a proprietary VPN built into the OS, that will provide privacy for communication. There are exactly twelve of those phones currently. So be careful with them. This is the fifth version and is extremely durable. The polymer front is the next version of the stuff he plans to use for his truck windows. Not indestructible, but you must work hard to break it. Once you are all setup, I'm turning you free to do research, or to do whatever you like. Meet at the Big House tonight at 19:00 for dinner? Again, Marcy, I apologize for my showmanship and getting carried away."

Chapter 54

Thursday, September 20th, 2018, 7:45 PM The Big House, Scotland

Dinner that evening was subdued. When they had the conversation, it was short and to the point. Several of Gus's relatives had heard that he was in town and had come by the Big House to meet him. Among them was a rather eccentric, older relative named Kier. "This is your cousin, Kier." Laoch said, and he and Gus shook hands. "You might have heard some howls during the evenings and nights."

"Was that you, Kier?" Gus interrupted with a smile, and all present chuckled.

"Nooooo, no lad," Kier said with a stiff brogue and an equally congenial smile. "What your grand is trying to get to is that I'm the strange cousin that raises wolves... or lives with wolves might be more appropriate. Since they run about, I thought it might be best to get you a little time with them and them with you. They are friendly if they know you are a friend, and I can make that happen. They mostly stay miles from here, but just in case."

"Sure, we would love to!" Marcy jumped in with the look of an excited child.

"We would enjoy that, I think," Gus said. "When would you like us to come by?"

"Oh, they are outside right now. They are my pack and, well, they follow most times." He said and looked up at Laoch. "Uncle, it will be just a minute or two and we will be right back?"

"Oh sure, not a problem. I think I will come to see them, too." Laoch rose and walked towards the door.

As the front door opened, they noticed the multitude of large animals milling in the front yard. All of them had distinct but similar patterns of dark brown hair, streaked with black. When Kier walked out, they came to him like they had been silently called. He sat down on the ground and roughed up several of their thick neck fur, as he called them by their names.

"They all seem quite docile," Marcy said.

"That is mostly because I am here and Laoch is standing there." Kier said. They are calm because I am calm. My calmness made it clear to them I tolerate you, so they reluctantly do the same. I need you each to sit. They will all come very close to you over the next few minutes. For now, don't extend any appendage until they recognize you, assuming you wish to keep them, that is. Preferably, you don't pet them or try to at all, ever, to be honest. These animals are not friendly pooches; these are wolves, not domesticated dogs. They perceive the world as totally different from how a dog does. They accept me as their leader because I lead them. I do not want you to put yourselves into their hierarchy. I want them to ignore you as they would a stone or tree because you are under my protection. The only command you need to know is "Go!". When you say that, they will leave, or at the very least, give you a comfortable space." Kier finished.

After several minutes milling around the group, the entire pack pulled back to the far side of the drive and noticeably relaxed. Some flopped on their side and took a nap, while others lounged near a large tree.

Six men in clean gardening coveralls walked from the large barn. All the men, save one, appeared to be in their mid-thirties, with the one leading towards the front a shade older. The leader, a tall, powerfully built, dark-skinned black man, with some graying at his temples, tipped his hat as they walked past. Three of the others were white men that looked like they could have come off a production line with consecutive serial numbers. Despite their loose coveralls, anyone could see that they were well built, and all were approximately five foot eight. The other two, walking near the back of the group, were taller and slighter in build. Both had olive skin and deep black hair. As they walked forward, Laoch called out to them, "Head inside boys, your dinner is waiting."

Gus looked at his grandfather, who, meeting his eyes, gave him a knowing nod as he rolled his eyes.

"Gus, could I speak to you for a minute or two?" Laoch said. To the rest he said, "We'll be in for tea... or coffee in a second."

The others walked inside and Laoch turned to Gus, "Yes," his grandfather said, "they are not gardeners. Do Marcy and Peter know that?"

"Uh, yes they do. It was part of the whole putting things together discussion a couple of days ago." Gus admitted, expecting a level of frustration.

With no apparent discomfort, Laoch simply nodded. "Ok, good. Let's introduce you to some people." he and Gus walked inside.

They walked in and found Peter and Marcy at the large table with the six men. Each of the men had healthy portions of meat pie and several were eating it as if they were being timed. Peter was watching like he had money on who would finish first. Laoch sat down at the table, reached to the center where a decanter of hot water sat, grabbed a prepared metal tea ball, placed it in a cup, and poured the steaming water over the top of it.

"Well, I guess this is as good a time as any," Laoch said, waving an open hand towards his grandson. "This is my grandson, Gus... he is actually Laoch the Fifth, as I'm the Third, but he has cleverly dodged the nomenclature. To his right is Marcy, his..." he stumbled clumsily to a stop.

"Girlfriend," Marcy said, "...unless this is a poorly planned rouse to make this moment extremely awkward."

"Girlfriend," Laoch continued. "To my grandson's left is Peter, Gus's lifelong friend. All of them, however, I see as family here. The men seated at the end of the table are the core of my trusted security."

"You mean they are not gardeners?" Peter said, clutching his pearls dramatically.

"Let me restate," Laoch said. "This is Peter. He is a bit of an asshole, but a pleasant chap." He smiled.

The older black man who led the group spoke in an unexpected Texas drawl, as he flashed a genuine smile, "Sounds like he will fit right in!"

"This is Dean," Laoch said. "His boys call him Dino."

"Because he is older than shit! And none of us had ever met a black guy named Dean before," offered the one of production model triplets as the other two made an almost identical chuckling sound.

"And this is?" Laoch asked, looking at Dino.

"Don't ask me," said Dino. "All of them white boys look alike to me. That's Buster, Wombat or Snow. All I can confirm is that they all came from different wombs and had different sperm donors. They must have all been in the same fraternity in college or something."

The person in question rose to his feet, leaned across the table to Marcy, extending his hand. "I am Lester, but they call me Buster, he said," as he shook hands with each of them after Marcy.

Following that lead, the second and third stood and similarly introduced themselves as "Wombat, "Walter Johnson, and "Snow" Sydney Larkin.

Taking the queue, the last two also introduced themselves. The first was "Jolly," he said in an almost too perfectly clean British accent. The accent was so absent of dialect as to seem fake. "My real name is Jafir Al-Amri."

Marcy squinted. "Al-Amri? Jordanian?"

"Yes mam," he replied simply and nodded.

The last, "Yoyo," introduced himself. "My name is Yoav Hipsher... and yes for the record, I'm from Israel." He said with a wide smile that seemed at odds with the almost dead appearance of his eyes.

"As Gus and I discussed earlier," Laoch spoke, "They are terrible gardeners, but some of the best retired operators in the business. Dino, Buster and Wombat both served with the U.S. Army's Delta, Chip and Snow are retired SEALs. Jolly is an inactive member of 'The King Abdullah II Special Forces Group' in Jordan, and Yoyo might have worked with Mossad and was a Silver Medalist in the Biathlon several Winter Olympics ago."

They spent the better part of a half hour speaking and getting to know each other. The security team was extremely friendly.

As they prepared to return to their bunkhouse in the old barn, Dino paused. He spoke to Laoch, "Hey, while we are taking your good money, you say these folks are here for a couple more days at least, right?"

"Yes, for the week, unless they want more time." Laoch replied.

"Well, there is something training wise I wouldn't mind putting them through. Nothing serious, but stuff we often must coach high value targets on in the field... that we always secretly wished they had trained with before. I'm thinking about things like, moving between cover and going where we say to go, when we say to go."

"Counter surveillance basics," piped up one triplet.

"I can show them how to avoid a sniper. I mean, show them what we see and how we think?" offered Yoyo.

"Hell, basics of how to handle a rifle and pistol," offered Dino

Gus nodded, "I have a bit of experience, but I would love to learn more. Peter might know what a gun is, but that is about it. Marcy has learned some in the last couple of months from me. I would defer in a second to any of you guys."

Laoch looked up with a smile. "Excellent. I will carve out time on the schedule!"

Chapter 55

Thursday, September 20th, 2018, 8:23 PM The Big House, Scotland

With discussions over, and the table cleared, Gus and Marcy returned to the living room with Gus's grandfather. Peter had struck up a conversation with Yoyo and both were chuckling over something as he walked with the security team back towards their barracks in the large, old barn. William sat in his normal chair, where he was reading the Times newspaper out of London.

Gus and his father discussed the day and came up with an idea of how to work out some time with the security team. After the quick talk, Laoch changed the subject. "So, son, the genetic test came back, and oddly, there does not seem to be a direct link to your mum. There is a small possibility of shared ancestors at some point, but it is not what anyone would call probable."

"That is oddly comforting," Gus chuckled.

Gus's grandfather smiled and nodded. "Agreed, but it poses an alternative problem or perhaps represents a lack of our understanding. Is it a genetic trait which we have passed down, as the lore suggests, or is it possibly just a genetic mutation that is simply not that widespread? The family going back to the start discussed this as an almost magic trait caused by the curse that created Scrios, but is it possible there is a more scientific reason, and the resistance is more widespread? So, that in mind, I wanted to ask you something."

"Sure," Gus replied. "What do you need?"

"Not to peel a scab, but the other obvious possibility is your mother's physiology and illness. I think we should dig into whatever the cause of your mom's death was in more depth. If the science exists, and test results remain, maybe we can see if perhaps her condition enabled her to resist him."

"I understand that," Gus said, "but they buried her years ago."

"I'm not talking anything as intrusive as that, I mean digging into her medical records that were recorded before she died. To do that, we would need your permission."

"Done. I have zero problem with that." Gus said, and they both nodded. "Hey, um, it's been a while. I'm going to go check on Peter. We don't need him distracting those security guys," as he rose and headed to the front door.

Gus crossed the yard and entered the old barn, where he followed the noise of laughter to find Peter lounging on couches with the security guys. As was usual, Peter was telling off-color jokes.

Peter noticed Gus as he rounded the corner in the barn. "Gus! These guys are great!"

"Yeah, I'm sure, but they need their downtime, too," Gus said in his fatherly party-pooper voice.

Peter nodded in agreement, as he got up off the couch. "Ok, I guess it is getting late."

They were waving goodnight as Gus was leading them out when Dino called to Peter. "Yo, Peter, when you have time tomorrow, come back, and we'll give you some beginner's gun safety training," Peter gave him a thumbs-up. From behind them, Dino called once more, but this time to Gus. "Hey Gus, is it true? Did you really swallow some five-hundred-year-old dude's junk?"

Gus stopped mid-step and snapped a look at Peter. Peter looked at him meekly, "What? We were trading stories, and yours was weak compared to some of theirs, but it was the best one I had."

"Oh, really?" Gus said. "Well, I think maybe we should sit down and discuss Hawaii and the hot little Asian hooker you were sure wanted you for you, and not your wallet?"

All conversation in the room screeched to a halt as Buster piped up, "Dude... there are no hot Asian hooker chicks in Hawaii in the bars that want you for anything but your money, and hand to my heart, all the 'hot ones'... those are all dudes in dresses. Very convincing dudes in dresses. Oh, no Peter," he laughed, as Gus nodded and indicated by touching his pointer finger on the tip of his nose.

A chorus started as the entire security team started singing, "...I know all there is to know about the crying game," and laughed.

"Wait, wait," Peter complained. "You can't give me any shit there, Mr. Balls... Buster's last name is Balls? Seriously? I mean, I was going to save that for later, but you forced this on yourself," as he tried to redirect the crowd, but it was pointless. The room had turned on him.

Chapter 56

Friday, September 21st, 2018, 6:24 AM, The Big House, Scotland

Gus woke early, as he attempted to adjust his internal clock to the new time zone. He had woken with a start that made Marcy jump. In calming her, the dream had faded into the ether. What had seemed so poignant moments before now simply evaded him. He slid from the covers, put on his running shorts and his running shoes, and slid on a tee shirt. Gus searched the end table and grabbed his phone and his ear buds. He reached in his bag and grabbed the fanny pack he wore to carry his phone and a small bottle of water and wrapped it around his waist as he walked. He quietly left the room and went down the stairs. As he passed the dining room, he saw William was already awake and looking at his paper. Across from him sat his grandfather, looking for guidance in the bottom of a coffee cup.

Laoch noticed Gus as he stopped near the doorway to the dining room. "Good morning, boy. You are up early?"

Gus began stretching the front muscles of his legs, alternating on one leg as he grabbed the ankle of the other behind him. "Good morning, grandfather."

"If you are going for a stroll, maybe I can join you," Laoch offered.

"Nah, I'm thinking a five-mile run," Gus said, "but I doubt I can do that, so more than likely three. When I run, my mind relaxes, and I solve a lot of things in my head."

Surprising both, William responded while folding down his paper, "I do most of my critical thinking in the loo." He said with a smile, and Gus and his grandfather both smiled too.

Laoch went back to his coffee, and William to his paper as Gus finished his stretches. "Be back soon." Gus received a nod from them both and he went out the large banded front door and entered a brisk fall morning.

The chill was cool enough for him to second guess his summer attire at first, but since there was little to no wind, he figured it might feel good in a few minutes.

Gus took off around the gravel circle at the front of the big house, made a loop down to the bridge, and ran along the stream that marked the edge of one of the enormous fields. This first field was vast. With the current edge he was following, he estimated at least a hundred yards. The family had been preparing to harvest potatoes in the coming days. The end of the field came quicker than he expected, as he entered a line of approximately 30 apple trees. Skipping high in his strides, he grabbed one and tugged it free as he ran. He continued along the creek after it took a ninety-degree turn to the west. In the distance ahead of him, he spied a fisherman by the creek, and as he closed, he swung out away from the creek so as not to disturb his fishing.

As he ran by, the elderly man watched him pass and they each raised a hand as a greeting. Five steps later, Gus winced as his mind processed the fisherman... He lacked a fishing rod and wore a green three-piece suit. Gus slid to a stop and spun back to the man and found only the babbling brook and an empty bank along it. There was nowhere the man could have gone in the three seconds that had elapsed. An icy shiver ran down Gus's back and he turned and, with increased speed, continued his now truncated run, which led him circuitously back to the circle drive and back to the front door in less than five minutes.

As Gus stepped inside the door, the two men at the table chided him about his speed, as William rose and walked to the kitchen carrying his coffee cup. When he disappeared, Gus quietly spoke to his grandfather. "Honesty, right?" as he looked sternly at his grandfather.

"Aye son. Always." Laoch responded.

"Okay... I'm pretty sure I just saw Pappy on my run... I thought he was a fisherman along the stream."

Laoch looked at Gus and asked with a sober tone, "What did he say to you?"

"Nothing. We each just raised a hand in greeting. Like I said, I thought he was a fisherman, so I swung wide of him to not disturb the fish... that's when I noticed as my mind replayed it, that he had no fishing equipment and was in an ugly green three-piece suit."

Laoch looked him in the eyes. "Any bad dreams recently, son?"

"I woke up with a start this morning, but I don't remember why. It had frightened Marcy, and after I calmed her, the dream was gone."

"In the future, document the dream first. There is plenty of time to calm after. It might be of life-or-death importance." Laoch said and offered, "Would you like some coffee, son? I can also whip up a mean omelet?"

"Seriously? That would be great!"

Laoch nodded his head and stood and strode to the kitchen.

Chapter 57

Friday, September 21st, 2018, 10:24 AM The Big House, Scotland

When Gus, Marcy, and Peter arrived at the makeshift training area the security team had set up, almost the entire team was waiting. The first area they had set up was in the side yard. They propped up sliding doors removed from some unused stalls in the yard at various locations. Stacked in piles were hay bales, later explained as representing parked vehicles. About 50 yards away, Jolly sat in a tree with a paintball gun that had a sinisterly long barrel. "That's Jolly," quipped Dino. "We have Jolly in the tree strictly to add realism to the drills. Most of the time it is one of his cousins shooting at us," he finished with a smile and a wink.

"I heard that!" Jolly said. "Looks like I have a new primary target."

Gus laughed. "Wait, who is missing?" he asked.

"Yoyo is out there somewhere," Dino said. "Heck, no telling where, but he kitted up all Rambo like and slid out an hour ago. So here is the drill. You can obviously see where Jolly is, and he is not that far away. This is because the paintballs he will shoot are slower than actual rounds. We have that gun of his cranked up to a scary speed, though. The shorter distance he is at should accurately simulate live fire from a sniper at a greater distance. Getting tagged with a shot, even though it's a paintball, will hurt like a bitch. Over here..." Dino pointed to the pile of heavy protective coats and a line of motorcycle helmets with full face protection. "Here is some safety gear. In the pile, you will also find some heavy scarves. These won't stop the impact of the paintballs completely, but it should help a lot. These things will come at you at around 300 feet per second, which is at, or a little higher than, 200 miles per hour. If you get hit, the pink paintballs will leave a distinctive splat, and you are dead. If they hit open skin, they will leave a nasty welt. In the beginning, Jolly is going to shoot near, but not at you for the first couple of practice runs. Keep your face mask down at all times, even while waiting. Basically, we will walk you through the process of moving between cover positions, and what it means to be in cover. When we tell you what to do, you do it, when we say to do it. Jolly will simulate his fire like he is using a bolt action weapon at first. Eventually, he will simulate semi-automatic and will honor clip sizes and reload times. We try to move in the shooter's reload if we can, but whatever you do, when you move, keep low, be fast and keep moving until you reach cover. We will apply suppressing fire to aid you in the move. Today, we will fire downrange with our paintballs to simulate that. We won't be shooting at Jolly, but jolly will pause when we are shooting like most targets will. Do not be a hero. We are going to practice a few times each type of move. Flat panels are walls and corners. Piles of hay are cars, note that they have space for you to hide between the bails... or in the car. One point, if you are covering a longer distance, you will want to vary your speed a little, especially just before reaching cover."

The team walked them through different scenarios, where they practice a low run and eventually, they moved on to live fire. The rules were, whomever got shot the most, bought the beer for the night. Ironically, Gus, the one with the only actual military experience, got hit eleven times across the drills that lasted until four in the afternoon. Marcy received eight hits, while Peter only received five hits.

The final drill of the day was a team drill. Dino signaled the patiently concealed Yoyo. The instructors equipped everyone with paintball guns for this exercise; they had to run from the starting point of the range to Jolly's tree without getting hit. That short fifty yards seemed like a simple ask to the novices, but the security team cursed when Dino told them about the exercise. They could shoot Yoyo, if they could find him, and in doing that, it would be an immediate win.

They started from a fence of panels that provided full cover. Dino turned off his microphone and drew out a plan in the dirt. "He will pretend to have a five-round magazine, but that still allows for one in the chamber. So, what we are going to do is send Wombat and Chip to two separate covers, while we send some rounds down range. Keep it to three-shot bursts for now," he said as he raised a small mirror higher than the fence to survey the wooded area towards the end of the range. They heard a tick from far on the other side of the protective wall and the mirror turned pink as it flew from Dino's hand.

"That bastard!" Dino said with a laugh. "I think that means game on! Buster, you stay back and help locate him. If anyone drops, you are next up for babysitting. Be ready to flank the sniper once we spot the path with the best cover."

"I think maybe we should send... um, someone else to draw fire. Just a thought." Chip said with a whimsical smile.

Dino flashed him a big fake smile. "Uhhh, No. I'm going to peek my helmet around the left side of the wall for just a sec and pull back. When I say go, you guys go, and go fast. When he shoots at you, I'm going to get a bead on him. Once you guys are in place, deploy smoke and coordinate cover fire as we move two pawns forward to join you. Marcy, Gus, you guys will be the first. Yoyo will expect me to hold back Gus, but we will let Peter be the target."

"Hey! What the fuck, man?" Peter said incredulously.

316

"Dude, you move like Spiderman," Dino said. "You only got hit three times in the drill."

"Five... Five times," Peter said.

"Everyone, check your gear, and tighten your scarves. Yoyo likes head shots and if he clips your neck, it hurts like shit, and you look like you made out with a lamprey for two to three weeks."

Dino called out, "Alright, getting ready to start this thing! Yoyo, are you ready?" Silence answered him. There was just a double click on the radio. "Shit, I was hoping he would answer back." He said with a laugh, and continued in a quiet, conspiratorial voice. "I'm poking my helmet out in three... two..."

Chapter 58

Friday, September 21st, 2018, 4:13 PM The Big House, Scotland

The calamitous run through had lasted just under forty-five seconds, thought Dino. The walk back to the house afterwards for dinner took more time and gave him time to run it back through his head to look for take aways.

Yoyo had not fired at all when Chip and Wombat moved to their first cover, and that signaled the start of the calamity. Chip was fast, "like a marsupial," Dino heard the voice of Kevin Pollock imitating Christopher Walken as he said it in his head. Chip paused, checked for wounds, and signaled his safe position behind cover. Next Chip and Wombat both rolled out smoke upwind to disguise the move of the first two HVTs, High Value Targets as they had designated Gus and his friends. As Marcy and Peter ran to join the first two in cover, the plan already showed symptoms of its inevitable unravel. It was supposed to be Marcy and Gus, but "what the hell," he thought, "at least they ran, and Gus stayed." As designed, the entire team opened fire with their paintball guns down range, firing into the wooded area intending to suppress the enemy sniper, Yoyo.

Chip raised his hands over his head and dropped his head. "Shit! I'm out!" as he turned to walk back to the waiting area. He was indeed out, with a pink splatter centered on the helmet and goggles between his eyes. A shot, ironically, that he had not seen coming.

Buster set his feet behind the barricade and sprinted out and made it almost two steps before a pink flower blossomed on his chest. "Out," he dropped his weapon and moved to the back to watch from the relative safety of the observation blind.

317

Dino noted the starburst splat seemed to blow outwards to the left side of Chip's face. He deduced that the deadly sniper must be to the right... somewhere, but he had seen nothing. The lack of muzzle flash with paintball guns made it even harder to find Yoyo, who he suspected was dug in like a tick somewhere.

Gus's question, for the second time, yelled with even more loud desperation, broke Dino out of his machinations. "Do I go now?!?" Gus asked.

"Hold one!" Dino replied, and Gus took off running like a shot. He stopped awkwardly halfway to the next cover as a paint ball whizzed past where his head would have been. After his inexplicable stop, he jumped into the air, turned 180 degrees and called upon his inner Shaggy as his feet ran in the air before they touched the ground, and Gus ran back to cover beside Dino.

"HE CAME THE FUCK BACK!" Dino would scream through a laugh while drinking beers, purchased by Gus, later that night... once the current calamity became funny.

The audible thump and spray of the sniper's second shot clipped the corner of the wood wall as he arrived back beside Dino. There was a sprinkle of pink dots on Gus's right shoulder. "I said, Hold One!!"

"Sorry, sorry. I heard Go, and I went," Gus said. "When my brain processed what you really said, I came back."

Dino looked at him like he was some kind of alien turd that was just crapped out of some larger alien's sphincter and landed on the ground beside him. He honestly didn't know if he should laugh or scream at him. This motherfucker had just 'Leroy Jenkins' himself into harm's way and dodged a sniper's bullet, came back, and apologized to him for doing it. Wombat's voice in his earphones broke him out of his momentary fugue.

"I think I saw him during Gus's goddamn magic trick, 20 feet to the right of the tree Jolly was in, under a... I'm out. Shit!" Wombat said as he stood and raised his hands. "Shit, that hurt!" he said as he walked to the back. Dino saw the shot that took him. It had hit him on his right side, in the armpit area. His earphone crackled as Dino heard Marcy speak up.

"I think they aimed that shot at me, but it hit Wombat," Marcy said. "I heard it pass right beside me."

Dino pictured the layout of the field in his mind. Where Wombat was, compared to Marcy, made the wound location on Wombat's side make zero sense. The shot had to come from the right, but Wombat's eyewitness location of the shooter was almost directly in front of him. Wombat might now know how it happened, but in the rules of this game, Wombat was now dead and could only

318

watch the mayhem unfold in the afterlife blind area. The problem with Marcy's report was that her wall should have protected Wombats right side. One thing was certain; this ex-fill was failing magnificently. Dino looked at Peter. "Count to three, and go to the cover where Marcy is. Fire at least three shots as you go. Jolly? I'm going the other way. You pop up and see after we move. If you can confirm the shooter's location, we will need to push forward."

After a three count, they moved. Gus and Dino split, with Peter taking three quick long strides and diving to cover to the right, and Dino moving left to an unoccupied wall to the left while Jolly prairie dogged a peek. Both sprinters arrived safely, and Peter somehow again dodged a paintball. This time, Jolly saw a puff of condensation and the ball traverse the distance, missing peter and skipping along the grass towards the Big House. Jolly called out his position when he saw a small tree to the left of the firing location shake, and another tree even further left moved just after.

"Sniper is moving left towards my old tree." Jolly called out. Suddenly, there was a loud crack on the right-side ear-phone cover of his ballistic helmet that made his ears ring. Hot lines radiated out from that spot where the paint had splattered his face and neck. He had not seen the shot coming. Dropping his paintball gun and raising his hands, Jolly announced he was out. He turned and walked towards the back.

To Dino, the numbers now were easy to calculate, and for all purposes, they were toast. He heard a repeated popping sound and peaked around his wall to see Gus running like a wild man, as round after round missed him by inches, as he reached successive covered locations. Seeing the location of the origination of the shots, Dino laid down fire. Gus's luck ran out, 20 feet from the tree, as a shot hit him and folded him like a realistic battle wound. After the shot on Gus, who now laid prone on the ground moaning, a smoke canister rolled from the firing location, quickly fouling the sightlines. Dino had seen enough and sounded a small piercing horn he carried on his kit to end the exercise. Cautiously, Peter got up and walked toward Gus, who still lay on the ground, now on his back. Others also converged on Gus, even a walking bush named Yoyo, carrying a long-barreled paintball gun in one hand and another short-barreled one in his right hand.

Peter was the first to reach Gus. "Dude, are you ok?"

"He shot me in the dick," Gus said as Peter collapsed to the ground like a felled tree and laughed.

"Wow, that is some kind of shot, to hit something that small while you were running!" Peter howled.

"Fuck you, Peter!" was all Gus could squeeze out.

"Aim small, miss small, I guess." Peter rolled around on the ground.

Yoyo walked up and apologized in his light Sephardic Hebrew accent, "Man, you are fast! I had to aim center mass and... man, I am so sorry," a slight rumble of laughter in his voice.

As they walked towards the house to grab food, Dino asked Yoyo, "How did you do the tree thing?"

"Oh that? Paracord. I tied it to a couple of trees to draw attention away from my spot." Yoyo said with a smile. "What was really cool, and probably unfair, my second shot, I had a paintball break in the barrel. Every shot after that was a curveball that broke about two feet to the right and after would dive like a Greg Maddox sinker. That was how I got both Chip and Wombat. It was beautiful! The one that hit Wombat I aimed at Marcy and it broke right about 15 feet, went past her and hit him behind a totally different blind. It was a complete luck shot. I had to switch to the normal, secondary gun after that, because the long barrel became totally fouled and inconsistent. The fifth shot from the other gun, hit Gus in the junk, and it was shooting hot rounds with a fresh, full CO2 tank.

Peter and Marcy flanked Gus as he walked with a John Wayne swagger. Peter relentlessly made jokes after confirming Gus was not seriously hurt, and as the pain faded, the jokes became funny. When they reached the door, everyone removed their footwear and padded covering and stacked them by the front entrance.

Chapter 59

Sunday, September 23rd, 2018, The Big House, Scotland 11:15 AM

It had been a lazy Sunday morning. Chores that needed to be completed, had been done. Breakfast was a spread, prepared with everyone kicking in to help where they could. Bynum had done the lion's share of the actual cooking, but others had all helped with the setup and cleanup.

Many people regarded this as one of the best times of the year in Scotland. The weather was cool, but not cold. The biting little midges, that had swarmed the highlands for much of the summer months had all but gone away. Gus and Marcy were sitting in the yard, taking in the midday sun, sitting on a horse blanket in the thick grassy side yard. They watched Peter talking and laughing with two members of the security team. "He is going to drive them fucking nuts, isn't he?" Marcy said.

"Oh yeah," Gus agreed. "He was like this on his fifth birthday when his parents got him a Teddy Ruxpin doll."

"A WHAT?!?" Marcy sat up and looked at him with a fantastic smile, the sunlight illuminating her hair like a halo and flashing off her eyes in a mental picture Gus would carry in his mind forever.

"Teddy Ruxpin... Picture this... A goofy faced teddy bear, wearing a red bodysuit and a tan vest, with 'Teddy Ruxpin' logo on the left breast. You basically shoved a cassette tape up his ass... well, into the tape player inside it."

"No damn way! Wait, I think I remember those!" Marcy said with a laugh.

"Oh yeah, it played music, and its mouth would move with the words and eyes would look up and down. He played with this damn thing for not weeks, but YEARS! I would go over to his house with my mom to play while they had tea or lunch, and all he wanted to do was play with Teddy fuckin' Ruxpin. So, fast forward a few years. We are in third grade, and I thought he had left Teddy behind. I walked to his house. Deb tells me he is upstairs in his room. I sneak up there planning to throw open his door and scare him, because when you startled him, he screamed like a little girl... and it was funny. So, I creep up the stairs and get to his doorway and the door is open just a little. I see his back is to me, and he is listening to baby music. I was prepared to throw the door open when I heard him sing with the music. That's when I realize the other voice is Ol' Teddy fuckin' Ruxpin, and it is like he is singing a duet. So, I throw the door open and say, 'is that Teddy Ruxpin Pete?' That was what I called him back in the day, Pete. He screeches and in one motion, throws the doll into the big drawer on his desk with a loud thump and slides it closed... He tells me. 'No, no!' He swears to me he just found it and it turned on." Marcy is rolling on the ground breathless as she listens. "So, I say. Wow, Pete, it sounds like the batteries are strong, as the muffled voice of Teddy is still coming from the drawer. Peter starts crying and I get in trouble for picking on him. But that's not all. I go to visit Peter at Stanford his freshman year because his parents are concerned, because he seems lonely there, and needs a friendly face."

"NO! Nooooo, say it's not... this cannot be true!" Marcy howls.

"We are sitting around his private dorm room, Peter is off taking a shower to get ready to hit the bars and I look in his desk drawer, and there he is... Teddy mutha-fuckin' Ruxpin loaded up with brand new batteries!"

"Ok, now that has gone from funny to super creepy." Her stern face melts into an evil grin as Gus can see her filing away this story in her head.

321

"You are the only one I have ever told that last part to, although I bet Deb knew." He said, as Peter strode towards them, his meeting with The Boyzzzz, apparently concluded.

As Peter got close, he waved his hands in front of himself in a lame imitation of maybe a rapper and said, "What's up mutha-fuckas?" he said, without missing a beat. "So, talking to the guys, Marcy, your new call sign is 'Sprite', and Gus, you, my friend, are 'Bullseye'. We all agreed." He said, all proud of himself.

Gus laughed, "Oh, and so what is yours?"

"I think I'm going to go with Reaper or, um... I don't know." Peter said introspectively with his eye cocked towards the sky.

"Hmm," said Marcy. "So, I'm guessing someone already took both Ruxpin and Teddy?"

Peter snapped his attention to Gus. "Dude! That was... That... Dude!" and he spun on his heal and stomped towards the house. He turned back towards them as he walked and gave two simultaneous middle fingers.

"Oh, I'm going to pay for that." Gus admitted.

Marcy laughed, "Hell, he is my boss!"

As Peter stomped towards the house, he almost brushed shoulders with Gus's grandfather Laoch, who was walking towards them with a sense of purpose.

As he closed within 15 feet, he asked, "Gus, can I have a moment?"

"Sure, what's up?" Gus asked.

"Well, this is regarding your mother's private information and medical records." The older man said looking at Gus.

"Oh, I'm fine with her hearing anything... unless there is something that worries you." Gus replied.

"A little, but nothing I think I would worry about. I asked more for your own privacy." He said with an almost formal accent and continued, sensing the implied permission from Gus's expectant look. "I need to confess. I told a white lie when I asked for your permission to access your mother's records. Your agreement came shortly after we had already secured the records, but it was much simpler to explain, after also receiving your permission. From analysis of DNA, well RNA more specifically, your mother was no direct relation to our family until she married your father. Her other tests were enlightening, however. Although most of the technology was rather crude by today's standards when she was in the hospital, she had many tests done. Before her hospitalization and diagnosis, she had extensive tests done to figure out the cause of the migraines

322

she suffered. When she went to the hospital for the last time, that hospital had the latest technology available for a PET/CT scan. They performed multiple scans on your mother in the days leading up to her passing. Here is where it got weird. When we received the scans electronically, we added them to our archive. At first, it was frustrating for our tech guys, because the AI, which correlates data, kept trying to assign the scan results as belonging to William. Later, when we examined the logic of the code, the geeks said that the program was trying to say there was an error because of the similarity to William's scan a decade ago. It wasn't a perfect match, but the areas of the hippocampus, limbic and Frontal Lobe, all showed very similar patterns with identical black dead spots, where there was no noticeable activity. Obviously, the tumor that your mother had was devastating. So, let's consider this next part as conjecture: Could looking the creature, Scrios, in the eye, physically change the brain functions of individuals without our bloodline traits? Or do people with our bloodline have a similar genetic mutation passed on through the X chromosome, which defines our resistance? Or, what if your mother's condition altered her brain's function somehow, and that tumor thwarted the beast? Maybe a combination of her condition combined with her natural pattern created a similar effect to us when Scrios attacked? Was the resulting effect something like what we have? Anyway, I think we should get tested and at least see if there is any pattern. Are you willing to have a PET/CT scan?" Laoch asked with a conspiratorial smile and a wink.

Peter asked from behind Laoch, having walked up during the discussion, "Since she was not a member of your family, why are you assuming the effect was the same? You said similar, not identical. Maybe it got her memories, too? Maybe, if what you are saying is true, what she wrote is what he wanted her to write and I am not saying that she was lying intentionally, but maybe it did, at some level, corrupt her thoughts, placing what it wanted you to know? I'm just saying, you now know she wasn't actually related to your family. Maybe we are assuming too much, all because we knew and loved her?"

Laoch looked at Peter with a totally different look in his eyes, "Peter, I mean this in the very best way. You sometimes remind me of an ass boil. However, you have an endearing quality about you, though as well. So, I mean this sincerely when I say it. Would you like a job? I need someone who will point out things and contradict me. I need an ass boil like you around."

"That is the worst compliment I have ever received, thanks, but let's talk later. I will certainly say something soon that will change your mind." Peter replied. "In theory though, could I get Executive Ass Boil on my business cards?"

"My counter to your hypothesis is simple however," Laoch said as he blinked away Peter's response. "Much like the situation with William. We are all here and Gus is alive. She had been to the Big House. She had seen the archives. This family would be dead, and Gus would have been a childhood friend you knew once who tragically died somehow."

Chapter 60

Monday, September 24th, 2018, 4:15 AM, The Big House, Scotland

A knock at their door startled Gus and Marcy. Neither noticed it had been the third attempt to wake them. With Gus, the knocking had melted perfectly into a dream he was having of his childhood, where his mom was listening to some oldies music of knocking three times on the ceiling, as they danced around the old living room before the storm. She would lift Gus up to let him knock on the ceiling... well, a doorway, and put him down and they would dance more.

Finally, the knocks penetrated the dream, and it faded as he woke up. The voice that came was his grand fathers and for just a minute, Gus could hear his father's voice in his grandfather.

"Gus... Marcy, are you decent?" he asked.

"Yes, grandfather, come in," replied Gus as Marcy pulled her bare leg under the cover.

"Marcy, dear," Laoch started, and Marcy cut him off.

"I'm not leaving."

"No, no, that was not what I mean. My girl, this is about your home in North Carolina. It is apparently on fire or so a contact there has notified us. 1503 Craig Street, in Raleigh?" Laoch asked her.

"Yes, that is the address of my house, but I don't live there. I have rented it out to the friends I used to live with... is everyone okay?" she asked, as her voice raised an octave?

"We know nothing yet, dear, just that the fire department is there, and reports are that the house is a total loss." Laoch said, as he looked into his grandson's eyes and Gus knew the answers were going to be gruesome.

Chapter 61

Monday, September 24th, 2018, 8:03 AM, The Big House, Scotland

As Laoch had conveyed in the stare he gave to Gus, the reports from Raleigh were indeed tragic. All three of Marcy's former roommates, her core of friends outside of work for years before she started dating, had perished in the fire that had consumed the house. One roommate had lived with Marcy since her first year in grad school. They discovered Eleanore, Marcy's oldest friend, on the floor in the master suite that Marcy had once occupied. She had attempted to crawl to the door of her room before succumbing. Eleanore was the name Marcy had mentioned as her maid of honor when they discussed their future together late in the night. It scared Gus that Marcy was remarkably calm as the news came in. It was as if she knew, as he did, what the outcome would be of the fire.

When Gus went to her and tried to put his arm around her, she side-stepped and escaped him and settled on the far side of the room near the window.

Two hours later, the landline rang again. Gus's grandfather answered the phone and spoke to the caller with a stern sharpness to his voice. Several times he cut the person off and said, "Tell Philip he needs to take control of this. The accusation is rubbish. Tell him to hire whomever he needs to on this and take control over it." As he listened, he nervously switched the balance to his other foot. The silence went on for several minutes as Laoch listened intently before speaking. "Well, tell them that Miss Kitchen is out of the country on business and will meet with them upon her return." Laoch again listened intently to the phone for a few moments. "It will not be until her lawyer and firm have collected all the information and we have a better idea on the way this will fall out... I know, but she won't be walking back into this circus. Also, I want ears to the ground. Find out where this is coming from... No, I know, the bloody fire department you git, but there is more to this than them. Someone is pushing the narrative. Find out who! I must go now." He smashed the handset onto the cradle.

"What the hell was that all about?" Gus asked.

"What time is it?" Laoch asked with a twitch like tremor of his eyebrow.

"A little after 10:00 O'clock AM... But what was the phone call about?" Gus asked again.

"Let's talk at the table," his grandfather said and walked a circuitous route past the liquor cabinet, grabbing a dusty old bottle and several glasses. "Marcy? You definitely need to be here for this."

Peter, seeing only three glasses in Laoch's hand, corrected the error and stopped by the cabinet for a fourth glass.

They all gathered at the table, and Laoch poured a deep glass for each of them. He looked up, shook his head, and spoke. "As you know, the fire destroyed the house. I don't know how to lighten this, dear. Two of your friends died in the house. The third died in intensive care at the burn unit at Duke University less than two hours after she arrived there." He said as Marcy released her first whimper. "An EMT allegedly heard her say during the life-flight that all the doors in the house were blocked, and escape was impossible. She told the EMT they had complained about the oven that would randomly turn itself on high, and how they had constantly complained to the homeowner about it."

"That's not true!" Marcy said. "I purchased a new oven last year when the old one stopped working. They all loved it."

"I'm not accusing you or agreeing with them. I'm only relaying the statement of the EMT who claimed this was her deathbed statement, during a life flight with the patient, who was on oxygen and suffering from terminal injuries." The grandfather said softly.

"That is complete bullshit!" Gus exclaimed, and everyone nodded in agreement. "I mean, the answer is right there. That she required oxygen and was on an evac helicopter suggests she was in serious distress. How could she possibly have made such a statement, or how could anyone hear her over the sounds of the rotors and through a mask? It just doesn't add up."

Marcy seemed to diminish in size like a cube of sugar melting in water as she leaned into Gus, "I don't know what to do. Should I go back? Should we go back?" she asked, looking up at him.

Laoch replied, "I would not advise that." He paused and added, "Son, I know where your head is going right now, and with all you have told us, and the information in the book and what the letter has confirmed, this creature is after you. Hell, all of you, and it will do this and more to get you to show yourself. If we are going to fight this thing, we need to take the fight to it, but first, we need to better understand it and plan. We have a lot of new information that we need to finish understanding. We have people researching around the clock what you all have brought here. Let see who is awake over there in the archives and get the latest. Meet out front in 30 minutes, and we will ride over to the archives?" Everyone agreed and went to get dressed. Marcy leaned heavily on Gus's arm; misery written on her face in silent tears.

Chapter 62

Each person at the table had a paper printout in front of them. The subject of discussion was the group of names that Gus's mother had mentioned in her first book entry. Laoch read and commented as the other read along.

"Allen Pinkerton - Died in 1884, I didn't expect to see that one. People say he experienced a stroke late in life that changed him. He seemed to focus on wild goose chases according to his wife. He was always drafting letters and sending telegraphs to people he referred to as 'friends in London' who, according to his wife, were bilking him of their money, and catering to his wild fantasies of finding a family for a client she never met, and she had never seen billed. She wrote in a letter to her friend, Ruth Burns."

"...He was obsessed and often forgot to eat or drink in his final year until I reminded him. He would ask me about families I knew or anyone that I might have known growing up in Duddingston that met the description of the focus of his obsession..."

Joan Carfrae Pinkerton

Summer of 1886.

Laoch moved on to the second name on the list, "John Milbrow, which was an alias for Jonathan Murphy, the nephew of the Tammany Hall gang's leader Charles Francis "Silent Charlie" Murphy, who ran a very successful private investigation and recovery firm in New York City. The emphasis there was recovery, as he was an enforcer and collected donations from the local neighborhood. In his youth, he was well known for his bare knuckles prize fighting. That was how he earned his reputation in his teens and early twenties. He made most of his money later, though, doing collections for his uncle. At 26, he served a two-year stint in Sing Sing Prison for manslaughter. They released him in June 1903. He punched his way into the Olympic heavyweight division trials, but officials disqualified him for cheating with a modified glove. The handlers had removed the padding in his gloves and soaked Jonny Milbrow's wrapped hands in plaster. Following that scandal, he established his own investigation and retrieval firm, which was deemed legitimate by law enforcement in a 1910 investigation. He had a team of over twenty people, including six investigators. In 1917, it was only he and a secretary left. Late paychecks led to several employees being fired or resigning. Over the next two years, several mysterious deaths and vanishings occurred within his family and business circle. His wife deliberately placed herself in the path of a streetcar while arguing with her husband. Former employees, during police interviews on the disappearances and suicides, characterized Mr. Milbrow as a troubled man. The majority thought he had something to do with the deaths, but had no evidence. Everyone agreed he had an unhealthy fixation on researching for a client who provided no compensation. Sound familiar?" Laoch said as he met eyes with the people around the table.

He continued. "He tasked the employees with pursuing leads for his research, which caused them to lose paying customers. Some individuals who expressed grievances met with horrifying deaths at their own hand, and a significant number perished alongside their loved ones. Jonathan Murphy, AKA John Milbrow, died in the fall of 1928."

Gus's grandfather took a deep solemn breath and continued, "One of the last to leave Mr. Milbrow's employ was an apprentice clerk in 1927, who was finishing his last year at Columbia Law. In his police interview, he spoke highly of Mr. Milbrow and regarded the investigation against him as unfounded."

"It gets a little confusing here," Laoch stated, "This last employee's name matches Jen's list, but appears to be the father of the person she names, Kenneth Riedling Sr. The person in Jen's list, however, is his first son and namesake, Kenneth Riedling Jr. born January 21st, 1931, and died on December 24th, 2010, at 79. His father, Riedling Sr., died in 1936 in a bar fight in a small-town, southeast of Munich, Germany, called Sauerlach. A court sentenced a teenage boy involved in the fatal confrontation with a choice of military duty or prison. His name, Ludwig Friedrich Keller."

Laoch paused and rubbed his eyes, shook his head and continued, "You probably don't recognize Keller's name. He is in our archives. Before the Dunkirk escape, William, as you know him, commanded an offensive in which his regiment defeated an elite German unit under Captain Ludwig Keller. War historians widely criticized the strategy of this elite team as poorly planned, to say the least. When William tried to accept their surrender, Captain Keller assassinated the flag waver with his sidearm and fought until all the Germans soldiers died. Many Germans equated the rise of Keller's fame during the early part of the war with that of General Custer. He had a daring and handsome demeanor, and the German ranks saw him as a fast riser. Hitler himself attended the funeral in the small Bavarian town of Sauerlach, and Joseph Goebbels used films and audio recordings from the service to motivate the troops in their push that kicked England from the continent."

Peter lifted a hand, and Laoch nodded. "So, William's troops killed this guy and his troops? Our William at the house?"

"Indeed. An embedded photographer for Life Magazine captured the victory in full color. This battle was during a time of deadlock near the French border with Luxembourg. Although a rather minor victory, it captivated the world's press, making William briefly famous. That action and his successes afterwards led to him being knighted after the Dunkirk retreat. The pictures of Keller, taken before his death, show something interesting. In most of those photos, he is carrying something in his right hand. We initially believed the object to be rolled-up papers; however, one color photo shows it reflecting a metallic gold color. Later analysis of colorizing black and white pictures, a process developed by Wilson Markle and later Hal Roach Studios, affirmed this theory. After the defeat of Keller's troops, William gained an item off that battlefield, allegedly previously owned by Captain Keller. People described it as a golden colored brass metal tube. William carried this item the duration of the war as a good-luck charm of sorts. After the great tragedy that ended his military career, he still carried it, and the records showed it was in his possession when he went to Bethlem Hospital after the war. Military brass confirmed that battle fatigue led to his error in judgement when Air Vice-Marshal William Atworth ordered the bombing of the ships in the Baltics. William had declared these ships to be filled with German troops, trying to turn the tide at the end of the war. When in reality, the Germans filled them with thousands of Jewish concentration camp survivors. There were many reports in William's hands which contradicted his belief. These reports stated factually that Jewish camp survivors were on the ship, yet he ordered the bombing, anyway. The bombs dropped on the ships, condemning about seven thousand souls. The SS Cap Arcona, was the largest individual loss of lives at nearly four thousand. William's status, and his connections, prevented the public release of his actions; only this archive has the evidence and references related to these facts."

The faces around the table all showed a look of shock, as Laoch continued, "With William's internment at Bethlem, the war's ending allowed the bad press surrounding the incident to fade. Similarly, the world eventually forgot about William. The artifact he took from Keller and carried disappeared without a trace. The hospital documented it as being sealed in box 45-G794538 with William's other belongings. However, the hospital staff discovered the damaged seal upon his release and, during the pre-release inventory check, found the item missing. We now think we know what happened to it." Laoch paused and turned the page.

Laoch took a deep breath and resumed. "The researchers found records of Kenneth Riedling Junior, with emphasis on junior, age 17 from Chicago, Illinois, USA entering the UK through Southampton Sea Ports. He had arrived on the Esso Oil Tanker Camden T2, registered as a Passenger/Guest, arriving May 7th, 1947. May 9th, two days later, the staff of Bethlem Royal Hospital in South London issued Kenneth Riedling Jr., age 17 from Chicago, Illinois, USA, a visitor pass to visit Alister Kornegay, an orderly at the hospital. They met at lunchtime for forty minutes and Kenneth turned in the pass and left the hospital. The standard procedure, both in the past and present, involves searching visitors upon entry to prevent any accidental introduction of dangerous items. However, they do not search for those guests leaving the facility. The cycle continues... Despite his short but successful career ascending to lead detective in Chicago in just eight years, Kenneth Riedling Jr.'s obsessive research of non-job-related topics as a lieutenant led to his eventual voluntary dismissal and divorce. Many people thought of him as on a career path that would have made him a police chief or mayor someday. He was the golden boy of the Chicago Tribune Newspaper for years, with the credit for solving multiple mysterious cold file crimes, including murder and robbery cases that had eluded his predecessors. Riedling left public service and retired from the Chicago Police Department in 1970, at forty, following concerns about his financial situation and the possession of items that appeared to be beyond his means. The paper that once celebrated him as a hero, accused him of grift and corruption as a public official. Over the ensuing two years, his ex-wife and only son died when the car she was driving went through a temporary guard rail at a parking garage that was under construction and crashed into the Chicago River. Six hours later, they recovered the car with both bodies still inside. Also in that same month, the writer of the exposé in the Tribune tied his own hands behind his back and hung himself in his own home. Kenneth Riedling Jr. received a life insurance payout for his ex-wife and son, retired to a spacious home near a new artificial reservoir, Lake Norman in North Carolina, north of Charlotte, after being cleared of any wrongdoing. There, his new neighbors were Walter and Emma Scandling. Their son Harold Emerson Scandling was in high school when Riedling moved in next door. The families were friendly with each other as both Kenneth and Walter, Harold's father, traded the presidency for the Homeowners Association for years. Harrold Scandling went on to..."

Gus interrupted. "He ran for State Attorney General when I was in college... and lost, but I think I voted for him. A girl I had a crush on was a big activist and I helped her hand out voting guides to students. I knew I knew that name when I saw it in my mother's first entry. It was so familiar."

Laoch nodded as he looked at Gus. "Your mom's notes mention him. He is the person currently employing a private investigation service out of London, led by Marcus Peige of Peige Partners Incorporated. Mr. Peige is a retired researcher from MI5, and the dossier states he is a very capable investigator, with friends in high and low places. He spent time in Iraq during the Gulf War with the British SAS. His time there overlapped with yours by six months, Gus, although he was mostly in Northern Iraq. He also spent two tours in Afghanistan. He is fluent in six languages besides English, including Arabic, Kurdish, Farsi, Pashto, Dari and Russian. If William's records existed anywhere in the British Archives, besides his basic direct service records, I would be very nervous right now."

Laoch took a deep breath as if resetting, and held up a picture of a white man, with green eyes and graying brown hair. "Back to Harold Emerson Scandling. This is him. He has an ivy league education and is a Georgetown Juris Doctor, passed the Bar in North Carolina, South Carolina, Virginia and the District of Columbia. After a successful stint as a criminal defense attorney, he switched sides and became an Assistant District Attorney for Mecklenburg County, which encompasses Charlotte, North Carolina. Following the current District Attorney's death in a car crash, they appointed him to the position. During that run as D.A., he ran for Attorney General in 2002 and lost convincingly. After completing eight years as the District Attorney, he ran for and won an election to become a judge in the North Carolina Superior Court Fifth Division, District 26. After just one year on the bench, he ran as a Democrat for Congress in the 9th Congressional district, after the incumbent unexpectedly stepped down, and he won. The following year, North Carolina's Republican-dominated senate redrew the districts, and Scandling made the choice not to run in 2012. He remained active in state and national politics and is a possible future candidate for national office as a senator or even a presidential candidate. He is a member of three prominent think-tanks and was a trusted advisor and friend to President Obama during his terms in office. Recently, he has taken a lower profile and has focused on the State of North Carolina with its growing political importance."

"That is great and all, grandfather," Gus said," incredible even with how it ties to what my mother wrote, but I am not sure I understand where you are going here."

"Yes, yes. I will cut to it. This is a story from the Raleigh News and Observer. It is a story about the funeral for Officer Corr, the person who killed Peter's father and tried to kill Marcy." There were two pictures in the article. One was a wide crowd shot showing the grieving wife being supported by an arm around her waist as she wailed. The arm was owned by the same person in the center of the second picture, Harold Emerson Scandling, who was politely shaking hands with members of the family.

"Holy shit!" and "Are you fucking kidding me?" came the chorus from Gus and Marcy

"Do you see it yet?" Laoch asked. "Do you see that what the creature is doing? It is trying to pull you out of hiding. He knows who you are. He knows who Marcy is and what she means to you. This fire is an attempt to pull you out.

Expect for him to escalate! The inane charges of Marcy being a poor landlord, is again trying to pull you out."

"What about my mom?" asked Peter.

"I have had Deb put on a plane and taken to a safe, undisclosed location," Laoch said. "She will move at least three times to make sure she is safe, with each previous air crew not being informed of the future move. Marcy, is there anyone you would like me to plan for? We can tell them they won a sweepstake or something and we can take them away somewhere safe."

"My relationship with my parents is strained." Marcy confided. "We haven't really talked in about a decade. We had a falling out over something silly. I was their golden child... excellent school, good grades and advanced degrees. They thought I was throwing my life away, working for Peter,"

"Rude!" Peter said, but Marcy ignored him.

"Hell, so I might have been at the beginning," she said as Peter sat there with his mouth agape in a shocked expression. "But, as my role grew, I got to use many of the skills I studied in university, and I loved the job... Anyway, one Christmas, there was a blowup. They screamed at me for wasting their good money and wouldn't let up. I called a cab, told them I loved them, and left. When I got home to Raleigh, Peter picked me up at the airport. He could tell I was still upset. I told him what happened, and he was mad. He jokingly asked me how much I had spent in school, and I told him. The next day, he sent them a check by courier for the whole expense and included a letter about how invaluable I was to Redwolf Solutions," she smiled to a much more content Peter. "Instead of Peter, however, his mother Deborah had signed the check and had written the letter."

"After we talked that day," Peter said, "I had dinner with my mom and told her about our conversation. She could see how mad I was. Honestly, she took it on herself to write the letter. The check she sent that day was her own personal check." He smiled with genuine pride at Marcy.

"Since that encounter," Marcy continued, "we talk occasionally. They both individually apologized, and I forgive them, but their words are hard to forget. If you could make them safe, I would appreciate it, but I do not know how you could get them to leave that home. It has been in our family for generations."

"How would they respond to a direct approach?" Asked Laoch. "Where we would tell them a version of the truth, maybe make it a bit more conventionally believable... Like instead of some mystical evil creature, hunting your boyfriend's family and perhaps their contacts, we say, some bad people," Laoch paused, as if he was tasting something bad in his own words.

"Before or after they laughed in your face? Also, my dad would probably produce his dove gun and hustle you off his property at first sight."

"Ok, what if we told them, you are in a hospital?" Laoch started.

"I had better be on death's door when they came or they would kill me outright!" Marcy said, with irritation filtering into her voice.

From behind her, Marcy heard a shuffle on the floor and turned to see Gus on a knee, holding out a gold ring with a diamond, "Would they come to a wedding?" he paused, "This isn't exactly how I pictured asking you this, but... Marcy, whether or not they come, would you marry me?"

"Yes... They would... I would... I will... Yes!" she said, jumping into his arms.

Chapter 63

Tuesday, September 25th, 2018, 7:07 PM 16312 Bell Island Drive, Lake Norman, North Carolina

Harold Scandling lounged in an Adirondack chair next to the pool at his luxurious estate, overlooking the lake. He had bought the two lots and destroyed the previous houses to build his enormous home. The gaudiness of the house was unmatched, even when compared to the other opulent houses nearby. For over two hours, he remained motionless, seated in the same place, with drool sliding down his chin and staining his expensive, custom-made white shirt. With empty eyes, he gazed toward the lake. The large bass jumping from the water went unnoticed as it struck the bug resting on the water, held up by surface tension. Hell, it wouldn't have mattered if he had seen it. The old johnboat beside the deckhouse hadn't touched the water since his wife had left him six years previously and took the kids with her. She knew to just take what he offered her, and hell, it was a great deal. He would provide for all the children's needs, including their education, freeing her from work forever. Harold Junior was a little piece of shit anyway, and he despised the fact that the fucking waste of good sperm shared his name. Despite his fight for women's right to choose, he felt let down. Hell, he never wanted kids, and Sarah fucking knew that. She was probably a goddamn Republican.

The lone, perfect sphere of ice in his whisky glass had long since dissolved, ruining the barely touched $600 pour of Rip Van Winkle, as a fly landed on his eyeball. It crawled before his involuntary reflexes blinked it away. Still, no focus returned to his eyes. The bottle of expensive hooch, as he called it, was a gift from an Asian lobbyist who was just hoping for a few minutes with one of his friends. He had lots of friends. Harold had looked at the case of rare whisky like an accountant receiving a pile of change to settle a large bill, pasted a fake smile on and thanked the man with the slight Mandarin accent, and scoffed at his request to speak to someone so high in the U.S. government that he thought, "that fucker couldn't breathe at that altitude and for a case of hooch? Fucking please!" He pushed the bottle back into the fancy box with the other bottles and slid it to the side. "Listen," he said. "There is no goddamn way that guy is going to meet with you. He is weighing a run for President, and I'm not even going to suggest it. There is absolutely no chance of that happening. I can arrange for you to meet his son. The kid is strange, so it's up to you to figure out how to charm him. I've heard he has a fondness for smack and significantly younger women. If he considered your offer worthy of discussing with his dad, that's a private matter between the two of you. If things do go well, I expect a thank you... that's all I'm saying. Make it clear to your uncle that if I choose to run for office, I will need his backing and strict adherence to campaign laws. The fucking cuckservatives are getting serious about that shit. Hence, we need to receive funds from different individuals. Read the fucking rule book!" As soon as he finished his diatribe, he discreetly pressed the button under his desk, silently signaling his secretary. She almost immediately stuck her head in the door after a courtesy tap. "Harold, I have an important call on line three. You really need to take it immediately. It sounds like an emergency involving your son."

"If only!" he thought and turned to his new bartender. He reached out to shake his hand as the man with the Mandarin accent bowed. Scandling tilted his head in a bow as the other man tried to recover and reach out his hand. Harold gave up and just waved, "Buh-bye," to him as he shuffled from the office.

Moments later, his secretary poked her head in and smiled, and he gave her a thumbs up. He stood up, cracked his back, walked around the desk to where the Asian man had just sat, flipped the chair over, and inspected it. Harold ran his hands down the rails of the legs of the chair, feeling the surfaces more than seeing them. He paused for a moment and thought. Walked to where the chair had sat, reached under the desk and found what felt like a fresh piece of chewing gum pushed up under the desk into the corner. He pried it loose with his fingertips. He could feel a single wire and a small box less than a centimeter in size, through the goo. "Fucking amateurs!" he shouted into the microphone in the gum. "You can forget the goddamn invitation, asshole!" He stuck the gum and device between two pieces of sticky note, reached to the gavel on the shelf behind his desk, and slammed it on the sticky note sandwich with enough force to make a circular impression on his antique wooden desk. Harold put the crushed remains of the gadget into the burn bin beside his chair.

Mosquitos were ravaging his comatose body and flying up the bowed cuffs of his shorts. His wife hated how he loved to go commando, but she was fucking gone now, so the boys were free roaming. In his non-drinking hand, an ancient golden metal tube sat. His thumb slowly caressing the raised section of the embossed snake where its head was. Though his mind was blank in fugue, as in, if his eyes were a TV from his childhood; looking into them you would see a big black and white circle test pattern, with an Indian head in full headdress in the middle above the large center circle. Though his conscious mind experienced a blank state, his brain was engaged at a level never achieved before.

It was a trick that Scrios had been practicing for... a few thousand years, maybe? He could not break the holds of this crystalline prison, but this was pretty damn close. He could feel the senses of the person he dominated. Touch, sight, hearing and he figured he could probably manage taste if he could get this meat sack to fucking move. He had never achieved that magic trick yet; however, some things worked. He increased Harold's sense of smell to the level Scrios had when he was a mortal roaming the earth. Scrios suspected all people had the capacity, but eons of security and farming had dulled their senses. Either way, he suspected that his interpretive ability of that sense probably belonged only to him.

This symbiosis was great for re-enabling his full ability to sense things only he could smell, but he did not miss the disgusting mortal smells of the world. With the smell came taste. He had to taste and smell this shithead's halitosis. But he knew that today was a day that he had hurt someone in the family or close to the family. The vagrant, who was so cold, just knew the only way to get warm was to build a fire. He knew if others knew about the warmth he had found, they too would want it, so he wedged the doors shut with chunks of wood. He turned on the stove to "High" and use the open flame to light some paper towels. Scrios's mind drifted back to the task at hand. If he had only been in this state when William's smell of loss had washed past. He might have been able to pinpoint where he was. William's scent had carried with it the tiniest taste of family. Was William with them? But something in William's essence felt different and new. It was probably because that geezer had to be pushing a hundred by now. He knew he would not likely get a repeat of that taste, except maybe when he finally faced the last moment of fear before death.

The third hour had passed without event and Scrios could feel the strain on his own considerable stamina. He could also feel and smell the blood that dripped from Harold's nose. Frustrated, he gave Harrold the memory of falling asleep in his chair and a certainty of how bad the bug bites were going to be, especially the ones on his balls. The creature retreated from Harold's mind.

Harold awoke. "Awe, Shit!" he said, and stood to go back inside.

Chapter 64

Thursday, September 27th, 2018, 4:45 AM The Big House, Scotland

Gus woke up in a cold sweat and rolled over to grab the diary inside his nightstand. Marcy turned the light on, on her side of the bed, as Gus dug into the drawer for his pen. Distractedly, he said, "Sorry if I woke you, dear. Let me write this down and I will tell you all about it. He scribbled notes out and cursed. Goddamn pen. He whipped it, holding it at the top, and went back to writing. Only a few seconds later, he cursed again, "Sweetheart, can you find me another pen?"

He heard rustling in her side drawer, which stopped, punctuated with a curse word. So, he tried the pen trick again. "This is a fairly new pen. What the hell?" He reached for his phone and pressed the power button on the side and a red battery light blinked on the screen and that was all. "Shit!" and he turned towards the now quiet Marcy.

She was there, sitting bolt like in the bed staring at him. "This damn pen and my freaking phone are both dead. Did you find a pen on your side?" Gus asked, knowing that the minimal time that had passed was dimming his memory of the dream. He looked at the cursed pen in his hands, and his mind flashed back to Marcy and her awkward stillness. When he looked back up, her eyes were totally wrong. Gone were the glacial green pools that he knew, replaced with the icy blue of a dead winter ocean, not unlike his own. However, in their own way, they seemed totally alien. Unnatural lights seemed to dance in these eyes and a menacing cold seemed to freeze in his chest. "Marcy?"

Gus heard a faint whisper like echo of her voice "I'm right here!" just barely audible over the rushing sound of blood in his ears. However, her mouth didn't move.

"Marcy?" he repeated, as a wicked smirk appeared impossibly twisting her beautiful features. The color of her skin seemed to blanch as wrinkles appeared like crows-feet at the sides of her eyes. Her face tilted to the left as the skin took on a drier, almost blue look, while her hair faded to blond and orange in the matter of a few seconds. The cruel weathering of her face continued until the rapidly transforming Marcy raised both hands to her hair at the top of her brow. Each hand grabbed a fistful of hair and pulled away from her head as the skin stretched and tore in a ragged vertical line. Some sort of pungent liquid fell from the gash in a cascade as the creature in front of him shed an outer layer like a molting crab. The hands came back to the edges of the wound and took Marcy off like a coat, revealing the creature of his childhood nightmares.

Scrios gave him a once overlook and said calmly, "Well, what now butter cup? This is your dream."

Gus woke up to Marcy almost sitting on his chest screaming at him, inches from his face, "I'm right here!!" His recognition coming only microseconds before he would have punched her in the head... hard. He changed the arc of his swing past her and grabbed her in a jarring hug.

"I'm so sorry!" Gus said. "Are you ok?"

"I'm fine... are you ok?" Marcy asked as Laoch and Peter arrived at the doorway. "You were screaming my name loud enough to wake everyone in the house, and you refused to wake up. I thought you were dying on me, you plonker!" as tears flooded her eyes.

"Dream! A terrible fucking dream. I need to write it down." He reached for his book and pen. He fully expected the pen not to work, but it did.

"Can you say it out loud lad," asked his grandfather who had run into the room. "It might help with the recall." So, Gus did.

He told them everything. He looked at Marcy apologetically as he described the dream. When he finished. They sat there in silence for a moment as Gus started writing. When he finished, he placed the book and pen back in the drawer. "What do you make of it, grandfather?"

"I dunno, lad. Seems different from most of mine. My dreams with Scrios, is him stalking me or me failing miserably to stalk him. It's different, that is for sure. You almost describe a classical shape shifter from the old books with the shedding of the skin, so that part is likely in your head from an old movie or show you have seen on the telly. However, I am not discounting that there has to be some significance to it."

"Ok, this shit is weirding me out. I just have to get that out there." Peter said. "I think it is early enough to wake up and get coffee. Can we leave the lights on, please?" he finished.

Peter and Laoch left to let Gus and Marcy get dressed, and they went down for breakfast.

When they got to the table, Laoch sat there in his normal spot at the end of the table closest to the front door. Bynum poked his head out of the door from the back stairs, "I will be right out to pull some food together."

"No, no," insisted Laoch. "We will be fine with coffee... go to sleep!"

"No bloody way I'll do that with all the howling outside!" Bynum replied.

That is when the sounds outside hit them. There was howling in the distance, and it was getting closer. "What the hell is that shite?" asked Laoch as he led people to the front door.

Almost as if a wave of noise crossing the landscape, the animals that usually ran so quietly arrived at the house, followed a minute later by a bedraggled man riding an off-road four-wheeler. The man was still wearing his sleeping cap and had a large double-barreled shotgun on his back. He killed the motor and stepped off the small vehicle. The wolves settled around him as if in ranks.

"Kier?" asked Laoch as he gave a stand down wave to whomever was over-watch for the security.

"Yes uncle. Everything alright?" Kier asked with his heavy brogue.

"Yes, I think everything is fine... why?" the grandfather asked warily.

"About 20 minutes ago, the pack came and woke me up. They tipped my bed over and took off this way. They were feart... scared, uncle. Something made them demand to come, and I just slid my boots and coat on and followed." Kier said with a shrug.

Laoch smiled. "Good, good. Let them satisfy their curiosity. When they are done, go to cool storage and get them a venison meal. Great job with them, lad," he said, and led the others back inside.

As they sat down for coffee, Peter looked up. "I'm just going to say it. The Scottish version of Lassie would kick the American version's ass."

Laoch, ignoring Peter, looked up at Gus. "That cinches it, my boy. Your dream was significant, and we better figure out why. Fast."

The voice came from inside the dark area of the great room. It was quiet and uncommonly meek. "It's looking for me," said the solemn voice. "I can feel him." William said with his voice gaining strength. "He ruined me, you know? First, I think he made me, only so he could ruin me."

"Who?" asked Laoch with a touch of innocence in his voice.

William turned on his reading light on and looked away from the light with sad eyes, ringed in red. The shadow from the light highlighted his age, showing the folds of his wrinkled skin. "I am standing in front of that bloody tiger again, I fear." He said as emotion colored his voice and stole its baritone. "There was something wrong with the baton I carried during the war. I didn't know it before, but there was something very, very, wrong with it. It would tell me things, or I would think of things and feel a certainty that I was correct. I can remember it now when I couldn't before. It's like when your glasses break, and you see two vases on the table. In one eye the vase is blue and in one it is red." William found his voice and grumbled. "But he tells you it is green, so it is green. He is looking for me. Somehow, he sensed me, but he doesn't know I sensed him too. For a moment the other day when we were at the table. He thinks I will lead him to you."

"Will you?" asked Laoch.

"I bloody well will not! I have cut my strings," he said with a small laugh. "I guess I'm back to being a real boy now," said the old man with a simple smile.

An outline of a plan formed in Laoch's mind.

Chapter 65 – Peter's Y

Thursday, September 27th, 2018, 11:00 AM, The Big House, Scotland

"Well, it cannot be here," Gus's grandfather insisted, his tone unwavering. "We must preserve this place as our abbey, a sanctuary we can escape to if everything falls apart."

Wedding planning was going GREAT Peter thought. The opening five minutes went without a hitch. Peter was fully expecting to be Gus's best man, but the anguish he witnessed in Marcy's eyes made him flinch inside when he realized that the fire had killed all the potential candidates for maid of honor. With a mix of recognition and sadness, Marcy attempted to rub her eyes discreetly. The recognition in Gus's eyes when he glanced at Peter clarified he had also seen it.

Peter's love for Gus was sincere, like that of a brother. Seeing him reach this milestone in his life, he momentarily longed for a companionship like his and Marcy's. He, too, had an affection for Marcy, but he felt she saw right through him from the very start. The idea was so amusing to him he couldn't help but laugh at himself.

There had been Bella, in college at Stanford. In his opinion, it was the one and only time he had truly fallen in love romantically. Isabella Nevirny had striking blue eyes that could rival those of a Sports Illustrated Swimsuit Edition model. Like the sky after a storm, her eyes were a brilliant shade of blue. Her tall and beautiful figure perfectly matched the beauty of her eyes. Her parents were apparently Ukrainian... or was it Romanian? He didn't remember for sure. Their relationship had lasted for more than a year, and it was the only one where Peter had ever entertained the thought of the "M" word. He had more than imagined it.

The situation couldn't have been better. He took her to some of the best restaurants in San Francisco, but her favorite was a small, cozy eatery tucked away in a quiet neighborhood. They called it Gazpacho's, an Italian place that had a cozy and welcoming atmosphere. Although it wasn't as renowned as the others, her fondness for the place transformed it into their own personal sanctuary. Armed with a ring in his pocket and a mind full of stupidity, he brought her there on their fourteen-month anniversary. He had a violinist ready to come in and hand her flowers when he gave the signal; he intended to get down on one knee and ask for her hand.

Peter's memories had engrossed him when Gus interrupted, asking, "Pete, what do you think?" Gus referring to him as Pete had cut off his introspection, as he couldn't recall the previous time Gus had used that name. Hell, it was probably before he was in college.

"Yeah, that sounds good to me!" Peter said, oblivious to the ongoing conversation. He traveled back in time through his memories, immersing himself again in remembrances of the past.

They were in the restaurant; they had gotten their drinks. As Marco, the waiter, set down the salads, Bella called him over and inquired, "I'm sorry to bother you, but could you point me toward the restrooms?" Peter thought to himself, counting the number of times they had been to this restaurant.

With a hint of a New York Italian accent, Marco apologized, "I'm sorry, miss, but the ladies' restroom is currently out of order. However, the owners have kindly offered to let customers use the bathroom in the apartment at the rear. Come, let me show you." He extended a helping hand to assist her to stand. She left with him, pointing the way past the out-of-order bathroom, to the hallway beyond.

Around six minutes later, according to Peter's watch, a busboy brought the food. Five minutes more passed, and Pete's concern grew as he pondered whether she had slipped into the toilet... and his beer bottle sat empty in his hand. It was 11:23 AM that his bladder reminded him he had two previous beers to pay the rent for. Rising from his chair, he informed the busboy that he would be back momentarily and to inform his date that he was using the restroom if she returned beforehand. Making his way down the slim rear hallway, he saw an older woman leaving the ladies' room and flicking off the light switch. Somewhere in the distance, the sound of a washing machine with an off-balance tub filled the air with a constant thump. The realization the old woman had wrecked the plumbing, hit his mind as he walked past, and Peter found amusement in the idea of phoning Gus to share the story later tonight. The odor emanating from the bathroom suggested that she had consumed three-day-old roadkill or some other foul substance.

340

Peter made a right turn, walked into the compact bathroom, secured the door with the lock, unzipped and pissed. He commended himself on the powerful stream and the booming sound it made as it struck the water in the ancient toilet bowl. After he finished, there was a peculiar sensation tugging at his brain stem. Something didn't feel right. A sound echoed through the vent, catching his attention. Someone was getting lucky, and they were getting loud! As the tank flushed, Peter heard a voice that was all too familiar, as it urged, "harder Marco! I'm about to cum!"

Like a drunk driver careening through a day care, the sudden awareness crashed through him, and the memory of the old woman leaving the supposedly broken bathroom triggered a wave of nausea. Desperate for respite, he pleaded for the tank above to be refilled, yearning for the clattering pipes and shrill whistle to overpower the surrounding noise. However, despite the cacophony, he couldn't escape the persistent thud of Marco's exertion, which reverberated in his mind and reverberated through the floor beneath him. Once the toilet finished refilling, Peter swiftly used toilet paper to wipe his face and the wall, eliminating any traces of his sickness. He flushed again, attempting to muffle the noise. He hurriedly washed his hands and rushed back to the table to stare at their cold food.

Another five minutes passed before Marco appeared, striding briskly across the kitchen. He leaned in close to a young cook, whispering something in their ear, and they exchanged a high five. Moments later, Bella emerged from the same hallway he did, her face glowing with newfound vitality. Peter put on his best fake smile. "I was about to send out a search party."

"Oh, yeah. Sorry it took a little longer than expected. The owners had these cute old pictures on the wall all the way back to the twenties and I think I kind of lost myself for a minute or two looking at them." Bella replied.

Peter's head swam with shame and anger, but he controlled it. He looked at Marco in the kitchen, who upon seeing him look up, instantly found a spot to clean on the metal serving window with a small towel. "I am guessing... twenty-four."

"Huh?" said the confused Bella. "Twenty-four what?"

Peter flushed red. "You said pictures from the twenties"

"Oh... yeah," she laughed distractedly with a honking sound that, until 15 minutes before, Peter would have described as endearing, but now...

Peter involuntarily scratched his head with both hands, trying to control his rage "You know, when you laugh like that, you sound like a beautiful swan," and she smiled. It was too late to stop the tidal fury coursing through him, "...a swan cumming on Marco's dick!" as loud violin music suddenly drowned out most of his statement and flowers appeared in Bella's stunned hands.

The involuntary head scratch had been close-enough to the signal that the violin guy, sensing he was late, busted in the door just five feet away and began playing loudly, and an assistant pushed flowers at his date. All that was audible to Bella was ...a swan" and she misinterpreted the wicked smile on Peter's face. She obviously thought the rest was some sort of compliment, so she smiled awkwardly.

The violinist leaned in and paused his playing for a split second. "To the lovely couple!" he said as Peter tried to wave him off. Peter's wave didn't work, so he grabbed the instrument and momentarily contemplated smashing it on the table.

The entire restaurant went quiet as Peter was now standing with his hand on the violin, spoiling the sound instantly. Peter saw as everyone looked at him... even the waitstaff and cooks paused, while something caught flame on the grill behind them.

Peter flushed a bright red, speaking with measured words, his mind pleading with him to maintain a modicum of composure. He altered his speech on the fly. "This is our fourteen-month anniversary," as patrons applauded lightly. "The first day we met, we talked, and I knew in the first five minutes there was no one else in the world like you," A chorus of coos came from the female patrons, while Bella glanced around the room uncomfortably. "I had set up this night, this table where we always tried to sit, a month ago. This is Michello on the violin," Peter said as Michello took one hand off the violin and tipped the small cap on his head and the crowd clapped.

Peter looked at Bella. "I had brought you here on this night, to this table, to get down on a knee and give you the ring in my pocket." Excited, deep breaths filled the room and Peter continued, "However, I want to thank Marco, our waiter, for helping me see the folly of this decision. I mean, I spent a lot on this ring. A whoooooole lot!" As the room somehow seemed to become more silent than moments before. "See, I too had to go to the bathroom, and I almost ran into that lady right there," Peter pointed towards the older woman at a table at the side of the restaurant, who kind of waived like this was her mini-shining moment, quickly realizing it was not about her. "...as she left, the apparently now WORKING lady's room. A total fucking miracle right there! As I went into the men's room to take a leak."

Bella found her voice, but it was only a squeak. "Peter?... honey?"

Peter looked at her with such intensity that she could have burst into flames, and she quieted immediately. Again, he continued. "Marco? You are the man! I flushed before I heard if you actually made her cum, but my money is on you, brother! I just hope you wore a raincoat, friend, because this is San Francisco, and she has a fuck-ton of favorite restaurants. Oh, and honey, tonight we are going Dutch... and Marco? She was your tip."

In the present, Peter heard Gus say, "So we are good? Security says they like this one the most and I think we go with their choice, with all else being the same."

"Yup, sounds good to me!" Peter said enthusiastically as Gus laughed to himself and shook his head.

Isabella Nevirny, Peter, would learn later from a Slavic neighbor his senior year, her last name, if you added a second "Y" to the end, literally translated to "unfaithful".

Chapter 66

Friday, September 28th, 2018, 4:00 AM The Big House, Atholl region, Scotland

The muffled sound of a phone ringing in the room woke Marcy. She heard it and was pretty sure it was her U.S. phone; however, she had no signal, and it surprised her it still had a charge. When she found it, it was her WhatsApp application that was ringing. Having attached it to the BigHouse's Wifi, she forgot about it after receiving a new phone from Laoch. The new phone would be capable of accessing her number once she got back to the U.S. She just had to get a new sim card for it, and the one from her old phone did not work.

When she looked at the phone, "Unknown Caller" was displayed, so Marcy almost ignored it. After answering, she wished she had. "Hello?" she said meekly.

"Hello," a stern voice said. "This is Detective Henry Brubaker with the Raleigh Police Department. Is this Marcy Kitchen?"

"Um, yes?" she said as Gus sat up beside her.

"Miss Kitchen, someone informed us you are currently out of town, and we have been trying to contact you for a statement regarding the fire at the home you own in Raleigh, at 1503 Craig Street? Do you have time today to come downtown to the station in Raleigh and give us a full statement?" The detective asked.

"I'm sorry. I am still currently out of the country, so that would be impossible," she said as Gus raised his shoulder and shrugged, miming, "who is it." Marcy twirled her finger over her head and mouthed "cops," and Gus leaned in to listen.

"Well mam, this is a very serious situation involving the deaths of three people, and I know you are eager to clear your name regarding this situation. Can I ask what country you are currently in and when you expect to be back in this country?" asked the man on the other end of the line. And Gus asked for the phone, so she handed it to him.

"Hello? This is her fiancé, Gus. Officer, um, what did you say your name was?"

"Brubaker sir, if you don't mind, I need to speak with miss Kitchen on this matter?"

"Oh, sure Officer Brubaker, just a couple of quick questions from me first," Gus said calmly. "What did you say your badge number is?"

"Sir, I don't see where that is relevant in this second," he said with his voice becoming crisper. I need Miss Kitchen to give me a timeframe for when she can meet to answer questions about the fire.

"Sure, sure. I get that. See, the problem is officer," Gus said, meeting his tone at the same level, "I know you have her lawyer's information and contact, and I also know that he has instructed you and your department to direct all inquiries through him. So again, I ask for your badge number and now also your supervisor's name. I'll be calling him in a second to pass on this information."

"Good, good and what will your lawyer say when I give him a third eye in his fucking forehead?" said the voice as the accent seemed to change from a good ol' NC country boy to a nondescript midwestern accent. Gus fiddled with his own phone and turned on the voice recorder and put Marcy's on speaker. "Better yet, when he goes to the press to admit your whore's guilt, with a written affidavit that says she rigged the house to burn down on purpose?"

"Wow, so I'm guessing this is you, huh?" Gus said with a slight crack in his voice that he cursed himself for.

"Look around. See all the people around you? They are all going to burn. But don't worry, I have special plans for your whore. I just thought I should clear the air. Tell William I said hello," and the phone battery on Marcy's phone died, ending the call.

If not for the quick, clear thinking from Gus, they both would have thought it was a dream. They immediately went downstairs to the dark, quiet dining room and sat. When Marcy was settled, Gus went to awaken his father.

When he came down, they told him about the message, and he shook his head. After his initial mortified reaction, he calmed. "That's a pretty clear recording," Laoch said. "I wonder if we can do a voice search on it and also maybe see if there is more we can learn about Officer Brewbaker."

Gus scrunched his face up. "I bet we find that Officer Brewbaker is a bullshit name. I'm pretty sure Henry Brubaker was the name of a character Robert Redford played in a movie in the early 80s."

Laoch looked at him wide eyed. "That is some pretty abstract knowledge to just know their son."

"Well, we used to play a lot of trivia at the bar after work," Gus explained. "We won a lot."

Chapter 67

Friday, September 28th, 2018, 9:07AM South Parking Lot, The George Bush Center for Intelligence, Langly, Virginia

Harold Emerson Scandling sat in his car. He turned off the slightly melted, bedazzle cased iPhone after closing the WhatsApp program. That fucker who grabbed the phone from that cunt had hung up on him? He didn't know why he had mentioned the, "pistol to the lawyer's forehead" thing. The compulsion had just come to him, so he said it... "and fuck him anyway. Hang up on me? Fuck you and your little prick!" he yelled at the now turned off phone and dunked it into the large compartment between the seats with a satisfying thump. Harold's face slackened and his neck drooped over his head into a stooper.

His eyes went blank and lost their awareness, as he said out loud, as if in a dream, "The cunt is with the boy... with William. William Atworth is somewhere in England; I can feel him in that direction."

This knowledge was not a lot to work with, Scrios thought, but with the evidence now piling up from his minions to show Gus being a likely terrorist, he will use his new group to find him.

Harold's face snapped to full consciousness as he took out his personal phone and dialed a number with a 919-area code. The phone rang twice, and a gruff voice answered. Harold spoke, cutting the gruff voices person off, "Jonathan? H. E. Scandling... I understand you have uncovered some important information

345

regarding Laoch Ferguson. I'll need you to send that information to the email address I'm getting ready to text you."

"Yes sir, Mr. Scandling, one second" Jonathan said, in a voice much younger than the one he answered with. Agent Jonathan Gilliam's mind questioned and immediately dismissed how Scandling could have known the information that he himself had discovered and typed on the computer, and forwarded to his Gmail account, was ready. He had literally just sent it there two minutes before his call.

H. E. Scandling, that politician guy, out of Charlotte, who walked through with the Governor last week as he visited the Raleigh Federal Building, had gone from "visitor badge jockey" to his unofficial boss in less than five minutes.

Jonathan didn't remember when, "Oh, call me Harold" let him see his relic from ancient Greece, that he had somehow carried through the metal detectors. He didn't recall the mind rape that occurred as he held the fascinating and ancient gold tube and involuntarily looked in to see the crystal it contained. He also didn't remember the trigger word that burrowed into his mind like a worm. The one that, if he heard it, would cause him to draw his service weapon, and kill everyone around him, eventually turning the gun on himself.

Minutes after Scandling introduced himself, a meeting created the "off the books task force" of which he was now a member. It comprised him and the other five members from the local Raleigh Federal contingent. The group included fellow researchers that carried a badge and gun for show, and all were just months to a few years out of training at Camp Peary. It was them and that Scandling guy. He beamed at finally doing something important.

Their first, and only, face-to-face meeting with Director Scandling, occurred as the Governor toured the facility and courthouse renovations, while the press cameras captured the footage for his reelection bid, starting in a few short months.

Each of the members of the task force, called "Blue King", committed the external URL, username and password to memory that Scandling gave them. This group could never write anything down. All findings were to be pushed up and disseminated through proper channels to ensure the legitimacy of the reports for other agency use. Duplicates were to be uploaded from non-work computers to the URL, with the credentials provided. The only thing they had to keep from their CIA management was the existence of Scandling as their boss, and that minor issue would be official soon enough.

Jonathan remembered how everyone in that meeting had been so on point, and each had helped build the consensus, through their own complimentary discoveries, that Laoch Kier Ferguson the Fifth was a dangerous person, with foreign connections that needed to be tracked down. He had family ties to Great Brittain, but none of those lead to an actual physical address.

The Governor, Mr. Scandling had apprised them, had been so concerned that he had called "friends in high places", to get Mr. Scandling clearance to act as the leader of this detail. The task force included access to the Highway Patrol, the NCDOJ, North Carolina's SBI and even contacts in British MI5.

Scandling had provided them with historical case files, related to this ghost family, that went back decades. They uncovered the treacherous roots of this family, even during the great westward expansion in the 1800s. None other than George Pinkerton documented and signed a report entitled "Bad Actions" about this family.

He remembered Scandling saying in the meeting, "While there is a presumption of innocence, I can't imagine it here. People seem to die around him a lot. A good friend and loyal member of the North Carolina State Patrol, who had been on my detail over the years, was setup by Mr. Ferguson and tricked into shooting the father of the owner of the company he worked for. When he figured out the circumstances, we believe he went to confront Mr. Ferguson, who murdered him in cold blood. You might have seen news reports that looked embarrassing to the Highway Patrol and my murdered friend, Trooper Stanley Corr. I assure you; those reports were wrong. To avoid prematurely alerting the family, the rumors were allowed to fester, ensuring their errors would be publicly addressed later.

Even though the research being performed for Scandling was off the books, this work was top priority for every member of the new team, and each of them knew it. It was important and "need to know only". It was so important that they were not to even discuss with their superiors. If questions came up, they were to notify H. E. Scandling, and he would handle the inquiry personally.

"Jonathan," came Scandling's voice from his phone. "Did you hear me? I asked if you emailed yet?"

With an audible click in the background, the agent replied, "Sent sir!"

"Excellent! Happy hunting Jonathan." Came the voice of his boss and the line went dead.

Hanging up the phone and turning off his car, Scandling opened the door and walked confidently towards the CIA headquarters for a 9:30 AM meeting with his contact in the Russian and European Analysis unit. He didn't know it, but he was about to hire him to lead the team he had assembled in Raleigh, even if that took handshake introductions up to the deputy director.

Chapter 68

Laoch sat at the head of the large table in the Cathedral room, with Gus, Marcy, Peter, Daniel and the security team. Laoch briefed them and played the recorded call aloud. Others, who were invited, stood around the table and listened. Some were noticeably unnerved.

"So," said Laoch. "Questions? Ideas?"

Thomas Finch, who Gus had originally met as an intern at Redwolf Solutions, flashed his hand in the air and Laoch nodded towards him. "Well, um, let me start with this message. It's totally fucking terrifying. I mean, I was glad to come work here with the crazy of what might be, but this call pushes the meter to... well, this is fucking real. I mean, I mean nothing bad, but I honestly hoped you guys were all just nuts and someday, we could open this information to the world. Now... I mean... Holy shit!"

"Indeed, and I understand your concerns and will be glad to speak with you later about them if you need," Laoch said, and paused and looked for hands. No one else raised their hands. "Okay, the standing people can go back to their work. I know some of you are looking for voice matches and are trying to clean up the audio as best as possible beforehand. So, get at that. Dino, you dropped me a note earlier about something you wanted to introduce. The floor is yours."

Dino sat up in his chair and leaned forward. Popped open his laptop and projected onto the screen a child video game called Bunny and Duck Farm. "You might ask why this old man operator might show you this silly kid's game. Well, the simple answer is communication, if all shit breaks loose. This game has a lot of things going for it. First, you can access it through your phone's VPN if this base becomes compromised or if you are unsure of its status. The IP addresses for this game are based in Romania. The game incorporates encrypted email; its one-to-one chats are temporary, self-deleting when either participant closes the chat. They also provide live, encrypted chat rooms with the same security for up to ten users. There is a rudimentary whiteboard built into the chat rooms... I mean, it is perfect. I have had friends check this out and they say it is solid. It has several million users already, so it is not just some unused game. I want everyone to take out their phones or laptops and go to this address on the external network." He waited a few moments and continued. "Setup an account and obviously, don't use your actual names, birthdays or ages. We will exchange the usernames, so we all know who we are talking to. I know the idea of kid's games like this one sucks, but play it a little to get used to the interface."

As the people around the table setup their accounts, Dino filled out a page in a text editor with usernames and their real IDs. The only person who was forced to change their user account was the giant Daniel, whose account was far too close to his love for the local Hearts football team.

Gus = FuzzyWabbit24

Peter = OI812

Marcy = Quackomatic71

Laoch III = SternEars

Daniel = Hearts_O_Mid#1 >> changed to >> Hearts_O_Gold

Kier = WolfWolf1

Dino = TyrannoRabbit

Buster = BrownPants

Wombat = FartBlossom

Snow = WhiteBunny6969

Jolly = GreenGiantDuck

Yoyo = DeadEyeBunny

After they figured out the accounts, they moved on to the next agenda item, still led by Dino. The subject was how to get Marcy's parents to the wedding location, decided on the previous day. A secondary factor was how to get them there without them knowing they were doing everything possible to ensure there was no one and no devices following them.

The wedding was going to be tiny, with the list limited to Gus's family, which was sizeable in the local community, but not all were going to be invited. Also, Marcy's parents and Deb, who were going to be coming from a different secure location. Altogether, there were just over 30 people, including the discreet security team, two or more members of which should remain unseen.

Marcy meticulously planned for her parents, devising ideas to avoid suspicion. The operation involved observing her parents for three weeks, focusing primarily on detecting any external surveillance. To ensure their safety, Laoch's funding supported the deployment of a Rapid Reaction Force (RRF) comprising experienced operators recommended to him by Dino and his team. The key stressed component was the complete lack of knowledge about the main home compound among all members of the force. Their assignment later on was to help with security at the wedding.

Chapter 69

Monday, October 1st, 2018, 9:00 AM The Archives, Scotland

The group got back together to check status on the previous meeting. All security plans looked good, and the progress seemed to be right along the lines expected.

The second point on the agenda was to check in on everyone with Bunny and Duck Farm to see if they were all comfortable with the game and its communications. All had touched it to varying degrees. They had gone through a tutorial and grown their starter gardens. They had learned how to turn away the big bad foxes, the bane of the Bunny and Duck universe.

Gus was joking about his seventh level and lording over the security team. "Let me know, guys, if you need a little help with those pesky foxes. I kind of have that part sorted. The highest member of the security team was at level four. Daniel swelled his chest and turned his laptop around to show his level 13 kingdom, and the room was in mock awe. Marcy had also made it to seventh and laughed with a shrug. Everyone had reported, except Peter. "Peter," Gus said. "We all showed ours. What is your level?"

"It's a stupid game," Peter said with a huff. "I have figured out the communications, though, and that's fine."

"Wait a sec," said Marcy "I saw something when I created a chat room with Gus. Everyone, accept the chatroom I'm opening." Peter closed his eyes and tilted his head back.

When the chat room opened, it showed the names of the people in the room. It also showed their level and title. The entire team except Peter were "Junior Farmers", However Peter was "Duke OI812" and level 713. Marcy saw it first and exploded in laughter. "Level 713!!!! Peter! What the hell?"

"I got bored, and I'm super competitive, alright?" Others laughed, and Daniel dramatically rolled from his chair onto the floor and laid flat.

"No, no," Dino said with a completely straight face. "This is fantastic! Peter is the leader of a top ten alliance with over two hundred members. Peter, we all need to join your alliance. This is perfect cover,"

Peter looked mockingly proud as others still snickered, but Dino was serious. "I hate to say this guys," said Dino, "but get with Peter and get some pointers. We all need to progress our bunnies and duck farms over time to create better cover. New users create red flags."

Albemarle Province of North America, 1708

It had been over two thousand six hundred years since Scrios had last experienced genuine sleep. That doesn't mean he never had dreams. He experienced dreams in periods best described as a trancelike state, where reality blurred and imagination took over. In those moments, time lost all meaning. Long, vivid dreams could pass by in a matter of seconds, leaving him disoriented in the real world. During the first five hundred years, trapped in the stone, hidden beneath a landslide of dirt, stones, and mud; he had single dreams that lasted for years. Some of them were beyond his understanding. There was a pattern to these works, as they consistently explored themes of death, dominance, and destruction. There were certain events in dreams that kept happening repeatedly, and surprisingly, they often turned out to be prophetic.

One of the prophetic dreams he had while buried was of being a passenger in someone else's body, experiencing their thoughts and knowledge. He couldn't grasp his situation yet, but this dream provided a glimpse of what turned out to be his own future.

November 1708, Nooherooka Village, on the Neuse River.

As Thomas Cary, a pale-skinned man, walked into the settlement, he could see the red, muddy river flowing nearby. People there built the buildings from a blend of wood, mud, and reeds. The construction of a solid wooden wall was underway, designed to imitate the forts constructed by European settlers. Bath, the town where Thomas lived, lacked one. Yet, he had encountered many during his journeys.

Edward Hyde, an idiotic individual expelled from Oxford, challenged Thomas for the Governorship of North Carolina. Cary's affiliation with the Quaker party led Hyde's supporters to push for his removal, as Hyde's party enjoyed the support of The Church of England. The supporters of Hyde were causing chaos and complaining about it to the Crown. His opposition expressed their dissatisfaction with the reasonable alterations Thomas implemented regarding land taxes. In his mind, they would even blame him for excessive rainfall if they could.

While Cary's party embraced pacifism, Thomas acknowledged the role of war in uniting people behind a leader. A strange golden scepter, featuring a snake design, which was given to Cary by a friend, evoked a feeling of unease. Upon receiving it, Cary tried to return it because of its high value, but if he was honest, there was something about it that repulsed him. His friend, its previous owner, assured Cary that he was worthy of the gift and would not take it back. Cary looked at the serpent on the side of the artifact. Following a compulsion, he studied the hole of the hollow cylinder at the eye of the gem inside, and clarity instantly unburdened his mind. Scrios's act of rearranging the man's priorities, like a rude guest rearranging furniture, provided Cary his first understanding, and made him truly grasp that war could unite his support.

This new understanding led him to the savage village the inhabitants called Nooherooka. The second lie Scrios silently imposed on Cary was that learning the language of the savages was simple. Cary had suddenly become fully fluent in their primitive grunts and strange sounds. Being an intelligent man from an excellent family, it just made sense that something primitive should be simple to him, and it was.

He walked up, as several of the adult males armed with clubs and spears ran forward to block his way. Speaking in their native tongue, Cary bewildered the savages and made them halt.

Thomas had encountered their savage leader previously, and he confidently stated, "No need to worry. My name is Thomas Cary," he said slowly so their primitive minds could keep up. "I am here to speak with your leader, Hancock. As you can plainly see, I am unarmed."

As the commotion reached his ears, Hancock emerged from a small building, his eyes meeting Cary's with a combination of shock and puzzlement. With a quick glance over his shoulder, he surveyed the pine forest behind him, searching for any sign of the troops that were a constant presence during their meetings. He looked around, but there was not a single companion in sight. He had never heard this person, a prominent figure in the world of the pale skins, speak his language before. However, although his word choice appeared peculiar, his pronunciation was flawless. Upon meeting Cary, Hancock felt trepidation about using the disrespectful name they had given him, and he worried that they may have spoken it in his presence before. Hancock just now had found that he could understand him. When in the past, he had always referred to him as "the bear with his hair burned off" because of his unbelievably pale skin, and the man's crooked yellow-brown teeth.

The white leader gave Hancock gifts. In his possession, he had a sizable, rolled up blue cloth and a petite wooden box equipped with brass fishing hooks. Since these were welcome gifts, he expressed his gratitude to him. As the day was cool, they gathered near the fire for a conversation while the rest of the tribe resumed their usual tasks.

With a determined gaze, Thomas addressed the leader, acknowledging, "I understand the anger that arises when my people encroach upon your territory. My intention is to halt that, but unfortunately, my people refuse to heed my

352

words. My purpose here is to convince them to put an end to what they're doing, and I cannot accomplish it without your help. I hope setting a few examples will intimidate others from attempting it." As an additional incentive, he promised to reward them with bracelets made from the same material as the hooks for their help in putting an end to this exasperating practice.

Without hesitation or any recollection of the act later, he instinctively reached into the pouch slung over his shoulder and revealed the golden artifact to Hancock. Invitingly, he offered to let Hancock hold it. Anxious yet intrigued, Hancock accepted, carefully examining the serpent's design and breaking into a smile as he pointed it out. Hancock rotated the cylindrical scepter horizontally and saw the hole at its end. Noticing something that caught his interest, he raised it up to examine with his eye.

Three days later, during the night, Thomas met a group of savages, as he saw them, near a small house deep in the woods. Their incredible silent movement amazed him as they skillfully navigated through the slightly wet leaves, avoiding any noise from the sticks. The bright moon hung in the sky as the wind swayed the trees, resembling waves in the ocean and causing the leaves to rattle.

A curious assembly of five warriors and a European approached the house, where a faint wisp of smoke was visible from the chimney. Upon receiving his instruction, the five warriors entered the home without making a sound. Scrios's position near the outer wall of the home aided him in hearing the muffled screams of the settler's wife as she witnessed her husband being mercilessly stabbed by two mysterious figures. As one of the two men finished with her husband, he turned his attention to her and silenced her scream by placing a hand over her mouth. Firelight glinted on the black gore splattered across the murderer's chest and face.

Following the European's instructions, they slaughtered her infant in her presence, while Scrios feasted on the woman's despair. Subsequently, the assailant with the knife, responsible for her husband's demise, forcefully thrust the blade into her lower abdomen, shattering her pubic bone, and sliced her open from pelvis to chin, tearing through flesh and sinew, bouncing off her ribs, and inflicting mortal damage. As the four men left the house, she laid there like a dissection. Lethally wounded, she twitched and spasmed as her oxygen starved brain begged her rendered abdominal muscles with desperate requests which they were incapable of fulfilling.

Moments later, the tall European figure stepped into the room and inspected the handiwork. When he smiled and nodded, he noticed the destroyed women's eyes looking at him. They froze on him, as if looking for an explanation. Scrios stared into her eyes with a butcher's grin and watched their light extinguish, drinking in that rarest of flavors.

With the golden artifact in Cary's hand, he turned on his heel and went outside. After giving the savages one final assignment, they went back inside the house and set it on fire. Afterwards, they received a pouch with their payment, as Thomas stepped back to watch the fire burn. As the blaze exploded from the roof and windows, Scrios sensed something behind Thomas. This was identical to the dream Scrios had so long ago. Without knowing why, Thomas turned around and studied the forest at a spot Scrios pointed him towards. The only thing present in that area were trees, yet Scrios was confident that something impossible was there based on the dream. From deep in his mind, Scrios heard or felt the words, "a singularity". Thomas stared at the space amongst the trees and spoke, "I guess this is when you see me."

Intense heat emanated from the scepter for just that moment, blistering Thomas's hand even through the woven glove he wore. He wouldn't experience the impact of the burns until the next morning.

Chapter 70

Saturday, October 20th, 2018, 9:45 AM River Kinglass, Northeast of Connel, Scotland

The brisk October morning was quickly giving way to what appeared to be an unnaturally warm fall day for this region. Perched halfway up a hill above the road that followed a large mountain stream, Dino observed the preparations from the cover of the fall foliage and contemplated. "It might even hit 60 today." As he looked at the sight below, he mentally reviewed the previous weeks of preparation.

The preceding three weeks had gone off without a hitch. Preparations had gone almost too well in Laoch's and the security forces' minds. There were no negative reports from the team watching over Marcy's parents. On the Wednesday before the wedding, the hired car arrived at her parent's home, driven by Wombat. The microphone he wore picked up the conversation with her parents as they loaded in the car and went to the private airport nearby. There they loaded on to a hired private two-propeller plane for the short forty-five-minute flight to Oban Airport, just north of the town of Connel. From there, another more rugged, large black American Suburban vehicle waited for them. This was driven by Buster, with Wombat hopping into the front passenger seat.

The car went to a large stone farmhouse overlooking Loch Entive, which Bynum and Nell, with help from other local family, had rented and staffed for the wedding guests. Bynum and Nell took on their familiar role as chef and host. Following a generous offer, they replaced the inn's entire staff in the large, quaint, former farmhouse. The well-appointed room melted Marcy's parents' initial skepticism. Bynum and Nell treated them like honored guests.

The security team rented and secured the area along the River Kinglass for the private wedding and reception. It was about six miles from the farmhouse, where the wedding and reception would take place at 1:00 PM later that day.

Yoyo and Jolly handpicked two prime spots overlooking the location from a multitude of potential options. "Snipers hate being in the perfect and obvious position. Everyone looks there." Dino reminisced about whispering to his date during their outing to see Saving Private Ryan years ago. "There is no goddamn way I would send someone to the only church steeple in town... unless I handed them a bouquet of fucking lilies," he finished as people around him made shushing sounds. As the night began, he completely captivated his date with his looks and military manners. However, by the conclusion of the movie's second hour, she had shifted her weight onto the armrest on the opposite side. When the Germans blew up the tower, he leaned over and confidently exclaimed, "I told you so!" She nodded, smiled, rolled her eyes, and mentioned that she had to use the restroom. He never saw or heard from Sandy again.

After searching the theater and bathrooms, Dino called to check if she was okay, and her sarcastic roommate answered, "She's home and apparently as dead as a sniper in the only steeple."

Dino chuckled at the memory, instantly transported back to when he had an epiphany. Civilian life wasn't for him. When that happened, he was 36 years old, but his knees were like those of a 60-year-old. Dino returned home from the theater, switched on his outdated laptop, and reached out to a few former team members who worked in personal security. Six years later, around eight years ago from today's date, he met a Scotsman through a Mossad contact named Yoav Hipsher, or Yoyo, who he eventually convinced to join this team.

The crackling of his earphone snapped him out of his thoughts, and Jolly's voice came through, giving him a detailed update on the preparations. The two snipers had taken their time and marked, ranged, and setup concealed motion activated remote cameras and sensors in areas of cover an enemy might try to occupy if someone were to sneak in. They thoroughly searched for all the favorable and acceptable positions, erasing any trace of their presence, mindful of leaving evidence.

Memories of leading advanced teams for President Clinton's appearances came rushing back as Dino observed the careful documentation and ranking of every point of egress into the wedding venue. This was a unique challenge for him, though, primarily because of the scarcity of intel available to him. According to the old man Laoch, if a chaotic situation unfolded, there would be no one to rely on for help except for the local authorities, who he claimed would likely be compromised.

Sure, they were kitted up with solid, modern equipment. Excellent stuff to handle about anything that came at them, but there were still just six on his team, and the five other guys supplementing them. In spec-ops, they had the advantage of having an eye in the sky and a Tactical Operations Center, feeding them real time information, but they were without these luxuries here. Instead, they had Yoyo and Jolly from their perches, Chip and Snow stationed up the road in each direction, and that was about it. They tasked one of the five additional support personnel to spot, scrutinizing the hidden sides of the hills surrounding the valley where the wedding and festivities would take place.

If a firefight broke out, Dino did not treasure the level of explanation that someone would have to provide for two well-armed snipers and nine other operators working on British sovereign soil without approval. Authorities inevitably would become involved, and that is where he hoped Laoch had some major pull.

The best-case scenario involved them swiftly clearing the area before the authorities showed up. However, lacking the support of the British government, they would become instant criminals if they departed, and face relentless inquiries about their arsenal if they remained.

Snow had meticulously planned three primary evacuation routes. The options for routes were west along the stream, east along the stream, or a mountain goat ascent up and over the valley wall to the north. All routes involved the strategic use of flashbangs and a cleverly positioned claymore mine as a last resort. They had hired and paid for a friend who could pick them up in a watercraft. The price tag was steep, but the hefty payment meant it was readily available should the need arise; a comforting thought.

Using, or hell, even possessing the claymore, with its trip wire mechanism, was illegal by international law. That alone would guarantee them a crappy life in a dark hole at best. Sure, laughter had filled the planning room when Snow suggested it in the design. However, Dino was firm in his belief the authorities would not perceive it as being nearly as funny, the irony that they used a claymore in Scotland, as the team had joked that night. Amid Dino's machinations of all that could go wrong, he prayed that the wedding and reception would simply just go off without a hitch.

The team's possible legal danger was a heavy weight on Dino's mind. These were HIS guys. He had gone through the process of recruiting and vouched for the abilities of everyone. The other five security also were his direct hires.

He told each of them he was providing a protection for a family haunted by their own shadows. Dino didn't really buy that "Great Evil" bullshit. However, the shit the other day happened, and he had no rationalization for it. Their employer had already provided them with a wealth of evidence, but the recorded phone call, acquired by Gus, was the final, damning piece of the puzzle. The weight pressing on his chest was as heavy as a 400-pound bench press bouncing off his sternum. It was the panic feeling of a live grenade being tossed into his foxhole. The overwhelming feeling of panic washed over Dino, as his doubt cleared. This was not a figment of the family's imagination. The Rangers and the Operator Training Course had supposedly eliminated this kind of panic from his psyche, or so he thought. Dino, now in his fifties, worried that he was finally losing his toughness and becoming a soft-ass pussy. He stood, brushing himself off, and muttered, "Next thing ya know, I'll be all cozy in a cardigan, sipping tea by the fire."

As he walked, climbing the large hill behind the wedding venue, he remembered thinking just a couple of weeks ago, "maybe Laoch's stories were an elaborate prank," as there were many inconsistencies that made little sense. Dino had finished college level calculus in 10th grade. He had a natural talent for numbers. "This bullshit, though, just doesn't add up right, and I fucking hate bad math."

His team felt uneasy as well. Yoyo had talked about the things that went bump in the Jordanian nights of his childhood. Initially, he mentioned a creature called a Djinn, and his father's claim to have encountered one. However, upon seeing the mural in the Cathedral room later at the briefing, he paused and uttered, "Oh shit."

Dino asked Yoyo a question about his reaction in the cave later that night. While shaving, Dino glanced at the worn-out mirror he had used for over two decades and questioned, "Hey Yoav," Dino said using his real first name to convey his sincere concern, "what happened to you in the cave during the briefing today, when you used that word?"

Yoyo directed his gaze towards him, as he cautiously confirmed there were no other listeners before stating, "I think the being menacing this family is most likely a specific type of Djinn referred to as a Qareen. That is disastrous, because, to kill one, according to custom, you must locate the box that stores its heart and destroy it. Anything short of that, you might as well be slapping it with your penis. Destroying the heart is the only way to kill it. There is no injuring it. The

357

family says this thing is thousands of years old, and I have heard no one say shit about a box with its heart in it."

"Damn," Dino said. "Is that slapping it with your penis or mine?" Dino nudged him and trying to lighten the mood.

"Fuck you!" Yoyo said, swatting his hand away playfully.

Coming back to the present, Dino watched from the least favored evacuation route that overlooked the wedding venue below on its climb up the valley wall. He paused a moment and watched the preparations being made. Yoyo and Jolly, his twin snipers, helped to place streamers that accented the decorations around the clearing. In addition, flower bouquets dotted the landscape around the designated parking area and the tree line in all visible directions. Dino laughed to himself and wondered if the decorators or guests would know the loose ribbons were there for the snipers to gage crosswind from a distance?

It was getting late, and he needed to get his wedding attire on, so he could blend with the small crowd that would arrive in just under two hours. Near the parking area, two trailers, or "caravans" as the locals called them, waited. They would eventually house the bride and groom before the ceremony, but would now give him a place to don his Sunday best. He hated not wearing more than the light ballistic vest under the suit, but it was better than nothing.

As he walked down the path to the clearing, he again tested the expensive communications equipment Laoch had provided at his spec. The old man, to his credit, didn't bat an eye at dropping 50 thousand pounds on communications and the latest optics for the team.

He had invested much more in three large vehicles, with windows and doors that would absorb most small arms, short of a tactical machine gun or 50 caliber rounds. The vehicles had run-flat tires, an enormous turbo diesel engine and a heavy four-wheel-drive suspension. They draped the black modified shell of a Suburban SUV around this urban armored vehicle, even though Chevrolet made very little of the car. Despite the well-furnished interiors, the external dimensions of the vehicle, excluding the space for modifications, limited the seating room for the occupants by several inches. Because of the heavy-duty tires and suspension necessary to support the vehicle's weight, every bump and unevenness on the road was palpable to the riders.

Interlude - The wings

In Scrios's dream, the sky turned red as the setting sun painted it with a crimson hue. The sky resembled the magnificent ground, drenched in layers of carnage. The army that once dreamed of defeating him was now slowly dying for miles in every direction. From an impossible distance, he sensed his father's pleasure. No, not that fearful, powerless man, with the fractured pelvis who had been reduced to dust countless centuries ago. His real father. It was beginning to make sense to him that the dreams he had been having were his father's thoughts. From the darkest reaches of the universe, the images were his speech, as he engaged in conversation with Scrios. His father was teaching him about his future, sharing his destiny.

Scrios was not trapped inside the stone in this reality. Once again, he possessed his own body, liberated from the crucible that had honed his gift by teaching him an unparalleled level of concentration. Scrios ascended the three-tiered pyramid of bodies that was near 50 feet high towards his throne. Most of the bodies that made up the mound of flesh were dead, but not all. He could taste the anguish of those still living. Before his throne came into full view, the enormous bat-like wings behind the throne dominated his view. Each enormous wing measured a hundred feet or more, and had patches of hair, or features like a flaccid penis, deflated breast or screaming faces distributed over the wings. Each wing, stitched from the skins of those who resisted him, was a lesson and a warning. Upon reaching the top, he turned and settled onto the grand throne, his gaze fixated on the breathtaking landscape of the tens of thousands impaled before him. Most of whom were not dead yet, as he was specific with a method learned a thousand years before. There they would stay until the birds picked them apart or their flesh rotted, and carrion carried away their bones.

Scrios reluctantly emerged from his dreamlike state, only to be reminded of his continued captivity.

Chapter 71

Saturday, October 20th, 2018, 12:45 PM, River Kinglass, Northeast of Connel, Scotland

The bride and groom were in separate trailers when a tiny microphone in Dino's ear alerted him to the imminent arrival of the three black and heavy Suburban SUVs coming over a small hill from the hotel. With them, followed several smaller cars belonging to some of the local relatives and a small activity bus rented for the occasion. "Right on time," said Dino to the team.

"All clear," came the calm voice of Jolly. "I also see the catering truck with Bynum and Donna about half a click behind them, as expected. No signs of distress."

"Can I get everyone to check in?" asked Dino, and one by one, they did.

"Chip is five by five," came Chip's voice as he watched the road extending to the east that, after 30 minutes, would lead to larger roads. However, before reaching the empty roads, the driver would be required to navigate a four-wheel drive with adequate clearance to ford streams, through some gnarly goat paths, with treacherous inclines along that path as well. Chip was in a fortified position, 600 meters east of the wedding location.

From his location, the same distance to the west, towards the small town named Connel... The only real clean way in or out came the next report. "Snow is five by five."

"Jolly here. All is excellent." His high British sounding voice sounding from somewhere above them on the hill, hidden among the fall colors.

"Yoyo is good." The other sniper checked in from his complimentary vantage point.

"Wally is ready to drink a brewski and chase some tail once this ceremony is over," said the stocky, blond-haired man, standing on the other side of the venue. He was in the direct line of sight of his boss, Dino. Dino was older, but still an imposing figure. The large black man, his dark brown eyes now laser-focused on Wally, giving him a dead man's stare. "Kidding!" Wally said with an innocent shrug and an awkward chuckle.

"Team B?" spoke Dino.

A sigh proceeded the next person to check in. "huhhhhh, Back-door man is five by... Do I really have to use this handle?" Victor Thomas, one former keeper of Marcy's parents, asked.

"Yes, for now you do, but I will also accept BD, cool?" said Dino with a smirk.

"Thanks, BD is five by five and has nothing to report."

"Bo-peep is five by... and my sheepdogs are coming home to me. Sheepdog-one, Sheepdog-two and Billy-Goat are in position, all currently driving the sheep to the corral. All three are ready to rumble if needed," said Bob Simmons.

"Sheepdog-one" came the voice of Tommy Smith, over noticeable engine noise.

"Sheepdog-two" said John Penick with a similar diesel whine in the background from the turbo kicking in as his vehicle climbed a small hill.

"Billy-Goat" said the deep voice of Phil Michaels, the person on the support team who was everyone's friend. He had the M240H in the very back of his vehicle, a 7.62 belt fed wrecking ball that Dino hoped he never had to fire. If he did, it meant plans were in the shitter.

Moments later, the caravan of cars and trucks pulled into the parking area, with the SUV's careful to back in and keep proper spacing between themselves. These vehicles served as the primary way out, so the drivers parked them with a purpose. The drivers backed in the SUVs and placed them at an operational distance from each other.

Dino hated this feeling in his stomach and popped two antacid pills from a roll in his pocket. Even with all the preparation, he couldn't shake off the feeling of being exposed in these mostly grass-covered hills. Back-door man was important. He focused his attention on the ridges behind them and into the wilderness. This provided a strategic vantage point for observing the ceremony for any bad guys in virtually every direction. BD was entrusted with some of the best handheld optics available and was checking in with Dino every five minutes. "BD clear," is all Dino wanted to keep hearing.

With the guests settled in their seats, Dino proceeded to his designated spot at the back of the venue, while the piercing sound of bagpipes playing a march and a solitary deep drum provided the rhythm. Playing this dirge, was a customary practice in the Ferguson Clan at weddings. Dino thought it was funny that they called it "March of the Damned," especially since it was almost identical to a dirge historically played during public executions. Dino totally understood this tradition when he thought about it.

When the condemned man joined Peter at the altar, the music transitioned to a melodious and enchanting song played by a stringed instrument and flute. This music, accompanying Marcy's entrance in a stunning white dress, quieted any murmurs in the crowd... Marcy's father led her forward, with a chaplet of locally picked daisies adorning her head, and fine white silk trailing to her waist, behind her. The silk, catching the gentle breeze of the early afternoon. Around her neck, she wore a simple plain stone that was threaded on to an ancient twine string for a necklace, which Marcy had found in the archives.

Gus had turned around to witness his bride's arrival. She looked breathtaking. Deb, Peter's mother, caught Gus's eye momentarily from the front row, and they exchanged a quick, genuine smile.

Even though they weren't there physically, Gus could sense his mother and Max, Peter's father, presence around them. Despite his memories of his father being faint, the smell of sandalwood drifting by instantly reminded him of being carried to bed, hugged by his father and smelling that same scent many years ago. Gus felt a torrent of emotions washing through him.

In his peripheral vision, he observed his grandfather to the right, who had a concerned look on his face as he checked his phone. Almost as if he knew Gus's eyes were on him, he looked up and his face softened artificially as he grinned his best "it's nothing" smile.

The world faded again to just Marcy's eyes, locked onto his, as she walked towards him. All concerns left him. He saw a world brimming with hope in her eyes, yet he also noticed a hint of melancholy. Her mother waited for her at the altar, standing beside the source of Marcy's sadness. The three simple wooden stools, each held a small bouquet for her recently lost friends. It was an idea Gus and Marcy discussed a couple of nights before the wedding, and while it was hard to see the flowers there, it felt right to honor them.

The wedding was a simple and quick ceremony comprising an abbreviated religious ceremony and the exchanging of custom vows that each had created. Peter smiled the entire time, like a proud parent. Noticing Gus's potential fainting spell, he casually grabbed his best friend's elbow, offering support and ensuring he didn't pass out. His action had been so subtle that it went unnoticed by the guests. Peter had leaned in, as he did it, and whispered, just loud enough for the wedding party to hear, "Nope, you don't get out of it that easy!"

Marcy smiled widely at Peter and Gus. The gathered crowd's only perception of Peter's behavior was that he had become overwhelmed with joy. He patted Gus on the back and resumed his pose, a wide smile on his face. Aware of Peter's actions and the humiliation he had spared him, Gus couldn't help but see it as a classic example of the many "Peter moments" that defined his life. Peter, like always, had Gus's back.

When Gus and Marcy finished exchanging their vows, they kissed, after the preacher gave the permission. Peter leaned in, as they were being introduced by the Preacher as Mr. and Mrs. Fergusson. He spoke when the priest paused for a breath, "I fucking love you guys!" in a heartfelt moment that was perfect, even if it caused a few people in the crowd to chuckle.

With the bagpipes in the background, their constant low drone provided a unique backdrop as the flutes joined in to play an extraordinary rendition of Mendelssohn's Wedding March. The newly married couple retreated down the aisle to the sound of applause and beaming smiles.

In a matter of minutes, the chairs were rearranged and positioned around portable tables that were promptly assembled from the back of a large truck. The tables were adorned with crisp white tablecloths, expertly arranged by the hired staff. As the guests mingled, they enjoyed their drinks from the bar, strategically positioned near the walkway to the parking area.

Everyone reported as clear after Dino performed a check in. The small smile he allowed himself vanished when he saw Laoch's face. His eyes locked on him. After switching channels, he turned to the older man and inquired if something was wrong.

"Aye, something is in the air," said Laoch. "A relative who owns a small gas and grocery store said police had come into her store with pictures of Gus, Peter and Marcy, asking if anyone had seen them. The officer had described them as missing and possibly in distress. She also identified a small line of military like vehicles had topped off their tanks at her store. Some troops came inside for drinks and snacks, and she overheard one asking another, since when does the U.S. direct us on breaching protocols on our sovereign soil?"

"What the hell?" asked Dino. "Americans?"

"I have no idea. Hold. I'm getting another call." Laoch said as he answered his cell phone. He chatted for about 15 seconds and hung up. He opened the comm back to Dino. "People are apparently searching and asking around at farms close to the PO Box address we use. Thankfully, it is about 15 odd miles from our home's location, in a direction that takes 30 minutes to get to by car. Most residents in the area are close friends or even extended family members."

"So, what's the plan?" Dino asked. "Do we call this thing? Maybe move it to the secondary location at the rented farm? We could say that it looks like rain is on the way."

"Hmmm. Are we safer here or more exposed?" Laoch asked. "I mean, obviously we are outside, but we are setup here."

"I say we send Sheepdog-One and Two to pick up Chip and Snow," said Dino, "and move them each a mile farther down the roads, east and west, to provide us more reaction time. Next, we have Jolly and Yoyo move to the secondary positions that prioritize the view of the roadways. If something happens, they could disable the vehicles and at least make the fuckers hike their asses in while we evac. Chip and Snow can go to ground and disappear until we can pick them up at a designated location... if things get sideways."

"That would take care of us, but what about the other guests?" Laoch asked.

"Yeah. Well, we know they are in ground vehicles and at least two and a half hours from here, right?" said Dino. "We do dinner and whatever we can do in an hour and a half. If you have anyone that can send them the wrong way, that will help our window. We can say that the weather is coming in and we will continue tonight at the hotel at 1900 hours. Get them to the hotel, break down the stuff here and just open the bar tonight. If some express a lack of interest in the late party, we offer them accommodations in Perth and get them safely out of the way?"

"I like the intent," Laoch said. "Let's see if I can sell it."

Fifteen minutes later, the buffet style dinner was set up, causing Bynum's frustration as he had meticulously planned a beautifully presented plated meal. When Laoch described the day's events in vivid detail, he couldn't help but consent. With a quick change to the food presentation, he transformed it into a self-serve setup, resulting in a swift moving line and attendees promptly finding their seats. As soon as everyone had found their places, Peter stood up to the melodic chimes of glasses and the harmonious notes of the flute and stringed band faded away.

"I will make this quick," Peter said, his words met with chuckles from the crowd, who were charmed by hiss warm and conspiratorial smile. "I have known Gus... well, all my life. He is not a friend; he is my brother. I love him as if he were my blood. I have watched him grow up and dragged him into doing things that probably should have ended with us in jail." Peter looked as if thinking and shook his head. "This is the part of the speech where you would expect me to reveal a secret that would embarrass and maybe even make him hide his face in his hands. However, that's not the person Gus is. Gus is the best man I know, someone who embodies kindness, empathy, and integrity. There is no doubt in my mind that any embarrassing story I try to relay will turn me into the Falstaff to his Henry IV, causing me to look foolish. No, his embarrassing times with me? Those are mine to keep and rib him about in private."

Peter shifted his gaze, "Marcy, as many of you know, worked for me for several years before she met Gus.

It was a few more years of pain before Gus finally had the courage to ask her out. The moment they met; it was obvious there was a connection between them. Once Gus grew the..." Peter paused briefly apparently overcome with emotion. When he continued, he stared at the couple, "It was insane how they would subtly enquire about each other, Marcy would ask, 'Hey, where's Gus today?' or 'Usually, you guys go out on Thursdays, right?'. Or Gus would ask, 'So is Marcy going to eat lunch with us today?' and I would roll my eyes. One day, finally!

The stars lined up or something and they accidentally found themselves both eating with each other, alone at the same table."

Peter looked at them both, "Thank God! You are the best people I know. You two are meant to be. To be honest, I fear what you two will unleash on this crazy world together." The guests laughed with Peter. "I love you both... To Mr. and Mrs. Ferguson!!!" Peter said and lifted his glass of champagne.

Moments later, Laoch garnered the attention of everyone present. "I wanted to thank all of you cherished friends and family for coming to this joining of these two wonderful kids. The merging of these families and these two individuals brings a necessary brightness to the world. I wanted to notify everyone that we are monitoring the potential for adverse weather that may affect the area. We might need to make our exit from here at some point. In the event of that happening, we'll reconvene the party at the restaurant at approximately 1900 hours. As we are Scottish, it could be long into the night and loud. If you'd like to stay in a different hotel, please inform us and we'll arrange a complimentary stay in a lovely hotel in Perth. Thanks for your ear and enjoy!"

Laoch's continuous receipt of updates about the search team's concentration in an area, several hours away, caused the party to go on for longer than expected. The plan underwent constant modifications by Laoch and Dino until it reached a point where no further modifications were necessary. Most of the guests, who were more interested in a peaceful night sleep, had accepted the offer in town and started their premature departure to the other hotel after three hours.

Chapter 72

Saturday, October 20th, 2018, 4:45 PM Druimeanach Inn, Loch Etive, Scotland

In the secluded dining area behind the bar, Laoch sat deep in thought. Peter, Dino, and Jolly were also present in the room. Each of them sat silently, lost in their own thoughts. They had shed their fancy suits and now wore comfortable clothes.

To prevent himself from over analyzing the situation, Laoch's mind wandered through the farm's rich history. It seemed unlikely that the owners fully grasped the real cultural importance it carried. Among the archives, as they planned the wedding, he discovered maps dating back to 317AD, when the Pictish King Vipoig ruled the area. Laoch had been searching for any potential advantages in the area in case of an emergency. The map detailed the construction of a stone tower at this exact location, which is now known for its beautiful, commanding views of Loch Etive. Its visibility of the loch and its strategic westward view towards the open ocean prompted its construction. Laoch's ancestors helped in the rise of the King, and had established trade with them and his successors, providing many trade goods not readily found on the western coast. Throughout the generations, members of Laoch's families fought for the King in skirmishes and wars alike, while assisting in the tracking of stories related to the Blue King terrorizing the large island to the South. In 827 AD, a community of Benedictine monks established a small cloister at this location, where they lived in seclusion. Here was the foundation of the Ferguson's family's monistic scriptoria. Where some of his ancestors had learned and imported to the archives their skills in scribing, which led eventually to Latin becoming the dominant language used in the archives. A Viking raid in 1221 destroyed the cloister. It is highly probable that this building's foundation, and the stones used in its construction, came from that place. Several monks survived the raid and helped establish the Ardchattan Priory under Duncan MacDougal. The room Laoch was sitting in, in the farmhouse, was the original single room, built in 1520. In 1560, British troops encamped here, on the way to the Priory under orders from Henry VIII, putting an end to the monastery and claiming its possessions for the Crown. These lands, later that same century, fell under Clan Campbell who, at times, were at odds politically with the Fergusons, although the family's quiet ways removed them mostly from the political landscape.

Laoch's ancestors were bitter, as they and other clans had provided aid, shed blood and sacrificed lives during the struggle for Scottish independence, while the Campbells had largely stayed out of the war. After 250 years of estrangement, an arranged marriage bonded the families in blood, peace and resumed commerce.

"There are certain places," Laoch mused to himself. "Locations that naturally accumulate history, regardless of their remoteness, much like dust on a top shelf of a cabinet." This was one of those places.

Today Laoch carried the burden of his family's history, the wait threatening to break him, as he searched for answers in the history and worried about the future of his family. He anxiously awaited news about the search happening just two and a half hours away, directly to the east. Laoch knew keenly that the archive was built upon his family's suffering and bloodshed. Hoping for one more unremarkable day, Laoch prayed. He asked only that today would be historically inconsequential.

As far as he knew, authorities had not found the "Big House", which was staffed with a skeleton crew of their work hands, with Kier overseeing them, with his four-legged family. Laoch had contacted the Archives and had them perform a full lockdown until further notice. Supplementary physical locks, heavy steel braces that locked the mechanism at the church entrance and made moving the elevator at the warehouse impossible, had been engaged to thwart entry. Even if they somehow located one of the two entrances, gaining physical access would take a long time.

Laoch decided the archive would be their next destination because of its unparalleled security measures, if they could only get to it.

He developed a plan with Dino and coordinated it with everyone else there, to discreetly access the Archives through the warehouse. However, they couldn't attract attention by driving up in a procession of cars. Some could also use the chapel entrance if needed, but that too would have to be coordinated with the inhabitants of the currently locked down location.

Laoch believed their continued presence at the inn was dangerous and made it more likely they'd be found. Finding them in this remote, treeless area would make escape nearly impossible if they used air resources with the few available roads. Gus and Marcy's honeymoon was going to be very boring, and that was if things went well getting to the archive. Laoch hoped for boring, because that meant they were still alive.

A sudden phone buzz from Laoch's phone on the table cut short the thoughts of everyone present. "Yes?" he asked, his eyes widening with anticipation. "Please hold on for a moment," he flicked the switch to activate the speaker.

"Uncle, as I was saying," came the gruff voice of Kier, "Initially, they reported the three as missing and expressed concerns about their wellbeing. Their tactics have changed, and now they report that Gus is being sought in the U.S. for a sealed indictment. There is a joint UK and American task force to locate and capture Gus and other family members, because of their alleged ties to terrorism and organized crime. If the weather clears, we can expect air support for the search by tomorrow morning. At present, the Big House has not been located, or maybe they have found it and are ignoring it. I'm uncertain for how much longer, though, that this will be the case. We have seen an American that is with them. A fat old bastard who appears to be the one in charge. He has some beady eyes, too. I'm sending you a photo."

As if on cue, Laoch's phone made the sound. "You've got mail!"

Peter snickered as Laoch flashed with anger at the new sound effect. He lifted heavy red eyes at Peter.

"Dude, it was an old man joke. I will fix it after the call." Peter said apologetically.

Laoch pivoted the phone, presenting them with an image of Harold Emerson Scandling. While the picture was clear, the American was a haggard and tired looking older man, standing alongside the road. His clear anger filled eyes locked in a stare with the camera. Clutched tightly in his left hand, an inch of a metallic tube protruded and reflected in the erratic light from the flash.

"Is that the fucking thing in his hand?" asked Dino.

"A-firm-a-tive," said Laoch phonetically, as he rubbed his stressed face.

"Run or hide?" Dino asked, with a tone of cold focus, as the operator in him emerged. "Either way, we need to get our dicks out of the wind. This place is so remote that I might be the only black man to set foot here. I have been in a Porta Potty with more and better exits than here."

"What's your call?" Laoch gazed at him.

"Shit, I would run for a beach in Bali right now, but something tells me the airports, even small ones, are being watched closely. We could still figure something out, but it would take time. Time, I doubt we have... the biggest thing is not to panic and do something stupid. I wish we were in your bunker right now, so we could wait and see if they lose interest."

"Is there a way to get us there safely?" Laoch asked.

"The best way would be to blend in with traffic," Dino advised, "so the big black trucks are out."

Jolly sat forward in his seat and suggested, "We could put some people in private cars, others in the catering truck. Fill the back with tables and such that, if searched, would cause no additional suspicion. Drive to areas near the warehouse entrance and go in that way."

Laoch nodded, "I like that. Some could also enter the other way, although it might be a little hike, but I prefer the warehouse."

"That's cool," said Jolly, "Either way, I kind of like a little walk in the woods."

"Another problem though," started Laoch. "We need to get the guests the hell out of here safely. I hate to take from our numbers, but who can we get to load them on a bus and drive them to an airport far away from here?"

"I might know someone," Dino said. "Let me make a call. He lives just a couple of hours from here. He is retired, about ten years older than me. He is a solid guy who can handle anything."

There was a light tap at the door, Laoch hastily ended the call, assuring the person on the other end that he would call back shortly if needed. "Come in," he said, his voice inviting and warm. Peter's mother, Deb entered the room.

Deb walked into the room sheepishly. "Hey guys, I know something is up and I know enough to not ask questions. I have the car that I rented, and I'm going for a drive to get out of your hair. I plan to get far away from here and a week later, I will be off to another random location that I feel is safe. To answer your next question, I have enough cash to go a long while and will use nothing trackable. Peter, tell Gus that I have transferred him to your division. I have notified his old boss by email and told him you were on a special assignment. To answer the question in your head, no, you are not his boss. If or when you need me, Laoch, you know how to reach me, and I will check in when I can. If things clear up, let me know so I can go home." Deb hugged Peter and kissed him on the cheek. She waved to the rest of the room and was gone.

"That is quite a lady," Dino said.

"You have no idea." Laoch replied. "Gentleman, we need a plan. I think it is only a matter of time before someone innocently points this way. We need to be gone when that happens. I hope everyone likes canned food, because we have enough for a year or more where we are headed.

Dino smiled comfortably. "Shit, I have eaten MRE's for longer than that. As long as there is a bathroom and a level surface to lie down on, I'm good."

Chapter 73

Saturday, October 20th, 2018, 6:13 PM On the road to the Archive, Scotland

The plans had been quick but carefully devised and mutually accepted. Everyone would make their way to the fortress that was the Archive. The group would divide into five vehicles, while Team-b members would receive cash and the big SUVs to drive to different locations and hold up within an hour of a specific coordinate chosen by Laoch. Their task was to find a room and wait. If there was no contact for over forty-eight hours, park the cars in long-term parking, dispose of the key fobs and get out of the country. Their specified accounts would receive their last payment automatically.

To get the others back to some place safe, Bynum and Donna would ride in the catering truck with Chip. Daniel's car would pair with their vehicle, carrying Laoch, Mimi, and Jolly. In case of a roadblock or a stop, they would keep half a kilometer between the cars.

A second group of cars would stay approximately three minutes behind the first. They would also maintain a staggard distance from one and other. In that grouping, a car driven by Nell accompanied by William up front and Wally in the back seat. A second car driven by Marcy, who had cut her hair short and used makeup to adjust the features of her face. Peter and Snow as her passengers. The fifth car, driven by Dino, with Gus and Yoyo riding along.

According to the rule, if the lead vehicle came to a stop, the others would stop too, provided they were far enough back not to be obvious and be prepared to intervene if necessary. Hoping to navigate any encounter smoothly, they aimed to exude a composed and rational demeanor. If reasonable didn't work, Laoch feared what the alternative would look like.

As prophesied throughout the records, the creature, Scrios, had returned, its sole intention being the destruction of his family. If successful in doing so, it would become an unstoppable force in the world. If it so chose, it could have dominion. Laoch understood this. Despite growing up with a deep understanding of the creature he now confronted, he couldn't help but grapple with the moral dilemma of taking the life of an innocent person, even if they were under the creature's control.

Laoch's face reddened as he chastised himself. The rules laid out by Sanura thousands of years ago seemed even more cruel now. Rule three said, "If a friend turns on you in battle, he is now your enemy." The Scandling person was no friend, but their presence served as a chilling reminder of the rule's decisiveness, hovering like a merciless blade, simplifying and validating deadly choices. Still, Laoch knew that the doubt he felt echoed the uncertainty felt by his ancestors. He had read their journals, yet somehow, the actual decision was falling to him. "Lucky me," he muttered under his breath.

The vehicles emerged from the locked up, dimly lit hotel and set off towards the A85, following the winding ancient roads. After driving east on the highway for nearly two hours, they continued straight onto A84 in Lochernhead. Considering that the traffic from the larger cities would come from the south along the A9 four-lane highway, they believed it would be advantageous to approach their destination from that direction.

The plan was simple: if they approached the old warehouse entrance, only William's car would proceed to the actual location. There was concern for the centenarian and his ability to cover a longer distance. They went to great lengths to hide their worry from the old man who had seemed to gain clarity in recent months. Instead of parking right at the destination, others would opt to park a short distance away and venture through the wooded area to reach their destination. Either Jolly or Yoyo, depending on who arrived first, would position themselves as a lookout, scanning the surroundings and guiding individuals towards the warehouse.

Chapter 74

"These are not the droids you are looking for..." **Obi Wan Kenobi**

Saturday, October 20th, 2018, 7:49 PM A84 Central Scotland

On A84, below Loch Lubnaig, by the Gaibh Uisge river, the road sharply bends eastward around a towering highland hill. Now right before the turn, officers were stopping cars in the right oncoming lane, flagging them down and using lights to conduct brief checks on each vehicle. As the team planned their approach to home, they had concerns about this specific area on the map, but they had limited options. Chip, driving the first car, slowly passed the checkpoint in the other lane, only to find another checkpoint in his lane after turning the corner three hundred meters ahead. Just as Daniel's car cleared the first checkpoint, Chip's voice crackled over the radio, revealing the next location and Laoch's stomach dropped. It was a perfect pinch point, a precarious spot wedged between a towering hill on their left and the rushing river falls on their right.

The follow car Daniel was driving slowed, when Laoch's voice came over the communication device each driver and security person wore, "Well, let's not invite trouble. If you're in the second group, try to stay behind a bit because it seems like they aren't checking cars too closely." Laoch spoke.

Chip, driving the lead car, activated his communication device's microphone, ensuring that everyone would hear the details of the encounter as he rolled up in the catering truck. The officer stood by as the truck came to a stop. He hopped onto the running board and addressed the driver with a friendly "Good evening. Be aware that there is a police search happening in the area you are about to enter. This side of the paper has our logo and a barcode sticker on it," he pointed out while scanning the barcode sticker. With minimal attention to the occupants, the officer typed on his handheld device and asked, "Three adults, two males and a female?"

"Yes sir," said Chip.

"American?" The officer asked with a quizzical smile.

"Yep," said Chip. "I moved here twelve years ago, but my accent still sounds like I just left Texas yesterday," Chip laughed.

"Lovely," the officer remarked. "Better late than never, I guess. Well, welcome to Scotland! Please place this paper with the logo side up on your dash. It will speed up your progress through any other subsequent stops tonight. If you come across another stop, use this sheet to show that you entered the area after the search had already begun. Once they scan this code and confirm everything is in order, they will send you on your way! Please refrain from picking up individuals on the roadside and ensure your windows and doors remain closed and locked. If you witness anything worth reporting, you can find a contact number and several other methods of contacting us on the back, along with the public statement about the search." He smiled with a nod, stepped down from the running board, and waved them forward.

Daniel's car, with Laoch and Jolly, cleared the checkpoint with similar ease, received handouts for their dashboard. This prompted Laoch to call the other cars forward. Within five minutes, everyone had passed the checkpoint. Laoch's optimistic smile faded when Gus expressed worry from the car behind Laoch's.

"This is great and all," Gus said, "but something feels off. Sure, we will get through checkpoints, but it will become pretty darn obvious that these five vehicles are traveling together if we all pass through the same checkpoints down the road and at similar times."

Peter nodded and casually replied, "Yeah, the whole nice and easy checkpoint thing is an analytics wet dream. Just like the process of tracking luggage through a large airport, it used to be overwhelming and confusing, but now automated systems with barcodes track everything and make sure items go where they are supposed to. Sure, we will appear initially as individual vehicles entering from outside the search area, so at first, they will ignore us, but if Laoch was right; that it was just a matter of time until someone put together the wedding location. Our entry into the area will flag us as possible or even likely as suspects. This is especially true when the same group of cars hits the same checkpoints. Those handheld devices are feeding raw data into something. If it is analytics based, we will appear at the top of any insight report." Peter said with a sigh.

"Bloody hell," said Laoch slapping the dashboard, "and this also means we cannot leave any of these vehicles near the warehouse."

Wally's voice broke into the conversation, "So, when Nell and William get out near the warehouse, I will trash the sheet of paper on the dash and dump anything that might get me detained at a later checkpoint. I didn't see anyone recording plate information, they were just handing out these papers with stickers on them. The worst thing they will find at a checkpoint is an American driving a car with nothing more threatening than a small folding pocketknife. I'll drive the car to Glasgow and leave the car in long-term parking at the airport. If you want, I can hike back across the countryside if needed. It might take me three or four days. Or I can catch a bus from Glasgow to Falkirk or Stirling, buy a bicycle there and be back late tomorrow?" Wally Finished.

372

"Excellent Wally," Laoch said. "Do that, but just find a place to stay somewhere, short term. However, let us get Jolly or Yoyo in a place near the warehouse before anyone else gets there, to provide some eyes on the area. The other priority is getting Bynum and Donna close. Chip, we will need you to do something similar, except you keep your paper and if asked, say you dropped off your riders... somewhere farther away. That way, if Peter and Gus are right, their data at least points in different directions. In the meantime, we should all take different routes to the warehouse."

The plan moving forward wasn't perfect. Like most plans, the original version did not survive the first real challenge, so Laoch and Jolly, after conferring with Dino on a private frequency, told all vehicles to slow their progress some, while they reworked the approach.

A few short minutes later, Laoch remarked to the team, "This car is going to keep on moving so we can get Jolly dropped off first. He will approach the warehouse overland and check to see if it is safe for others to approach. Mimi and I will exit the car with him and wait near the drop off point for his word that the approach is clear. If he likes what he sees, he will find a secure position and take on overwatch and direct in the vehicles to drop off William, Nell, Bynum and Donna. Wally and Chip, we will need you two to linger about ten minutes out and wait for Jolly's call. On your phones, everyone will receive the general locations to park your vehicles. After you park, start hiking while maintaining as much cover as you can. You will each need to coordinate with Jolly once he is in place. Find a safe covered location when you are ten minutes out. Notify Jolly and he will coordinate so we can get all to arrive at the warehouse in a similar time window. When Jolly says come Wally and Chip, you both come, so we can make one trip down on the elevator. I have already coordinated with the people in the Archive, and they have moved the elevator to the top in the warehouse and reengaged the locks. They will release them when we get there. One trip down the elevator people, no dawdling in the warehouse."

Chapter 75

"Beware the autumn people." **Ray Bradburry**

Saturday, October 20th, 2018, 8:53 PM Warehouse Entrance to the Archive, Scotland

Three hundred yards away from the Warehouse, Daniel slowed the car on a country lane that led to the area and turned at a ninety-degree angle away from the large building. He traced the perimeter of a farm field, covered in harvested corn stalks that made a crackling sound in the light breeze. Jolly reached forward from his seat in the back and disabled the interior lights of the vehicle, grabbed the large, long black bag beside him, opened the door and rolled from the car, somehow nudging the door softly shut as he fell out.

As Daniel turned the sharp turn to follow the road, and sped up to a normal pace, Laoch peeked over his shoulder to see if Jolly was making it into the woods. To his surprise, there was absolutely no sign of his presence. "That is one spooky bastard," Laoch said under his breath as he and his wife Mimi readied themselves to exit the car at the next covered spot, which was coming up soon.

Daniel peeked up into the rearview at Laoch, "Uncle, you and Mimi take it slow."

"We love you too Daniel," Mimi said, patting him on the shoulder.

"Son," said Laoch, "Try again to reach Kier through the bunny game. He may have gotten the message, but it would be very helpful to know, if he got the..." Laoch paused as he heard howls in the distance. "Never mind, I think he got the message." Laoch reached to key his headset. "People, by the sound outside my window, the pack is out and about. Remember, they know you and you are safe with them... others, not so much."

Laoch and Mimi exited the car, and Daniel quickly pulled away. It was dark except, with only a little over half of the moon lighting their way through a fading cloud layer. The term, "waxing gibbous," came to Laoch's mind as he led Mimi by the hand into the woods beside the road. The first dry leaves of fall descended from the canopy around them like tear drops, shaken loose by the light breeze that rattled through the trees. About five minutes into their estimated 15-minute hike to the warehouse, a shadow grew in front of Laoch near the base of a tree as a large four-legged animal stepped out, a base growl that would terrorize most people, comforted Laoch, as he squatted down and called the large wolf over. It was one of the new broods that was close to two years old, and it immediately calmed and glided over when it heard his voice and caught his scent. After greeting him with a head rub across his chest, it disappeared into the woods to his left with barely a sound. Laoch's work with Kier throughout the years allowed him to know that the animal would stay close unless he called it, and Kier had trained it to pace them through the woods to his left.

"Christ," said Mimi, "That bloody thing is enormous."

"Yeah, and it is still growing." Laoch replied, as he quietly led them forward.

Jolly's voice came through the earphone, notifying everyone through the general channel that he had dipped into the warehouse, found it clear, as well as the streets nearby and was now in a clean, overwatch position.

After only ten more of Laoch's steps, while he was contemplating checking in with Jolly as he was nearing the ten-minute point, the general frequency picked up in his ear.

Snow's voice came through a calm yet edged tone. "So, I think we are about to get stopped." He was riding with Peter in the car, driven by Marcy.

By Snow's description, they were about eight hundred meters to the north of the warehouse, nearing the car drop off location. Jolly could locate them by the reflection of the headlights on the ridge, from his vantage point above, and he could hear both car's engines. Through his scope, he scanned ahead on their line. He saw what he dreaded seeing: a small barn a hundred yards ahead concealed a large official looking Land Rover, or perhaps even two vehicles sitting in a row. His angle made it hard to be certain. They sat along the far side of a barn with lights off and engines idling. The only option Marcy had would be to turn towards the warehouse. That was if they let her get to the turn, to avoid driving in front of the concealed vehicles.

"So," Jolly spoke softly, "I can see your lights on the ridge. Be aware the barn on your right in one hundred meters is concealing one or maybe two large official looking vehicles that appear to be Land Rover SUVs." There was a silent pause, long enough for Snow to relay the information.

The sound of Laoch huffing with effort came through the earphones. "You are going to make that turn. Everyone needs to get to the warehouse now. Stay concealed if you can but MOVE quickly! I need to know how close people are based on your new speed. Tell Marcy to make that turn nice and slow and try to act normal."

"I'll direct," came Jolly's voice, calm and in control. "Chip and Wally, find places to park a couple hundred yards west of the warehouse, in or near the woods. Lights off approach and skirt the trees with your packages on the way in if possible."

Chip notified Bynum and Donna of the new plan, while Wally, who had taken over driving, did the same with William and Nell.

"Chip, two mikes out."

"Wally, two mikes out, taking some undocumented shortcuts."

William looked up into the rearview mirror, catching Wally's eye, "Keep your wits about you lad," William said. "The beast is close. I can feel him."

Wally keyed his microphone. "Shiiit, Laoch, be advised, William has just gone all Key-master of Gozer on me and is saying he can feel the beast is close."

When Marcy reached the road before the barn, she turned right towards the warehouse, as Laoch directed. After covering close to 600 of the 800 yards down the hill, towards the warehouse, the lights and siren of the police vehicle behind her turned on. "Should I stop?"

"Yes dear," came the voice of Gus, as he breathed with obvious exertion. Dino and I are closing in from the east. Yoyo is off to be Yoyo. Just stay calm, you got this," Gus spoke to convince himself as much as her.

As Marcy pulled slowly to the side, two larger vehicles pulled on to the grass on either side of the police car, one plowing through a light wooden fence along the road to do so. Both large vehicles angled in, in front of, and dwarfed the small Nissan Qashqai SUV she was driving.

"They just blocked my view; I have no line. Repositioning." reported Jolly as Snow opened his microphone. A rustling sound came through the microphone as Snow put his communication rig in the seat.

Moments later, they heard the distant sound of a voice with a thick Scottish accent. "Good evening," said the unfamiliar voice. "I'm officer Chatterley, and I need the IDs of everyone in the vehicle. As you see, there are two other vehicles with us. They are assisting in the stops this evening."

"Yes sir," said Marcy. "They informed us about the stops going on. On the dash, you can find the paper that was given to us at a checkpoint not too long ago. Our instructions were to inform anyone who stopped us."

"Oh, perfect," officer Chatterley exclaimed, "that's exactly what I needed. Are there any items in the vehicle that could be dangerous or sharp?

Snow's voice was clear and closer to the microphone. "Yes sir, I work in private security and I am licensed to carry the weapons I have in the car. I'll be glad to supply you with that documentation as soon as I can get to it."

"Excellent," the officer replied. "You, sir, in the front. I need you to open your door and, while keeping hands in plain view, exit the vehicle. Officer Guidry is going to pat you down. If you will please follow his orders. Hopefully, we can get you back on the way momentarily."

The door chime sounding as he opened the door. "Yes, sir," Peter replied, , stepped out, and then closed it with a thump, ending the chime.

"Mam," came the voice of officer Chatterley, "would you do the same?"

Again, the door chimed as Marcy climbed from the car.

Each headset picked up Yoyo's voice clearly as he confirmed, "I'm set, 300 yards east, and I have a clear visual. They've restrained Peter with zip ties and placed him in the west side SUV, away from me. They're also taking Marcy in the same direction. There is someone else in the back of the car besides Peter. The tinted glass is making it difficult to see clearly. They are taking Snow out too," Yoyo echoed the narrative heard through the open microphone. "If they inspect the back of that car, things will turn ugly."

In what seemed like a premonition, Officer Chatterley made his way to the rear of the car, holding the keys. With some fiddling of the fob, he made the trunk pop open a little, as he redirected his focus to the opposite side of the car. They used a similar manner to restrain Snow and placed him in the other large SUV closest to Yoyo. Observing the scene, the sniper described the door closing and heard the thump sound with a slight delay. Observing the grass illuminated by the headlights, the sniper calculated the speed of the north breeze, estimated his distance, and made a small modification to his scope. The unlocked trunk of the car Marcy was driving went unnoticed as the opening door of the vehicle holding Marcy and Peter briefly diverted the officer's attention. While he was reaching for the loose trunk lid, a voice interrupted the officer. Jolly heard a voice amidst the background noises but couldn't understand the words.

The officer nodded briskly, and went back to his cruiser, settled into the driver's seat, and closed the door. Making his way to the left side, Officer Guidry also entered the vehicle.

From the west of the warehouse, walking along the wood line, were Bynum, Donna, Nell, and William. They could see Laoch in front of them. In an awkward manner, he unlocked the warehouse's side door while discreetly holding a pistol in his armpit to have both hands available. From the tree line, Wally watched Laoch and shook his head in disbelief. Moments later, Mimi stepped from the woods into the middle of the group of her family, causing Donna to flinch visibly. Both Wally and Chip were about 30 feet ahead and behind the group. Abandoning the idea of being clever with hiding the vehicles, they both brandished assault rifles.

"Wally, Chip. Packages in position." Wally said quietly

To the east of the traffic stop, Gus carried an HK416, which was very similar in weight to the M16A2 he had in the Gulf War and on his hip, a Baretta 9mm as a sidearm, as he followed Dino. Yoyo had crept south, to the left, as they exited the car.

As they abandoned the vehicle, Dino had smiled a confident smile and handed Gus the rifle. "Stay on my six kid and don't shoot me in the ass!"

"No, no. It's cool. Last time I held one of these, I was a 2nd, Lieutenant." Gus said as Dino flinched and glanced back at him. "Kidding!"

"You hang around with Peter way too fucking much," Dino said.

It was so strange to Gus. Dino had smiled... and it wasn't a fake smile. It was a warrior smile. Unlike the fake bravado Gus had tried on, Dino smiled like a Viking, excited about a chance to see Valhalla.

The two large vehicles and the police car crept forward toward the warehouse. It was at that moment that Jolly's voice came through the radio, "We have more company coming." As at least two, maybe three more cars were driving at breakneck speed across the ridge above with blue, white, and red lights flashing. As the three vehicles with Marcy, Peter, and Snow slowed to a stop 20 yards in front of the warehouse's main entrance, the other cars slid around the corner at the top of the hill. "More on the way, too. Looks like they are about one mike out. Make the call Big Daddy."

Three cars on the hilltop broke through the fence, spreading out 150 yards past the vehicles near the warehouse.

Once Laoch opened the door, Wally swiftly took hold of Mimi's arm and guided her to her husband, instinctually protecting her with his own body. Donna had a similar encounter with Chip, and Nell went through a similar situation with Wally. Only Bynum was present when Chip got back, contrary to the expectation of both Bynum and William. Chip quickly closed the gap and asked, "Where did the old man go?"

Confused, Bynum spun around, "He was right here!"

"Fucking shit!" Chip said and keyed his microphone, "Does anyone have eyes on William? He must have just teleported somewhere. I mean, he was right here 30 seconds ago."

"Find him!" came the voice of Laoch.

Without keying his microphone, Chip grabbed Bynum's arm and led him to the door, mumbling, "No shit, grandpa!" as Wally passed him going the other direction with a purpose.

Chapter 76

"The goat grieves over his life and the butcher over his meat." **Afghan Proverb**

Saturday, October 20th, 2018, 8:53 PM Warehouse Entrance to the Archive, Scotland

The doors of the vehicles, now stopped in front of the warehouse, opened. A helmeted head emerged from each driver's side door of the bigger vehicles. The vehicle carrying Snow opened its rear door, revealing him and another person wearing a military helmet. It was clear that the second person was using Snow as a shield. Stepping out of the other large vehicle were Marcy, Peter, and a third person, who appeared older and on the portly side. That person stayed directly behind Peter. With the people in front emerging, and three vehicles farther up the hill activating their roof-mounted lights, the area became brighter. The bumps in the tall grass of the uneven meadow created odd shadows that coursed in the northern breeze. The drivers of the large vehicles nearer the storeroom, reached into the vehicles and turned on a switch, instantly illuminating the area directly in front of the warehouse as bright as day. Facing them, directly in front of the warehouse, stood William, leaning on his cane. William focused on the portly old man, who seemed to cower behind Marcy and Peter.

"Well, it is about time, you wretched piece of deceitful shit." William said in a voice that carried easily as if projected, as everyone else on each side of the line paused in utter surprise.

Laoch watched helplessly from the corner of the warehouse, along the western side. Tears formed in his eyes, seeing his new granddaughter, his grandson's best friend and an employee who had become family over the last several years, and William all standing there in peril.

His mind flashed back to earlier in the day where he questioned himself. He questioned if he could make the call that was materializing in front of him right now. These good people... People he loved. The fate of their lives rested on his decision to make the call. In his newfound self-awareness, Laoch discovered that there was something that frightened him even more than the creature.

Determined, Scandling brushed past the trembling Marcy, carelessly bumping Peter, with his eyes focused on William. Scandling's face portrayed a mixture of curiosity and amusement as he prepared to speak.

Jolly's calm, flat tone came over Laoch's earpiece. "I have a clear line on Scandling."

Scandling's advance caught Laoch's attention as he lurked in the shadows beside the warehouse. Realizing the magnitude of his responsibility, he concluded nothing was more crucial than exterminating the creature, even if it meant paying a high price. With the cold calculation of a butcher, Laoch condemned Marcy, Peter, William and Snow as acceptable losses. Laoch felt the weight of damnation as he depressed the microphone button and coldly said, "Take him."

The shot from Jolly came with no delay and was impossibly loud. Scantling's head was there one second and deflated balloon the next with a red cloud backlit by the many bright lights behind. The body of Scandling faltered in its stride and fell face first, as if it had a face, to the ground.

In almost the same instant, Snow's face exploded outwards, and his body listed to the left and collapsed.

Laoch threw his back against the side wall of the warehouse and closed his eyes as reports rang out from close and far. When he opened them, the face of Pappy stared into his eyes with a look of pained resolve, and he turned and walked towards William.

An angry wasp flew past Marcy's ear, the military man nearest to Marcy, who had just murdered Snow, swiftly turned, aiming his pistol at her. Before he could pull the trigger, Yoyo's bullet from the northeast collided with the assassin's chest, causing his body to catapult over the car hood and whiz past her like a surreal Saturday morning cartoon scene. Another soldier came around the back side of the other truck as Dino popped up and double-tapped him to the chest. The force of the shots, making him stumble back. Dino, without delay, snapped his rifle up and fired a single shot to the face just below his left eye.

Gus appeared from a shadow and pulled Marcy to the ground, while Peter, who appeared to be looking for a piece of ground tailored for him, stood there just looking. He frantically scanned the ground, searching for a less bloody, less muddy spot, oblivious to the gore already splattered across his clothes and face.

William, with the pageantry of a gentleman walking casually in the park, ignored the frenzy of gunfire landing all around him as he calmly strolled through the chaos, moving forward with the stride of a younger man.

"Are you guys fucking seeing this?" Jolly asked. "What the hell is William doing?"

In the relentless rain of bullets thumping into the vehicles and punching irregular holes in the warehouse, William glanced at Gus and Marcy as streaks of tracer fire flew between them, a fearless smile spreading across his face, as he nodded to them as if it were all some inside joke and continued to stride forward. He pointed at them sprawled on the ground as he walked, his finger trembling slightly with urgency. He gestured sharply towards the open doorway, silently mouthing the word, "Go!" while a fiery determination blazed in his eyes. With a swift motion, he seized the paralyzed Peter, delivering a sharp slap to his face, startling him awake. "Good boy!" said William. He smiled at Peter with a mixture of pity and concern, his eyes conveying a sense of understanding of the poor lad's condition. Without further hesitation, he firmly grasped Peter's lapels, and tugged down and to the side forcefully, propelling him towards the ground near the newly married couple. While pulling Peter out of the way, a bullet grazed the outermost edge of William's coat at the shoulder, causing a fray spot to appear that looked like a large caterpillar.

In the distance, the unmistakable sound of a powerful diesel engine filled the air between the gunshots, its distinct whistle echoing as a massive vehicle descended from the ridge and gained speed downhill.

"Everyone, make for the warehouse, right fucking now." Came the voice of Dino. "Some kind of armored personnel carrier is coming down the hill. The plan now is, run!"

Gus looked over towards William and blinked his eyes, when, for a moment, he saw two men there. William and the impossible figure of Pappy walking in front of him, his features blowing backwards, as if facing a gale of wind. When he blinked again, Pappy was gone, and William was standing over the destroyed body of Harold Emerson Scandling. With no sense of urgency, he bent down leisurely over the body.

"Noooooo!" came the voice of Laoch from the far side of the bullet riddled warehouse and with a slight delay, Gus also heard it over the earphone.

William crouched and plucked up the ancient artifact from the dead man's left hand. The hand of the corpse still grasped the artifact as it tried to keep it, even in death. William tugged it away and deposited it casually in the pocket of his coat, as Scandling's ruined body jumped with the impact of small arms fire. The line of automatic fire that stitched Scandling's body continued off, tearing up chunks from the earth beside William's right foot. William seemed to admire the blooms of dirt caused by the errant shots, as he looked up and to the right as something caught his attention.

A beam of intense light suddenly emanated from the top right side of the enormous armored vehicle coming down the incline. At first, the cone of light moved erratically, casting strange moving shadows that seemed to race up the hill from the southeast and southwest, the beam briefly illuminated the sky, before it settled upon William, like he was about to perform a solo at center stage.

Less than three heartbeats later, another thunderous boom erupted from the roof of the warehouse, dwarfing the other gunfire sounds and the bright light on the APV exploded as sparks flew from where the light had been, like in a Hollywood movie. While the sparks settled, Jolly scurried for cover knowing, the attention that shot would bring to his position.

Dino could not shake the playback in his mind of the shadows running on the hill, as he had seen them again, moving up the hill, cast by the last light emanating from the explosion and sparks. The bullets came in like an angry

381

squall on the North Sea, as Jolly laid as prone as he could behind the air recycling unit on the roof.

Gus got up on his right knee and pulled Peter over in front of the large Land Rover as the rain of bullets intensified from the vehicles stopped back on the ridge behind them.

Gus popped up to a crouch, his heart pounding in his ears, and urgently said to Peter to keep low and make a run for the door, "and don't look back! Just go!" Gus helped Marcy up to a crouch, as bullets fell and chewed the roofline of the warehouse like a hailstorm, while Peter scrambled to the door in a low crouch.

Next, he looked at Marcy, "Ready?" as they crouched in front of the large truck. They watched Peter disappear into the door when suddenly the lights on the grill of the vehicle they took refuge behind, and on the racks above it, turned off and Dino appeared beside them.

"You two go NOW! I'll grab William," Dino spoke with an unnatural calm.

"No," Gus replied. "William has the artifact... I will get him... you get her in there safe!"

There was a moment of silent understanding between Dino and Gus as they locked eyes. Dino blinked, recognizing the warrior spirit in Gus. He nodded, affirming, "Keep your head down and move fast!"

Over the earpiece, everyone heard Yoyo as he said, "Seriously, are you guys seeing this? The old man is walking through live fire like fucking C3PO. Someone, grab his ass!"

"Gus is going to go reel him in." Dino answered. "No one else touch William, he has... IT! The artifact."

Yoyo voice crackled over the radio almost apologetically. "Guys, let me know when everyone is in the warehouse. I'm going to disable all the vehicles I can, cover your ex-fill as much as possible, while keeping their heads down. The moment you guys are in, I'm going dark. I'll be in touch... later... and good luck..." Moments later, Yoyo re-keyed the microphone, "What the hell is that?"

The number of bullets seemed to ebb some as the sound of howls seemed to come from multiple directions. The shots still were coming, but the reports were sporadic and had lost focus and direction.

Jolly checked in, "I'm making for the warehouse. I'll be inside in forty-five seconds."

"Good to hear your voice, Jolly," Yoyo said. "Nice shot on the light."

With the exertion of motion in his voice, Jolly chuckled, "Saw that, huh? My fan club noticed it too, apparently."

Once William had retrieved the item, he turned and casually walked back towards the warehouse, with the urgency of someone retrieving the morning paper. Gus stood and pulled William in front of the Land Rover as he passed and looked towards the warehouse just in time to see Dino and Marcy disappear in the doorway.

The large, armored vehicle was getting worryingly close by the sound of it and the shaking of the ground.

"Yoyo?" Gus asked. "How close is the big thing?"

"You have time if you go now," he replied. "But this should get their attention, too."

The shot Yoyo took had a zero chance at penetration, but he knew it would make the driver piss himself when a circular fracture appeared beside his head. He also knew it would keep anyone they had onboard in the vehicle for a couple of extra seconds. The shot flew true and had an immediate effect as the armored urban assault vehicle turned its nose towards him before it came to a stop as Gus and William entered the warehouse.

When Gus entered, he pulled William to the side, behind the heavy steel girder that formed a ribcage like support for the building. William reached into his pocket and grabbed the artifact and handed it to Gus with eyes clouded with what appeared to be grief. "I'm sorry to make you take this," William said, "but he wants you to have this less than you do."

When Gus touched the metal, it seemed to crackle with electricity. Despite feeling a powerful urge, he resisted the temptation to peer into the hole like countless others had done before him. With a quick motion, he tucked it into the pocket of his cargo pants and secured it by buttoning the pocket.

Leading William towards the large industrial elevator, he placed a comforting arm around him, and they ventured through the scattered beams of light that penetrated the metal walls. Donna was lying motionless on the floor of the elevator, her body sprawled out. As Chip applied CPR, the surrounding pool silently testified to the futility of his efforts. When he and William stepped on, the entire floor descended, as the duplicate of the space they stood on dropped to cover the hole.

Outside, final shots were being fired towards the bullet riddled warehouse. One innocuously vile shot skipped off the sidewalk outside, tumbled through the thin metal wall, ricocheted off a forklift, which bled off much of its speed... and hit Bynum behind the left ear as the elevator dropped below floor level. He had been leaning over, watching the lifesaving attempts on house managing partner and lifelong lover, Donna. Before his brain could register or react to the approaching "Vvvvp" sound, the final thing he heard, he dropped to the floor, lifeless. Minutes passed as they treated him for a heart attack until someone noticed the small amount of blood in his hair behind his ear.

William heard the Reaper's voice too as it came for Bynum, and the sound made him think of his dear friend Tom, dead nearly 80 years now. He had heard Grimm back during the war many times, but the reaper had never come for him, and he wondered why.

On the hill outside, a whistle no human could hear, recalled the wolves that had disrupted the men on the hill. They had appeared like a wave of shadows, knocking some people to the ground before evaporating back into the darkness. One bite wound required a medical evacuation, but the victim would likely live. The other three had raised weapons while spinning to see the commotion, only to have an arm clamped on to by an animal they didn't see until too late. The bites, while savage, were a controlled response to a threat. As the pack cleared the area, the animals let go and broke to catch up with their family. The three less serious bites were deep, but superficial wounds to a forearm, elbow, and shoulder, respectively.

Future inquiries would record that, "The damage was not as traumatic as what any of them had expected." And "Each task force member who encountered the wolves expressed they thought they were going to die." They each credited their equipment, training, and luck for their survival.

Early reports from the police showed that some had thought herd animals that the gunfire had frightened stampeded them. Those individuals estimated the "herd" that attacked to be from, "... at least a hundred" to, "... fifty or more" when the number of animals was seven-teen.

Some detail members declared they were mastiffs because of their size, while others described what they thought were feral pigs. Only one person had seen one of them clearly enough for certainty, and she insisted they were wolves. At first, others laughed at her, but she insisted with conviction, and her certainty changed the group's opinion. When others disagreed, she asked them if they also heard the howls on the recordings just before the attacks, showed them the pictures gathered later of the large canine prints, and the debate stopped. So, the others guessed it was a wolf hybrid... probably with a mastiff.

Chapter 77

"I'll huff, and I'll puff..." **Joseph Jacobs**

Saturday, October 20th, 2018, 9:21 PM The Archive, Scotland

Once the elevator arrived on the ground floor, security measures immediately reengaged, securing the lift. Anyone trying to use the mechanisms while locked would find the effort futile, because they had physically jammed the mechanism, preventing any kind of operation. Every time the elevator descended, steel doors would block any access to the shaft, completely sealing it off at multiple levels. Because these doors were integral to the lift mechanism, someone would need a cutting torch and considerable time to unlock them.

As he looked on, Gus watched members of the engineering team use a six-pound sledgehammer for delicately tapping the color coded, fabricated steel wedges into the elevator's mechanisms. After the engineering crew was done, they placed their equipment in the closet and departed. Gus lingered. After the room cleared, he requested Dino to monitor the door while he shut it.

He took out the artifact from his pocket, feeling the tingling sensation of contact and the urge to look at the open end, yet he resisted once again. Holding the sledgehammer, he cautiously laid the artifact on the stone floor. As he set it down, he heard a doubtful thought that passed through his mind that he dismissed as self-doubt. "Cute," came the voice, "but that will not do it."

He cleared his mind of the wayward thought and, with every ounce of his being; he lined up his shot, swinging the hammer through the air with incredible force. With the powerful swing, he struck the golden scepter, creating a resounding "thwock" that reverberated through the room. The artifact went skittering across the floor, spinning wildly like a bottle at a rowdy teenage basement party.

Gus walked over to it, hoping to admire his handiwork, but disappointment waited for him. There was nothing to see. Using his foot, he gave it a gentle push to the other side, but there was no sign of damage. "Hmmm," he thought, as he furrowed his brow, "I must have missed it." Determined, he nudged it into the recently chipped depression on the stone floor and gave it another shot. After 27 unsuccessful attempts to even make a scuff mark on the object, he finally gave up in frustration. He looked at the damage he had done to the floor and shook his head. The absence of any mark on the metal caused him to sigh and return it to his pocket. As he stepped from the room, he glanced at Dino and muttered, "The sledge didn't even make a dent in it."

As he left the elevator's mechanical room, Gus saw the blood covered floor of the elevator. The vein attempts to save the lives of the two members of the family; family in all ways except blood, had gone on for ten minutes beyond what was reasonable. Now they laid there, with their upper bodies covered with discarded jackets. Mimi sat on the floor beside them, ignoring the gore, with her face in her hands as Marcy hugged her shoulder, apologizing for being caught.

A hundred and fifty odd feet above his head, the police were diligently searching the warehouse and the surrounding land. Laoch closely monitored their every move on the security cameras, observing as they entered and eventually exited through the back door. Gus entered the conference table area of the Cathedral room.

In a way, they had won. However, Gus could not reconcile that this should be what winning should feel like. To him, it sure felt a lot like losing, and they had never discussed what they would do if they got to this point. How they would destroy this artifact, that took a beating with a six-pound sledge like he had lovingly caressed it with a rose petal.

Laoch watched the large flat screen television from the conference room table. The searchers above had traveled about 50 feet through the woods behind the warehouse until they reached the precipice overlooking the deep valley below. Given the steepness of the area, it would be evident that attempting to traverse it at a fast pace, in the dark, would be unfeasible, making it an improbable escape route. It would be immediately clear to the police and government investigators that they hadn't fled in that direction. Gus approached the table and pulled out a chair, joining his grandfather. Their gazes met briefly as he settled in his seat.

Laoch gestured towards the large flat screen. "Only five of the nine warehouse security cameras are operational." The screen displayed one main window and eight smaller ones below. However, four of the smaller windows displayed nothing but static. "I guess bullets or other damage," he mumbled, recalling the chaotic moment a few minutes ago, when the large, armored personnel carrier crashed through the office wall. "They drove the beast through the bloody wall, and it got stuck between two beams of the building. It's wedged so tightly that they can't open the front doors. If they tried to back it out now... if they even could get the needed traction, it would jeopardize the integrity of the entire structure," spoke Laoch with a sad yet whimsical look. With his fists tightly balled, he hit the tabletop. He declared, "It's all falling apart, son. The warehouse is like some twisted analogy to this situation we are in!"

Gus noticed how his knuckles were a stark white against the flushed redness of his neck and face.

They both sat there for a full minute while Laoch's breathing calmed. He turned to Gus in his black office chair, "I hear you have it."

"I do," Gus said simply. "I tried a minute ago to see what a sledgehammer would do to it. And it did nothing. It didn't even scuff it."

Laoch looked Gus in the eyes. "You need to get photos of it for the archive and immediately after, you need to go. Destroy that fucking cursed thing. Kill that fucker and end this family's responsibility. I need to protect the workers down here and the survivors from upstairs by defusing this situation. We are about three hours from something terrible happening and the clock is ticking. The current situation here is untenable. We have dead bodies lying on the floor of the elevator. The workers here didn't sign up for this. Even before we descended in the elevator with the dead bodies of Donna and Bynum, the workers, cloistered here, were getting restless. They are seeing the news reports too and are rightfully worried about their own families and livelihoods. The way I see it; we have a brief period where we can get you out of here and uncork this bottle before it explodes and more people get hurt." Laoch spoke as he pointed at the ceiling, "Eventually they will breach the archive... once they find it. Forensics will eventually lead them along a blood trail that ends with a clean floor that conceals the elevator shaft."

"Alright, where am I going to go?" asked Gus.

"That's just it my boy," said Laoch, "I don't want to know. Dino will go with you, but that is just to help you get clear of here and out of the country. He said he will tell you some rules and review common mistakes with you. After that, you will need to figure it out. In the weeks you have been here, we had someone make a second set of identity papers that should pass muster most anywhere. I have those, and their associated credit cards, which you should never use if possible. I have a belt with money, mostly American dollars, English pounds and some Euros... quite a bit, if you were to add them all together, but not inexhaustible. We can communicate through the game, assuming we are not all in prison after tonight," Laoch said with an awkward, stressed laugh.

"With all the police and the news coverage?" Gus asked. "How will we get out of here? The chapel entrance is right over there, what 50 feet that way? I mean, that is basically the same footprint of the center of their search above us."

"There is another way out of here," Laoch said. "I used to play in there as a kid, but it is a tight fit and very unpleasant, so you will travel very light. As you have only the clothes on your back and whatever you can find in a locker or lost and found anyway, that should not be a big issue. Dino can advise you way better than I can on what you need to know. I will hold out here until you are ready to exit from the small cave and I will get their attention on me... well, us, while you slip away. I'm so very sorry to put this on you, son." Laoch's mind briefly drifted back to the night Gus was born, when the clouds seemed to talk to him. "Have you ever gone spelunking before?"

"Um, I have heard of it. Are you freaking kidding me?" Gus asked incredulously.

"Most of the cavern is very uneven and involves either walking through water or climbing over boulders, but it is walkable; but the last 30 meters are... special. It will involve either pushing any packs ahead of you or pulling them behind you. Normally you can use flashlights, but you won't be able to use them much today, as any light might give you away. Dino suggests glow sticks and NVG's. I also have pictures and a video you can watch from when we were surveying it."

"You will take care of Marcy." Gus stated.

"The family will. I assure you." Laoch said with an earnest stare, "I will probably be quite busy or incarcerated, as I'm going to take the responsibility for tonight," as a sad smile crossed his face. "Don't worry, I have a plan to say that security forces acted under my standing orders to defend the family. The police had not identified themselves before the gunfire started. I have already spoken to the lawyers briefly about all of this. The Scandling shooting was close to simultaneous on the video with the execution of Snow."

Laoch stood and walked around the table and grasped his grandson by each shoulder. He dipped his head a little to look eye to eye with him. "I deeply apologize for the unfortunate turn of events that has marred your special day. Go see Marcy now. Please extend my sincere apologies to her as well. Pack your things and use the time wisely. Take a moment to explain the plan and gather her input. While you do that, I'm going to address the staff down here and calm their fears. Our lawyers are already working to help ensure a safe and peaceful resolution, when we are ready, and you are away."

Gus hugged his grandfather and quietly left the conference area. As he walked towards the back, Marcy met him, handing him a cup of coffee. In that moment, Gus locked eyes with Marcy and saw an unmistakable expression of sorrow. He instinctively took his coffee and wrapped his offhand around her and asked softly, "Marcy, are you okay?"

Despite her brave smile, her eyes betrayed her true feelings as she assured him, she was. Gus saw it and mentally noted it as a topic to discuss later in private.

"We need to talk," he told her. His words hung heavy in the air. Again, sensing Marcy was at the edge of tears. For some level of privacy, Gus and Marcy ducked into the London room lock area. As the outer door of the lock that separated the hallway from the artifact storage area closed, Marcy melted.

"I should never have stopped when I did," she said, her tone dark. "It is all my fault that Snow, Bynum, and Donna died. I should have delayed my stop and given Bynum and Donna a chance to get to safety." Marcy said as large tears rolled down her face.

Gus shook his head. "That was not you, dear," his tone filled with reassurance. "You did everything you could reasonably do. You had to stop, or those larger vehicles would have stopped you and things would have been worse. Plus, the bullet that hit Donna came through the wall of the warehouse with no one even aiming it at her. Someone shot Bynum while he was on the elevator platform. We were incredibly lucky that more of us were not injured or killed."

"Yeah, but if I didn't turn towards the warehouse, everyone else would have been okay." Marcy appealed.

"No dear," Gus kindly corrected her, "it was our call for you to turn there," his voice filled with patience.

For a moment, Gus held her tightly, feeling her body relax against his shoulder. A thought occurred to him, "What happened when you entered the other vehicle?"

"Other vehicle?" Marcy replied.

"When they removed you from your car," Gus answered.

"Oh, they tied my hands and put me in the big truck thing," Marcy said. "I sat in there for a minute, and they pulled forward towards the warehouse. It was like they knew we were trying to get there. It was probably my fault for turning that way. Poor Donna, did you see the look on her face? She kept trying to say something to me... She was staring right into my eyes, trying to say something."

"Sweetheart," Gus said. "She was gone almost immediately. If you saw anything, it was involuntary muscle spasms."

Gus paused; something was different. He had seen in Iraq how battle changed people and the violence he saw there had changed him. "Babydoll," Gus said with a firm even tone, trying not to allow his own emotions to drive her further down the damaging path she was on. "What happened when Peter got put in the car?"

"Peter?" Marcy said. "Honestly, I didn't even notice him getting in the car. I think I was looking out the far window. I honestly don't remember him getting in the car... although I remember him when we left the car, so yeah... he was in there. We were only in there a minute or two. I was afraid we were being arrested."

Gus felt something was off. He was not sure it was the trauma or if there was something else, but there was no real time to get into it.

So, he changed the subject. "Love, the man you were in the vehicle with was the man who had the artifact... Scandling. During the chaos that unfolded in front of the warehouse, someone took his life and somehow William retrieved the cursed thing and gave it to me. I have spoken to my grandfather, and I must figure out a way to destroy it before..." he paused, looking for the right words. "Before they blast their way into this place, arrest us all, and take it away from us." He lowered his head to look directly into her eyes. "I have to go before they figure out where we went. That is why I needed to speak to you."

"You are leaving me? Here?" Marcy asked with a panicked sob.

"Grandfather is going to protect you," Gus said, "while I find a way to destroy the creature. He assured me he would protect you at all costs. At this moment, he is having a conversation with his lawyers. His plan is to deescalate the situation outside and submit to the police before it becomes more violent. Right now, he is planning that path. Before that can occur, I must go. After I finish the task and kill the creature, I will return. I promise. Peter will also be here with you, and he would rather die than let anything happen to you." Gus instantly regretted his choice of words.

"Why can't I come with you?" Marcy said.

"Because I need to disappear, and that is exponentially harder with two people." Gus explained. "Dino will accompany me for a while, but eventually, I'll be on my own. We will have the game where we can talk, and I will write you regularly on there. My dear, I love you dearly and I will be back. I promise."

Marcy stared into his eyes, and he into hers. There was something unusual that Gus noticed in her eyes. He noticed a deep well of sadness in them, but there was something else he couldn't identify.

In his eyes, Marcy could only see distrust, and it broke her heart.

She replied with a simple "Okay. I understand." In her mind, the words with all the rich meanings and intents the words could carry, she meant them. Intents that Gus did not and could not comprehend.

Sitting in the room holding his bride, Gus spotted a warm forest green fleece pullover and rose to check its size. "Adult Large," on the tag, and Gus tucked it under his arm. "I think I'm going to borrow this from whomever left it here."

Peering through the changing room window, Gus caught sight of Peter, who was standing in an indentation in the stone hallway, scrutinizing the people passing by. He observed each passerby with a dissecting gaze reminiscent of a trap-door spider. The corners of his mouth curled into a smirk of dissatisfaction, as if he had caught a faint whiff of something disagreeable. Gus went to the door and called for Peter, who shifted uncomfortably and seemed taken aback by the sudden attention. As soon as Peter saw his old friend, his face underwent a rapid change, breaking into a wide, carefree smile. The smile on Peter's face seemed oddly juxtaposed with the weight of the events that had transpired over the past few hours as he made his way towards the door leading to the cramped changing area of the London archive.

Gus embraced his lifelong friend in a quick hug. "Hey," his voice filled with warmth. "I need your help. I'm getting ready to leave here and won't be back until I complete my job. My Grandfather asked me to destroy the artifact and kill the fucker inside it." Gus finished.

"Okay Frodo, so what is the plan?" Peter said with a wry smile.

"Holy Shit!" Gus laughed. "Well, it includes you as Samwise. Doesn't it?"

"Right, so you are off to Mordor, to toss this asshole into a volcano, huh?"

"Well, maybe... last resort. Yeah, maybe." Gus admitted. "I hit the fucker with a sledgehammer about 30 times and it didn't even scuff it."

"Really? Let me see it. Can I look at it?"

"No!" said Gus, "It is far too dangerous."

"Too dangerous to look at???" Peter said. "I mean it is right there in your pocket, right" he said, pointing and reaching towards Gus's pocket.

Gus jumped back and parried Peter's half effort reach. "Hey, totally not funny!" Gus flashed.

Peter took on a spider like pose momentarily. "I musts haves the Precious!" and stood and smiled, while Marcy barely seemed to notice. He looked at Marcy, "Tough crowd!"

Marcy rose and kissed Gus on the cheek. As she left the room as she said, "I need to find something to eat. My stomach feels weird... sorry."

"I'll find you before I go, Marcy," Gus said as she left.

Gus closed the door and looked at his old friend sincerely. "She is a total wreck right now. I really, really need you to keep a close eye on her for me. I'm worried about her. She thinks the whole thing up top was her fault."

"Yeah, I saw the look in her eye," Peter said, "I mean obviously, I will do anything you ask, but women... women are like that sometimes... right?"

Gus snorted, "Man, I'm so glad she left the room, or she would have slapped the taste out of your mouth. Your mom, wherever she is, would have felt that slap." As Gus laughed, Peter's reaction was noticeably different. A faint chill seemed to surround him as he pondered Gus's words. It lasted only a moment, before Peter seemed to relax, superficially engaging a smile, like a child manufacturing a Halloween mask, before reacting to Gus's joke. Peter's late smile sparked concern in Gus, but most of that burned away when his friend looked at him. Gus thought to himself, "Peter has been through a trauma too... and for that matter, so have I. Maybe this is just me overreacting." Gus did his best to just let it go, and move forward.

Peter, as if sensing the heightened tension in Gus, leaned in. "I'll take care of her for you, if you need, brother. You know I will."

"Thanks," said Gus. "Oh, one other thing. What happened when they took you out of the car and put you in the other car with that Scandling guy?"

"Well, it was a blur. For a couple of seconds, I thought we were dead, to be honest." Peter said. "It was like some kind of calmness came over me. In situations like that, it's as if you never truly know who you are until you face them. If you had asked me yesterday about it, I would have guessed I would have been in a puddle, begging not to die. Oddly, I think in that car I understood myself finally. When they took us out of the car, near the warehouse, I knew I was still alive and energized by a strange sense of self-realization. Even when I was wearing Scandling's brains all over my face and I felt the shockwave of the bullet that caused the rain of his brains and teeth, I felt alive and excited. I think I got carried away with the elation of being alive until William tossed me on the ground like Raggedy Andy. Is he alive? Damn, he is stronger than he looks! Did he make the elevator?"

"He is alive," Gus said. "The guy walked nonchalantly through a rainstorm of bullets somehow without getting touched. Over the radio, Yoyo jokingly remarked about his resemblance to C3PO as he waddled his way through the firefight without a care in the world. It was just like that."

Gus checked the time on his phone. "Shit!" he said. "I have to run and gather a couple of things. Keep her... and you! Safe."

"I will Gus." Peter said, "Now go save the world."

Part 4 – The Fall

Interlude - Perthshire

Monday, October 22nd, 2018, 9:00 PM

Thank you for watching BBC One. In Perthshire, the search continues for the focus of a joint U.S. and British Task Force. You may remember Saturday night reports of a dramatic and failed attempt by the team to detain Laoch Kier Ferguson, the Fifth, in a traffic stop in a region near his grandfather's estate.

During the apprehension attempt, reports surfaced of a shootout with a level of violence unseen on the British Isles since the 1970s unrest in Northern Ireland. The U.S. and British Task Force's crossfire tragically killed three employees on the fugitive's family estate. Also killed were four members of the Police Service of Scotland, and a prominent United States political advisor, recently assigned by the American government to head up efforts to apprehend Ferguson. The gun battle also resulted in seven more police officers being injured, aside from those killed. American suspicions of racketeering and murder against Ferguson and his Scottish family surfaced in previously sealed documents. Reports surfaced that the United States government was working to suspend the family's bank accounts.

The battle, which roused nearby residents and sent them scrambling for cover as thousands of bullets flew, immediately followed. The family's patriarch, Laoch Kier Ferguson, the Third, surrendered to police in a highly orchestrated and public appeal for calmer heads. We know little about the next eight hours except that the family cooperated with the investigation, and surprisingly, police released the patriarch a few hours after processing. Even more confusing was a complete lack of charges against him personally.

The target of the joint effort, the patriarch's grandson, is still the focus of an enormous search area that includes virtually all of Europe. As you see on the screen, the task force has released several photos of Laoch Kier "Gus" Ferguson. The squad describes him as a strongly built man in his mid to late thirties, who stands six feet and one inch, and weighs between fourteen and fifteen stones. He has reddish-brown hair, blue eyes, and was last seen in the Perthshire region.

If you see Ferguson, please call the task force hotline below and report it. The group's representative emphasized no one should approach or confront Ferguson under any circumstances, as he is armed and extremely dangerous.

Stay tuned to BBC One for details in this highly unusual case. You can also follow us and this story as it unfolds on the web.

Chapter 1

"Oh, won't you
Gimme three steps, gimme three steps, mister
Gimme three steps towards the door?
Gimme three steps, gimme three steps, mister
And you'll never see me no more

Show me the back door" - **Allen Collins / Ronnie Van Zant**

Saturday, October 20th, 2018, 10:30 PM The Archive, Scotland

With just a small assortment of essential supplies, consisting primarily of a single bottle of water and a handful of granola bars, Gus and Dino followed Laoch as he led them back to the very room where he had previously tried to obliterate the artifact by pounding it with a sledgehammer. As Laoch observed the floor with its pitted surface and the scattered chips of stone, he couldn't help but shake his head.

Gus and Dino both had backpacks slung over their shoulders. Dino's bag seemed fuller than Gus's. Dino glanced at him and suggested, "Before we do anything else, let's examine what you've got." Gus carefully emptied his pack onto a clean section of the floor, avoiding the scattered debris of rocks and dust.

Gus packed his bag with two t-shirts, a pullover fleece, an extra pair of underwear, shorts, a bottle of water, Band Aid like bandages in a Ziplock bag, eight snack bars, a Leatherman tool, his custom phone from his grandfather, and a black disposable rain poncho.

Dino's critical gaze swept over it, and a small smile crept onto his face as he nodded and declared, "Not bad."

Dino dumped out his bag. His pack contained a list of basic items that were almost the same, but with some extra duplicates in Ziplocks that he shared with Gus. Dino narrated the additional bags. "Carefully packed in this bag is a two-ounce bottle of povidone iodine, an essential item for any first aid kit. Besides its effectiveness on cuts and wounds, this stuff can also purify water with just a few drops. The bag also contains 50 alcohol pads for disinfection. These things are also great! Everything from scratches to lighting a fire in stubborn environments. Everything here is warmth or water. You can go without food for a while. It sucks, but water and warmth are what we need, baby. Water and warmth. In that light, in the next baggie, wrapped up in that loverly toilet paper, and no, that is not for your ass. In that paper is a nine-volt battery. You can use a small piece of that TP to help start a fire. Warmth baby! In addition, there is a small jar of petroleum jelly. There are countless possibilities for using that. Fire is just one...

cuts and blister treatment etc. Inside the final small baggie, you'll find steel wool and extra TP. If you use the TP on your ass, I will use the steel wool. Here is a small four-ounce bottle of hydrogen peroxide. If you mix it with iodine on wounds, you'll end up regretting it. Also, I have a normal disposable lighter and four, one gallon, Ziplock bags for who knows what. If you are crossing deep water, you can protect stuff with two bags and blow two up and put them in the pack to make a float bundle. Two more things." Dino said with a smile. "Some nice person donated you their day-old socks. Always carry an extra pair of socks. Wash the ones you wore as often as possible." The very last thing he gave Gus was a flashlight.

Dino pushed the pile towards him, and Gus packed them in his bag.

After that, Laoch drew their attention to the closet. He cleared the tools from the closet and reached down and grabbed an old nail off the floor. To the back left of the space was a small nail sized hole in the wall about waist high. It wasn't the only hole of similar size, but it was the only one that, when Laoch forcefully inserted the nail, triggered the spring release that allowed the entire left side of the wall to come loose, making the entire back wall removable.

Removing the back wall exposed a hidden space between the manufactured wall and the ancient cave's natural imperfections. Despite being narrow, they navigated the walkway made of weathered wooden planks around the elevator's control room, until they arrived at a more significant gap in the wall.

Gus's grandfather stepped past the fissure and turned to them, "This is where I leave you. You have watched the videos. Take your time and be careful." From a bag, Laoch produced two pairs of night vision goggles and a plastic bag full of light sticks. "Be careful!" he reiterated. "Traversing this cave can break ankles easily. Even the water has rocks at angles and deep spots. When you get to the other end, remember, temps outside are near freezing and might get below later."

"How deep is the water would you guess?" asked Dino.

"Knee, maybe higher in spots." Laoch said.

"Did you ever break any bottles or anything in it?"

"No!" Laoch said incredulously, almost like he was answering his own father.

"Good," said Gus. "When we get there, we will put our pants and socks in your bag and tie your shoes together so we can keep stuff dry. How far do we have to cover in the water? Seemed like about 50 feet in the video?"

"That is my memory, yes," said Laoch.

"Let's do this!" Dino said.

"Ok, let's do it!" Gus agreed.

Laoch hugged his grandson, "God's speed, my boy."

"Yes sir. We will let you know when we are in position to leave the cavern... as we discussed." Gus said.

With that, the long, careful walk began.

Chapter 2

Sunday, October 21st, 2018, 12:41 AM The Archive, Scotland

With Dino leading the way, they pushed their backpacks through a narrow hole in the cavern and emerged into a wider space. As they turned a corner, a dark spot, suddenly glowing in their NVGs, mesmerized them. Countless stars seemed to have huddled around the hole that was their exit from the cavern, beckoning them forward. The stars, visible through the NVGs, cast a luminous, green glow marking the end of their subterranean journey.

Slowly, Dino cautiously poked his head out of the hole, taking in his surroundings. "Well, kid, get ready for a bit of an uphill adventure. The climb is not too technical, but I think you shouldn't notify your grand-pops until we see we can go somewhere, which means about 20 feet of a climb. You're familiar with the three-points rule, right?"

"I used to do free climbing," Gus said, "and received some training in the Army."

"Cool," said Dino. "Climbing with NVGs is a novel experience, and without them, it's pitch black out there. The saying goes, "seeing is believing," but it's not until you touch something that you truly trust it. You don't put your entire weight on something until you test it. Got it? I don't want to climb down, set your leg, and have to carry your ass out of here. Feel me?"

"Oh, shit." Gus exclaimed.

"What?" Dino said as he turned towards him.

"I think I left the evil world ending monster in my other pair of pants, back at the Archive." Gus said, holding both hands up in an "oops" look.

"Fuck you!" Dino said with a smile that showed below his goggles. "You are lucky I don't just toss you out this hole for trying to make me believe that shit!" he said as he shook his head and smiled, and looked back at Gus and loudly whispered, one last time, "Fuck you! That is a damn Peter joke!"

As Gus slowly made his way to the opening, Dino skillfully scurried up the rocks, the sound of his movements echoing in the quiet surroundings. Moments later, Gus peered out. Dino vanished, having successfully made the climb to the top, surveyed the views, and ascended the hill above the cliff face.

Gus cautiously ascended to the top in just a few minutes. Dino's large black hand extended to assist him up the final few feet. Settling under a large oak 20 feet away, Gus used the game to contact his grandfather.

FuzzyWabbit24: Yawn! I'm leaving my hole to go play with TyrannoRabbit. I hope it is a nice day!

A few seconds later, came the note from his grandfather.

SternEars: Good morning FW24. It is clear and sunny today here. But I hear there might be storms soon. So, stay low and keep your ears to the ground and be safe. Storm will be starting here in one hour, I hear from SolicitorDuck.

Gus looked at Dino. "Shit is hitting the fan in about one hour. We need to make some tracks." Gus turned the brightness on his phone to the lowest setting, cursing himself for not thinking of it when they were underground.

"Are you good?" asked Dino. "I have seen you run. What is your normal distance?"

"I'm feeling fine, I usually run about five miles, but can stretch to maybe seven or ten if I had to."

"Ok, cool, we are going to get some distance before sunrise, and it will probably help us keep warm. If you get sweaty, or if I do, we will walk until we cool off. We will stay near tree cover as much as possible, and when we see dawn, we will get into some wild area, if we can, and hunker down for a rest," Dino said as he stretched his hamstrings.

Gus noted his stretching and performed his own stretching routine as well. When they were both ready, they moved at a comfortable pace along an ancient dirt road.

Crossing the River Dee just west of Braemar, their phones' GPS showed they had moved southwest as they intended. The sparse lights of the town were visible from afar. From there, they headed straight south until they reached the hilly, forested region, where their pace slowed as they continued in a southwestern direction. Following a few additional miles, they arrived at a cultivated and well-groomed forest. All the trees in the rows were of similar age and size. While walking through the trees, they discovered a dilapidated cottage that was mostly in ruins, just as the eastern sky brightened. The roof showed signs of deterioration, with sagging areas and noticeable gaps. However, one room escaped the damage and remained mostly intact. The place seemed frozen in time, abandoned and untouched by the outside world. Despite being neatly made, the bed had patches of moss and indications of wildlife living in the bedding. By careful testing, Dino determined that the floor comprised tiles placed on top of packed earth. He began gently exploring the chest of drawers, hoping to find something beneficial. In a single, spacious drawer, he discovered a weighty blanket tucked away in an old, zippered bag made of plastic. The zipper fell apart when he pulled it back, but the dark green blanket was still intact.

"Here," Dino said. "Wrap up in this and get comfortable. I'll take first watch. You good with no fire?"

"Sounds good," Gus said, as he found a comfortable spot, placed his pack under his head, and drifted off to sleep.

After a few hours, a shoulder shake, gently awakened Gus, pulling him out of a nightmare of a world consumed by fire and a triumphant blue-skinned demon dancing. Gus felt the familiar bulge of the artifact in his pocket when he touched it. He handed the blanket to Dino.

"What time do you want me to wake you up?" Gus asked.

"It's roughly 11:00AM right now," Dino said. "So, give me to until 1500 or 1600. If you see anyone or anything that makes you tingly, wake me up."

Dino nestled into the cozy spot that Gus had warmed up and soon drifted off to sleep. Meanwhile, Gus surveyed the ruins, the milky sunlight casting eerie shadows, before retrieving his phone from his bag and searching for a signal. There was none, much as he expected.

Gus searched the area that was once the kitchen and found remnants of a sink, now rusted and overgrown with vines. In an unexpected twist, Gus struck gold in a collapsed corner. Despite the destruction, he found an unbroken bottle nestled inside a broken wooden case, defying the surrounding chaos. Despite the weather damage, the label on the bottle was legible enough to make out the word "Macallan," and upon closer inspection, he could also clearly see the number "17." Setting it down gently on the ground in Dino's sleeping area, he pressed on with his search.

Over the next couple of hours, Gus explored the house, finding intriguing relics while the sky outside turned from sunny, to gloomy overcast, to a deluge of rain. It was a stroke of luck that they discovered a dry spot amidst the ruin, as the rest of the house resembled a picturesque scene from a post-apocalyptic world, with waterfalls flowing in every direction.

This sight transported him back to a distant memory of a trip to Orlando with his mother when he was in middle school. His mother took him to The Rainforest Cafe. Although the food was mediocre and the atmosphere cheesy, he adored the place for its rain sound effects and jungle ambiance that ignited his imagination. "God, I miss you mom," he whispered.

In a couple of hours, Gus improvised a solution to a broken table by using a stack of deteriorating books as a replacement leg. In that same chest of drawers, Gus stumbled upon a yellowed but spotless sheet, likely white at one point. He came across a box of candles and set them aside because of their worth. Inside the old cupboard were two usable earthenware plates and, in the rear, a set of delicate bone-china teacups, all of which he carefully washed. When it was time to wake Dino up, a chair made of old books and a bucket served as seating.

Gus carefully nudged Dino, who went from full sleep to aware between heartbeats. The seamless transition to alertness amazed Gus. There was no blinking the sleep out of his eyes or yawn, just awareness where there had been none a moment before.

"Are we good?" Dino whispered.

"Yup, all good," Gus replied as he offered his companion a hand up.

Dino stood and saw the table set and glanced at Gus with a flicker of amusement. "Are we going on a date?" Dino asked with a chuckle.

Gus nudged the bottle of Macallan into view with his foot and tilted his head towards Dino in a conspiratorial look.

"Holy Shit!" Dino said with recognition. "Do you know how much that bottle of hooch is probably worth?"

"I know it's worth taking with us, and worth us drinking when we need a nip along the way." Gus replied.

Dino looked at the set table with the earthenware plates and bone-china cups. Each plate held a still packaged granola bar. "Shit, you went all domesticated and made us a three-course meal. Thanks, honey," Dino said. "This beats the shit out of walking through that shitty rain outside. I say we eat and see what happens with the weather."

"And to hell with the value of this bottle," Gus said towards the bottle now in his hand. "Let's see if it is still any good."

So, they sat, ate their meal slowly, and sipped on the Scotch Whisky from the bottle with the red top. The faded label on the bottle's top, bearing the words "Distilled 1941," was difficult to make out because of its tattered state. Smooth and chocolate like, the 79-year-old whisky had a pleasant burn.

As Gus was getting ready to pack the still full bottle, Dino halted him. "Wait a second," he said in a calm and sincere tone. "We've both lost people close to us." He stood and looked around the small cottage. Gus, anticipating his need, pointed him towards the cupboard and Dino dodged the falling rainwater getting there.

On the top shelf, behind a collapsed piece of wood, was a Christmas themed cup. The cup featured a hand painted Christmas tree that seemed to be from an ancient era, with its simplicity and imperfections. A mother, father, and son sat near a fire. A snow cap like edge encircled the top of the cup. Using the water from the roof, Dino washed off the dirt from the cup, cleaning it. The scene unfolding reminded Gus of the ritualistic postmortem body cleansing he'd witnessed in Iraq. Dino walked back to the table and used his shirt to finish cleaning before placing the cup next to the others. "For Snow," he said, his eyes filled with a mix of parental responsibility and sadness.

"The tradition in my squad," Dino explained, "was to honor our fallen comrades by pouring their favorite drink at our bar," he said, as moisture made his eyes seem to burn. "This will have to do for the bar... and it's way better than the shit Snow drank," he laughed, but it came out as almost a desperate gasp. "The drink sat there, untouched, until it evaporated or turned rancid, and eventually someone cleaned it up."

Gus nodded, understanding, and opened the top of the Macallan bottle. When he finished pouring, he placed the remaining three quarters of the bottle in his backpack, wrapped in a tee-shirt, and shook Dino's hand. "I'm sorry for your loss, and so unbelievably thankful for people like you and Snow."

Totally unpredictably, Dino pulled him in and gave him a hug. "Sorry for failing you and losing Donna and Bynum. I promise, man, I won't fail you."

Gus was prepared to parry Dino's degrading self-assessment, but the look on Dino's face pleaded with him not to, so he just answered with a simple nod.

The rain increased outside in its intensity, as if it was a challenge to them, and even a rumble of thunder in the distance warned them. The two men looked at each other and laughed and pulled the disposable ponchos from their bags and carefully dawned them as to not make a rip. They turned and walked into the downpour, leaving behind the three silent toasts on the table for their fallen family.

Chapter 3

Monday, October 22nd, 2018, 10:25 PM Cairngorm National Park Wilderness, Scotland

As the cold fall storm raged on, Gus and Dino trudged through the wilderness for nearly six hours, their steps faltering as they crossed the roaring, swollen creeks. The slogging sucked, and they both embraced it. However, when they came across the large stream that seemed to flow higher than the land they stood on, it felt like they were watching an enormous, endless serpent pass. The water was thunderous when Dino asked, "Do you hear that sound in the roar? That sound, like enormous balls from a pool table?"

Gus concentrated on the roaring rivers and, sure enough, he heard a noise that resembled a colliding pool or bowling ball. "I hear it, yes. Are those rocks?" Gus asked.

"Those are boulders, friend. We stop here and hope the rains stops and the stream slows, or tomorrow we go up, and see if we can find the source and go around it or find a safe crossing."

They surveyed their surroundings for a place to take cover and finally settled on a low, stout, and wide pine tree. The ground beneath it was slightly damp, but it became drier as they approached the trunk. Dino gathered the pine needles and small sticks, separating out most of the sticks and piling them up. He inserted thicker sticks into the rugged terrain while constructing a small ring of rocks. Stacking much higher on the far side of the circle, he described his every move as he went along. "This will do two things. It will reduce the glow from the fire and direct some of its heat towards us, hopefully, because we are already wet. Shoes off!" He said and took the shoes and stood them heel down on the edge of the circle. He took a handful of the dryer needles, stood up, and collected some dead branches from above, making sure not to disturb the tree. Braving the rain, he went to gather more wood from other small trees nearby.

On a different excursion, he brought back a sizable mat of moss and placed it near the fire pit. Next, he retrieved a nine-volt battery and a small steel wool fragment from his bag. Using his knife, he shaved a little of one candle Gus had found at the ruin earlier in the day onto the pile of dry needles. He held the candle up to Gus, "This is the shit!" he said. "Great find!" Next, he inserted the steel wool into the pile and contacted the battery, causing the wool to glow brightly and a small fire to ignite almost instantly. Within minutes, the fire was a stable size. "If we get nervous, we do this." He picked up the pelt of moss and placed it over the fire, immediately snuffing it. Moments later, he picked it back up and blew life back into the hot coals. "If we ever need to evacuate, pouring water on the moss will greatly reduce the smoke, but it's the mud that actually puts out the fire. However, if there are sufficient coals, the moss might eventually dry and catch fire." Dino finished.

Gus took the blanket from his pack and spread it over the pile of needles, while Dino took their shoes and stood them on the sticks to the side of the fire.

"Gimme your socks," Dino said, and he spread them too on the branches near the shoes, as he did the same for himself. He noticed Gus checking his feet, "There you go, Lieutenant Ferguson! Feet first baby!"

Gus relaxed and looked at his phone. Still no signal.

The rain gradually slowed and came to a stop in the early morning. The absence of the rain sounds woke Gus, prompting him to tend to the fire, add wood, and rotate the shoes. Since the socks were warm and dry, he wore them as gloves. He gazed at the sky, witnessing stars emerging amidst the clouds. A bright spot towards the west resolved itself for a moment. It was an almost full moon that seemed to look down at him like an eyeball. Sleep had become Gus's new enemy. He assumed that his possession of the artifact was the reason.

Gus was cognizant of the fact that the small scepter containing the creature that had instilled fear in his family for thousands of years was now sitting in his pocket. Yet it seemed surreal to him.

Despite his efforts to ignore it, the damn thing was always on his mind. Carrying it in his pants pocket, he was constantly aware of its weight, which felt like a rhythmic drumbeat on his leg with every step he took. Occasionally, he swore he heard whispers and rustling sounds emanating from it. Contrary phrases would flash through his mind, mirroring his inner voice but contradicting his true feelings. The thoughts mimicked stereotypical self-doubt, but were hollow of any real meaning to him. He thought about his next action for a moment and decided it was time. "Fuck it!" Gus said.

In a swift motion, he snatched his shoes from their spot near the crackling fire. After slipping on his cozy socks, he effortlessly slid his feet into the warm boots. Taking cautious steps, he made his way to another tree, mindful not to wake Dino. Heading towards the far side of the tree, he undid his pocket, inserted his hand, and sensed a spark when he touched the ancient artifact. He had so much he wanted to say to this fucker... if this wasn't some cosmic joke. "The slowest goddamn joke in history if it is," he thought. When he grasped the relic, the compulsion grasped him to investigate the end and see the crystal. He did not resist the urge this time, and his world changed forever.

Chapter 4

Monday, October 22nd, 2018, 3:15 AM Cairngorm National Park Wilderness, Scotland

Under the faint moonlight, Gus gazed into the end of the tube; flashing scenes filled his vision as an unrecognizable scream echoed in his ears. He immediately grasped the significance of the unknown words and eerie languages in which the voice cursed him by name, causing a shiver to run down his spine. Like a flood, memories inundated his mind, each carrying its own imbedded emotional burden.

Watching the farmer named Tadgan work the small field with a wooden tool stirred up memories that felt both intimate and commonplace. Gus observed him laboring in the field all day, absorbing the sounds of the clanging tools and the smell of freshly turned earth, before he figured out how to pull back from the memory.

It was as if, conflicted by his urge to stay, he forced himself mentally, to climb out of a pit that was this man's life. This odd person who had lived a life as a simple farmer, married someone he truly loved and had seven children, and died terribly. Tadgan's lifetime was a collection of memories, and within them lay the end of not only himself, but his whole family. Faced with the unsettling conclusion, he attempted to push aside the horror, as Tadgan's memories, emotions, and fears washed over Gus. The experiencing of them was as if they engulfed him. Tadgan's lifetime of clear recollections, and those of thousands of other individuals, poured into Gus. They were now his own.

No, these memories were sharper than his own, and Gus momentarily panicked that their weight might displace his, leaving him trapped in one of them. He vividly remembered the field from thousands of years ago, feeling the sun's heat and the soft breeze in the air. He felt as though he was present in the field, but he also knew he wasn't.

A swirling mass of crows and ravens, their raucous calls filling the air, heralded Tadgan's demise. From the depths of the forest, a small band of men appeared, led by a figure with an eerie, pale blue complexion. Riding on horses, they found shelter under a shadow formed by the swarming black birds. Gus averted his mind, focusing on someone else in a separate distant memory, instead of what was about to happen next to Tadgan and his family. He didn't want to go any further. He already knew every horrifying damn detail of the gruesome ending, and didn't feel the need to live it.

Another ghost's voice echoed in his mind, adding to the cacophony of thoughts swirling within him. Gus had no trouble understanding the ancient language; it was plain to him, and he consumed it. He remembered counseling a young follower about wisdom. "The old possess wisdom..." he said, "they earn it through time, pay for it with blood, and bear it in their missing fingertips, limping gait, and in both visible and unseen scars," the man counseled a follower. "A humble man's pain and embarrassment marks his path to wisdom. So much pain that few truly ever find it. Embracing embarrassment is essential to transform pain into a valuable lesson, gaining wisdom through the forge of experience. Those who are incapable of understanding their own faults define themselves as the fools."

Gus recognized the voice, its haunting echo stirring memories of a distant past, but he chose not to unravel the mysteries of Myang Tangshu's mind or revisit the tragic events of his death in 672 AD. Death found him at the monastery he managed, nestled in the majestic Himalayan region of Northern India. The chaos of a Chinese invasion disrupted the serene setting, with a figure at the forefront holding the exact item Gus had in his possession. Gus wondered how he knew the year with such certainty.

An eternal spring of memories, each containing the intimate thoughts and self-doubts of countless individuals, swamped Gus's mind. As Gus looked at the surrounding people, their auras seemed to resonate with importance, magnifying his own feelings of insignificance as their intense suffering frayed his sanity. Gus felt a sense of impending doom with each memory, as if a dark cloud hung over them all, forcing him to retreat. These memories, unwanted yet unavoidable, had now become his to carry.

With sheer willpower, he finally disconnected from the artifact and took a mental step back. Anticipating a world transformed by the passing of days, no time seemed to have passed. Everything around him remained unchanged.

He could visualize Dino perfectly in his mind, standing there with his trademark grin and nonchalant pose. The panic surged through Gus as he reached the present, imagining the possibility that Dino had also gazed into the artifact's end.

With his mind settling, as he noticed the moon up above, the sustained, deep rumble of one of Dino's diabolical farts rumbled from under the distant tree. Dino's teammates had warned Gus, but nothing could prepare a person for that... filth, which that human could emanate.

Gus felt reassured that only a brief period had passed. Minutes? Maybe just seconds. Like a Tsunami the memories of thousands of people crashed over his consciousness, overwhelming him and causing him to vomit on the ground in front of him.

With his hands resting heavily on his knees, Gus stood there, taking deep breaths. As he gazed at the artifact in his right hand, a sense of certainty washed over him, dispelling any doubts about the creature's existence or nature.

Gus heard the creature's voice. "Well, that was interesting, in an ass-raping monkey sort of way." The voice in his head quipped.

"What the hell is that?" Gus said, spinning around, looking for the source of the voice he heard.

"From my point of view? I consider this connection between us to be highly unfortunate, but feel free to assign it any label you prefer," the creature said.

Gus realized the lack of echo or location and determined the voice was in his head. "Can you hear my thoughts?" Gus thought to himself and looked up at the moon that seemed like a solitary eye that stared down at him with pity. Gus waited to see what he would hear next.

"There is nothing on the moon that will help you either, if my destruction is your actual goal," said the voice in Gus's head.

After flashing a brief knowing smile, Gus sensed another wave of nausea coming, which led him to swiftly put the artifact back into his pocket. Just as he was performing the action, he noticed the soft sounds of a protest starting, but they were immediately hushed when the item slipped from his grip.

The throbbing pain in Gus's head brought back memories of the time he had foolishly neglected to stay hydrated in the scorching Iraqi desert during his second week of deployment. Or, even worse, the pain he went through on his birthday years ago with Peter and Marcy, approximately 30 linear miles away from this pile of vomit.

As he gripped the sides of his head, he was once again flooded with memories. It felt less dramatic, as though the information was struggling and succeeding to find a comfortable position in the small area called his brain, even though his head was too small for the added burden.

Memories flooded back to him in a dreamlike haze as soon as he heard Peter's voice. It was Gus's own twelfth birthday party at Chucky Cheeses in North Raleigh. Peter excitedly watched as Gus unwrapped his gifts, looking forward to Gus opening his own. Gus's new SlingKing water-balloon slingshot guaranteed a fun-filled time for them. Peter sat at the table, with twelve kids from school around him, none of whom he considered friends. The only one he cared about was Gus.

The thought of others getting stuck in the poop tunnels that ran overhead, resembling a Habitrail for giant hamsters, didn't bother him at all. "I mean, who

405

would willingly crawl into those disgusting, filthy things?" Gus could hear Peter's thoughts as he vividly recalled the time the previous year when they played tag in the tubes.

Everything was going fine, until Peter noticed a foul smell, and realized that he had unknowingly crawled through a child's freaking turd while trying to get away. It was all over his knees and the side of his leg where he had slid through the tube sideways...

The sound of Dino's voice snapped Gus back to the present. "You ok bud?"

"Yeah, yeah, I just got up to take a leak," Gus lied.

"Cool. If you need to do more than that, bury that turd and cover it with some ashes from the fire. I'll be back in a minute after I pinch one off myself." Dino said, as he walked towards a distant tree.

Gus forced a smile. "Try to banish that evil ass-demon while you are at it."

Dino waved and laughed... and, in the moonlight, Gus was certain he saw a flash of toilet paper in his other hand. "That motherfu..." Gus started, as a wave of panic rushed over him.

"Peter!" Gus said out loud as he dropped to a knee. And as soon as he focused on him, Peter's memories rushed into his consciousness and there was something terribly wrong. Some memories that Peter had seemed familiar to Gus, while others appeared to be corrupted. There was the Peter at his wedding, proud and happy, gushing even, over Gus and Marcy's union. Alongside that memory, there was a different version. Peter's mind, in the other version, was a chaos of shadows and inconsistent memories. Gus knew immediately these were the scars of the monster's corruption.

The shift in Peter's feelings towards Gus was subtle, yet Gus could sense that Peter now likened him to a cherished tool in a carpenter's workshop. The same way a carpenter would think of his favorite hammer. He was a tool in Peter's altered mind. The tool that helped him with his attempts to look human.

With Gus around, no one questioned how few friends Peter had. He had no one else, except for maybe Marcy, who was close to Peter. Marcy fulfilled a comparable role, lending credibility to his connection to the normal world, even if she was receiving payment for it. She was the "woman friend", that people with the fetishes like he had, needed to have around to avoid notice.

Peter believed Gus had to know. He was around before, when he was Pete. Gus was smart, and he knew Peter. At Stanford, he witnessed the transformative moment when Pete became Peter. As the whore shattered his innocence and danced upon the remnants of his good nature. She had embarrassed him!

Peter remembered how Gus flew out and found him in his apartment. Him settling down next to Peter on the couch. Gus had encouraged him to rebuild himself, and he did. Gus helped put Peter back together by explaining to him how he was way too good for that bitch. When the weakling, limp-dicked Pete cried and wished her dead, Gus had wrapped his arms around him in a comforting embrace and whispered, "It's not your fault, Peter. You're built different, bro. You have honor, dignity and a great family... Fuck her! Let her define herself for what she is. It does not define you!"

Gus had almost never called him Pete again. Peter was born that day and Gus had buttoned up his armor, aimed him by his shoulders and shoved him back towards the world. Pete was dead.

"Holy shit," Gus mumbled to himself as he continued to review the event that twisted Peter's reality. The revelations were terrifying.

Gus, in Peter's memory of that day in San Fran, had continued laying out the prophecy for Peter. "She will get hers, bud. People like that always do. Someone will hurt her and rip out her heart the way she did yours. You will be fine. Hell, brother, you always have me covering your six!"

"Isabella got hers, too," Peter remembered as Gus screamed "No!" in his memory. "So did fuck-boy Marco," Peter thought, as he remembered stuffing that dude's love sausage in his damn mouth, silencing his scream as he sprayed blood. That was just before he rolled him screaming over the bridge rail of the bridge, where he seemed to fall forever into the fog. He tossed Bella's lifeless body off the bridge to follow him. The San Francisco Chronicle featured a silly story about "Lover's Leap," a spot where the couple reportedly jumped to their deaths.

The coroner never discovered his pecker inside his mouth, or that Peter had indeed cut the heart out of that cunt bitch Bella. That first time around, when Peter popped his cherry, his performance was rather sloppy. The ocean, with its currents and inhabitants, played a crucial role in covering his mistakes and offered him a chance to grow and perfect his craft.

"Of course, Gus knew," Peter believed. He could tell by how Gus spoke to him, and by the subtle glances they exchanged when they went on trips together. Sometimes, unfortunately, bad things happened that made it to the news, but no authority had ever questioned either of them.

Gus panicked with the newfound understanding of the Peter that Scrios had ruined. The Peter Gus spoke to in the changing room had seemed different. When Gus asked him to "Take care of Marcy," what would the newly configured Peter think he meant? The multiple meanings of the request visibly confused Peter, he could see it in his eyes that day. Gus had never asked for a favor so overtly before. How was the monster that Scrios created going to grant that favor? "Marcy!"

The thought of her, and he immediately saw her perspective, talking from the driver's seat of the car to the officer as he asked her to exit the vehicle. He could feel the cool plastic of the zip ties as they tightened on her wrists and the chilly breeze that seemed to drift down the hill gently tossing her hair. A quick glance from her revealed a dark warehouse downhill from them. Although there was no one in sight, she had the certainty that someone was there.

As she entered the large vehicle, Peter calmly sat in the seat on the far side, staring out the window like he didn't know or notice her. He didn't seem distressed at all. She sat in the seat across from an older, chubby, and exhausted looking man.

"Marcy! It is a pleasure to meet you finally." The older balding man said, as he glanced up and down her slowly, subconsciously wetting his lips with his tongue like a lizard, as he covetingly took her in. "Peter tells me you were just married. How wonderful! If only we had more time, I would introduce you to the famous local tradition of Prima Nocta, but alas, no time for any real fun. Instead, I just need you to look at something for me." Gus, an invisible witness in her dream, boiled at the threat.

"Fuck off, Scandling!" Marcy said with spittle flying from her mouth in wild droplets as tears formed in her eyes.

"I mean, I guess we could make more time and even have a threesome... or you can just be a good girl, and look into this," Scandling said as he held the open end of a golden artifact towards her face.

In her mind, Marcy was preparing to say something else, when Scandling held something up, and out of normal human reaction, she glanced towards his hand. She saw a flash of green that she would never remember. But Gus would be the witness for her. Gus would be the vengeance for her. Because Gus knew what it did to her and the rage warmed him.

The beast had changed her understanding of herself. The way she spoke in the changing room and the sorrow in her eyes all made sense now. Such a simple, subtle change in her had cracked her foundation. Just to be ugly, the creature Scrios had given her a shadowy memory of a night of wild drinking in Scotland, at Gus's crazy birthday celebration, where a drunken Peter had raped her. It added to her guilt by convincing her she wanted it.

Although it never occurred, her recollection of it made it tangible for her. The weight of her perception of the events of the day, where she had a certainty now

408

that it was her fault, hung over her like a dark cloud. Marcy, Gus knew, pondered on how she could atone for her mistakes and make amends to the world.

Gus heard a rustle of branches, and Dino stepped out with an awkward swagger, "Do NOT go in there... Whooo!" and waved his hand like Jim Carrey as Ace Ventura. The joke fell flat when he saw Gus on a knee, looking like a person who had been gut shot. Without hesitation, Dino sprinted to Gus's side and asked, "Dude, are you okay?"

"No. I lied to you a few minutes ago. I got pissed off at the world. So, I checked on the little monster in my pocket. I know this might sound unbelievable, but I experienced a similar thing to what my mother described." Gus shook his head. "Except, I think I saw more. She saw events of importance, or at least that was all she ever described. I saw the entire memory of thousands of his victims. They poured into me in the matter of a few seconds. Worse, I don't think I even touched the reservoir of awful shit this thing has done and souls it has stolen. In those same few seconds, I spent an entire day watching some dirt farmer, thousands of years ago, break up a field with a wooden sticklike tool. It was like I was standing beside him or riding piggyback. I saw the creature Scrios, before it became trapped in the stone, ride up with a group of men and do terrible shit to this simple farmer and his family. When it arrived, there were black birds that followed him. I mean, thousands of them." Gus finished.

Gus took a second, while Dino tried to absorb what he was saying. After a moment, he continued. "The fucking thing has Peter and Marcy's memories. That means he touched them! This thing can change people, like Laoch said, but worse than I imagined. Anyway, he changed Peter to believe that he is, and has always been, some type of woman hating, serial killer. The creature gave him memories and experiences, probably from actual killers as lessons. My sweet Marcy, he ruined differently. Her, he put the weight of the world on. Basically, every bad thing that has happened or will happen are logically, to her, her fault by commission or omission."

"If she is involved, and something wrong happens," Dino said.

"It's her fault. And if she sits back and does nothing," Gus said.

"It's her fault. That mother fucker! Your gunna kill this piece of shit, right?"

"You bet your ass, but we need to get somewhere so I can contact my grandfather. Someone must get a hold of those two and keep them from hurting themselves or others!" Gus said with a sense of urgency.

"Alright, you good with some up-hill?" Dino asked. "We are going east towards the highway and cell reception. Pack your shit."

"Ready in five." Gus said and shuffled towards camp. "You wouldn't have any aspirin, would you? My head is pounding."

"The natural doctor will get you fixed up along the way. First, drink some water and eat a power bar." Dino said. As they followed the large, still swollen stream up the hill, Dino walked up to a willow tree, flicked out his knife, and cut several strips of bark. "Here. You chew on the inner part of the bark. It tastes like shit, but it has salicin in it and works just like aspirin. Next fire we do. I will make you some tea. It is better than chewing and works faster if you think you are going to need it."

As they walked, to distract Gus some from the phone he was constantly checking, Dino started playing a game he called, "Edible, and will kill you," when it became light enough to see the details. While he did that, he gathered some edibles for later consumption, without breaking pace.

As they got close to the top of the hill, Gus's face brightened. "I have a signal!"

Dino pointed at a metal tower on a distant hill. "I would hope so,"

Once the phone connection was complete, Gus entered the game.

FuzzyWabbit24: Yawn and stretch. It is a wonderful day.

The line was one of the many used to mean that there was no pressing imminent danger, and they were not currently running away from something chasing them. They waited for almost ten minutes before there was a reply.

Wolfwolf1(Kier): Good morning, boys. I'm tending to the sheep this loverly morning.

FuzzyWabbit24 (Gus): Is SternEars around.

Quackomatic71(Marcy): It's lovely to hear from you, Fuzzy. Keeping warm?

FuzzyWabbit24 (Gus): Oh yes. I have been playing in the garden with Tyranno. All the fences are in place to keep the foxes out.

Wolfwolf1(Kier): Stern was in timeout for being a bad bunny for a while, but he is back in his hole now after playing in his field... Oh fuck it. He is out.

FuzzyWabbit24 (Gus): Ha, Quack! Wonderful, have you seen OI812 around? (Gus asked about Peter)

Quackomatic71(Marcy): He is around. He is off to give a statement later today. (Marcy replied)

On the side, Gus opened a Private Room in hopes Laoch, AKA SternEars would get online soon.

--Private Room – BunnyRoom2895423

--FuzzyWabbit24 enters room

--SternEars enters room

--SternEars: Good to hear you, Gus. Are you safe, my boy?

--FuzzyWabbit24: I am, but there is a big problem. That is why I searched out a cellular signal. I have communed with the creature, and the stories are true about how we can see its memories. But more. I see the memories of those he killed or dominated (for lack of any better term). Grandfather, I can see their entire life stories unfold before me. Literally from birth. I can even feel the gentle wind of a sunny day and the warmth of the sun beaming down on them. It has made me a witness to the senses they felt so many years ago that were just a part of a day in their lives. So many people were involved, maybe tens of thousands, and I feel I've only just begun to understand... there are so many more victims.

Two of those affected by it were Peter and Marcy. Scrios affected both Peter and Marcy, and they need help. They need to be protected for the sake of themselves and in Peter's case, for others.

This is hard to say. Peter needs to be confined, likely in a hospital setting until... I don't know, maybe permanently. Scrios has manipulated his beliefs, leading him to see himself as a woman-hating murderer, and equipped him with the skills and information to become even more dangerous than the Ripper.

Marcy needs to be watched as well, but for different reasons. Scrios made her believe that all things that are wrong are her fault. If she takes part in something and it goes wrong, it's her fault. If she chooses to not be involved and it goes wrong, it is her fault for not helping. Understand? I don't know what to do, other than keep her close and watch her for me until I get done with this awful assignment. She somehow needs to be made to believe that you are helping her and will be there for her. I don't think any amount of professional help will benefit her. Her programming leads her to believe she is damned, and that her presence damns everything around her.

--SternEars: I'm so sorry, son. Maybe the destruction of the creature will undo its effects? I will do whatever needs to be done for both.

--FuzzyWabbit24: That is my hope as well grandfather. I need to speak to her. Keep her there, please. I will work to make her stay as well. Grandfather? Thank you. And make sure the people that handle Peter are capable and know to be prepared and careful. This version of him is extremely dangerous and cunning.

--SternEars: Will do. Oh, add a name to your list of friends in the game. Add FunnyBunny47, Peter's mum. I will tell her of the developments, but it will require me to read her in on so much more that it is daunting. Godspeed, son.

--Private Room – BunnyRoom2895423 has ended

Gus exited out of the private room and wrote that he loved everyone, but his availability was short. His battery, too, was below 20%. He turned off his phone and looked at Dino, "Which way?"

"Well, here is the good news," Dino replied. "We have bypassed the stream and are now descending downhill, heading back towards the tree line. Unfortunately, the descent is going to be more dangerous, but we need to move with a purpose to find shelter before full daylight. This means we need to move the proper speed, so no running and breaking an ankle. Might as well give those crayon eating SEALs their due. They loved to say, 'Slow is smooth, smooth is fast.' We need to do that." He turned and walked down the incline, throwing his pack on his back.

Chapter 5

Wednesday, October 24th, 2018, 4:45 AM Cairngorm National Park Wilderness, Scotland

The duo embarked on a challenging hike that lasted for a day and a half, navigating only through the darkness of the night, before encountering their first modern obstacle. Ironically, the hurdle came in the form of the rural, yet somewhat busy, A9 highway corridor that they had driven on several days before. The only other truly modern thing they had passed were lines of small plastic flags that seemed to radiate out from a point to the east of them. Dino had commented on the flags.

"What in the hell is someone making flag lines like this for, out here in no-where town? Dino asked. "It looks like they are surveying or something."

"Do you really want to know?" Gus asked tentatively, with a knowing look in his eye. Dread washed over him as he anxiously awaited the response following his inquiry. Because if Dino responded yes, he would have to explain how he knew what happened at the center of the circle about three miles northeast over 2500 years ago. Because, as he walked, the feeling of déjà vu was crashing on him like waves on an ocean. This place was remote, but 2500 years is a long time and at least three people's memories included parts of the area they walked through. The older memories of the area where entire forests had grown or retreated here. One memory, from a soldier in World War 2, who found himself under the command of Lord William Atworth, had trained in an area they recently crossed. Gus expected to see a large tree when they crossed the hill they were walking over, but only found the moldered rotten stump of the tree the young trainee had sat under during meals. Time erased the tree that he and his platoon had carved their initials into, leaving only the pitted base of the once glorious shade tree.

In his usual witty manner, Dino retorted, "Alright, oh wise Swami, enlighten me on the mystical ways of these bad teeth motherfuckers, with their high hip boots and little metal wires adorned with colorful flags, and why they are up here planting them in circles... I'm all ears."

"The answer is over there," Gus said. "At the center of these circles is where the battle took place against this fucker." He patted the bulge caused by the artifact in his pocket. "A couple of years ago, when the big storm hit... and an earthquake too... amid that storm, the combination of the events uncovered parts of where that battle took place. The flags are markers for distance from the blast that Laoch talked about. Let me tell you, the blast was enormous." As he tapped his head. "The land here has changed some over the millennia, but not a lot. Over there, though, it looks very different. You see that peak over there that looks like something took a bite out of it? Something did, and it buried this thing for half a millennium. Somehow, the creature coaxed some asshat to dig him out," Gus said as a change in weather brought a line of clouds swallowed the sun as it rose in the east. Gus caught the emotion that he crept into his own voice, so he took a breath and reset himself and calmed.

"Sorry," Gus said. "The researchers that are somewhere in that direction are doing some kind of search. These flags must mark a range or something important to them." The gathering clouds to the east broke apart, allowing the early rays of sun to once again cast their long shadows.

Several hours later, the pair stood in the woods near a highway. They waited for an open opportunity to cross the road undetected. The primary other issue was the larger, fast-moving river they could see directly on the far side of the road. Even if they crossed the road, they had to make it past the river safely. Gus opened his phone and found signal and a battery at 18%. He pulled up a maps page and zoomed in. "There is a place where the highway crosses the river about a mile to the south." Gus said, as an alert popped on his phone from the game. He clicked on the game. "One sec, I have a couple of messages. Let me see if there is anything important.".

He opened the game and there was a message, eight hours ago from FunnyBunny47, Peter's mother. It read:

Subject: FunnyBunny47 sent you an invitation to become friends!

413

Message: Hi! I joined the game. SternEars invited me and it's so fun! He said we should become friends. If you get this, ping me back. I have an alert setup to tell me any time anyone tries to contact me.

So, Gus accepted the invitation and wrote, "That would be great. Thanks!"

There were other messages, including one from Marcy. In his response, he assured her he was fine and that he loved her. As he prepared to shut down his phone, an alert pinged again. FunnyBunny47 was reaching out. He reopened the app and told Dino what was going on. Dino came over and shoulder surfed as Gus opened a private room.

--Private Room – BunnyRoom2897238

--FuzzyWabbit24 enters room

--FunnyBunny47 enters room

--FuzzyWabbit24: Hey Deb, what's up?

--FunnyBunny47: Hey you. I guess we can talk here, so. I spoke to your grandfather some. I'm scared as shit, but I know your grandfather well enough. I know you also well enough that whatever is going on, you are protecting Peter as best you can. My real reason for the call is to give you some updates. There is still a manhunt for you. Your face is pretty much everywhere on TV and in newspapers. They think you have left the country. The shootout at the warehouse and the discovery of a rumored clandestine hideaway are the subjects of much discussion. Anyway, I haven't seen a single police checkpoint in the area, so if you can acquire a vehicle, you could likely drive to wherever you are going. If you need a ride, I'm staying in Glasgow and debating my options. If it fits your plans, that is.

Gus purely expected to hear Dino squash the idea, but he piped up, "Hell yeah, your ass needs a bath!"

"What should I tell her?" Gus asked.

"Tell her to come up the A9," Dino said as he consulted his own phone, zooming in with two fingers. "When she crossed the River Tay... the only big river she will cross, there is what looks like an access road along the river. Unless we cancel, I mean there might be a campground there now since this satellite picture is from several years ago. We will wait for her there, but we need a 30-minute window or else we will need to move on."

Gus relayed the details, and they made plans.

At 6:04 AM, Deb pulled off the A9 and picked up two very dirty men in her nice white Volvo SUV. She took the men to a guesthouse in the country that she

414

had rented several days before. It offered privacy and seclusion. It offered a hot shower and a warm bed. Also, there was food there that did not comprise granola bars and "edibles" that Dino had gathered. Some edibles Gus could not complain about, because they tasted pretty good. Others... the freaking Meadow Sweet, for instance, is neither sweet nor grows in a meadow. Dino had spied it near a stream they had crossed. He sold it as an "old friend he had eaten many times in the field," and there're was only enough really for Gus. It smelled ok, but the first and only bite tasted like something used to sterilize a doctor's office.

"Holy shit!" Gus had choked out as Dino laughed and Gus tried to brush the mush from his tongue.

Chapter 6

Wednesday, October 24th, 2018, 7:39 AM Cottage off Kilsyth Rd. Queenzieburn, Scotland

Now, Gus was in a small cottage, with real food. A fruit bowl sat on the table, and Gus greedily took an apple and bit into it.

"You two boys, go take showers and I will whip up some breakfast and you get some sleep," said Deb.

Gus heard her say almost that same thing frequently when he and Peter were growing up. Gus reached into his bag, grabbed his charger and plugged it in, and plugged in his phone. He looked at Deb, and she saw his stare and met his eyes. "We need to..."

"Later," Deb said, "Get a shower, some food and some rest first... you can fill me in later, okay? I'm not sure if I am ready for it yet."

"Later," Gus agreed. Dino had gone up the stairs of the cottage to one of the two upstairs bedrooms and the shower they shared. Gus got to a standing position and prepared to follow Dino.

"If you don't want to wait, you can use my shower." Deb said. "There are extra towels in the small closet there. Also, toss me your dirty clothes and I will put them in the shitty little washer they have here. When they are done, I will hang them to dry... Tell your friend to do that too."

"Sorry," Gus said. "Did I introduce you? I mean, you probably saw him around, but that is Dino... well, that is his callsign. His real name is Dean, Dean Williams."

415

"It's fine, sweetheart," Deb said. "Tell Dean to throw his clothes down and I will get them all washed and ready for when you guys wake up. I'll swing out and get a couple of things to eat, too."

Gus went to the staircase and called up to Dino. He told him what Deb had offered, and a pile of clothes dropped to the bottom of the stairway. "Thank you so much, Mrs. Smith, for everything." Dino called down.

Gus gathered his dirty clothes and made a pile, and set the others on the pile with a toss from the bathroom door.

When Gus finished his long shower, he dried himself and wrapped in a bath towel. When he left the bedroom, Deb and the car were gone. He could hear the small laboring clothes washer churning in the mudroom. He turned and grabbed another piece of fruit as Dino came down the stairs, similarly dressed in a large towel.

About an hour later, Deb's car pulled back into the front drive. Deb carried in a bag of fresh food from the store, with the odor of warm bread torturing Gus's nostrils. In a second bag, Deb pulled a package of men's underwear, two warm blue long sleeve fleece shirts and a pair of gray and a pair of black sweatpants. She also had scarves from the local football club, the Rangers. "There is a game tomorrow, boys. With these, you will blend in if you need to." She spoke.

They ate, and they slept, and Gus dreamed terrible dreams.

Interlude – Pain and confusion

The pain Scrios felt at the invasion of this one, Gus, was unique. It had been so long since he experienced actual pain; he was uncertain that he could. The boy's mother had been uncomfortable, but to call that pain, compared to this, was unfair. This was unlike anything he had felt, ever.

With his sister, when he was in his mortal form, it felt like mentally she had held his unusual additional sense down with a heavy immovable blanket. Losing his unique perception of those around him, the blindness he felt was terrifying for him at his young age. He had been so young and dependent on it and its insights that he was unprepared for the suppressive power his sister had over it... and him. He hated her, when he figured out it was her doing it. The feeling of that day had shaped him, and there was also the assassin the family had sent to kill him. Although, that attempt had come well over a hundred years after he was born.

When he thought about it, he had gone back to her house with a small army, only 6 years after meeting her, intent on killing her... only to find she had left. He

416

had been pretty sure Lil sensed his intent that first day. "Ah family," Scrios thought, "You can't live with them."

The assassin they sent was a naïve child... barely a man. That attempt had been thankfully sloppy. When the assassin arrived at his keep, his approach and familial relationship had again blanketed Scrios's perception. All his attempts to prepare for that exact occurrence had fallen apart. It was only Scrios's own cunning that saved him that time.

He was much more prepared for the next encounter hundreds of years later, and the battle had gone much the way he had hoped, until he touched the artifact that now contained him.

His imprisonment had changed the rules a bit. Maybe it was the lack of his corporal form that changed them, Scrios pondered, as he had for thousands of years. His family's presence could still be sensed, but there was not the suppression and the feel of pressure he had felt before when they were near.

When he finally compelled Gus to look into the crystal that was now his home, Scrios was not sure what to expect. The pain he experienced was tenfold of anything he predicted. The pain was as if the action of Gus looking into the gem had eviscerated him, cutting him into pieces, each moment that he stared. He felt pain so searing; it reminded him of the torturing he had doled out. Next, it was as if someone had driven a metal rod between his ribs and wrenched him open. He swore, despite no longer having a corporeal form, he felt it as muscle and sinew ripped, bones shattered, and entrails spilled from the fresh wound. The unexpected pain strobed through him like a lightning, but the torment receded just as swiftly when Gus pulled away.

He had also connected with Gus. But it was not the type of connection he could leverage or read. There was communication that frustratingly seemed to disappear when Gus dropped his artifact back into his pants pocket. He watched him as he vomited on the ground and wondered what had caused that, only to have Gus explained it to the black-skinned man... he traveled with. The one he called Dino.

So, Gus knew about Peter and Marcy, "Good," he thought. "I hope it hurts! I hope it hurts a lot!" Scrios wondered, though, if Gus understood the depth of her sorrow he had given her. He wondered if he knew or suspected that she carried Gus's spawn. Scrios's, some vast number of great, grandnephew, in the English language and tradition. He wondered if Gus could sense the changes he made. It surprised Scrios when he could affect the tiny child she carried. He hoped that hurt most of all!

Scrios had tried and failed to reach out to this Dino, whom he guessed to be a descendent of the Moors, he thought with disdain. He thought Dino had looked at Gus's pocket once when he called, while Gus slept, but he had never approached. Scrios couldn't put a finger on why he thought less of Dino, but knew that his memories, as he stole them, their accumulation seemed to hold some influence on him.

He took a moment to reflect on that clinically, examining the silliness of the inclination. Scrios examined himself and his own memories. He decided that his preference, as it had started, was as old as the contact with the other shades of human and the upright walking monkey race he was once a member of. He had discovered quickly that his leverage of this basic tribal instinct made manipulation of even people he did not personally dominate, easier.

While he could control individuals, the concepts of tribalism, controlled the masses of people. The people wanted to believe that someone who looked different from them, was less than they were.

He felt the influence of the Romans and their careless dominance over every society they stumbled upon, and he had learned a lesson. They had somehow conquered and successfully, over time, converted their subjects to Romans. They did this by feeding their tribalistic tendencies.

The Germanic tribes dominated their neighbors for a millennium before the Romans came. They too had found focusing on the smallest physical attributes that defined them, empowered their tribe to commit glorious atrocities. Later, the Romans came and crushed them into subservience... for a while. Scrios thought as he remembered the fate of General Varus and eventually Arminius.

To Scrios, that key manipulation of Arminius, even unknowingly to Scrios, set the stage for the wars that continued through present day. He had caught the Germanic tribes in the precarious balancing point between independence and subservience to Rome and nudged them back to rebelliousness. The great wars of the last century, where he had feasted, would have still happened, even without his later influences, of which there had been many. However, he had felt certain that his efforts had sped up the timeline of the insurrection with the critical nudges of influential individuals.

Christians credited the Devil with such treachery, he thought to himself with amusement. If that beast existed, he had never encountered it. Maybe they swam in different pools, he mused. Also, his father never sent him dreams of such a potentially powerful ally. Scrios sat with a certainty that anything with the darkness ascribed to the human's devil, his true father, would know of it.

He was even proud of the things that happened without his direct intervention, because he had helped sow the seeds of their inspiration. Death camps. The sound of that word as it seemed to echo in his mind and brought satisfaction. Not his direct idea, but boy, was it a powerful concept? So much so that other countries imitated it on both sides of that second enormous war. Nothing tasted better than innocent suffering.

Those conflicts, he wished he could have bottled the wine like flavors for future consumption, but alas, that was not how it worked. He ate all he could, but so much went to waste.

Scrios now could choose to be a picky eater. Instead of feeding on the general despair of any moment in existence, he ate only the pain he directly created. He picked flavors of pain with the discernment of a sommelier.

Marcy was going to be a meal when she finished cooking. Each time Gus contacted her on his little phone, it was to Scrios, like a cook tasting the broth of a hearty stew. The worry he caused Gus with both her and Peter was better sustenance than what Gus had been eating during his volksmarch through the Scottish countryside.

Gus impressed Scrios when he used the memories that he had stolen from him to understand why someone had placed the small flags in the wilderness.

When Gus placed his clothes out to be washed, Scrios cringed when he remembered the artifact, and wrapping it in a towel, before placing the clothes in the hallway. Still, it had tried to lure the Deborah lady, when she stopped to check in on the sleeping Gus, to no effect. The influential effect Scrios tried to employ seemed to work best on simpletons, and frustratingly, neither she nor Dino, despite his dark skin, fit that description.

Scrios's newest appetite was how he longed for the pain that politics could inflict. Politics had been a constant of the human condition, but never had it been so divisive or powerful. It was a unique type of suffering it could cause. It had the power to affect the interpretation of, or even corrupt, the findings of science.

It was like simmering a roast, only to pile it on to the table of a glutton. The politics of the modern world caused more despair than he could consume in a thousand years. It flowed past him like pastries on an enormous carrousel.

The same drawn tribal lines determined what entire groups believed science to be. Some sought to infer that man held sway over the workings of the universe, because their tribe said it to be true. While the opposing tribe would over run common sense to prove them wrong. At the root of it all, was the dreams his father had given him, with him on his throne of pain. His father was right. What the humans needed was a king to unify them as one tribe. They needed... him.

Chapter 7

Wednesday, October 24th, 2018, 4:15 PM Cottage off Kilsyth Rd. Queenzieburn, Scotland

Gus woke to the aroma of a home cooked meal cooking. The smell had drifted up the stairs and lifted him by his stomach. It had been enough to rip him from a nightmare in which the world had ended in a nuclear fire or something. It was gone now, and good food was just down the stairs.

At the end of his bed were his clothes, dry and folded. He felt like he was home from college again. He dressed, went to the drawer of the bedside table, and unwrapped the monster from the towel. As he reached for it, he heard the voice of the creature narrating to him, "So I guess you had a good..." the voice said, and he pulled back his hand, silencing it again. He had not touched it and he could hear the evil little shithead. Gus shook his head and reached for the item and again heard the voice as it rose in volume as he reached for it. "Yes, that is part of the deal. As you and I become in tune, it will get better. No, I don't know why or how it works... it just does."

"Fucking great!" Gus said.

"What's up?" came a concerned voice in the hallway.

"Nothing Dino. Apparently, I'm hearing this shithead now without touching it. That little trick just started. It is like a mini goddamn radio station, WGAS, Who Gives A Shit radio."

Gus started towards the stairs. "I have a deal for you, asshole. It goes like this. You don't talk to me."

"And what," came the voice in Gus's head.

"That's it," he said under his breath, "you don't talk to me, that's the best deal you get," as he descended the steps towards a small table in the kitchen, piled with food.

"You still talking to that thing?" Dino asked.

"Yes," Gus said, "I told him I had no interest in hearing anything from it."

"Funny," Scrios said in Gus's head, "I think soon you will have the..."

"Dude, I swear to freaking God," Gus grumbled low, with a sense of promise filling his voice. "I will take you, weld you into a metal box, and submerge that box in six feet of cement, at the center of Disney World!"

"Disney World?" Scrios said incredulously.

Dino tumbled from his chair, landing on the floor in laughter as Deb watched, concerned he might be injured, until his first strained laugh. "Did you just threaten to entomb a fucking, excuse my language," he said as he turned quickly to Mrs. Smith, "Did you just threaten to entomb that mythical motherfu... that thing that feeds on human misery, in the middle of the happiest place on earth?" Dino laughed while lying on his back, kicking his feet like a dying cockroach.

Deb snorted a short laugh, too. She put the glass of water down on the counter and placed both hands on her knees, and enjoyed the moment.

"I will capitulate to your request." Came the voice of Scrios in Gus's head.

"A first," Scrios mused to himself, realizing that he was yielding to someone for the first time. A cascade of images overwhelmed Scrios's thoughts. With an intensity that felt like a dream, they embodied anger and disappointment. Father was speaking to him in a way he had never had before. Previously, it had always occurred while he was meditating. His normal dreams were orgasmic, filled with chaos and a sense of grand purpose.

In his mind, vivid images of despair and torture played out, but he was not the one inflicting them. They tied Scrios to an altar in a place filled with unending bright light and sunshine, where pure happiness starved him and prevented him from fulfilling his destiny. Understanding the lesson, Scrios humbly apologized to his father.

Feeling a connection over the vast distance, he sensed the creature, his true father, turning his enormous head away in scorn. The tentacles of the gigantic beast's head seemed to linger, shooting with a jolt as the slack disappeared, to catch up with the disdainful glowing blue eyes as they turned away. The motion, snapping tightly through the tentacles like a hundred enormous whips cracking with monstrous potential. One of the many tentacles, smashing a subservient planet that orbited its enormous form. As the planet shattered, molten yellow light escaped its core, momentarily breaking the darkness only the titan's blue eyes had lit, briefly highlighting the massive dust vortex in his gravity.

Scrios realized too late that apologizing, a second novel action for him, was a second sign of weakness. Scrios felt alone, unilluminated by the blue glow of his father's observation. For the first time in his unnatural life, he felt the true terror of being removed from his father's awareness. He had lost his father's favor and attention.

He inherently understood this was the consequence of displaying this weakness. With determination, he resolved, "I will regain your attention, father," he declared to the vast universe. Scrios shouted into the void without a care for who heard, he proclaimed, "I will endure this disgrace."

With an angered and defiant surge of power, Scrios declared, "I will seize my destiny, with or without your notice. I will no longer seek your approval," he screamed in adolescent rage.

Sitting at the table consuming the best meal he could remember eating, suddenly, Gus's nose bled, like it did when he was a child.

Chapter 8

Thursday, October 25th, 2018, 9:25 AM Cottage off Kilsyth Rd. Queenzieburn, Scotland

Dino had a busy night contacting some old friends. Friends he had spilled blood with and knew would help just by his asking. More importantly, they would do it without asking questions. Gus needed help. As Dino watched the news on his phone after dinner, Gus's picture was everywhere. Multiple witnesses saw Harold Emmerson Scandling perish at the warehouse. However, only one police officer among the first three cars that stopped Marcy's survived the incident. In an ironic twist, friendly fire from the three cars on the hill saved Officer Guidry during the first moments of pandemonium after Scandling's death.

Officer Guidry, interviewed in the hospital, told an impossible story of the American, Laoch Kier Ferguson the Fifth, referred to by the alias, "Gus". He painted an unfeasible scene where the accused had appeared from the shadows, placed a large pistol to the forehead of the U.S. politician, appointed to lead the American effort by the head of the CIA, and pulled the trigger. The story continued, describing Gus as a "highly trained and dangerous individual" and asking the public to report any sightings. They cautioned the public to not approach Mr. Ferguson. The reporter cut to a prepared part of the story, and Dino turned up the sound to his earphones.

"A solicitor for the Fergusson family," said the narrator, "refused comment as to the whereabouts of Laoch "Gus" Ferguson, stating, "He's not here and I have no information on his whereabouts," said the tall lanky man in a suit and a tan overcoat.

The wiry solicitor continued, "The story being told by the officer, however, is false. Officers did not identify themselves prior to the family security team's intervention. The security personnel saw and documented with close circuit video the execution of one of their team by a now deceased officer and reacted. They shared that footage with the British Government, police, and American contacts. It puts to an end any of this speculation, and you should push authorities for its full release. I mean, obviously they will need to protect the families of the deceased, as the video is quite graphic. However, it also shows the police firing approximately a thousand rounds down range with complete disregard. The only living witness for the police, who in the mayhem's fog, misremembers the sequence of events, and," the solicitor alleged flatly, "fabricated memories. His own comrades shot him. Friendly fire also hit several of the slain, including the CIA liaison, Harold Scandling. The jackbooted acts of this task force were shockingly unprofessional and deadly; their heavy-handed tactics, reminiscent of the infamous Bonnie and Clyde ambush, resulted in unfortunate and unnecessary fatalities. The exchange of gunfire concluded only after the private security team had accomplished the safe evacuation of most of the family, who were returning from a family wedding, to a safe-room. This band of dragoons barbarically and without provocation gunned down two unarmed and beloved members of the staff; these two individuals posed no threat and were defenseless against this violent act. I offer my condolences to all the families affected, and the Fergusons have already generously started a fund to support the bereaved families on both sides of the conflict," said the solicitor, as the crowd of reporters lobbed questions.

The solicitor waved his hands like wings to bring order to the rabid throng of paparazzi before he continued. "It is important to add that Laoch Kier Ferguson, the third, showing remarkable self-control, surrendered himself in on the day of the ambush in a carefully planned manner that helped prevent additional injuries or casualties. He was the voice of reason here, and when investigators took his statement and examined the evidence, they immediately set him free to return to his home."

As the paparazzi streamed questions and flashes from cameras created a strobe effect on the advocate, the BBC Scotland camera panned back, showing the bullet ridden warehouse, with the armored personnel carrier still lodged in the structure, framing the argument. "Brilliant," Dino said as he watched the spectacle.

The BBC showed airport security and the Chunnel both at a heightened level of awareness. As they displayed a picture of the handouts for passersby, Dino used his phone to capture a screenshot. "Now, we have to make Gus look nothing like this. Good news," he thought, "the last couple of days had cut some of that fat ass off of him." So, he already looked thinner than the pictures and the drawing. Looking up at Gus, Dino said, "Jesus, my boy, we've gotta do something with that reddish hair. It's like a damn Where's Waldo hat." He reached into his bag and retrieved a small pad of paper and a pen, and started writing a list. As he finished, he heard a rumbling noise in the gravel drive and stepped to the side of the window to see who was driving up to the house.

Arriving was a small DHL truck with a petite woman driving it. She popped out of the small sprinter van carrying an envelope. The bell rang at the front of the house as Dino scanned the horizon for movement and saw none. He heard Deb greet the delivery driver and accept the package; the door closed, and the driver returned to her vehicle. She started the van, turned around, and left.

Satisfied everything was alright, he went downstairs, taking another apple from the fruit bowl on the table. "What was that?" Dino asked non-accusingly.

"That was a delivery from the States to the current resident... me," she said, showing him the DHL logo on the envelope. "I had it sent from a friend overnight yesterday. The envelope contains marketing materials for timeshares across the United States and Canada. It came from a group that mails out hundreds of like packages worldwide each day. One page will have a dog-eared corner. It will also have a phone number on it for a real company in the town where a storage facility is located," she said as she looked at Gus, who was paying attention with interest. "In that location, or there will eventually be, a box that will contain enough resources for you," she stared at Gus, "to rebuild your life. For immediate needs, there will be cash. There will also be identification, which is being assembled now, a lifetime worth of investments for you to live a quiet life, wherever and however you choose."

"A drop. Nice!" said Dino. "If you want, I can give you a list of things he might need."

"Please do," she said, "and I will convey that to the person handling this. There will also be papers for Marcy."

Gus's eyes shone a little as he tried to speak. He swallowed hard and shook his head.

"No need to say anything, dear. This is not me giving you something. This is from what I owe your mother and for what your grandfather has done for my family. If this all somehow just works out, and I hope with all my heart it does, I look forward to welcoming you back to Redwolf."

Gus could not speak. All he could do was stand and in an awkward gait that reminded Deb of the toddler waddling through the door of her crappy temporary office all those years ago, he walked towards her.

Every attempt to speak caused Gus's eyes to burn, so he walked around the small table and hugged her for a long time. He dried his eyes on her sweater while his shoulders shook. Gus felt embarrassed, totally unmanly and reduced to adolescence, in front of the warrior that was with them in the room. That was until Dino joined the hug, his enormous frame and long arms enveloping both of them.

"Brother, down the line, if there is anything I can do," Dino whispered into the huddle.

The group hug ended, and they sat back down at the table. "There are other preparations underway. Great Britain is not the place for you," Deb said as Gus's mind drifted to the playful argument Gus had with Peter and Marcy years before. The Great Britain or England debate memory made him smile, while simultaneously causing his heart to ache.

"I won't tell you where to go," Deb said, "but wherever that is, if it is safe to contact me, I will help you in any way I can. To that, I am setting up locations at multiple university gymnasiums that have long-term rentable lockers, using the identity that your grandfather has shared with me. In those locations, distributed across the U.S. and Canada, there will be cash. I cannot make this easy for you, but I can hopefully take some of the risk away from you as you do what your grandfather shared with me. The combination to the lock will be a version of your actual birthday, using the last two digits of the year as part of the code. "Those universities," she said, sliding him the unopened DHL envelope, "are mentioned in passing, in the literature inside, discussing timeshares and rentals."

"Thank you, so much... again," Gus said. "Dino has been adding to my knowledge about what not to do."

"Yep," Dino said, "and to that Deb, here is a list of things we need before we head out. Foremost, we need to change your look some. That dern red hair. I say brown or dirty blonde."

"I can do blonde highlights in whatever color you choose," Deb offered as Gus glared at her.

"Only if you can make them look like they have been there a while," Dino responded.

"Oh, if you mean a crappy job," Deb said, "that's right in my wheelhouse. Honestly, my best effort would not look very professional. This is high school trips to the beach, knowledge, and very low tech."

Ignoring Deb's next comments on his hair and even eyeliner recommendations, Gus opened the stiff envelope, trying to tune them out. Sometime later, Deb stood up and patted Gus on the shoulder to get his attention.

"I'm making a store run and will be back. Anything you want or need?" she asked.

"I was thinking," Gus said extra loud so Dino could hear him, "maybe to help disappear, we can get Dino an outfit that makes him the biggest, loudest cross dresser... you know? Everyone will look at him and no one will notice me."

"Hey!" came Dino's voice from upstairs, "I totally have the ass and legs to carry that off! But I would hate to be responsible for all the catcalls that might cause a stir."

Deb laughed and walked towards the front door, grabbing her keys off a low half wall.

An hour and a half later, Deb was back from the store. For the next hour, Deb's Beauty Shop opened briefly, for the first time in over forty years, at the kitchen's large deep basin sink.

Deb carefully washed his hair, colored it the chosen dirty blond color, and they waited forty-five minutes for it to set. Following that, Gus took a shower and washed his hair several times until the water at his feet looked clear. After that came phase two, "blonde fucking highlights," Gus grumbled as he walked down the stairs towards the kitchen.

As Deb worked on his hair, Dino looked at his phone and asked Gus, "Are you ok with step one being Paris?"

"Uh, sure. Is that a good place to start?" Gus asked.

"Yes, you would be with the team from there, whom offered me their services," Dino said. "They are the best of the best. You just listen to what they say and you will be fine. After that, you tell them where you want to go, and they will get you there, legally even," he said while wavering his hand in the air side to side, "well, they will get you through customs. Oh, and Deb, this won't be cheap."

Deb didn't even lose concentration on her work as she made the sound of air leaving a bike tire, "Psst." And waved her empty gloved hand dismissively. "Just let me know how they want it paid, and I will figure it out."

"That sounded exactly like Peter," Gus noted silently and smiled to himself.

"It will be a Bitcoin transaction, I'm guessing... or cash." Dino said.

"If we can do it while endangering no one more than we are now, let's make it happen." She spoke.

"There will be a van here in about two hours," Dino said, as both Deb's and Gus's eyes shifted to him. "Gus, you break out that bottle for a toast. If I can suggest it, I think the bottle should stay with Deb and someday we will all get together and salute with it."

"Yes Dino... Gus, dear, is it safe for him to get the bottle out of your bag?" Deb asked.

"Uh, yes," Gus responded patting his buttoned pocket, "it's safe."

"Dino," she said with a pained look, "Can you get that and give us the room for a couple minutes?"

"Yes mam," Dino said emphasizing his Texas drawl. "You guys just call upstairs when you are ready for that drink." He stood and climbed the stairs, taking them three steps at a time. As he entered the room, he closed the door for their privacy.

The delicate, motherly Deb, transformed in front of Gus in to the CEO of a large corporation between heartbeats. Her posture became more rigid, and she carried herself differently. Gus thought to himself that the transformation in her was like watching a time-lapse of concrete setting and becoming stonelike, except Deb had done it faster. Her eyes took on the look of a jungle predator as she looked into him.

"Tell me about my son. Tell me about my Peter," she said, and plowed the conversation forward. "Tell me everything you know and what I need to do."

Gus didn't hesitate or soften his words. "The creature has affected him... actually, it more accurately infected him." Gus said. "It twisted his memories of a breakup in college with a woman. A woman named Isabella, who cheated on him with a waiter named Marco. Even in his genuine memories, it was bad, but Scrios twisted those and used them as a leveraging point. Peter thinks that after that indecency... he murdered them both and threw them off a bridge into the San Francisco Bay. Her last name is Nevirny, or was... she might be married by now, and I hope she is fat and grown warts," Gus said, nervously trying to elicit a smile as Deb's eyes sharpened.

"Go on," Deb said with a tone of impatience. "What did he lever?"

Gus continued. "After the fake memory of the murder, the monster built multiple fake memories and surrounded them with actual events. These memories plus something the creature calls 'understandings' have convinced Peter that he is a woman hating serial killer."

"Understandings? Explain." Deb said.

"They work like this," Gus explained. "The creature, when you look into the crystal, if you are not protected like I thankfully am, sees everything about you, instantaneously. I think it has access to the subconscious recall that most humans don't. Deb, I have thousands of these memories in my head from people this monster destroyed. I can recall the terror of their birth until the last moment of domination by this beast. Scrios sees their intimate feelings and can mold their desires and create a need... a compulsion to do horrible things. The monster changes the meaning of love and hate for entertainment. He convinced a man that drowning his daughter in a goddamn stream was an act of kindness."

Deb finally broke, "WHY!!! Why the hell would anything do that!" she screamed as tears of rage exploded in her eyes.

Gus softened his voice, "Because he feeds off of the misery he creates. The piece of shit feeds off pain, misery, and death." Gus said matter-of-factly, "and I swear to you, I'm going to destroy this motherfucker... somehow."

Deb regained her professional distance and wiped the tears from her face with a dish towel. She looked at Gus again with the fire back in her eyes, "What is it? A vampire?" she asked.

"No, among the memories of the people..." Gus said as he heard a voice in his head that was not Deb's

"I wouldn't go there, sport," Scrios said as Gus ignored him.

Gus had paused for a second, and Deb had tilted her head as if getting ready to ask a question. "Sorry, the buffoon was begging me not to tell you his origin story." Gus said and smiled, "But this dumb fucking monkey doesn't run the zoo," he said as Scottish sunshine fell outside of the house in large droplets. "Among the memories of the people are the memories of the creature's mother. Who he killed. Well compelled her to jump off a cliff into the ocean, while his father begged her not to. That little-bit was also in the archives, and I had dreams of that before I even knew the creature existed. Before she invented cliff diving, after losing most of her children and placing the other, a daughter, my direct blood relative and source of my resistance, with a friend. That woman named Srene, called down a curse. This must have been back in the days when that kind of shit mattered, because something, what Scrios calls his father, granted it. Scrios is that curse. This was not some simple demon. This is something way far away, real, ancient, and alive right now. Scrios calls it his 'real father', and speaks to him, kind of. Gives him vivid dreams similar to the ones myself and my family members have. Except his dreams seem to convey convoluted and violent messages to him."

There was something there, in that conclusion, that troubled him, but he could not put his finger on why a chill ran through him. His pause caused Deb to grab his hand.

"What is it, Gus?" she asked.

"I don't know," Gus said, taking the discussion on a tangent. "I solve problems weirdly. I basically gather information and read everything I can about a problem. At some point, my brain will build a model, and I get a sense... No, not a sense. I get a clarity, after my mind boils down the information. After the boiling process, all that's left is the clarity, which is the ultimate solution. Except I have no control over when that clarity will happen. It almost happened a

428

moment ago, and I know I am close to something. That knowledge is supported by the fact that the inmate has shut his good little monkey mouth."

"The good little monkey is waiting to see if daddy noticed you," Scrios said as Gus ignored him.

Adjusting his seat a little, "I hate to say this, but Peter is changed, and I don't know if it is reversible. I hope that when this fucker ceases to exist, things get put normal. But I don't know if they will. He also changed Marcy by making my sweetheart perpetually depressed. I'm not sure how much of her will remain after I finish, and thinking about it is tearing me apart. When I chat with her through the game, I'm so glad to read something from her and I simultaneously feel so terrible for her and the pain she is in, and utterly helpless to do anything about it."

"Is my Peter dangerous to me?" she asked.

"Honestly?" Gus said, "Yes. Peter is dangerous to everyone, and no one should underestimate him. He is still brilliant. He still has all of his charm and social skills. However, he would slit yours or my throat if he thought it would help his purpose." Gus said with a sense of sadness. "Worse yet, I know with complete certainty that he loves you with all of his heart. That is why I advised my father to take no chances when they apprehended and restrained him. I suggested they sedate him and not confront him. With detaining him, they need to be exceptionally careful and never give him an avenue of escape or he will disappear. I do not know how they can do that long-term." Gus spoke.

Deb interrupted him, "The creature, it's here and can hear us?" she asked.

"Yes," Gus said.

She took a piece of paper she had used for Dino's shopping list out of her pocket, and a pen off the table, and wrote on the back, "Can it read this?"

Gus shook his head, closing his eyes gently to signify, "No."

Deb cursed the creature, calling it many names as she wrote something completely different on the paper. "You need to know this. I don't want the creature to know. Peter went to the police station to be interviewed after the event at the warehouse. After his interview, he left the police station and disappeared. Your grandfather and team are looking for him, but he has disappeared. Less than a day later, he appeared on security cameras at Redwolf. He went to his office and took a bag he had there. Went to my office and emptied my personal safe. He took tens of thousands of dollars, jewelry Max had bought me over the years, Max's gold coin collection, and a Rolex watch Max had left to him in the will. He left a note in the safe," She wrote. Next, she removed her phone, opened a picture, and turned the phone on the table for Gus to read.

Mom,

I need to leave. The events of the last few days have been traumatic. I feel confused and that I need to do something about it. I overheard a discussion I was probably not supposed to hear, where I think others thought they could help me. So, I needed to leave. Sorry if this inconveniences you.

Please don't search for me and know that I love you. If you talk to Gus, tell him the same. I have something I need to do. Consider this note a resignation of my role in the company and sorry for the credit card bill you will get soon. Ha ha, same ol' Peter, right?

Peter

Gus read the note, trying desperately to control his breathing. He nodded his head curtly as his determination to destroy the artifact and kill the monster it contained intensified. "I need to go pack," Gus said, "and tell Dino he is ok to come out, if you have no more questions."

Deb looked into his eye again with the heat of a furnace, "Kill that thing!"

"Yes mam," Gus replied, mimicking Dino's drawl, and climbed the stairs. Packing his remarkably few items took almost no time at all. He prepared to leave the small bedroom, and he looked down at the bulge caused by the artifact in his pocket. He reached into it, touched the cool metal, and felt the dance of electricity on his fingertips. The urge to investigate the green gem it contained was completely absent. "I thought so, you fucking coward!" he said. "You must have more of your 'real dad' in you than my family's lineage. I'm just guessing that the stone in there is a damn sapphire, all blue and beautiful until your craven yellow ass got sucked into it. So much fucking yellow turned it green." He said with a sneer.

He heard a sort of scoffing sound in his head and, "No eye contact is necessary for this one, big boy. I'll give you this for free... Tell your wife congratulations for me. You are going to be a daddy. That is assuming she can actually successfully do anything correctly... right?" Scrios said sarcastically.

Gus ripped the artifact from his pocket and stared into the crystal as the monster screamed in agony and a fresh tide of souls flowed into Gus's consciousness. There was so much, too much, and eventually Gus pulled away. As he did, he heard the echo of a simple priest in his head, a Father Tristain of a small parish near Chicago 1880's. In the priest's head, Gus watched as he prayed the Rosary. His fingers moved from the small bead as he finished the "Hail Mary" and on to the larger bead, as he began the "Our Father". He prayed for a reason that the Lord had taken his last brother. Why did such a thing as tuberculosis even exist? Suddenly, Gus was back in the bedroom.

"Wow," came the voice in his head. "I swear, I thought that actually would hurt less this time. Checking the box that says, 'WRONG' on that one."

"Good, now go back to shutting the hell up, because Disney is still on the table." Gus said as he grabbed his bag and walked downstairs where the bottle of Macallan sat on the table with three small glasses.

As he reached the bottom stair, Deb stood and came to him, holding the dish towel. "Honey, your nose is bleeding again."

Gus touched his face and sure enough, blood. Deb held out a rag for his face, and he took it from her, rolling his eyes at the inconvenient timing.

They toasted to Gus's journey and the ones they had lost. To friendship and love. Gus toasted to the fact that their feeling of love, and friendship was irritating Scrios in the same cringeworthy way that everyone else not involved in child beauty pageants, saw child beauty pageants, and the hovering mothers attempting to live a childhood they felt denied of somehow.

Chapter 9

Thursday, October 25th, 2018, 3:00 PM Cottage off Kilsyth Rd. Queenzieburn, Scotland,

Precisely at 3:00, a delivery van, like the DHL one earlier, pulled into the drive. It drove up the drive parking close to the door. On the side of the van was a name of a company, "Lowland Exterminators," with a tag line, "The Ex will na get oot? Call a Solicitor. Got Bugs? Call us." A skinny man with a ponytail sticking out from under his cap, wearing a pair of loose-fitting coveralls, came to the door with a clipboard and a bag. He rang the bell. Deb answered the door and let the man in. As he entered, Dino turned towards Gus, "You ready?"

"Yup!" said Gus as the new person in the room took off the hat with the attached ponytail and unzipped the coveralls. He handed the hat to Gus, and the coveralls soon followed. Inside of a minute, Gus had them on as Gus realized the similarity of height and build of the pretend exterminator.

Dino embraced the new man in the room in a big hug, while saying, "Spider!" as Gus adjusted the cuffs on the pants to go over his boots.

"We'll chat in a few. Hell, as long as you want," said Spider as he spun to Gus. "When you walk out the door, take a second out front to look at the house like somehow you got the wrong address and head to the van. You will meet Billy in the car. He is a good guy for a squid. He will drive you out of here. There is a false floor in the back if needed, but I doubt you will. Listen to Billy and get familiar with how it works when you leave. Got it? We informed everyone on the team; you're responsible for yourself and your own luggage. Not sure anyone understands, but whatever package you are carrying, it's on you. Dino explained that."

"Got it," Gus said as Dino and Spider ushered him towards the door and handed him the clipboard. He walked out, looking down at the clipboard, glanced back at the house once and shook his head. Entered the passenger seat and looked as if he was complaining, as he said, "Hi Billy, I hear you are my ride."

Gus's driver, Billy, looked as if he must have lost his razor several months ago and the gristly beard that had taken root reminded Gus of swampland after a hurricane blew through. His beard mostly concealed what Gus could see when he got up close. Billy's features hid many old, deep scars. Near and in the scars, the hair was heavily flecked with white. Once he noticed that, he noted the other areas that had that same characteristic in the hair on his head. He tried not to stare.

"Yup," Billy said. "When we clear the drive, hop in the back and make yourself familiar with the mole hole. It's tight, but you will fit with your bag if needed. Also, back there you have another bag. Dino specified some shit for you. Don't bother with your real name. I don't want to know it. Think up something and I will call you that, cool?"

"Uh, sure," Gus said as he climbed into the back.

"When you get back there, the release is near the wheel-well on the right, facing the back. What you are looking for is a tie-down, like where a strap would connect to. It doesn't look like it, but it twists, and it is not supposed to be easy."

"I think I got it. "Holy shit, that's a tough turn," Gus exclaimed, as he felt the ground he was squatting on rise.

"Don't worry," said Billy, "the release from the inside is a lot easier. In there, you will find earphones that are hard-wired into the sound system. You can hear the radio or me talking up here. I cannot hear you, so I won't be asking you questions. If you think you hear a question, it's not me... How about Oscar?"

"Oscar?" Gus asked, with a confused look on his face.

"For your name." Billy said.

"Oscar works," Gus said with a nod.

"Cool, so you know where you are going?" Billy asked.

"Paris, right? Who knows where after that, though." Gus replied.

"Ha!" Billy said, "Paris is where everyone goes, but no one goes to Paris, yah dig? Someone says they are going to Paris, that means they don't know or don't want to know where they are going. When your man got you this ride, he specified Paris. That meant, I don't want to know where he is going. We are heading to a transport plane that is going to take you to Calgary, Canada."

"Ok," Gus said with a tentative sound to his voice. "Joking, right?"

"Nope, Canada," the driver said plainly.

"Behind my seat, said Billy, you will see a bag. In it there is a change of clothes. They are intentionally a little big. Take your shit off and toss it on the seat beside you or pack it. There is even underwear and socks too, if you need them. Put on the stuff in the bag. Undies first,"

"I know how to get dressed..." Gus started.

"Man, just listen a sec! After the undies, you will see a ballistic vest at the bottom of the bag. That goes on next. It will stop small arms and shrapnel. Well, most small-arm rounds... not mine, but hopefully theirs. After that, you will see a black long-sleeve shirt that is stiff and uncomfortable. Put it on next. After that there is a matching pair of long shorts, they are next. After that, the normal shirt, pants, socks and boots. They should all fit you. Do you know how to use a pistol?"

"Um, yeah?" Gus said with his head swirling. With, "What the hell is going on?" rushing through his mind. "I have concealed carry in the states, and I served four years."

"Good," said the driver, squinting his eyes a little, "Navy, right?"

"Hell no," Gus said, "Army."

"Damn son, you look too pretty to be Army," Billy said. "Must have been an officer."

Gus shrugged his shoulders, "Yup, got me."

Back on task, Billy said, "There is a coat back there too, but before that, you will see a shoulder rig designed for a right-handed draw. There are three spare clips in the rig. The pistol has a clip in it but not chambered. Do not chamber that round unless shit hits the fan."

"Got it," Gus said. "I'm guessing if I ask if I'm going to need this weapon, you are going to say to always be prepared."

"Were you an Eagle Scout?" Billy said with a smile as he looked at him through a large mirror mounted on his sun visor.

"I was not much of a joiner when I was a kid," Gus replied, "and the one meeting for cub scouts I went to was enough for me to say, Hell No!" he said with a laugh.

"Ok General, anything you don't want, put in that plastic bag and it will get burned," the driver said. "If you have any possessions that you are uncertain of, toss them in there too."

"Uncertain?" Gus asked.

"Some people we pick up have a watch that was given to them and later we find them dead, because it had a tracker in it. So, I tell people anything they are uncertain of goes in the bag. Most of the time, nothing goes in there, but hey, I tried, right?"

"One quick pit-stop," Billy said as he pulled off into a secluded parking area. I need to change the signs. Back in the back, you will see a plastic tube that is about a foot in diameter. Bring it up here to the back door," he said as he dawned plastic gloves. A couple of seconds after he exited the vehicle, Gus heard a tearing sound on the outside of the van as Billy removed the exterminator sign from the driver's side. Next, he removed the one from the passenger side.

When he came to Gus's door, he took the large tube, "Also, give me the coveralls you wore," he said, "and take the patch off the hat." Gus complied.

With speed and efficiency of someone who had done this before, Billy placed the new magnetic signs on the vehicle with surprisingly few curse words or re-seating. He took the old signs, Gus's coveralls and patch and threw them into a steel drum that Billy did not seem surprised to find at their pull-off location. He followed them with his own coveralls and the patch from his hat. Billy returned to Gus's door. "Hand me that red plastic bag right there," he said, and Gus handed him the heavy bag that contained a plastic bottle of something. He walked to the can, tossed his plastic gloves on top of the pile, and soaked the steel can with the contents of the plastic bottle. Billy picked up some dry leaves and lit them with a lighter and tossed them into the can. The flames grew and Billy tossed the remaining bottle of lighter fluid into the flaming bin and walked back to the van, and they drove off.

Interlude – The Strange Case

Monday, October 25th, 2018, 9:00 PM

Thank you for watching BBC One. In Perthshire, the search continues for Laoch "Gus" Ferguson, the focus of a joint U.S. and British Task Force. The case, however, has taken many strange turns over the last five days. With many residents, and even prominent figures in British government siding with the Ferguson family.

There have been statements of support for the family, from several prominent members of Parliament.

Chapter 10

Thursday, October 25th, 2018, 11:19 PM East Midlands Airport, Near Derby, England

Six hours later, they arrived at an enormous airport. "Where are we?" Gus asked.

"This is East Midlands Airport. This airport ranks among the world's largest airports and specializes in worldwide shipping. Put this patch on your hat," Billy said, "and here is your ID card," as he handed him the card. "Your name now is Oscar Johnson, and you are from Paduka, Kentucky. Congratulations on your new job at DHL!"

"You fucking planned the Oscar name, didn't you?" Gus asked.

"Oh yeah," Billy said with a smile. "Hop up front and smile. If they ask you to roll down your window, don't do it all the way. Just about a hand's width. The inside of each of the passenger windows is coated with a tint that fouls up cameras. Basically, just washes out the picture with reflection. I have papers that say we are picking up medical perishable goods and they will check out if checked. They will think transplants most likely. But after that, I will hand you off to the team tasked with getting you to your next stop. Let's get through the gate and we will shake hands. Deal?"

"Deal." Gus said.

When they pulled to the gate, following a short line of similar vehicles, the guard stepped to the window and asked for IDs as a second guard walked around the car with a mirror on a pole, inspecting the undercarriage and wheel wells. After about 30 seconds, the arm of the gate opened, and they drove in. "Easy-peasy," Billy said with a big smile.

They drove, following the other similar vehicles towards the enormous warehouse on the Western side of the airport. Billy turned the car and drove right past a sign that said, "Restricted" in several languages, and pulled in next to two identical vehicles.

"Oscar? It has been a pleasure," Billy said to Gus. "Let's get you inside and let you meet the crew that will take you from here."

"One question," Gus asked, "When I get in there and say Calgary, when they ask, are they going to laugh like you did about Paris?"

Billy smiled and patted Gus on the shoulder, "Oscar, if I said you are really going to Calgary, would you believe me?"

"Probably not," Gus replied.

"Wise man, but you are going to Calgary," Billy said, waggling his eyebrows in a Groucho Marx imitation.

Chapter 11

Friday, October 26th, 2018, 8:19 AM Calgary International Airport, Calgary, Canada

Fourteen hours later, and six time zones west of England, Gus stood outside of the Calgary airport, after being dropped off by a work shuttle, to an employee parking lot. Gus stood in the shelter of a bus stop; it was a chilly morning even with an indecisive breeze generally out of the south. He sat on the metal stylized bench inside the plexiglass and plastic structure, its metal ribs showing the exposure to the harsh elements for several years.

A person who had also been on the bus that dropped them off, pulled up to the shelter and rolled down the window of his late eighties Chevy Impala. "Hey buddy," he said, "You, uh... okay?" he asked with a genuine concern that kind of shocked Gus. "You need a ride somewhere or somethin'?"

"Seriously? That would be great!" Gus said. "I got sent here for a week, last minute, and I think my phone completely died," he said with mock frustration.

"Where can I take you?" the nice man asked, as Gus opened the passenger side door to get in.

"Is there a like, a Goodwill shop or anything? I came here kinda quick, and this is all I really had for warmth," Gus explained. "I don't really need anything for that long, since I go home in a couple of days, so no reason to empty the piggy bank on a brand-new coat."

"Ah, you are from the States?" The man asked and reached a hand over to shake. "Teddy Kaspernevitch, please to meet you. I think I might know the perfect place for you. It's a nice little thrift store on 5th Avenue Southeast. What part of the states are you from?"

Gus shook his hand. "Oscar Johnson," he said. "I'm from the southeast. I grew up in Georgia, north of Atlanta, a little way. In high school, I moved to Paduka, Kentucky. Good stuff at this place?" Gus asked, getting the topic off him and his thin cover story as quick as he could.

"Well, my daughter buys all her clothes there and raves about how she finds even new stuff she can buy on her babysitting money." Teddy said. "Its downtown, and less rural than up here near the airport. Up here you can catch a two-mile hike real fricken, excused my language, quick between populated areas. Especially at night, I tell ya. I had a breakdown up here one night in February... minus forty and that is freaking Celsius, not your fairy Fahrenheit." Teddy said as Gus did the numbers in his head and decided not to point out the number's being exactly the same. "Any-who, here I'm walking along the road, people driving by and probably not even seeing me because the wind is making it hard to see, so I'm staying away from the road as much as possible to not get hit, right? Right out of the snow squall comes my lovely Martha, in the Suburban. She had gotten my text message and saved my life, I tell ya. Saved it. So, I get in the car, close the door and I look at her with my cheeks all puffed up, like this." He said and turned to Gus with his cheeks blown up. "She says, she says, 'Teddy, why are your cheeks all puffed up like that?' So, I says, after a big fake swallow, Honeybun, I was just keeping my testicles warm. Get it? Testicles warm! I mean it, we laughed the entire way home," he said as he laughed, with a far-off look.

"So, down in the U.S., carpooling is a big thing. Do you guys do that up here much?" Gus asked.

"Oh yeah, saving gas and all. We did it for a while. Two guys I work with live close to me, kind of on my way home. We did it for a couple of weeks, but one day, they both said they had saved up and bought cars for themselves. I think they thought I talk too damn much. I probably was driving them nuts," he said.

"Please! You are just good at pleasant conversation. Some people aren't." Gus said as the car stopped at a light after taking an exit from the highway. Gus could feel Teddy looking at the side of his face and glanced that way.

"Thank you so very much. My Martha says I always talk too damn much," he spoke.

"Wow, that would be an easy push to get rid of ol' Martha," came the voice of Scrios in Gus's head. "Talk about your easy layups."

Gus wanted to respond to Scrios, but obviously couldn't, so he tried to pick up where he had left off. "On top of being fun to talk to, you saved me a cold ass morning in that bus stop. So, you are nice too. Martha is a lucky lady."

"Actually, that lovely lady left my life last summer," he said in a much calmer and solemn voice.

"Oh, I am so sorry," Gus said. "How did she pass?"

"Oh," Teddy said. "She didn't pass. She left me for a guy who sells carpets and flooring in Edmonton. I wondered why she was looking at new carpets in Edmonton several times a week."

"So was the bloke in Edmonton," Scrios said to Gus, causing him to choke.

"Are you okay?" asked Teddy.

"Oh yeah," he said. "I was stuck between breathing in and swallowing saliva, and the breathing won out."

"Please, please, please, you must let me do my civic duty and empower this guy to do the right thing," the monster said in Gus's head.

"Ah, So the place is right up here, on the right," Teddy said. "No proper places to park, so I will have to drop you off."

"That will be great Teddy. Thanks so much."

"I meant to ask you," Teddy said, "but I felt awkward... that bulge in your pants pocket there. Don't worry, I won't make the old happy to see me joke. Just wondering."

"Oh, that is just my toothbrush holder. I forgot I had it in my pocket and should have put it in my bag." Gus explained.

As the car pulled up, Teddy's face twisted as he awkwardly asked, "Can... uhh... do you mind if I see it?" he asked.

"Well, it's kind of a private item... and it's pink, my daughter gave it to me, so I would be too embarrassed, but thank you for the ride. Do you need any gas money or anything?" Gus asked.

Teddy seemed to brighten up like someone waking from a daydream, "Oh no. This is right on my way home. Glad to have helped."

Gus closed the door and waved, and Teddy waved back, as he drove away. He watched for a second as he drove to the next intersection and turned left. Gus turned and walked into the nice sized thrift store, that was indeed full of very nice items.

He had listened well to Dino during their walk and talks. Dino had talked to him about changing his appearance. Gus knew that for actual change, it would take time. Gus was not anyone's definition of fat, but the several days he spent with Dino had changed his appearance by melting some of the thickness to his frame that, even with exercise, his diet and sitting in front of a computer, had added.

Thirty minutes later, he left the thrift store carrying a framed, black backpack. He also carried several plastic bags with various heavier clothes in them and under his arm he carried a small, expensive sleeping bag and bedroll. A bag overflowed with useful knickknacks: flashlight, multi-tool, extra batteries, ready for the backpack. When he left the store, he turned right and right again at the small paved alley that went between the building and a Greek restaurant.

He walked behind the building and set about repacking his bags. It had been awkward, when he paid with American dollars, but the store was fine with it when he rounded to the nearest twenty and said to consider the rest a donation. When he finished repacking, he walked past the Greek restaurant, which was still closed, and entered the gas station portion of the building. He found a kiosk for cell phones that included an inexpensive knockoff phone. And grabbed it, and grabbed three prepaid SIM cards for the phone his grandfather had given him.

Gus knew that if he could find a Wi-Fi hot-spot, he could use the good phone, but out beyond Calgary's sprawl, the endless expanse of flat grasslands he'd glimpsed from the air seemed to mock his hope of regular connection. While he felt confident that there would be cellular coverage, he was uncertain if it would expand to where he planned to travel. He liked, however, the idea of having a burner phone in his pack as a backup.

Gus walked south and found an open bank in the not too pleasant area he was currently in. I mean, it was not Detroit bad, but the signage reminded him of more dangerous areas of Raleigh. From his grandfather's money belt, he retrieved 500 British pounds. Wearing a Calgary Flames red logo hat and sunglasses from the thrift store, he entered the bank like he owned it. Making his way to a small desk, he asked the lady seated there about the possibility of exchanging foreign currency. She mentioned they did, and asked if he was an RBC customer. He replied he was not, but he was seeking a bank. So, she helped him setup an account under the name Oscar Johnson, the last use of this brilliant and disposable cover that had gotten him to Canada. Twenty minutes later, he left with just under 800 Canadian dollars. He left 50 dollars in savings, which was much more than the minimum required.

When he walked outside the bank, he took the roads south and occasionally east. He was glad to see the phone from his grandfather had activated and checked the internet for a place likely to offer an inexpensive place to stay. He found the answer to that question was along Highway 2E, also named Macleod Trail, which made him laugh thinking of Highlander and the Spaniard played by Sean Connery, a Scot with his unbridled Scottish accent. The reference in his mind made him smile and pushed him back just over a couple of months in time. He thought about that dang piece of paper on his refrigerator. "Holy shit," he mumbled, "has it only been two months?"

During that period, his home had been the scene of a violent altercation with a police officer. After fleeing to Scotland, he learned he had inherited a unique natural immunity from his father. He had gotten married. He unsettlingly found out that monsters are real. The monster had ravaged Peter's world and reduced Marcy to a mere shadow of her former self. "Marcy!" he said.

"And there it is," came Scrios's voice in Gus's head. "It finally, finally sank in."

He tried to ignore the damn monster's taunting in his head, but couldn't. Gus dropped to a seat on the ground and took out his phone. Powered it up, waited for a signal, and pulled up the bunny game. In his mailbox there was one message from his grandfather, one from Peter and 37 from Quackomatic71, his Marcy. He started going through the in-game emails from Marcy.

In the letters from her, he heard tones in his head as he read the messages. Sadness and apologies for her many mistakes. Another email would apologize for the tone of the previous email. Sometimes there had been hours between the emails and other times, just seconds. The notes appeared in his mind like that of the woman he loved, unraveling like a ball of yarn with a cat in the room. His heart ached as he read through them and the cool dry breeze made it feel like icy lines where the tears rolled down his face. The feeling of helplessness was overwhelming. He looked at his grandfather's letter for some kind of solace.

His grandfather wrote to him with great concern over the disappearance of Peter and apologized to him for his failure to protect him from himself. The letter talked about how he had slipped the tail of Buster and Wombat in a manner that they did not think anyone was capable. They had even tried an electronic tracker, only to find it being carried by a schoolboy on a playground who said a secret agent gave it to him.

The note from Peter beckoned. So, he opened it.

Gus,

I'm sorry about my failure to do as you asked. My love for you, as my brother, will never waver, but amidst recent confusion, I have to leave and find myself. With that, I have resigned from the company and have taken my show, packed up my nest egg... and maybe a little of Mom's. Hope she doesn't get too mad. Let's face it, Redwolf was nice, but it was never really my thing. I'm deleting my account on here, but I'm certain we will see one and other again sometime.

I am forever your brother.

Peter

The normalcy of the letter, transposed over what Gus knew to be true, was disturbing. When he tried to hit reply, just in case, he saw a pop-up screen that read, "This account has been deleted and won't receive any responses."

Gus wrote Marcy a quick note and told her he would be back online by 9:00 PM her time to text in a live chat. His writing took on a glum sound, so he erased those lines. He found he sounded excited and happy, and that also did not work. So, he told her, "Marcy, I love you to the moon and back. I look forward to when this bullshit is over, and I can hold you in my arms again. I will try to fulfill my task as fast as I can manage. You should know that I'm safe. I will speak to you soon." He wrote and hit the send button and exited the game.

He brought up a navigation app, wiped the drying tears from his face, and gathered his belongings. As he stood, a police car pulled up beside him. The officer smiled at him, "Hey Pal, are you ok, eh?"

Gus laughed and nodded cordially. "Yeah, thanks. Chatting with my girlfriend back home, and I miss her."

"Okay, just saw you sitting there and decided to check on ya. You have a good day there, my friend." The officer said as he slowly drove away as Gus raised his hand in the common sign for "Thanks."

Gus began walking at his normal steady pace towards the district that seemed to have the inexpensive hotels. He was not looking for a nice place. Just something with a door, and he found that on Macleod Trail. As expected, they did not give a shit for a credit card deposit. They just wanted cash, and he just wanted a room that did not have bugs or blood stains.

Chapter 12

Friday, October 26th, 2018, 2:04 PM A Cheap Hotel on Macleod Trail, Calgary, Canada

Gus got one of his two requirements; the door was solid. When Gus inspected the bed, by lifting the pillows, he cringed. "Wow," he said, "You would think a hotel with Best in its name would be... better." When he looked at the wall at the front of the room, which faced the busy highway out front, he could see gaps in places where he could see daylight through. Gus nodded his head in surrender, "Wow," he said again. "This place makes the ruin in the woods that Dino and I stayed in look like the Hilton," as he scanned the room for anything redeemable.

Everything about the place screamed Howard Johnson's but no, it was not. Daring himself, He pulled back the covers on the bed and saw nothing. Next, he pulled back the sheets, and still nothing. Unconvinced, he lifted the mattress from the bedsprings, discovering worrying signs and opting for a night in the bathtub. Still, it was a roof.

"What a shithole," a voice in his head said.

"You are not helping," Gus said, "nor is your opinion wanted."

"You know," said Scrios, "I have the account numbers and access codes to millions, maybe billions."

"Thanks to you," Gus replied, "So do I... along with a shit-ton of baggage I never wanted."

"Really?" Scrios said with genuine surprise. "How does your monkey brain access such things?"

"I'm not talking to you about this, or anything." Gus replied.

"No, no. I'm just asking, wondering if your brain is anything like mine?" Scrios said in ancient Greek.

"Yes, I can understand you," Gus said, and I'm still not talking about it.

"Interesting and unexpected. Bravo!" Scrios said.

"Ok, do I need to submerge you in the toilet bowl before or after I take a shit to get you to shut up?" Gus asked.

"Zipping!" Scrios replied and went silent.

Hmm, thought Gus, not a bad idea. So, he walked into the bathroom, lifted the back of the lid off of the tank and lowered Scrios into the elbow deep water. "Better this than the bowl. That is the only other choice. If I hear anything, I'll assume you prefer my turds, because I know you can't fit down the hole if I flush.

Scrios thought to himself, "I have sat in throne rooms covered in glorious blood...," however, this time he decided it would be unwise if he challenged his descendant's resolve.

Gus made himself comfortable with the new sleeping pad and sleeping bag in the tub while he prepared to talk with Marcy. He knew from her memories, his goals of boosting her spirits were near impossible, but he had to try.

His discussion with her lasted for over 30 minutes. He dreaded her telling him about the pregnancy. She never brought it up. Somehow, she didn't know. He couldn't and wouldn't dare say it, or he would have to explain how he knew.

He dreaded her describing how her happiness depended on him. Dependent on him being there for the process, and the sadness of him missing the experience. He knew from her memories how she would respond. She would beg him to finish his task quickly and come home, and he would promise her he would try.

He was so caught up in the discussion that didn't happen in his mind; it distracted him from the one he was having. She thought he was tired and told him to get some sleep.

The discussion over, he checked his kit, aware of the hard month ahead walking south, hoping for pleasant weather until he could enter the U.S. The brutal Iraqi winters and intense California mountain training for the army showed his ability to withstand the cold. He prayed he would not have to use much of the bushcraft he had learned there, and from Dino.

From his large pack's side pocket, he retrieved the book he'd unexpectedly discovered at the back of the thrift store. The TM 31-210 Improvised Munitions Handbook, 1971 version was just sitting there on the shelf. Inside the cover, which someone had reinforced with duct tape, were over 200 dog-eared pages. Many of the pages had places where the previous owner had used a highlighter or pencil to write in the margins. Gus read it for 30 odd minutes, mostly browsing parts he thought might be helpful in the task in front of him. Not long after that, the jet-lag was dragging him down, so he pulled his hat down to block the light from above.

Gus woke to his phone alarm at 5:00 AM and climbed out of the tub. He grabbed the golden artifact from its watery resting spot, dried it with a towel, and placed it in the pocket of his pants. Once he stowed all his belongings, he checked the shower, expecting the worst. However, the water came on hot and clear. So, he removed his clothing and took a long shower to burn the pain of the tub from his muscles. When the shower was complete, he dressed and walked to

443

the door. He checked the peephole, and all looked clear, so he walked out into the chilly morning. To prepare for his hike to the south, he was on the lookout for a nice coffee and a hearty breakfast.

Chapter 13

Saturday, October 27th, 2018, 7:04 AM Corral Restaurant, Calgary, Canada

Gus checked the local reviews and found a place with a great breakfast and strong coffee. He sat and ate food that reminded him of home. All was going great, and he was prepared for the hike that awaited him. He checked his phone one last time before he headed out.

In the game's email, was a message from Deb. The subject of the email was, "Places with bags already in place... should you need it." By that she meant money. He examined the list. From a long list of fifteen cities, Calgary seemed to jump out at him. The University of Calgary campus Kinesiology-A men's locker room was listed as the location. Checking the Google map on his phone, he saw heartbreakingly that it was close to eight miles away. So, he counted his current funds, and kicked himself for not doing that sooner. On the bench seat beside him, in the booth he was in, he counted the money. There were 2000 British pounds sterling, 2500 U.S. Dollars and 2500 Euros. A pretty good stash, "but not inexhaustible," he heard in his grandfather's voice. So, he looked at other active drops, and none of the others seemed workable in the near term. Places like UW, in Seattle and UNLV in Las Vegas and other large cities. In the note, Deb had promised more cities to come. He weighed the thought to himself, "how much could there really be?" as he packed the money back into the belt.

Moments later, a server brought him his bill. He asked the pleasant young man, "what is the best way to get to the University of Calgary?"

"Oh, that's easy?" said the server. "We are right on the Red Line, buddy. You don't even have to switch. Just go to the kiosk where you get on at Chinook station, buy a day or weekly or heck, even a monthly pass and you are good to go!" The waiter as he handed Gus his bill. In appreciation for excellent service and assistance, Gus paid the server 30 Canadian dollars, covering a 15-dollar charge.

Gus walked to the station, bought a pass, and rode in comfort to the university on the light rail. When he arrived at the first stop for the University, he exited and asked someone who looked like a student for directions. After, Gus stopped under a tree to pull out his alternate ID that Deb had used for the drops. He walked into the Kinesiology building that was right next to the stadium used for speed-skating at the Winter Olympics. He followed the signs to the locker room. There, he ran into a helpful staff person who asked for identification, which Gus provided. The man nodded and Gus walked in. As he walked, he checked his phone for details in Deb's message and found the locker. He tried and failed the first time on the black and silver Master Lock, before remembering the proper spin cadence. The lock popped open.

Inside the locker was a large gym bag. Leaving the bag in the locker, he unzipped it and looked inside, seeing an obscene amount of violet strapped bundles of $20 bills. He was thankful that the locker was off to the side of the mane causeway of travel. There had to be a hundred thousand dollars in that bag. Just for safety, he felt compelled to load it carefully into the bottom compartment of his large backpack, feeling the anxiety of fear that came with the stupidity of carrying the kind of money people would kill him for, after they robbed him and found it. His panic was genuine; what if they found a single bundle in the locker during a routine check? They had seen his face. After moving the money over, he took a piece of paper from the notebook he purchased, and his pen and wrote a cartoon worthy "I.O.U." and placed it in the bag in the locker. Taking a clean shirt from his gear, he casually wiped the locker down where he had touched it while he fidgeted with the pack. He used the shirt to close the door and placed it back in the pouch pocket, and left the area through a different exit. Fifteen minutes later, he was back on the Red Line and heading back towards south Calgary. He took the line till its end and exited.

He had only lost about a half hour. He exited the station, checked his phone's GPS and started walking south, while drifting away from the A2 highway, taking a more cross-country approach to his hike. While the walk along the highway might have been easier, he didn't want the attention it could bring.

Chapter 14

Tuesday, October 30th, 2018, 9:15 AM Sheep River basin, East of Okotoks, Canada

Gus sat beside the campfire on the millions of rocks that made up the riverbanks. He sat there nibbling on some jerky and drinking some warm tea. In his hand, was his notebook as he brainstormed ideas to destroy the artifact. Part of him did not want to believe the experience a week before when he tried to hit the relic with the sledge.

With the cursed object in a pouch next to him, he wrote in his book and glanced at it. "That fucking thing," Gus thought, "What could make it so invulnerable?" He had searched the internet for the hardness of metals and found that they followed a similar model as gemstones. Everyone knew diamonds had the hardest rating. They rated at a 10 on the Mohs scale. In Okotoks, a town seemingly stuck in the 1970s, Gus bought a tungsten carbide chisel, a three-pound hammer, and diamond-coated files the previous night.

He had spent the last hour again trying to cut, smash, or scratch the golden tube. None of which were successful. The hardness of the metal was uncanny. "That's fucking impossible!" Gus said to himself.

He quickly gave up on the chisel when it broke. So, he placed the artifact on a larger, flat boulder and used it as an anvil. He slammed the heavy hammer onto the scepter almost 300 times. As his arm ached, he had pushed through the weariness that made his hand and arm numb. The impact pulverized rock beneath the artifact and even chipped off large chunks of stone. Cracks appeared between layers of the rock anvil. It wasn't until he saw the handle beginning to bend that he gave up on it. He examined the golden colored tube, wiping the rock dust from it. It was clean without even an abrasion. Trapped inside of it, the determined punishment he had delivered surprised even Scrios. All that effort without a single result. Gus didn't know it, but both he and Scrios were concerned for differing reasons. Gus looked at the weathered appearance of the serpent that coiled around the rod and could not justify how any weathering or wear could have happened. He surmised this thing must have been forged with the weathered look, because nothing thus far had produced any effect.

Gus looked at the plastic bag from the hardware store, knowing what it still contained. He had a sense of dread at trying the diamond files. What would he do if they failed? If they failed, it took so many possibilities off the table with the use of most any conventional tool.

The file did nothing, its diamonds seeming to skim across the surface of the artifact. Gus howled in frustration, throwing the destroyed hammer that sat beside the large stone 50 feet away. He picked up large rocks and slammed them on the object of his ire. He didn't honestly expect any results, but the exertion allowed him to slam away the frustrations with the artifact. The effort allowed him to pour his anger about Marcy and Peter into action until he was physically exhausted. The watermelon-sized rock he was smashing split in his hands, revealing the undamaged artifact and marking his moment of utter exhaustion.

Across the river from him, on a natural glacial ridge, a family from the Blood Tribe of the Kainai Nation, watched the rabid display. Their house was behind them, a small, weathered building with multiple creative repairs apparent from the outside. They stood and watched the crazy white man on the far bank of the Sheep River.

The youngest, a small boy of ten, moved from the family and walked forward intending to yell to the foolish man smashing rocks who was screaming an obscenity laced tirade. The ancient, prune like wrinkled and weathered grandmother placed a crooked fingered hand on his shoulder and stopped him.

In an ancient language, she told the children to go inside, and they unquestioningly followed her command. She told her daughter, "Evil walks over there! Leave him to it." The old women chanted to her ancestors to keep the evil away from her family. She walked back into the house, where they immediately sealed the doors and windows, both physically and spiritually.

Gus looked at his hands. They had scratches and raised blue and purple locations where he had destroyed the blood vessels. As he looked at them, he said, "Well, shit! That's going to hurt for a while."

Dino's discussions rang in his head, where he was told to never take silly chances when he was alone. He had said, "Most people have issues when they do something stupid, and to make up for it, they do something even dumber."

Gus had done step one, so now he needed to avoid making it worse. While his hands were sore and bloody in spots, he didn't think he had broken either of them. So, he took it easy and rested for a day. He walked to the river, squatted and stuck his hands in the icy water until they were numb, mentally beating himself up for his lunacy.

Interlude – Sunsets

Wednesday, November 1st, 6:30 PM The Big House, Atholl region, Scotland

William sat in his chair in front of the warm fire in the great room. The evening was freezing outside and the fingers of the cold reached in through the ancient walls. Gusts of wind outside pushed the dead leaves into dancing vortexes off towards the west.

"Old man," said Daniel as he added another log to the fire, "You seem awful quiet tonight. Do you need anything?"

"Oh no," William replied. "I'm fine. I am just thinking of the events of the recent days. Thinking about how quiet it is around here. How I truly miss Bynum and Donna. Growing old is strange. You spend your younger years wishing you were just a little older and at some sneaky point. The table turns, and you wonder how you got so old. I used to ask the Good Lord why. Why was I put here to grow so old? God, I miss Tilly. Do you know how long ago she left us? Fifty bloody years ago. We were supposed to do this getting old thing together. I was never one to do it myself. I have seen enough death and felt enough pain before she passed."

"Christ, I'm sorry," offered Daniel. "I didn't mean to push you into a melancholy."

"Oh no," William said with a genuine smile, "You didn't. I'm just stating a fact. I frankly didn't know my purpose was to be anything more than to carry the guilt of actions I had no control over. Through the years, when I was just more than a boy playing army. I thought the war was a game until Thomas died." He said as Laoch wandered into the room and sat quietly.

"You knew," William said, looking at Laoch. "You knew what happened to me when I touched that cursed thing the German commander carried, didn't you?"

"I suspected," Laoch admitted with a nod.

"It bloody scrambled me," William said. "Tried to ruin me. Succeeded in many important ways, but not completely. Now Gus is going to give it what for."

"We only have it because of you and your bravery," Laoch said as Daniel nodded.

"Bravery?" William laughed. "I have been a bloody coward my entire life. I pissed myself with the tiger, cried in and after every battle. That is hardly bravery. With that bastard, I needed it to know he had not beaten me. You are going to think I'm crazy."

"We already do that!" Daniel said with a laugh.

"Laoch, your grandfather... he was indeed there that night," William said. "He bloody walked with me to retrieve that thing. Pulled me along, if I was honest."

"I know," Laoch said. "When it all started, and I gave... the order, he appeared beside me and gave me that look. You know that one of determination he always had... and next he walked out towards you."

"I picked the cursed thing up, and I heard the creature's voice in my head," William said. "It talked like we were old friends and now he was back. I laughed at him and told him to sod right off! I had never done such a thing before. I placed the scepter in my pocket and walked back inside with Gus and handed it to him. He had no hold on me anymore. None," he said with a genuine smile.

The three talked for several more minutes before William excused himself to bed. William stood and Laoch stood as well, intent on the evening handshake he was so accustomed to. Williams' bypass of the handshake and immediate hug surprised Laoch.

"Thank you!" William said. "For taking me in. For believing in me. For giving me a home. I don't feel I have ever adequately expressed that."

"You are so very welcome, William," he replied.

William turned and walked to his room, where he changed into his nightclothes. He sat where Nell had pulled back his covers not long before, slid his feet under the sheet and blanket and laid back on his pillow.

Sleep came to William quickly this night. He dreamed of Tilly and of Thomas. He dreamed of all those he commanded that he had written condolence letters to their families during the war. Their faces seemed clear to him now, as if they were showing up for a party. From a corner of the great room, a band played lovely music, and everyone was in sharp attire.

He saw her, his lovely Tilly. She was not sick, but full of life like their wedding day. She ran to him and they hugged as they walked to the dance floor. As they began their second dance on the parquet squares, a twinge of pain hit William in the chest for a moment and faded quickly away. Tilly looked at him and smiled.

"That happens to everyone," she said and kissed him.

Chapter 15

Sunday, November 11th, 2018, 8:00 AM Near Belly River Campground, Alberta, Canada

From Calgary, Gus trekked south, devising a plan to demolish Scrios's fortified dwelling. He had been walking, camping, checking messages and keeping in touch in the game, eating and drinking for twelve days. He spent each night adding to his notebook's collection of creature-destroying ideas.

In later pages, where there were complexities, he wrote out needs. He began his list with a jackhammer, knowing it was likely useless, and escalated in destructive potential from that point. Some things he felt comfortable he could make happen, other things he would need help with, and the idea of involving others, scared him.

Inevitably, each night he would hear Peter's voice in a memory from the last time they talked, "Right, so you are off to Mordor, to toss him into the volcano, huh?" The first few times he would choke a laugh, and he would notice the tears running down his face.

"Dammit Peter. Why did you have to run away like that?" he would think as his thoughts would wander to the darkness and Peter's likely activities. Gus was not really the praying type. Even growing up going to church with his mother had not really stuck. However, Gus bargained with the Big-Guy more often than he ever had lately.

He prayed Peter wouldn't hurt anyone, because if someone could help him later, or if he regained his center after Gus successfully destroyed the monster; Gus knew he would find it hard to live with the knowledge he hurt someone. He knew this with a supernatural certainty of being able to feel the understandings of both versions of his friend.

Gus constantly weighed the suggestion of tossing the artifact into a volcano. He decided it would be a last resort, because he doubted it would kill the monster or destroy the artifact. Much like his being buried in the wilderness for half a millennium, inevitably in the future, a pig-faced Liam would find him.

The enormous time scale of how long before someone would recover him, if he pitched him into a fiery caldera, was the one reason he kept the idea on the list as Project Frodo. Internet searches narrowed down the locations of open lava pool calderas with visible lava pools to just seven. To reach either Hawaii or Vanuatu would require traversing a significant open ocean, with Vanuatu presenting the most favorable access to the open crater. There were trails that overlooked the crater in Vanuatu, whereas Hawaii had restricted access and additional security.

When there was a signal, he would check email in the game and have discussions with his grandfather or Marcy. He even spoke to Dino once, who asked him how the baguettes were in Paris. They chatted and joked, pretending how Gus had sent him pictures from various tourist spots. Gus had taken pictures of his travel, but he kept them private.

Some places were so breathtaking, with cascading waterfalls, vibrant wildflowers, that he knew he needed to bring Marcy back to share the stunning scenery. He had walked along the foothills and, in some places, the views of the towering mountains, when it was clear, were magical. Someday he would come back and go throughout these incredible mountains with his wife and their child.

He thought, even though Marcy had not brought up the child, he reasoned Scrios was evil and despicable, but he had no evidence of him really being a liar. Sure, the changes he made to people could easily be described as lies, though, he thought. Not that he thought the creature was above uttering a falsehood. If the circumstances met the need; however, as he searched the memories gained from the creature, he was not sure if the fiend had ever felt the need to deceive.

Gus knew he could not tell her what the monster told him, because the trauma response of Scrios knowing before she did might push her over the edge, if it were true. Gus's mind chewed that thought, "If it were true," as Marcy wrote him her next text message.

"So," she said as if she sensed his current thoughts, "Maybe not the best time, because it rips my heart out. I was feeling sick, so Nell took me to the doctor's office. I thought I was coming down with a cold or gastrointestinal infection... and I am not. God, I wish you were here, because I'm pregnant... We are pregnant," she corrected herself in the next message.

Gus didn't know what to type, so he just typed anything. "That is fantastic! God, I wish I was there to go get a nice dinner and celebrate. Soon, I promise!" he typed and hit send and immediately regretted the "soon" part.

"Me too, I'm so sorry to do that to you," she wrote. "My doctor estimates my due date as April 15th. That feels like forever to me right now."

"Honey, this is fantastic. The timing of this adventure is terrible and totally outside of anyone's control."

When they finished talking, and Gus shut down his phone, he was a mix of emotions. To get his mind off the current emotional spin, he evaluated his current situation.

He had found this camping place on the online map when he had decent service. He was glad he had taken screenshots. When he got to the campground, he found it had closed for the season, which he had somehow missed in his research. "That's fine," Gus thought as he sat there. "Fewer people... ok, no people... even better," he said to himself. As to not break any rules that might capture unwanted attention, he moved over a mile away from the actual campground. Looking at the maps, he was close to the Alberta Highway-6, which was to his east a short way. Occasionally, he could hear a car or truck pass by on it.

While there were signs of wildlife, other than seeing a distant bird or two, he had seen very few animals. It was like they were avoiding him. He was thankful for not running into a bear, as signs both human painted ones on warning signs; and trees that were scratched with deep gouges that shredded the bark at places higher than his head as he walked. Numerous bear droppings were found in piles during his hike. The weather had been dry and cold for an extended period of days, he thought optimistically. "Maybe they are all just taking their long winter nap?" he said quietly.

He knew that when he walked to the road and head south; in just a couple miles, he would come across the border and the border crossing. That made him nervous. There could be several challenges. They might choose to search his pack for contraband, and the $100,000 might be a little hard to explain. Also difficult would be the fact that the United States passport he had, had not legally entered Canada. Although unlikely to be cross-referenced, that ID had been used at the University of Calgary when he accessed his locker. If that tripped an additional flag, his exit could be a lot more interesting. What if in a search they found Scrios? What would be the logical, critical path that would happen after that?

He thought about crossing the border using the stream beside his campsite, but the flow of strong current went the wrong way and the water, even in summer, was cold as hell.

As he had hiked from Calgary, Gus and run across several bands of "homeless hikers", as he liked to call them. They were not truly homeless, he theorized, but simply on an extended break from the world. He noticed a trend in the men. Most were wiry, as Gus had become over the past several weeks. That had been part of the goal when he had purposely cut his diet to help to achieve that exact look... It changed his appearance, as Dino had suggested. Strangely, he felt healthier, too. His hair length had obviously not changed terribly, but the blonde highlights looked much more of a distant summer decision than an effort to change his appearance.

He didn't know why he had purchased the yellow bandana that he had seen in a bin at the thrift store, but after seeing the popularity of them in the fellow homeless wanderers he now emulated, he was glad he did. He wore one on his head much of the time, emulating the others he had seen. The other pattern he took on, at least when in sight of others, was what he thought of as the "opportunistic big-balled walk," combined with the outgoing "everything is great" personality. His three weeklong facial hair had finally passed the always itchy point, and it completed his look.

An idea crept into his mind. He remembered looking at the border's satellite photos on Google Earth to find the crossing he wanted to use. Now he was considering going back into the U.S. through the wilderness. Between entry points, the woods appeared to have been cleared, and he noted the shadows of poles that dotted the open area. A bulge in the shadow near the top of the pole was either a light, which seemed improbable, or some type of active surveillance. Surveillance made sense. So, he guessed that the cameras, probably multiple, one for daylight and one for nighttime and motion detection to alert for movement, with 24x7 storage of the streams.

Nighttime would be best for him to cross, and the more remote, the better. In his pack, he searched for an emergency supply he had picked up just in case he needed it. In his pack was a clear plastic package, segmented into ten pouches. Each pouch contained a disposable mylar blanket, which Gus had purchased just in case he needed to make an emergency shelter. He remembered a security blind spot that he and a fellow lieutenant in Iraq had discussed and tested with such a blanket and standard issue NVGs. When the person with the blanket completely covered themselves, they had virtually disappeared... and Gus had ten such blankets and a roll of duct tape.

Chapter 16

Monday, November 12th, 2018, 9:45 AM Chief Mountain Highway, Montana, USA

Gus sat in the woods where he made camp. Yesterday and last night had made for a long day. He had broken camp yesterday morning, and hiked northeast, crossing the Belly River, again. He had picked the place that would be the least convenient for any border patrol to get to, hoping they didn't have a helicopter.

The path took him across Highway- 6 in view of the entrance to the campgrounds to the north and into the hills east of the road. He followed the gentle slope upwards as the hills grew dramatically steeper to the north and the south. Gus trekked along the valley between the two large hills for close to three miles before the hill to the south dropped in elevation. That elevation change he had seen on the maps marked where he made his way south.

After walking due south for another mile and a half, near lunch time he reached the meandering Middle Fork Lee Creek, where he refilled his water bottles and treated the water with iodine. He sat down and ate some jerky and granola bars from his provisions while he debated if he could cross without getting his feet wet, since the creek was so low. After breakfast and drinking all the water he could, he refilled the water bottles again in the clear water. Finding a spot in the creek narrow enough to cross safely, he continued southwest.

The new heading took him up a gentle ridge, which he expected, choosing the route to avoid other water crossings if possible, and entered the heavier forest as he climbed. Not long after carefully crossing a rural dirt road, he reached a point where he could see a clearing in the woods, which he was certain was for the boarder clearing and peered hard through the gaps in the trees, looking for the poles that he believed held the surveillance equipment. After traversing east about 50 feet, he saw a pole about forty feet further to the east. He mentally marked the spot and went west until he found another pole. They were not as far apart as he had thought, more like 50 yards between the two. "It will have to do," Gus said to himself.

He went back west, counting his paces until he was near the center point between the poles and settled down against a tree. As he took out the folded sheets of mylar and made a long poncho like cover with a deep hood. It had to be big enough to cover him and his pack, so he was extra generous with the silvery fabric as he taped the seams with the duct tape. He placed the silver side of the mylar on the outside for maximum heat reflection. When satisfied with the hooded poncho, he slid it over the backpack frame and picked up the backpack and slid his arms into the straps in a dry run. It went on easily, and the hood stuck out nearly a foot in front of him, like blinders. In his mind, he had pictured how it would look through infrared and saw the hood area would glow white. So, he took the contraption off and crated a mask to wear under the hood, with holes for his eyes. He created a long dress to wear to help conceal his feet. It took until almost sunset to complete the outfit. When the sun went down, it got dark fast.

The minimal moonlight from the moon that looked like a fingernail in the west told Gus the later he waited, the darker it would get. While that was great for his costume, it was bad for his ability to see the uneven ground, and those things called sticks that he occasionally tripped over at mid-day.

At 6:50, it was dark, with barely any ambient light to the west where the sun had set over an hour before. Gus had mentally marked the first 30 feet. After that, he just had to take it slow and hope there was no open mineshaft. "Why the hell did I think that?" Gus had thought immediately after.

Sounding like a windstorm inside the thin metal costume, Gus slowly crossed the open area. The 30 feet took nearly five minutes as he placed each foot as he went. It was so loud inside the outfit that a tank could have driven up to him and he probably would not have noticed. He maintained discipline and kept from looking to the side for either tower. The last thing he wanted to do was to make two eyes appear, making whoever might watch, have a Predator movie moment.

When he made it to the far wood line, he sped up his steps slightly. Once he was 20 feet in, he slid off his pack and took off his hood. "Man, was it getting cold outside?" he thought. He took off the dress and carefully folded the material until it was the size of a standard envelope. Mentally reminding himself to find a hole in a tree or something to dispose of it when he could see, he continued south, listening to hear if there were the sounds of any vehicles. He heard nothing and when he got far enough into the woods as to feel safe, he used the light from his phone screen to light his way enough to increase his pace.

Last night, or in the early morning anyway, he heard the road ahead of him before he could see it, so he settled into the ground, unfolding his costume for insulation from the cold ground. It had fallen from around freezing when the sun went down, and the cloudless sky had allowed the bottom to fall off the thermometer. Gus estimated it was somewhere in the teens. It had been fine when he was moving, but the chill had been apparent as he waited for the light. He stood and grabbed the part of the costume he had used as a dress and placed it back on the ground and pulled the poncho over his head again and, using a couple of sticks, made it into a serviceable tent. He debated keeping it for just this purpose. Inside, the temperature grew remarkably fast once he weighed down the edges with small stones. The life-threatening temperatures outside stayed outside. He set an alert on the phone in case he fell asleep and woke up four hours later as the sun lit the sky.

While he waited for the sun to rise this lovely Monday morning, he ate some food and finished his reflection of how he had arrived here. At about 9:30, he packed his bags and folded the costume, stowing it away in a side pocket, and walked to the road, following it south. He walked with the big-balled walk of an avid hiker and attempted to catch a ride to the next town from each truck that passed. Eventually, one stopped, and he climbed in with a great big smile. "Hi," Gus said, "Jonathan Colthwait, they call me John. Thanks for picking me up."

Gus put his pack in the small couch like area behind the seat, as the driver of the 18-wheeled logging truck said, "Where are yah going, friend? My name is Purvis... You can call me Purvis," and smiled.

"Well, I'm hoping to get to Helena," Gus said, "but anywhere in that direction is much appreciated."

"I can get you to Browning," Purvis replied. "That will get you about 60 miles in the right direction. It's a bigger town, so you might have better luck there or maybe there is even a bus. I'm heading east from there to Minot."

"That would be outstanding!" Gus said with a genuine smile.

The hour passed with pleasant conversation. Gus liked Purvis. He found out that Purvis had retired from working with the North Dakota State Police eight years before. He had taken a job as a driver to pass the time until he reached retirement.

When they got to Browning, Gus grabbed his bag and thanked Pervis, and shook his hand before leaving the truck.

Purvis pulled away and Gus pulled out his phone. A proper bed and an actual shower would be great. On the north side of town, Gus found an inexpensive motel that rented out small cabins on North Boundary Street. It was a half-mile walk. Gus slid the bag on his shoulder and started walking, hoping they were not seasonal. He stopped after 10 steps when he saw a restaurant sign for Nations Burger Station, and his stomach growled at him.

"Was that you?" the voice of Scrios said in his head, and Gus ignored him.

455

He walked into the small restaurant and the smell of cooking hamburgers were like the entry to paradise. He ordered two double quarter pound classic burgers with one as a combo, paid, and asked if they had a bathroom just as his eyes saw the sign.

After relieving himself, he changed up the IDs in his wallet. Grabbing more American dollars, he removed the Canadian currency and placed it in the money belt. He put 500 U.S. dollars in his wallet, hoping to rent a room with cash only. He washed his hands. Noticing a dark mark on his wrists, he pulled up his sleeves and washed his arms and his face. When he finished, he cleaned the sink of the dirt buildup and left the restroom. He sat and ate one burger outside at a picnic table, and it might have been the best thing he had ever eaten. He couldn't remember ever eating good food after his long journey from Calgary. Ok, maybe that was overstating the facts a little, but the food was excellent. When he finished the burger, he resumed his walk to the hotel on Boundary Street.

When he arrived at the hotel, he went into the larger house that had an old weathered "Office" sign. He knocked and entered. A Native American woman in her 20's sat at a desk, and asked, "Can I help you?"

"Yes," Gus said, "I'm looking to rent one of your cabins."

Ten minutes and 500 dollars later, he was in the cabin he had rented for three nights. Originally, he wanted to get a week, but he had the feeling he had scored a deal because of the town's proximity to Glacier National Park. His offer to pay cash helped some on the price, too.

When he got into his nice little cabin, he sat and went on his phone and checked messages. There were many vague requests to contact him from Marcy around November 2nd and that concerned him. When he responded to his father, he used a catch phrase they had discussed and gave a vague update. That was the rule. The message said simply, "Safe at Samuel's house." The use of the name Samuel was for Uncle Sam, so his grandfather knew he was in the U.S. Other countries also received similar invented names, such as "Dieter" for Deutschland. Canada had been Dudley, as in Dudley Do-Right from The Rocky and Bullwinkle Show... of which Gus's grandfather was shockingly a fan.

Gus set a time to chat with Marcy and told her he loved her.

There was still nothing from Peter, and he kind of expected that there wouldn't be.

Gus pulled out the other burger and the now cold fries and ate until he felt a nap coming on. So, he plugged in his phone into the charger beside the bed. Plugging into a wall outlet charged his phone so much faster than the small solar charger he carried in his pack. He also plugged in the solar charger to top off its battery that rarely went above 30 percent on his journey. He set an alarm on his phone to wake him up at 4:00 PM, roughly three hours from now. As the feelings of bees buzzed in his head, like they always did when he was super tired, Gus went to sleep.

Chapter 17

Tuesday, November 13th, 2018, 1:07 AM Glacier View Cabins, Browning, Montana, USA

Twelve hours later, he woke up in the complete darkness of his room. He checked his phone and cursed. He'd set an alarm for 4:00 AM by accident and slept through his planned meeting with Marcy. When he entered the application, there were messages that grew in frantic fear from her, as they asked if he was there and if he was okay. He wrote a quick response, and she immediately answered.

She had been up the entire night in a panic. He had never missed a meeting time before, and she was sure that something had gone terribly wrong. They entered a private chat room and wrote to each other.

In the private chat, Gus asked Marcy how she was doing. She said that she was doing ok, and that she missed him terribly and that the morning sickness was dreadful. The smell of certain foods would send her running for the bathroom.

Marcy asked Gus, "Have you heard anything from Peter?"

"Not a thing," Gus confessed.

"It was so strange the day he left," she said. "He came by our room and told her he was heading out to meet with the police. He didn't seem nervous or anything. However, right before he left, he said something weird. He expected the interview to take a while, and he walked up to me like he was telling me something in confidence. It was something like, 'I think I'm doing what Gus meant when he asked me to take care of you. You know how Gus is. He never says what he really means. So, I may go away for a bit... Peter was acting really strange."

Gus replied with, "Wow, that is strange," as he changed the subject. "How are things around there with the craziness a couple of weeks ago?"

"Well, the funerals all took place the week after you left," she said. "Laoch suggested I rest because of the morning sickness and the weather getting a lot colder over the last couple of days, so I did. The police thing seems to have calmed down somehow. The police searched the house the day after the shoot-out at the warehouse. Other than that, not much happened here related to the incident. I'm sure there will be more legal talks, but I haven't been told what's going on."

"What was with all the vague questions on November 2nd?" Gus asked.

"Oh, crap, I thought you knew," Marcy said. "William passed in his sleep that night. I tried for days to get in touch with you... I'm so sorry; I probably should have said in the message."

"Oh, Wow," was all Gus could muster at first. "How are people there handling it?"

"It was a shock," she said, "but at 104, it was not totally unexpected."

Something tickled Gus's memory, and he marked it in his mind to come back and think about its meaning.

Gus and Marcy chatted for another 30 minutes before she decided she could actually get some sleep, and they disconnected.

Gus turned on the TV and surfed for the first time in a month. He was flipping past Fox News when he saw his own face. He had turned to the channel late in the story.

"... manhunt continues in Europe for the suspect in the murder of Harold Scandling, a prominent North Carolina political advisor. The officials in the British Police and Interpol, do not state why they are searching for Laoch "Gus" Ferguson, a resident of Raleigh, North Carolina, who was visiting family in Scotland, or if he is the only suspect in the case. They do, however, refer to him as a man of interest in the slaying. When asked who else was on the list, the officials declined to comment. Ferguson's whereabouts have been unknown for over a week, and investigators believe he is in the British Isles or on the European continent. Thus far, a location described as a bunker on his grandfather's land in Scotland has been a keen interest to investigators. It is said to house an amazing collection of artifacts from multiple ancient cultures. Experts have deemed many items culturally significant. The family claims that the archives have long been a private collection and were not secret. Any concealment to the public, they claim, was simply an execution of prudent physical security. The collection provided contracts where they had worked with several large public projects, including assisting with the deciphering of Dead Sea Scroll fragments. Contacts in Isreal, who were reached for comment, expressed that they have long partnered with the family and their private collection, sharing techniques and co-training personnel. When asked for a statement, the retired archaeologist, who was instrumental in the early discoveries of the scrolls, David Kats, admitted to working closely with the Ferguson Archives."

The video on the screen switched to a gray-haired man, *"Of course we partnered with 'zhem. I'm certain very few people knew of 'zher work, but we did. Just because a group prefers 'zheir privacy, it does not make 'zhem a covert and evil entity. We were introduced to 'zhem by zhe British Museum for crying out loud. 'Zhey surely knew about zhem,"* Kats said with a sound of incredulity.

Gus turned the channel, stood up, and walked towards the bathroom. He looked in the mirror and compared his features to the pictures he had just seen on the television. Sure, there were similarities, but his face had changed so much. Both the elements, weight loss and facial hair, changed the shape of his face. The blue eyes, though, he would need to keep his sunglasses on when it was appropriate. He also needed to be more mobile. The hiking had served its purpose.

Something was bothering him, and the conclusion was just outside of his consciousness as he worked to figure it out. It had to do with the way Teddy had taken an interest in the artifact while it was in his pocket. Even when he had not seen it. All he had seen was the bulge in his pocket, and yet he felt compelled to ask. It seemed illogic even for a personality like Teddy. There had been other times, but not as clear as that one.

When he was on the light rail train, going to the university in Calgary. A lady sitting on the train kept staring at that pocket. It was unnerving him so much that he had turned to face a different direction. The action seemed to break the trancelike state she was in.

Gus, to protect his own soul, had mentally put up a block to Scrios's own memories. Although he was unsure if he had put them in place consciously, or if it was his mind's attempt to protect itself from the trauma that came with the way the creature thought.

Gus met people who claimed to have a heightened or different perception of the world around them. Researchers referred to their perception as "synesthetes". It was where certain smells to them carried an associated color or number. Marcy was one of those people, as ironically, so was Gus's own mother. It was reportedly an extremely rare trait, but somehow two of the most important people in his life had won that lottery. The memories of Scrios sitting in Gus's head elicited a similar feeling.

If memories could carry a smell or taste, and to Gus, the creature's most certainly did. These carried the smell of death that he could only relate to an event he witnessed in Iraq. In the aftermath of a suicide bomber, who had detonated his vest in a school for girls between five and twelve years old, the air was thick with the same smell and inevitably the acrid taste, that its memories educed.

Perhaps the reason for that association also had to do with the abject horror he endured walking into the partially collapsed school and helping to find survivors. Some few that he helped survive, probably cursed him and the other responders now, for saving the shredded life that their actions had cursed them to living. Most poignant in Gus's memory the little girl, caught at the edge of the blast, with blackened, smoldering clothing, righting herself and stumbling to the corner of the room, attempting to retrieve an arm among the bloody bits and pieces, only to realize hers was not there.

Gus was helping a medic who was working on the dying teacher as he watched the insane puppet show from across the debris strewn room. She shopped another edge of the room, like a person looking through bargain bins at hell's thrift store, leaving a trail of dark blood, until she found her missing part. She looked at it and tried to place it back where it was supposed to be as she wobbled and collapsed to the floor from blood loss and died.

Opening his mind to Scrios's memories was exponentially worse than that moment. There was no innocence in his thoughts. There was no remorse. Gus braced himself and cracked the sarcophagus door to the creature's memories and lived the monster's experience looking for answers.

He felt the moment Scrios had become trapped in the artifact's prison 2500 years ago. The monster didn't understand what had happened. It had happened so fast. It found itself buried in soil and debris from an enormous explosion that coincided with its imprisonment and trapped it for hundreds of years.

Gus felt it as over the centuries the feeling of starvation led to desperation as the creature became sensitive to the smallest forest creatures above, in the woods that grew over the once devastated battlefield. Gus lived the feeling as the creature beckoned to the animals for centuries to help dig him from this grave. With a small measure of success, they did, as a small indention grew above his location. The day the creature reached out, catching the interest of a wandering hunter named Liam. Liam became fascinated by the indention, and dug relentlessly over several days, before he plucked the artifact from the dirt, rinsed it off in the creek. Once clean, he peered into one of the open ends of the artifact and became the first victim of this new era for the creature.

He had reached out to Liam... somehow, attracting his interest and concentration.

Gus closed the sarcophagus and tried to breathe, as he lay in the bed with tears streaming onto the pillow beneath his head. He tried to forget the other intrusive memories that came as part of the package. "Fucking hell," he said, exasperated.

A few minutes later, he realized he had answered another question that nagged at him since talking to Marcy. Scrios did not know that William had passed. There had been no "sweet reward" at the end of his life for the creature to enjoy. His smile betrayed him.

"Well, I'm glad that was good for someone," Scrios's voice rang in his head. Care to share what the smile is for?

"Absolutely!" Gus said in a chipper voice. "Do you really want to know?"

"Great, games huh? Is it 20 questions?" Scrios asked.

"Nope!" Gus replied. "I'll give you this one for free, because I want you to take in the full meaning of this. William died almost two weeks ago."

"Ok," the monster said, "And?"

"...And you didn't know it. No last morsel of goodness as you seem to think of it." Gus said with a giddy voice. "Why would that be? Hmmm? Because the only thing I can think of is, he died happy and without regrets or fear... He fucking beat you!" Gus said as he rolled around in maniacal laughter for minutes while Scrios remained silent.

Chapter 18

Tuesday, November 13th, 2018, 2:35 AM Glacier View Cabins, Browning, Montana, USA

When Gus recovered from the nausea that accompanied the visitation to that mind, he pulled out his phone and went about accessing some of the social media that was created for his identity weeks before. He was shocked to find a generic Facebook page in his new name that had a much earlier date than he expected. Someone created the page several years before. There were no pictures other than generic scenery that could be Alaska or Scotland or Siberia for all he knew.

The identification page from his passport encoded the account password. A mathematic progression based on his birthday pointed to the ten characters in the password. Gus hated math, but he had figured it out and got connected.

In the Marketplace application on Facebook, Gus started looking in the area for cheap but dependable cars. Gus had his favorites, but he was not totally stingy and hung up on any single brand. He needed something that was capable of minimal off-road or inclement weather driving. So, it needed to be an SUV of some sort. Jeep? Maybe.

He searched an area within 80 miles of Browning, because it would include the Kalispell area on the far side of the Glacier National Park. He didn't really want to go that far and enter a place with so many people. This was because of Dino's reinforcement of common sense.

He had said as they hiked, "What you are embarking on is not much different from being undercover in an op. You must stay in character, no matter what happens. The world is a tiny, tiny place, bro. Stay out of busy areas, because that is where you will probably run into someone you know. I was in Egypt... Some Muslim Brotherhood things. I was sitting in the back of some shithole tea and hukkah bar, all dolled up with a keffiyeh on my head, sitting with two other operators, thankfully just getting a drink. When my high school world history teacher walks right through the fucking place. This was not a very U.S. friendly part of town, and in strolls this Where's Waldo American, looking for a bathroom. He walks in and I hear him ask the guy running the place if they have a bathroom. I hear that voice, and I cringe. Sure enough, it is Mr. Smith. The guy was also my J.V. Football coach. I hid my face as he brushed against my back as he walked back to the hole in the floor that served as a toilet, in the small hut in the back. That is just the way shit happens, man."

So, Gus was not eager to go to a more populated area and further tempt fate or show up on some tourist's social media in the background and have some facial recognition application pop him with a location and a timestamp. It was dangerous enough in this little town.

It was as if some ray of sun came in the window at 2:42 AM, from the dark sky outside and illuminated a listing that was right there in Browning. Someone was selling a one-year-old Toyota Highlander Hybrid, Limited. It said it had all-wheel drive, and a salvaged title, which almost made Gus close the link. When he read on in the expanded description, he was glad he hadn't. The note encouraged people to come see the car and decide for themselves if they thought it was a piece of junk. So, Gus sent the man a message, asking about looking at it.

At 6:35 AM, Gus got a message back. Illias Branson, the owner, said that he would be around all day if Gus wanted to stop in to look at the car. Gus replied he could be there by 1-2 PM and Illias gave him a thumbs-up emoji. In the few messages planning the meeting, Mr. Branson admitted to being a Toyota mechanic for over 30 years in Kalispell. He described this car as being "returned to premium condition" by his own hand.

Still, the price he had of $27,000 seemed high for one with the obvious title issues, like this one had. However, if the car was as mentioned, it might be worth something close. Especially if it was reliable. He also had no intentions of ever trying to sell the car if he bought it. He similarly wanted as little paper trail as possible.

Gus went to find breakfast and to do a little shopping. His machinations about the creature last night had inspired an idea.

After a quick breakfast sandwich, as he walked. Gus went to a thrift store he had noticed on 1st Avenue, near downtown. When he walked in, he saw piles of clothing, in which he found a heavy dark-blue hoodie.

In the back left corner of the small store, he found piles of antiquated computer parts in boxes. He found three random motherboards on the $1 shelf, wrapped in their clear gray, static protection plastic envelopes.

A voice popped into his head, "Building a computer, are we?"

Gus flushed with a little anger as the voice confirmed a suspicion. He had seen Gus grab that. Even in his pocket, Scrios could see or sense the world around him. Not an optimal situation, but Gus shook it off and ignored the bait. He walked past an area piled with discarded old hospital equipment and other related items.

In the pile he found the remains of a heavy lead apron, like those used in an X-ray department. Someone had broken the neck strap and re-sewed it, but it had broken a second time in a different location. Gus picked up the well-worn apron and looked at it contemplatively, and tucked it under his arm.

"Interesting... that looks heavy and like a total waste of energy," Scrios said with a snicker. Gus remained silent.

He looked on the shelf to the right and saw an older white lacquered metal bedpan. He picked it up also and walked towards the front of the store. As he walked past a bin, he saw a small overnight backpack and grabbed it. When he got to the cash register, an older woman of Native American descent checked out his weird pile and shrugged her shoulders. She looked at the tags on the items while typing numbers on a small calculator.

"That comes up to $10.50 but today is a 50% discount day, so, $5.25" she said. Gus smiled and handed her a $20 bill, and she blanched. "I will need to go get change. I'll be right back."

"No, no," said Gus, "just count the rest as a donation. That's fine."

"Oh, thank you! Hey those are some cool pants. Were you in the military?" she asked as she pointed at the pocket that contained a monster trapped in the artifact.

"Oh, these?" asked Gus. "Nah, I got these at a different thrift store last year."

"Can I see what's inside that pocket?" She asked, with eyes that burned like that of a homeless meth addict that begged for a fix.

463

"No, I'm sorry I have to go, but thank you," he said and snatched up the things he bought and blew out the door.

As the door swung shut behind him, the older woman clerk said, "Fucking rude!"

When he got away from the door, and saw no one near, he asked, "Was that bullshit you?"

"Gotta try, right?" said the creature.

"Yeah, about that..." Gus said as he stepped off the road and behind a nearby abandoned house. Gus dumped the motherboards onto the ground, "Let's see how this works... yah know in the spirit of gotta try." He pulled the artifact from his pocket and felt the electric tingle that now carried no compulsion. Gus gave the artifact a sarcastic glance, glimpsing the green stone inside as he casually briefly glanced into the hole. Shaking his head from the flash of contact, he carefully wrapped each bag consecutively around the ancient scepter. Noticing that when he touched the metal through the bag, he felt no tingle like with bare skin.

Spreading the lead apron on the ground, he heard a slightly muffled, like a bad AM station on the radio, "Hey, what the hell?" Scrios said, as Gus tightened the wrapping of the crinkly bags. Gus folded the crinkly bagged creature up in the lead apron and swiftly pulled a sharp folding knife from his pocket to cut away excess material. He used the remains of the apron strings to tie it tight, took the bundle and stuffed it into the bedpan. He placed the bedpan in his pack and experienced true silence for the first time in weeks.

Gus's mind snapped back to that brief instant of contact that had made his head momentarily swim. He had witnessed the view of hundreds of rudimentary crosses staggered across a desolate landscape overlooking an old stone city. Gus knew with clarity it was the year of the Consulship of Sabinus and Rufus, and somehow that equated to 4 BC. The Romans, by his command, were punishing the Judeans for their revolt and the death of Herod the Great. Acting on the orders of Publius Quinctilius Varus, he rounded up two thousand Jews in the ancient city of Jerusalem and had them executed by crucifixion.

Gus saw the scene from the eyes of a young Roman of Germanic descent. His name was Arminius, who had stood at attention in front of the General, before receiving the commands that came from the cruel mind of the creature he held.

The General stared into Arminius's eyes, "If they force you to drag them to the cross, cut the tendons on their heels and the others won't resist," he said with a wicked smile. Right before the contact ended, the general licked his lips, and

Gus understood the general was only voicing the creature Scrios's salivating thoughts.

Chapter 19

Tuesday, November 13th, 2018, 1:17 PM Glacier View Cabins, Browning, Montana, USA

When he arrived at the seller's house at the designated time window, the seller, Illias, greeted him. As they walked around the side of the house, Illias told him the story.

It was a story that could probably only happen in the expanse of the Western United States. The seller had purchased the car 14 months before. One day on the way home from Whitefish, where he worked at the dealership, he was sitting at a stoplight. The back gate of the truck in front of him swung open and clunked hard against his front bumper, as Illias cringed. Three large steers, on their way to a slaughterhouse, poured out of the back, landing on the hood of his car. One slipped and fell, coming out of the truck, landing on, and ravaging the hood. The weight of the animal destroyed several parts of the engine and broke the engine mounts. The insurance company declared the car a total loss, but Illias bought it back from them at a fraction of the cost.

Illias showed Gus the car, which he had housed in an old barn like garage. The door to the garage was one solid piece, which was counter weighted and lifted on well-greased hinges to the roof. Old and new Toyota parts littered the garage. "I just finished the touch up paint last week and hit the whole thing with Toyota's paint sealing product. That would cost you 500 bucks at the dealer." Illias said with a hopeful sound in his voice.

When walking up, Gus had noticed the home was for sale and had a small banner at the bottom that said, "Motivated Seller!". Gus looked at him and back at the car. "What were you asking?" Gus asked.

"I'm looking to get 29k," Illias said. "It's a fantastic car. He only has nine thousand original miles on him."

"Him?" Gus asked.

"Well, his name is Seamus... you know, it's Scottish and I like the name." Illias said.

"Well, the problem I have is that is about two grand over bluebook for this car, without a history of it being declared totaled and a salvage title. Do you have any wiggle room?" Gus asked.

"A bit..." the man said, sounding encouraged.

"Let's come to a number we are both comfortable with," Gus said, "and hopefully when we reach it, I can do cash if that works for you. Right here and now, I could swing 22,000 cash. To me, that is higher than the estimates for any car with a salvage title. Frankly, if I ever try to sell this thing, I'm going to get scalded. Would that work for you? I mean, I don't want you to take a bath or anything either. You see, I'm hoping you got a much lower cost when you bought it back from the insurance people. I just got paid out for working the oil fields for this past summer." Gus waited for several quiet seconds and continued. "So, where does that leave you?" Gus asked.

"That frankly is pretty tight," Illias said. "But I'm not looking to make anything. I'm just trying to get back what I put into fixing it. Frankly, I spent too much doing that, and that is not on you. Can you swing five hundred more?" the seller asked.

Gus rubbed his chin pensively; he was trying to calm and cover a nervous smile. "I appreciate your honesty. How about I just round it up to 23?" Gus said as the man's face in front of him grew an enormous grin.

"That would be great, but you have to let me feed you dinner tonight. I'm making steaks... I have to clear out my freezer." He spoke.

"That sounds fantastic. I saw the sign. Are you moving?" Gus asked.

"Yes sir! I'm retiring to Yuma, Arizona."

"Well, I have one more request," Gus said. "I see you have a lot of tools. Can you sell me a set of tools that I can take care of most things in this car myself if I need to? I can add another grand to the total?" Gus said with a sideways look.

The man whose face already had an impossible smile somehow grew wider. I sure can and if you want, I can give you the mobile carrying rack I used twice, before cow-ma-geddon. It will carry the tools and whatever else you got. You just have to fold down the back row to fit it." The man said with all his teeth showing.

"Well," Gus said with a smile, "let's get the signing done so I can get you paid."

"Let me go grab my neighbor Nadine," said Illias. "She is a notary."

Ten minutes later, the car was his. Forty-five minutes after that, he was eating a steak the size of his plate with Illias and Nadine. It was a substantial amount of food, but he exerted an extraordinary effort and completed it. An hour later, he was on the road back to his motel with Seamus and a trunk full of useful tools.

Two days later, Gus packed up the car and headed south.

Chapter 20

Sunday, March 24th, 2019, Lander County Nevada, USA. East of Mt. Tobin.

"I should be in Vegas watching a basketball game with my girl and my friends instead of here with you!" Gus said as he trudged across the barren salt basin. He looked like he was contemplating throwing the ancient golden artifact in his hand away in disgust. Even with the cart carrying the most weight, the heavy backpack still cut into his shoulders through the heavy parka he wore. The cart idea had become a total fucking failure. It might have even been comical if it were just him and Marcy trying to carry gear onto a summer beach. Sure, it was still rolling... some; but half sliding and clogged with the wet sandy clay. "I can't believe it! A goddamn snowstorm in the freaking desert! Seriously, what the hell!" he exclaimed.

Sand accumulated on the rubber tires of the cart and had also affected the bearings, causing everything to get stuck. Soon, the salty sand and mud would trap the tires once more. Pausing momentarily, he kicked the tires vigorously, hoping to dislodge the thick layer of mud, but it stuck there like a paste. The kick served as a harsh reminder of the freezing cold weather, numbing his feet. Although he didn't directly feel the impact, the resulting ache was undeniable. Dressed appropriately for the cool weather that was in the forecast, he was wearing warm clothes, but the winter storm he encountered today had been absent from the predictions. Occasionally, a gust of wind would uncover a small window of clear sky amidst the storm, making him hopeful the relentless weather would ease up.

Scrios, the ancient evil entity confined to the golden artifact in his hand, communicated directly into Gus's mind, "You could be in Vegas by now if you and your family had abandoned this nonsense generations ago. Hell, you could end this now and still make it to Las Vegas by tonight. I could make you richer than you could ever imagine." The creature inside the green gem proclaimed, "If you desire, we could rule this entire planet together."

"Stop!" said Gus exasperatedly. "This is the end. You evil piece of shit, you are done! Also, you wouldn't make me rich or work together with me. You killed most everyone you encountered, and you would kill me, too. My family hid from you, because you hunted us."

"That was nothing but war," the entity's voice declared. "A war you have won, and I have to admit, among very few losses... at least not the ones I intended to win. But you... you are safe. My wiles don't even work on you. You know why, right? Have you pieced all that together? Have you deduced our familial relation? Sure, it was a little way back, but one of my siblings, born before me, slipped the fucking fence. Sorry, I mean, survived. It was tough in the

467

Bronze Age. No In-and-Out burgers back then." The monster imprisoned in the short scepter shaped artifact droned on, stating, "I'm pretty certain blood relates my bitch sister's kids to you."

Stopping momentarily, Gus stared intently at the artifact he was holding. "Oh my God, can you please shut the fuck up? If I wanted to know more, I could take one of those GodIHopeWeAreNotRelated.com tests and find out more, but I don't give a shit why your bullshit doesn't work on me. I do care about why you hunted me and my family for ages. I do care about why you killed my friends, why you killed my family... Why you ruined Peter... Why you ruined my life and my family's life?" Gus said as his voice hinted at cracking and quieting to an exasperated mumble. "Why do you want to destroy the world? I would take an answer to that!"

Gus experienced a moment of complete silence, during which he heard his footsteps squeak on the fine, wet sand. The monster eventually replied sheepishly. "It seems like you've got the wrong impression of me. I don't want to destroy this world. You know I'm being honest with you here, because I think you can tell when I am lying. I have no desire at all. By destroying the world, I would destroy myself. I have the same desire as you to live," soothed the soft voice of the creature.

"What?!?" Gus said incredulously. "I have seen your thoughts asshole and now I'm forced to carry those memories too. I saw some of the terrible shit you did and felt the satisfaction you had doing it! No, I'm not looking into your damn crystal anymore. You fed off the deaths of those people... Fed! OFF THE DEATH OF PEOPLE!!!"

"That's not true. Why would I want to eliminate everyone when I've been patiently waiting for this world to ripen? If I killed EVERYONE, I would starve like the plants in this awful place. I have killed no one. I'm a farmer, not a murderer. No, no, NO, I leave the hating to you. I leave the jealousy to you. I leave the murdering..." Scrios said, "I can sit here, doing nothing but watch what man does to man in this world and let it nourish me."

Gus's hand wildly flailed towards the heavens, as if he were reaching for an elusive imaginary item to smash as Scrios spoke, "The living ones sustain me. Sure, there is a delicious burst near the end when they embrace that last breath, but..." said Scrios, sounding like a sommelier pairing a wine to exotic meat.

"I don't care how you parse it, you evil asshat. You kill people. When you give them their new understanding, and because of that, they kill their own families and themselves... that is you killing them."

"You say potato..." the creature started before Gus cut him off.

"Just one question," Gus asked. "Am I currently providing you with nourishment?"

The creature in the stone appeared to be holding its breath during the extended period of silence. Scrios did his best, and Gus sensed the monster's discomfort in his thoughts. "Goddamn it!"

"Wait," the creature said calmly. "I recall you making a stop at the In-and-Out restaurant for two double-doubles gorilla style," Gus heard the order in his own voice transmitted in his head like a recording. "I didn't notice any sign of you feeling sadness for the cows becoming your burgers. Plus, let's be real. Like I said, today, I could just do nothing, and the human species would overwhelm my hunger daily just by being human. If I get peckish for a nice, tasty treat, all I need to do is have someone mis-gender someone else or violate their safe space and it's like apple pie à la mode. Three thousand years ago? Finding a sustenance among people who expected tragedy??? Now that was a challenge! Today? Pfft! I mean, one presidential election and look at you fucking monkeys."

Thoughts of his departed loved ones, Scrios's impossible lifespan, and the suffering he caused, overwhelmed Gus. Gus's jaw tightened. Having had enough, Gus said, "If all you had to do was nothing, and you had done nothing, we would not be here right now!" Again, silence met Gus's observation.

He spun around as if gathering a full view of the area. "This looks like as good a spot as any... Yup, looks like this at long last, is your graveyard asshole!" With a mixture of disdain and determination, Gus started unpacking and assembling the device, hoping it could finally destroy this thing.

The hollow artifact had the appearance and texture of gold. Experts confirmed it was an electrum construct, although not a conventional alloy. Upon receiving the electron microscope results, a metallurgist accused him of lying and alleged that it was data from a meteorite. The electron microscope readings revealed gold, silver, copper, iron, palladium, bismuth, and three unidentified elements.

"Either show it to me or shut the hell up," said Randy Cooper, his online metallurgist friend, "because this belongs in either a Marvel or Middle Earth universe, not our reality." Gus liked Randy.

"Randy, I would love to let you see it, but if I did, I would probably have to kill you." Randy did not know the irony of the joke but took it as if it must be some top-secret thing or something.

"Wait a sec, this isn't like little green men stuff, right?" Randy asked.

"No, nothing like that."

"Riiight," Randy said.

Over the last six months, Gus made various comedic attempts to destroy this artifact. To be honest, if this attempt didn't work, he wasn't certain anything less than launching it at the sun would be effective. Perhaps "Operation Frodo" involving an open caldera volcano was the only alternative?

His efforts thus far with fire, including forges and the acetylene torch technique, only resulted in heating the object until it glowed. The heat from the torch dissipated unnaturally fast, with no visible change in the object's malleability.

He tried heating it in an electric furnace to a white glow, then quickly plunged it into liquid nitrogen. The nitrogen erupted explosively, but no damage was done to the artifact.

He attempted to hit it with a hammer, but it remained unscathed. So, Gus tried a real big hammer... like a goddamn mechanized hydraulic hammer of Thor used to shape and cut girders... nothing.

When he combined the electric furnace, heating it until it glowed white and quickly striking it with a massive hydraulic hammer, finally he noticed a scratch and a small dent. He actually screamed in delight. Later, still smiling to himself after finally creating a lasting mark, his mind transitioned to the thought of explosives.

In a different attempt, Gus tried enough C4 to shoot the artifact 6 feet into the ground. He debated leaving it there, but he knew somehow, someone would find it and he had to ensure its destruction. After digging it up, it remained intact. It did, however, scuff it with another small abrasion on the metal cylinder, so that too gave him some hope.

Late one night five months ago, as Gus stayed in the string of awful hotels that took cash and asked no questions, a TV show caught his eye. He found himself engrossed in an old MythBusters episode on a vintage Zenith CRT TV with a digital converter. The beginning of an idea sparked in Gus's mind. It caused a smile to grow on his tired and bearded face. To evaluate its destructive effects, the show employed a shaped charge to penetrate a U.S. Army tank.

The episode started off by talking about some movie with Tom Hanks and a sticky bomb. In their typical fashion, they exceeded expectations to the point of ridiculousness. With his fists raised in the air, Adam Savage proudly paraded around the watch bunker as the shaped charge blast ripped through the dummy in the driver's seat. "Myth Confirmed!" yelled Adam with a geeky squeak of excitement.

The hotel TV, with a manufacture year as ancient as Gus, appeared to have a hidden message just for him. As MythBusters ended, the upcoming preview for the next show was a documentary on Oppenheimer and the development of the first nuclear bombs.

Gus's mind briefly drifted back to the current task at hand in the desert. He couldn't help but notice the irony of being hundreds of miles away from White Sands, now in a similar, desolate area in northern Nevada.

The day after MythBusters, Gus reached out to an old college friend using a disposable phone. At Western Carolina University, Jack, like Gus was involved with the ROTC program. Jack, his old friend, had gained a reputation on campus for his practical jokes in the dorms, many of which involved minor explosions. He, later becoming a demolitions specialist for a career in the Army, was... let's just say, a predictable outcome. Jack Caldwell's level of military commitment far surpassed Gus's.

They had reconnected in the past, when they unexpectedly met while attending a homecoming football game at WCU. To be honest, in those years at Western, the event was more of a home band performance with a miserable beat down of a football game surrounding it.

Gus searched the small notebook he kept in his bag and found Jack's contact information. When they talked, Gus steered the conversation towards the TV show he had seen with MythBusters and the Oppenheimer documentary. Bingo! Jack took control of the conversation.

Jack was absolutely obsessed with this subject of shaped charges and their use in nuclear weapons and had a wealth of knowledge about the physics involved. He talked about the technology employed in New Mexico in 1944, which primarily involved shaped charges like the ones on that Mythbusters episode. Jack described how one bomb specifically used a charge to fire an enriched uranium slug into a uranium core. He shared with Gus how he would regularly construct makeshift shaped charges now during his retirement, using smaller ones to blow up tree stumps, while doing side work for a landscaping company.

Jack laughed while describing how easy they were to make and shared how they got him arrested on a drunken Fourth of July night. Sensing his interest, he quoted a link to Gus with a step-by-step video which, two years before, resulted in his YouTube account getting suspended. Watching that video and thumbing through an old, dog-eared copy of The Anarchist Cookbook, a plan formed in Gus's mind.

Gus's design employed a shaped charge to push a 50-caliber depleted uranium slug and force it down the about 40-caliber hole that ran the length of the tube-like artifact, which contained the green crystal he believed to be preserving the essence of Scrios. He had an optimistic vision, likening it to splitting a log.

471

"Let's raise a glass to hope!" Gus said, while enjoying a zero-calorie soda, toasting the drawing in his notebook.

Returning to the present, Gus turned his gaze to the cart he had hauled through the cold desert rain and snow squall. The planning in the notebook led to a load of close to 300 pounds, with some in a heavy backpack and the rest on a wheeled cart. The cart had transformed into a sled on the wet sand, which he pulled across three to four miles of hills and salt flat, constantly annoyed by the cart's wheels, "That keep getting clogged with goddamn MUD!!" he yelled in frustration as he kicked the useless wheel on the cart one last time.

Once assembled, Gus placed the artifact upright on the high grade layered steel base that measured 16 inches square and 2.5 inches thick. The base alone weighed about 180 pounds. A small steel, 3-inch nub of sanded rebar, stood up in the center, welded to the plate to hold the creature's tube vertical from the inside. The artifact that contained Scrios slid on to the sanded rebar with a satisfying click. The purpose of the shaped charge was to propel the slug into the tube, wreck everything in its path, and potentially destroy the plate of steel below.

His friend Jack had sheepishly reviewed his blueprints, "The key is to force the blast in one direction," and he thought Gus's plan would do that, "but you should bolt all the other metal structure pieces in place," he emphasized. Jack paused, and stared at him on the Skype screen with a troubled look on his face. "Are you, like, really building this?" Jack asked. "Because, if the D.U. slug passes through the steel plate, someone in China might receive a slightly radioactive colonic."

In an unconvincing bland tone, Gus replied, "Oh no. I just like designing crazy stuff like this."

In the northern Nevada desert, Gus removed from the backpack, a sandbag filled with 30 empty sandbags and a crappy old military shovel remake. "This piece of crap deserves a one-star review if I ever have the chance to write one up online." The job became more challenging when the shovel broke about eight bags in, and Gus's language turned just as expressive as his level of frustration.

After three hours, with two breaks to warm his hands in his armpits, the build was finally done. Through pure determination, he ignored the pleas and promises of power and wealth from Scrios. Even with the creature customizing Miley Cyrus music and making DJ call outs for mercy, Gus ignored Scrios, the wonder tube. Until that point, he did not know of Scrios' ability to make him hear other voices, but it made sense when he thought about it.

After the build was complete, he unpacked and inserted a new battery from his pocket and powered up the wireless detonator. Gus gathered the remains of his gear, specifically selecting the items he wanted to keep. He left the cursed wagon behind and incorporated it to further back the charge before leaving.

Gus moved back approximately 100 meters. Positioned well within the radio's three-mile detonator range, he prepared to activate the switch and hit the button. In his epic application to the Darwin Awards, he had a premonition of a loose bolt or shrapnel flying at him like a bullet. He mused, "How about we step back a bit more?"

As he retreated to 300 meters, Gus noticed that the ancient monster's voice had ceased in his mind and observed how the drizzle and light snowflakes seemed to create a private domed cloud surrounding the creature. "That motherfucker! No goddam way! That has to be freaking impossible," he said aloud as he paced back and forth, staring at it.

While again contemplating whether to press the button, Gus spotted a gentle slope in the ground about 50 feet further back, along with a dry stream bed at the base. He shrugged his shoulders and nodded to himself. Listening to his inner voice, he quickly moved towards the ditch. Even without the sandbags, previous test fires of smaller test models were not excessively loud. However, he was still glad that he had come all the way to this ancient desolate lakebed.

With dusk approaching, he took a moment and consulted his phone's GPS. Scanning for the ridge where, just beyond, his car was located, he felt reassured that he could make a speedy three-mile escape once he finished the job.

Settling into the ditch, Gus found amusement in his little trigger device. The red button had a flip up cover and a green light. "Just like MacGyver!" Peter's voice and maniacal laughter echoed in his head. He smiled and barked a small, sad laugh. Gus readied himself, "This is for you, Peter," and pushed the trigger. He attentively listened for the expected loud pop that would accompany the explosion as he pushed the button.

Gus's next memory was a green flash, with no noise. It appeared his entire chest was being compressed by something heavy and soft, comparable to the force of a three-story tall stuffed animal bouncing against him. Chaos erupted silently as a blast wave swept through his hiding spot. In Gus's memory, the sand and pebbles appeared to briefly defy gravity before disappearing away from the explosion.

A scraggly chunk of scrub-brush at the top of the ditch across from him flattened for a moment, before it suddenly burst into flames... "It fucking caught fire," he reflected later.

Instead of the blast continuing to push towards him, it reversed, causing a suction effect, dragging sand, rocks, and burning plant fragments from the area, towards its glow. While Gus watched outward, the shockwave propagated towards the distant mountains, climbing up the banks of the desolate lakebed, and causing the mountains several miles in front of him to release clouds of dust, reminiscent of an old woman vigorously beating a dirty carpet.

Just a few seconds later, he could feel a rumbling sensation beneath him as the wave echoed off the walls of the valley. The never-ending rumble beneath his feet caused the wash edges to collapse around him. When he stood, Gus felt dampness on his cheek and upon investigation, discovered a mysterious dark liquid. There was complete silence for him, he couldn't hear anything, but the ground still shook.

He rose into the green unnatural light, his flickering shadow stretching from the explosion site. As he glanced behind, he witnessed a small yet iconic mushroom cloud ascending into the sky, accompanied by peculiar green lightning streaks. Although not as enormous as the clouds in the old 1950s explosion videos on YouTube, it was still large enough for him to utter a silent "Holy Shit!" After standing in a daze for what seemed like an eternity, he quickly realized, "It's time to go!"

He put his hand in his pocket and took out his phone. Tapped the screen and... Nothing! Gus pressed the power button, but it also did nothing. He was grateful for checking directions earlier and having a clear idea of where his car was. In the fading light of the cloud, Gus could see the ridge that concealed his car.

Gus dismissed the possibility that his car, like his phone, was completely dead. Hearing his long-lost mother's voice as she said, "You're in enough trouble without buying more". He walked briskly... the walk soon became a jog... the jog became a sprint. When the fatigue outpaced the panic, he slowed back down to a jog and soon after, a walk again. His legs felt like they were made of sponge and his hands were shaking.

Once he reached his car, he pressed the keyless entry button, but there was no response. He collapsed onto the ground, momentarily defeated, before smacking his head and rising to his feet. With a shake of his head, he removed the manual key from the fob; put it in the lock and the doors locks clicked when he turned the key. Upon opening the door, the interior lights illuminated inside his dependable old Highlander. Seamus became animated as soon as the key was stuck in the slot close to the start button. Inside the glove box, there was a burner phone. The one he had purchased months ago. As soon as he inserted it into the dangling USB cord, the screen turned on. He powered on the phone, brought up a navigation app, and got the hell out of the area.

He made it east, to Highway 305. While traveling north on the highway towards Interstate 80, he witnessed multiple police cars passing by, heading in the opposite direction. While driving east on I-80, he came across a sizeable convoy of military vehicles racing in the opposite direction as well. The speed at which they were traveling underlined their urgency. Like the other few cars on the highway that night, he slowed to watch the procession pass.

In the meantime, he reached into the glove box and pulled out a pouch of wet naps to tidy up his face. He noticed blood at some point had trickled out of his ears, while looking at himself in the rearview mirror. He observed he was now experiencing a persistent ringing sound.

Another fear gripped him, and he started getting concerned about being exposed to radiation. "Was that some kind of nuclear explosion?" he asked the empty car.

He felt a calm, as the ringing in his ears returned, and he realized he had just heard himself speak. Once again, he was hearing things. Also on the positive side, he felt assured he had completely obliterated Scrios.

He intended to call Marcy soon, and his grandfather, and inform them about the destruction of the monster and its cursed prison.

Emotion over the battle being over, raced through him. The thought of Marcy not wanting him back brought tears to his eyes. Things had grown distant over the months. Frequently, he had no ability to contact her. Rarely did they chance an actual voice call. He knew she was due to have the baby any day now, and he had been gone for all the events that bond a couple. Sure, it wasn't his fault, but that did not matter to him or her.

The destruction of Scrios did not ease the issues that awaited him, either. He had not killed Scandling, as the reports had said, but he had run like a criminal. He had evaded like he was guilty. Who will believe him at this point? "Hey, this is Gus. Yeah, I have been dodging you guys for the last six plus months because I had to kill the family monster," he thought. "Sure, that will go over great!"

Given his legal troubles over the past year, even if they don't expose his connection to the enormous explosion, he was driving away from... Again, the voice he heard was his mother in his head, like when he was stuck on one of those goddamn word problems in math, "Work one problem at a time, sweetheart," his mother said in his head as he drove east towards Utah.

Epilogue

Tuesday, April 2nd, 4:04 PM Infirmary of Edinburgh, Edinburgh Scotland. 2019

Gus arrived at the hospital, accompanied by two U.S. Marshals. His legs and hands were in chains. He struck a deal to resolve the hunt, with his only request, to be allowed to be with Marcy when she had the baby. Laoch and Deb's legal teams collaborated to ensure full legal compliance and signature acquisition prior to the surrender.

The manhunt for Gus was a continuous effort, but reduced priority and resources hampered the recovery effort as investigations in England and the U.S. rapidly fell apart under scrutiny. They cited "facts" that Scandling had sworn to, but these facts, were thinly fabricated or never existed. The entire management line at the CIA that had coordinated the effort to capture Clan Ferguson, citing them as a crime family, passing the information to the FBI leading to a racketeering investigation, had their case similarly withdrawn. Under pressure, signers of the warrants recanted their agreement. It was probable that Gus would eventually walk free. Multiple news sources, after being fed the flimsy case by the Furgeson defense team, had inquired in press conferences and received "no comment" as a reply. Quietly, the charges were being dropped, falling like dominoes.

When Gus, for expediency, offered to surrender, the FBI kept it low key and agreed to the deal quickly. It would take weeks, however, now with Gus present, the defense team expected these charges also to go away.

Once at the hospital, the Marshals removed the chains and handcuffs before taking him upstairs to be with his wife. The mood was somber when his grandfather met him in the lobby and waited patiently for the restraints to be removed before he hugged his grandson. Deb was there too. Her eyes were red with recent tears. Gus knew the prognosis. He had heard yesterday that the tiny baby in Marcy's stomach had not moved in over a week, and yesterday, they had again failed to find a heartbeat. The coming hours were a brutal guarantee. It was coming at Gus like a fist to his face as he walked the hallway from the elevator towards Marcy's room.

He turned the corner and saw his wife for the first time since October. Despite the growth of her abdomen with the baby, she looked frail. She had dark rings below her eyes, which now seemed to have the look of a startled animal. She saw him and melted as he ran to her.

"I'm so sorry," she said.

"Honey, nothing is your fault here, darling. Nothing," he said as he consoled her.

After 30 minutes, the doctor came in and introduced himself, while the nursing staff cleared the room of unnecessary people. Gus sat on a stool, staring into her eyes as they adjusted a liquid drip beside the bed, and strapped her stomach with a belt that had a wide disk on it, with a wire that led to a machine beside the bed. The main line on the display didn't even seem to notice being hooked up. It stayed flat.

An hour and a half later, Marcy was feeling hard pains in her stomach as the contractions built both in regularity and intensity. An hour after that, she reported an inordinate need to push to the nurse, who reached between her legs and under the gown. Moments later, the nurse faked a gentle smile, "It looks like you are ready. I will notify the doctor."

She stripped her glove and disposed of it in the blue trash bag beside her elevated bed, as a flurry of activity started, which led to the bed being transformed into a birthing station.

Two more hours passed, as the epidural took effect, and the waiting became noticeable and painful to endure. Eventually, things moved in the somber room. As Gus stared into Marcy's eyes, her memories surfaced in his mind. He used them as a guide to read her face and understand her misery. He knew her pain was deeper than he could fathom, and he could not take it from her, but he could hold her and help her endure it, so he did. For the first time, Gus felt buoyed by the wisdom of the thousands of consciousnesses that he had in his head as they helped him form a consensus. Instead of being drawn in by each lost soul into their emotions and memories, he could leverage their knowledge without engaging in their tragedy. Rather than refuting her as she expressed her sadness, as he normally would have; he focused on the curse the creature had inflicted upon her, and simply embraced her while he told her he loved her.

As an enormous contraction hardened Marcy's stomach, Marcy actually managed a small smile at Gus as the doctor commanded her to "Push!" The instruction startled both him and Marcy. She did as she was asked. Several minutes later, the crown of a dark-blue head appeared. Moments after, the tiny, limp baby slid out into the doctor's waiting hands. The doctor quickly transferred the child's corpse to a waiting towel, as Gus glimpsed his daughter.

She was so tiny, with black fingernails and purple lips. The baby had a matted mane of orange-brown hair that was almost an inch long. As he watched the medical personnel work, Gus realized from the corner of his eye that Marcy, too, was watching. Her first wail shattered the room, and they both broke down into sobs.

As the doctor handed the corpse of their child, now partially wrapped in the towel, to the nurse; the baby suddenly arched its back in a spasm and an amber clear liquid ejected from its mouth in a stream. Before the liquid hit the floor, the baby gasped and squealed, a sound reminiscent of a parrot's screech. The loud cry startled everyone in the room, including the doctor, who almost dropped her as he fought the compulsion to pull his hands back.

Gus, though, recognized the sound instantly; it was the echo of memories forced into his mind during his first encounter with the artifact in the woods that day. The horror threatened to tear Gus's mind apart, shocking him into a motionless stare.

The doctor quickly recovered from his surprise and immediately issued orders to the nurses and requested an incubation crib. The mood in the room lightened immediately as Gus reached over, trying to hide his own reaction from the room as he hugged a stunned Marcy.

From Gus's left, he heard as the doctor said, "Wow, she is a strong one!"

When Gus's red eyes looked to see the baby, it impossibly appeared to be trying to sit up in the doctor's hands. Gus looked at his daughter's face. The baby's sea-blue eyes were open. Strange lights seemed to dance in them as they dreadfully focused and fixed on his own eyes.

The child in the doctor's hands squealed, causing everyone in the room to flinch, except Gus, who heard the sound in his head and through his ears at the same time.

In Gus's mind, a single set of memories entered. There was darkness and muffled noises and the strong constant thump of a heartbeat. There were moments of singing and music in the darkness. In the last memory, there was compression and pain and a sudden light that hurt her eyes. Everything was blurry until Gus saw himself from across the room. In her, he felt it as her fear lifted when she saw him and Marcy. She felt safe and tired.

Jennifer Delilla Ferguson 5 lbs. 6oz. 15 and ½ inches long. Born 8:23 PM April 2nd, 2019.

Epilogue 2

Monday, March 25th, 2019, 9:00 AM Lander County Nevada, USA. East of Mt. Tobin.

In the middle of the dry lakebed, people walk around in heavy protective suits scouring samples around the perfectly spherical half circle taken from the lakebed, measuring 1.57164 meters. It was as if someone used a gigantic ice cream scoop and removed lake bottom. The edges of the scoop mark were hardened and had a microscopic layer of a gold like material that seemed impossible to remove. Outside of the five-micron thick solid foil, the lakebed showed signs of a great explosion, with heat extreme enough to form glass, but was not apparently nuclear. The scientists measured the area they called "the scoop" and found that there was a small offset. As if the center of the circle was approximately 15.24 centimeters, or roughly six inches above, the golden-colored scoop mark.

In their heavy protective suits, the workers walked around in the middle of the dry lakebed, carrying various detectors and finding no sign of radiation. Cameras were setup to capture live pictures that were beamed back to their command center while a drone flew overhead collecting a high resolution lidar image of the entire area for a mile in every direction.

A crust of green glass covered the sand for a hundred and 50 yards in every direction. Several of the scientists remarked about the glass, asking if this was Trinitite? Others agreed it appeared to be.

"Something happened here," one said. "I just cannot understand why there is zero trace radiation."

The winds were sweeping the area from the south on the wintry day, but coming off the mountains, it stole precious warmth even through the suits.

"Did you see that flash?" a different researcher near the scoop asked.

"What flash?" asked another.

"Right at the center of the scoop. I swear I saw something," he replied, "control, did anyone get anything on the cameras?" he asked with urgency.

Several other researchers at the center of the blast area each reported seeing something out of the corner of their eye, but thought it was a reflection.

"I think they did witness something," said a voice from the command center tractor trailer a mile away, "but it happened so fast, and without a pause it is simply there, and the next, just gone. I slowed the frame rate on one of the HD cameras down one thousandth of a second. At that rate, you can see green dust come together, like a giant sucking in breath. The dust instantly congealed into a solid stone about two centimeters across and shot to the east, rapidly speeding up in a blur, even at that frame rate.

People gathered around screens to watch the video. It was like a reverse explosion. The digital speed reduced, told the story, albeit not as clearly as they would have liked. Sure enough, some kind of green cloud came together, swirled quickly into a stone... a crystal, as in the brief 13 milliseconds it was stationary, before it blurred out of frame. For a moment before it moved, we could see light passing through it. The light in one area refracted by an imperfection. The next frame it was gone. A slight green blur was the only indicator of its trajectory.

Within 30 seconds, the team leader ordered everyone to remain silent about the incident under penalty of treason. They removed the golden bowl from the scoop in the sand and similarly assigned it the same secrecy level. Despite its thinness, its feather weight that caused issues in the wind because of its gigantic size, initial tests showed it to be impervious to gentle attempts to damage it, as it rang like a bell in a perfect deep C.

Later tests at a clandestine desert research facility, about 375 miles southeast of the scoop, also near a dry desert lakebed, would find the material remarkably resistant to almost anything. Simulated small arms fire didn't even mar the perfect dome. Electron microscope results were interesting. They revealed gold, silver, copper, iron, palladium, bismuth, and three unidentified elements. The finding resulted in an archival search of internet traffic, which led to the detainment of a metallurgist by the name of Randy Cooper, who immediately copped to talking to someone on the internet, and said, "Holy shit! That was freaking real?"

Randy signed a paid non-disclosure agreement that was revokable with severe penalties if he ever mentioned it, or let it become known.

Epilogue 3

Monday, March 25th, 2019, 9:00 AM Viana do Castelo, Portugal

The ancient woman, who could pass for 30, sat on the porch of her small home in the hills of Portugal, north of Viana do Castelo. She had been there for nearly 20 years now and the view of the ocean seemed familiar to her somehow.

Oh, her memories, but she had somehow forgotten where she was born. As far as she knew, she was born in pain at just a few years younger than she appeared now. She remembered waking up in agony as she was being towed on a makeshift sled through high grass by a man leading an ox. When she got to the town, everyone there talked outside of the room she was in, in a squat hut. Some talked about aiding her in death, while others agreed she would find death on her own. But she didn't.

The same morning, she stood up and left the room, searching for water and something to eat. Her recovery was so profound and impossible that the community ushered her away at spear point. The many horrifically damaged areas of skin sloughed off revealing pink, new, healthy and unmarred skin. They were certain she was a demon. Some called her a foundling.

At the edge of town, she ran away in confusion, and the cycle started for her. She would find a town, make a home and, after a blink of an eye, suspicion would rise, and she would leave. Hundreds of years passed, and those extended into thousands. She befriended and later abandoned people.

She had a warrior spirit; she knew that, but was afraid of how that would raise attention to her. All the while, she would change her name and where she lived as if it were by the seasons to her. Things got much easier once banks became common, but she found the world exceedingly boring.

She didn't fit in anywhere and had to hide her true self. The times she didn't, the people would stalk her like a monster. That word, "monster," it stuck with her every time she heard it in the many languages she knew. Something about it. It was there like a concept that was just out of her reach. She would dream of older times and even flashes of battles, but nothing made sense. The invention of TV, she thought, resembled her dreams. The odd dreams of battles were like she was watching it on a television.

During the times of great strife, she would help where she could, often as a nurse. She had a knack for helping people and that, too, stuck in her head.

The sun was setting on a warm day, when a sense came over her, she didn't recall having before. Something was coming at her and it was almost there. She could feel its promise as it came closer, summoning to her like a lost lover. She stuck out her hand and, as if a magician's trick, a green round crystal appeared.

A friend she knew, but more. In less than a blink, she said the word, "Sanura," and she knew who she was.

She immediately dropped to her knees as a great sadness rolled over her, as she finally grieved her fallen friends. Anguish overcame her, and she collapsed to the floor, wailing for them as in days past. When she was done, she stood.

Enki gave her an understanding that the evil was loose in the world, and it feared it was about to get worse. Something had freed the creature from the walls of his crystal, and even he wasn't sure what that meant, but it could still sense the evil that had stained him for so long. The Scrios that had corrupted his purpose and imprisoned him unknowingly, to witness its dark obsessions. Enki knew it was a witness by nature, but this entrapment again allowed him to feel new emotions, and this one was called anger.

Sanura boarded a plane in Lisbon and landed at Heathrow. She exited the plane and rented a car at 7:00 PM local time. 57 minutes later, she arrived in front of the almost completely dark UCL Institute of Archaeology at the University of London.

She parked in a no-parking zone, not caring what happened to the automobile. It was only money, and she had lots of that. She walked up to the overhang that covered the door in front of the mostly brick six story building that was wrapped with a black, head high steel railed fence. The design of the outside made for an area inside the fence which reminded her of a mote, as she had seen throughout her life after the great battle.

She walked to the large door of the building and found it locked. Sanura placed Enki to the door and the door soon buzzed. She pulled the now unlocked door open. She went to the stairs and somehow knew to go to the basement. A man in a white coat approached her as she walked down the hall.

"Hello, it is after hours. Is there some way I can help you?" he asked. "Oh no," she said, we are just here for a minute. The smile she gave him disarmed the wormy academic, who tilted his head and continued down the hall after watching her walk away for an extra moment.

She knew the smile, and the bit lip, might have been too much and she could feel his eyes on her backside as she walked away, as he lost his ability to think rationally. She turned the corner in the hall and went to a set of double doors on the left. Again, an electric ID pad was beside the door. She ignored it. Sanura placed Enki on the locking mechanism and the door opened immediately.

She walked in to see a startled Doctor Sebastian Blane, sitting at a table with a lighted magnifying glass, and cotton gloves, examining an ancient sword on the table, which was sitting in a blue felt lined case with the lid opened. "Can I help you miss?" said the man with "Dr. Blane" embroidered on his jacket.

"Yes," said Sanura. "That belongs to me, and I'm reclaiming it." She snapped her fingers with an impatient, "give it to me now," look.

The doctor bristled and reached to close the case when Sanura said, "Tell you what. If you can keep a secret, I can give you context to this sword. I can tell you where to look for things lost for up to four thousand years. I can give you places and locations of cities and palaces, lost to history.

I know you think it is crazy, but I will keep the sword, and you can get that in return or not. Plus, I will make the sword privately available when it is not in use. Better than that, I can tell you when and where I had it made and by whom.

Epilogue 4

In the deep void, a spherical puddle of blackness rippled as it, along with entire planets, orbited the impossibly gigantic creature. The blackness of the pool was almost invisible in this dark place, only illuminated by the blue glowing eyes of the titan that peered out through its mane of tentacles. It felt it when its child's essence appeared in the pool, but the creature showed it no recognition.

For years, the puddle struggled to take a form. Some kind of avatar with which it could communicate. The embarrassing excuse for a child tried for years to will the thick, viscous blackness into a familiar form. A form like a homunculus is what it aspired to. It once even achieving the shape of a gingerbread man before collapsing back into the rippling sphere as its father looked on with disdain.

It had traded one trap for another, not the escape it had plotted for centuries as it waited for the world it was born into, to become destructive enough to end its imprisonment. The creature knew destroying the crystal would likely kill it. However, it acknowledged its unsustainable situation, realizing that staying in its prison was not viable.

Now, after his destruction, he found his awareness here. Although he felt a lack of presence, sensing he wasn't substantively in this place, he viewed his surroundings in an immersive way. The pool was a communication medium of sorts. He knew that somehow, although he never remembered learning it. He had no awareness of where his real self was or if it still existed. Going back to it was not an option. So, he found himself in a new prison, constantly bathed in the palpable disappointment emanating from his father.

Years passed on Earth, before Scrios finally reached a familiar form. The human form it chose was a reasonable facsimile of his adult human form, except in its monotone obsidian sheen.

A moon sized eye swayed in his direction, its dim blueish light shining as it took in the human form. It twitched its enormous, clawed appendage at him in dismissal. The wave of gravity generated by its hand motion sent Scrios's tenuous form back to a wobbling sphere.

In frustration, Scrios pouted like a petulant child for a moment before a newer, simpler form popped into his head. From the pool emerged an elongated serpentine head. A long, scaled body that continued to grow until it consumed the entire pool, followed it. Scrios marveled at how simple this form came to him.

Years passed before his father again gave him the slightest attention. The attention brought a flood of scornful images from his father into Scrios's mind. This time, Scrios didn't flinch. He paid attention to the admonishment without apology. The flood of images shifted as he bombarded his son with images of torment, impressing the experience of ages and the absolute correctness of power. The lessons continued while the earth, an impossible distance away, swam laps around the sun.

Then suddenly, the lesson stopped with a feeling of completeness. From his vantage point, Scrios couldn't see the enormous claw reach across the vast distance at relativistic speeds, making it suddenly appear in front of him as it reabsorbed the pool that contained his perspective. A last series of images gave him the information he required, dispatching him back to the place of his failure. He knew no vessel was there to receive him; he understood his father had assigned him to handle this matter alone. Scrios could flourish as his father had or fail.

The End

If you enjoyed the book, I would love it if you took a moment to give it a review. Reviews are the lifeblood of independent books like this. Stay tuned for Book 2 – **The Man Who Knew Too Much**. Thank you for reading this novel.

The next page contains a scannable QR code that will take you to a page where you can review the book.

E. J. Josephson